Praise for *The American Heiress*

"Ms. Goodwin . . . writes deliciously."

—Janet Maslin, *The New York Times*

"Smart, emotional, entertaining writing . . . Like Henry James and Edith Wharton, Goodwin delves into this seemingly gracious world of opulence to uncover its harsh side, and brings a cast of fascinating characters into a delicious tale that captivates."

—*RT Book Reviews*

"A propulsive story of love, manners, culture clash, and store-bought class from a time long past that proves altogether fresh."

—*Publishers Weekly*

Praise for *The Fortune Hunter*

"Finely drawn characters and intriguing plotlines . . . Although readers who enjoyed *The American Heiress* will be first in line to savor Goodwin's new novel, they will be followed quickly by others who appreciate engaging and thoughtful historical fiction."

—*Library Journal* (starred review)

"A sophisticated blend of money, class, history, misunderstandings among lovers, spirited women, and unpredictable but irresistible men."

—*Kirkus Reviews*

"A luxurious indulgence . . . Goodwin writes with effortless grace, and her dialogue's subtle wit is delightful."

—*Booklist*

"A sumptuous, scrumptious confection, with country houses, Austrian empresses and Victorian glamor galore."

—Lucy Worsley, chief curator at Historic Royal Palaces

The American Heiress

The Fortune Hunter

Also by Daisy Goodwin

Victoria
Victoria & Albert

The American Heiress

&

The Fortune Hunter

DAISY GOODWIN

 St. Martin's Griffin ⚞ New York

THE AMERICAN HEIRESS. Copyright © 2010 by Daisy Goodwin Productions. THE FORTUNE HUNTER. Copyright © 2014 by Daisy Goodwin Productions. All rights reserved. Printed in the United States of America. For information, address St. Martin's Press, 175 Fifth Avenue, New York, N.Y. 10010.

www.stmartins.com

The Library of Congress Cataloging-in-Publication Data is available upon request.

ISBN 978-1-250-25996-7 (trade paperback)

Our books may be purchased in bulk for promotional, educational, or business use. Please contact your local bookseller or the Macmillan Corporate and Premium Sales Department at 1-800-221-7945, extension 5442, or by email at MacmillanSpecialMarkets@macmillan.com.

The American Heiress and *The Fortune Hunter* first published in Great Britain by Headline Review, an imprint of Headline Publishing Group, an Hachette UK Company

First Edition: June 2019

10 9 8 7 6 5 4 3 2 1

The American Heiress

For my father Richard Goodwin – my ideal reader

That's my last Duchess painted on the wall

'My Last Duchess', Robert Browning

The American girl has the advantage of her English sister in that she possesses all that the other lacks

Titled Americans, 1890

Part One

LADY FERMOR-HESKETH.

MISS FLORENCE EMILY SHARON, daughter of the late Senator William Sharon, of Nevada.

Born 186—.

Married, in 1880, to

SIR THOMAS GEORGE FERMOR FERMOR-HESKETH, seventh Baronet; born May 9, 1849; is Major of Fourth Battalion, King's Regiment; has been Sheriff of Northamptonshire; and is a Deputy Lieutenant and Justice of the Peace of the County.

Issue:

Thomas, born November 17, 1881.

Frederick, born 1883.

Seats: Rufford Hall, Omskirk, and Easton Neston, Towcester.

Creation of title, 1761.

The family has been settled in Lancashire for seven hundred years.

> *Titled Americans, A List of American Ladies Who Have Married Foreigners of Rank*, 1890

CHAPTER 1

The Hummingbird Man

Newport, Rhode Island, August 1893

THE VISITING HOUR WAS ALMOST OVER, SO the hummingbird man encountered only the occasional carriage as he pushed his cart along the narrow strip of road between the mansions of Newport and the Atlantic Ocean. The ladies of Newport had left their cards early that afternoon, some to prepare for the last and most important ball of the season, others so they could at least appear to do so. The usual clatter and bustle of Bellevue Avenue had faded away as the Four Hundred rested in anticipation of the evening ahead, leaving behind only the steady beat of the waves breaking on the rocks below. The light was beginning to go, but the heat of the day still shimmered from the white limestone façades of the great houses that clustered along the cliffs like a collection of wedding cakes, each one vying with its neighbour to be the most gorgeous confection. But the hummingbird man, who wore a dusty tailcoat and a battered grey bowler in some shabby approximation of evening dress, did not stop to admire the verandah at the Breakers, or the turrets of Beaulieu, or the Rhinelander fountains that could be glimpsed through the yew hedges and gilded gates. He continued along the road, whistling and clicking to his charges in their black shrouded cages, so that they should hear a familiar noise on their last journey. His destination was the French chateau just before the point, the largest and most elaborate creation on a street of superlatives, Sans Souci, the summer cottage of the Cash family. The Union flag was flying from one tower, the Cash family emblem from the other.

He stopped at the gatehouse and the porter pointed him to the stable entrance half a mile away. As he walked to the other side of the grounds, orange lights were beginning to puncture the twilight; footmen were walking through the house and the grounds lighting Chinese lanterns in amber silk shades. Just as he turned past the terrace, he was dazzled by a low shaft of light from the dying sun refracted by the long windows of the ballroom.

In the Hall of Mirrors, which visitors who had been to Versailles pronounced even more spectacular than the original, Mrs Cash, who had sent out eight hundred invitations for the ball that night, was looking at herself reflected into infinity. She tapped her foot, waiting impatiently for the sun to disappear so that she could see the full effect of her costume. Mr Rhinehart stood by, sweat dripping from his brow, perhaps more sweat than the heat warranted.

'So I just press this rubber valve and the whole thing will illuminate?'

'Yes indeed, Mrs Cash, you just grasp the bulb firmly and all the lights will sparkle with a truly celestial effect. If I could just remind you that the moment must be short-lived. The batteries are cumbersome and I have only put as many on the gown as is compatible with fluid movement.'

'How long have I got, Mr Rhinehart?'

'Very hard to say, but probably no more than five minutes. Any longer and I cannot guarantee your safety.'

But Mrs Cash was not listening. Limits were of no interest to her. The pink evening glow was fading into darkness. It was time. She gripped the rubber bulb with her left hand and heard a slight crackle as light tripped through the one hundred and twenty light bulbs on her dress and the fifty in her diadem. It was as if a firework had been set off in the mirrored ballroom.

As she turned round slowly she was reminded of the yachts in Newport harbour illuminated for the recent visit of the German Emperor. The back view was quite as splendid as the front; the train that fell from her shoulders looked like a swathe of the night sky. She gave a glittering nod of satisfaction and released the bulb. The room went dark until a footman came forward to light the chandeliers.

'It is exactly the effect I had hoped for. You may send in your account.'

The electrician wiped his brow with a handkerchief that was less than clean, jerked his head in an approximation of a bow and turned to leave.

'Mr Rhinehart!' The man froze on the glossy parquet. 'I trust you have been as discreet as I instructed.' It was not a question.

'Oh yes, Mrs Cash. I did it all myself, that's why I couldn't deliver it till today. Worked on it every evening in the workshop when all the apprentices had gone home.'

'Good.' A dismissal. Mrs Cash turned and walked to the other end of the Hall of Mirrors where two footmen waited to open the door. Mr Rhinehart walked down the marble staircase, his hand leaving a damp smear on the cold balustrade.

In the Blue Room, Cora Cash was trying to concentrate on her book. Cora found most novels hard to sympathise with – all those plain governesses – but this one had much to recommend it. The heroine was 'handsome, clever and rich', rather like Cora herself. Cora knew she was handsome – wasn't she always referred to in the papers as 'the divine Miss Cash'? She was clever – she could speak three languages and could handle calculus. And as to rich, well, she was undoubtedly that. Emma Woodhouse was not rich in the way that she, Cora Cash, was rich. Emma Woodhouse did not lie on a *lit à la polonaise* once owned by Madame du Barry in a room which was, but for the lingering smell of paint, an exact replica of Marie Antoinette's bedchamber at le petit Trianon. Emma Woodhouse went to dances at the Assembly Rooms, not fancy dress spectaculars in specially built ballrooms. But Emma Woodhouse was motherless which meant, thought Cora, that she was handsome, clever, rich and free. That could not be said of Cora, who at that moment was holding the book straight out in front of her because there was a steel rod strapped to her spine. Cora's arms ached and she longed to lie down on Madame du Barry's bed but her mother believed that spending two hours a day strapped to the spine improver would give Cora the posture and carriage of a princess, albeit an American one, and for now at least Cora had no choice but to read her book in extreme discomfort.

At this moment her mother, Cora knew, would be checking the placement for the dinner she was holding before the ball, tweaking it so that her forty odd guests knew exactly how brightly they sparkled in Mrs Cash's social firmament. To be invited to Mrs Cash's fancy dress ball was an honour, to be invited to the dinner beforehand a privilege, but to be seated within touching distance of Mrs Cash herself was a true mark of distinction, and was not to be bestowed lightly. Mrs Cash liked to sit opposite her husband at dinner ever since she had discovered that the Prince and Princess of Wales always faced each other across the width not the length of the table. Cora knew that she would be placed at one end sandwiched between two suitable bachelors with whom she would be expected to flirt just enough to confirm her reputation as the belle of the season but not so much that she compromised her mother's stratagems for her future. Mrs Cash was throwing this ball to display Cora like a costly gem to be admired but not touched. This diamond was destined for a coronet, at least.

Directly after the ball the Cashes were leaving for Europe on their yacht the SS *Aspen*. Mrs Cash had done nothing so vulgar as to suggest that they were going there to find Cora a title; she did not, like some other ladies in Newport, subscribe to *Titled Americans*, a quarterly periodical which gave details of blue-blooded but impecunious young men from Europe who were looking for a rich American bride, but Cora knew that her mother's ambitions were limitless.

Cora put the novel down and shifted uncomfortably in the spine harness. Surely it was time for Bertha to come and unbuckle her. The strap across her forehead was digging in; she would look ridiculous at the ball tonight with a great red welt on her brow. She wouldn't mind in the least discomfiting her mother but she had her own reasons for wanting to look her best. Tonight was her last chance with Teddy before she had to leave for Europe. Yesterday at the picnic they had come so close, she was sure that

Teddy had been about to kiss her, but her mother had found them before anything could happen. Cora smiled a little at the thought of her mother sweating as she pedalled to catch up with them. Mrs Cash had dismissed bicycles as hoydenish, until she realised that her daughter could use them to evade her, and then she had learnt to ride one in an afternoon. She might be the richest girl in America but surely she was also the most persecuted. Tonight was her coming-out party and here she was strapped into this instrument of torture. It was time she was released. In one stiff movement she rose and rang the bell.

Bertha was in the kitchen with the hummingbird man. He came from the same part of South Carolina as she did, and every year when he came up to supply the Newport hostesses with their favourite party trick, he would bring Bertha a message from what was left of her family. She had not seen any of them since the day ten years ago when she had been picked by the Reverend to go North, but sometimes when she walked through the kitchens on baking day and smelt the hot sweet smell, she thought she saw the swish of her mother's blue and white striped skirt. These days she could barely remember her mother's face but that smell would knock her back into the old cabin so fast it would bring tears to her eyes. She had sent letters at first with the presents and the money, figuring that her mother would find someone to read them to her, but now she had stopped, she didn't want some stranger reading aloud to her momma the secrets of her heart.

'Your momma said to say that your Uncle Ezra passed,' said the hummingbird man, removing his bowler hat, perhaps as a sign of respect, perhaps to impress Bertha with the noble planes of his skull. Bertha bowed her head; she had a dim memory of being carried into church on Uncle Ezra's shoulders and wondering if it was safe to hold on to the hair coming out of his ears.

'It was a fine burial, even Mrs Calhoun came to pay her respects.'

'And Momma, how's she doing? Is she wearing the shawl I sent her? Tell her that the mistress brought it back from Europe.'

'I'll be sure to let her know . . .' The hummingbird man paused and looked down at the shrouded cage on the floor where the hummingbirds slept. Bertha knew there was something wrong; the man had something to say that he didn't quite have the words for. She should help him, ask him the question that would let him reveal what was troubling him, but a strange reluctance came over her. She wanted her mother to stay in her blue and white striped dress, warm and sweet and whole.

There was a crash from the kitchen behind and the hummingbirds stirred, their short futile flights disturbing the air like sighs.

'What colour are they this time?' asked Bertha, welcoming the distraction.

'I was told to make 'em all gold. Wasn't easy. Hummingbirds don't like to be painted; some of 'em just give up, just lay themselves down and don't fly no more.'

Bertha knelt down and lifted up the cloth. She could see flickers of brightness moving in the darkness. When all the guests sat down for supper at midnight they would be released into the winter garden like a shower of gold. They would be the talking point of the room for maybe a whole ten minutes; the young men would try and catch them as favours for the girls they were flirting with. The other hostesses would think a touch grimly that Nancy Cash would stop at nothing to impress, and in the morning the maids would sweep the tiny golden bodies into a surrendered heap.

'Did Momma give you any message for me, Samuel? Is there something wrong?' Bertha asked quietly.

The hummingbird man was speaking to his birds, making small popping noises with his mouth. He clucked his tongue and looked at Bertha sadly.

'She told me to tell you that everything was fine, but she ain't fine, Bertha. She's so skinny now she looks like she might blow away in the hurricane season. She's wasting away, I don't give her another winter. If you want to see her again, you should make it quick.'

Bertha looked down at the birds fizzing like Roman candles in their cage. She put her hands to her hair, which was smooth. Her mother's hair was frizzy – it had constantly to be suppressed under headscarves. She knew that the hummingbird man was expecting emotion from her, tears at least. But Bertha had not cried for years, ten years in fact, since she had come North. What would be the point? After all, there was nothing she could do. Bertha knew how lucky she was, she knew of no other coloured girls who had become lady's maids. From the moment she had been made Miss Cora's maid, she had tried to speak, dress and behave like her as far as she was able. She remembered her mother's calloused hands and found she could not look at the hummingbird man.

The Blue Room bell rang again. One of the maids came out of the kitchen and shouted, 'That's the second time Miss Cora's bell's gone, you had better get up there, Bertha.'

Bertha jumped. 'I have to go now. I'll come and find you later, once the ball gets going. Don't go until I see you.' She tried to conceal her relief at the interruption with the vehemence of her tone.

'I'll be waiting for you, Bertha,' the hummingbird man said.

The bell jangled again. Bertha walked as fast as she dared up the servants' staircase. Running was forbidden. One of the housemaids had been dismissed for going down the marble staircase two at a time. Disrespectful, Mr Simmons the butler had called it.

She knocked on the Blue Room door and went in.

Cora was almost crying with frustration. 'Where have you been, Bertha? I must have rung three times. Get me out of this infernal thing.'

She was tugging at the leather bands encircling her body. The spine straightener, which had been made to Mrs Cash's special design, had all the buckles at the back and so was impossible to remove without help.

Bertha tried to appease her. 'I'm sorry, Miss Cora, the man with the hummingbirds had news from home, I guess I didn't hear the bell.'

Cora snorted. 'It's hardly an excuse that you were listening to gossip while I was trussed up here like a chicken.'

Bertha said nothing but fumbled at the buckles. She could feel her mistress twitching with impatience. As soon as she was free of the harness, Cora shook herself like a dog trying to get dry, then she spun round and grabbed Bertha by the shoulders. Bertha braced herself for a telling off, but to her surprise Cora smiled.

'I need you to tell me how to kiss a man. I know you know how, I saw you with the Vandemeyers' groom after their ball.' Cora's eyes were glittering with urgency. Bertha drew back from her mistress.

'I don't think kissing is something you can tell,' she said slowly, playing for time. Was Miss Cora going to let Mrs Cash know about her and Amos?

'Show me then. I have to get this right,' Cora said fiercely and leant towards Bertha. As she did so, a low shaft of light from the setting sun hit her conker-coloured hair, setting it ablaze.

Bertha tried not to shrink away. 'You really want me to kiss you the way I would a man?' Surely Miss Cora was not serious.

'Yes, yes, yes.' Cora tossed her head. The red mark from the harness was still visible on her forehead.

'But Miss Cora, it ain't natural two women kissing. If anyone were to see us I'd lose my place.'

'Oh, don't be so squeamish, Bertha. What if I were to give you fifty dollars?' Cora smiled enticingly as if offering a child a sweet.

Bertha considered this. Fifty dollars was two months' salary. But kissing another woman was still not right.

'I don't think you should be asking me this, Miss Cora, it just ain't fitting.' Bertha tried to sound as much like the Madam as she could; she knew that Mrs Cash was the only person in the world that Cora was frightened of. But Cora was not to be put off.

'Do you imagine that I actually want to kiss *you*? But I must practise. There is someone I need to kiss tonight and I have to do it right.' Cora shook with determination.

'Well . . .' Still Bertha hesitated.

'Seventy-five dollars.' Cora was wheedling now; Bertha knew she wouldn't be able to hold out for very long when her mistress wanted something that badly. Cora would just persist until she got her own way. Only Mrs Cash could say no to her daughter. Bertha decided to make the best of the situation.

'All right, Miss Cora, I will show you how to kiss a man, but I would like the seventy-five dollars now if you don't mind.'

Bertha knew quite well that Mrs Cash did not give Cora an allowance, so she had every reason to ask to see the money. Miss Cora was a great one for making promises she couldn't keep. But to Bertha's surprise, Cora produced a purse from under her pillow and counted out the dollars.

'Can you set aside your scruples now?' she said, holding out the bills.

The maid hesitated for a second and then took the money and tucked it away in her bodice. Seventy-five dollars should stop the hummingbird man looking at her like that. Taking a deep breath, she took Cora's flushed cheeks gingerly in her hands and bent her head towards her mistress. She pressed her lips against hers with a modest pressure and drew back as quickly as she could.

Cora broke away impatiently. 'No, I want you to do it properly. I saw you with that man. You looked as if, well,' she paused, trying to find the right phrase, 'as if you were eating each other.'

This time she put her hands on the maid's shoulders and pulled Bertha's face towards hers and pushed her lips to Bertha's, pressing as hard as she could.

Reluctantly Bertha pushed her mistress's lips open with her tongue and ran it lightly around the other woman's mouth. She felt her go stiff for a moment with shock and then Cora began to kiss her back, pushing her tongue between her teeth.

Bertha was the first to pull away. It was not unpleasant kissing Cora, it was certainly the most sweet-tasting kiss she had ever had. Better than Amos, who stank of chewing tobacco.

'You taste quite . . . piquant,' said Cora, wiping her mouth with a lace handkerchief. 'Is that all you have to do? You haven't left anything out? I have to do this correctly.' She looked earnestly at Bertha.

Not for the first time, Bertha wondered how anyone could be as educated as Cora and yet so ignorant. It was all Mrs Cash's fault of course. She had raised Cora like a beautiful doll. She wouldn't mind having Miss Cora's money or her face, but she sure as hell wouldn't want to have Miss Cora's mother.

'If it's just kissing you're having in mind, Miss Cora, then I reckon that's all you will require,' Bertha said firmly.

'Aren't you going to ask me who it is?' Cora said.

'Begging your pardon, Miss Cora, but I don't want to know. If the Madam was to find out what you're about . . .'

'She won't, or rather, she will but by the time she does it will be too late. Everything will be different after tonight.' She looked at the maid sideways as if challenging Bertha to ask her more. But Bertha was not to be drawn. So long as she didn't ask questions, she couldn't be made to answer them. She made her face go slack.

Cora, however, had lost interest in her. She was looking at herself in the long gilt cheval glass. Once they had kissed, she was sure that everything else would fall into place. They would announce their engagement and she would be a married woman by Christmas.

'You'd better get my costume ready, Bertha. Mother will be here in a minute, checking that I have followed her instructions *à la lettre*. I can't believe I have to wear something so perfectly hideous. Still, Martha Van Der Leyden told me that her mother is making her dress like a Puritan maid so I suppose it could be worse.'

Cora's dress had been copied from a Velázquez painting of a

Spanish infanta that Mrs Cash had bought because she had heard Mrs Astor admire it.

As Bertha took the elaborate hooped skirt from the closet, she wondered if the Madam had chosen her daughter's costume as much for the way it restricted the wearer's movement as for any artistic considerations. No gentleman would be able to get within three feet of Miss Cora. The kissing lesson would have been in vain.

She helped Cora out of her tea gown and into the farthingale. Cora had to step into it and Bertha had to fasten the harness like shutting a gate. The silk brocade of the skirt and bodice had been specially woven in Lyons; the fabric was heavy and dense. Cora swayed slightly as the weight of it settled on the frame. It would only take the slightest pressure to make her lose her balance entirely. The dress was three feet wide so Cora would have to go through all doorways sideways. Waltzing in such a dress would be impossible.

Bertha knelt and helped Cora into the brocade shoes with Louis heels and upturned toes. Cora began to wobble.

'I can't wear these, Bertha, I will fall over. Get the bronze slippers instead.'

'If you're sure, Miss Cora . . .' Bertha said cautiously.

'My mother is expecting eight hundred people tonight,' Cora said. 'I doubt she will have time to inspect my feet. Get the slippers.'

But Cora's words were braver than she felt; both girls knew that the Madam never missed anything.

Mrs Cash was making one last survey of her costume. Her neck and ears were still bare, not through austerity on her part but because she knew that any minute her husband would come in with a 'little something' which would have to be put on and admired. Winthrop had been spending a lot of time in the city lately, which meant that a 'little something' was due. Some of her contemporaries had used their husband's infidelities as a way of purchasing their freedom, but Mrs Cash, having spent the last five years shaking Cash's Finest Flour from her skirts, had no desire to tarnish her hard-won reputation as the most elegant hostess in Newport and Fifth Avenue by something as shabby as divorce. So long as Winthrop was discreet, she was prepared to pretend that she knew nothing of his passion for the opera.

There had been a time once, though, when she had not been so sanguine. In the early days of their marriage she could not bear to let him out of her sight, for fear that he would bestow that same confiding smile on someone else. In those days she would have thought jewels no substitute for Winthrop's unclouded gaze. But now she had her daughter, her houses and she was *the* Mrs Cash. She hoped that Winthrop would bring her diamonds this time. They would go well with her costume.

There was a tap at the door and Winthrop Rutherford II came in wearing the satin breeches, brocade waistcoat and powdered wig of Louis XV; the father might have started life as a stable boy but the son was a convincing Bourbon king. Mrs Cash thought with satisfaction that he looked quite distinguished in his costume, not many men could carry off silk stockings; they would be a handsome couple.

Her husband cleared his throat a little nervously. 'You look quite magnificent tonight, my dear, no one would think this was the last ball of the season. May I be permitted to add a little something to perfection?'

Mrs Cash moved her head forward as if readying herself for the axe. Winthrop pulled the diamond collar from his pocket and fastened it round her neck.

'You anticipate me, as always. It is indeed a necklace,' he said.

'Thank you, Winthrop. Always such taste. I shall wear the earrings you gave me last summer; I think they will make a perfect match.' She reached without a moment's hesitation for one of the morocco leather boxes on the dressing table, leaving Winthrop to wonder, not for the first time, if his wife could read his mind.

The opening bars of the Radetsky March floated up from the terrace. Mrs Cash stood and took her husband's proffered arm.

'You know, Winthrop, I would like this evening to be remembered.'

Cash knew better than to ask what she wanted the evening to be remembered for. She was only interested in one thing: perfection.

CHAPTER 2

A Spirit of Electricity

HERE WAS A MOMENT AS THE VAN DER LEYDEN family stood at the top of Sans Souci's famous double staircase, waiting to be announced, when Teddy Van Der Leyden thought his mother might have regretted her choice of costume. To be wearing plain dimity and fustian in a room full of satin, velvet and diamonds took an effort of will. But Mrs Van Der Leyden had wished to make a point and it was a point worthy of sacrifice. The family's sober dress was a silent reminder to the assembled guests and particularly their hosts that the Van Der Leydens could trace their lineage all the way back to the *Mayflower*. Their lineage did not peter out in a floury dead end. The sombre black and white was a sign that even here in Newport, some things could not be bought.

Teddy Van Der Leyden knew his mother's purpose and was amused by it. He was quite happy to wear a starched white neckband and black cloak, although he would have preferred to be one of the founding fathers, Jefferson perhaps. He understood her need to distinguish herself from all this unvariegated opulence. Every corner of the mirrored ballroom glittered, each jewel reflected into infinity.

He had been coming to the resort every summer for as long as he could remember and had been happy enough, but this year was different. Now that he had decided to go to Paris, he felt impatient with the observances of the Newport day. Every hour was accounted for – tennis at the club in the morning, carriage drives in the afternoon, and every night there were balls that started at midnight and did not end till dawn. Day after day he met the same hundred or so people. Only the costumes changed.

There was Eli Montagu and his wife dressed as Christopher Columbus and what Teddy took to be Madame de Pompadour. He had already met them that morning at the Casino, and yesterday on the bicycle excursion which had ended so precipitously. He would meet them again tomorrow at the breakfast given at the Belmonts and then at the Schooner picnic. He didn't wince as his mother did when he heard Eli's vowels or shudder at the brassy tint of Mrs Montagu's hair; he rather liked the fact that when she smiled she showed her teeth. But he didn't want to talk to them nor did he want to make a point by not talking to them. He looked around for Cora. She was the only person he wanted to see. She was always surprising. He remembered the way she had blown the hair out of her eyes when she was cycling yesterday, the way the offending tendril had fluttered and then rested on her cheek.

He moved out of the receiving line and over to one of the champagne fountains. A footman in full Bourbon livery offered him a glass. He drank it quickly, watching the arrivals flooding in through the great double doors. Most of the guests had chosen to come as *ancien régime* French aristocrats – he had seen three Marie Antoinettes and innumerable Louis already. Perhaps it was a compliment to the Versailles-inspired surroundings; perhaps it was the only period of history that matched the opulence of the present. Now he felt glad of his Puritan clothes. There was something uneasy about railway barons and steel magnates dressing up in the silk hose and embroidered tailcoats of another gilded age.

And then he saw Cora and his discontents were forgotten. Her dress was ridiculous; her skirts stuck out so far on either side of her that she would clear a path through the ballroom like an oar through water when she danced, but even in the absurd costume she was radiant. Her red-brown hair hung in ringlets against her white neck and shoulders. He thought of the small beauty spot he had noticed yesterday at the hollow of her throat.

She was standing just below her parents who were installed on a velvet-draped dais. She was surrounded by young men and Teddy realised that he must ask Cora for a dance or he would never get a chance to talk to her. He walked towards her, passing a Cardinal Richelieu and a Marquise de Montespan. He waited for an opening among the young men and then he caught her eye. She squinted a little to make sure it was really him and then went back to her dance card, but Teddy knew she was waiting for him to approach. He walked round the scaffolding of her skirt and stood behind her.

'Am I too late?' he asked her softly.

She turned her head in his direction and smiled.

'Much too late for a dance. They all went ages ago. But I guess I might need to catch my breath after a while. Maybe around here?' She pointed to a waltz on her dance card with her little ivory pencil. 'We could meet on the terrace.' Her eyes flickered towards where her mother was standing in majesty. Teddy understood the look – Cora did not want her mother to see them together.

Did Mrs Cash think he was a fortune-hunter then? He shuddered to think how horrified *his* mother would be if she imagined that he was making advances to Cora Cash. Mrs Van Der Leyden might attend a ball given by Mrs Cash but that did not mean she saw Cora as a suitable wife for her son, no matter how rich she was. They had never spoken about it but Teddy sensed that his mother thought that his desire to go to Europe and paint was the lesser of two evils.

In the winter garden, Simmons the butler was inspecting the supper tables. Down the length of each one ran a stream contained in a silver channel, agitated by tiny pumps so that it sparkled with an effervescent current. At the bottom of the stream was pure white sand and Bertha was pushing stones into the sand to look like submerged boulders. Each of these boulders was in fact an uncut gem – diamonds, rubies, emeralds and topazes. Beside each place setting was a miniature silver shovel so that the guests could 'prospect' for these treasures. Bertha had been told by the butler to make sure that the 'boulders' were distributed evenly. Despite the enormous wealth of many of the guests, there would be fierce competition among the 'prospectors' to amass the most rocks. There had been an unseemly scramble for the Fabergé bonbons at the Astor ball the week before.

Bertha pushed sand artfully around a 'boulder' so that a crystalline spar just punctured the surface. Simmons had told her not to make them too easy to find. He was meant to do this task himself but Bertha knew he felt it beneath him. He hadn't told her what the rocks were but Bertha well understood their value. She would wait until they got to the end of the last table before taking one. Supper was to start at midnight when Mrs Cash would go on to the terrace to light up her costume and lead her guests into the winter garden like a star. At the same time the humming-birds would be released to create the illusion that the guests were entering the tropics. Bertha reckoned that Simmons would be so involved in ministering to this procession that he would hardly notice a missing gem.

Teddy waited for Cora on the terrace. It was a hot, still night. He could hear a cicada somewhere near his feet. An orange moon lit up the pale stone surrounding him. The slabs of marble covering the terrace were not smooth but had been worn into grooves by generations of feet. The entire terrace must have been brought over from some Tuscan villa, reflected Teddy, so that the Nine Muses who stood on the balustrade would not look their age. He could only admire Mrs Cash's thoroughness. Nothing, in her world, was left to chance. And yet here was Cora, screwing up her eyes to find him on the terrace, unchaperoned and uncaring. He knew from the way that Mrs Cash had pedalled after them yesterday when they had pulled ahead of the cycling party, her marble complexion turning quite pink, that she would not approve of her daughter being here. He knew, too, that he should not be alone with Cora, she was not part of the future he had decided on, yet here he was.

As she walked towards him through the apricot-hued pools of light cast by the Chinese silk lanterns hanging in the trees, he could see a red filigree dappling her collarbone and throat. She stopped before him, the panniers of her skirt making it impossible for her to stand anywhere but straight in front of him. He could see a faint prickling of flesh on her forearms that made the soft golden hairs stand up like fur. There was, he knew, a tiny scar on the underside of her wrist. He would have liked to take her hand to reassure himself it was still there.

'It is the most beautiful night,' he said. 'I was worried this morning that there would be a storm.'

Cora laughed. 'As if my mother would allow bad weather on the night of her party. Only inferior hostesses get rained off.'

'She has a remarkable eye for detail; she has set the standard very high in Newport.' Teddy spoke lightly. They both knew that the old guard like Teddy's mother thought that the parties thrown by incomers like the Cashes were over the top and vulgar.

Cora looked directly at him, her eyes scanning his face. 'Tell me something, Teddy. Yesterday, if Mother hadn't caught up with us, what would you have done?'

'Continued our charming conversation about your chances of winning the archery and then cycled home to dress for dinner.' His tone was deliberately light, he didn't want to think about the colour in Cora's cheeks yesterday or the gold flecks in the iris of her right eye.

But Cora was not to be deflected.

'I think that you are being . . .' she frowned, searching for the right word, 'disingenuous. I think that you were going to do this.' She put her hands on his shoulders and leant towards him, swaying unsteadily against the counterweight of the dress. He felt the warm dry touch of her lips on his. He knew that he should stop this now, draw back and pretend that nothing had happened and yet he wanted to kiss her so much. He felt her toppling in her ridiculous costume and he put his hands on her waist to steady her, and then he found he was kissing her back.

When, at last, they drew back from each other, neither smiled. Cora said, 'I was right then.'

'You were right about the intention. Of course I want to kiss you, what man wouldn't? There are fifty men out there who would give anything to take my place, but I had promised myself not to.' Teddy smiled at his good intentions.

'But why, if that was what you wanted?' She sounded suddenly much younger than eighteen.

Teddy looked away from her at the horizon where he could see the moonlight playing on the sea. 'Because I am afraid.'

'Of me?' Cora sounded pleased.

He turned to face her. 'If I fall in love with you, it would change everything, all my plans.' His voice trailed away as he saw that the flush had spread down across her chest; down, he was sure, beneath the infanta's modest neckline. He picked up her hand and turned it over, pressing the scar to his lips.

Cora trembled and the shudder ran through the construction of her dress.

'Do you know I am going away to Europe?' she said in a strained voice.

'The whole of America knows you are going to Europe, to find a suitable consort for the Cash millions.' Teddy tried to bat away her emotion but Cora did not respond in kind. She leant towards him, her eyes dark and opaque. When she spoke, her voice was almost a whisper.

'I don't want to go, you know. I would like to stay here – with you.'

Teddy dropped her hand and felt the heat of Cora's stare. He wanted to believe her, even though this would make his choice so much harder. She kissed him again, more fiercely this time. It was hard to resist the foxy smell of her hair and the downy smoothness of her cheeks. He could hardly feel her body through the architecture of her costume but he could feel the pulse beating in her neck. Who was he to resist Cora Cash, the girl that every woman in Newport envied and every man desired? He kissed her harder, grazing her lip with his teeth. He wanted to pull the combs and jewels out of her hair and take her out of her prison of a costume. He could hear her breathing quicken.

The music stopped. Then came the crash of the supper gong rippling out into the still night air.

For the first time Cora looked nervous. 'Mother will notice I have gone.' She made a gesture as if to go back inside, but then she turned back and spoke to him in a torrent of urgency. 'We could go now to the city and get married. Then she can't touch me. I have my own money, Grandfather left a trust for me which is mine when I am twenty-five or when I marry. And I'm sure Father would give us something. I don't want to go away.' She was pleading now.

Teddy saw that it had not occurred to her that he might refuse to accept her proposal.

'You are the one who is being disingenuous now. Do you really think that I can elope with you? Not only would it break your mother's heart, it would surely break my mother's too. The Van Der Leydens are not as rich as the Cashes but they are honourable. People would say I was a fortune-hunter.' He tried to take his hands from her waist but she held them there.

'But they would say that about anyone. It's not my fault I'm richer than everyone else. Please, Teddy, don't be all ... scrupulous about this. Why can't we just be happy? You like kissing me, don't you? Didn't I get it right?' She reached up to stroke his cheek. And then a thought hit her, amazing her with its audacity. 'There isn't someone else, is there? Someone you like more than me?'

'Not someone, something. I want to be a painter. I'm going to Paris to study. I think I have a talent but I have to be sure.' Even as he said it, Teddy realised how weak he sounded against Cora's passionate intensity.

'But why can't you paint here? Or if you have to go to Paris, I could come with you.' She made it all sound so easy.

'No, Cora,' he said almost roughly, afraid she might persuade him. 'I don't want to be that kind of painter, a Newport character who sails in the morning and paints in the afternoon. I don't want to paint pictures of ladies and their lapdogs. I want to do something serious and I can't do that here and I can't do that with a wife.'

He thought for a moment that she would cry. She was waving her hands in front of her face as if trying to push away his words, swaying clumsily in her galleon of a dress.

'Honestly, there is no one I would rather marry than you, Cora, even if you are too rich for me. But I can't now; there is something I want more. And what I need can't be bought.'

She looked back at him crossly. He saw with relief tinged with regret that she was not so much heartbroken as thwarted. He said firmly, 'Admit it, Cora, you don't really want to marry me as much as you want to get away from your mother. A sentiment

I can fully appreciate, but if you go to Europe you will no doubt find yourself a princeling and then you can send her back to America.'

Cora gave him an angry little shove. 'And what, give her the satisfaction of being the matchmaker? The mother who married her daughter to the most eligible bachelor in Europe? She pretends she is above such things but I know she thinks of nothing else. Ever since I was born my mother has chosen everything for me, my clothes, my food, the books I can read, the friends I can have. She has thought of everything except me.' She shook her head sharply as if trying to shake her mother out of her life. 'Oh Teddy, won't you change your mind? I can help you; it wouldn't be so very terrible, would it? It's only money. We don't have to have it. I don't mind living in a garret.'

Perhaps, he thought, if she really cared for him . . . but he knew that what he principally represented to her was escape. He would like to paint her, though, angry and direct – the spirit of the New World dressed in the trappings of the Old. He couldn't resist taking her face in his hands and kissing her one last time.

But just as he felt his resolve weaken, as he felt Cora's shudder, the Spirit of Electricity exploded into the darkness and they were illuminated. Mrs Cash stood like a shining general at the head of her legion of guests.

There was a ripple in the air as a sigh of surprise was expelled across the terrace.

The radiant bulbs cast harsh shadows across the contours of Mrs Cash's face. 'Cora, what are you doing?' Her voice was soft but penetrating.

'Kissing Teddy, Mother,' her daughter replied. 'Surely with all that candle power, you can see that?'

The Spirit of Electricity brushed her daughter's insolence aside. She turned her glittering head to Teddy.

'Mr Van Der Leyden, for all your family's pride in your lineage, you appear to have no more morals than a stable hand. How dare you take advantage of my daughter?'

But it was Cora who answered. 'Oh, he wasn't taking advantage of me, Mother. I kissed him. But then my grandfather *was* a stable hand so you wouldn't expect any better, would you?'

Mrs Cash stood in shining silence, the echo of Cora's defiance ringing in the air around her. And then, just as Mrs Cash was about to deliver her counter blow, a tongue of flame snaked round the diamond star in her hair, turning her headdress into a fiery halo. Mrs Cash was all at once ablaze, her expression as fierce as the flames that were about to engulf her.

For a moment no one moved. It was as if the guests had all gathered together to watch a firework display, and indeed the sparks springing from Mrs Cash's head shone prettily against the night sky. And then the flames began to lick her face and Mrs Cash screamed – the high keening noise of an animal in pain. Teddy rushed towards her, throwing his cloak over the flaming head, and pushed her to the ground, pummelling her body with his hands. The stench of burnt hair and flesh was overwhelming, a gruesome echo of that hint of feral musk he had smelt on Cora moments before. But Teddy was hardly aware of this; later, all he remembered was the band striking the opening bars of the 'Blue Danube' as Cora knelt beside him and together they turned her mother over to face the stars above. The left side of her face was a mess of charred and blistered flesh.

Teddy heard Cora whisper, 'Is she dead?'

Teddy said nothing but pointed to Mrs Cash's right eye, her

good eye. It was bright with moisture and they watched as a tear made its way down the smooth stretch of her undamaged cheek.

In the conservatory the hummingbird man took the cloth from his cage. The gong had sounded, that was his signal. Carefully he opened the door and then stood aside as his birds scattered like sequins over the dark velvet of the night air.

A minute later Bertha found him standing in front of the empty cage.

'Samuel, I have something I want you to take to my mother. This should take care of her while I am in Europe.' She held out a little purse with the seventy-five dollars. She had decided to keep the 'boulder', it was not the sort of thing her mother would be able to sell easily.

The hummingbird man said, 'There was nobody to see them fly out. They looked so fine too.'

Bertha stood there with her hand still outstretched. Slowly, Samuel turned to face her and without haste he took the purse. He said nothing, but then he did not need to. Bertha filled the silence.

'If I could leave now I would, but we sail at the end of the week. This is a good position. Mrs Cash, she's looked after me.' Bertha's voice rose, as if asking a question.

The hummingbird man's stare did not waver. 'Goodbye, Bertha. I don't reckon I'll be coming up here again.' He picked up his cage and walked into the darkness.

CHAPTER 3

The Hunt

Dorset, England, January 1894

'BE CAREFUL WITH THAT NEEDLE, BERTHA. I DON'T want to be blooded before the hunt has even begun.'

'I'm sorry, Miss Cora, but this wash leather is tough to work and you keep moving so. If you don't want to get stuck, I reckon you'll have to keep still.'

Cora tried to stand motionless in front of the oval cheval glass as her maid stitched the chamois leather bodice together so that it was perfectly moulded to the contours of her body. Mrs Wyndham had insisted that the only riding habits worth having were from Busvine, 'He shows the form to perfection, my dear, almost indecently so. There's something quite naked about his tailoring. With a figure like yours, it would be a crime to go anywhere else.' Cora remembered the gleam in Mrs Wyndham's eyes as she said this and the way the widow's bejewelled hands had speculatively spanned her waist. 'Nineteen inches, I would say. Very nice indeed. Made for a Busvine.'

In order to ensure that the habit had the requisite smooth line, Cora could not wear her usual corset and stays. She wore a specially cut undergarment of chamois leather which she had to be sewn into so that no hooks or bumps would disfigure the unforgiving tailoring. Cora almost thanked her mother for the hours spent in the spine straightener when she saw how fine and upright she looked in her habit. Her chestnut hair had been pulled back into a high chignon, exposing the tender nape of her neck. As she adjusted the brim of her hat so that it tilted at just the right angle over her left eye, she felt quite equal to the day ahead. It was only when she pulled the veil down over her face to see whether she should stain her lips red as Mrs Wyndham had advised, 'Just a spot of colour, dear, for snap,' that she thought of her mother and the way the left half of her face was now shrouded in a gauzy white veil to conceal the devastation beneath. Cora knew that her mother would expect her to go in and submit herself for approval, but she hated the sight of her mother's naked, maimed face before she had put on her veil. Of course her mother's accident had not been her fault precisely, but she felt responsible nonetheless.

Cora reached for the cochineal stain and dabbed a little on her lips. That woman was right again, the splash of colour made all the difference. Cora had not liked the way that Mrs Wyndham had looked her over as if pricing horseflesh. She had felt ashamed when her mother had brought her in, 'to introduce us to the right people'. She was almost sure that her mother had paid Mrs Wyndham for her services. Still, Mrs Wyndham had been right about the Busvine. The leather felt warm and soft against her skin. She bent forward, intoxicated with the freedom the habit gave her to touch her toes. As she straightened up, she found the loop on the left side of her habit, which allowed her to lift it up out of the way as she walked. The left side of the skirt was about three feet longer than the right so that her legs would be covered at all times as she rode side-saddle. The trick was to hold the excess fabric across the body with the right hand so that it looked like Grecian drapery. Cora fiddled with the material until she had achieved the desired effect.

Bertha looked on with impatience; she wanted Miss Cora out of here so that she could have some breakfast. Her stomach was rumbling and breakfast for the upper servants was served promptly at seven thirty at Sutton Veney.

There was a knock at the door and one of the housemaids walked in shyly.

'If you please, miss, the master says that your horse is being brought round from the stables.'

'Tell Lord Bridport I will be down directly.' Cora turned to Bertha. 'Can you tell Mother that Lord Bridport insisted that we leave promptly, which means I didn't have time to visit her this morning.'

'She won't be happy, Miss Cora. You know how she likes to make sure you look the part.'

'I know, I know, but I don't have time to stand there while she picks over me. It is bad enough being sneered at by all those English ladies with their red hands and their small blue eyes looking at me as if I was a savage. I don't need Mother telling me how her whole happiness depends on seeing me splendidly married.' Cora picked up her ivory-handled crop and brandished it at her maid. Bertha looked at her wearily.

'I'll pass on the message to the Madam. What do you want to wear tonight?'

'The pink mousseline from Madame Fromont, I think. It will make all those English hags green with envy. Shame I can't wear the bill around my neck. I would like to see their faces when they realise that I can spend more on one dress than they spend on their clothes in a year. They're all so dowdy, and yet they dare to look down their long dripping noses at me, even though they're all desperate for me to marry one of their namby-pamby sons.' Cora brought the crop down on the bed with a thwack.

She smiled when she saw Lincoln waiting for her in the stable yard, twitching his head impatiently. A sixteen-hand grey stallion, Lincoln was the finest product of her father's stables. Cora was not ready to admit that she might find a British horse to suit her, so she had brought her favourite hunters with her, walking them every day on the deck of the SS *Aspen*, her father's steam yacht. Lincoln's breath condensed in a white cloud in the chill January morning. There had been a frost and the ground was white and hazy with mist. But the sun was beginning to break through and for the first time since she had come to England, miserable and guilty about her mother's accident, Cora felt excited at the thought of the day to come. To ride as hard as she could, with no conversation to make or customs to observe, was an irresistible prospect. She felt as if she had taken off more than her corset. She felt unbound.

The Myddleton considered itself the finest hunt in the southwest. Lord Bridport, the Master, was stingy when it came to his house and children but stinted nothing on his beloved hounds. His mother had been one of the first society ladies to ride to hounds and the Myddleton was now as famous for its 'Dianas' as for the quality of the sport. Mrs Wyndham had looked Cora over in her drawing room in Mayfair and had declared, 'The Myddleton for you, my dear. I think you will keep up.'

At the time Cora had not been quite sure of the older lady's meaning, but now, as she rode up after Lord Bridport, she understood that the competition had already begun. So far her exposure to smart British womanhood had been restricted; Cora and her mother had arrived in London at the end of the season when all the people of fashion had left for the country, or else were lying low so as not to draw attention to the fact that they had no estates to go to. Lord Bridport's wife and daughter were not in Cora's view 'smart' even if they could trace their lineage back to the Conqueror. But here were women whose Busvine habits fitted as closely as her own. Her appearance did not cause the ripple of anticipation that always heralded her arrival anywhere in her native country. Not a single shining head turned in her direction as she followed Lord Bridport into the throng. Cora was not sure how she felt about this, to be anonymous was an unfamiliar sensation.

'Ah Charlotte, may I introduce you to Miss Cash. Miss Cash, my niece by marriage, Lady Beauchamp.'

A blond head turned fractionally in her direction and gave her the faintest of nods.

'And here is my nephew Odo. Miss Cora Cash – Sir Odo Beauchamp.'

Odo Beauchamp put even his wife's elegant habit to shame. His pink coat and white breeches were immaculately tailored. His hair was as blond as his wife's but her chignon was tight, while a suggestion of a curl had been allowed to escape over his collar.

He turned his wide face with its limpid blue eyes and flushed cheeks to Cora. 'How do you do, Miss Cash. Is this your first time riding to hounds? I suspect you have wilder sport in your country.'

His voice was surprisingly high and light for such a big man, but it had an unmistakable edge. Cora replied in her most American drawl.

'Oh, we hunt foxes at home right enough, but we find them pretty tame after the bears and the rattlesnakes.'

Odo Beauchamp lifted an eyebrow. 'You American girls are so spirited, let's hope you feel as plucky after a day with the Myddleton. That's a very large animal you have there, I hope you can remount without help.'

'Where I come from, Sir Odo, a lady would be ashamed of herself if she rode out on a horse she couldn't manage herself.' Cora smiled.

'An Amazon, no less. Charlotte my angel, you must come and admire Miss Cash. She is quite the thing.' Odo waved a gloved hand at his wife. The blond head turned; Cora got the impression of wide-set blue eyes and a certain hardness to the mouth. Her voice was unexpectedly deep for a woman.

'Come, Odo, you mustn't tease Miss Cash. You don't want to spoil her first impressions of the Myddleton. It must be quite unlike anything you are used to, Miss Cash, although I know that American girls like nothing better than to give chase.'

Cora heard the sneer and narrowed her eyes. 'Only when there is something worth pursuing,' she replied.

Further hostilities were halted by the yelping of the hounds picking up the scent.

The huntsman blew his horn and the riders followed Lord Bridport as he cantered up after the hounds. Cora dug her heels into Lincoln's side. He took off at a smooth pace, pushing his way to the front. He cleared the first hedgerow without hesitation, and Lord Bridport gave her an encouraging wave.

The hunting country of Virginia where Cora had learnt to ride was flat and open, but here the landscape was thicketed with fences and coverts. The pace was hard and Cora was soon breathless. But Lincoln was enjoying himself, he took fence after fence without even breaking his stride. He, at least, had no reservations about this unfamiliar terrain. The field began to thin out. Cora found herself alone at the front, until a substantial young man in a pink coat came alongside her.

'Pleasure to watch you taking those fences. Lovely, quite lovely.'

Cora smiled but spurred her horse on. It wasn't altogether clear from the young man's tone whether his pleasure was directed at her or Lincoln and she didn't care to find out. But her admirer kept his horse abreast of hers.

'I've been hunting with the Myddleton since I was a nipper. Best pack in the country.'

Cora nodded in her most dismissive manner. The man in the pink coat was not be rebuffed, though.

'Saw you from the off. There's a girl with spirit, I thought. A girl who could appreciate a sportsman like myself. A girl who would like nothing better than to see what I have to offer.' He caught Lincoln by the bridle and slowed the animals down to a walk. Cora began to protest but he shushed her and, holding her bridle tightly, took off one glove and began to roll back his sleeve. To her astonishment she saw that his hand and arm were covered by a detailed tattoo of the huntsmen, the riders and hounds of the Myddleton. The portly figure of Lord Bridport was unmistakably cantering up the man's forearm. Cora could not help but laugh.

'Fine piece of work, eh? Took three days and a quart of brandy. The work is remarkably detailed. Can't see all of it myself of course, covers my whole back. Take a closer look if you like. Don't be shy.'

'I can appreciate the detail quite well from here, Mr . . .?'

'Cannadine's the name. Won't you at least have a look at the fox? People tell me it is remarkably true to life.'

Mr Cannadine put the reins in his other hand and started to pull off the other glove. Cora could see the red nose of the fox peering out from the man's sleeve.

'I'm sure it is, Mr Cannadine, but perhaps some other time, I don't want to lose the scent.'

Cannadine looked downcast. 'Giving me the brush-off, eh? People say the fox is worthy of Landseer. Don't show it to everyone, of course. But don't often see a gel who can ride like you.' He let go of Lincoln's reins to put his glove back on and Cora took the opportunity to pick them up and pull the horse's head up.

'So nice to have met you, Mr Cannadine.' And she dug her heels into Lincoln's side so that the horse went straight into a canter. Cora heard Mr Cannadine shouting as he set off after her.

The hunt was approaching a spinney. Mr Cannadine veered left after the rest of the pack, so Cora took her chance and turned right. She had no desire to see any more of Mr Cannadine's fox. If she went round the wood from the other side she would lose him.

It was a handsome beech wood, the trees were mostly bare but the lower branches were hung with mistletoe and ivy. A pheasant suddenly shot up in front of Lincoln. He stumbled and slowed. Cora let him walk for a while to check that no harm was done. She steered the horse into the wood itself, thinking she would catch up with the others faster. The air was quiet apart from Lincoln's heavy snorting and the strange rattle of the leaves still clinging to the branches. And then she heard it: a low exclamation, somewhere between pain and pleasure. Was it animal or human? she wondered. Cora rode on a few paces and then she heard it again, louder this time and somehow thrilling. It was coming from a dense piece of undergrowth towards the centre of the wood. She could see green fronds of bracken and the handsome smooth trunk of a great beech tree. Without quite understanding why, Cora turned her horse towards the sound. It was more urgent now, then there was a sharp cry that made her start. It was a sound she recognised even if she had never heard it before. She should not be here, this was a private place. She tugged Lincoln's reins, pulling his head sharply to the right and dug her heels into his flanks, desperate now to get away. The horse responded to her urgency and took off so swiftly that Cora had no time to avoid the low-lying branches coming towards her. The first knocked her hat off and the second struck her on the forehead and she knew no more.

The first thing she saw were the branches arching over her like a ribcage. Stunned by her fall, she sensed every detail sharply but she could not put them together. Bones and the smell of leaves and a hot wind blowing in her ear.

Wind? Cora turned her head. She realised she was lying on the ground. The breath tickling her cheek was from a horse, her horse, she fancied, who was pawing the ground impatiently, and snorting. The sound reminded Cora of something else, another noise she had heard but she could not place it. Her head felt muzzy, why was she lying on the ground? She saw a dark shape lying next to her. A bucket, or a chimney pot – no, it was a hat. Cora tried to raise her head but the effort was too much. She lay back and closed her eyes but at once opened them again. She must not sleep, there was something she had to remember. The horse whinnied. Something about a play, how did she enjoy the play, Mrs Lincoln. Lincoln was the name of the horse, her horse. But why was she lying on the ground? What was the sound that was pushing against her consciousness? She couldn't grasp it, it kept slipping out of reach. Other things were crowding in now – a crown of flames, a face she couldn't see behind a veil, a kiss that was not a kiss, a half-glimpsed fox. And then a voice.

'Can you hear me?'

Was is it a real voice, or just part of the jangle in her head?

'Are you hurt? Can I be of assistance?'

Cora tried to find the voice, and there was something leaning over her – a face, she thought, not the fox man, someone different. His eyes were looking at her, looking for something, she thought suddenly, but then he spoke again.

'Can you hear me? You have fallen from your horse. Can you move your limbs?'

My limbs, thought Cora, in limbo. I am in limbo, always in limbo. She smiled and the man, who she saw now was a young man, smiled back. It was not an easy smile, but a hard-won smile of pure relief.

'Oh, thank God, you are alive. I thought for one minute when I saw you that you were . . . Here, let me help you.' He put his arm under Cora's back and helped her to sit.

'But this,' she said, 'is not my country. I shouldn't be here. I am an American girl.' She didn't know why exactly but for some reason it was very important to say that now. There was something she knew that she did not want to be taken for. The young man nodded his head in acknowledgement.

'No indeed, this is my country. This is my wood, my land. My family have lived here for seven hundred years. But you are most welcome, Miss. . .?'

'Cash. I am Cora Cash. I am very rich. I have a flour fortune, not flower you can smell but flour you make bread with. Bread, you know, is the staff of life. Would you like to kiss me? Most men want to, but I am just too rich.' And then she felt the darkness coming again, and before the young man could answer, she fainted into his arms.

CHAPTER 4

Hot Water

THIS TIME WHEN CORA OPENED HER EYES SHE saw a wooden angel looking at her with vacant eyes. She was in a bed, a bed with a roof and curtains. But she awoke clear- if sore-headed. She was Cora Cash, she had fallen off her horse and now she was where? And wearing what? She gave a little scream of dismay and suddenly there was a flurry of movement and heads male and female bending over her.

'Miss Cash – you are Miss Cash, I think,' said a voice she recognised. It was the man in the wood. Something had happened there. But what? There were things there she could almost feel, sounds she could almost hear, shapes she could almost distinguish but they lay behind a veil she couldn't penetrate. This was irritating, there was something important there, if only she could remember. Like her mother, Cora had no patience for obstacles.

'Miss Cash from America I believe,' said the voice again with a suggestion of meaning that Cora found vaguely troubling. This man with dark hair and clear brown eyes seemed very well-informed, and why was he smiling?

'I found you lying on the ground in Paradise Wood. I carried you back here. I've called the doctor.'

'But how do you know my name?' Cora said.

'Don't you remember our conversation?' The man was teasing her, but why?

'No, I don't remember anything since riding out this morning – well, nothing that makes sense anyway. I remember your face but that's all. How did I fall? Is Lincoln all right?'

'You mean the fine American horse? He is in the stables where his Republican opinions are causing my groom much anguish,' the man said.

'And how long have I been here? What about Mother, does she know where I am? She will be furious. I must go back.' Cora tried to sit up, but the movement made her feel nauseous, she could feel hot bile flooding into her mouth. To vomit in front of this strange Englishman would be unbearable. She bit her lip.

'My dear Miss Cash, I'm afraid you must stay here until the doctor arrives. Head injuries can be treacherous. Perhaps you would like to write to your mother.' The man turned to the woman beside him; Cora guessed that she was some kind of servant.

'Perhaps you could get some writing paper for Miss Cash, Mrs Softley.'

The housekeeper left in a rustle of bombazine.

'You know my name, but I don't know yours.'

The man smiled. 'My friends call me Ivo.'

Cora sensed that he was holding something back. She felt annoyed. Why was nothing in this country straightforward? She felt as if she was being forced to play a game where everybody knew the rules but her. She decided to attack.

'Why do all you Englishmen have names that sound like patent medicines? Ivo and Odo and Hugo. Bromides and bath salts, every one of them.' She waved her hand dismissively.

The man made her a little bow. 'I can only apologise, Miss Cash, on behalf of my compatriots. Men in my family have been called Ivo for many hundreds of years, but perhaps the moment has come to move with the times. Would you like to call me Maltravers? It hasn't been my name for very long, but I suppose I must get used to it, and I don't think it has any medicinal properties.'

Cora looked at him in bewilderment. How many names did the man have?

His voice was not the strangulated roar that she had begun to think was handed out to all upper-class Englishmen at birth. It was very low and he spoke quietly so that the listener had to lean forward to catch every word. Cora realised that this man must be important, not many men could mutter and be completely confident that every word would be listened for and understood. She felt awkward. Did this man know who she was, that she was not just any American girl? She came back at him with as much dignity as she could muster.

'You are laughing at me for daring to question perfectly ridiculous things about your country that you take as quite normal. You do what you do not because it is the best way but because that is the way you have always done it. Why, in the house where I am staying, there are ten housemaids whose job it is to carry hot water up long staircases and endless corridors every morning so that a guest can take a bath in front of the fire. When I asked Lord Bridport why he didn't have bathrooms like we do in the United States, he said they were vulgar. Vulgar! To wash. No wonder all the women here look so grey and dingy. I have seen girls, quite pretty girls, with dirty necks. At least where I come from we keep ourselves clean.' She looked at her host defiantly.

She might be confined to bed in a strange house but she would speak as she found.

Her host did not look offended by her outburst; in fact he was smiling.

'I will have to take your word for that, Miss Cash. You were not at all clean when I found you in the forest and I regret that I have never visited your country. I am afraid you will be equally disappointed with the washing arrangements here. I have no moral objections to bathrooms, quite the contrary, I only object to their cost. But I can assure you that I wash very thoroughly. Perhaps you would care to inspect my neck?' He leant forward and proffered his neck to Cora as if to the scaffold. It was indeed clean and though the dark curls were longer than would have been acceptable in America, Maltravers did not smell, as so many Englishmen seemed to, of wet dog. No, he had another scent entirely. Cora couldn't quite describe it. She felt an urge to push her fingers through his hair. Again she bit her lip.

'Your neck is immaculate. I congratulate you.' Cora tried to hang on to her indignation. She was definitely not going to be charmed.

'But tell me, how many housemaids do you need to bring the hot water for the hip baths? How many steps do they have to climb? How long are the corridors they have to struggle down? Surely piped water would be more economical in the long run, not to mention kinder to the servants?' She tried to sit up so that she could hear his answer clearly and in an instant he was behind her with another pillow.

'Is that better? Excellent.' He paused. 'If we had running water, we wouldn't need so many housemaids and that might upset them mightily, not to mention their families who rely on them to send them money.'

'There are plenty of things for girls to do these days besides carry hot water and lay fires. They could teach or make hats or learn to use typewriting machines.' Cora knew that her mother was always losing her maids to shops and offices. The wages were better and they could have all the admirers they liked.

'Indeed they could, Miss Cash. But I suspect that most of them just want to earn a wage until they get married, and a big house like this is a very good place to find a husband.'

'Yes, I've heard about the marriage market in the servants' hall from Bertha.'

'Bertha is your maid?' The man's tone was amused.

'Yes, she came over with me from the States.'

'And as an American girl, she has no objections to being in service?'

Cora almost laughed. Hadn't she given Bertha three of her old dresses last month? How could Bertha be anything but happy.

She said in her most dignified tone, 'Bertha, I assure you, is very grateful for the opportunity to work for me. I wonder if you can say that about any of your maids?'

Maltravers' reply was lost as the housekeeper came in with a writing desk which she arranged on the bed in front of Cora. She had brought a quantity of thick cream paper. Cora picked up a sheet with a crest at the top and the single word Lulworth underneath. She had been in England long enough to understand that understatement was all. Lulworth was clearly an 'important' house and its owner must have some kind of title. But then why hadn't he told her when he gave his name? The English were infuriating. Everything was designed to put an outsider at a disadvantage. If you had to ask, you didn't belong.

The man walked to the end of the bed and looked down at

her. 'I shall leave you to write to your mother in peace. But before I go, satisfy my curiosity on one point. Why, if you find the English system so distasteful, are you here? I thought you Americans rather liked our quaint customs and antiquated ways, yet you don't seem to find us charming at all.'

Cora looked at him. His tone was light and yet there was an edge to his voice. She was pleased that she had nettled him. He had the advantage, but still she had piqued him.

'Oh, I would have thought that should be obvious. As an American heiress I have come here to buy the one thing I can't get at home, a title. My mother would like a prince of the blood, but I think she would settle for a duke. Does that satisfy your curiosity?'

'Perfectly, Miss Cash. I hope you will invite your mother to spend a few days here at Lulworth. I won't hear of you leaving until the doctor has given you a clean bill of health. And I rather think your mother will like it here, despite our lack of bathrooms. You see, while I may not be a prince, I am the Ninth Duke of Wareham.'

Cora felt the bile rushing into her mouth again. She waved her hands in front of her face.

The Duke was all concern. 'Mrs Softley, I think Miss Cash is feeling unwell.'

Cora managed to contain her nausea until the Duke had left the room.

CHAPTER 5

The Black Pearl

MRS CASH WAS ARRANGING FOLDS OF TULLE around her neck. By candlelight, in the foxed silver of the pier glass, the effects of the accident were almost unnoticeable; only the shiny tautness where the flesh had been burnt showed up in this forgiving light. For anyone sitting on Mrs Cash's right side there would have been no reason to suspect there was anything wrong; it was only when she turned her head that the ravages of the fire were revealed. At least, thought Mrs Cash, her right profile had always been generally the more admired. She had been lucky, the flames had not actually reached her left eye, although the area around it had been singed. The scars as they formed had pulled the skin tight, so that in this half-light the damaged side of Mrs Cash's face was a grotesque facsimile of youthfulness. She half closed her eyes and through the blur she could see the spectre of the girl she had been. She pulled at the hairpiece of curls she wore so that the tendrils covered the misshapen lump of flesh that had been her left ear. As she felt the waxy smoothness of the scarring, she flinched. The doctors had told her that she had been fortunate that her skin had healed so quickly, but she hated touching its smooth deadness, which she minded even more than the shooting pains she still felt. She straightened up and began to dust her face with powder.

There was a knock at the door and the butler came in with a letter on a silver salver.

'This has just arrived for you, ma'am. From Lulworth.'

Mrs Cash had not heard of Lulworth but judging from the little pause the butler made before he pronounced the name, she guessed that it was a place of some significance. She took up the letter and recognised, to her surprise, her daughter's loopy scrawl.

'But this is from Cora. Why is she writing to me? I thought she was hunting?'

The butler bowed his head. Mrs Cash's question was rhetorical, although as the letter was unsealed, every servant in the house could have given her an answer.

To the butler's surprise Mrs Cash did not gasp or reach for the sal volatile when reading her daughter's letter. Indeed, if the butler had been on Mrs Cash's right, he might have seen the beginnings of a smile.

In the servants' hall, Bertha was mending a lace nightgown that Cora had torn because she was too impatient to undo the buttons before pulling it over her head. It had been one of those nights when Cora had come upstairs from dinner noisy and truculent after an evening spent listening docilely to Lord Bridport's views on crop rotation. Bertha hadn't unlaced her fast enough and Cora, snatching the nightgown from her, had pulled it over her head, ripping the two-hundred-year-old Brussels lace that covered the bodice as she did so. Cora hadn't even noticed the tear but Bertha, who looked forward to the day when the nightgown and the lace would be passed on to her, had felt the ripping cloth as a laceration. The lace had been made by nuns, the work so fine and exquisite that it was almost an act of worship. It was taking all her concentration to sew the jagged cobweb edges together seamlessly. She had been so absorbed in joining one filigree flower to its mate, marvelling at the intricacy of the net showing white against her brown fingers, that she had missed the entrance of the groom from Lulworth with the letter for Mrs Cash, but now she caught Cora's name in the conversation between the housekeeper and the cook and she looked up from her sewing.

'Miss Cash was lucky that she didn't break her neck like the poor Duke that was. It was the new Duke that found her. Lucky he was in the woods, otherwise she might have been out there all night,' the housekeeper said.

'I don't think it was luck that put the Duke in that wood. Remember what day it is.' The cook looked at Mrs Lawrence the housekeeper with meaning. The housekeeper gave a gasp of remembrance and bowed her head.

'Is it the anniversary today? I'd almost forgotten. That poor young man and so soon after the old Duke's death too.' She closed her eyes for a moment and when she opened them she saw Bertha looking at her.

'Looks like you'll be going over to Lulworth, Miss Cash.' Bertha started at the name. Mrs Lawrence had told her when she arrived that all the visiting servants were known by the name of their employer, but still it felt strange.

The housekeeper continued, 'Your lady had a fall out hunting and she's been put to bed over at Lulworth. The groom came over with a letter for your young lady's mother. Mr Druitt is up there now waiting for a reply.' At the sight of Bertha's face, the house-keeper softened her tone. 'She'll be all right. If there was anything wrong, the Duke would have come himself.'

The cook chuckled. 'I expect he didn't want to leave Miss Cash's side. There's an awful lot of holes in the roof.'

'The Duke's not married then, Mrs Lawrence?' Bertha felt that the cook's hint had given her licence to ask. But she knew she had to be careful, the line between an innocent question and a liberty was a fine one. Soon after she arrived she had asked Lady Beauchamp's maid what her wages were and had been made to realise her mistake. As Miss Cash's lady's maid she was accorded a certain seniority in the servants' hall – she took precedence over the parlourmaids going into dinner, for instance – but her status did not allow her to ask questions. Mr Druitt had taken her aside and told her that while such things as wages and so forth might be the subject of much talk where she came from, here in England some things were kept private. Bertha had bowed her head and learnt her lesson.

Despite her lecture from the butler, Bertha was enjoying her stay at Sutton Veney. At home she ate at the bottom of the servants' table with the other coloured girls. Here she went into dinner every night on the arm of Sir Odo's valet. The first night she had retreated to her room, but Mrs Lawrence had sent one of the housemaids up to tell her that her presence was required in the servants' hall. Jim the valet had blushed when Mr Druitt had told him to take Miss Cash's maid into dinner. Their conversation was limited as Druitt liked to hold forth, but every time Bertha glanced his way, Jim would be looking at her. He was handsome enough; at least he looked as if he had been raised in the fresh air, unlike so many of the servants whose pasty complexions suggested they had spent all their life underground. Since that first night, Jim had been waiting for her every evening to take her into dinner and she found herself bumping into him on the servants' staircase two or three times a day.

Bertha looked at the two women, waiting for them to rebuff her. But the cook did not draw back at Bertha's question; in fact she looked rather pleased at the opportunity to show off in front of her rival, the housekeeper.

'No, the new Duke's a bachelor. I used to work in the kitchen over at Lulworth before I came here. Slave labour that was. They still cook over an open range in the kitchen there and forty people sitting down for dinner. Things are better here even if Lord Bridport is always asking after yesterday's joint. I was there when Miss Charlotte came to Lulworth. They were always together, Lord Ivo and Miss Charlotte, playin' with their bows and arrows. They used to come down to the kitchen begging for food to take out on their archery expeditions. Shame she had no money, Miss Charlotte would have made a handsome duchess.'

'Some more tea, Mrs James?' interrupted the housekeeper, clearly nettled at this exhibition of superior knowledge of the Duke.

Bertha picked up her work basket and went up the back stairs to Cora's room. The room was in the right-hand wing of the house and looked over the park at the front and the stable block at the side. The light was beginning to fade and Bertha could see the footman walking round the stable yard with a torch, lighting the lanterns. The yellow balls of light hung in the grey dusk like jack o'lanterns. The lamplighter had reached the lamp nearest the entrance to the arch when a rider came in. As he put his torch up, Bertha could see a gleam of blond hair under a riding hat.

Bertha pressed her forehead against the cold glass. She wanted a glimpse of the blonde woman's face but the hat was tilted too far down for her to see anything but the curve of a smooth cheek. The rider flung her reins to the groom and swung down from her horse, revealing a glimpse of white beneath her blue habit. As she turned, the lower half of the woman's face became visible and Bertha saw that her mouth was curved upwards in what might have been a smile. Bertha shivered. The room suddenly seemed empty without Cora.

For the first time since she had arrived in England, Bertha felt homesick – not for the half-remembered smell of her mother, she had long ago learned the futility of that – but rather for the well-lit certainties of her American life, where she had one hundred and fifty dollars in her sewing box and she knew the price of everything.

She went to the wardrobe and began to take out Miss Cora's most elaborate costumes. Whatever happened next, she knew that her mistress would want to look her expensive best.

Mrs Cash had wanted to leave Sutton Veney as soon as she had received her daughter's note, but Lord Bridport had persuaded her that it would be better to go in the morning. As she sat down to dinner, Mrs Cash was grateful for the opportunity to find out something more about the man she now thought of as Cora's duke.

'You must be beside yourself with worry about your daughter,

Mrs Cash,' said Odo Beauchamp, who had been seated tactfully on her good side. 'What an unfortunate accident, and your daughter such a fine horsewoman too. Charlotte and I saw her riding out this morning looking splendid. Quite a number of people said they would have thought she was English.'

Mrs Cash sighed. 'Cora assures me that she is unhurt, merely a little shaken. So kind of the Duke to insist on her staying at Lulworth till she is recovered and to invite me to stay with her. I shall go over there tomorrow,' she smiled. 'I am quite intrigued to meet an English duke. We were lucky enough to entertain the Duc de Clermont Tonnere when he was in Newport last summer, and he could not have been more gracious, so much more so than the Grand Duke Michael of Russia. He travelled with his own plate as if he didn't think there would be anything sufficiently magnificent in America. But I fancy he saw the error of his ways by the end of his visit.'

Mrs Cash's ducal reminiscences were interrupted by the footman serving the soup. Lord Bridport insisted on dinner taking no more than an hour, so each of the seven courses remained for only a short time in front of the diner. Mrs Cash, who found that the prospect of Lulworth had awakened her appetite, realised that she must focus on the lobster bisque. As she concentrated on conveying the soup to the undamaged side of her mouth, Odo took his chance. As the sole heir to a considerable fortune and due to inherit even more from his maternal grandfather, Odo was not abashed by Mrs Cash's wealth, nor was he in the least interested in her catalogue of foreign titles.

'I quite envy you going to Lulworth, if it weren't under such dramatic circumstances. It's a lovely house, one of the few really fine houses around here. It's not a great big dukery like the ones up north, it's more subtle than that. Lulworth has charm,' Odo tittered, 'if a building can be said to have charm. And you must see the chapel, it's exquisite, a little rococo gem.' He made a circle in the air with a finger to indicate the curves of the chapel. 'Of course I haven't been there since the old Duke's funeral, but I gather things have gone downhill since then. Wretched death duties I suppose.' Odo looked down the table to where his wife was sitting and raised his voice a little.

'I almost feel sorry for Ivo. He was such a perfect younger son, excellent shot, popular with the ladies, clever. There was some talk of the Diplomatic after he came out of the Guards, but then Maltravers, his elder brother, broke his neck eighteen months after the old Duke died, and it all came to Ivo. That was about a year ago, and since then he has become such a bore. He's shut himself up at Lulworth and won't come out to play. Didn't come to town for the season, nobody's seen him for months. Even Charlotte can't tempt him out and they used to be *such* friends.'

At the mention of her name, his wife began to talk with unchar-acteristic animation to the Rural Dean on her left. If Mrs Cash had not been in the habit of only observing what was directly connected to her own interests, she might have noticed the flush spreading across Charlotte Beauchamp's cheeks. But Mrs Cash's attention was all with Odo.

'So there is no Duchess at Lulworth?' she said as nonchalantly as she was able. She didn't remember seeing Wareham's name in the list of noble bachelors in *Titled Americans*, a magazine she would never admit to buying, though she was exhaustively acquainted with its contents. She was certain she would not have missed an eligible duke.

'Not even a dowager,' said Odo, looking at Mrs Cash directly, his exophthalmic blue eyes glistening. He had noticed his wife's animation and the sudden colour in her cheeks. His tongue darted over his lips involuntarily. He paused to drink some claret. He knew he had Mrs Cash's full attention, and he was aware, too, that she was not the only listener; his wife was still chattering to the clergyman but she would hear every word.

'No, the moment the old Duke died, Duchess Fanny was off. Barely out of mourning before she married Buckingham. Of course everyone knew what special friends they were, but still . . . She was probably worried that someone else would snaffle him up, although who else would want poor old Buckingham, God knows. But the Double Duchess couldn't be happier.'

'The Double Duchess?' It was the closest Mrs Cash had come to a squeak since childhood.

'First Duchess of Wareham and now Duchess of Buckingham, first woman I know to have done the double.' Beauchamp smiled. 'Some people think that poor old Wareham died just in time. Duchess Fanny had spent a fortune on Lulworth. She even had a branch line built so the Prince of Wales could get there faster. But now she entertains him at Conyers – Buckingham's place. The shooting is better at Lulworth, but dear old Buckers has the wherewithal.'

Mrs Cash pulled at the tulle covering her damaged left cheek and wondered why her neighbour was being so forthcoming. At home she knew to a cent how much her friends and enemies were worth and whether they figured in the Social Register or were on Ward McAlister's list for the Patriarchs' Ball. But things were different here. Mrs Cash had taken great pains to learn the order of precedence among the English nobility – she liked nothing better than a set of rules. But she had been astonished, not to say shocked, to discover on her arrival in London that she was as likely to encounter an actress like Mrs Patrick Campbell as a countess at the smartest society events. In Newport or even New York you might engage such a person to perform at a party but it would be quite unthinkable to entertain them on equal terms socially. When she made this point to Mrs Wyndham, whom she had persuaded, at some cost, to introduce Cora and herself into society, Mrs Wyndham had reacted in such a way that Mrs Cash had felt the unfamiliar and unwelcome sensation of being laughed at. 'Oh, you can go pretty much anywhere now if you are amusing enough,' said Mrs Wyndham. 'Or rich enough,' she added, narrowing her gaze at Mrs Cash.

Mrs Cash had resented the implication very much and had considered breaking off her relationship with her sponsor. But, as Mrs Wyndham knew very well, Mrs Cash needed her help. Cora was rich enough and beautiful enough to be sought after, but only Mrs Wyndham was prepared to tell her that Lord Henry Fitzroy had syphilis or that Patrick Castlerosse had been named as the co-respondent in the Abagavenny divorce. So Mrs Cash was surprised and delighted to find Lord Bridport's nephew so willing and indeed eager to satisfy her curiosity about the Duke of Wareham.

'But when you say that the Duke has shut himself away, is there any reason why he should? Is he ill?' Mrs Cash was wondering whether the Duke of Wareham's health was another of those topics that was common knowledge only among those who belong.

'Nothing wrong with him at all physically. Mentally, well, I really couldn't say. He's a Catholic of course, like all the Maltravers, so Lord alone knows what twisted Papist fancies are at work. Oh, don't worry, Mrs Cash,' said Odo, seeing the expression on her face. 'It's a very old Catholic family, they're not converts. No, I think the Duke is having money troubles. Lulworth is a huge estate but rents are down. Duchess Fanny spent every penny and more on entertaining Tum Tum, and then old Wareham and poor Guy died so close together, which meant paying death duties twice.' Mrs Cash assumed that Tum Tum was the Prince of Wales, and that this was a nickname that, as a foreigner, she would not be safe in using.

Odo was still speaking. 'No wonder Ivo is lying low. Shame really, because what he needs is a nice rich wife. Who knows, Mrs Cash, perhaps you will spirit him back to Newport and find him a lovely young heiress? She'll have to be beautiful, though. Ivo is very particular.'

Mrs Cash was deciding how to reply when a small hubbub erupted at the other end of the table. Charlotte Beauchamp, who had been fingering the choker of black pearls around her throat, had inadvertently touched upon a weak link in the stringing, and the necklace snapped, the pearls exploding across the table, rattling across plates and ricocheting off the crystal glasses. Charlotte, making a sound somewhere between a shriek and a laugh, was trying to recover the pearls as nonchalantly as she could. The Rural Dean found one in his claret and embarked on a long-winded allusion to Cleopatra's dinner with Antony.

'She said she would give him a priceless dinner, so he was very surprised to be given indifferent food and then Cleopatra took off one of her pearl earrings, dropped it into her glass of wine where it dissolved and she offered him the glass to drink. What a magnificent gesture. I can't claim to be Antony of course but, my dear Lady Beauchamp, you are surely a modern Cleopatra.'

The Dean stopped, rather amazed at where his unexpected eloquence had taken him.

Charlotte was busy trying to retrieve the pearl with a teaspoon when her husband called out, 'I hope, Dean, that you are not suggesting that my wife should have herself delivered to you in a carpet, the better to seduce you. You really mustn't put such fancies in her head.'

The Dean looked rather pleased with himself. 'Age cannot wither, nor custom stale her infinite variety.'

'Eighteen, nineteen, twenty,' said Charlotte as she counted the pearls rolling about on her dinner plate. 'Only one missing. Is it in your waistcoat pocket, Dean, I wonder?'

'I will ask Druitt to have a thorough search afterwards,' said Lady Bridport hastily, alarmed equally by the thought of Charlotte going through the Dean's pockets as by the Dean's willingness to quote Shakespeare at a civilised dinner party. She rose and gave the signal for the ladies to withdraw.

When Odo went to visit his wife's bedroom later that evening, he found her in her peignoir at the dressing table. He noted the blue veins that threaded her slender arms as she pulled the silver hairbrush through her long fair hair. Cleopatra was altogether too coarse an image for Charlotte, he thought. She had the head of an Italian Renaissance beauty. When he had last been in London, Snoad the dealer had shown him a painting by the Sienese painter Martini of Bianca Saracini. She had long fair hair and a high forehead like Charlotte's, in her hand she held a snowball to signify her purity. He must have Charlotte painted, although he could think of no one who could do her justice. Meanwhile, he would buy the Martini and give it to Charlotte for her birthday. She liked presents.

'I'm sorry about your necklace, Charlotte. Such an exotic colour. Have I seen it before?'

Charlotte's hair flickered in a sudden storm of static. Odo took the brush from her and began to brush it himself. He liked to pacify it into a shining sheet. Charlotte flinched and avoided his eyes in the mirror as she said, 'It belonged to my great-aunt Georgina – you know, the one who was in India. I never thought to wear it before but, faced with all those American sparklers, I didn't want to appear dowdy.'

'Pearls before swine, eh?' He put the brush down, and pulled back her hair so he could kiss her neck. 'Such a pity I lost you today at the meet. Where did you get to?' Odo began to pull the fastenings of her peignoir.

'Oh, I don't know, my stirrup kept twisting and by the time I had fixed it, you had gone. Had to spend hours dodging that buffoon Cannadine.'

Odo squeezed her nipple hard. 'Cannadine indeed. Poor Charlotte. But you know I don't like it when you disappear. I shall have to punish you.'

He picked up the hairbrush.

In the servants' hall, Bertha was finishing her supper. She was eating some kind of pudding laced with currants. It was a dish that everyone else seemed to relish, but she found it hard going. She longed suddenly for an ice-cream sundae. That had been her treat on her afternoons off at home, ice cream from the drug-store in Newport. She would go there dressed up to the nines in one of Miss Cora's fanciest cast-offs, with a parasol and a bonnet with a veil. Bertha could just pass for white, and in her second-hand Paris finery the man behind the counter was not about to question her colour. It was the combination of cold ice cream and hot chocolate sauce that made her gasp with pleasure. She couldn't understand why Miss Cora, who could have all the sundaes she wanted, didn't eat them night and day. That was luxury all right.

There was a tap on her shoulder. She looked up and saw Jim. 'Think you dropped this, Miss Cash.' He put something in her lap. It was a handkerchief, not one of hers, inside which was a tiny screw of paper. She hid it up her sleeve as she knew that Druitt and Mrs Lawrence were watching her.

As she walked out of the hall, she unfolded the note and read it by the light of her candle. In careful rounded script she read:

Meet me by the stables. I have something for you.
Yours ever,
Jim Harman

He was waiting there by Lincoln's stall, stamping his feet in the cold. When he saw her, his face relaxed into a smile.

'You came then. Good girl. You won't be sorry.'

'I should hope not, I could lose my place for this.'

'Look.' Jim held out a clenched fist to her. Bertha hesitated. 'Go on, open it'.

Bertha pulled back his fingers one by one. There, on his outstretched palm, was a black pearl. Under the lamplight she could see its faint iridescent sheen like a slick of oil on a puddle. It was as big as a marble and almost perfectly spherical. Bertha took it and rubbed it against her cheek.

'It's so smooth. Where did you find it? You did find it, didn't you?' She looked at his face, hoping he would meet her eyes. He didn't flinch.

'I was waiting at table tonight, on account of it being such a big party, and just as I was coming round with the savoury, one of the ladies went and broke her necklace by fidgeting with it at the table. She thought she picked 'em all up but this one rolled under my foot and I stood on it tight until all the ladies went upstairs. I wanted to give it to you. You're a black pearl, Bertha, that's what you are and it's only right that you should have it.'

Bertha looked at him, astonished. No one had ever talked to her this way before. Honey talk, that's what her mother would call it. 'Honey talk is fine and dandy but make sure you get the ring first.' Bertha's mother had never had a ring though. The man who had seduced her had been white, so there was no question of marriage. Mrs Calhoun had kept her on in the laundry after Bertha was born. The Reverend called it an act of Christian charity, but Bertha's mother never looked grateful. But Bertha did not pull away as Jim leant down to kiss her. It was different from all the other kisses she had had, softer, more tentative. His hands were holding her head as if it was made of glass.

When he drew back she said, 'Don't you mind?'

'Mind what?' he whispered.

'My skin. Don't you mind kissing a coloured girl?'

He didn't answer but kissed her again, this time with more urgency.

Finally he said, 'Mind? I told you, you're my black pearl. When

I first set eyes on you in the servants' hall I thought you were the most beautiful thing I had ever seen in my life. When old Druitt told me to take you into dinner I thought I'd died and gone to heaven.'

There was no mistaking the sincerity of his tone. Bertha was touched. She felt for his hand and squeezed it. She saw Jim's blue eyes go round with concern.

'You're not cross, are you, that I kissed you? You just looked so fine standing there, I couldn't help myself. It wasn't that I thought I could, I don't think you're fast or anything.' He looked so worried that Bertha laughed and swung his hand.

'No, I'm not cross. Not at all.' She leant towards him, the better to show him how far from cross she was, but they heard footsteps and Jim drew away.

'I must go. Save this for me.' And he touched his finger to her lips and was gone.

Bertha turned back towards the house, rolling the pearl between her fingers. It grew warm in her hand. She slipped it into the bodice of her dress and as she walked into the house she could feel the glow somewhere just above her heart.

CHAPTER 6

A Link in the Chain

IF MRS CASH HAD BEEN EDUCATED AS ELEGANTLY as her daughter, if she had read Byron, or had pored over Doré's engravings of Dante, she would have recognised Lulworth with its turrets and its twisted chimneys silhouetted against the shining sea as a glorious example of the Picturesque. But Mrs Cash was the daughter of a colonel of the Confederate Army, and when she had been growing up, there had been no call for poetry. Mrs Cash was a crack shot and could command an army of servants but she had not had a sentimental education.

After the Confederate surrender at Appomatox, Nancy Lovett, as she then was, had been sent North to stay with her aunt in New York. She was a handsome girl with dark hair and a delicate but firm jaw. Her mother had sent her into enemy territory with misgivings, but Nancy had not looked back. She liked the rich colours of her aunt's house, the wide skirts, the elaborate pelmets. She enjoyed the plentiful food and rosy prosperous company. When Winthrop the Golden Miller's son had proposed, she had accepted gladly. Her mother had sighed and thought about what might have been, but her father was by then in the institution where he would die three months later. Later, as Nancy the bride solidified into Mrs Cash the society matron, she had felt some of the lacunae in her education; she could not speak a word of French, for example. But for a woman with such a natural talent to command, her inability to talk to the French Ambassador in his native tongue was the faintest of setbacks. Colonel Lovett had been a keen disciplinarian before his 'indisposition' and he would have appreciated his daughter's ability to impose order.

So Mrs Cash did not gasp, as so many visitors had before her, at the romantic charms of Lulworth. The house with its four turrets flanked by lacy Jacobean wings studded with mullioned windows was imposing but delicate, like a queen whose coronation robes cannot disguise the slenderness of her waist or the fragile tilt of her head.

No, like the commander she was, Mrs Cash sized up the strengths and the weaknesses of her new billet. She could tell from the irregular façade with its towers and battlements that the food would be at best tepid by the time it reached the dining room. Driving in through the park gates, Mrs Cash looked up only briefly at the bronze stag over the cast-iron gates; she was far more interested in the dilapidated state of the gatehouse windows. By the time she was halfway up the drive of two-hundred-year-old elm trees she had made a realistic assessment of Lulworth's plumbing.

But even Mrs Cash could not fault the magnificent matching pair of footmen who handed her out of her carriage. The Lulworth livery of green and gold was certainly elegant, she had never seen shoulder tassels of such splendour. She would have smiled with appreciation, if it hadn't been so painful. She had to husband her smiles for more important occasions. Perhaps the Duke might give her the name of his livery maker.

A voice murmured in her ear, 'Welcome to Lulworth, Madam. His Grace has asked me to take you to see Miss Cash and then he hopes you will join him for lunch.' She followed the butler up the stone steps through the great arched door into a vaulted hall with a carved stone chimney piece at one end. The blackened oak of the roof timbers was not to Mrs Cash's taste, she preferred her wood gilded, but she felt its weight.

'If you would like to come this way, Madam.'

Mrs Cash followed the servant up a wide wooden staircase lit by a glass lantern roof. There were fantastical beasts on the newel posts: gryphons, salamanders and lions. Mrs Cash admired the carvings but noticed that they had not been carefully dusted. At length they reached a wide gallery and the servant turned left and proceeded until he reached a door about halfway down.

Cora was lying in an immense wooden bed hung with green damask with carved angels at each corner. She looked pale and, to Mrs Cash's irritation, rather plain. Much of Cora's charm lay in the vividness of her colouring: the bright chestnut curls, mossy green eyes and rosy skin. Lying there with dark circles under her eyes and with her hair limp and unkempt against the snowy mounds of linen, she did not look at all like the belle of Newport. Mrs Cash, for the first time since her daughter's accident, began to worry about the extent of her injuries. She hoped that her daughter had not been, in some way, damaged.

'Hello, Mother.' Cora smiled.

'Cora, I am so relieved to see you.' Mrs Cash bent over to kiss her daughter's cheek and stayed there for a moment before sitting down on the bed, making sure that her daughter had her right side and saying, 'What an unbecoming nightgown, it makes you look quite sallow.'

Cora's smile vanished. 'It belongs to the Duke's mother.' She started to play with one of her limp ringlets. 'Mother, did you bring Bertha with you?'

'You would think that a duchess, a duchess twice over, would be ashamed to wear something so shabby. The cheapest kind of cotton and not a scrap of lace. I wouldn't even give this to my maid.' Mrs Cash pinched the cuff of fabric round her daughter's wrist. Cora pulled her hand away.

'Mother, did you bring Bertha?'

Mrs Cash was looking at the canopy above the bed. She lowered her head slowly and met her daughter's gaze. 'Bertha is following in the Bridport governess cart. You surely didn't expect her to travel with me.'

Cora sighed, and lay back against her pillows. She had found it difficult to sleep last night in this strange house that creaked and shivered in the dark, prey to fears she could not give shape or name to. The doctor had said she might feel some light-headedness for a few days, but had said nothing about hallucinations. But the irritation and annoyance that pecked at her the moment her mother began to talk was reassuring. Her mother was real enough. This part of her mind, at least, was unharmed.

Mrs Cash was wandering through the room on a tour of inspection. She turned to Cora. 'These English houses are so haphazard. There is no planning, nothing matches. I could do so much with this house.' Mrs Cash paused and narrowed her eyes a little as if mentally remodelling their surroundings. Those casement windows with leaded frames – so antiquated and dismal. The English had lived in their houses so long that they no longer noticed them. It took a New World eye like hers to see them as they really were. The situation here was really quite good, if a little isolated. How long, she wondered, would it take to build a new house worthy of an American duchess?

Cora read her mother's thoughts. 'Mother, you know that my being here is nothing more than an accident.'

Mrs Cash chose to misunderstand her. 'My poor girl, how frightened you must have been. Still, it was really most fortunate that you should have been rescued so promptly. And by such a Samaritan.'

Cora realised that nothing would prevent her mother from believing that her accident and subsequent rescue was a sign that Providence was supporting her ambitions for her daughter. Cora might think she was a free agent but Mrs Cash and the Almighty knew better. Indeed, Mrs Cash was prepared to concede that Fate's method of bringing her daughter within proposing distance of a duke was more ingenious than anything that she might have engineered. The only blemish in the divine plan was that Cora's injury was not so serious that she would be obliged to stay at Lulworth indefinitely. A broken ankle would have been so much more definite. Really, there was nothing more appealing than a pretty girl confined to a sofa. Still, it couldn't be helped. The important thing was to get Cora out of that hideous nightdress into something more becoming. She began to regret leaving Bertha behind, perhaps it wouldn't have been so bad to have brought her in her coach. But she didn't want the Duke to think that she was the kind of woman who travelled with the help. A pointless scruple it turned out, as the Duke had not been there to greet her in person. Was that intended as a slight, or was there something in the impenetrable English rule book which meant that hosts above a certain rank never waited at the door to welcome their guests? It was one of the many things she would ask Mrs Wyndham.

She turned to Cora. 'I must leave you now, Cora, the Duke is expecting me at lunch.'

'I don't think you'll be disappointed, Mother. Maltravers is everything a duke should be. But I wouldn't make your dissatisfaction with the décor too plain. I have the feeling that he is very attached to this house.'

'As if I would do anything so ill-bred! Really, Cora, sometimes I think you forget that I am mistress of a house quite the match of this one.'

'I am not sure the Duke would agree. I don't think he is in the habit of comparing himself with others.'

Mother and daughter glared at each other. Cora closed her eyes in feigned weariness. But Mrs Cash was not to be silenced so easily.

'Even dukes can count, Cora,' she said, sweeping from the room.

Cora lay back, imagining her mother's impatient progress through the house. Unconscious when the Duke had brought her to Lulworth the day before, she had so far only seen the inside of the bedroom and a glimpse of the dark corridor beyond. If only Bertha were here. She needed to see the house for herself, but she couldn't very well wander the corridors in the Duchess's second-best nightgown. Not for the first time, Cora cursed her mother's notions of propriety.

Mrs Cash found a footman waiting outside her daughter's room, ready to escort her to the dining room. The wide oak boards creaked as she walked carefully down the polished steps.

The footman opened the library door.

'Mrs Cash, Your Grace.'

Mrs Cash wondered if she should curtsy, but thought on the whole not. She had been expecting one of those milky Englishmen whose youthful slimness was almost a reproach to the corpulence to come, but the Duke was darker almost than any Englishman had a right to be, his hair was black and his slightly hooded eyes were a golden brown. She couldn't make out his age. She knew he couldn't be more than thirty but there was nothing youthful in the grave way he took her hand. Deep grooves ran from his nose to his mouth and there were flecks of grey at his temples.

'Mrs Cash, welcome to Lulworth. I hope your stay will be a pleasant one even if the reason for your visit is not.' His words were cordial enough but he did not smile or meet her eyes. For the first time in many years, Mrs Cash felt awkward. She had come here expecting to assess the Duke's suitability as a match for her daughter, but the man before her was not acting like a suitor. Perhaps he was not aware of the prize that was within his grasp. But from what she had seen of Lulworth, he could not afford to be indifferent.

She replied in her most gracious tones. 'Your Grace has been most kind in taking in my unfortunate daughter. Who knows what would have happened if you hadn't found her. A young girl, alone and hurt and so far from home.'

The Duke replied, 'Oh, I don't think she would have come to much harm in an English beech wood, and from what little I have seen of your daughter, she seems more than able to take care of herself. American girls have so much spirit.'

Mrs Cash was not encouraged by this speech. It sounded as if the Duke had judged her daughter and found her wanting. She felt at a disadvantage, an entirely unfamiliar and unwelcome sensation.

The Duke led the way into the dining room where they were joined, rather to Mrs Cash's surprise, by a priest.

'Mrs Cash, may I present Father Oliver. He is writing a history of Lulworth and the Maltravers.'

The priest, whose face was as perfectly round and smooth as a balloon, advanced towards her beaming. 'Delighted to make your acquaintance, Mrs Cash. I am so fond of your country. I was in New York only last year staying with Mrs Astor. What a peerless woman. Such manners! And taste!'

Mrs Cash smiled weakly. She wondered if Father Oliver knew that her acquaintance with the fabled Mrs Astor was not as intimate as she would like. Was everyone here determined to wrong-foot her? She might throw the most talked-about parties in Newport but so far Mrs Astor had never accepted one of her invitations. It was one of the reasons that she was so anxious for Cora to marry splendidly. Even Mrs Astor could not look down on a duchess, or the mother of a duchess.

But despite the Duke's apparent indifference to her, she noticed that he beckoned her to sit at his left so that the undamaged side of her face would be turned towards him, even though as the only woman present she should have been on his right. Mrs Cash was surprised and grateful at this tactful gesture. Father Oliver sat on the other side of the table. Father Oliver said grace, to which the Duke said Amen very loudly. The food was, as she had predicted, barely lukewarm.

They ate their soup in silence and then the Duke said, 'I'm afraid you will find us very quiet here, Mrs Cash. My mother used to entertain on a grand scale, but now that she has moved to Conyers the parties have gone with her. My mother is so wonder-fully energetic.' He said the word 'mother' with a peculiar emphasis, almost as if he was calling their relationship into doubt.

'Why, the quiet couldn't be more delightful,' Mrs Cash assured him. 'Cora and I came to Europe after a hectic summer in Newport. We had nearly a thousand guests for Cora's coming-out ball. People were kind enough to say that it was the event of the season. But after my accident,' Mrs Cash fluttered her hand towards her cheek, 'the doctors said I must rest and recover my strength.' She watched the Duke's face carefully but he did not react to the mention of the thousand guests.

'Did you have a pleasant crossing, Mrs Cash?' asked Father Oliver solicitously. 'No storms in the Atlantic, I trust. My last journey was so rough that some of the passengers were asking me to hear their confessions! I became quite the parish priest for the upper deck.' Father Oliver was talking too much and too fast, but he had been at Lulworth for six weeks now, and too many meals had been eaten in silence. There had been few visitors and none like Mrs Cash. He had been asked to write the history by the Duke's brother. It had been a handsome commission but he sensed that the current Duke was not as eager as his brother had been to commemorate his family's past.

He leant towards the American woman. 'Which boat did you come over in, Mrs Cash? I believe there is a new vessel on the White Star line that has its own tennis court.'

Mrs Cash's smile of triumph spread over the good side of her face. Here was a chance to make her place in the world quite clear.

'We have our own steam yacht, the *Aspen*. My husband Winthrop had it built five years ago, after a bad crossing on a steamer. He has a dread of being cooped up with strangers.'

Father Oliver was silenced, but the Duke looked up, interested.

'Oh, that explains it. I was wondering how your daughter had brought her horse over.'

'Horses you mean, Duke,' Mrs Cash said with a little trill of satisfaction. She decided that it was time to use the more familiar form of address – 'Your Grace' felt altogether too subservient. 'She brought three hunters with her and insisted on walking them on deck morning and evening whatever the weather. There were days when I thought all four of them would be washed overboard. But Cora is so headstrong. She takes after my father the Colonel. He had more decorations for gallantry than any soldier in the Confederate Army.'

'You are from the South then, Mrs Cash?' enquired Father Oliver.

'My family, the Lovetts, is one of the oldest in Virginia. The original Delmore Lovett came over from England two hundred years ago. Not many families can go that far back. Our family place L'Hirondelle was one of the finest plantations on the Chesapeake River.'

'Two hundred years? I had no idea you Americans had so much history,' said the Duke, but before Mrs Cash could answer, the priest broke in.

'"Was", Mrs Cash?'

'It was razed to the ground by Sherman. I don't think my father was ever in his right mind after that.'

'How savage,' murmured the Duke.

'It is only through God's grace that Lulworth did not suffer a similar fate in the seventeenth century, Your Grace,' said Father Oliver. 'Think of what Cromwell's armies did to Corfe Castle just twenty miles away from here. They could so easily have marched to the coast. Indeed, it is very surprising they did not, given that the Second Duke was such a close friend of the King. But like so many families, they had a foot in both camps. Your namesake, Lord Ivo, the Duke's younger son, was in the Protector's army. He must have been the reason that Cromwell didn't head south. So fortunate.'

'Fortunate indeed,' said the Duke without enthusiasm. Mrs Cash looked at him in surprise.

'But without ever relinquishing the true faith, Your Grace,' said Father Oliver unctuously. 'The Maltravers are one of the very few aristocratic families that can claim an unbroken allegiance to Holy Mother Church since the Norman Conquest. To a convert like myself it is an extraordinary achievement. You are, if I may say so, Your Grace, a living link to a simpler time when the whole country was united in one faith.' The priest folded his hands at this last remark as if giving a blessing.

The Duke pushed his plate away with a hint of impatience and turned to Mrs Cash.

'You must forgive Father Oliver's enthusiasm, Mrs Cash. He is very attached to his subject.'

'Oh, I understand. We have a great respect for family history where I come from, even if our stories don't go back as far as yours.' She lifted her chin a little as she said this and for the first time she met the Duke's eyes. She stared at him coldly. He might feel ambivalent about his ancestry but she did not. She had not liked the way he had dismissed her proud family history as colonial pretension.

The Duke saw the annoyance in her face and smiled at her, a charming smile that made him look much younger.

'My father used to call himself a link in the chain. I suppose we all have our chains, Mrs Cash.'

Mrs Cash gave a dignified little nod. 'Yes indeed, Duke. And now if you will excuse me, I must go and see Cora.' She rose and the men got to their feet. The Duke walked over to the door and held it open for her.

'I hope Miss Cash will soon be able to join us downstairs. I am looking forward to meeting her properly.' He sounded sincere and Mrs Cash gave him another nod. Perhaps he was, after all, interested in her daughter.

'Cora is not the kind of girl to stay in bed for a moment longer than she has to. But I will decide when she is ready to get up.' Having asserted her maternal rights, she swept past the Duke towards the great staircase.

On her way up to Cora's room, Mrs Cash walked through a gallery lined with pictures of the Maltravers family. She stopped in front of the Second Duke, resplendent in blue satin with long dark curls falling over his lace collar. He was framed by a great damask curtain and behind that the ramparts of Lulworth. At his feet were two brown dogs lying on silk cushions with gold tassels. His face had a melancholy cast, his eyes were a little too moist and the lips a little too full for Mrs Cash's taste, but the man in the picture had a look she knew well: the complete indifference of inherited position. It was something she saw rarely in New York but she recognised it instantly; it was the quality she herself most aspired to. She knew that unlike her hall of mirrors or the cedar-lined yacht, this was not something that could be acquired or even reproduced. It had to develop over time, like the patina on bronze. It was a coating that meant you had no doubts at all about your place in the world or concern about the world's perception of you. Mrs Cash knew that she gave a good imitation of this indifference, but as she looked at the Second Duke she was aware that her celebrated composure did not have the authenticity of this long-dead aristocrat standing quietly but splendidly in the centre of his world. She wondered if Cora's children would ever gaze at the world with such serene lack of interest.

She put out a finger and ran it over the gilded moulding of the picture frame, caressing its baroque curlicues.

It came up black with dust.

CHAPTER 7

Bows and Arrows

ORA STAYED IN HER ROOM FOR THREE DAYS. ON THE fourth the doctor said she was well enough to get up. The Duke hadn't been to see her since that first day, and she had been forced to listen to her mother's interminable accounts of his attentiveness as a host. But he had not been attentive to her. For an instant, Cora wondered if the Duke might actually prefer her mother's company, but this thought was dispelled when she looked at herself in the cheval glass. She was wearing her prettiest evening gown, pale green silk with silver embroidery on the bodice. She had made Bertha lace her even more tightly than usual, so that her waist appeared to vanish beneath the confection of lace and silk above. The diamond drops in her ears sparkled against the warm brown of her hair. She pinched her cheeks and bit her lips to give her face some colour. The Duke, of course, had not seen her looking like this, at her best. It was possible that he had not quite taken in the extent to which she, Cora Cash, was as beautiful as she was rich.

'What do you think, Bertha? Do I look well enough to go downstairs?'

Bertha did not even look up from the petticoat she was folding.

'I think you know the answer to that question already, Miss Cora, judging by the way you've been gazing at yourself in that mirror.'

'Yes, but sometimes I look at myself and all I see is the bump in my nose and the mole on my neck. I admit that tonight I can see other things as well but if I can see things so differently, then maybe other people do too.'

'I think the other people will think you look just fine, Miss Cora. No one is going to be looking at your bump.' Bertha straightened the folds of the petticoat with a snap.

'So you can see it? The bump? You know, if it wasn't there, I would have a perfect classical profile. I wish I could just shave it off. Mother has a friend who had paraffin wax injected into the bridge of her nose to make it perfectly straight. Perhaps I should do that. It's awful to think that I could be really beautiful if it weren't for that one little thing.'

'Don't forget the mole on your neck, Miss Cora, and that scar on your knee you got falling off your bicycle.'

'Oh, but no one can see the scar on my knee!'

Bertha was now threading a satin ribbon through the eyelet edging of a cambric chemise. She looked up at Cora for a moment with a gaze so steady that Cora was forced to laugh, even if it was a little uncertainly. They both knew how she had come by that scar. Teddy Van Der Leyden had been teaching her to ride a bicycle. He had been running along beside her, steadying the saddle, and then he had let go. She hadn't noticed at first and had sailed along freely, but then she had looked around, expecting to find him. Realising that she was cycling unaided, she had promptly fallen off, skinning her knee. She had cried then, more from the humiliation than the pain. Teddy had laughed at her tears, which had made them come even faster. Finally he had taken pity on her and had whispered into her ear, 'Get back on the bike now, Cora. You can do it. Don't you want to be free?' And he had given her his handkerchief to bind up her knee and had helped her up as, still trembling, she got back on her machine and slowly wobbled off. She had been scared at first but then suddenly it all came together and she pedalled faster, feeling the breeze lifting her hair and drying her tears. Teddy had been right, she did feel free. When she rode out she had to be accompanied by a groom but there were no rules about bicycles – now she could simply pedal away. She realised that Teddy had seen and understood this and she had liked the feeling of being noticed.

Cora shivered impatiently. 'I know you think I am being ridiculous but it would be awful to think I was beautiful if I really wasn't. I would be no better than those dreadful English girls who think they are so fetching when really they look like simpering carthorses with their flaring nostrils and their bulging eyes.'

'And they ain't as rich as you neither, Miss Cora,' Bertha said.

'Then why hasn't the Duke been to see me for three whole days? He must know that I have been bored to tears up here. Even Mother has hardly been to see me. Out of sight, out of mind.'

'I'm thinking that the Madam seems a lot like her old self since we've been here. She ain't bored to tears. She was wearing that diamond necklace with the sapphire drops the master gave her. I ain't seen her wearing that since—'

Cora held up her hand. She hated to have that night mentioned. Especially now. That evening in Newport had started so well, she and Teddy had come so close to an understanding – and then it had all changed from hope to disaster in a second. Even now when Bertha accidentally singed her fringe with the curling tongs, she would feel bile rising up into her throat as she remembered the terrible stench of her mother's burning hair. If it hadn't been for Teddy, she thought, her mother could have died.

She remembered how when the bandages were removed, Mrs Cash had asked for a mirror. Cora had brought her the tortoise-shell-backed hand mirror that had once belonged to Marie Antoinette. Her hand had trembled as she handed it over, she didn't want to see her mother's reaction to her ravaged face, but Mrs Cash had not flinched when she saw what the flames had done. Mrs Cash had looked at this unfamiliar countenance with the same glacial indifference as she might regard one of her husband's operatic 'enthusiasms'. Apart from the careful dressing of tulle and net she employed to disguise the livid side of her face, Mrs Cash made no concessions to her misfortune and such was the control she had over herself and others that when strangers met Mrs Cash, it was her eyes that held them, not the mystery behind the veil. Later they might wonder and make discreet inquiries, to which they received whispered replies: 'Some kind of accident at her daughter's coming-out ball, her head a ball of flame, Cash's comet, the New York wags are calling it. Teddy Van Der Leyden is the only reason she wasn't fried to a crisp.' A sad story but no one who had encountered the adamantine surface of Mrs Cash's composure would have had the temerity to feel for her anything resembling pity.

Her mother had never mentioned the scene she had witnessed on the terrace before her dress had caught fire, and Cora saw no reason to bring it up. It was possible that the shock of the conflagration had affected Mrs Cash's recall of the minutes preceding the accident, possible but not likely; Cora suspected that her mother remembered every detail but had chosen to put her memories aside as long as it suited her to do so. It was wrong that Teddy's part in saving her life had also been put to one side, but Cora could only feel relief that her mother had decided not to blame her. It was hard enough to face the possibility that it had been her fault. She could not help feeling that her kissing Teddy had been the spark that had started her mother's blaze.

The dinner gong sounded and Cora allowed herself one more glance in the mirror. Perhaps the bump wasn't so very prominent on her left side if she pulled the curls of her fringe down a little. Was the green silk really appropriate, or was it just a little too frivolous? Perhaps she should change into something more interesting. Something that suggested that she could be fascinating as well as decorative. The blue velvet with the square neckline that Teddy had once said made her look like a Renaissance duchess, Isabella Gonzaga. But did she want to look like a duchess?

The blue or the green? The Old World or the New? Cora didn't know. A week ago she could have made the decision without a qualm but now . . . She turned to Bertha in appeal, but the maid was standing by the door.

'All right, I'm coming. Don't look so cross, I'm the one who is going to be late, not you.'

'And when do you think I get my dinner, Miss Cora? You may not have worked up an appetite lying in that bed, but I'm famished. The sooner you're downstairs sparkling at the Duke, the sooner I can eat.'

Cora suspected that English servants would not talk to their mistresses so frankly; indeed, Mrs Cash would have been horrified if she had heard the exchange, but that was precisely why Cora put up with her maid's tartness.

As she walked down the wide steps, the train of green silk and lace carefully looped over her left hand, she found the house both grander and more intimate than she had imagined. She passed any number of ducal portraits on the stairs but she stopped when she saw an arrangement of small detailed oils of grey lurcher-like dogs, clearly beloved pets. Beneath each canvas was the name, date and motto of the animal. 'Campion' in the lower left-hand corner had died only three months previously. She wondered if the animal described as '*semper fidelis*' had belonged to the Duke. She hoped her mother had not seen them; Cora could imagine only too well how much she would enjoy the notion of dynastic pets.

At the end of the staircase lay two double-height intricately carved oak doors flanked by a pair of perfectly matched footmen who flung them open as Cora approached. As an American heiress, Cora had grown up under high ceilings but even so she could not help but be impressed by the scale of the vaulted gallery, running the whole length of the south front. Cora could see the Duke and other guests standing by the carved chimney piece in the middle of the room at least forty feet away. The Duke was in the middle of a story when Cora walked into the room and as all the listeners were straining to catch every word that he delivered in his low voice, no one looked round. Cora paused. Normally she would feel no qualms about joining a group in a strange house. Normally she would stride into the throng, her hand outstretched, her bright American charm at full tilt. But something about the way the Duke commanded the attention of his half-dozen listeners, including Cora's mother, made her hesitate. Cora could not hear what he was saying but she could tell that this was not just polite attention on the part of the listeners, the Duke held his little audience in thrall. A moment later, he reached a hiatus in his story, looked up and caught sight of Cora. He raised an eyebrow, and then resumed his tale. She saw him lift his arm and swing it down suddenly, and she heard the word 'chukka' – he was talking about polo apparently. But why was he ignoring her?

Cora stood like a pistachio ice melting in her mint frills and Brussels lace. She had spent the last three days imagining the moment when she would reveal herself in her full splendour to the Duke. She was expecting that look in his eyes that she had seen so many times before in other people, the look that meant they were not seeing her but all that she represented, the marble palaces, the yachts, the gilded hummingbirds. She could not blame them for this, for she was all these things. Would she be Cora Cash if she wasn't dressed by Worth, and surrounded by luxury? Of course she was as pretty and amusing as any of her contemporaries, but Cora knew that it was her money that produced that little pocket of hush which preceded her whenever she walked into a strange room. It was her money that triggered all those sideways covert glances, the conversations that faltered when she approached. No one was unaffected by the money – even Teddy who did not want it had let it push him away.

So she had come fully prepared for the brief moment of disappointment when she would see the Duke shaping himself around the bulk of her inheritance. She was almost looking forward to seeing him moulded by its weight. It had not occurred to her that he could be indifferent.

She could feel a cold rivulet of sweat running down the inside of her corset and the heat of a flush burning its way across her chest. Could she steal away back to her room? She did feel rather faint. But the Duke had seen her, he would know that she was retreating. Stiffly and without any of her usual jauntiness, Cora advanced into the room, her steps making the wide oak floor-boards creak as if in pain. She forced herself to smile as if she had noticed nothing amiss.

And then she heard her name being announced by the butler. 'Miss Cash, Your Grace.'

And all at once Maltravers broke off from his story and advanced towards her as if seeing her for the first time.

'Miss Cash! How delightful to see that you have recovered so . . . fully.' The Duke's gaze took in the green silk, the Brussels lace, the artfully curled fringe, the perfectly matched string of pinky pearls, the faint flush beneath them. Had he really ignored her just now? thought Cora. Did she really have to be announced by a flunkey before he could acknowledge her in his own house? This was a degree of formality at which Cora, despite growing up in the codified atmosphere of New York and Newport, could only marvel.

She did her best to give Maltravers her most charming smile. She did not want him to see her confusion. Whether his hesitation was deliberate or not, she would not give him the satisfaction of watching her falter. He was being perfectly attentive now but she could see nothing, not a dent in his manner, that suggested he knew that she could buy him and everything he possessed and hardly notice it.

He was leading her into the circle around the fire, introducing her to the assembled company as the miraculously restored, the indomitable Miss Cash. His tone was light and if there was a touch of irony, it was lost on Mrs Cash, who accepted this praise of her daughter's powers of endurance as a fitting tribute to her talents as a parent. Cora realised that Bertha had been correct in her assessment of her mother's return to form. Mrs Cash was looking particularly regal in a gown of purple brocade with gold passementerie. A diamond and sapphire parure sparkled at her neck, her wrists, and her undamaged ear lobe. Cora did not need to look at the other women in the room to know that none of them could match her mother's display. In this world of hidden meanings and unspoken rules, there was no mistaking Mrs Cash's value. Her mother's queenly mien was emphasised by the priest at her side, who listened to her every word with all the attentiveness of a cardinal.

Cora found herself talking to the Hon. Reggie Greatorex, the younger son of Lord Hallam, a young man in his late twenties who had been at Cambridge with the Duke.

'Maltravers tells me you brought over your own horse from America and that it puts all our domestic animals to shame. It really is most unfair of you Americans, Miss Cash, to outclass us so effortlessly. You come over here so magnificently equipped that I fear we have nothing to offer you, except of course our undying devotion.'

Cora laughed, she had had years of practice at dealing with the Reggies of this world. Polished, blond and, she suspected, idle, Reggie probably knew more about the exact magnitude of her inheritance than she did.

'Oh, come, come, Mr Greatorex, are you telling me that your

family can't trace their lineage all the way back to William the Conqueror? Something that you know full well we newly minted Americans can never match.'

Reggie replied in kind. 'Oh, I would trade all the Ethelreds and Athelstans in the Greatorex lineage – Saxons being, you know, so much smarter than mere Normans – if I could belong to a nation of such magnificent creatures!'

'Yes, but you look down on us all the same. I have read your Mr Wilde. What is it he says? American girls are as good at concealing their parents as English women are at concealing their past.'

Reggie threw up his hands in mock horror. 'Not my Mr Wilde, I can assure you, my dear Miss Cash. Not only is he Irish, but he is an Oxford man. Moreover, he is quite wrong. Who would want to conceal your mother, for instance? She is quite magnificent. She would give any of our duchesses a run for their money.'

Cora looked at him, suddenly curious.

'Do you think so? I've never met an English duchess. Are they very formidable?'

'The old guard perhaps, but it is quite fashionable these days to be charming rather than regal. There are duchesses about who can be positively kittenish. Ivo's mama, for instance, has quite the girlish laugh.'

Cora stopped short. 'The Duke's mother? Is she here?' She wondered if she had made some terrible faux pas by not recognising her.

Reggie laughed at her confusion, 'Don't worry, if Duchess Fanny were present, you would know it. Although I'm surprised she isn't here. Maybe she doesn't know that Ivo has stumbled across an American heiress. You are an heiress, Miss Cash, aren't

85

you? I just assume that all Americans are rich these days, though I suppose that can't be true. Judging by the jewels your mama is sporting, it must be in your case.' He opened his blue eyes so wide to show how dazzled he was by the Cash fortune that Cora laughed.

'But where is the Duchess? Doesn't she live with her son?'

'Oh no. Duchess Fanny married again as soon as she could after Wareham died. Not ready for the dower house.' Reggie looked around to make sure the Duke was out of earshot and then said in a lower voice, 'Ivo didn't like it one bit but then he's a moody cove, I don't blame the Double Duchess for taking off.'

Cora looked at him curiously. 'You are very indiscreet, Mr Greatorex.' Her tone was light but she was testing him.

Reggie simply smiled. 'Do you really think so? It must be you drawing all these secrets out of me. Normally I am the soul of discretion, but I feel the urge to confide in you.'

'I am flattered. I wish I had something interesting to tell you in return.'

'Well . . .' He narrowed his eyes a little. 'You could tell me how you got here. Ivo hasn't had company at Lulworth since he got the title, and then this morning I got a telegram summoning me to a house party.'

'That's no secret. I was hunting with the Myddleton and I got lost.' Cora was not about to tell her new friend about Mr Cannadine and his tattoos. 'I was in a wood and something startled my horse, I must have hit my head on a branch. The Duke found me unconscious. When I woke up I was here in the house.'

'A damsel in distress, eh. Well, lucky old Ivo.'

'Oh, but surely I was the lucky one. If the Duke hadn't found me, who knows what might have happened,' Cora protested, but Reggie looked at her assessingly.

'No, I still say he's the lucky one,' and then he smiled and Cora smiled back, showing her small white teeth. After the strange encounter with the Duke, it was reassuring to find herself in familiar territory. She was used to being admired by charming young men. Reggie clearly understood her value even if the Duke did not.

Mrs Cash could sense a flirtation at a hundred paces. She beckoned to her daughter with a hand glittering with sapphires.

'Excuse me, Mr Greatorex, I am being summoned.'

'You must go. I believe your mother is about to give me a look and I will certainly crumple.'

Cora moved over to the chimney piece supported by carved caryatids whose proportions echoed those of Mrs Cash.

'Cora, I want you to meet Father Oliver. He is writing a history of the Maltravers family. Such a fascinating subject, so much tradition, so much self-sacrifice. I think it is just the sort of thing that you like.' She raised her voice slightly so that the Duke, who was standing close by, could not fail to hear her. 'My daughter is a great reader. She has had every kind of tutor and has outdistanced them all. You must ask the Duke to show you his library, Cora.'

This had the desired effect of making it impossible for the Duke not to be drawn into the conversation.

'As to the library, I am afraid that Father Oliver is a guide far more suited to a lady of Miss Cash's intellectual gifts than myself. My brother was the scholar in the family. He was fascinated by the vicissitudes of the Maltravers – it was Guy who asked Father Oliver here. Guy was very proud of our recusant status. He felt that the Maltravers family's refusal to accept the tenor of the times and leave the Church of Rome was proof that we were somehow of a finer moral weave than others.' He smiled wryly.

'I think if Guy had not been the eldest son, he would have followed his true vocation and become a priest. When we were children we were always playing Crusades. He was the Knight Templar and I was always the Saracen. Guy would fire his infernal toy arrows at me through the arrow slits until I surrendered. I always did surrender, of course.' The Duke halted. Cora was about to make some droll comment but realised with a sudden hot gust of embarrassment that Guy the older brother must be dead. She looked at the Duke, but he had recovered himself and addressed her with exaggerated gallantry.

'So, Miss Cash, you must let Father Oliver show you the library, but I will show you the best places to play Crusaders!'

'Do you still have the bow and arrows?' Cora responded in the same tone.

'Of course, you never know when you might have to repel marauders.' The Duke smiled at Cora when he said this but she heard the warning there. She felt his words like a slap. She was there by pure accident, after all; how could he imply that he was under siege? She wondered if she could persuade her mother to leave in the morning.

The butler appeared to announce that dinner was served and Reggie, smiling and uncomplicated, took her into dinner.

Cora found herself seated between Reggie and Father Oliver. The Duke had her mother on one side and Lady Briscoe, a stout lady with an ear trumpet who was evidently a neighbour, on the other. Reggie flirted with Cora over the fish; Father Oliver told her about the Reformation over the entrée. The food was neither plentiful nor particularly appetising. As one of the footmen bent over her to serve her, a large white globule fell from his powdered hair on to her plate. She looked at it astonished. The footman gasped in horror and snatched the plate away. Reggie, who had seen the whole thing, winked at her.

'That's the problem of staying in a house without a mistress. The servants can get awfully slack. Things were a good deal sprucer when Duchess Fanny was here.'

'I can't say I envy the future Duchess if her duties consist of making sure the footmen powder their hair properly. I think it is a ridiculous habit anyway. Why make the servants adopt a fashion that their masters gave up a century ago at least. I think there is something of the tumbrils about it.' Cora's tone was rather strident. She had conveniently forgotten that her mother's own footmen had equally antediluvian hairstyles.

'Oh, Miss Cash, what a modern girl you are. But I think you underestimate how much we English enjoy our traditions. I'm sure that the footman takes great pride in his snowy white hair and knee breeches. The whole point of being a footman is to look magnificently *ancien régime*. They have enormous cachet in the servants' hall and get paid according to their height. Do you really want to bring these glorious creatures down to earth by forcing them to go unpowdered in drab broadcloth?'

'I just think they might prefer it.'

The footman in question was handing Cora some gravy. She turned to him and said, 'What is your name?'

The footman blushed and said, 'Thomas, miss.'

'Can I ask you a question, Thomas?'

'Certainly, miss,' he said with obvious reluctance.

'Do you enjoy powdering your hair every day? How would you like it if you could wear your hair naturally?'

The footman looked at the floor and muttered, 'Very much, miss.' Cora looked at Reggie triumphantly, but then the servant continued, 'It would mean I had been made up to butler. Now if you'll excuse me, miss, I need to finish serving.'

Cora nodded, feeling not a little foolish. But Reggie was too tactful to press home his advantage and changed the subject deftly.

As the meal drew to a close, the Duke looked at Mrs Cash and said, 'In the absence of a hostess, Mrs Cash, I wonder if you would be so kind as to lead the ladies to the drawing room. I apologise for the imposition but it will only be for one more day. My mother will be arriving the day after tomorrow with my step-sister Sybil.'

'Oh, how delightful, Duke, I would so much like to meet them, but I fear that Cora and I cannot impose upon your hospitality any longer. As you can see, she is quite recovered and we really should return to Sutton Veney.' Mrs Cash's words were more emphatic than her tone.

The Duke took up the challenge.

'But my dear Mrs Cash, my mother is hoping so much to meet you and your daughter. She will be quite disappointed not to find you here after she has made the journey from Conyers. And to be honest, Mrs Cash, my mother's disappointment is not an easy thing to endure. Unless you have some very pressing engagement, perhaps I can prevail on you to stay for another week or so. I would so much like to show Miss Cash more of Lulworth than the wood where she met her accident.'

Although there had been no doubt in Mrs Cash's mind about her intention to stay, the Duke's last remark was reassuring. She took it as a declaration of interest and looked over at Cora to see whether she had registered this too. But Cora was talking to the young man on her left, altogether too animatedly in Mrs Cash's view, and had not heard. Mrs Cash cleared her throat and rose to her feet.

'In that case, Duke, you leave me no choice but to accept your very kind invitation; I would hate to be the cause of a duchess's disappointment. I shall write to Lord Bridport tonight. Ladies, shall we?'

The Duke rose to his feet to open the door. As Cora passed him, he looked at her and smiled, this time without reservation.

'You must allow me to show you over Lulworth, when you feel well enough, Miss Cash.'

'I would like that very much, but I insist on having the bows and arrows.' Cora picked up her train and followed her mother up the stairs.

As the footmen cleared the rest of the dishes from the table and brought in the port, Father Oliver stood up and bowed to the other two men.

'If Your Grace will excuse me, I would like to get back to the Fourth Duke. Such a devout man, quite an inspiration. Goodnight, gentlemen.'

The Duke rolled his eyes as the well-fed figure of the priest left the room. 'He has the zeal of the convert. Takes it all very seriously. Guy and he were very thick.' He paused and Reggie moved up to sit next to him. Silently, the Duke passed him the decanter. The room was empty now apart from the two men.

The only noises were the crackle of the fire in the stone fire-place and the tapping of the Duke's fingers as he inflicted an invisible rhythm on the polished surface of the table. Finally he spoke.

'Thank you for coming down at such short notice. I promise the sport will be tolerable, if nothing else.'

'It's been too long, Ivo. I haven't seen you since . . .' Reggie stopped. The last time he had been at Lulworth was for Guy's funeral.

Ivo looked at him, reading his thoughts. 'It was a year ago this week. Feels longer.'

'Is that why the Duchess is coming?'

'She would like me to think so, but she only sent the telegram yesterday.' The Duke did an imitation of his mother's breathy tones. 'I felt such an urge to be with you.'

Reggie nodded towards the door. 'The Americans?'

'Of course.'

'But how did she know?'

'At first I suspected Father Oliver of writing to her, but actually it was Charlotte. She was at Sutton Veney when the accident happened and felt that Mother ought to know.'

'And how is Charlotte? I have hardly seen her since she married Beauchamp. Never cared for him much at school. Used to keep a diary full of his ghastly "observations". Still can't understand why Charlotte accepted him.'

'Isn't it obvious?'

'But Beauchamp, of all people. I mean, he collects *china*.'

'He loves beautiful things and Charlotte has always liked to be admired.'

'But we all admired her, Ivo.'

'But none of us had the means to display her properly.' The Duke's fingers, which had not stopped moving to their invisible rhythm, suddenly hit a fortissimo chord and the glasses rattled.

There was another silence. Both men drained and refilled their glasses.

'Quite a thing, finding Miss Cash like that,' Reggie said, looking at his friend speculatively. 'Something of a windfall, you might say.'

Another rattle from the glasses. Finally Ivo said, 'Well, I couldn't very well leave her there. I had no idea that she came with all this . . . this stuff.' Ivo picked up a silver coaster and sent it flying down the table. Both men watched it as it circled and slowly grew still.

'Do you think she knew who the wood belonged to?'

'I did wonder, especially after I met the mother, but I don't think the daughter is a schemer. No, I think Miss Cash's arrival at Lulworth was entirely accidental.'

'And?' Reggie let the monosyllable hang between them.

'Oh, don't be absurd. You're as bad as my mother. Miss Cash is American . . .' Ivo's voice trailed away in disdain.

'And spectacularly rich.'

'As Mrs Cash never stops reminding me.' Ivo filled his glass again and turned on his friend. 'Have you taken a fancy to Miss Cash then, Reggie? I saw you whispering to her at dinner. Poor Sybil will be heartbroken.'

Reggie laughed. 'I'm afraid that Miss Cash has no interest in me. But I like her, Ivo. As windfalls go, you could do a lot worse.'

But Ivo was looking up at the portrait of his mother that had been painted at the time of her first marriage. Blonde and creamy, she gazed serenely down at her son. He raised his glass to the portrait and said with sardonic clarity, 'To the Double Duchess.'

Reggie realised that his friend was drunk. He wasn't sure that he wanted to hear Ivo talk about the Duchess. Ivo had always been his mother's favourite and their relationship had been relaxed and mutually admiring. Mother and son were never more aware of their own beauty and charm than when in each other's company. But that was before his mother's remarriage. She had been barely out of mourning when the marriage took place. There were those who would have enjoyed a spell of disapproval, but that would have been a luxury when the Duchess was so charming, so hospitable and so close to Marlborough House. But if society was prepared to overlook the Duchess's haste, her son, it seemed, was not.

Reggie repeated his friend's toast but without the ironical inflection.

Ivo caught the reproof and got to his feet. 'Time to join the ladies, I think, before Mrs Cash starts rehanging the pictures.'

In the servants' hall, Bertha accepted a glass of madeira from Mrs Softley the housekeeper. She was grateful for the warm length of it spreading through her chest. Lulworth was a good deal colder than Sutton Veney. There she had had the occasional sight of Jim to keep her warm. Here there was nothing to heat the chilly corridors.

The green baize door swung open with a clatter as the footmen came in carrying trays loaded with plates and cutlery.

As soon he got through the door, Thomas the footman burst out, 'Did you hear what the American girl said to me when I was serving her? Said did I like having my hair powdered, like I was some kind of performing monkey. It's not correct.'

Thomas's handsome face was red with emotion. The other footman laughed.

'You should be careful what you say, Thomas, she might be your new Duchess. His Grace is taking her round the house tomorrow. Do you think he's going to show her the holes in the roof?'

The housekeeper frowned and got to her feet. 'Thomas, Walter, that's quite enough from you. Are the ladies still in the drawing room?'

'Finishing up, Mrs Softley'.

She turned to Bertha. 'In that case, Miss Cash, you will be wanting to go upstairs to your mistress.' She paused and gave the keys on her belt a little shake. 'Thomas and Walter are foolish boys. They mean no disrespect.'

Bertha thanked the housekeeper and began the long climb to Cora's room. The stone flags were cold and unforgiving under her feet.

She wondered what kind of mood Cora would be in. She wouldn't tell her what the footmen had said. Miss Cora would be quite put out to think that in the servants' hall her destiny had already been decided. She liked to make up her own mind. But as Bertha climbed the carpetless back staircase, feeling the chill draughts from the uncurtained windows, she wondered if this was to be her new home.

The next morning a thick sea fog drifted in over Lulworth, muffling its towers and crenellations and concealing the shining view that gave even the dingiest rooms a splendid point. Cora felt the damp chill as she opened her window. She had hoped to take Lincoln out, to ride away some of the uncertainties that hung around her like cobwebs. But this was not weather to be riding in unknown country. She told Bertha to put away her habit and put on a morning dress of dove-grey wool with black frogging. It was as modest an outfit as she possessed. She remembered Reggie's eyes flicking over her mother's jewelled magnificence the night before.

There was no one about apart from the odd housemaid. At Sutton Veney the ladies of the house had gone to the morning room after breakfast to write letters and gossip but in this house there were no ladies to join. Cora knew she should look for her mother but she did not feel ready for the conversation that she guessed would follow.

Retracing her steps from the night before, she found herself again in the long gallery where the Duke had seen her and not seen her the night before. The stone walls reflected the light from the sea, bathing the room in a pearly haze. There was no fire lit and Cora could smell the chalky sweat of the limestone. She sat down in one of the mullioned embrasures and looked out at the grey sky. The fog had suppressed everything, even the sound of the sea was muffled.

Cora was looking up at the carved vault of the arch, trying to make out the carved motif at the apex, when she heard music. Someone was playing the piano. She walked to the end of the gallery in the direction of the sound. Cora stood for a moment and listened. It was dark choppy music, full of false starts and minor chords, lacy pianissimo passages and startling crescendos. Cora could play the piano well enough, she had the young lady's repertory of Strauss waltzes and Chopin nocturnes, but she knew that whoever was playing was in a different class. It was not just the technical difficulty of the piece, she had the feeling that the player was completely submerged in the music.

A set of chords faded away into silence. Cora pushed open the door a fraction. The room was another stone chamber – like the gallery it seemed older and more austere than the rest of the house. In the centre of the room under a narrow arched window was a grand piano and at the keyboard sat the Duke. He was frowning down at the keyboard as if he was trying to remember something. Then he started to play. Cora recognised the piece, it was a Beethoven sonata – but she had never heard it played like this. The opening was allegro con brio, but in the Duke's hands it was not just fast, it was dangerous. The Duke had taken off his jacket and had rolled up his shirtsleeves. From where she was standing, Cora could see his bare forearms, the tendons stretching and tensing as he reached up and down the keyboard. She stood motionless, not sure whether she wanted him to look up and discover her. Was she listening or intruding? This was private music and yet she could not bear to look away. She was fascinated by the way he swayed towards the keyboard as if he was embracing the instrument, and his complete absorption. He was, she felt sure, in another place entirely. The long glissando passage at the end of the first movement finished and he looked up for a moment. At first he looked straight through her and then she saw him register her presence with a wary smile.

She said nothing, she did not know whether she should apologise or praise his playing.

In the end he spoke first. 'Do you know the piece?'

'It's Beethoven, isn't it? My music master used to play it for me, but never like that.' Cora was being quite truthful. She was amazed that the same piece of music could sound so different.

'The "Waldstein". Beethoven was in love with Countess Waldstein, but there was no question of her marrying a musician. He wrote this for her but dedicated it publicly to her brother. He was almost completely deaf when he composed it.' He looked down at the keyboard and played a passage where the music seemed to grope for a resolution. 'Can you hear how he seems to be looking for something? Some satisfaction?'

Cora was about to say how sad it was that Beethoven never heard his own piece but in the end stayed silent. She realised that this was the obvious thing to say and she did not want to appear obvious. She knew that she was here on sufferance. What she had taken at first for the music room was clearly the Duke's personal sanctum. There were piles of books on the window ledges and a desk at the far end covered with papers. There were no chairs or sofas apart from an uncomfortable-looking metal campaign bed.

'You play very well,' she said.

He shrugged. 'You're too kind. I play adequately, that's all. But I play very well for a man, certainly.'

Cora smiled. He was right, she had been surprised at the Duke's playing at all. In her experience, the drawing-room piano as opposed to the concert hall instrument was an exclusively female instrument.

'My mother taught me to play when I was very young. She had no daughter and she needed someone to play duets with. She would summon me after dinner and we would perform for her guests. The house was always full then, I got a lot of practice.' He started playing a Brahms lullaby with exaggerated sweetness. 'This was my finale. I played my own lullaby and then I was despatched upstairs to bed.'

'Do you still play duets?'

'No. As I grew up, we could never keep the same time. My mother always wants everything to be charming. She is all about effect, while I simply like to play.' He pulled his finger down the keyboard in a soft glissando. He looked up at her. 'And you, Miss Cash, do you like to play?' The question ended in a minor arpeggio.

'Yes,' she said firmly, 'I do.' If there was challenge in his question, Cora would meet it.

'Well then, what about a little Schubert?' He stood up and rummaged among the piles of music on the floor until he found the piece he was looking for. He set it up on the piano and gestured to her to sit beside him on the stool. She walked towards him slowly, conscious that she had not played properly since leaving Newport, hoping that the piece he had chosen would not be too difficult.

The Duke gestured towards the music and said, 'Which part would you like?'

Cora looked at the music, and felt her heart pounding in panic. The semiquavers exploded across the page. He certainly hadn't chosen something easy. The lower part looked marginally calmer so she pointed towards it.

As he sat down next to her on the seat, she felt herself tense. But he was careful not to touch her. He spread his fingers out across the keys and she did the same.

'When you're ready, Miss Cash.'

Cora nodded and began. The piece started cantabile sostenuto in her part for a few bars and then the treble part came in with the melody. She played softly at first, hoping to muffle her mistakes, but as she grew more confident, her side of the piece met the melody in the upper register and suddenly they were playing together – their hands weaving round each other in the elaborate dance of the music. At one point the Duke's left hand passed over her right and she felt the heat from his palm cross hers like a flame. But she could not afford to be distracted; to play the piece 'adequately' needed all Cora's reserves of concentration and skill. The Schubert was just outside her level of competence but her desire not to fail meant that she was playing as well as she had ever done in her life. As the music reached the finale, there was a sequence of chords that were played in unison and to her surprise they played them in perfect synchronicity. Without thinking, she reached for the sostenuto pedal to hold down the final chord, only to find the Duke's foot already there. She pulled her foot away but he had felt the pressure and as they finished, he turned to her with a smile.

'I'm sorry I forgot to negotiate the pedals with you. It's been a long time since I played a duet.'

'And me. I've never played with anyone as good as you before.'

'Duets are not about individual skill but about the relationship between the two players. The whole must be more than the sum of the individual parts.'

'And were we?' Cora could not stop herself asking.

'It's perhaps too early to say entirely, but on the whole I think we will do very well. Shall we have a go at the second movement?'

But Cora knew she must retreat now. She did not want to play again and be found wanting.

'I think I have been lucky so far. I would like to practise before we play again.'

The Duke smiled. 'As you wish, Miss Cash. But as I say, I think we will do very well.'

As Cora left the room, she heard him start the 'Waldstein' sonata again. It was clearly a favourite piece. As she listened to him play, she remembered his remark about Beethoven looking for satisfaction.

CHAPTER 8

We Have a Rubens

*A*S AN UNDER-HOUSEMAID AT LULWORTH, Mabel Roe started her working day at five in the morning. It was still dark so she had to dress and wash herself by the light of last night's candle. Her hands were red and chapped, her knuckles swollen from years of scrubbing. It was not so cold this morning that she had to break the ice on the handbasin, but Mabel could see her breath issuing in frosty plumes across the unforgiving air of the attic bedroom.

Usually Mabel would linger in bed for a precious five minutes before getting up. But Iris had gone home for her mother's funeral, so there was no extra warmth in the bed to ward off the chill, no one to grumble with about the rigours of the day ahead. Still, Iris's absence meant that Mabel could spend more time than usual in front of the tiny square of mirror above the chest of drawers, adjusting her cap to sit becomingly on her thin brown hair. On the chair lay the thick brown holland apron that she wore in the morning while she was doing the fires, but Mabel picked up the light cotton apron that she wore in the afternoons and tied that round her waist. She wanted to look her best.

Mabel had been startled the first time she found the Duke in his dressing gown, sitting on the window seat, looking out to sea. When he had been Lord Ivo he had never been an early riser, except when he was hunting, but things were different now. Her job was to get the fires lit in the bedrooms without waking the occupants. Under-housemaids like Mabel were not meant to have anything to do with the 'family'. The housekeeper had told her that she must turn and face the wall if she met any of them in the corridor. To reveal that the Duke now woke with the lark would have given Mabel some status among her fellow house-maids, who discussed the family endlessly, but she had said nothing. This silent audience with the Duke was Mabel's talisman, the antidote to her aching knees and stinging hands. It had made her nervous at first to go through the lengthy ritual of cleaning out the ashes of the night before, polishing the grate and laying the new fire with His Grace sitting there so still. Once she had dropped the poker on to the marble hearth; the noise had been calam-itous, it felt like the loudest sound she had ever heard, but the Duke had hardly stirred.

He was there on the window seat this morning as usual. She wondered what he looked at so hard. There was nothing to see out there but the green hills leading down to the sea.

Mabel finished laying the fire, building a neat little pyramid of kindling that burst into obedient flame the moment she put a match to it. She gathered together all her tools – the stiff hearth brush, the tin of blacking, the matches – and put them back in her work box; she wiped her hands on her apron and stood up slowly, her knees cracking as she did.

The Duke said softly, 'Thank you, Mabel.'

Mabel very nearly dropped the ash bucket. She scraped her knees together in something like a curtsy and mumbled, 'Yer Grace.'

He had never spoken to her before, and yet he knew her name. She felt herself going scarlet and backed out of the room as speedily as she could. She stood in the corridor, her heart pounding and the palms of her hands clammy with sweat. She leant against the wall and closed her eyes. The Duke knew her name. She felt like a character in a *Peg's Paper* story. He had noticed her; surely this was the start of something.

Her reverie was interrupted by Betty who was coming from the Cash girl's bedroom.

'What you doing, Mabel?' she said in a fierce whisper. 'Don't you know the old Duchess is coming today and we've got to turn out those rooms this morning? If you don't get on you'll miss breakfast. This isn't the time to be daydreaming, and how come you're wearing your best apron and it's covered all over with smuts?'

Mabel looked down at the black smears on the white cotton. They were, she knew, impossible to remove.

Cora decided that she would go down to breakfast that morning before meeting the Duke for her tour of the house. As she walked along the corridor that led from her bedroom to the staircase, she saw a maid with a crumpled and soiled apron running in the other direction. Cora was enough of her mother's daughter to notice the dirty apron.

As she walked through Lulworth she was torn between her admiration of the pictures, the walnut furniture, the faded brocade curtains, objects which looked as if they had been always been there, and her awareness of a rank, musty smell that lingered here in the less frequented parts. Cora had grown up in a dust-free world that smelt of fresh flowers, furniture polish and wet varnish. Only rarely in her native country did she enter a building that was older than she was. But here she was surrounded by an unfamiliar odour, one she was too young and too American to recognise as a mixture of damp, decay and disappointment. She did notice the chill, though, and wondered that the Duke could bear to live in such a cold house.

He was not at breakfast. Cora ate alone and then decided that she would not wait on his whim; she would go to the stables and see Lincoln. She was walking down the immense flight of stone steps at the entrance of the house when she heard the Duke calling her name.

'Miss Cash, don't tell me you have forgotten our arrangement?'

The Duke had evidently been riding already, he was hatless and his cheeks were flushed from the cold.

'Not at all. I thought you must have found other business to attend to when I didn't see you at breakfast.'

'I went for a ride. Early morning is the best time for it. It clears my head for the rest of the day.'

'I envy you your freedom. I wish riding were such a carefree business for my sex. You can just jump on your horse and go. I, on the other hand, have to spend at least quarter of an hour being laced into my habit and then I have to find a groom to ride out with me, and in my experience no groom has ever wanted to ride at my pace.'

The Duke made her a bow. 'Miss Cash, I accept the challenge. I will ride out with you and I promise not to baulk at your pace, however reckless. If we break our necks, at least we shall do so together.'

Cora bridled at the implied criticism, she knew she was an excellent horsewoman. 'I assure you, Duke, I am not in the habit of falling off my horse. What happened the other day was completely out of character. Unfortunately the fall has destroyed my memory of the moments leading up to it, but I am sure that something quite untoward must have happened for me to lose control like that.'

'Perhaps you saw a ghost. Lulworth is full of them: headless cavaliers, wailing monks, medieval chatelaines rattling their ghostly keys. You won't find a housemaid who will go into the gallery after dark in case she bumps into the Grey Lady.'

'The Grey Lady?'

'One of my ancestors, Lady Eleanor Maltravers. It was in the Civil War. Our Civil War, we had one too . . . The Maltravers were Royalists of course, but Eleanor fell in love with a neighbour's son who went to fight for Cromwell. When she was told that he had been killed at the battle of Marsden, she fell into such despair that she threw herself off the cliffs. Turned out that the boy she loved wasn't dead after all so she can't leave the house till she finds him.'

'And why is she grey?'

'Oh, because she started wearing grim Puritan clothes – to please her lover or to annoy her family, who's to say?' The Duke gave Cora a knowing smile that suggested she might know something about the latter situation.

Cora was wondering whether to smile back when two rangy grey dogs raced between them, yapping shrilly and jumping up on to Cora's skirts, leaving a pattern of dirty brown paw marks.

'Aloysius, Jerome, stop it at once.' The Duke spoke with an authority completely unlike his usual quiet tone. The dogs subsided instantly. 'I'm sorry about your skirt, Miss Cash. Would you like me to get a maid to sponge it down?'

Cora shook her head. 'No indeed. I want my tour. But I am curious about your dogs' names. Back home we call our dogs things like Spot or Fido. These must be very special animals to warrant such fancy names.'

The Duke leant down to one of the dogs and pulled its ears. 'The Maltravers have been breeding Lulworth lurchers for God knows how many generations but I think I am the first duke to name them after medieval popes.' He stood up and the dog ran lightly to the bottom of the steps. 'And now, Miss Cash, you shall have your tour.' He bowed to her and raised his hand in a mock flourish.

'Lulworth was originally built as a hunting lodge for Edward the Third. The long gallery, the dining room and the music room where you found me yesterday,' he gave her a half smile of recognition, 'were part of this original building. In 1315 he gave it to my ancestor Guy Maltravers as a reward for his services in the Hundred Years War. The front of the house and the great hall were built by my namesake Ivo, the First Duke. He was a favourite of James the First, who made him a duke and gave him the monopoly on sealing wax so he was able to build all this. Ivo had very good taste, he got Inigo Jones to do the designs. They ran out of money – the Civil War was very bad for the Maltravers – but with the Restoration things improved, except for poor Eleanor, and they were able to finish it. After that things went downhill rather. The Maltravers stayed Catholic when the rest of the country went Protestant so they spent a lot of time down here, praying. The family has only become smart again since my mother married into it. She had no intention of being a dowdy duchess. She spent a fortune on the place, put in the new servants' wing and built the station so that her smart friends could get here easily from London. Very energetic woman, my mother, she did more to Lulworth in the last twenty years than had been done in the last two hundred.' The Duke's voice trailed off. They were walking along a paved path that led up a small hill to the right of the house. At the top was an elegant white stone building. The Duke paused on the steps flanked by two weathered stone pillars.

'And this is the chapel, which as Father Oliver will have no doubt told you is the oldest consecrated Catholic site in continuous use in England. This chapel was built by the Fifth Duke who had a French wife who was very devout. She didn't like saying her prayers in the draughty medieval chapel, so she ordered her husband to build her something modern, and this is the result.' Ivo held open the grey painted door for Cora. As she walked past him, her hand brushed against his. It was the tiniest contact, as fleeting as a moth's wing brushing her cheek, but it sent a tremor through her arm. She gave a gasp and Ivo looked at her.

'It's beautiful, isn't it? A French bonbon in deepest Dorset.'

Cora nodded. The chapel was perfectly proportioned. The main body was circular. A gallery ran round the top beneath a domed ceiling painted with voluptuous saints and attendant cherubs. The walls were white, and the woodwork a pale greyish-green picked out in gold. The pews were upholstered in the same shade of velvet. There were two padded armchairs in the front row, with coronets and the ducal W embroidered on the backs. The altar was covered with a green velvet cloth decorated with elaborate gold embroideries. An ivory prie-dieu hung between two gold candlesticks. The overall effect was rich but graceful – rather, thought Cora, like the Duke himself.

Cora had never been in a Catholic church before. Catholicism was something she associated with the Irish maids at home. On Sunday mornings they would be taken in a shiny-faced, giggling bevy to Mass at the local Catholic church. The Irish girls always looked so excited, as if they were going to a ball rather than to a place of worship. Cora, who found attending the Episcopal church on Sunday mornings an ordeal only mitigated by the knowledge that of all the exquisite examples of the milliner's art on display, hers was undoubtedly the finest, had envied the maids their gleeful high spirits.

She tried not to stare as the Duke dipped his fingers into the stoup at the entrance of the church and knelt down and crossed himself. This automatic act of devotion surprised her. She wondered if he expected her to do likewise. But he got to his feet and walked towards her without constraint.

The Duke gestured towards the ducal chairs. 'Embroidered by Duchess Mathilde herself. Must have been rather reassuring to sew your own coronet when all your friends were losing their titles and even their heads. Her mother was one of Marie Antoinette's ladies-in-waiting. Her brother lost his head to La Guillotine.' The Duke gave a theatrical shiver.

Cora noticed that in the alcove behind the altar there was a rectangular patch that glowed whitely against the faded paint that surrounded it. She guessed that a picture, quite a large one, had hung there until quite recently

The Duke noticed the direction of her gaze. 'Yes, there should be a picture there. Rather a fine one actually, my father always said it was the finest Rubens in the country even if St Cecilia was a touch on the fleshy side.' He voice trailed into silence as if he had forgotten his reason for being there. His hands absentmindedly picked at the gold tassel hanging from the ducal cushion.

'We have a Rubens,' said Cora brightly. 'Mother bought it last year from Prince Pamphilij. She is very proud of it but I find it a little overpowering. But where is yours? I know Mother would love to compare them, although of course hers will be the superior.' She smiled but the Duke did not smile back.

'Not possible, I'm afraid. The Rubens was sold, along with a very pretty set of Fragonard panels that were part of Duchess Mathilde's dowry. My mother had some royal guests to entertain and the house needed to be brought up to scratch. My father was quite cut up.' He wrenched the tassel so hard that it broke off. 'But now, fortunately, she has married into another Rubens. I'm sure she will be only too happy to tell Mrs Cash about it.'

Cora felt her face burn. She thought of the picture gallery in Sans Souci and the faded outlines of past glory that its magnificence represented. She tried to imagine what it must be like to have to give up something because you needed the money. She saw that the Duke, too, was flushed and instinctively she put her hand on his arm in mute apology – for her lack of tact, for her Rubens, for underestimating him.

'You have every right now, Duke, to think of me as the worst kind of vulgar American, but I can tell you that while there is much – so much I don't know, I am a quick study. I never make the same mistake twice.'

Ivo said nothing. For a moment Cora thought he was about to shake her hand away but then he took it in his own, turning her palm upwards.

'What a crisp line of destiny you have.' He traced the line that tapered round the mound of her thumb with his finger. Cora felt as if her whole being was concentrated under his fingertip. 'You are going into an unblemished future, Cora. A bright, confident, American destiny. You will have no faded patches on your walls, no missing pictures. There is nothing you need to learn from me, unless of course you want to.' He hesitated and then slowly raised his eyes to look at her. Cora felt she could not meet his gaze; she stared hard at the ducal W embroidered by a dead French duchess, but she could not ignore his hand on hers and the warmth she felt in the cold morning.

At last she turned to him and then quickly before she lost heart she said, 'I would like to learn how to make you happy. I think I could, you know.' Cora could feel her heart beating, her face scarlet. She had spoken before she had a chance to think and yet she knew this was what she wanted.

Ivo raised her hand to his lips and kissed the soft white skin of her wrist. 'Is that really what you want, Cora? All this?'

This time she did not look away. 'If this is what makes you happy, then yes.'

She spoke more loudly than she had realised, and the bright ring of her voice hit the clear chill air of the chapel. Ivo looked at her so intently that she felt transparent, that he could see through her, but she had nothing to hide. And when she thought she could bear it no longer, he put his hand behind her head and put his mouth on hers. His lips tasted of honey and tobacco. It was not a tentative kiss.

Cora smelt the musky scent of his neck and ran her fingers through his springy curls. She felt the length of his body pressing against her through her clothes. His arm was round her waist, his mouth moved down to kiss the inch of neck that escaped from the high collar of her morning dress. And then he pulled away from her abruptly.

'But I am making an unwarranted assumption here.'

He stepped back, his eyes searching her face. Cora stood motionless. She saw the corner of his mouth twitch; was he going to laugh? Then he dropped on to his knees.

Ivo cleared his throat. 'Cora, will you do me the honour of accepting my hand in marriage?'

Cora looked down at him. She saw that the tips of his ears were red. This had come before she was ready, everything he did seemed to take her by surprise. Surely there should be more of a courtship, a period of mutual discovery and delicious anticipation. She remembered the long summer in Newport when Teddy had seemed to hover about her consciousness. She remembered the words he had whispered in her ear the day she had fallen off her bicycle. He had seemed to understand her, but he had not made her free. At least Ivo was offering that. She wondered if she was giving in too quickly And yet, and yet . . . that kiss had been too urgent to be contained for long. She wanted the sequel as much as she regretted the lost dance of courtship. And by marrying the Duke, she would at once dispatch her mother and the lingering burden of guilt that she had carried since that evening in Newport.

Not that Cora's thoughts were quite so cogent in the minute that she made the Duke wait, kneeling before her on the stone floor of the chapel; but those were the strands which swirled around in her head before resolving into the force that made her slowly but definitely reach out her hand to pull him to her.

'Yes,' she whispered into his coat. There were tears in her eyes. Tears for the speed of her surrender, tears for all the other futures there might have been. But then he kissed her again.

They only drew apart when the chapel bell started striking

eleven. The noise was so loud and unexpected that they both laughed, as if guilty at having been caught out.

'I suppose we should go back and speak to Mother.' Cora dragged out the last word.

'And will your mother approve?'

Cora smiled. 'I think it will be the first time that she and I will agree about my future. But what about your mother? How will she feel about your marrying an American girl?'

'Well that, my dear Cora, you are about to find out. She is coming here expressly to take charge of the situation. But we have forestalled her.' Ivo took Cora's arm formally and walked down the aisle with her out of the chapel. It was an oddly solemn moment until the lurchers, who had been waiting patiently on the steps, sensed the change of situation and began to bark and lick their hands.

CHAPTER 9

The Double Duchess

THE STATIONMASTER'S STIFF COLLAR WAS DIGGING into the back of his neck. It was new and so full of starch that he could only move his head by turning his whole body. He tried to put his finger between the hard fabric and his skin but the extra pressure only made the collar even more like a garrotte. He gave up and tried to stand as still as possible. He could only look straight ahead but he could hear the distant whistle of the train. He lowered his eyes to the red carpet that lay across the platform – a little threadbare in parts but he knew that the Duchess would be pleased with the attention. The red carpet had last been taken out when the Prince of Wales had come for the old Duke's funeral. The stationmaster wondered if the Duchess would remember; perhaps the red carpet had not been such a good idea after all. Was it too late to remove it? Yes, the train was seconds away from pulling in. The stationmaster turned ninety degrees so that he could face his former mistress.

Duchess Fanny looked out of the compartment window as the familiar gingerbread-house fretwork of Lulworth Halt slid into view. She had thought it might be amusing to make the station a little more *orné*, perhaps an Oriental pavilion or something with shells, but the Directors of the South Dorset Railway had been firm: stations were of a standard design and not subject to the whims even of duchesses. She had been quite put out, even mentioning it to the Prince. This had been a mistake. Bertie had looked bored, his heavy eyelids drooping and the corners of his mouth beginning to sag. Fanny had changed the subject swiftly; she could not afford to be tiresome.

Duchess Fanny had always known, even as a little girl, the importance of not being tiresome. She was the second oldest of four sisters, daughters of a bad-tempered Somerset squire whose moods were as terrifying as they were unpredictable. Fanny was her father's favourite. She, alone of her sisters, had noticed that when her father was growing irritable, he would start to twist the buttons of his waistcoat. As soon as she saw his fat red fingers pulling at the straining mother-of-pearl discs, she would shoo her sisters away and make a point of asking her father if she could bring him something from the kitchen – a hot toddy perhaps, with cinnamon, just the way he liked it. Her father had appreciated her tact, and so when his rich widowed sister had offered to bring out one of his girls in London, he had sent Fanny.

Before she left, Fanny had considered telling Amelia, the third sister, the secret of the buttons, but decided against it. If, heaven forbid, her debut was not the success she hoped for and she was forced to return, unmarried, then it would be as well to keep this precious lever to herself. Indeed, it was only after her wedding to Lord Maltravers, the heir to the Duke of Wareham, a match that had astonished everyone that season (everyone, that is, except Fanny herself), that she felt she could afford to impart this precious piece of information to her sister. Amelia had been helping Fanny to change into her going-away outfit. Amelia's transparent envy at Fanny's good fortune, the titled husband, the beautiful clothes and jewels, the great house and position that would all be hers, had been most gratifying to Fanny. She had whispered to her sister that she wanted to give her a present. Amelia leant in eagerly, hoping for some jewelled cast-off from her sister's new magnificence and when she received her 'gift', she had laughed a little bitterly. Fanny had tried to explain to her sister the importance of being able to manage their father, but Amelia was too glassy-eyed with covetousness to understand the significance of the buttons.

Amelia never had learnt to manage men, thought Fanny. It was inevitable, perhaps, that her husband Sholto would take a mistress, but Amelia should never have allowed him to be so publicly besotted. If Amelia had ignored Sholto's infatuation with Lady Eskdale, it would have passed – no one could stand Pamela Eskdale for more than a season – but to allow herself to look wounded and reproachful had only prolonged the affair. Amelia had been tiresome; it was lucky for her that the Eskdale was even more tiresome and even Sholto had grown tired of her. She really must invite Amelia and Sholto to Conyers. To one of the larger parties, of course.

The carriage jolted and came to a stop. The Duchess smiled when she saw Weld, the stationmaster. Such a handsome man, he had been quite her favourite footman – his calves had been spectacular. She rarely took lovers outside her class – the risk of blackmail was too great – but Weld had proved as discreet as he was muscular. When he had announced he was marrying one of the housemaids, it seemed entirely appropriate that he should be nominated to the South Dorset Railway as a stationmaster. It was necessary, of course, that the stationmaster should understand the needs of the house. Weld had been quite satisfactory. The brass buttons on his tunic were always shiny and he even looked handsome in that cap (such a shame that the uniform was, like the station, standard issue).

The Duchess smiled when she saw the red carpet laid out on the platform. She guessed that this had been the stationmaster's idea, rather than her son's. This was her first visit to Lulworth since her marriage to Buckingham, it was only fitting that it should be marked out as a special occasion. The Lulworth staff had always worshipped her. She beckoned to Sybil, her step-daughter, to follow her.

'Weld, how splendid everything looks.'

'Welcome back, Your Grace.' Weld attempted his best footman bow but the collar defeated him. The Duchess was smiling, she was gliding across the red carpet, the fur trim of her pelisse brown and rich against the faded pile.

'Is the train early, Weld? I can't see the Duke.'

'No, the train is on time, Your Grace. I believe that is the Lulworth carriage drawing up now.'

The Duchess knew that the late arrival of the carriage was a declaration. She was not entirely surprised to see that the man getting out was not her son but his friend Reggie Greatorex. She turned to her stepdaughter.

'Sybil darling, look how popular you are.'

She was rewarded by the sight of Sybil blushing. There was nothing artful about Sybil. If the girl had been the Duchess's own daughter she would, by now, have learnt to blush entirely at her own volition; but by the time Sybil had come into her care it was too late to teach her even the most basic strategies. There had been moments when the Duchess had thought that Sybil might do for Ivo, but as Ivo had quite refused to come to Conyers or to Belgrave Square, there had never been the chance to put them together. She really must give the girl some powder, that blush against the red hair was so unbecoming.

'But where is Ivo, Mama? I thought he would be here to meet us.'

Fortunately Reggie had reached them before the Duchess was forced to answer Sybil's tactless question.

'Duchess, Lady Sybil, what a magnificent sight on such a grey morning. You must forgive me for taking Ivo's place but I begged him to let me come. Life at Lulworth is positively dull without you. Ivo has not inherited your genius for entertaining. I just couldn't wait to bask in some feminine company.' Reggie's beam embraced both women.

The Duchess looked at him, her pale blue eyes open wide with disbelief. 'But Reggie, from what I hear, there is no shortage of female companionship at Lulworth.'

'Oh, you mean the Americans. Well, the mother is unspeakably dignified and the daughter is pretty enough but such a modern girl. Not restful, either of them. I want to sink into female company, I want to be soothed and indulged, not buffeted about by opinions.'

For a moment Reggie thought he might have gone too far, but then the Duchess smiled and allowed him to help her into the carriage. As he helped Sybil up, he squeezed her hand and was rewarded by an almost imperceptible wink.

The Duchess settled her furs around her and nodded to Weld, who still stood to attention by the red carpet. Then she leant forward to Reggie and asked him in her most intimate tone, 'Do we *know* anything about the Americans? Charlotte wrote to tell me that the girl had fallen off her horse and that Ivo discovered her unconscious in Paradise Wood. Can she really have had such a convenient accident?'

Reggie understood now why Ivo had begged him to go to the station in his place. The Duchess was quite relentless in the pursuit of information. Nothing would infuriate her more than her son entertaining two Americans whom she couldn't quite place.

'From what I hear, she is quite the heiress. They came over to Britain on their own yacht. I don't think she is the sort of girl who would throw herself in anyone's way. I would imagine her approach to be a good deal more direct. My impression is that Miss Cash usually gets what she wants.'

'She sounds quite . . . terrifying,' said the Duchess, mollified by the mention of the steam yacht. 'How lucky for Ivo that Sybil and I were able to come to his aid. Direct Americans! My poor boy.' She rolled her beautiful eyes in mock sympathy.

'Is Miss Cash very elegant?' asked Sybil anxiously. 'My dressmaker says that she never gets any work from the American ladies as they go straight to Paris for their clothes.

'Such an affectation,' said the Duchess. 'Paris does not have the monopoly on fashion. London is full of beautifully dressed women.' She smoothed the grey broadcloth of her travelling dress with one white beringed hand.

Reggie searched for the right answer. 'She certainly looks very smart. But how would I know, since until you came I had no one to compare her to.' He smiled at Sybil. The Duchess was looking out of the window and tutting at the state of the lodge as they turned through the gates to Lulworth. Reggie hoped that Ivo would be there to welcome his mother.

The staff of Lulworth were lined up on the grey stone steps as the carriage drew up, the male servants on the left, the female servants on the right, from the butler and housekeeper right down to the scullery maid and knife boy. Reggie looked for Ivo in vain, but fortunately the Duchess was too busy composing herself for her triumphal return to notice her son's absence.

As she got out of the carriage, there was a rustle like wind blowing autumn leaves as the female servants sank into their deepest curtsy. Bertha, who was observing the scene from Cora's bedroom on the second floor, wondered if the servants here knew automatically which step they were meant to stand on to form a perfectly symmetrical inverted V, or whether they had had to be told. Did the scullery maid assume that her place was at the bottommost right-hand step, or had she settled herself a few steps higher and then been sent down to her correct station? In America there would have been all kinds of jostling for position; as a lady's maid her own position was at the top, just below the housekeeper, but that wouldn't stop the Irish housemaids from pushing themselves to the front. In England everyone knew their place.

She heard the door open and Cora's voice, high with excitement, calling her.

'Bertha, I need you now! The Duchess is here and I must be ready!'

Bertha turned from the spectacle at the window to see that her mistress had succeeded in getting out of her bodice and was tugging at the strings at her waist.

'I want the blue costume, the one with the high neck. Please hurry, I don't want to be late for lunch. Damn, these petticoats are muddy. I will have to change completely.'

Bertha went to the armoire and took out the blue costume. She had to use both arms to lift it as the skirt was a heavy broadcloth with an elaborate frogged border. Bertha looked at the row of tiny mother-of-pearl buttons on the back of the blouse and sighed. This was not a dress that could be hurried.

Her mistress was standing in a foamy sea of cotton and lace, pouting at herself in the cheval mirror. She wriggled into the petticoats that Bertha held out. At least the blue dress was in the very latest style and did not have a full bustle; there was only a small horsehair pad to hold the skirt out at the back. Arranging a bustle, Bertha knew from experience, could take half an hour. This dress had the new sleeves that ballooned out from the shoulder to be caught into a tight sleeve at the forearm. The skirt was gored, flowing out to a wide hem. The proportions were designed to narrow the waist, but Cora was tugging at the belt unsatisfied.

'Bertha, can you lace me a little tighter? I think I could go down an inch.'

'Not if you want to be ready in time for lunch, let alone eat anything.'

'Oh, I don't want to eat. . . Oh Bertha, can't you guess what's happened?'

The maid looked at Cora steadily. The girl's colour was up and there was a certain bruised quality to her mouth as if she had been eating raspberries.

'Can't you guess? The Duke, Ivo, has proposed! We were in the chapel and all of a sudden it happened.'

'And how did you answer?' Bertha fastened the nineteenth button.

'What do you think I said? Yes, of course.'

Bertha found her knees buckling beneath her and fell to the floor rather heavily. She had not fainted, rather the ground beneath her feet had simply seemed to give way.

'What are you doing, Bertha? Are you all right? Shall I fetch my smelling salts?' Cora was genuinely anxious, Bertha was her confidante and, moreoever, the only person capable of confecting the hairstyle she had determined to wear that night at dinner.

Bertha looked about her blankly and then pulled herself up on to Cora's bed where she sat down heavily.

'I'm fine, Miss Cora, it was just a turn, that's all. I guess if you're going to be a duchess and all, you'll be needing a fancy French mamselle not a Carolina foundling.'

'Oh, don't be so dramatic. When I am Duchess I shall have whoever I like. I'm not going to change just because I'm getting married, except that Mother won't be able to nag me all the time. Are you feeling better now? I really must go downstairs and meet my future mother-in-law.'

Bertha rose slowly to her feet and with clumsy, unresponsive fingers fastened the last buttons at the back of Cora's high-necked blue silk blouse. She freed a couple of chestnut tendrils from the stiff boned collar. She knew why Cora had chosen this costume, she could feel the red flush of her skin under the thin silk. As she finished, Cora squirmed away from her and rushed to the cheval glass to inspect herself. No need to bite her lips or pinch her cheeks, she looked vivid enough. Bertha watched as she leant forward and kissed her reflection in the speckled mirror. Cora saw Bertha looking at her in the mirror and she laughed a little foolishly.

'Wish me luck, Bertha. It's all beginning now, everything,' and Cora swept out of the room to her future. Bertha watched her go and then moved to the window where she pressed her face against the cold glass. A mist was rolling in from the sea, shrouding the view. She watched her warm breath turn the glass cloudy and without thinking she pressed the black pearl lying close to her heart.

Cora stood at the top of the stairs; she caught sight of her reflection in a gilt mirrored sconce. Almost perfect, but . . . she looked to see if anyone was about and then adjusted her bosom under the blue silk blouse. She was squaring her shoulders for the descent when she heard a voice that sliced through the dusty calm of the house so confidently that Cora knew that it could only belong to the Double Duchess.

'Darling Ivo, it is so lovely to be back at Lulworth. I had almost forgotten how thrilling that view of the sea is when you first come over the hill from the station. But you look pale, darling. I hope you aren't taking your responsibilities *too* seriously. You've been buried away down here for so long.'

'Well, now I have you to entertain me, Mother.' Ivo's voice was flat.

'And your Americans, of course,' the Duchess cooed. 'I can't wait to meet them. Charlotte says that Miss Cash is quite the thing.' She paused for a second and then said in a lower tone, 'Dear boy, I realise how lonely you must have been. I wish you had come to see me at Conyers. I could have made things more comfortable for you.'

'And how is your husband?' Ivo replied.

'Oh darling, there's no need to be like that. Buckingham was saying only the other day how much he looked forward to your maiden speech in the House. He is a great admirer of yours, you know.'

Ivo said nothing.

The Duchess tried again. 'I think you might have told me that Reggie was here. I should hardly have brought Sybil with me if I'd known.'

'I don't remember asking you to come, Mother,' Ivo said without emphasis.

There was a pause and Cora wondered what would happen next. Was Ivo going to tell his mother about their engagement? They had only come back an hour ago and yet that scene in the chapel already seemed unreal. Had Ivo really proposed or had she somehow imagined it? Was there some kind of secret English code that she had missed? It was all so unlikely – that sudden connection, as if from nowhere. She heard footsteps coming down the gallery; she must go or be discovered eavesdropping.

'I came because I thought you might need me, darling.' The Duchess's voice was soft but Ivo did not yield.

'I'm touched by your concern, Mother, especially when I know how busy you are with all your new duties. I'm surprised Buckingham can spare you.' He looked up and saw Cora coming down the stairs. 'But here comes Miss Cash now. Miss Cash, please come and meet my mother, she wants to inspect you.'

Cora saw a blonde woman, younger and more chic than she had expected. This was not the dowager in dirty diamonds that she had vaguely imagined but a beauty who hardly looked old enough to be Ivo's mother. Only as she got closer did she see the web of lines around the eyes and the faint weathering of the skin that betrayed the Duchess's real age.

'My dear Miss Cash, Ivo is so uncouth.' The Duchess's voice had dropped into a thrilling coo like a seductive wood pigeon. 'I want to assure myself that you have been looked after. Such an unfortunate accident . . . All alone in a strange country. I dread to think what might have happened if Ivo had not happened to be riding through Paradise Wood that morning. And now forced to put up in my son's bachelor establishment. I feel for you. Ivo really has no idea of comfort. His tastes are positively Spartan.'

Cora found that she had the advantage of at least two inches over the Duchess. Normally her height was a cause for self-consciousness but here she was glad of it.

'Oh, Your Grace, I could not have been better looked after. Your son has been the most attentive host.' Cora gave her best American smile and her eyes flickered over to Ivo.

The Duchess looked at her carefully. The girl was certainly presentable. Tall, with chestnut hair and greenish eyes, she had the carriage and the neck to carry off the fashionable silhouette of the season. Some women looked puny and cowed in those enormous sleeves. Reggie had been right, she was used to getting her own way; this was not a girl whose future had depended on the close observation of waistcoat buttons. She saw her glance at Ivo. They smiled at each other. The Duchess wondered if her son realised what sort of girl she was. All the prospective brides Ivo had encountered, that she had placed in his way, had known the rules, had been inducted from birth in the rituals of their world. But this American miss was from a different world entirely.

'And I believe your mother is here also? How fortunate that she was able to join you. But like all mothers she knew that her place was with her child at the hour of need.' The Duchess looked meaningfully at Ivo.

Cora caught the look and felt the colour rising to her face. Was the Duchess hinting that she had come to save her son from an unfortunate marriage?

But the Duchess smiled sadly and continued, 'It was three years ago that Guy, my eldest son, died.' She placed her hand on Ivo's arm briefly. He made no answering movement.

They heard voices coming down the hall

'And how did you get here, Lady Sybil? At home we always take our own train to Newport. Even with two separate establishments, there is still so much stuff to be carried back and forth. My husband had to buy the railway in the end so that there would be no difficulties with the timetable.' Mrs Cash entered the hall with Sybil at her side.

Cora noted the way the Duchess's eyes lit upon the brooch her mother wore pinned to hold down her veil; it was a huge ruby in a nest of diamonds. Perhaps for the first time in her life, Cora was grateful for her mother's sense of her own magnificence. She looked at Ivo and thought she saw his lips twitch, but before she could catch his eye properly there was a flurry of introductions and they were being ushered into the dining room.

The Duchess made a great display of hesitating before she took the seat that had once been hers at the opposite end of the table to her son. Cora saw that this uncertainty was aimed at Ivo but he refused to rise to the bait. When, in desperation, the Duchess said, with a quaver in her voice, 'How charming to find myself once more at Lulworth at my end of the table, and yet of course how poignant it is when I remember how things were,' Ivo simply nodded and without looking at his mother asked Mrs Cash whether her private train had loose boxes.

Cora was seated between Reggie and Father Oliver, with the Duchess on Reggie's other side. She could see that Reggie was to be monopolised by the Duchess so she began to ask Father Oliver about the history of the Lulworth chapel. As the priest recounted in detail the various vicissitudes of Catholicism at Lulworth, Cora was able to watch the Duchess talk intimately to Reggie and the effect this was having on her stepdaughter Lady Sybil. Cora thought that Sybil was quite good-looking for an English girl, despite her dowdy clothes and miserable hair. They must be about the same age. Cora wondered how the girl liked having the Duchess for a stepmother.

At the end of the meal Cora observed a curious ritual which had puzzled her the night before. One of the footmen was scraping all the contents of the serving dishes into a series of tins. This was quite indiscriminate: fish, eggs in aspic and trifle were all piled into the same receptacles which were then stacked on top of one another in a wicker basket. She turned to Reggie and asked him where the food was going.

'Oh, I suspect it must be for the poor and infirm of Lulworth. Is that right, Duchess?'

The Duchess turned her blond head. 'Yes, there is such a tradition of charity at Lulworth, the poor man at the gate and so forth. Really quite a lot of work for the servants, but it is so counted upon . . .'

Cora looked at the Duchess. 'But is there any reason why all the food is jumbled together? I just saw the remains of a raspberry soufflé being thrown into the same dish as the mutton. Surely it would be no trouble to put the food into separate dishes?'

Duchess Fanny put down the spoon she had been holding with a clatter. At the other end of the table her son looked up.

'My dear Miss Cash, the villagers at Lulworth are not gourmets. They are quite happy to have a meal even if it isn't as cooked by Escoffier.' The Duchess's tone was light and there was a hint of a laugh in her voice, but her eyes were cold.

'But it would take so little to make the food more palatable,' Cora protested. 'There is no reason why charity should be indigestible.'

Before the Duchess could reply, Ivo spoke.

'Indeed there isn't, and when you are chatelaine of this house, Cora, I suspect that we will have the most contented parishioners anywhere in the kingdom.'

The table fell silent. Mrs Cash, who was raising a glass to her lips, froze. Ivo rose to his feet.

'Mother, Mrs Cash, I apologise for the scant ceremony, but this morning I asked Cora to marry me and I am delighted to say that she accepted.'

There was a pause. Even the servants stopped weaving around the table.

Then the Duchess put her head on one side and smiled at her son. 'Ivo darling, how perfectly romantic. Dear Mrs Cash, you must forgive my impulsive son. He, of course, needs to consult with Mr Cash.' Then her blue eyes opened wide and she said in mock dismay, 'Oh, I hope there is a Mr Cash?'

Mrs Cash moved her head by a fraction. She could find no words to express her feelings; shock, pleasure, outrage mingled in equal measure. 'My husband is in New York.'

'Then, Ivo, you must telegraph at once.' With a great swish of satin, the Duchess rose to her feet. A footman scurried to pull back her chair. She ignored her son and looked at Mrs Cash. 'Ladies, shall we?' And with her blond head held high, she moved towards the door. As she walked the length of the table, the ladies got up one by one to follow her; even Cora was pulled to her feet. Only when she reached the door did the Duchess stop and look back at her son.

He stood up and opened it for her.

As she walked past him, she laid one gloved finger against his cheek. 'Dearest Ivo, I should have come sooner. I never realised how much you minded.'

It was much later before Cora realised what she meant.

Part Two

LORD BENNET.

Eldest son and heir of the sixth Earl of Tankerville.

The entailed estates amount to 31,000 acres, yielding an income of $150,000.

The Earl owns the only herd of wild cattle to be found in Great Britain.

Lord Bennet, who at present has nothing but a very small allowance, has served in the navy and the army, and is thirty-six years of age.

Family seat: Chillingham Castle, Northumberland.

Excerpt from 'A carefully composed List of Peers, who are supposed to be eager to lay their coronets, and incidentally their hearts, at the feet of the all-conquering American Girl'

Titled Americans, 1890

CHAPTER 10

Mrs Van Der Leyden Pays a Call

New York, March 1894

M RS VAN DER LEYDEN LOOKED AT THE LETTERS lying on the silver salver. She recognised her sister's handwriting, the quaver in the way she wrote the words 'Washington Square', and her heart sank. Poor Effie, her husband's 'accident' had been so unfortunate. To clean your gun with fatal consequences at the moment when there were widespread rumours about the bank was an unhappy coincidence. She knew that Effie's letter would pain her. Her sister had let herself go and she dreaded the covert appeals for money on every page. She would help, of course, it was her duty; but it would be in a time and manner of her own choosing.

Mrs Van Der Leyden put her sister's letter aside and picked up a thin envelope that bore a foreign stamp. She recognised her son's handwriting and duly picked up the silver paper knife that had been a gift to her from Ward McAlister on the occasion of her marriage. Her son's letter was affectionate but brief. He would be returning from France on the *Berengaria* which docked on the fourteenth; he vouchsafed nothing about his plans for the future or the reason why he was returning months earlier than he had originally planned. She hoped that he had finished with painting and had come back to claim his rightful position in the family law firm, but Teddy had always been such a stubborn boy and she doubted whether, having fought so hard, he would give up so easily. And then a ghastly thought came to her and she rapidly scanned the page again. No, he made no mention of a companion, nobody that he was anxious for her to meet. That, at least, was a relief. A foreign daughter-in-law from God knows where would be a drawback even for a Van Der Leyden.

Still wondering about her son's state of mind, Mrs Van Der Leyden picked up the last envelope on the salver: a heavy slab of pasteboard – an invitation of some sort. She picked up the paper knife. Mr and Mrs Winthrop Cash request the pleasure etc. at the marriage of their daughter Cora to His Grace the Duke of Wareham at Trinity Church on 16 March. So Nancy Cash had found a title for Cora after all. Personally, Mrs Van der Leyden found the desire to link American money with European aristocracy rather vulgar, but then if you were fortunate enough to bear the name Van Der Leyden, a title was superfluous. She couldn't really blame Nancy Cash for wanting a duchess for a daughter. The Cashes were rich all right and Nancy, of course, came from a fine old Southern family, but they weren't quite the thing. Cora had only been chosen to dance the quadrille at the Patriarch's Ball after one of the Schoonmaker girls had fallen ill with rheumatic fever. Isobel, of course, had been in the original eight, which was her birthright as a Van Der Leyden. It didn't hurt Nancy Cash to be reminded once in a while that money couldn't buy everything.

It could, however, secure a duke. Martha Van Der Leyden had never heard of the Duke of Wareham. But that was probably to his credit: last season there had been quite a clutch of English lords looking for heiresses. There had been the Duke of Manchester who had made quite a play for Isobel at first but had married a sewing machine heiress from Cincinnati. It was quite clear what he was after. No, she had never heard of Wareham, but no doubt he had a crumbling mansion in need of repair. Still, Cora was a handsome girl, who would make a perfectly creditable duchess. She was headstrong and perhaps a little fast (there had been that business with Teddy at the Cash ball in Newport – Teddy had never explained to her satisfaction why he had been alone on the terrace with Cora). No, Cora Cash would do very well and really the family was not an embarrassment. There was that business with Nancy Cash's father killing himself in the asylum but, after all, thought Mrs Van Der Leyden looking at poor Effie's letter, these things could happen in the very best families.

It was only when she rang the bell to have the breakfast things cleared away that it occurred to her that there might be some connection between her son's arrival and the Cash girl's impending nuptials. But surely Teddy would not be foolish enough to imagine that he could prevent Cora from marrying this duke. Mrs Cash would let nothing come in the way of that marriage and for once Mrs Van Der Leyden agreed with her. Cora Cash might make a passable duchess but she was not a suitable candidate to be Mrs Van Der Leyden Junior. Really, she hoped Teddy had not come back with romantic notions. She would turn a blind eye to his artistic ambitions; she had heard some quite shocking things about artist's models but she was prepared to ignore this, provided it was all safely in a foreign country. But to pursue an engaged girl, that would be a scandal that even a Van Der Leyden would have difficulty rising above.

She put the paper knife down on the salver and noticed, to her disappointment, a speck of tarnish in the moulding. Pursing her thin lips, she went up the stairs to her bedroom and told the maid to fetch her hat and cloak. Her visiting dress was very much in last year's style but she was of the generation that thought it was vulgar to be in fashion and she regularly packed away the new season's clothes until the moment when to wear them would not be seen as ostentatious. It was time to pay a call on Mrs Cash. For a moment she considered walking the half mile or so to the Cash mansion at 660 Fifth Avenue – really, it was barely civilised up there – but when she thought of the marble entrance hall and the footmen in their matching livery, she decided to take the carriage.

Fifteen years ago the Winthrop Cashes had been universally mocked for their audacity when they unveiled their plans for a town house in the far north of the island. But now the Cash mansion that occupied the whole block at 60th and Fifth was at the beginning of a strip of fashionable buildings that stretched as far as 70th Street. Although the Cash mansion no longer stood in isolation, it was still the most magnificent. In a city of brownstone houses, 660 Fifth was built of honey-coloured stone. It was Mrs Cash's first house and she had, in her youthful enthusiasm, asked Spencer the architect to build her a castle, and had been delighted when he showed the plans complete with turrets and gargoyles. His designs for the interiors had come complete with tiny figures wearing doublet and hose and farthingales. Mrs Cash, who had visited the Loire Valley on her honeymoon in Europe, adored the whimsicality of his design, so different from the neoclassicism of the South or the drab narrow town houses of her adopted city. Winthrop had raised a few objections to living in the 'wilderness' above 44th Street but he soon realised that his bride was not to be deflected. She had shown the plans to his father the Golden

Miller, who had goggled at the turrets and the eighty-foot dining room and had asked who was going to pay for all this. Nancy had turned to him, put one small white hand on his arm and, looking him straight in the eyes, had said, 'Why, you are, Papa.' There had been no more discussion. The house had been built and Nancy's campaign to become 'the' Mrs Cash had begun.

As the tall footman in the full Cash livery of purple and gold held the door of her carriage open for her, Mrs Van Der Leyden felt a shiver of irritation. She had grown up in a house where the door was opened by maids in stuff gowns and white aprons. This fashion for male indoor servants dressed up like peacocks was one of the many things brought over from Europe by the new rich of which Martha Van Der Leyden disapproved. To her Knickerbocker mind, men did outdoor work looking after the horses or tending the garden, they did not prance around in knee breeches doing the work of housemaids.

A moment later Mrs Van Der Leyden sat erect on one of the Louis sofas in Mrs Cash's drawing room. A lesser woman might have been intimidated by the sheer scale of the room with its original French *boiserie*, Flemish tapestries and an Aubusson carpet that was reputed to be the largest ever made. But Mrs Van Der Leyden sat secure in the knowledge that without her presence, no social gathering in this city was considered truly respectable. She had no fear of finding Mrs Cash 'not at home'.

Her hostess sailed across the Aubusson towards her. Mrs Cash did not, as a rule, receive callers so early (it took so long to arrange her veils and gauze to her satisfaction) but this was an exception. She was looking forward to seeing her new status as the mother of a future duchess acknowledged by the redoubtable Martha Van Der Leyden.

'Dear Mrs Van Der Leyden, what an unexpected pleasure. I have hardly seen a soul since we returned from Europe, we have been so busy with the preparations with the wedding. I hope you received your invitation. It is quite the wrong time of year to get married, as everyone is so busy with the season, but Cora and Wareham are so impatient, dear things, that they would not wait. I am sure that dear Isobel would not be as inconsiderate as my headstrong girl!'

Both women knew, of course, that Isobel Van Der Leyden's matrimonial prospects looked increasingly remote with each passing year.

'I must congratulate you, Mrs Cash. Tell me about the Duke, I am so ignorant of the English aristocracy. I don't recall seeing him here.' Mrs Van Der Leyden lowered her gaze.

'Oh no, Wareham has never been to America. Cora and he had a notion to be married in the chapel at Lulworth, which is the Maltravers country seat, but I was determined that Wareham should see something of his bride's country. Sometimes I believe that the English think we still live behind stockades.'

Mrs Van Der Leyden nodded gravely, not by a flicker did she betray her understanding of just how much the wedding of her daughter to a duke meant to Mrs Cash.

'It is only fitting that Cora should be married from her family home.'

Mrs Cash smiled gratefully. If Mrs Van Der Leyden thought it was fitting then all was well.

'But forgive me for all this wedding talk. How is dear Mr Van Der Leyden? Is he still bicycling in the park? Such youthful vigour. I would be quite alarmed if Winthrop took up anything so energetic.'

'Cornelius has always been the first to try things. I believe we were the first house in the square to have electric light. Personally I see nothing wrong with the way things are, but the Van Der Leyden men are all for Progress. When Teddy returns from Paris next month I shall be quite outnumbered.' Having introduced the real reason for her visit into the conversation, Mrs Van Der Leyden observed her hostess closely, but Mrs Cash did not seem perturbed.

'You must be so happy that he is coming back. Cora, I know, will be delighted. And of course I owe your son so much.' Mrs Cash gestured poignantly towards the veiled side of her face. 'I hope he will be back in time for the wedding.'

'Yes, his ship gets in on the fourteenth.'

'The *Berengaria*? Why, that is the vessel that the Duke and his party are on. The Duke is bringing his mother, who is Duchess of Buckingham now. I am so looking forward to showing her New York.'

But Mrs Van Der Leyden had no interest in duchesses, her business with Mrs Cash was finished: she had warned the other woman of her son's return. She pulled on her gloves and made to leave.

'Do give my regards to Cora. I am sorry not to see her today, but I shall look forward to seeing her as a bride.' And Mrs Van Der Leyden walked the length of the Aubusson, reassured that Mrs Cash, who surely had the most to lose, had not shown even a flicker of concern over the imminent arrival of Teddy.

As she walked down the wide marble steps, she saw Cora coming in with her maid, followed by a footman bestrewn with parcels. Even to Martha Van Der Leyden's disapproving eye, the girl looked radiant. She was wearing a brown tailor-made costume of such severe cut that on another girl it would have looked quite forbidding, but on Cora with her conker-coloured hair and shiny eyes it was simply a frame. The older woman understood why Mrs Cash had not been concerned by Teddy's arrival. For the first time in many years, Mrs Van Der Leyden, who had seen everything, was surprised: Cora Cash was clearly in love. That look was unmistakable. Mrs Van Der Leyden was so used to seeing it in unbecoming places that she was almost touched at the idea that a girl of such beauty and wealth might actually be marrying a Duke because she loved him.

Cora looked up and saw her.

'Mrs Van Der Leyden, I am so glad to see you. Now I know I am really in New York. Everyone else tries so hard to be European, I hardly know where I am, but now I have seen you, I know exactly which country I'm in. How are Isobel and Teddy?' Cora could not help but smile when she said Teddy's name and for a moment Mrs Van Der Leyden felt her misgivings return.

'They are both quite well and looking forward to seeing you married. Your mother has been telling me all about the wedding. It will be quite the spectacle.'

'Oh, you know Mother, everything has to be the best. But did you say that Teddy would be coming to the wedding? I thought he was in Europe. I was planning to look him up on our wedding trip. Why has he come back so soon? I thought he was going to study in Paris.'

Mrs Van Der Leyden smiled faintly. 'Who knows what makes young men change their plans? Perhaps he has lost his heart to a French marquise and has come back to ask for my blessing. You young people seem to find Europe so romantic.'

She was rewarded by seeing Cora flush and the wide smile falter.

'When is Teddy coming back? I would so like to see him. Ivo and I are leaving directly after the wedding. I hope I don't miss him as I really don't know when I will be back.' For a moment she looked a little forlorn as she felt the width of the Atlantic between Fifth Avenue and her destiny.

Mrs Van Der Leyden patted her on the arm. 'I received Teddy's letter this morning, I'm sure he will be here for your wedding.' She saw no reason to mention that Teddy was travelling on the same boat as Cora's fiancé. She would leave that to Mrs Cash. 'Goodbye, my dear.' Mrs Van Der Leyden pecked her on the cheek. She could feel the heat of Cora's skin against hers. The girl was burning up. It was high time she was married.

In Cora's bedroom, Bertha was unpacking one of the thirty trunks that had arrived yesterday from Maison Worth in Paris. After the engagement, Mrs Cash had not lingered in Lulworth even though Cora would have liked to stay longer. Mother and daughter had gone to Paris where they spent a month having fittings at Maison Worth and buying shoes, hats, gloves and jewels. Mrs Cash had been planning for this moment for years. A year ago she had had Worth take Cora's measurements so that he could start creating her trousseau. When Cora had found out just how far her mother had been planning in advance, she asked her how she could have been so sure that she would marry within the year. 'Because that had always been my intention,' said Mrs Cash.

Bertha picked up a tissue-wrapped parcel and opened it carefully. It was a corset. As she held it out, Cora walked in carrying a magazine.

'Bring that here, Bertha. Is that the one Mrs Redding writes about in *Vogue*? "The bridal corset is made of pink satin, embroidered with tiny white carnations and trimmed at the upper edge with a deep pointed border of Valenciennes lace. The clasps, the large hook, and the buckles on the attached stocking supporters are all made of solid gold studded with diamonds." All correct except for the diamonds of course. Why would anyone put diamonds on their corset? I am embarrassed that anyone would think me so foolish.'

Bertha said nothing. It was not her place to point out that Cora's corset even without the diamonds would pay her salary for the next twenty years. The clasps were fashioned from twenty-one-carat gold and the silk from the corset had been woven to order in Lyons. And this corset was only one of five in Cora's trousseau. The lace alone on the numerous nightgowns, peignoirs, wrappers, bedjackets, and petticoats was probably worth more than diamonds, as all of it was handmade, some of it worn by the French queen who had had her head cut off.

And then there were the dresses, all ninety of them. Each dress packed in yards of tissue paper and suspended over a tape frame so that it would not be crushed. There were plain day dresses for writing letters in the morning, riding habits in dark blue and bottle green, visiting dresses with the widest of leg-of-mutton sleeves and passementerie fringing around the hem, strict tailor-mades for yachting with no ornament but braid, tea gowns frothing with lace and with such a forgiving silhouette that they could be worn without a corset; there were theatre dresses with high necklines and long sleeves, and opera dresses with lower necklines and short sleeves, dinner dresses with half high necklines and elbow-length sleeves, and ball dresses with full décolletage and trains; and of course the wedding dress itself which had so many pearls sewn on to its train that when it swept along the floor it made a faint crunching noise like fairies walking across gravel. Not to mention the furs: Mrs Cash had ordered a sable cloak for Cora modelled on one the Grand Duchess Sophia had worn in Paris. It was so heavy that it could really only be worn sitting down. Bertha remembered the damp chill of Lulworth and thought that Cora might be grateful for the cloak, and for all the other stoles and fur-trimmed dolmans, muffs and mantles that Mrs Cash had thought necessary for a duchess.

Mrs Cash had wanted to order Cora's state robes as well, but when she wrote to the Double Duchess about this, Her Grace had replied that 'robes were never bought, but inherited'. Mrs Cash, who suspected that robes inherited at Lulworth would be as musty and damp-smelling as everything else there, had tried to protest but Mrs Wyndham had taken her aside and told her that damp and mustiness were much prized among the aristocracy as they showed that the title was of an old creation. Only new titles had freshly made robes. Mrs Cash had allowed herself to be overruled but she still could not understand why the British liked things to be shabby. It had taken weeks before she could persuade Wareham to install a proper bathroom for Cora at Lulworth. He had seemed to think there was nothing wrong with a duchess having to wash herself in a copper hip bath in front of the fire. Bertha had heard the whole story as Mrs Cash had unburdened herself to Cora. Cora had laughed at her mother for her American passion for progress but underneath Bertha knew that her mistress was secretly relieved. Cora loved the romance of Lulworth, but Bertha had seen her shiver as she went down for dinner in a low-cut evening dress and her look when she had found ice on the inside of the mullioned window of her bedroom.

Here in Cora's bedroom it was pleasantly warm. The Cash house had had the latest steam heating system installed when it was built. Even the servants' bedrooms were heated. Bertha thought of the draughty attic she had slept in at Lulworth and wondered not for the first time whether her destiny really lay in England, but then she thought of Jim and that night in the stables at Sutton Veney. He had written to her once at Lulworth. It had not been much of a letter, but it was the first letter of a sentimental nature that Bertha had ever received and she carried it with her everywhere tucked round the black pearl.

Cora was reading aloud again. She was fascinated by all the stories about her wedding in the newspapers. In public it was very bad form to admit that you had read any of the scandal rags but in private Cora devoured them.

'*Town Topics* has pages about the wedding. It says my departure for Europe broke hearts all over New York and that my marriage will deprive New York society of one of its brightest stars. "What a pity that one of the greatest heiresses that we have ever produced should take her talents and her fortune abroad to the benefit of some dilapidated English castle, instead of bestowing her beauty and wealth on one of her fellow countrymen. *Town Topics* has heard that Newport last summer had fully expected Miss Cash to announce a more patriotic match. We can only assume that the ever ambitious Mrs Cash is responsible for her daughter's change of direction. Mrs Cash has long sought to become the pre-eminent hostess of her day, and having a duchess for a daughter can only bring that day closer." They couldn't be more wrong, of course, Mother had nothing to do with my marriage. Why don't people realise that I have a mind of my own?'

Again Bertha said nothing. Cora tossed the paper on the floor. Bertha was counting kid gloves, thirty-two, thirty-three, thirty-four, there should be fifty pairs. Cora's gloves never lasted longer than an evening. Skin-tight and so thin that the fingernails were visible through the translucent leather, they took an age to get on and off and Cora would quiver with impatience as Bertha tried to roll them off without damaging them. Most evenings Cora would push her away and rip the gloves off with her teeth. Bertha was used to it but it always pained her, as used kid gloves of this quality fetched 25c a pair at the dress exchange where Bertha went to sell Cora's cast-offs. Mrs Cash always demanded receipts for the dresses, but the gloves were beneath her notice. Bertha wondered whether there was a trade in kid gloves in London.

The door opened and Mrs Cash came in carrying a large blue leather box in both hands. Cora did not get up. Since the engagement, Bertha had noticed that Cora was far less in awe of her mother. But Mrs Cash did not appear to notice.

'I am delighted you are back, Cora. I have something to show you.'

She sat down on the sofa next to Cora and touched the clasp of the blue leather box. It sprang open with a heavy click and from the other side of the room Bertha could see thousands of points of light dance across the ceiling as a ray of light hit the contents.

Mrs Cash took the tiara out of the box and placed it on Cora's head. It was a diadem of stars that twinkled against the rich brown of Cora's hair.

'Thank God you didn't get your father's hair, dear. Diamonds are wasted on blondes.'

Cora walked over to the mirror to see what she looked like,

and faced with her reflection she couldn't help smiling.

'Oh, it's beautiful, Mother. Where did you get it?'

'I had Tiffany copy one belonging to the Empress of Austria. She has chestnut hair like you. You will need a tiara when you are married and I wanted you to have something light and graceful. I saw some really hideous jewels in London, huge gems but such dingy settings. Really, what is the point of dirty diamonds?'

Cora turned her head to the side. 'I feel quite the Duchess when I'm wearing this.' She made a stately curtsy to her reflection. Her mother reached over and tucked in a strand of hair that had escaped from the tiara. Cora looked at her mother, and was astonished to see that her mother's good eye was wet.

Forty-eight, forty-nine, fifty, fifty-one. There was a pair of gloves too many. A new pair of gloves would fetch at least a dollar and in Bertha's opinion, taking what was surplus to requirements was not the same as stealing. Bertha looked up to see if the women were watching her, but they were too absorbed in each other. She took the gloves and stuffed them in her pocket. She might want to get married herself one day.

CHAPTER 11

Euston Station

TWO WEEKS AFTER HIS MOTHER HAD MADE HER way up Fifth Avenue, Teddy Van Der Leyden found himself making the same journey. But after ten days on board ship, the young man was happy to walk in the bright cold morning. He told himself that it was the exercise he wanted but there was another reason for walking – he needed to think. When he had heard of Cora's engagement he had felt an immediate, unreasonable sense of loss. He was not surprised exactly by the engagement, such a match had only been a matter of time; what he had not expected was how much he would mind. He heard the news from an English acquaintance in Paris who had been buzzing with the serendipity of it all. Wareham is a lucky fellow, the artistically inclined baronet had said, the American girl fell into his lap, literally. Came off her horse hunting and Wareham found her. A week later they were engaged. Couldn't have come at a better time for him – Lulworth is a terrible old barn and Wareham had to pay all these death duties, first the father then the brother. But they say the girl, Miss Cash, has pots of money, so she should be able to set all that straight. What, you know her? Is she really as rich as they say? Richer? Wish I'd been in that wood when she had that tumble.

Teddy drank absinthe that night and spent the next day in a queasy fog underpinned by the feeling that something was badly wrong. It was only in the evening that he realised that it was Cora's engagement that had brought on this feeling of dread. He had sent her to this and now he didn't like it. He had gone to London to look for her, to talk to her, but she had already left for New York. He knew, even as he bought his ticket for the SS *Berengaria*, that it was a mistake – that he had made his choice that night in Newport and now Cora had made hers. But still he carried on. If Cora really loved this duke then he could do nothing, but if she was being forced into a dynastic match by her mother, he would rescue her. He must talk to Cora once before she disappeared into a world of stately homes and coronets.

He had spent a few days in London in a haze of impatience. Once he knew that the Cashes had gone back to New York, he wanted nothing but to get back to America himself. He had made his way to Euston Station to board the train for Liverpool automatically; he just wanted to be at his destination. But there was one scene that had pierced his numbness: a couple on the platform at Euston, a man and a woman looking at each other with such intensity that Teddy felt almost scorched by it. The woman, he thought, was beautiful, he could see the gorgeous curve of her cheek beneath the deep brim of her hat. The man was tall and dark and Teddy sensed there was tension in the square of his shoulders and the set of his jaw. The couple stood there motionless, an island of stillness in the frantic bustle and clamour of the boat-train traffic. They were not speaking, all communication was in their gaze. And then Teddy saw the woman take the man's hand with a small, almost feral gesture and pull it into the fur muff she was carrying. She looked up at him with challenge in her eyes. The man leant forward stiffly, he whispered something in the woman's ear. He withdrew his hand from the muff and stood tall, although his eyes never once left her face. She turned and walked down the platform, the man looking after her. Teddy wondered if she would look back at him but she kept on walking. There was a scream from the locomotive and the man started and began to move towards the train. Teddy continued to watch the woman and was rewarded by a glimpse of her veiled face looking back at last. But the man had disappeared on to the train. Teddy wanted to tell her that the man had waited as long as he could, that there had been no loss of faith.

The scene had stayed with him as he boarded the *Berengaria*. The way the woman had placed the man's hand in her muff suggested intimacy but not, Teddy thought, marriage. Married couples would embrace openly; that gesture spoke of concealment. She had wanted something from him, but had he given it? Teddy could not be sure.

The crossing had been rough and Teddy had spent most of it in his cabin as the ship lurched nauseously from one swell to the next. But on the fourth day, the weather cleared and Teddy ventured out on deck. He was walking rather unsteadily to a group of steamer chairs when he saw the man from the station talking to two women. Teddy almost greeted him as the man had been such a big part of his thoughts for the last few days, but of course the man had not seen him and had no idea who he was. The steward with Teddy saw the direction of his glance and asked him if he knew His Grace the Duke of Wareham. Teddy shook his head –

he felt a return of his earlier queasiness as he realised that this was Cora's fiancé. He tried to walk away, but the steward was determined to tell him about the Duke, his mother the Duchess and his stepsister the Lady Sybil and how they were all going over to attend the Duke's wedding to an American girl, the richest girl in the world, they said. Nice gentleman, the Duke, very civil to the crew, and as for his mother the Duchess, well, she was something else, a real lady. Teddy could bear no more and dispatched the steward for some broth. Wrapped in rugs in his steamer chair, his book covering his face, Teddy was able to observe the Duke unseen. He was dark for an Englishman and spare in build. His features were mobile but saved from weakness by a strong Roman nose. As he listened to his mother tell some story, the Duke smiled but Teddy thought that he seemed detached, as if he was thinking of something else. His mother clearly noticed this as well and tapped him on the arm with her parasol. The Duke started, collected himself and offered both ladies his arm so they could make a circuit of the deck. They made a graceful trio.

For the rest of the journey, Teddy hid in his cabin. He didn't want to see the Duke again. He dreaded an introduction that would inevitably result in a conversation about Cora. When they reached New York he lingered in his stateroom until he was sure that the ducal party had disembarked. The last thing he wanted was to encounter Cora on the quay.

Now, as Teddy approached the park, he was still no clearer in his mind. He had come back from Europe because he wanted to give Cora a choice. But did he have the right to tell her what he had seen on the platform in London? He was sure that what he had witnessed was a lovers' farewell. Would that give him an advantage, one that he did not merit? He had had his chance with Cora after all, but he had been too scared then of all her paraphernalia to take it. Did he have the right to spoil the chances of his rival? Did he really want Cora on those terms? He was on the corner of the block that was occupied by the Cash mansion. As he walked up the street he saw Mrs Cash and the Duchess get into a carriage. He rang the bell and gave his card to the footman.

Presently there was a rustle and a vision in green swept down the stairs. His first impression was that Cora had changed, in a way that he could not immediately define. She rushed towards him and took his hands.

'Teddy, I am so glad you are here. How clever of you to come when Mother is out. All she talks about is the wedding.' She took his arm. 'Let's go into the library, the drawing room is full of wedding gifts. You look very fine, very Continental and distinguished. How is the painting? Shall I come and sit for you when I am a duchess? Or are you too grand to paint society ladies? I hear Sargent regularly turns people away if they don't interest him.'

Teddy could see she was nervous, trying to fill the room with chatter so that there would be no space for awkwardness. She looked beautiful but feverish, he could see red spots of colour on her cheeks and neck.

'Paris was everything I had hoped for. It is so far ahead of New York. I was lucky enough to work with Menasche for a while. He said I had some talent.' He looked at his hands.

'That's wonderful, Teddy. I know how much you admire him.' Cora smiled.

There was a silence. The fact of her marriage lay heavily between them. At last Teddy plunged in.

'Cora, I came here because I wanted to be sure that you were happy. I have no doubt that your mother is happy and your Duke and your dressmaker but I just wanted to be sure that you were.' He paused, realising that his tone was too light, Cora would think he was teasing her. 'I came today because I realise that last summer you offered me something precious that I was too foolish to accept. No, please, let me speak.' Cora was trying to bat away his words with her hands as if they were bees about to sting her. 'Now you are engaged to be married, I have no right to say anything at all, but Cora, can you tell me that this is what you want, that you love this man and you want to be with him?'

Cora hung her head. She picked at a green bobble that hung from the fringe on her bodice. But when she looked at him at last, her face was scarlet and her eyes were fierce.

'How dare you come and offer to rescue me! Last summer you wouldn't help me when I asked, but now that I don't need your help, you have come back. It's too late, Teddy.' She pulled at the green bobble so hard that it came away in her hand. Teddy tried to speak but she rushed on. 'Do you really think I would marry a man I didn't care for to please my mother?'

'Do you love him?' Teddy forced himself to ask, even though he dreaded the answer.

'How can you ask me that?' Cora turned her head away.

'I just want you to be sure. If you answer yes then this conversation will stop and we can pretend it never happened. But if you can't say yes, then I am here.'

Cora still looked away. Without thinking, he put out his hand to touch that flushed cheek. He felt her flinch. How could he tell her now what he knew about the Duke? She wouldn't believe him. After all, what had he seen? A parting, a passionate one but a parting nonetheless. If the Duke had to put his affairs in order before his marriage, surely there was nothing so terrible in that – any more than there was in Cora saying goodbye to him now. Anything he said would seem motivated by jealousy. He tried to put things right with her.

'Cora, I know how fine you are, don't be angry with me. I only came here because I care for you.'

Cora heard the catch in his voice and her face softened. She was about to speak when the library door opened and the girl Teddy had seen with the Duke on the boat walked in.

'Oh, I am sorry, Cora. I didn't realise you had a visitor.' There was a pause.

Cora shook herself and when she spoke her voice was light.

'Sybil, this is Teddy Van Der Leyden. Teddy, this is Lady Sybil Lytchett, she is the Duke's stepsister and one of my bridesmaids.' Her voice was a little too high. Teddy felt the warning in it.

Sybil held out her hand awkwardly. 'I just came to ask you whether you could lend me something to wear tonight. I know it's a frightful imposition, but you all dress up so much here and I have worn my best evening dress three times. Your mother gave me one of her eyebrow raises last night. I could have died. It's all very well for Mama to say that breeding shines through, but honestly, Cora, I would much rather be well-dressed than well-bred.'

Cora could not help smiling, there was something very appealing about Sybil's lack of guile, 'Of course, you are more than welcome to take anything in my wardrobe. I will come and help you find something. As it happens, Mr Van Der Leyden was just leaving.' She turned to Teddy. 'I hope you will come and see us on your next trip to Europe. I don't know what I will do over there without all my old friends.'

She looked at him then and he thought he saw some trace of doubt in her eyes. He wondered again about the scene on the platform: what did Cora really know about her duke? For a moment he forgot about himself and felt apprehensive to think of this bright American girl entering Old World shadows. But she was smiling, a bright, taut, social smile for her future stepsister's benefit, and he knew he must leave.

'Certainly I will come and see you in Europe. If nothing else I must deliver your wedding gift. I thought perhaps a bicycle? I know how fond you are of cycling.' Cora caught his gaze and he knew that she, too, was thinking of that day in Newport when she had fallen off her bicycle. They were both thinking of what might have been. He walked to the door and turned.

'If you ever need an old friend, I will be there.' Teddy could not say more. He bowed to Sybil and shook Cora's outstretched hand and left.

Out in the sunshine he felt foolish. He had wanted to rescue Cora from a ducal cage but it seemed that she was entering it willingly. He had handled things so badly. What Cora wanted, he now realised, was love, and all he had offered her was protection. And now it was too late, the wedding was in less than a week. He must write to her. At least then she would know how he really felt: that he didn't want to rescue her, he wanted to tear her away.

He walked down Fifth Avenue, his hands in the pockets of his ulster, framing the letter in his head.

He was so preoccupied that he did not notice Mrs Cash's carriage as it returned to the house. She noticed him, though. She hoped she had not been too confident. Perhaps it would be as well to monitor Cora's visitors and correspondence until the girl was safely married. Cora was so impulsive and the Duke could be so prickly.

If they were to have some ridiculous tiff and Cora were to seek solace with Teddy Van Der Leyden... Mrs Cash shivered. If only the Duke had stayed in New York instead of going on that absurd hunting expedition. It was very strange behaviour so close to the wedding, especially after all the unpleasantness over the marriage settlement. Winthrop had not wanted to tell her all the details but apparently the Duke had been quite put out by the fact that the money had been settled directly on Cora. He said he found the presumption behind it insulting. How could there be separation of property between husband and wife? But Winthrop had been firm, Cora was his only child and he had to protect her interests. Immediately after this conversation, the Duke had announced that he was going hunting. Mrs Cash had expected Cora to object, but her daughter had made no protest. Only the Duchess had remonstrated with her son but without success. Wareham had gone off upstate with his best man Reggie, and his valet, to shoot canvasback duck. It had made the numbers at dinner quite uneven. What a good thing she had seen Teddy leaving the house, she had almost made up her mind to ask him to dinner to amuse poor Lady Sybil. Smiling as she always did at the sight of her tall footmen waiting to hand her out of her carriage – really, they were quite the finest specimens in New York – she began to review her list of amusing bachelors who could be summoned to dinner that night.

CHAPTER 12

Two Cigarettes

*I*N THE SERVANTS' HALL OF 660 FIFTH, THE departure of the Duke and the visit of Teddy Van Der Leyden was the subject of much speculation. The butler, who was English, held that the Duke was a sporting gentleman who preferred duck shooting to being put on display in Mrs Cash's drawing room, but the housekeeper was convinced that he had left in a huff because he wasn't getting his hands on all of Miss Cora's money – every detail of the row between the Duke and Mr Cash in Mr Cash's study having been overheard by the footman. A full report of the row was even now being turned into a spiky little column in *Town Topics* – Colonel Mann the editor had let it be known that he was prepared to pay handsomely for anything to do with the Cash wedding. Indeed, Colonel Mann was probably better informed about the disagreement between Cora's father and her future husband than Cora herself. Winthrop Cash had no desire to upset his daughter and the Duke did not talk about such things with anyone. He had told her he wanted to get away from 'all the people gawking at him' and she, having read that morning's *Town Topics* which contained a list of all the paintings and fine furniture that the Duke had sold in the past year, could only agree. If she was insulted, she could only imagine how he felt.

The argument swirled on with all parties taking sides. Only Bertha said nothing. This was not unusual. As the only coloured upper servant, her position was a strange one; no one would ask her opinion directly but as Cora's maid she was privy to all the information they craved. But Bertha was not silent from loyalty to Cora, she simply did not hear the hubbub around her. She was still replaying the scene of the day before yesterday at the New York Customs. Cora had wanted to meet the Duke's party at the docks and had taken Bertha as companion. Mrs Cash had thought the whole expedition unseemly but she had been unable to deflect her daughter. It had been cold standing in the Customs Hall and Bertha wished that she had a fur stole and muff like her mistress. At last the ducal party could be seen at the far end (the *Berengaria* disembarked its passengers in order of precedence). Cora gave a cry of excitement and started towards the tall figure of the Duke. Bertha knew she should restrain her but she was frozen by the sight of another figure standing a little to the right of the party, carrying a valise. The height and the blond hair reminded her of Jim, he had that same catlike way of walking – and then the man drew closer and his face was lit by a shaft of light from a hole in the roof above. It was Jim. Somehow he was here and he was smiling at her. She wanted to run to him as Cora had done, but of course she had to stand modestly behind her mistress. All she could do was raise one gloved hand in greeting and see Jim wink in return. No one else saw this exchange as everyone was looking at Cora launching herself at the Duke. As she did so, there was a flash and the sharp, dry smell of magnesium in the damp air of the Customs Hall. The photographer for the *Herald*, who was sent to cover all boats arriving from Europe, had got the picture of his career: Miss Cora Cash, radiant in fur, arms outstretched, and the Duke of Wareham standing to attention, his arms raised as if to ward off a blow. It was a trick of the camera, of course; the Duke had raised his arms to embrace Cora by her enormously exaggerated shoulders, but the camera only saw the defensive arms and the look of surprise on the Duke's face.

To Bertha's relief, her face was masked by Cora's furs in the published photograph. Only the raised gloved hand was visible in the corner.

After the commotion in the Customs Hall subsided, Cora leant on the Duke's arm and shepherded him to her carriage, with the Double Duchess, Reggie and Sybil following in her wake. Bertha hung back to supervise the loading of the luggage on to the wagon. Cora, she knew, would not miss her for hours and there was so much she had to say to Jim. He found her and caught her by the wrist. But she moved away from him, conscious of the witnesses all around them.

'Pleased to see me?'

Bertha nodded, she could not find the words to describe her feelings. Instead she said, 'How did you get here?'

'The Duke needed a valet and when I heard, I left Sir Odious right away and asked him for the job. I told him that I had always wanted to go to America. Course he didn't know why.' He looked at Bertha and she knew he wanted to kiss her, but she kept her distance. She was overwhelmed by his presence and what it meant. Jim felt her silence and carried on.

'Turned out his old valet suffered from seasickness and didn't want to go abroad, so he took me on right away. Oh Bertha, you should have seen your face when I came through that door. Your mouth was hanging open so wide.' He smiled at her, gleeful. But Bertha could not smile yet. There was so much to understand.

'I can't really believe you're here.'

'Didn't you get my letter?'

'Why yes, I have it here.' She patted the bodice of her dress. 'And the pearl, that's where I keep precious things. But you never said you were coming over.' She was half angry with him for not warning her.

'It was all decided at the last minute. I thought of writing to you but then I knew I was going to be seeing you, so I thought I would surprise you.' Jim put his hand on hers, right over the spot where the pearl was sewn into her dress. 'Did I do right then to come?'

Bertha heard the tremor in his voice and realised then that none of this had been easy for him. When she spoke she found herself talking in Cora's voice.

'Why, Jim, I couldn't be happier.'

He looked at her for a moment and then laughed. This was safer territory.

'The Duke could hardly believe it when she flew at him like that,' he said.

'Oh, he'll have to get used to it. Miss Cora don't hang back when she wants something.'

After they had gathered together the numerous trunks, hatboxes and valises and had them loaded on to the wagon, Bertha decided to call a hansom. Normally she would have taken a tram, but Jim and she would have to sit separately. This way she would be able to explain what was what before they got back to the house. She was pretty sure that Jim did not understand the way things worked over here.

She was right. As they left the Customs Hall together, Jim's arm around her waist, there were shouts and catcalls from the porters on the docks. Jim looked puzzled and put out, he was about to respond when Bertha stopped him.

'Don't pay them any mind, Jim, they just don't see many white folks walking around with people like me. They don't know you're not American.'

Jim subsided grumbling. This was new territory.

In the hansom, Jim held her hand in his and she found it hard to concentrate on the unpleasant realities they faced. But as the cab crossed Broadway, she pulled herself up and looked at Jim strictly.

'I can't say I'm not pleased to see you because I am but things are different here. No one is going to take kindly to us being together. They don't think it's right for white and coloured folk to keep company. That's the way it is. And if the Madam gets to know, I'll lose my place. She won't stand for any goings-on in her house.'

Jim smiled at her stern manner. 'I promise to behave, Miss Bertha.'

She wondered if he really understood. In England they would face dismissal without references if their relationship was discovered. Here in New York a white man could not have a respectable relationship with a coloured woman. It wasn't illegal to marry as it was in South Carolina, but it never happened. And Bertha was determined to have a respectable relationship.

It had almost been a relief when Jim came to tell her he was leaving town. He said that the Duke had come back to the hotel in a foul temper and had thrown a brush at him when he had put out the wrong waistcoat. He had been surprised, he hadn't thought the Duke was that kind of gentleman. Then Mr Greatorex had come in and the Duke had started playing the piano, 'Angry music,' said Jim. An hour later the Duke had sent for him and told him they were going on a hunting trip, returning the day before the wedding.

Now he was gone Bertha could collect her thoughts. It had been exhausting trying not to look at Jim, even worse showing no reaction when he touched her as he passed her on the stairs or in the corridors. She didn't know how much longer she could keep it up. It was lucky that the household was all over the place trying to keep the Madam happy. Bertha's biggest worry was the maids who had come with the Duchess and Lady Sybil; they had been quite put out when Jim had stayed behind with her at the Customs Hall. On the voyage over they had waited to see which one of them he preferred, so they could not help but notice his interest in her. Now they were constantly running after her, demanding curling papers, pincushions, the best place to procure carmine, all the while trying to find out how exactly she had come to know Mr Harness, the Duke's valet.

They were looking at her now. One of them was mending a petticoat that Bertha would have discarded long ago as beyond saving. She knew they were talking about her and she felt uncomfortable under their pale stares. She decided to leave them to their gossiping and get on with sorting out Miss Cora's trousseau.

As she pushed open the door to Cora's room, she was struck by a blast of cold air. Who had left the windows open? She walked through the sitting room to the bedroom to close the window when she noticed Cora sitting in the twilight, smoking a cigarette. She didn't know what was more surprising, Cora smoking or that she was alone.

'Sorry, Miss Cora, I didn't know you were in here. Shall I close the window? It's getting pretty cold now. What do you want to wear for dinner tonight? Shall I put out the lilac silk? You haven't worn that one yet.'

But even the promise of a new dress did not rouse Cora. She inhaled on her cigarette (where had she got them from? wondered Bertha) and blew the smoke out of the window.

Bertha went to the closet to fetch the lilac dress, which smelt of lavender and cedarwood. Every Worth dress had its own pomander, which gave the dresses their own individual perfumes.

'Oh, leave it, Bertha, I don't think I will go down tonight. I have a headache.'

'The Madam won't like it.'

'I know, but I can't face them all tonight.' She tossed her cigarette out of the window where it fell in a rainbow of tiny sparks. And then she began to speak, looking out of the window, anywhere but at Bertha.

'I was so sure before . . . about Ivo. I've wanted him to be here so much but since he came to America . . . he isn't the same. He used to touch me all the time, I mean he couldn't stand next to me without putting his hand on my arm or my waist, and if we were ever alone he would kiss me – so much sometimes that I had to make him stop. But since he came he hasn't touched me once, not properly, not unless it's expected of him. I've tried to get him alone but he is always with somebody, and now he's been gone for a whole week. Oh Bertha, do you think he's coming back?'

Bertha looked at Cora's frowning face and felt a little sorry for her. She was so used to getting her own way and yet she could not control the Duke. But it was not Bertha's role to sympathise with her – she had her own reasons for wanting Cora married and back in England. 'I do, Miss Cora. And as for the rest of it, you'll be on your honeymoon soon and you can be alone all you want.'

'Yes, but that's what I'm scared of. Suppose we don't like each other? Suppose everything that happened before was a mistake? Teddy came here this morning and offered to take me away and the awful thing is that for a moment I was tempted. Teddy loves me, I can see it in his face, but when I look at Ivo I don't know what he feels.'

Bertha knew to say nothing.

'At Lulworth it was all so easy, we understood each other. But it is all so different here. Everyone thinks he is marrying me for my money, even his mother. But I know he liked me first. I know he did.'

Cora's voice was not as certain as her words. Bertha again remained silent. She wondered if Cora knew about the row over her marriage settlement.

'Don't worry, Miss Cora, every bride has doubts before the wedding. It's only natural. Why don't you let me bathe your head in eau de cologne and then you can get dressed and go down for dinner. You don't want all those English ladies to be asking where you've got to.'

'Oh Lord, Sybil came in while I was with Teddy this morning. I'd better go down and be cheerful, otherwise she might say something in front of Mother. Poor girl, I had to lend her two dinner dresses. I don't understand why the Duchess doesn't get her some nice things.'

The lamentable state of the English girl's wardrobe seemed to cheer Cora. Bertha hustled her into the lilac dress. Once she was downstairs being admired and fussed over, her mistress, she knew, would start to feel much better. To distract her while she did her hair, Bertha told Cora about the English lady's maids and their superior ways. Cora was laughing as Bertha described their attempts to conceal their amazement at the size and splendour of Cora's trousseau. They had looked down their noses and wondered aloud if there were any dresses left in Paris.

'Oh, they was actin' like it was nothin' but I saw them put out their hands to touch your furs. They ain't seen anything so fine. I made out I didn't notice but I could see 'em swallowin' their envy. I hope you don' mind me showing 'em all the clothes and stuff, Miss Cora, but it gave me no end of satisfaction.'

'I don't mind, Bertha. I'd like to do the same with the Duchess, except she would think it vulgar.'

The dinner gong rang and Cora went downstairs. Bertha sprayed cologne in Cora's bedroom to mask the smell of the cigarette. Mrs Cash often came in to say goodnight and she would make an almighty row if she thought Cora had been smoking. Bertha was just about to go to her dinner in the servants' quarters when Mrs Cash stopped her at the door of Cora's room.

'Bertha, a word.' Mrs Cash was at her most stately.

'Yes, ma'am.' Bertha curtsied, praying her legs wouldn't wobble. She could only hope that all the smoke had gone.

'You don't need me to remind you how unusual it is for a girl of your type to be working as a lady's maid. The money you send home must mean a great deal to your mother.'

Bertha looked at the floor. She had not heard from her mother since coming back from England.

'You have worked hard and I know that Cora has great confidence in you. Indeed, she confides in you in a way that is perhaps not entirely fitting but because we have given you so much, I know you will always be discreet. That is why I chose you instead of a professional lady's maid. I knew you would soon pick up your duties, but the habit of loyalty cannot be bought.'

Bertha curtsied again. What was the Madam up to?

'Tell me, did Cora seem distressed today? Does she seem unsettled in any way?'

'No, ma'am, just nervous about the wedding, as is only natural for a bride.'

'Yes indeed, her whole life is about to change. By this time on Thursday she will be a duchess.'

And by this time on Thursday you will be the mother of a duchess, thought Bertha. She realised that Mrs Cash was as nervous about the wedding as her daughter.

'It would be quite dreadful if anything were to happen to prevent that. So, Bertha, I am asking you to be especially vigilant. If any letters come for Cora, I want you to bring them straight to me so I may judge their suitability. I don't want anyone or anything to upset her at this delicate time in her life. Do you understand me?'

'Yes, ma'am.'

'Good. And Bertha, I don't need to tell you not to speak to Cora about this. I don't want her to be . . . distracted.'

Bertha nodded.

When Mrs Cash had left, Bertha went into the bedroom and looked until she found the cigarettes. She lit one, and stood as Cora had done, blowing the smoke into the street below.

Next morning, a note was brought up to Cora's bedroom by a footman. Bertha put it in her pocket and left it there.

CHAPTER 13

The Coiled Serpent

'REALLY, I DON'T UNDERSTAND ALL THIS excitement.' Duchess Fanny tapped the wooden pew for emphasis. 'I've had two weddings and never felt any need to rehearse. All you have to remember is not to gallop up the aisle, so people have time to admire your dress, and to speak your vows clearly. Hardly taxing for a girl of your intelligence, Cora. And as for your bridesmaids, Sybil has done this many times before, she can lead the way. If you really want to practise, why don't you walk up and down a few times now, to get the timing of the thing. But not too much, you don't want to appear drilled.' The Duchess smiled at the assembled company, her pale blue eyes candid with the air of someone who has found the missing key that the whole household has been searching for. Her audience, however, did not share her conviction. When Mrs Cash at last found her voice, it was tight with suppressed emotion.

'I have not had the experience of an English wedding, Duchess, perhaps they are simpler affairs. Here it is customary to rehearse with all the members of the wedding, including the groom.' Mrs Cash was trying to control her irritation but without much success. She looked up at the great stained-glass window over the altar for inspiration. She had gazed at this window at so many society weddings in the past, imagining the moment when it would be Cora at the altar, that she knew every detail. There had never been any question about which church to use. All the smartest weddings were here at Trinity. There were airier, more spacious churches further uptown, but Mrs Cash had never even considered them. Trinity was the church used by the Astors, the Rhinebackers, the Schoonmakers and the rest of Old New York. Although Mrs Cash was pleased to think that none of them had ever seen the church looking so splendid.

Built of native granite, the building could be a little gloomy but the great arches of ivy and jasmine that hung over the congregation, echoing the stone vaulting above, made the stern church feel almost boudoir-like. She was particularly pleased with the cloth-of-gold carpet that she had had laid from the altar all the way down the nave. It was embroidered here and there with the bridal couple's monograms in silver. Even the Duchess, who had deemed the church quite 'forbidding' from the outside, had gasped at that. Mrs Cash glanced over to where the Duchess was seated under an enormous floral representation of the Maltravers coat of arms on the groom's side of the church, looking completely unconcerned by her son's absence, and felt the scar tissue on the left side of her face begin to ache.

When the Duke and his party had arrived in the country, she had given them itineraries that had made it absolutely clear that the rehearsal was a formal event. It was bad enough that he had missed nearly all of the dinners she had arranged to introduce him to New York society, but for the groom and the best man to miss the rehearsal, that really was too much. The bishop was there, the bridesmaids and ushers, even the editor of *Vogue*; only the groom was missing. And the Duchess, who really should know better, was acting as if this was some tiresome piece of American nonsense. Duchess Fanny took no notice of the stiffness in Mrs Cash's reply and continued regardless. 'Ivo would be mortified to think that you were all here waiting for him.' She lingered on the word mortified, somehow implying that Ivo would be quite the opposite. 'I'm sure he had no idea that this was such an event. He probably thought it was a women's affair.'

Nobody spoke.

The Duchess looked up at her future daughter-in-law, who was standing at the altar steps next to her father. 'Don't worry, Cora. I'm sure he will remember to turn up tomorrow.' She gave her most adorable smile.

Cora tried to smile back. Her cheeks ached as she tried to match the Duchess's breeziness, even though she could feel her eyes stinging. Suppose Ivo really had changed his mind? But she forced herself to sound as if, like the Duchess, she found his absence simply amusing.

'Oh, I hope so, Duchess. It would be so tiresome to return all the wedding gifts, and to waste all these flowers would be criminal.' She gestured at the banks of orchids, the tuberose garlands and the columns of myrtle and jasmine. The air inside the church was so thick with floral scent that Cora felt as if she could fall back and be supported by the fragrant undercurrents.

The Duchess looked at her with something like approval. If only the mother would stop making such a fuss. She decided to bring the proceedings to a close.

'When I see Ivo I will scold him roundly for being so inconsiderate, but for my part I am delighted to have had the chance to admire this church and the magnificent floral arrangements at my leisure. I don't think I have ever seen such a profusion of flowers or such tasteful arrangements. Reassure me, Mrs Cash, that this is an exceptional display even by New York standards. Our poor London posies feel quite primitive by comparison.'

Mrs Cash was somewhat mollified by this overture. It was the first time that the Duchess had admitted that anything in America was superior to its British equivalent. She was about to speak when her husband forestalled her. Standing at Cora's side, he had noticed the tears in his daughter's eyes.

'Well, as we have now been here for the best part of two hours, I think the ladies should conserve their strength for tomorrow. I expect Wareham to come back with a mountain lion at the very least. Duchess, would you allow me to escort you to the carriage?'

The Duchess lowered her eyelashes at him. Really, Cora's father was quite gentlemanly for an American. She placed her kid-gloved hand on his proffered arm with a look of complicity that made Winthrop stroke the ends of his mustache.

As they walked up the aisle of the church to the entrance, Duchess Fanny could not resist saying, 'Really, this makes me feel a little emotional, Mr Cash, walking up the aisle on the arm of a man. I feel as if I were the bride myself,' and she gave him a sideways look that made it clear that she considered him quite a suitable partner.

'Well, anybody could be forgiven for mistaking you for a blushing bride, Duchess. Why, I could scarcely credit that you were old enough to have a grown son. When I first saw you I thought you must be your stepdaughter.'

'Oh Mr Cash, you are teasing me, but I shan't pretend I don't like it. I hope you will come to England soon, I think you would enjoy it. If you come to Conyers, I promise to entertain you.'

Winthrop Cash wondered if the Duchess was really flirting with him. The little squeeze she gave his arm as she invited him to England held the promise of greater intimacy. He was not used to such signals from women of his own social class; his tastes ran to rather simpler transactions. But the Duchess was a beautiful woman and it tickled his vanity to have her look up at him with such invitation in her eyes. He found the Duchess altogether more to his taste than her son. The disagreement they had had over Cora's settlement still rankled. The Duke had expected Cora's fortune to be handed over to him; he had been astonished when Cash had explained that the money he would settle on Cora would be hers to control. 'Do you mean to say that you expect me to ask Cora for money?' Ivo had said loudly and slowly, as if speaking to someone with an imperfect command of English. Winthrop had replied that in America women retained control of their fortune when they married, he saw no reason to change things because his only child was marrying an Englishman, even such a distinguished one (the last remark made with a stiff little bow to the Duke). The implication was not lost on Wareham, who went silent. The pause lasted for some minutes until the Duke managed a smile of sorts and tried to speak with some degree of warmth.

'You must excuse me, Mr Cash, I had no idea that our ways of doing things were so very different. I should probably have brought some adviser with me but I did not foresee the need. I am not a fortune-hunter, Mr Cash, I am merely an Englishman who shrinks from burdening his future wife with the cares of running an estate. I won't pretend that my affairs are unencumbered. The depression in prices has affected me greatly. I don't want to marry Cora for her money but there is no doubt that money will be needed. We English don't mind so much being shabby but Cora has been brought up to all this . . .' he gestured round the library in the Cash mansion. In its decoration and furnishings, the American library was in every way similar to its English equivalent on which it had been closely modelled; the difference was not in the furnishings but in the absence of damp and the general air of comfort that lay across the room like a cashmere stole.

Winthrop looked at the younger man with a degree of scepticism. He knew that dukes did not marry American heiresses for love alone; moreover, this union was a transaction on both sides, even if Cora would never admit it. He could protect her fortune but he wondered if by doing so he would condemn their marriage; he thought of how much he would dislike having to ask his wife for money. He decided to make a concession to the Duke's pride – his father the Golden Miller had taught him that it was bad business not to let the defeated party walk away with honour. He would make a settlement on the Duke as a wedding gift, but he would make his gesture on the day of the wedding. He had not quite forgiven the Duke for his assumption that Cora was getting the best part of the bargain.

But thoughts of the son evaporated as the mother cooed in his ear about the splendours of Conyers and how much she would like to introduce him to the Prince of Wales. As he handed her into the carriage, Winthrop noticed that on the sliver of skin visible between the Duchess's sleeve and her glove there was a blue marking. If it had been anyone else, he would have sworn it was a tattoo.

The Duchess caught his look and laughed throatily. 'I see you have found the serpent, Mr Cash.' She peeled back her glove to give him a closer look at the tattoo of a snake that coiled itself round her wrist, the tail disappearing into the serpent's mouth on the tender white skin beneath the mound of her thumb. It was delicate work, a world away from the pictures of sweethearts and mothers that adorned the biceps of Mr Cash's mill hands.

'It is very . . . particular,' he said.

'You have no idea how true that is. There are only four tattoos like it in existence. And when you come to Conyers, I will explain its significance.'

'I don't know that I can wait that long.' Winthrop felt unreasonably excited by the Duchess and her secrets, but the moment was interrupted by the arrival of his wife, daughter and a clutch of bridesmaids all complaining about the cold and in urgent need of a carriage. By the time all the women were accommodated, Winthrop had been separated from the Duchess but not from the image of the tattoo. He felt a sudden spike of desire mixed with something like alarm. Was Cora, he wondered, ready for this world of coiled serpents and secret symbols?

The rehearsal dinner was to go ahead that night, even if as yet there was no sign of the Duke and his best man.

Only the Duchess was entirely serene. As she walked into the drawing room before dinner, she surveyed the members of the wedding and drawled in her throatiest tones, 'This is like *Hamlet* without the Prince. It really is too naughty of Ivo to neglect his duties so.' But her smile suggested that she felt that her presence more than made up for the non-appearance of her son. Only Winthrop smiled back with genuine warmth.

Cora tried to concentrate on her bridesmaids who were peppering her with questions about England. When would she be presented at court? How many rooms did Lulworth have? What would people call her? Were all the English girls as tall as Lady Sybil? Cora answered them as best she could, although she knew the only thing that would satisfy them would be Ivo himself. She was not above looking forward to seeing her bridesmaids' faces when they saw that her future husband was a handsome man as well as a duke. But her smile became more and more fixed as the last of the guests arrived and there was still no sign of Ivo. At last her mother announced that they must go in to dinner. Cora did her best to sparkle as if completely unconcerned and declared that Ivo was probably confused as to the hour, as in London no one dined before eight.

'Oh, you know men and their shooting,' the Double Duchess said helpfully. 'We should be grateful really that they have something to get them out from under our feet. Really, I don't think I could endure a man I had to lunch with every day.'

Winthrop laughed, but Cora's smile was thin and her mother's non-existent.

Cora went in to dinner with Sybil, as they were both missing their partners. The width of their enormous leg-of-mutton sleeves made it difficult for them to talk easily but Sybil turned her head sideways and said, 'You are an angel for lending me the frock. One of your friends asked me where I had got it. I said from Maison Worth as if I went there all the time!' She laughed and then she saw the expression on Cora's face. 'Don't worry, Cora, he'll be here. I'm sure he's only doing this to annoy Mama.'

And then, just as they were walking into the long candle-filled dining room, each girl felt her arm being taken by the elbow. The hunting party had returned. Ivo and Reggie were there, faces ruddy from the shooting, looking delighted with themselves, and boasting about their tally.

Cora tried not to show how relieved she was to see him and how furious she was with him for having stayed away so long, but Ivo caught the flicker of emotions on her face and said in a lower voice, 'Are you angry with me for missing the rehearsal? Your mother sent a note to the hotel saying how disappointed she was.' Ivo's tone was hardly contrite. Cora tried to temper the pleasure she took in seeing him with the coolness appropriate to his behaviour. But Ivo's hand was caressing the inside of her arm, and as he pulled out the chair for her to sit down, his hand brushed the nape of her neck.

'I had to field some searching questions from my bridesmaids. The ones that credited your existence at all were most curious about your habits. A duke is excitement enough, but a missing duke is even better. So I don't know who is more put out with you, me because you missed the rehearsal or my bridesmaids because you've spoiled a promising mystery.' Her tone was as unconcerned as she could make it.

Ivo sat down next to her. He took her hand under the table and squeezed it. The gesture was enough to make her eyes fill. She smiled, desperately trying to make the tears disperse through sheer will. She took her hand away and had a sip of Ivo's champagne.

'You know, I wondered last night if you were ever coming back. I thought perhaps you might have gone home.' She said this in a very fast muttered undertone so that only he should hear.

'Gone home?' Ivo opened his eyes wide in exaggerated astonishment. She saw that he was trying not to take her comment seriously. 'But why would I do that, when I have come all this way to marry you?'

Cora felt her mother's stare, but she had to talk to Ivo about this now; tomorrow would be too late.

'Because you feel differently. Ever since you arrived you have been . . . distant. Not like you were in Lulworth.' Her words tumbled out, all her attempts at insouciance abandoned.

Ivo heard the change in her voice and said quietly, 'But that's because we're not at Lulworth. You forget, I am a foreigner here. So many things seem strange to me here. Even you.'

Cora looked at him in astonishment. 'Me? But I have not changed. I am the same girl you proposed to.' She put her hand to her chest as she said this as if to emphasise that, underneath, she was the same.

Ivo looked at her directly and she felt she was seeing a part of him she had never seen before. 'But when I see you here amidst all this, I realise that I proposed to a very small part of you. I thought I was giving you a home and a position, but here I see that I am taking you away from so much.' He looked down at his plate which was made of gold and chased with the Cash monogram, and lifted it, exaggerating its weight. She was about to tell him how little she cared for any of it when there was a chink of metal on glass and Winthrop stood up to make a toast.

All eyes were on them now. Cora looked at Ivo anxiously but to her relief and joy he took her hand and raised it to his lips. There was a little sigh of envy from the bridesmaids. Cora felt the tightness behind her eyes loosen; this, after all, was what she had wanted.

The dinner ended promptly at nine. Mrs Cash's direction had been quite clear, there was to be no lingering. Cora stood at the top of the stairs saying goodbye to Cornelia Rhinelander, her mother's favourite bridesmaid (to have a Rhinelander as a bridesmaid at the wedding of her daughter to a duke was almost at the summit of Mrs Cash's social ambitions). Cornelia, who was twenty-four, congratulated Cora with a creditable display of enthusiasm, given her unmarried status. 'You look very well together, I think it will be the wedding of the season.' She was about to go on but then she saw the Duke approaching over Cora's shoulder and made her goodbyes. Even Cornelia could see that the Duke wanted to be alone with his bride-to-be.

A touch on her shoulder. She turned to face him. He took one of her hands in his and used the other to trace the curve of her cheek. 'I am glad I came back.' He looked as serious as she had ever seen him, his dark brown eyes deep with emotion, his mouth soft.

But Cora stiffened. She was disturbed by the implication of his remark. He had spoken as if he had overcome something, that he had come back from the brink. She had been right – he had been having second thoughts. But then she thought of the way he had lifted the gold dinner plate – it was her money that was coming between them. She almost smiled in relief.

'Did you have a choice?' She looked at him with all the longing and disappointment of the last week in her eyes.

'Not any more,' and he raised her hand, opened the buttons of her long kid evening glove and kissed her exposed wrist. 'Not any more.' He looked at her fully with what Cora felt was love and she swayed towards him. But then there were footsteps and he straightened away from her.

'Oh, there's Reggie, we must go. I don't want to annoy your mother twice in one day.' He gave her back her hand like a gift. 'Sleep well, Cora.'

Cora watched him walk down the stairs to the door. Would he turn and look back at her? But here was Reggie bidding her good night before following his friend to the Astoria Hotel where they were spending the night. When she turned back, Ivo had gone.

Shaken, she tried to slip upstairs to her room before she had to talk to anyone. She wanted to be alone to think. She rubbed the wrist he had kissed against her cheek. But as she turned towards the staircase she heard the Duchess's voice. Cora had no desire to talk to her future mother-in-law. She opened the door behind her.

She turned into the dark drawing room just as a beam of moonlight struck the table in front of her. The ceiling was pierced by a hundred points of light and then as a cloud moved across the moon, the brilliance was gone. Cora walked over to the long table where the wedding presents had been laid out ready for inspection by the guests the next day. The sparkle had come from one of the antique crystal and bronze candlesticks that had been sent by Mrs Auchinschloss. Cora flicked one of the brilliants with her finger and watched the shower of light it made in the mirror opposite. She could still hear the Duchess's husky voice on the other side of the door.

The presents had been arriving since the engagement was announced. The display had been set out on three long tables, each gift with a card announcing the giver. The more magnificent the gift, the more likely it was to have come from a friend of the bride. Cora looked at a Louis boulle clock of tortoiseshell and gilt which was about two feet high – a gift from the Carnegies. There was an alabaster bowl set with gold and gems from the Mellons, a silver punchbowl – so big that it would happily accommodate a small child – from the Hammerschorns. There were no dinner services or cutlery, as it was tacitly assumed that a duke would have no need of such things.

Cora moved restlessly around the table. There was too much here, she thought; all these glittering objects shining in the moonlight made her feel slightly queasy. Hitherto she had felt bolstered by the size and splendour of this tribute, but now it seemed worrying. So many things and for what? She stopped by a pair of boxes that lay side by side on the table. They were beautiful things made from walnut with mother-of-pearl inlay and her and Ivo's monograms in silver on the lid. She opened the box marked CW and found it was a dressing case whose sides opened out like arms to reveal crystal bottles with chased silver tops and sets of ivory manicure instruments and glove stretchers, tortoiseshell-backed hairbrushes and combs, a porcelain box for rouge, a pair of tiny gold scissors shaped like a crane with its legs turning into the blades, and a golden thimble. Every item from the thimble to the hairbrush was engraved with her monogram. Even Cora, who was no stranger to such things, was struck by the luxurious preciseness of the case, the way in which every feminine need was accommodated and allowed to nestle in its red velvet hollow. Cora looked at the card which accompanied it: From Sir Odo and Lady Beauchamp. She remembered the couple at the hunt and the chilliness of their attitude towards her; perhaps they regretted their behaviour now that she was to be a duchess. Then she lifted the lid of Ivo's box – it was like hers except that the linings were in green morocco leather and velvet, not red, and the rouge pots and tweezers were replaced by ivory-handled shaving brushes. Cora thought for a moment that it was a curiously intimate present, it disturbed her to see Ivo's bodily needs anticipated so neatly by a stranger. She noticed that unlike her case, this one had a set of drawers for cufflinks. She pulled at a tiny golden handle and the drawer came out smoothly to reveal a set of black pearl dress studs and a card. Cora picked up the card. Written on it in cramped italic writing were the words '*May your marriage be as happy as mine has been*'. Cora wondered which of the couple from the hunt had placed it there, Sir Odo with his shiny face and high voice, or his handsome, sulky wife? She was about to put the note back but then, angry with everything British and mealy-mouthed, she tore the card in two.

She pushed the drawer shut. Looking about her for distraction, she saw a birdcage with a tiny gilded bird on a perch in the middle. There was a key at the base of the cage. Cora gave it a couple of sharp turns and the golden bird began to chirp its way through 'Dixie'. This was a present from one of Mother's cousins in South Carolina – who else would send something so eccentric? But the jaunty song roused Cora. At once the pressure in her head lifted and although she could still hear the Duchess's voice, she opened the door.

She waved at the assembled company and walked up the twenty-four marble steps to her bedroom. At the top she remembered the bicycle that Teddy had offered her as a wedding present and the thought of its rude practicality amongst all the gilt and glitter downstairs almost made her smile.

CHAPTER 14

Florence Dursheimer's Day Out

LORENCE DURSHEIMER'S NOSE WAS BEGINNING
to run. She had been standing on the corner of Wall
Street and Broadway since six o'clock that morning. She had gone
early from her home in Orchard Street thinking to be the first
outside the church, but to her annoyance there was already a small
knot of women established there. Florence had taken up her place
beside these women, who were occupying what she considered to
be her rightful spot, with the barest of greetings. None of these
interlopers had her connection with the bride. Florence had
trimmed the hat that Cora Cash had worn in the photograph
that accompanied the notice of her engagement in *Town Topics*.
It was Florence's deft fingers that had pinned the gold hummingbird just below the ostrich-feather plume. It had been the bird
that had caught Cora's eye when she had entered Madame Rochas's
millinery establishment.

Florence had worked hard on the Coruscator, harder perhaps
than was warranted as she was paid by the piece but she had felt
uplifted when Miss Cash, the heiress of the season, had raised
her hand on seeing her hat. She had tried it on in the shop and
Florence had been allowed to place the hat at the precise angle

on Miss Cash's head and had pushed the diamond-headed hat-pin into Miss Cash's warm brown hair. Miss Cash had smelt faintly of orange blossom which had made Florence only too conscious of her own unwashed state and the sharp stink of sweat that escaped as she lifted her arms to place the Coruscator on the heiress's head. But Miss Cash had not wrinkled her nose or reached for her handkerchief as other rich girls might have done, but had smiled at her reflection in the glass and said, 'What a charming hat! Did you make it?' And Florence had nodded and had followed Miss Cash from that point to this spot on the corner of Wall Street and Broadway.

Florence would have liked to dab her nose with her handker-chief but at eleven thirty the crush was now so great that she could not move her arms. She was hemmed in on all sides by women like herself, desperate for a glimpse of the Cash wedding. A number of the women were clutching newspapers with Cora's picture on the front. They talked about her while they were waiting as if she were a sister or a friend, exchanging details of shoes, her hats, even her gold-plated bridal underwear. Florence had wondered whether she should announce that she had actually met Cora but it was easier to listen to the chatter that swirled around her and content herself with merely feeling the glow of ownership. The general feeling among the crowd was that it was a shame that she was marrying an Englishman, even if he was a duke. But Florence had seen Cora twisting her engagement ring and smiling while she waited for her hat to be boxed up. She knew it was a love match, whatever the papers might say. Florence had seen enough engaged girls pass through Madame Rochas to know the differ-ence between the ones who looked forward to married life and the ones who could not see beyond the wedding.

There was a big swell from the crowd: the bridegroom's party was arriving. Florence fought her way to the front of the crowd, wedging her head under a policeman's elbow. She saw two men getting out of the carriage, one blond, one dark. Florence knew from *Town Topics* that the dark man was the Duke and the other was his best man Reggie Greatorex. She screwed up her eyes, which had been made shortsighted by years of fine sewing in bad light. Prompted by a remark from his friend, the groom turned his head and looked at the crowd. The crowd roared and the Duke smiled and waved his hand and pointed at the white gardenia in his buttonhole. Florence could not be sure of the expression on his face but she thought she saw his hand shake as he reached to touch the flower in his lapel. The Duke's acknowledgement pleased the crowd and there was a general agreement that he was a fine-looking man. Then the coach containing Mrs Cash and the bridesmaids arrived and there was a high-pitched coo as all the women in the largely feminine crowd sighed over their clothes.

Mrs Cash was in gold brocade trimmed with sable. On her head she wore a fur toque pinned with a brilliant diamond aigrette and a delicate lace veil. Florence had made the hat after a photograph that Mrs Cash had shown her of the Princess of Wales, and although she had not been specifically asked, she had reinforced the side of the veil that would lie over the damaged part of Mrs Cash's face. The six bridesmaids wore gowns of peach satin with wide hats trimmed with ostrich feathers, and each had a pearl choker round her neck that had been presented to them that morning by Winthrop Cash. There was one bridesmaid with red hair whom Florence did not recognise and she frowned, put out that her encyclopaedic knowledge of New York society women should be found wanting; but then she remembered that one of the bridesmaids was a relation of the Duke. She felt sure that she would have remembered hair of that particular hue, rather an unfortunate contrast with the peach satin. Florence felt the droplet on her nose fall and another one well up to take its place; her eyes, too, were streaming. If only she could reach her handkerchief. Then there was a loud cheer as the crowd further up Broadway caught sight of the bridal coach pulled by four matched greys.

At last the coach drew up in front of the church. Mr Cash got out and turned to help his daughter. Florence found herself being pushed forward by the surge of the crowd. She was edging closer and closer to the entrance of the church. She could smell the lilies in the great wreath that hung over the carved doors. Florence felt someone put their foot through the back of her skirt, but she dared not turn round – she would never forgive herself if she failed to see Cora. There was another sigh from the crowd as the bride was handed out of the coach. Florence craned her head to see but her view was blocked by the coach. She stood on the tips of her toes, pushing her head up until she felt her neck would break, but at just under five feet she was too small to see the bride's face. Two women behind her were talking about the dress.

'Now would you say that satin was oyster or more cream, Edith?'

'It looks cream to me. Wonderful lace on the bodice, Brussels or Valenciennes?'

'Brussels. It's a Worth dress, he only uses Brussels lace.'

Hearing this exchange, Florence felt she would burst. Cora was her property, not theirs. Did they have pictures of Cora on every wall of their bedrooms? She, Florence, had even been born in the same year as Cora nineteen years ago and on the same day, if not actually the same month. How dare these women dissect the dress that was Florence's by right? The policeman standing over her heard her snort and looked down, amused.

'All right there, miss?' He had an Irish accent and red, protuberant ears.

'I can't see the bride and she's the only reason I'm here.' Florence's eyes were wet. The policeman had left three younger sisters behind him in County Wicklow, so he knew feminine desperation when he heard it.

'Well, we can't have that now, can we?' and with a swoop he picked Florence up by her waist and lifted her on to his shoulders. She made a little scream of protest that turned into a gasp of delight as she caught sight of Cora. The bride was standing on the red-brown granite steps of the church, her train spread out behind her like a puddle of cream. The dress was in the latest fashion with wide leg-of-mutton sleeves, a tiny waist and a flowing skirt. The fabric was a heavy duchesse satin set with pearls. As custom dictated, the neckline was high and the sleeves came right down to the wrist. On each shoulder were epaulettes of white flowers – Florence thought they were gardenias – otherwise the dress had no ornament, no bows, frills or flounces, nothing that would detract from the lace veil with its intricate réseau of fruit, flowers and butterflies. That kind of lace could not be had for love or money these days, *Town Topics* had told its readers. This veil had originally belonged to the Princesse de Lamballe who, the article went on, had lost her head in the French Revolution. Florence knew nothing about the French Revolution but she knew enough about lace to know that Cora's veil was worth enough money to buy the whole of Madame Rochas several times over. But she felt no revolutionary fervour, quite the contrary – Florence would have felt cheated if Cora had settled for anything less.

Florence had seen at least ten brides stand on the steps of that church, but she couldn't recall any of them now as she looked at Cora, whose arms were raised, trying to adjust the tiara on her head, while her father stood by rather helplessly. Florence could see the frown of concentration on Cora's face and longed to rush forward and fix the tiara so that it would frame Cora's white face and not ride too low and give her a headache. Florence sometimes worked in the cloakrooms at DelMonico's and she had helped debutantes with red weals on their foreheads where their hired tiaras had cut into their flesh. The trick was to dress the hair so that no part of the metal would touch the delicate skin around the temple. Surely Cora would have had someone to fix her hair who knew that.

At last Cora was satisfied and lowered her arms and shook her head a little to test her handiwork. As she turned, the lace veil over her face fluttered and Florence saw how white her face was and how she chewed her lower lip. She looked different to the smiling girl who had played with her engagement ring in Madame Rochas: more serious but less confident, and there were purple shadows under her eyes that hadn't been there before. Florence felt disappointed, even a little irritated. She had come here to see a radiant bride – purple shadows she could see in the mirror. Florence put two fingers to her mouth and let out the most piercing whistle she could manage. The Irish policeman pulled her leg.

'Hey, do you want to get me into trouble now? I'm meant to be keeping the peace here.'

But Florence was deaf to his protests. Cora had heard the

whistle and turned in her direction. Florence waved her arms wildly, so much so that the policeman had to put his hands on her thighs to keep her steady. The milliner had never allowed a man such liberties before, but at this moment she was oblivious to the intimacy. Cora looked right at her and she started to smile, the same smile she had given Florence when she had tried on the hat. Florence felt triumphant; she had restored the situation, she alone had given the world what it wanted, a radiant bride. Proprietorially she watched as Cora was handed her bouquet by one of the bridesmaids. The flowers had come, Florence had read, all the way from Lulworth, the Duke's home in England. Florence didn't really understand why such a fragile thing as flowers had come all that way; jewels she could understand, but not flowers. But *Town Topics* had said that all the duchesses carried flowers from Lulworth and it was a tradition that the Duke was determined not to break just because he was marrying an American girl. Florence could barely remember her journey to New York from Germany – the roll of the ship and the smell. She imagined Cora's flowers on a white cushion in their own cabin and thought of her mother clutching her shoulder as they huddled on deck.

But now Cora was taking her father's arm with her free hand. The sound of the organ came out of the open doors of the church. Florence watched as the pool of satin and lace was drawn up the steps. As it disappeared and the great carved doors swung shut, Florence felt her body go limp. She slid into the arms of the policeman, who held her upright as the crowd surged around them.

Florence Dursheimer was not the only woman to faint that day. As *Town Topics* reported later, there were four faintings, one minor concussion and a woman who went into early labour. The paper commented that it was a relief to all concerned that the New York police had managed to keep the injuries among the crowd to the bare minimum.

CHAPTER 15

'That Spot of Joy'

'WOULD YOU LIKE ME TO WARM THE PEARLS for you now, Miss Cora?' Bertha had tried to get into the habit of calling her mistress Your Grace, but she did not always succeed. Cora had corrected her at first but now the first thrill of her new title had worn off, and she did not altogether mind this reminder of her girlhood.

'Yes, thank you, Bertha. The Prince will be there tonight. Ivo says that he notices what women wear. Ivo's aunt wore the same dress twice during one week and the Prince said, haven't I seen that before, and she had to go and change into something new, and when she didn't have anything new she had to pretend she was ill and have meals on a tray.'

This was not a problem that was likely to affect Cora, who had come to Conyers with no less than forty trunks. But tonight Cora was wearing a dress she had worn before: her wedding dress which had been cut down at the neckline and at the sleeves so that it was now a dinner dress. In New York it was the custom for a bride to wear her wedding dress for the first round of visits as a newly-wed. As this was the first time she would go into society proper after the honeymoon, it seemed the perfect time to wear it. It did no harm to remind people that although she was now a duchess she was also still a bride.

Putting on the dress had brought her wedding day back in all its chaos and glory. Although Cora was used to being written about in the papers, the crowds lining her progress from the Cash mansion downtown to Trinity Church had amazed her. So many people shouting her name as if they knew her. Her father had shaken his head and said, 'It's like a royal wedding.' But Cora had worried what Ivo would think. She could imagine his mother's words: 'Crowds of people waiting for a glimpse of the bride, no wonder Cora didn't want a quiet country wedding.' Yet it was exciting that all these people had come out just to see her, not because she was going to be a duchess but because she was Cora Cash, the Golden Miller's granddaughter and probably the richest girl in the world. Her father had taken her hand and said, 'This is quite something, Cora. There was nothing like this when I married your mother. Look at those women over there screaming. Don't they have families to look after? I hope Wareham realises he is marrying an American princess.'

Cora had smiled at this but all she could think of was Ivo's horrified start when she had embraced him in the Customs Hall in front of the photographers. She knew that the roar that greeted her as she got out of the coach would be heard inside the church. The thought of Ivo wincing had almost ruined the moment but then she had seen the little girl from the milliner's sitting on a policeman's shoulders whistling and waving for all she was worth and she had felt buoyed up by the girl's enthusiasm. These people were here for her, why should she feel guilty? As she walked up the aisle she could just make out the back of Ivo's head through her veil. She thought of their first meeting and how he had shown her his neck. She willed him to look round at her but he kept his eyes straight ahead. She remembered that moment in the gallery at Lulworth when he had seen her but had pretended not to. At last she drew level with him and caught a glimpse of his face. His profile was hard and set and Cora wondered for a moment if this had all been a terrible mistake Then her father took her hand and placed it in Ivo's and she felt him hold it fast. His touch, as always, reassured her. All she had to do was hold on.

The dinner gong sounded. Cora put out her hand for the pearls. Bertha took them from her bodice where she had been warming them so that they would be at their most lustrous. It was a trick she had learnt from the Double Duchess's maid, who had been amazed at Bertha's ignorance. 'Ladies are always cold in their evening things, so you need to warm the pearls so they shine – cold pearls on cold skin, spittle on a turkey gizzard.'

Bertha fastened the necklace round her mistress's long white neck. Their dark iridescent sheen made the skin glow. The Duke had given them to Cora in Venice on their honeymoon, and Cora had worn them every night since.

Cora's hands went straight to her throat. She loved the smooth weight of the pearls against her skin. She knew that white pearls would be more usual with her dress but she liked the contrast between the white and the black, it made her feel worldly, brazen even. Every time she put them on she remembered the first time she had worn them: naked but for the necklace under the sheets of their canopied bed in the Palazzo Mocenigo. It was the fourth week of their honeymoon and they had been in Venice for three days. Cora had not known what to expect of married life. She had some inkling of the physical side of things from Ivo's more fervent embraces, but she had not realised that her old self would be so completely obliterated. After their first night together, when he had got up from the bed, she had felt the parting of their flesh as pain, it was if she had lost a skin. And that feeling had only intensified with every passing day and night; she only felt at peace when he was in her arms, when his skin covered hers. Never in her life had she been so aware of all her senses; every morning she smelled the sweet dark smell of his skin and was glad. When she was with him she had to touch him, when he was apart from her she would hug herself so as not to let the flesh that had been warmed by him grow cold.

That morning in Venice he had disappeared after breakfast. It was too hot to go out and Cora had wandered about the palazzo aimlessly. She tried to read her Baedeker but she could not concentrate on anything while he was gone. He didn't come back for lunch and Cora had gone for her siesta in a frenzy of impatience. She had undressed completely, feeling that only the cool white linen sheets would dampen the heat coursing round her body. But the sheets, too, began to twist and grow hot, so she had thrown them off and had lain there with the warm air on her skin and the sounds of the Grand Canal floating in through the open window. She must have fallen asleep because the next thing she remembered was Ivo's hand on her breast. She put up her arms to draw him to her, but he had held back. 'Wait, my impatient darling, there is something I want you to wear for me.' And he had taken a worn leather box out of his pocket. 'Open it.' Cora had leant over him and had squeezed the lid of the box open. Inside were the pearls, as big as quail's eggs and all the colours of the night from bronze to midnight purple. She picked them out of the box and held them to her throat, where they had lain, as they lay now, heavy with promise. She lifted her arms to reach for the clasp, half expecting Ivo to take over, but he simply watched her as she tried to fit the golden hook into its sprung clasp.

He leant back a little from her to admire his gift.

'Black pearls are so rare that it can take a lifetime to collect enough to make a necklace. I thought they were a fitting tribute.' He reached forward and ran his fingers along the pearls and then put his mouth on hers.

Later, he had whispered in her ear, 'I wanted you to have them, only you.' And she had kissed him and put his hand to her throat.

'Feel how warm they are now. Every time I wear them I will think of this.'

Cora felt the warmth of that remembered afternoon sweep through her body. It had been hard coming back to England after the honeymoon, not just because she now had a title and a great house to run, but because she could no longer be with Ivo all day and night. Lulworth had eighty-one servants and even though they had not begun to entertain, it felt as if they were never alone. She was no longer as certain of Ivo as she had been when they had sailed around the Mediterranean on her father's yacht. Then they had both been loose and shapeless, constrained by nothing but the weather. The occasional dinner they had taken with ambassadors and minor princes had been adventures that they had dressed up for, laughing and complicit, catching each other's eye throughout the evening, longing for it to end so that they could be alone together again. But now when Cora looked up hoping to exchange a glance with Ivo, she could not be certain that his eyes would be waiting for her. Only at night could she be sure of him. It had been quite a shock to discover that here at Conyers they had been given separate bedrooms. Ivo had laughed at her evident dismay.

'Darling, you will never pass as a duchess if people think that you actually want to share a bed with your husband.'

Cora had made him promise that he would spend the nights with her.

'But I will have to leave at crack of dawn or the servants will talk.'

Cora had pouted but Ivo had laughed her out of it.

Now she was waiting for him to take her downstairs. Where was he? Maybe she should go to him, his room must be on the same corridor. But Conyers was so cavernous that she might get lost. She thought of that poem where the bride hid in a chest and was never found, until much later when a skeleton with a veil was discovered. Not that the Double Duchess would look very hard, she thought. Her mother-in-law was invariably charming to her but Cora was not deceived. She knew that Fanny was making the best of what she considered a bad job. Fanny's ideal daughter-in-law would have been a girl she had chosen, a girl of good family, pretty but not spectacularly so, wealthy but not too rich, a little bit dowdy, who would defer to her mother-in-law in all things. Instead she had Cora who was not only American, but beautifully dressed, indecently rich and only erratically deferential. Cora suspected that the Double Duchess had organised this royal party at Conyers to remind her daughter-in-law just how much she still had to learn.

She opened the door of her room and looked down the corridor. The door had a card inserted into a brass holder on which was written 'The Duchess of Wareham'. Cora looked at it stupidly. It was still hard for her to connect this edifice with herself. But if her name was on the door then surely it would not be too hard to find Ivo. She walked down the corridor, which for an English house was almost warm. She could hear muffled voices through the door that said 'Lady Beauchamp' and then a peal of laughter. Cora moved on in search of her husband. She found his room right at the very end of the corridor (really, Duchess Fanny might as well have put them in separate buildings). There was the name card, 'The Duke of Wareham' in the same spidery hand. She turned the handle.

'Ivo, are you there, darling? I want you to come and put me out of my misery. If I wait around any longer practising my curtsy I will turn into a pillar of salt. Ivo?'

But the room was empty. Ivo had evidently dressed, his collar case was empty on the dressing table. Cora saw that Ivo had brought the travelling case from the Beauchamps; she felt irrationally annoyed that Ivo should be using it. She remembered the dress studs that had also been in the drawer, they had been black pearls too. She opened the drawer where they had lain, and found it empty. She felt suddenly desolate without her husband. On the bureau lay a shirt that he must have taken off before putting on his evening clothes. She picked it up and buried her face in it, finding reassurance in that familiar scent.

'Darling, what on earth are you doing?' He was standing in the doorway, laughing at her.

'I was missing you!' said Cora defiantly. He went over to her and kissed her on the forehead. She put her face up to his.

'Why didn't you come and get me? I got so bored of waiting I came to find you.'

'Oh, I got waylaid by Colonel Ferrers the Prince's equerry, some very tedious question of protocol. Can't think why Bertie puts so much store by all that stuff. But because he's here we will all have to play by the rules. Which means that you, my little savage, are the senior duchess present and will go in to dinner with the Prince.'

'But surely your mother is more qualified. I shouldn't take precedence over her,'

'Oh, infinitely more qualified, but sadly the Buckinghams are an eighteenth-century concoction whereas the Warehams go all the way back to James the First, so you are number seven and poor old Mama is number twelve. Ferrers has looked it up in Debrett's so there is no getting around it. Everyone has their number and those are the rules. The only person who can play around with precedent is the Prince, which I suppose is what Mama was counting on.'

'Oh Lord. Well, you had better kiss me for good luck, I feel as if I am going into battle.'

'You are, Cora, you are.'

The Double Duchess was in the Chinese room. Conyers had been built in the 1760s when the fashion for chinoiserie was at its height. This octagonal room with its lacquered furniture and hand-painted silk wallpaper was so famous that it had never been modernised. Every detail – the faux bamboo window frets picked out in gilt, the dragon's head sconces, the pagodas on the octagonal silk carpet – had been perfectly realised. Even Cora, who took splendour for granted, was impressed. Each wall showed a different scene from life in the Imperial Court. The Duchess Fanny was standing in front of a wall that showed a group of exquisitely dressed courtiers grouped around an empty throne.

Buckingham, her husband, stood slightly behind her, ready and waiting to obey his wife's every whim.

'Cora, my dear, how fresh you look. Is that your wedding dress remodelled? How charming. So few of Ivo's friends were there for the wedding. I am sure they will all be delighted to see you in your bridal finery.' The Duchess's words were warm, yet it was evident to Cora that wearing the wedding dress would not 'do'. But it was too late to change.

The Double Duchess introduced her to the assembled guests. Everybody had been told to be there at seven thirty as the Prince of Wales would arrive promptly at a quarter to eight. There was no social crime more heinous than arriving after the Prince.

'Lord and Lady Bessborough, my daughter-in-law the Duchess of Wareham. Colonel Ferrers, my daughter-in-law the Duchess of Wareham, Ernest Cassel . . . Sir Odo and Lady Beauchamp, my daughter-in-law the Duchess of Wareh—'

'Oh, but we've met the Duchess before,' said Sir Odo, his face gleaming rosily over his white tie, his large pale blue eyes sparkling with malice, 'when she was still Miss Cash. We were hunting with the Myddleton, the day that Your Grace had your accident. We feel almost responsible for the match.' Odo giggled and Cora looked around for Ivo but he was on the other side of the room talking to Ferrers the equerry.

She turned to Charlotte Beauchamp, who gave her a small tight smile and dropped the very faintest of curtsies. 'Your Grace,' she said ever so slightly, inclining her smooth blond head.

Cora nodded, doing her best to smile. Unconsciously she put her hands to her throat, seeking reassurance from the glowing pearls round her neck.

Odo noticed. 'But what a magnificent necklace, Duchess Cora!

You hardly ever see pearls of that colour and size. And such a charming contrast to the dress.'

'Ivo gave it to me when we were in Venice on our wedding tour.'

'Didn't you have a necklace with pearls that colour, Charlotte, that your aunt gave you? You and Duchess Cora must be careful not to wear your black pearls at the same time or people will think that you both belong to some secret society.' Odo was almost squeaking with pleasure at his conceit. But Charlotte did not rise to his bait.

'My necklace is far inferior, Odo. Anyway it is broken, so there is no danger of duplication.'

Odo did not reply. Cora was struck by the evident tension between the couple.

There was a sudden dip in the hum of conversation and a rustling sound that spread through the room like the wind through dry leaves. Cora turned and saw the Prince of Wales standing in the doorway. He was of average height but even the immaculate tailoring of his evening clothes could not disguise his enormous girth; she understood now why his nickname was Tum Tum. He looked older than the photographs she had seen of him and they did not convey his florid complexion or the coldness of his pale blue eyes. She realised that the rustling had stopped with her, and then she caught her mother-in-law's scandalised eye and realised that the whole room was waiting for her to curtsy. But her knees refused to bend. It was only when she saw the slow smile on the face of Charlotte Beauchamp that the spell was broken; her knees obeyed and she sank into the most graceful curtsy she could manage.

'Your Highness, may I present the Duchess of Wareham.'

Duchess Fanny stopped short of a full endorsement of her daughter-in-law.

Cora was conscious of the Prince's heavy-lidded eyes looking her over with the scrutiny of experience.

'I think your son has made a very wise choice, Fanny. I've always liked Amerrricans.' The Prince had an almost French habit of rolling his 'r's.

Cora wondered whether she could safely rise from her curtsy, or was she meant to hover in obeisance while the Prince inspected her? She decided to stand up. This meant that she now stood an inch or two above the Prince. He smiled at her, revealing uneven yellow teeth.

'I have very fond memories of your country. I saw Blondin walk across the Niagarrra Falls, you know. My heart was in my mouth the whole way.' The Prince nodded at the memory.

Cora had no idea who Blondin was, but smiled back. She guessed that the Prince must be in his late fifties; if Blondin had been famous in his youth then she knew better than to remind him of his age.

'You have the advantage of this American then, Your Royal Highness. I have not yet visited the Niagara Falls.'

'But that is a shocking omission. You must make a point of going there when you return to your country.'

'Is that a royal command, sir?' Cora said as pertly as she dared.

The Prince laughed and turned to the Double Duchess. 'I hope I am sitting next to your daughter-in-law at dinner, she can amuse me.'

The Double Duchess smiled and nodded, not betraying by a flicker her dismay at this casual destruction of her carefully considered placement.

The Prince moved on and Cora felt Ivo's breath tickling her neck.

'You've made an impression on the Prince. Mother must be thrilled.'

'But where were you, Ivo? I shouldn't have to face all these people alone,' Cora said sharply. Her heart was still pounding from her encounter with the Prince.

'Nonsense, Cora, you are quite indestructible and besides, the Prince likes to have the pretty ones all to himself.' He bent down and whispered into her ear. 'But remember that I shall be watching you.'

Cora blushed and looked down in confusion. When she dared to raise her gaze, she caught a glimpse of Charlotte Beauchamp staring at them.

'Ivo, why does Charlotte Beauchamp stare at me like that?'

Ivo hesitated, then he took her hand and kissed it. 'Cora, my love, you must be used to staring by now. Poor old Charlotte is probably feeling put out that she is now no longer the reigning beauty. Don't worry about her.'

Ivo's tone was breezy but Cora felt there was something out of place that she couldn't quite identify. She noticed that he did not look over at Charlotte but kept his eyes on her.

Cora had no time to puzzle over her husband's evasions during dinner. She was fully occupied with entertaining the Prince, who had the most disconcerting habit of changing the subject the moment he grew tired of it. Cora was in the middle of describing the alterations that she was making to Lulworth when the royal eyelids flickered and he interrupted her with a question about the hunting in her native country. It was only during the serving of the fish course, when the Prince turned to talk to the Double Duchess on his other side, that Cora was able to look down the table and see that Ivo was sitting next to Charlotte Beauchamp. They were talking not to each other but to the people sitting on either side of them. Cora wanted to see how they spoke to each other but here was the ptarmigan and the Prince was turning back towards her.

'I shall look forward to seeing Lulworth again. The shooting there has always been good. As soon as you have got the house to your liking, we will visit. I know the Prrrincess would like you.'

Cora remembered what Ivo had told her about the building of the railway line and how it had almost bankrupted his father. She wondered how pleased Ivo would be to entertain the royal couple.

'I look forward to entertaining Your Royal Highnesses at Lulworth, although being an American I feel I cannot have anyone to stay until we have sufficient bathrooms.'

The Prince rumbled with laughter. 'Hear that, Fanny? Your new Duchess thinks Lulworth is unhygienic.'

The Double Duchess smiled at him lazily. 'We seemed to manage, though, didn't we, sir. Perhaps I am just set in my ways but I cannot help but think there is more to life than hot water. But Cora has grown up with every convenience, so it is only right that she should mould Lulworth to her own taste. I just hope the character of the place may be preserved. It is such an atmospheric house.' The Duchess's voice dropped to its most thrilling timbre. 'Although I love it here at Conyers, I do miss the romance of Lulworth, the mist on the trees in the morning, and the Maltravers ghosts. Poor Lady Eleanor and her broken heart. I do think there is something peculiarly English about Lulworth. It is as if a little bit of England's soul had been frozen there forever.'

The Prince leant over to Cora, and raised an eyebrow. 'The question is, can Lulworth have soul and hot water?'

Cora did not hesitate. She was tired of Duchess Fanny's condescension. 'Most definitely, Your Highness. In my country we have houses that have history *and* bathrooms. We even have ghosts.' She flashed her most jaunty smile at the Prince and her mother-in-law. The Prince gave her an appraising glance. The American girl had spirit.

'Well, there you have it, Fanny. The voice of the New World,' and he shot the Double Duchess a malicious glance, to show that he thought that she had been bested by her daughter-in-law. And then, as if suddenly bored of the rivalry between the two women which he had stirred up, he began to drum his fingers on the table. The Double Duchess saw this with alarm and hastily changed the subject to the composition of the bridge fours after dinner.

Cora leant forward in the hope of seeing Ivo. He was still talking to Lady Bessborough even though by rights he should be talking to Charlotte. As she turned back to her plate, she noticed that Odo Beauchamp was staring at his wife. Despite their rancorous little exchange earlier, it struck Cora that he was looking at Charlotte as if he could not bear to let her out of his sight.

The meal went on and on. The Prince tackled each one of the nine courses with relish and teased Cora, who found she had lost her appetite, for not doing the food justice.

At last the Double Duchess gave the signal for the ladies to withdraw. When the ladies had followed her into the drawing room, Cora was surprised to find that Charlotte came to sit next to her.

'So have you survived the ordeal?' Charlotte's voice was friendly.

Cora smiled uncertainly. 'I think so. It was a very long dinner.'

'The Prince likes his food. Anything less than nine courses and he thinks you are trying to starve him. I simply dread the day he decides to stay with us. Everything, the guests, the menus, the seating plans, even the sleeping arrangements have to be approved before he comes. Even Aunt Fanny gets nervous.' Charlotte looked over to the Double Duchess, who was drinking coffee with Lady Bessborough.

'I didn't know she was your aunt. Does that mean you and Ivo are cousins?' Cora was curious. Ivo had never mentioned that he was related to Charlotte.

'No, aunt is just a courtesy title. My mother and Aunt Fanny were friends as girls. Then they both got married.' Charlotte gave a little shrug. 'Aunt Fanny married a duke and my mother married an army officer who died when I was a baby. But they remained friends. My mother died when I was sixteen and Aunt Fanny took me in. She had promised my mother that she would bring me out. She kept her promise.' Charlotte's smile had a slightly hard edge to it.

Cora tried to imagine what it would be like to have no family.

'I can't think what it must be like to be an orphan.' She thought of the way her mother had monitored every minute of her life until her marriage.

Charlotte gave her a half smile. 'I hope you won't be shocked if I tell you that it is liberating.'

Cora was shocked, but then she thought of the endless afternoons in Sans Souci and she nodded at Charlotte. 'I think I understand.'

Charlotte put her hand on Cora's arm. 'Good. I hope that means we can be friends.'

Cora was surprised at this but tried not to show it. She said in what she had come to think of as her Duchess voice, 'I hope so too.'

Before Charlotte could say any more, there was a flurry of activity as the men arrived. The guests were organised into bridge tables. Charlotte was summoned by the Double Duchess and with a rueful backward glance at Cora she was swallowed up into the card players.

And then to Cora's relief she saw Ivo's tall figure coming towards her.

He sat down next to her in the place just vacated by Charlotte. She was about to tell him about her conversation, when he said quietly, 'In a minute my mother is going to ask me to play the piano. When she does I want you to come with me. We'll give them the Schubert.'

Cora looked at him in dismay. 'But Ivo, I haven't been practising. I can't play in front of all these people.'

He smiled at her. 'Don't worry, no one here is going to notice if you hit a wrong note. We will do very nicely.'

Cora swallowed and tried to smile back.

As Ivo had predicted, a moment later the Double Duchess approached them.

'Dear Cora, would you mind awfully if I asked Ivo to play for us? It would be such a treat.' She turned to her son. 'I don't remember the last time I heard you play.'

'Don't you, Mother? It was a long time ago.' Ivo stared at his mother, who lowered her gaze.

Ivo stood up and kept Cora's hand in his so she had no choice but to follow him. Cora saw the flicker of incomprehension in her mother-in-law's eyes as he took her with him to the piano, and then as they sat down together in front of the keyboard, she watched the Duchess turn her face to the side suddenly, as if she had been struck.

Ivo's hands were poised over the keys. He looked at Cora gravely. 'Are you ready? One, two, three . . .'

They plunged into the Schubert. Cora played harder than she had ever done before. She could feel the Duchess watching her. As they played, the room grew silent, even the card players paused to listen. Her part supported his rippling arpeggios with a succession of minor chords; if her timing was a fraction out, the piece would sound discordant and harsh, but Ivo was with her, hovering above the foundation she was laying with his own comments and inter-polations. A few bars before the end, Cora had forgotten the other people in the room, she was completely caught up in the music. She could feel Ivo's leg pressed against hers and she found herself swaying with him as they reached the finale. As they came to the last bars, she knew they were perfectly in time and she gave her last chord every ounce of feeling she possessed. The sound faded away and she leant against him.

Ivo whispered in her ear, 'I told you we would do well together.'

And then he was up, smiling his acknowledgement of the applause that greeted the end of the piece. He turned to her and lifted her hand and kissed it. The applause grew louder still. Cora felt herself blushing.

She heard the Prince saying to Ivo, 'So you've found yourself a new parrrtner, Wareham. I rrremember you used to play with your mother. But I think your new Duchess is quite capable of keeping up with you, what.'

'You are very perceptive, sir.' Ivo made a little bow to the Prince.

Duchess Fanny approached in full throaty flight. 'My dears,

what a musical honeymoon you must have had.' She turned to Cora. 'I hope Ivo didn't make you practise all the time?'

Cora smiled but said nothing. She knew that her mother-in-law was furious at having been upstaged. As Fanny moved on, Cora caught a glimpse of Charlotte Beauchamp, who was sitting very still, her arms folded. As the Prince went back towards the card table, Charlotte rose to greet him and Cora saw that she had four red marks on her smooth white upper arm where the nails had dug into the skin.

That night, Cora sent Bertha away as soon as she was out of her dress. Before her marriage she would have told her maid everything about the evening, but Ivo had made it clear that he did not think that a duchess should be gossiping with the servants. He had even wondered whether Bertha was an altogether suitable maid for a Duchess, but Cora had refused to listen, Bertha was the only familiar thing in her new life. But out of loyalty to Ivo's wishes, she no longer confided in her maid as she used to. Now as she sat in front of the dressing-table mirror brushing her hair, she felt lonely. She thought of writing to her mother. Mrs Cash would want to know every detail of her encounter with the Prince. She wondered what her mother would think if she wrote what she really thought, which was that the Prince was fat and alarming and that he had pressed his foot against hers several times during dinner. She ran her hand over the smooth skirts of her wedding dress lying on the chair; she would not wear it again.

She was tired, but she was too anxious to sleep. She wanted desperately to see Ivo. If only she could go and find him. She sat on the bed, twisting her hair, waiting for the door to open. At last she heard his step outside. He looked flushed and before she could tell him anything he was kissing her bare neck and shoulders and tugging at the strings of her peignoir and she was caught up in the urgency of the moment.

When he finally reared up, giving a yelp of what was both pain and pleasure, she pushed herself towards him, willing him to continue. She wanted him to stay deep inside her forever – only by keeping him there would he be really hers. As he collapsed, spent, she still yearned for him. She lay in the dark for a while, listening to him breathe; once he stirred and pulled her to him, whispering her name. She moulded herself against him and at last she, too, fell asleep. But when she woke in the morning, he was gone.

CHAPTER 16

Madonna and Child

I T WAS THE FIRST REALLY COLD DAY OF THE YEAR and the track leading down to the sea was beginning to be covered by fallen leaves. This was Cora's favourite part of the ride: going down the narrow pathway through the wood where the undergrowth was so dense that she could see only a few feet ahead, and then about halfway down the rumble would begin and she began to smell the salty tang of the sea air through the rotting smell of leaf mould. The wood ended and then she was on the cliff overlooking the cove. She thought that it looked like a lady's drawstring purse, a weighted oval with an opening through a break in the cliffs into the sea. The mist that had lain over Lulworth all week had finally been blown away. Today the sea beyond the cliffs was dark blue and here in the shallower waters of the cove it was almost turquoise. The sun had turned the sandstone cliffs a warm gold. But for the bite in the air, it might have been summer. There were sheep grazing on the fields surrounding her, their white shapes echoed by the stray white clouds in the sky. Cora loved the scale of the cove, the coastline was so charming here compared to the rocky outcrops and pounding surf of Rhode Island. She looked at her pocket watch – eleven o'clock. She should turn back, Ivo might return tonight and she wanted to make sure that everything was ready.

After their week at Conyers they had come back to Lulworth, but Ivo had almost immediately been called away to his estates in Ireland. There had been a rent strike and Ivo did not trust his steward to handle it alone. She had wanted to go with him but there had been Fenian activity in the area and he had declared it too dangerous. The last seven days were the longest they had been apart since their marriage six months ago in March. Ivo had suggested, almost seriously, that she might go back to Conyers while he was away but Cora had chosen to stay at Lulworth. She had wanted to get to know the house, to make it hers. When Ivo was there she was always conscious of his relationship with the house; every inch of it, she knew, had meaning for him. On their return from their honeymoon, Cora had been shown the Duchess's rooms, a set of exquisitely panelled rooms on the south side of the house facing the sea. She had been delighted with their proportions, their lightness and the distant glimpse of a triangle of sea through the shouldered hills. She had at once decided to make these rooms her own and had ordered new furnishings, jettisoning the red velvets and beaded fringes that the Double Duchess had favoured in favour of a Liberty fabric with birds and pomegranates. The first night after the rooms were finished, Cora had got ready for bed and waited for Ivo. He had been late, it was past eleven, and when he came in, instead of embracing her, he had skirted round the room, touching the curtains and the walls like a dog getting to know unfamiliar territory. In the end she had taken his hand and led him to the bed but there he had been restless and angular and had left her in the small hours. He had even smelt different, there had been a sour undercurrent to his normally warm sweet skin. This behaviour had gone on for three nights, with Ivo behaving as normal during the day but turning into a twitchy facsimile of himself at night. Cora had tried to talk to him about it but he had been evasive, so the next night she had gone to his room, the Duke's room, and Ivo had fallen on her before she had even closed the door. Clearly no amount of new curtains could erase his mother's presence from her rooms. After that she only used the Duchess's apartments during the day when Ivo was out on the estate.

Cora tilted her face to the sun and closed her eyes. It was not warm, thanks to the south-westerly wind, but she enjoyed the light burning through her eyelids. The sun was the thing she missed most; at home she had always taken it for granted but here every sunny day felt like a blessing. She opened her eyes and looked out to sea and saw a flash of white in the waters just beyond the mouth of the cove. She kicked Lincoln's flanks and trotted along the cliff for a closer look. As she grew nearer she saw that it was a pod of dolphins lacing through the waves. There were about five of them moving in unison as they spiralled through the water. Cora had seen individual dolphins before in Newport but this was the first time she had seen a pod and she found herself smiling till her cheeks ached.

Usually, about halfway back to the house, Lincoln would prick up his ears and she would let him canter home. But today she did not let him have his head but reined him in tightly as they walked sedately back up the hill. Lincoln snorted in protest but Cora did not relent. Normally she liked to be shaken up but today she wanted to prolong her state of dreamy content. As she approached the stables a groom ran out to take Lincoln.

'Good morning, Your Grace.' The groom touched his cap and led Lincoln over to the mounting block.

'What a beautiful day! I saw some dolphins in the bay. Is that common round here?'

The groom scratched his head. 'Well, I'z bin here close on seventeen years and I ain't never seen no dolphins, Your Grace.' The groom clicked his teeth and held out his hand to Cora as she dismounted. 'They say as dolphins are lucky, and Lulworth ain't had much luck lately, though I reckon that's changin'.' And the groom smiled, showing a row of broken brown teeth, his eyes moving across her body.

Cora's understanding lagged behind as she struggled to decipher the man's thick Dorset accent, but then she felt herself flushing. What did he mean? How could he possibly know? She had only begun to suspect herself these last few days. No one else knew, except possibly Bertha, and she was unlikely to start gossiping to the grooms. She threw down her whip and gloves and stalked off towards the house. As she reached the garden entrance, the butler appeared with a telegram on a silver salver. She tore it open.

'It's from the Duke, Bugler, to say he will be here for dinner. Have they finished in the chapel?'

'Yes, Your Grace. I think the men are only waiting for you to come and approve their work.'

'Have you seen it? Do you think the Duke will be pleased?'

Bugler looked at her from under his hooded eyelids. He had worked at the house for thirty years, starting as a footman, then under-butler, and he had been in his present position for the last ten years. He had many duties: the upkeep of the family silver, the maintenance of the cellar, upholding good behaviour in the servants' hall, even the conveying of bad news (it had fallen to him to tell Duchess Fanny about her older son's death) but he was not paid to have opinions. The new American Duchess should know better than to ask.

'I really couldn't say, Your Grace.'

'But you saw the old one, do you think this one is as good?'

'They both seem to be of the same size, Your Grace.'

Cora gave up. 'Tell them I will be up there directly I've changed.'

Bugler noted with disapproval that the new Duchess ran up the stairs to her rooms, holding her habit so high that he could see her legs nearly to her knees. Cora was running because she had felt an overwhelming desire to be sick. If only she could reach her room first. But her door was a good hundred yards away. To her horror she found herself on her knees retching on the carpet in the corridor. She prayed that Bugler had not seen. Feeling clammy and shaky, she got to her room and rang for Bertha.

Before Bertha reached the Duchess, the mess on the carpet had been cleaned up by Mabel the housemaid, who had seen the whole episode. By the time that Bertha had sponged her mistress's temples with eau de cologne and had helped her into her morning dress, and the cook had sent up some dry toast and weak tea, the news of the Duchess's indisposition had spread through the servants' hall, much to the jubilation of the second footman, who had drawn May in the downstairs sweepstake on the birth of an heir.

Aloysius and Jerome, the Duke's dogs, followed Cora as she walked up the path to the chapel. It had been nearly a year since she had first seen the chapel. Every time she had entered it since then, she had felt reproached by the rectangle of light paint above the altar. In Venice she had written to Duveen Brothers, the art dealers who her mother used, and asked them if they could trace the painting of St Cecilia that had hung there. In July she had received a letter telling her that the painting had been sold to one Cyrus Guest of San Francisco, who was not minded to sell. Undaunted, Cora had asked the dealers to find another painting by Rubens that would fit in the alcove above the altar in the Lulworth chapel. Two weeks later Duveen wrote to say that there was a Madonna and Child by the same painter being offered for sale by an impoverished Irish earl. Was the Duchess interested in viewing it? Cora decided to buy the painting on the spot. A Rubens was a Rubens, after all. The price had been higher than she had expected but she had found that reassuring.

She told the dogs to stay on the steps of the chapel. They did not mind her as they minded Ivo, so she went into the chapel quickly, shutting the door behind her so they would not follow her in. At first she could not see anything, but then a shaft of light broke through the windows in the cupola and fell directly on the altar and lit up the painting. The Madonna, who was wearing an orange robe, was clutching the infant Jesus to her with one arm and looking at an illuminated book that rested in the other. They were in a bower of pale pink roses, and the book that Mary was looking at lay on an intricately patterned Persian carpet. Cora was struck by the picture's tenderness, the way that Jesus, blond and naked as a cherub, was resting his head so trustingly on his mother's breast. She could not help noticing that the Madonna had hair of the same chestnut hue as her own.

A voice behind her said, 'They say that Rubens used his wife and baby son as models for this picture. I think that gives the picture its intimacy.'

Cora turned to see a small dark man in a very white collar, smiling at her.

'Ambrose Fox, Your Grace. Mr Duveen asked me to come down with the painting to make sure you were happy with it.'

Cora held out her hand and after a moment's hesitation the man shook it.

'Tell him it is perfect. I think it looks very well here in the chapel, don't you, Mr Fox?'

'Yes indeed, Your Grace. It looks quite settled.'

'I am so relieved. You see it is a surprise for the Duke. There was another Rubens here before, but it was sold and I wanted to replace it. The other one was of St Cecilia but I think the Madonna and Child is just as good, perhaps even more appropriate. I wonder, have you seen the other picture? I never did but if you have you could tell me whether this one is as good.'

Cora knew she was talking too much to someone whose status was not clear – was he someone you invited for lunch or sent to the housekeeper? But she felt overwhelmed by the painting. She had not known when she had agreed to buy it how apt it was. She had never had much to do with children, but there was something about the way that the baby's hand was spread out so possessively on his mother's breast that made her realise, for the first time since her suspicions began, where she was heading. Would her baby lean on her like that, claiming her for his own?

'The St Cecilia is generally regarded as one of Ruben's finest works but I would have thought it a little imposing for a chapel of this size. I think that this work is of the right scale and, dare I say it, the right mood for this place.'

Cora looked at him sharply. Was he suggesting anything? But Mr Fox gazed back at her unblinkingly. His confidence impressed her, she would ask him for lunch. There were, after all, plenty of other pictures that needed replacing.

The dogs were waiting for her outside, and they began to bark when they saw the stranger with her.

'Please don't mind them, Mr Fox, they will calm down once they realise you are with me.'

'These are the famous Lulworth lurchers I suppose, I recognise them from the Van Dyck portrait of the first Duke. Splendid creatures.' But in spite of his confident words, Cora couldn't help noticing that Mr Fox looked extremely nervous. She batted the dogs away with her hand and motioned for him to follow her back to the house.

Ivo looked surprised when Cora suggested they visit the chapel after dinner.

'Of course, if you want to go, but wouldn't you rather go in daylight? There is no gaslight in the chapel.'

'Oh, but there are candles, it will look much prettier.' Cora had already asked Bugler to have the candles lit.

She rushed through dinner, twitching impatiently as Ivo cleared his plate. At last he put his napkin down and she stood up.

'Shall we go now? Up to the chapel?'

'Can't it wait until I have had a cigarette?'

'I really don't think so, Ivo. Please, darling.'

With exaggerated slowness, Ivo got up and started to move towards the door. Cora was by now in a frenzy of impatience. She took him by the arm and pulled him through the door.

'You American girls are such hoydens,' he said, laughing at her vehemence, but he took her arm and they walked up the path. He teased her all the way about being an American bully until they turned the corner and he saw that the chapel was lit up inside. Cora felt his hand tense around her arm.

'Is there something wrong?'

'No, it's just that I haven't seen the chapel lit up at night for a while. The last time was when Guy was laid out here.'

Another evening Cora would have shuddered at her thoughtlessness. But tonight she was too full of the revelations to come to pay complete attention to his mood. As they reached the chapel doors she stopped.

'I have something to show you, but I want it to be a surprise, so close your eyes.'

'Do you have the Holy Father in there, or the Holy Grail? Really, Cora, we will make a Catholic of you yet.'

'Ssh, stop talking, just shut your eyes and come with me.'

At last Ivo closed his eyes and she guided him into the chapel. The Madonna and Child glowed in the candlelight. Cora felt she would burst with her own cleverness; she was making Lulworth magnificent again.

'You can open your eyes now.' She turned away from the painting to look at Ivo's face.

He opened his eyes and looked around him puzzled, and then he saw the Rubens and went very still, gazing at the painting with an expression that Cora could not read. She waited for his set face to crack open with surprise and pleasure. When he did nothing but stare, she thought perhaps he did not know what it was.

'It's a Rubens, you know, like the one you had before.'

Still Ivo was silent. She put a hand on his arm, but he did not move. He was gazing at the painting, his face completely motionless. The muscles of his arm were hard under her hand. Part of her knew to be silent but another piece of her wanted to scream. This was her surprise and he was not playing his part.

She willed herself to wait, watching a rivulet of wax run down the side of one of the candles. Finally when its warmth had gone and the drop had stiffened, she spoke again.

'I did try to get the other Rubens, the one that was here before, the one of St Cecilia, but the man who bought it was American—'

'And he didn't need the money.' Ivo's voice was flat, this was a statement not a question. Could it be that he was angry because she had not been able to buy the original painting?

'Of course I haven't seen the painting of St Cecilia but Mr Fox, who brought the painting down from Duveen's, has, and he thought that the Madonna was actually better suited to this position.'

'It is a fine picture.' Ivo's voice was still colourless.

'Rubens used his wife and baby as his models.' She moved closer to the painting. Every time she looked at it she saw more in it. There was a basket of fruit in the lower right-hand corner, with grapes and plums. Some of the grapes had been eaten. Behind the Virgin's right shoulder there were trees opening on to a rural landscape that looked green and cool. Underneath her orange robe the Virgin was wearing a sleeve of damask pink. She wondered if she might have a dress made up in those very colours when she had her baby.

'Look at the baby's hand, Ivo. See how tightly he is holding on to his mother.' She reached out her own hand to him, willing him to come forward.

But Ivo did not move. 'I know the painting.'

Cora was astonished. 'Really? But how? Duveen's said it had never been on the market before.'

'No, it hasn't.'

'So how did you . . .' Cora trailed off when she realised where Ivo must have seen the picture.

'It was in the Kinsale family for two hundred years. It used to hang in their chapel.' Ivo's voice was expressionless.

'I didn't realise you knew the owners.' Cora began to feel cold. She persisted. 'But does it matter, Ivo? They needed the money. I gave them a good price and now you have a Rubens over the altar again.'

Ivo raised his arms. For a moment Cora thought he was going to embrace her, but then he dropped them and was once more still.

'Ivo, what's wrong? I only did this because I thought it would make you happy. You minded about the other picture, I know you did.' Cora ground her shoe into the stone floor in frustration.

'Of course I minded! But Cora, you can't make everything better just by buying a new picture. The Lulworth Rubens had been here since the Fourth Duke. When I came into the chapel I used to think of all my ancestors who had knelt in front of the same painting saying the same words. Now St Cecilia is in California and we have a lovely new Rubens courtesy of my very rich wife.' He looked at her face and shook his head. 'You don't understand what I'm saying, do you? And why should you? My scruples must seem absurd to you.'

'Not absurd, just puzzling. I thought you wanted my money for what it could do here.' She peered at him, trying to read his face.

'No Cora, I needed it. There's a difference, but I see you don't understand.'

It was true she didn't understand. She had bought the picture to show him how she would make Lulworth great again, but instead of pleasing him she had offended him instead. How could she have misjudged him so badly? She realised that she really knew very little about the man she had married.

At last he walked over to her and looked down at her. She put her arms on his shoulders and after a pause he reciprocated by putting his arms round her waist.

'Oh Cora, can you believe that there are some things in life that can't be bought?'

She looked up at his dark face and noticed the light creases that ran between his nose and chin and the flicker in his eyelid. She was relieved that whatever had made him so sombre was passing. She had felt for a moment, there, that he was a stranger.

'Of course I know that. Would you like to hear about one of them?' She smiled, having won the conversation back on to her territory.

He looked at her closely and his glance moved down her body. 'Do you mean that you are . . .'

'Yes I do – well, I'm almost certain. I was sick this morning, and my corsets won't lace properly.' She put her hands to her still tiny waist.

He took a step away from her as if he had been pushed backwards by the force of her news, put a hand on one of the pews to steady himself, but missed it and almost lost his balance. Cora looked at him bemused, it was unlike Ivo to be clumsy, but then he straightened up and his face re-formed into a smile.

'I am glad. It was too melancholy being the last of the Maltravers. Have you seen a doctor?'

'Not yet, I wanted to tell you first, although some of the servants seem to have guessed.'

'They always know everything first. Do you have any idea when it will . . .'

'May. Well, at least I think so. I can't be sure until I have seen the doctor.'

'My clever girl.' He bent his head and kissed her on the forehead.

'So you see, I had my reasons for buying a Madonna and Child,' she said a little reproachfully.

Ivo hung his head in mock supplication. 'Of course you did. Everything you do is perfectly reasonable. I have been churlish, Cora, and you must forgive me. We do things differently, that's all.'

He put his arms round her neck and pulled her to him. She remembered the first time they had kissed, here in the chapel. He had been unexpected then, the speed of his proposal, the certainty of his embrace; and now, did she really know him better? Physically perhaps, when they kissed now it was a communication, not an exploration, but there was a part of him that was still opaque. But she dismissed this from her mind. Whatever he thought about the Rubens, there could be no doubt that he wanted an heir.

It was days later before she allowed herself to think about the scene in the chapel again. She thought of his cold, still face and the way he had not looked at her but only at the picture. Afterwards it was all right, although Cora could not help noticing that now when he entered the chapel he never looked straight ahead; he would enter, dip his fingers in the stoup of holy water and walk to the altar with his head bowed. It was only when he approached the altar to take Communion that he would raise his head and look at the picture, as if it was his own particular cross to bear.

CHAPTER 17

Bridgewater House

THE DAYS WERE BEGINNING TO DRAW IN NOW. Cora watched the lamplighter make his way down Cleveland Row to the park, adding his punctuation to the light that spilled from doorways and from behind curtains into the gathering gloom. She was tired from the journey up from Lulworth but she had felt her spirits lift when the carriage had drawn up outside the limestone pillars that flanked their London house. Bridgewater House, with its façade by Barry, had been a wedding gift from her father, although, of course, it had been chosen by her mother, who had been surprised to find that the Duke had no permanent residence in town. This house, with its enormous central hall and colonnaded gallery was, in Mrs Cash's view, on the right scale. She had thought it entirely fitting that it had been built by the same man who had remodelled Buckingham Palace.

There had been a Maltravers house once, in St James's, but the Duke's grandfather had sold it. Cora had wondered whether she should try and buy it back, but after her experience with the Rubens she was wary of offending her husband. Besides, she liked this house with its drawing room that had six long windows overlooking Green Park.

She saw a carriage draw up outside the house and a liveried footman walk up to the front door. Who would be calling now? wondered Cora. She hoped it was Sybil. At least then they could talk about clothes. With Sybil she could forget about being a duchess and return to the serious business of sleeve width. Cora thought they could not get any wider but then she had thought that six months ago, and had been proved quite wrong.

The footman brought in Lady Beauchamp's card.

Cora was surprised and pleased. The Beauchamps had left Conyers the day after Charlotte had expressed the hope that they would be friends, on account of a death in the family. Cora had been sorry not to see more of her. Cora had no female friends in England apart from Sybil, and while Sybil was charming, her awkwardness and her awful clothes meant that she was more Cora's protégée than her equal. Charlotte was in a different class. There was something intriguing about her and she was one of the few English women who Cora regarded as a worthy sartorial rival. She wondered how wide Charlotte's sleeves would be.

She was not disappointed. Although Charlotte was dressed in half mourning for one of Odo's cousins, her dress made no concessions to grief, bar the colour, and the lavender tones of her gown were a spectacular foil to her blonde sleekness. She had abandoned the full sleeve of the summer for a puffed shoulder that tapered into a tight cuff. The cuffs and hem were covered in silver braid. Around her shoulders she had a silver fox fur and she wore a hat with mauve and grey plumes. She glided towards Cora and took her hands.

'I am so pleased to find you at home, Duchess,' Charlotte's voice was warm. 'I was driving past on my way home from the

Lauderdales' and I saw that your shutters were down. Have you been in town long?' She gave Cora's hand a little squeeze.

'No, we've only just arrived. Ivo has decided to take up his seat in the Lords.' Cora felt proud at being able to say this. She gestured to Charlotte to sit on a gilt Louis Quinze sofa. The other woman sank into it gracefully.

'Well, now you are here, we must introduce you to some amusing people. If Ivo is going to take up politics you will need some distraction. You mustn't think that everything is as dull as Conyers. Of course, if the Double Duchess asks, you have to go, but the Marlborough House thing is so *vieux jeu* now. I think it all used to be tremendous fun, gambling and divorces and what have you, but now Bertie is only slightly less stuffy than his mother.'

Cora smiled. 'I wouldn't say that Conyers was dull. Americans like me can't be blasé about royalty. But it was certainly exacting. So much to remember, I was so worried about saying the wrong thing. I was sorry you had to leave, I was relying on you for guidance.'

Charlotte adjusted her sleeve. 'Oh Duchess, I don't think you need any help from me. You seemed to have everything in order. I hear the Prince is quite smitten.'

Cora couldn't disguise her pleasure. 'I wish you would call me Cora, I am still getting used to being a duchess.'

Charlotte nodded. 'Very well, Cora it is, and you must call me Charlotte. I will never get used to being Lady Beauchamp.' This last remark was thrown off with a laugh, but Cora was surprised nonetheless. Charlotte noticed Cora's expression. 'Oh dear, have I shocked you again? I keep forgetting that Americans marry for love.'

Cora looked back at her steadily. 'Well, this one did.' She smiled self-deprecatingly. 'But the title is quite hard to get used to. Sometimes I find it difficult to believe they are talking about me.'

'Whereas every English girl has been dreaming of being called Your Grace since the schoolroom. You won't get an ounce of sympathy from me on that score, Cora.'

Cora laughed. She found Charlotte dangerously good company.

'But English girls are trained for this life. So many things I should know. Ivo is quite tolerant but the servants are merciless. Every time I ask for something, they say just as you wish, Your Grace, and then I know I have sinned. I asked Bugler to light the fire for me in the library and he looked as if I had hit him. He said I will send a footman to take care of that, Your Grace. By the time it was done, I was shivering with cold.' She made a little pout of mock distress.

'You asked the butler to light the fire? But that is a serious case of lese-majesty. I am surprised Bugler didn't hand in his notice. To be a duke's butler is only a little less important than being a Duke.' Charlotte gave an accurate impression of Bugler's most stately expression.

Cora rang the bell for tea. 'Well, at least the servants here in London are new, I don't have to worry about hurting their feelings.'

Charlotte leaned towards Cora. 'I am having a small party on Thursday. You must come. Louvain will be there.' She looked at Cora through her lashes to see if the name registered.

'The painter? I thought he lived in Paris. My mother tried to get him to do her portrait but he said he was too busy to come to America. She was furious.' Cora remembered her mother's wrath vividly. Louvain had not been too 'busy' to paint the Rhinelander girls earlier in the year.

Charlotte smiled. 'He is very choosy about his subjects. I sat for him earlier this year. Fifteen sittings in his draughty studio by the river. He absolutely insisted on painting me in my riding habit – and he called me Diana all the way through the sittings. I would have given up but Odo was adamant I continue, and Louvain can be very charming when he wants to be.' Charlotte shrugged, causing the feathers on her hat to quiver. 'He has told everybody that he won't do any more portraits, but I am sure if he were to meet you,' she gestured towards Cora who was wearing a gorgeously beribboned tea gown from Madame Vionnet, 'an American duchess, how could he resist?' She stopped for breath as the footman brought in the tea things. 'Oh Lord, is that the time? I must fly. So, Thursday then.' Charlotte stood up, shaking out her mauve skirts so that the little train at the back fell perfectly on the floor behind her.

Cora thought about Louvain. His portrait of Mamie Rhinelander in her peignoir had divided New York society last year. Her mother had called it vulgar but Teddy said it was a masterpiece.

'Well, there are things I have to attend to, but as far as I know we have no other engagements that night.' It sounded rather ponderous but Cora was not minded to confide the news of her pregnancy to the other woman. Charlotte appeared not to notice the evasiveness, gathered her furs and left.

As the Double Duchess's ward, Charlotte was almost an honorary member of the Maltravers family, hence her presence at Conyers; yet Cora could not remember Ivo ever talking about her. She had tried hard to find out more from her husband but Ivo, she was learning, could turn a conversation in any way he pleased, and it did not please him to talk about the Beauchamps.

Cora rang the bell for the footman to take away the tea things and went over to the bureau. She took out a sheet of writing paper which had an embossed coronet on the top (her mother had ordered the paper to go with the house) and wrote a note to Mrs Wyndham asking her to call. She had found the older woman rather alarming when she had first arrived in London, but now she could do with some of her unrelenting worldliness. She knew it was time for her to start taking on the mantle of Duchess; she remembered with dread the Prince's threat to visit Lulworth. In New York she would have known exactly where to begin, but here she was nervous about making a mistake. Mrs Wyndham, she felt sure, would know where to start, and Cora had no qualms about asking her because she knew that her goodwill was essential to Mrs Wyndham's 'business'.

Cora had never asked her mother how much money she had paid for procuring their invitation to Sutton Veney but judging by Mrs Wyndham's carriage and her charming house in Curzon Street, it had not come cheap. Mrs Wyndham was a woman who put a price on everything, a quality which Cora was coming to appreciate. The English were so peculiar about money. There had been Ivo's reaction to the Rubens and then there was the matter of Sybil's birthday present. Cora had sent her a sable wrap. Sybil had been delighted but the Double Duchess had pulled Cora aside for a word. 'You really mustn't give such extravagant presents, Cora dear, there is a fine line between generosity and bribery.' The Duchess had even tried to make Sybil return the furs, but her stepdaughter had refused. The Duchess had been equally caustic when Cora had appeared at Conyers wearing the tiara that her mother had given her, instead of the Maltravers 'fender', a heavy edifice of diamonds which was impossible to wear without getting a headache. When Cora pointed this out and explained that her tiara had been modelled on one worn by the Empress of Austria, the Duchess had sighed and said that she had always been proud to wear the Maltravers tiara when she had been Duchess of Wareham. Cora, with Ivo's permission, had sent the 'fender' to Garrards the jewellers to be remodelled, and had been astonished when a polite note had been sent back regretfully informing her that the tiara was not worth redesigning as the stones were not real. When she had told Ivo, he had laughed bitterly and said that he supposed that his mother must have sold the gems to pay her dress bill.

Even her charitable schemes had been found wanting. At Lulworth, Cora was full of ideas to improve the estate. Her first act was to separate the food left over from the Lulworth table into different courses before it was distributed to the poor. The servants had grumbled about the extra work, and the poor had done nothing to express their gratitude. She had proposed building a school for the children of the village – a scheme which Ivo had originally encouraged; but when she had had plans drawn up and started designing uniforms, he quashed the whole idea as too expensive and troublesome. When she replied that the money was not a problem and she was quite prepared to take on the running of the school, he sighed and said that there some things about English life that she didn't yet understand. But because Ivo put his arms round her and kissed her as he said it, Cora had let it go. There would be time enough for philanthropy after the baby was born.

When the footman arrived to take away the tea things she asked him to take the note directly to Mrs Wyndham. With any luck she would come tomorrow. There was much that Cora needed to discuss.

Bertha was delighted when she found that she and Jim were to travel to London together alone. Even though they lived in the same house and saw each other every day, they were rarely able to be together for more than a moment. They had to be so careful. She felt constantly watched. Most of the Lulworth servants had been there for years so they were wary of newcomers, particularly foreign ones. Only butlers were allowed to marry and remain in service. Bertha was fairly confident that Cora would protect her, but she did not want to put Jim's future in jeopardy. If he lost his post without a reference he would find it very hard to get another job, and if they were to marry, then his experience as the Duke of Wareham's valet would be invaluable. The fashion for the new palace-type hotels meant that there was always work for experienced servants with impeccable references. If Jim could get a job at the Savoy, and she could find work at a milliner's, they might be able to afford to get married. And Bertha was clear that marriage, rather than these fumbling encounters in corridors and shrubberies, was what she wanted. She liked Jim's kisses, and the feel of his hands on her body, but she had no intention of letting things go any further without a ring.

Today was Bertha's chance to raise the idea of the Savoy with Jim. They were travelling up to London together alone, as they were the only servants that the Duke and Duchess were bringing with them from Dorset. Mrs Cash, when she bought the house, had also engaged a full household staff, including a French chef and a Swiss laundry maid. But Bertha's hopes of a conversation with Jim faded when she saw that they were the only occupants of their third-class carriage. Within minutes of the doors closing and the train leaving the station, Jim pulled down the blinds and pounced on her. Bertha tried to resist him but he was so sweetly eager that she soon lost any desire to do anything but enjoy the present moment. And later on, when other people got into the carriage at stations along the way, she was too aware of his leg pressed against hers, the hand that kept brushing her fingers and the kisses that he would steal every time the train went through a tunnel to think about anything else. So she had suggested that instead of taking a hansom they go on foot to Cleveland Row from the station. The walk would be a good time to talk uninterrupted.

But Jim was excited to be in London. He sniffed the air around him like a dog. As they walked across Waterloo Bridge, he was enchanted by the view of Parliament in one direction and St Paul's in the other. He bought her a bunch of violets from an old gypsy woman, who told him he had a lucky face but glared at Bertha. Although London was better in that respect than New York, at least no one jeered at them in the street. Bertha knew that Jim did not notice these things; it was what she loved about him – he thought she was magnificent and he expected everyone else to feel the same. They walked through Trafalgar Square and along the Strand, until they came to the Savoy Theatre and the hotel which stood next to it.

She pointed towards it. 'They pay good wages in there, you know. We stayed there our first week in London, and the head waiter told me he was getting a hundred guineas all told, together with his tips.' Bertha pointed out a magnificently dressed employee to Jim.

'It'd be hard, though, getting used to all those different people.

Everyone wanting things to be done differently. Lord knows His Grace is bad enough with his soft collars and hard collars and his bathwater just so, but fancy having a new master every week and some of them foreigners.' Jim fingered his stiff collar.

'Foreigners ain't so bad, are they, Jim?' Bertha put her arm through his. He smiled at her.

'Some of them are tolerable, I suppose.' He jerked his head back towards the hotel. 'So this is what you have in mind for me? Is that the way of it then?'

'Well if you found work there and I took a job trimming hats, we could make a living.'

Jim stopped and looked at her. Bertha realised she had gone too far and she laughed it off. Perhaps marriage wasn't on Jim's mind.

'We will both need jobs if we lose our posts for being late!' she said, pulling at his arm. A garden bus went by on the Strand. 'Come on, this will be quicker than walking.' They got on to the platform at the back and climbed up the stairs to the top deck. It was cold up there but the fug on the bottom deck was unbearable. They found seats at the front behind the driver. She looked at Jim's profile; behind him there was a hoarding advertising Pear's Soap, 'For a Pearly Complexion'.

'I'm sorry, Jim, I didn't mean to presume.' She put her hand on his arm. He squeezed it by way of reply and they sat in silence until the bus reached Pall Mall.

As they walked up Cleveland Row, Jim said slowly, 'It's not that I don't want to be with you, Bertha, but service is all I've ever known. I was the boot boy at Sutton Veney and then when I grew tall they made me a footman and now I'm valet to a duke. I never thought I'd come this far. But I'm a lucky man. I met you, didn't I?'

They were too close to the house for Bertha to be able to kiss him, but she stroked his arm and said, 'We've both been lucky.'

As they approached the house, and began to draw apart from each other, they saw a lady in furs hurry down the steps. Jim recognised her at once.

'Good thing she didn't see us. She's a mean one, Lady Beauchamp. There were two housemaids as lost their place at Sutton on account of her. Said they were rude to her, as if that were likely – they were local girls who wouldn't say boo to a goose. No, I reckon as they saw something they shouldn't, they were sent off that quickly. Still, I suppose anyone would go sour married to that Sir Odious. I'd rather go back to being a boot boy than work for him again.' Jim's handsome face was grim at the thought of his former employer.

Bertha realised that she was fortunate. Miss Cora was hard work but they'd been together for eight years now and so she was Bertha's hard work.

They walked down the area steps to the tradesmen's entrance. Bertha could see M. Pechon the French chef piping rosettes of cream round a glistening mountain of aspic in which anchovies and sprats had been suspended as if swimming in a gelatinous sea. There were many days when Bertha envied her mistress, but today was not one of them.

Cora had been right in thinking that Mrs Wyndham would respond swiftly to her summons. Madeleine Wyndham was delighted when she saw the Wareham crest on the seal. Cora had been her greatest match to date, although in all honesty she could not take credit for having introduced her to Wareham. What, Mrs Wyndham wondered, did the young Duchess want her for? Cora had been different to most of the young American girls and their parents who came her way. Most of them were quite 'au naturel', beautifully dressed hoydens who had the manners of farm girls and had nothing to recommend them apart from youthful high spirits and, of course, money. But Cora had arrived already 'finished', there was nothing to improve. Indeed, the only thing that separated Cora from a well-bred English girl was her confidence. Serene in the knowledge that she was the heiress of her generation, she had an air of assurance quite unusual in a girl of her age. She was spoilt, of course, most of the Americans were; but on the rare occasions she failed to get her own way, she looked amazed rather than petulant.

Mrs Wyndham wondered if Cora was having trouble with her mother-in-law. She had met the Double Duchess at countless gatherings over the last twenty years, but every time they encountered each other the Duchess pretended never to have seen her before. She wondered if the Duchess would keep this up now that her son had married an American. When Madeleine had first arrived in London fifteen years ago, she had quite often been asked about the Natives in her country as if she had herself only recently emerged from a wigwam. She had once, in jest, gone to a masquerade ball dressed as an Indian squaw, only to have a number of dowagers ask her if she missed wearing her native costume.

But that had been at the end of the seventies, before the heiresses had started arriving. Mrs Wyndham did not come from a very wealthy family. Her father had owned a hotel in Manhattan and there was gossip that he had met his wife when she was working there as a chambermaid. Both her parents had always denied this but the rumour was enough to place a cloud over the family's social prospects. Madeleine was well-liked at Miss Porter's Academy but her friendship with the Rhinebackers, Stuyvesants and Astors stopped at the school door. It had been Mr Lester, Madeleine's father, who had proposed going to Europe; he wanted, he said, to look at how they ran hotels over there. Within a month of arriving in London, Madeleine had met the Hon. Captain Wyndham, and within two months they were engaged to be married. Madeleine found the captain with his beautiful manners, resplendent moustaches and aristocratic family (his father was an Irish baron) far superior to any of her American beaux and accepted him gladly. She knew that when he proposed he had hoped that she was rich, but he had not flinched when he realised the modest scale of her fortune.

They had been very happy for the ten years of their marriage, which ended when the captain had taken a fence too fast and had broken his neck. He left his widow with a son and a small annuity which would hardly support them. But providentially her father had sent her a family from Philadelphia, who had stayed at his hotel in New York and who were curious to meet his aristocratic daughter. The eldest girl had been a beauty, thankfully a quiet one, and extremely rich and Mrs Wyndham had introduced her to Lord Castlerosse, an old friend of her husband's. The marriage received huge attention in the American papers and soon Mrs Wyndham found herself a necessary stopping point on an American belle's grand tour – somewhere between a visit to M. Worth and the Forum by moonlight.

At first she had not asked her charges for money, relying instead on 'presents' from the grateful milliners, jewellers, and dressmakers to whom she directed her American friends. But after a while she realised that her scruples were unnecessary. The American families that relied on her to introduce them into the best English society were happy to pay her; in fact the fathers preferred a commercial transaction to an unseen web of obligation and favours. And she soon learnt that the higher the price, the more her new friends valued her services. Mrs Wyndham had taste and tact, and she knew how to get her girls, and on not a few occasions their mamas, to look their best. There was a difference, she would tell them, between dressing smartly and overdressing. American girls were, on the whole, far more fashionable than their English contemporaries, but it did not do to rub their noses in it. Even though many of her young charges had sable cloaks and diamond tiaras, that did not mean they should wear them. Such things were best left for married ladies and even then she could not really countenance diamonds in the daytime.

When she had first come to London, Mrs Wyndham had been as bemused as her protégées, but having been punished by knowing glances and raised eyebrows every time she did something perceived to be 'American', she was now more English in her habits than the crustiest of dowagers. Growing up in a hotel, she had acquired a good memory for names and faces; after fifteen years in London she knew everybody and her command of Burke's Peerage was unmatched. No genealogical nuance of the aristocracy was lost on her; she could talk with authority about the Spencer red hair or the Percy chin or the Londonderry madness, and she had long ago learnt never to comment on a likeness in a younger child when visiting an aristocratic nursery. Mrs Wyndham knew to within a sovereign every single girl's portion and every man's income. Her network of lady's maids, French chefs and butlers, whom she was in the habit of 'recommending', kept her supplied with the kind of information that made her invaluable to her friends. She always knew the latest gossip, often before the participants themselves were aware of it. At a society ball, she was probably the only person, apart from a jeweller with a loupe, who could tell which jewels were real and which were paste.

But even Mrs Wyndham had very little to teach the Cashes. They had come to her because Mrs Cash wanted entry to the very choicest circles. Mrs Wyndham's friendship with the Prince of Wales meant that in London at least, she was received everywhere. When Mrs Cash had heard about the royal connection, she had made hints about introducing Cora to one of the younger princes but Mrs Wyndham had refused to understand her. At last, exasperated by Mrs Cash's persistence, she had told her that she could buy Cora pretty much any husband she chose within the ranks of the British aristocracy except for a royal one. If she wanted a prince she would have to go to Europe where you could find royal titles by the score.

As Mrs Wyndham drew up outside the neo-classical façade of Bridgewater House, the clock at St James's Palace chimed eleven. It was early in the day for a call but Cora had implied in her letter that she wanted a tête-à-tête. Mrs Wyndham knew the house well: she had housed many of her American protégées there, and she had received a handsome commission when she had persuaded Mrs Cash to buy it for her daughter.

Cora was standing at the top of the long marble staircase. Looking up at her Mrs Wyndham saw at once that the girl was different to the one she had met the year before. Some of those changes were physical; Mrs Wyndham assumed that the Duchess was by now pregnant, but the new softness was more than corporeal. The bright stare had gone. Something had dented that air of ownership. Mrs Wyndham was surprised, she had not put Cora down as the type to be altered by her marriage, she had seemed so self-possessed.

'Thank you so much for coming to see me, Mrs Wyndham,' said Cora.

'Oh, my dear Duchess, you can't imagine how thrilled I was to get your note. I rushed over here as soon as it was decent. I hope you are pleased with the house. Such a pleasant aspect, I always think. It would be hard to find a more elegant street in London. And how is the Duke? I hear there was some trouble in Ireland.'

'Yes, there was a rent strike and the bailiff was held up at gunpoint. Ivo came away most disheartened. I think he should sell the Irish estate and buy something in Scotland but he won't hear of it.' Cora's tone was light but there was a note of petulance.

'Well, no, Dunleary has some of the best fishing in Ireland. No sportsman would want to give that up. You know how attached gentlemen are to their sport.' Mrs Wyndham smiled wistfully, conveying in her glance the dead husband who had fallen while hunting with the Quorn. A reference that was lost on Cora.

'Ivo is attached all right. He missed the rehearsal for our wedding because he decided to go on a hunting trip. My mother was scandalised. Of course American men like their sport too but they have their occupations, they can't just take off in the middle of the week. Only today Ivo has gone all the way to Windsor to look at polo ponies.'

'Such a noble game, but I hope he will be careful. I remember what happened to his poor brother.' There was a pause as both ladies reflected on the death of the Eighth Duke.

Cora gestured to Mrs Wyndham to sit in one of the Louis

fauteuils by the fire (Mrs Cash had had them sent over from America).

'It's interesting that you should mention Ivo's brother, Mrs Wyndham. I know so little about Ivo's earlier life. And he so rarely speaks of it. Did you know the family well?'

Mrs Wyndham lowered her eyelids, she hated to admit ignorance. 'Not well exactly, but I saw the Warehams from time to time in London, and I was there for Charlotte Vane's coming-out ball, which of course was given by the Duchess. Such a beautiful girl, she did very well for herself, considering. Odo Beauchamp is independently wealthy even beyond what he will inherit from his father.' Mrs Wyndham noticed that Cora looked suddenly alert when she mentioned Charlotte's name.

'You say that Charlotte Vane did well for herself, considering. Considering what?'

'Oh, her complete lack of fortune. Her father was a gambler and lost it all at the tables. She was lucky that the Duchess took her in after her mother died, I don't know what she would have done otherwise. Far too pretty to be a governess. But the Duchess and Charlotte's mother were cousins on the Laycock side, and I suppose not having a daughter, she thought it would be nice to have a girl to dress up. She was very kind to Charlotte, I dare say she would have settled something on her if she could. Instead she did the next best thing and saw her well married. Odo is not to everyone's taste but he dotes on Charlotte and gives her everything she wants. Of course with her looks she might have done better than a baronet, but better a baronet with money than a marquess with mortgages.' Mrs Wyndham looked in her reticule for her lorgnette, so she could see clearly what effect her conversation was having on Cora.

'She looks like she enjoys spending money. She is quite the

fashion plate,' Cora was going to add, 'for an English girl', but stopped as she wasn't sure how Mrs Wyndham, who by now had almost completely lost the American twang in her speech, would take this remark. Sometimes it was hard to remember that Mrs Wyndham had grown up in Manhattan not Mayfair.

'Indeed, I believe her picture was in the *Illustrated London News*. Most regrettable. A respectable woman's name should only appear in the newspaper three times in her life: when she is born, when she is married and when she dies.'

Cora smiled faintly, thinking of the many newspapers and magazines which had printed her own picture in the last few months. *Town Topics* had doubled its circulation at the time of her wedding. She had not enjoyed the articles about her trousseau but she had found it hard to object to the photograph of her that had run in the paper with the caption: 'Is this the definitive American Beauty?' Mrs Wyndham really had become quite British. Ivo had the same disdain for the press.

'Charlotte Beauchamp was here yesterday, asking me to a musical evening. She seemed quite anxious that I should go. I wondered if I should accept.' She looked anxiously at the older woman. Mrs Wyndham realised that, for all her poise, Cora was nervous of getting it wrong. She would be delighted to advise her. It had taken her twenty years to learn how to get it right.

'Well, of course! You are the catch of the season. She, no doubt, is anxious to claim you as her own protégée. I am sure every hostess in London will feel the same. But you must be careful, my dear, to bestow your favours equally. You can't afford to make any enemies so early in your career.' Mrs Wyndham tapped the table for emphasis and continued.

'Everyone will be watching you to see what kind of Duchess

you will make. I'm sure most of them will be grateful for a new young, charming hostess, but you must remember that there are some who will be only too happy to see you fail. Your age, your wealth, your nationality make you conspicuous, not to mention your rank. Just take care you get yourself noticed for the right reasons. So by all means go to Charlotte Beauchamp's, but make sure the next time you appear in public it is with someone who is unquestionably old school like Lady Bessborough or even your mother-in-law. Keep them all guessing until you have decided where you want to be.'

Cora grimaced at the thought of her mother-in-law, but she understood Mrs Wyndham's point.

'But surely Ivo has already been identified as one thing or another?'

'When a man marries, my dear, it is for his wife to set the tone. If the Duke is thinking of going into politics – I heard he is taking his seat in the Lords – then the biggest asset he can have is a wife who knows everybody.'

Cora looked a little daunted by this, so Mrs Wyndham changed the subject. 'Now you will think me very indelicate for asking but I claim my privilege as your fellow countrywoman. Are you expecting a happy event? You have a look that suggests that you might be.'

Cora admitted that she was right.

'And when do you expect the little Marquess? I feel sure you will produce an heir. The Maltravers are so good at boys.'

'Sir Julius thinks May.'

'A spring baby. How delightful! Of course you will miss the season but there is plenty of time for that. I am so glad you are with Sercombe. Such a superior physician, and very liberal with the chloroform. Really, when I think of the agonies we women had to endure before. Why, Milly Hardcastle who had twin boys said that she hardly felt a thing. Luckily there are no twins in the Maltravers family, unless of course they run on your side.'

Cora shook her head. She felt her stomach churn and the bile rising up her gullet.

'Will you excuse me, Mrs Wyndham.' Cora rushed out of the room.

Mrs Wyndham tutted sympathetically. Poor child. Perhaps she should not have referred to the dolours of childbirth, it had clearly alarmed her. She wondered if she should wait for Cora's return. No, she had a luncheon in Portland Place. She would leave a note. She picked up a piece of monogrammed paper and wrote,

'I am very conscious that you are without a mother's care and guidance at this delicate time. Please allow me to assist you in any way that an older compatriot can. Your friend, Madeleine Wyndham.'

Perhaps, thought Mrs Wyndham as her carriage turned into Pall Mall, she should have warned Cora to be on her guard with Charlotte Beauchamp. There had been rumours earlier this year of a liaison with Louvain the painter; given that Charlotte had not yet produced an heir, this was hardly prudent behaviour. But then Mrs Wyndham's attention was distracted by an intriguing display of parasols in the window of Swan and Edgar and the moment passed.

CHAPTER 18

An Ideal Husband

THE CARPET OUTSIDE THE BEAUCHAMP HOUSE IN Prince's Gate, Cora noticed, was green instead of the usual red. It looked as if a roll of turf had been laid out between the door and the pavement. As she stepped on to the carpet in her silver slippers, Cora wished that Ivo was with her. When she had told him about Charlotte's invitation, he had grimaced. 'At home with the Beauchamps and all their artistic friends? Honestly, Cora, I can't think of anything worse.'

Cora had pleaded, but Ivo had not been persuaded to change his mind. Every time she mentioned the party, he laughed and said he was too much a philistine to go to the Beauchamps. So she had come alone, although now she was at the house, she wondered why, a feeling that intensified as she walked up the stairs to the drawing room. She heard a swell of noise and laughter as the door opened. Inside she caught a glimpse of yellow walls and black paintwork as Charlotte greeted her.

'Cora, I am so pleased you are here.' She took Cora's hand in hers and gazed into her eyes with such intentness that Cora flushed. 'Don't look so anxious, I promise you, it will be amusing, not like Conyers at all. Louvain is here, and Stebbings the poet, you know, and he's brought some men who are publishing a new magazine.'

Cora followed her hostess into the room. She could see at once that Charlotte was right, this was a very different kind of party. There were no diamonds here, even dirty ones. The lighting was quite dim, there was no chandelier, only wall lights with coloured glass shades that bathed the interior in a curious yellow light, as if the whole room were set in aspic. The men seemed paler than normal and several of them, Cora noticed, had hair that touched their shoulders. Charlotte was as smartly dressed as ever in mauve chiffon with black lace but Cora noticed that some of the other women were wearing oddly limp garments that bore no relation to any fashion that she was familiar with. She was amazed to see that some of the women were smoking in public.

Charlotte led her over to two men who were looking at a periodical with a yellow and black cover. She heard one of the men say, 'They wouldn't have him, you know. He wanted to contribute but Aubrey said no.'

'Not serious enough, I suppose. Poor Oscar.'

Charlotte clapped her hands. 'Gentlemen, may I present you to my new Duchess. Mr Louvain and Mr Stebbings.'

Cora held out her hand and smiled brightly. 'Why, I am delighted to meet you both. I never saw your picture of Mamie Rhinebacker, Mr Louvain, but I heard of nothing else in New York last year. And Mr Stebbings, you mustn't be cross that I haven't read your work yet, but I'm new to this country.'

Charlotte laughed. 'Goodness, no one here has read Stebbings' book, although we all fully intend to.' She gave the poet a proprietorial glance.

Cora saw the poet flinch and she tried to shake his hand in

such a way as to show her sympathy. He had sandy hair and his skin was so covered in freckles that she could hardly see the blush creeping over his face.

'I shall certainly read it, Mr Stebbings. I am very fond of poetry.' The poet blinked his colourless lashes and murmured something inaudible. Cora felt she had embarrassed him, so she turned to Louvain who met her eyes and gave a faint smile. As she stepped back to speak to Charlotte, she was aware of the painter's eyes still upon her.

'I have been looking forward to seeing your portrait, Charlotte,' she said.

'Well then,' Charlotte replied, 'you have only to turn your head.' Cora turned and saw the painting on the wall behind her. Louvain had painted Charlotte wearing her riding clothes, her hat in one hand and her whip in the other. Cora realised at once why Louvain had insisted on painting Charlotte as a contemporary Diana. The dark costume was a foil to the pale intensity of Charlotte's face, whose expression was alert, defiant and, despite her gentle colouring, predatory. The hand that grasped the whip looked ready to strike, the curve of her mouth was about to declare the *coup de grâce*. She looked slightly dishevelled as if she had just dismounted. She was beautiful, but, Cora thought, alarming as well. But then she looked at Charlotte, who tonight was all smiles and softness, and wondered if she was right in sensing an edge to the portrait.

'You have done Lady Beauchamp justice, Mr Louvain. I have seen her in the field and she is fearless.'

'Thank you. A portrait is all about the exchange between the sitter and the artist. In Lady Beauchamp's case, I saw at once that I could only be her prey.' He made Charlotte an ironic bow.

Charlotte laughed and moved away.

'And did she catch you, Mr Louvain?' Cora risked asking.

'I'm not sure she wanted to, Duchess,' Louvain replied.

Cora felt again the heat of the painter's gaze. She looked up at him and saw that his eyes were a pale blue, so pale as to be almost colourless. Cora was well used to being looked at but usually, she felt, people were looking at her clothes or her money; Louvain was looking at *her*. His eyes were slightly narrowed; she saw in them neither admiration nor envy. No, he was taking her measure. She crossed her arms protectively, and forced herself to speak.

'You had a lucky escape then. The subject of your painting looks as if she would show no pity. I am surprised you did not give her a bow and arrow,' Cora said. She hardly knew what she was saying, her only thought was to keep going – she found the pale gaze unsettling.

'Do you think she needs one?' Louvain smiled.

He had, Cora noticed, quite a beautiful mouth, the upper lip finely drawn into a masculine version of a cupid's bow. He was soberly dressed in a dark suit, the only indicator that he was an artist was the yellow carnation he wore in his lapel.

'Well, perhaps not, her intention is quite clear.' Cora was about to continue when a voice spoke behind her.

'And what intention would that be, Duchess?' Sir Odo was standing next to her, his skin as shiny as ever with a red spot on either cheek. He had let his hair grow to aesthetic lengths and it lay like two spaniel ears on either side of his face.

'To carry all before her.' Cora smiled painfully. She felt on edge.

'Yes, she likes to be at the head of the pack.' Sir Odo laughed and a little spray of spittle fell in the space between them. 'Shame that Louvain here won't do any more portraits. Ivo must need some new pictures to replace all the ones that Duchess Fanny sold, eh?' To Cora's relief the baronet went off to speak to a footman.

Louvain was still looking at her. Cora felt the hairs on her arms prickle. The painter nodded. 'Actually, I do want to paint you.'

'Already? You flatter me.' Cora tried to look away from him but found she could not. 'And how would you fill the space between us, Mr Louvain? I worry that you might reveal me in all my shallowness.' She laughed nervously.

'Do you really think so? I think I might see other things that you would prefer to keep hidden, but I don't think you have anything to be afraid of. And it is not my intention to flatter you, I assure you. I am sure you are quite adequately flattered elsewhere. No, when I say I want to paint you, I say that not to appeal to your vanity, but to your interest in truth. I think you would like to be seen instead of always being looked at. Am I right?' His eyes never left hers as he spoke. She felt her heart flutter in her chest.

'It sounds very,' Cora paused, trying to find the right word, 'intimate. I hope I can withstand your scrutiny.'

'If you want absolute fidelity you can go to a photographer and get it. I won't paint you just as you are, but as I see you.' Louvain narrowed his eyes again as if trying to distil her image in his mind.

'And what do you see?' she said faintly

'I can only tell you with my brush, Duchess. I don't want to put my thoughts into words. I try to keep my impressions as colour, light and shade for as long as possible.'

'I see,' said Cora. She would have liked a more definite answer.

'When you come to the studio, wear something simple. I want

to paint you, not all the fuss that surrounds you. Shall we say next Monday morning?' Louvain spoke as if there could be no doubt that she would make herself available.

Cora knew she should not let this continue unchecked. 'I'm not sure that will be convenient, Mr Louvain. I may be returning to Lulworth next week.'

'Bury yourself in the country at this time of year? Surely not. No, you must come to my studio on Monday,' Louvain said firmly.

Cora bridled. 'Really, Mr Louvain, I can't rearrange my whole life at your whim,' she said as haughtily as she could.

Louvain opened his arms in a supplicatory gesture. 'Please, Duchess. A week is all I need to start with.'

Cora raised an eyebrow. 'You work very fast, Mr Louvain.'

Louvain pulled out his watch from his waistcoat pocket and, consulting it, he said, 'Thirty-four Old Church Street at eleven o'clock. Don't be late or I will lose the light. And remember, wear something simple. Goodbye, Duchess.' And he walked away.

Cora wanted to think about this encounter, and wondered if she could leave, but before she could move she saw Sir Odo approaching accompanied by a woman who was wearing a clinging gown of purple and green, unsupported, as far as Cora could see, by stays.

'Duchess, you must meet Beatrice Stanley, the actress. She was in *A Woman of No Importance* last year, you know. She has promised to recite for us later. Too thrilling.'

Cora held out her hand, she still had not acquired the English habit of bowing. The actress took it with a languid clasp. She had a very long white neck, on which her small head with its cloud of black hair balanced precariously. She had huge dark eyes which gazed mournfully at Cora.

'How do you do, Mrs Stanley,' Cora said. 'I came to London just too late for the play, but I hope I will see you on the stage soon.'

'Mr Wilde has two plays coming in the New Year, so you won't have to wait too long,' Mrs Stanley replied coolly.

Cora paused, at a loss. 'You know, I've never met an actress before.'

'Really? I have the advantage then, as I have met a number of duchesses, although never an American one.' Having established the upper hand, Mrs Stanley smiled at Cora. 'Do you like England, or am I asking you to betray a confidence?'

'I like very much what I know of it, but there is still so much I haven't seen,' Cora said.

'Have you been to the *Second Mrs Tanquerary* yet? Mrs Pat gives the performance of the season.' The actress waved her arm languidly.

'No, I haven't, but now you have recommended it I shall force the Duke to take me.' Cora smiled at the thought of forcing Ivo to do anything.

'Oh, I don't think you will have any trouble, Duchess. Your husband was always a great fan of the theatre.' Mrs Stanley lowered her lashes at Cora.

Cora felt the blow but knew she must not show weakness. 'The Duke has so many interests, but we shall certainly make a point of seeing you in your next play. What is the name of it?'

'It is called *An Ideal Husband*, Your Grace.' And having delivered her exit line, Mrs Stanley glided off to prepare for her recital.

Cora hoped that this exchange had not been overheard, but Sir Odo was behind her and cleared his throat.

'You mustn't mind Mrs Stanley, Duchess. She only does it to annoy because she knows it teases. I'm sure Wareham barely remembers her.' He giggled and Cora was furious with herself for being there. She guessed that the story of the ideal husband would be everywhere by the end of the evening. But she must not give Odo Beauchamp the satisfaction of appearing humiliated. She smiled in what she hoped was a worldly manner.

'I've made it a rule never to ask Ivo about his past. That way he can't ask about mine.' It was the best she could muster.

Sir Odo gave her a condescending smile. 'Some more tea, Duchess? Mrs Stanley is to give us her Ophelia. Such a treat.'

Cora smiled back, drank her tea, and sat on a conversation seat upholstered in mauve velvet as Beatrice Stanley performed the mad scene from *Hamlet*. She had a melodious voice and, when acting, a sweetness of expression that surprised Cora. When the performance was over, she clapped as loudly as her kid gloves would permit and made herself congratulate the actress warmly. Then she looked around for Charlotte to say goodbye. She was standing under the portrait, smoking a cigarette and laughing at something that Stebbings the poet had said.

'Goodbye, Charlotte, such an interesting party. Thank you so much for inviting me.'

'Oh, I hope you found it amusing.' Charlotte exhaled a long plume of smoke. 'Tell me, did Louvain ask you to sit for him? He left before I could ask him.'

Cora laughed. 'Not so much ask as command. He assumed I would have nothing better to do.'

Charlotte gave her a slow smile. 'And do you?'

Inexplicably, Cora found herself blushing, but before she could reply, Charlotte said, 'I don't think you can refuse to be Louvain's last portrait.'

Cora laughed a little nervously. 'Well, I would certainly have to find a good reason. And now if you'll excuse me,' and she made her way to the door. As she walked down the stairs to the black and white checkered hall, she heard footsteps behind her.

'Duchess!'

It was Stebbings. He smiled at her shyly. In his hands he had a book bound in yellow.

'May I give this to you, Duchess? I would like you to read my poem. You seem to be a woman of feeling.'

'Thank you, Mr Stebbings, I am flattered you think so.' Cora took the book, which had a woman wearing a masquerade mask on the cover. She appreciated the contrast between the vivid yellow of the cover and the dark green of her dress.

'No one in there has read it, they just talk about it. But I thought that you might be different.'

Cora felt sorry for this anxious young man and touched by his interest in her. 'I will certainly read it and I will write and tell you what I think.'

'You can find me at Albany. I shall wait for your letter.' And he took her hand and wrung it so fervently that Cora felt quite worried about her wrist.

'Goodbye, Mr Stebbings.'

'*Au revoir*, Duchess.'

Her encounter with Stebbings had taken the sting out of her visit to the Beauchamps and she found herself smiling as she got into her carriage. She was grateful to have at least one admirer.

She arrived at Cleveland Row just in time to change for dinner, and asked Bertha to fetch her the apricot mousseline dinner dress with the black ribbon trim as she considered it particularly fetching.

Reggie Greatorex and Father Oliver were in the drawing room with the Duke.

'Darling, how very charming you look. Did you enjoy yourself at the Beauchamps?' Ivo kissed her cheek.

'It was certainly interesting,' she said brightly.

'Did Charlotte throw you amongst the lions, Duchess?' Reggie smiled at her.

'Well, I met Louvain, and a poet called Stebbings. He gave me a copy of *The Yellow Book*. Have you seen it? It is quite beautiful.'

'Good Lord, Cora, one visit to Charlotte's salon and you have come back an aesthete. Promise me you won't start wearing rational dress and drooping everywhere.' Ivo put his arm round her waist as if to assure himself that she was still wearing a corset.

'I have seen *The Yellow Book*,' said Father Oliver. 'There is something rather febrile about it, don't you think? As if they are trying just a little too hard to be modern. I always feel that nothing palls faster than a book that is trying to shock.'

'Are you saying that this book is unsuitable, Father Oliver?' said Ivo. 'Should I confiscate it from Cora in order to preserve her moral character? I don't want her to be a decadent duchess.' He smiled and gave Cora's waist a squeeze.

Cora longed to lean into him and let it go, but she was annoyed by the way they were all talking over her as if she had no thoughts or opinions of her own. She drew herself a little apart.

'I think I am quite capable of deciding for myself whether a magazine is suitable or not. And from what I have seen of *The Yellow Book*, I think I am quite safe.'

'Of course, Duchess,' said Father Oliver soothingly. 'I didn't mean to suggest for a moment that you shouldn't read it. I think the Duke may be exaggerating for effect.' He smiled knowingly at Ivo.

Ivo laughed. 'The idea is preposterous. But Caesar's wife and all that. A duchess, especially a young and beautiful one, has to be seen to be virtuous. A woman's reputation is a fragile thing, and a duchess's is like gossamer.' His voice was light but there was an edge to it.

Seeing the look on Cora's face, Reggie broke in.

'Did you hear the story about the drawing of Mrs Pat in *The Yellow Book*. There is a picture of her done by this chap Beardsley that looks like a wraith. Ricketts, the editor of the *Morning Post*, gets a copy and says he likes the magazine but where is the portrait of Mrs Patrick Campbell? Beardsley thinks there has been a mishap and sends him another copy. Ricketts writes back and says, I still can't see anything in the book that resembles Mrs Patrick Campbell!'

Cora laughed and the tension dissipated as Ivo laughed too.

At dinner Reggie entertained them with stories about his time as a page at Windsor Castle. But Cora was tired and thankful that she had instituted the sixty-minute rule here at Cleveland Row. She had to conceal a smile as a footman whisked away Father Oliver's *oeufs en cocotte aux truffes* while he was in the middle of a long and elaborate story about intermarriages between the Maltravers and Percy families in the sixteenth century.

She went to bed early. She hoped that Ivo would not stay in the smoking room forever. Bertha helped her out of her dress and corsets, which were getting increasingly uncomfortable, and she sat at the mirror brushing out her hair, enjoying the respite from stays and hairpins. It was only when she got undressed at night that she realised just how trussed up and pinned down she had been during the day. There were red welts under her breasts where her corset had dug into her expanding flesh. Her scalp was sore from the pins that held the diamond and feather aigrette to her head. The back of her neck was red from the diamond clasp of her pearls.

But then she heard Ivo whistling a tune from *The Mikado* in the corridor and she forgot about the lacerations of the flesh.

'You see, I didn't linger. Here, let me do that for you.' Ivo picked up the hairbrush and began to pull it through Cora's thick brown hair. He did it well, applying just the right amount of pressure to smooth out the tangles without pulling on her scalp. There were times when Ivo said things that Cora did not understand but every time he touched her she felt that they were in perfect accord. She looked at him in the dressing-table mirror. His thin face was soft, it didn't have the creases and angles tonight that sometimes made him look so stern.

Ivo whistled a few more bars from *The Mikado*. Cora tried to catch his eye in the mirror.

'You know, I realised today how little I know about you,' she said.

Ivo's whistling turned into singing. 'Three little maids from school are we, full to the brim with girlish glee, three little ma-aaaaids from school.'

Cora persisted. 'I mean, I know nothing about your childhood really, or your youth or how you lived before you met me.' She caught his free hand and kissed it. Ivo carried on brushing, his dark eyes glittering.

'But Cora, I was nothing before I met you. Simply a cipher with strawberry leaves. Do you really want to hear all about Nanny Hutchins who drank, and Nanny Crawford who didn't. Or the time that I threw a stone into the hothouse at Lulworth and was chased round the pond by the head gardener. Or how Guy and I used to spend days tapping the panelling looking for the priest's hole with the secret staircase that leads down to the sea. Or the day that the under-butler got the keys to the cellar and got so drunk that he climbed into my mother's bed at two in the morning. Or my inability to master the finer points of Latin prose and being beaten for same, or my first pony, or my dear departed dog Tray, or my first Communion, or the first time I tasted ice cream . . .' As he spoke his strokes with the brush got faster and faster so that Cora's hair was beginning to flicker with electricity. She put up her hands and seized his arm, laughing in spite of herself.

'Ivo! Enough. My head is going to explode,' she said in mock exasperation.

'But I thought you wanted to know about my early life,' Ivo said reproachfully. He got free of her restraining hands and went back to the brushing, albeit rather more gently.

Cora was grateful for the mirror, somehow it was easier to talk to his reflection. She said carefully, 'I want to know everything, even the things you might not want to tell me.'

'Such as?' Ivo stopped brushing and raised an eyebrow at her.

Cora wondered if she should leave well alone, but she thought of the uncorseted actress and she went on. 'Well, your past . . .' she struggled to find the right word, 'liaisons. I mean, I am not so naive as to suppose that there were no women in your life before you met me.'

'Women, Your Grace? The very idea!' Ivo drew up his hands in mock horror.

Cora persevered. 'It's just that if I don't know about them, I look foolish. I was mortified today at the Beauchamps.'

Ivo stopped brushing for a moment and then brought the brush down hard on a particularly sensitive part of her scalp. He had stopped whistling.

'And why was that?' His voice was quiet.

Cora found that she did not dare meet his eyes in the looking glass. 'Because Odo Beauchamp introduced me to Mrs Stanley and of course everybody knew except for me that you and she were once . . . friendly.' She dared look at him now and saw to her surprise that far from looking angry, he looked relieved.

'So you met Beatrice.' He began to brush her hair again with long rhythmic strokes. 'She was very kind to me once.'

Cora looked at him sharply. She thought he might be a little more contrite. She turned round to face him. 'I'm sure she was kind to you once, but she humiliated me today.'

Ivo gave a look of genuine astonishment. 'But honestly, Cora, I don't know why you should feel humiliated. You are a duchess with youth, beauty and everything you could ever want, while Beatrice is nearly forty, with no husband to speak of and an uncertain future. I am sorry if she made you feel foolish but I think she is the one who deserves sympathy.'

Ivo's tone was unexpectedly serious, Cora could not understand why he was taking the other woman's side.

She stood up, her hair crackling with static as she turned her head. 'Well, I still think you should have told me. I don't want us to have secrets from each other. I hate walking into a room and feeling that everyone there knows more about you than I do.'

Ivo looked down at his hands. 'I'm sorry, Cora, that you felt unprepared. I have never wanted to burden you with my past, just as you,' he looked Cora in the eyes, 'have not disclosed everything to me.'

Cora took a step backwards in amazement. 'What do you mean? I have nothing to "disclose".'

Ivo shrugged. 'So the Newport swain that your wretched papers kept comparing me to unfavourably was purely a fiction then?' he said lightly.

Cora felt something close to anger. 'But that was before I met you,' she said.

'Precisely,' said Ivo, and he put the hairbrush back on the dressing table, lining it up with the hand mirror and the boxes of pins and powder.

Something about his careful movements infuriated her.

'But they were laughing at me, Ivo!' Her voice was petulant.

Ivo turned round and spoke so quietly that Cora had to lean towards him to hear every word. 'Do you really want me to feel sorry for you? You can't accept the privileges of our rank and not understand that you will also be stared at and gossiped about. You didn't mind it when there were crowds outside the church for our wedding, did you? There were pictures of you in the New York papers as well as all kinds of articles about the most intimate details of your trousseau and fortune. I bore all that without complaint even though I found it vulgar beyond belief because I knew that in your world these things were quite normal. So I'm sorry if you felt embarrassed today but perhaps now you understand how I felt every day in your country, being spoken of quite freely in the press as a penniless fortune-hunter.' His voice was almost a whisper but Cora felt the chill in his words. She was more alarmed by his quietness than she would have been by a more obvious display of anger. She wondered how things had come to this point.

She had pictured Ivo making a tender confession which she accepted with exquisite tact, but instead they were having a quarrel with no real purpose. Ivo was angry with her when clearly it was her prerogative to be angry with him. She looked at him and saw no softness in his face at all, and she started to cry. She tried to check herself but every time she attempted to hold back, she felt another wave of tears demolishing her self-control. She heard a violent heaving noise and realised that it was the sound of her own sobbing.

At last she felt his hand on her face, smoothing the hair away from her cheek. He gave her a big white handkerchief to dry her eyes. She blew her nose in it viciously. He laughed.

'Poor Cora, I won't let you go out alone again. I thought it might amuse you to be the toast of the town.' He led her over to the chaise longue at the end of her bed and made her sit down.

Cora knew she should leave well alone but she couldn't help herself saying, 'Did you love her?' She spoke through a curtain of hair.

Ivo paused and spoke carefully. 'I was fond of her.'

'Did you want to marry her?' Cora knew that the question was absurd but again she couldn't resist.

'Dearest Cora, you're the only woman I have asked to be my duchess.'

Cora wiped her face with the sleeve of her peignoir. She felt very tired. 'And how did it end?' she whispered.

'End?' He looked surprised. 'It wasn't like that.' Ivo picked up the black pearls on Cora's dressing table and started to feed them through his fingers like a rosary. 'No, things ended when my brother broke his neck.'

'What do you mean?'

Ivo put the pearls down with a clatter.

'Everything changed when Guy died. It was the worst day of my life. My brother was dead and I was the Duke.' Ivo stood up and went over to the bell pull. A footman appeared almost immediately. 'Get me a brandy and soda.'

When the footman returned with the decanter and soda siphon on a salver, Ivo poured himself a stiff drink and began to pace up and down the room, talking as much to himself as to Cora.

'Guy was the only thing I have ever believed in. He was a good man, almost a saint. If he hadn't been the oldest son I think he would have been a monk. He only ever did the right thing and yet he was dead and I was the Duke. It made no sense at all.'

Cora said nothing, she had never seen Ivo like this before. He moved restlessly around the room, not looking at her but talking with quiet insistence.

'I never wanted to be Duke, never. There are younger sons who think of nothing else but the health of their older brother. But I was glad that I was not going to inherit. I saw what happened to my father – he pretty much bankrupted himself trying to behave in the way he thought a duke should and all he got for it was the dubious pleasure of being cuckolded by the Prince of Wales, among others.' He drained his glass and went back to the decanter.

Cora could hardly believe what he had just said. 'You mean your mother and the Prince are . . . more than friends?' She tried not to sound shocked but she couldn't help herself. Duchess Fanny and the Prince, why hadn't she realised?

'Oh, I don't think they are now, but when my father was alive . . .' Ivo broke off as if in pain.

Cora was bewildered. 'Did your father know?'

'Of course he knew,' Ivo said bitterly. 'Everybody knew. My mother made sure of that. She even had that snake tattooed on her wrist to show she was part of "the club", as she called it.'

Cora was struggling to understand. 'But couldn't your father stop her? He could have threatened to divorce her.'

Ivo shook his head. 'Catholics don't get divorced and, besides, you can't name the Prince of Wales as co-respondent. No, my mother knew exactly what she was doing. My poor father, all he could do was stand by and let it happen. The worst thing was that he really loved her. Plenty of women would have consoled him but he wasn't interested. And all the time my mother was acting as if she was doing him a favour by becoming a royal favourite. I didn't understand what was happening at first, but now I can hardly believe how callous she was. She would open her love letters from the Prince in front of him, and he would sit there and watch.' Ivo bowed his head in an unconscious imitation of his father's acquiescence. 'In the end, of course, the Prince got bored, which she accepted gracefully enough – I don't think she ever cared for him deeply – and simply replaced him with Buckingham. When my father realised what had happened, he just gave up. He died a year later.' He shook his head, as if trying to shake off the memories.

Cora felt a surge of pity. She saw the naked hollow at the base of his skull – when he turned his head there was a vulnerability in Ivo she had never noticed before.

'And the worst of it was that Mother never understood what she had done. If anything, she was proud of herself. She was the reason that Guy was so devout. I think he was trying to atone for her sins. God knows there are enough of them. It wasn't just the Prince, although he was the most public. She always had admirers – I think she even amused herself with the servants.' His voice was bitter.

Cora put her hand on his arm. 'But don't you like being Duke now?' she said.

'It is not about liking. I am a link in a chain that stretches from the past through me into the future. Even though I never wanted it, I don't have a choice.' He looked down at her and his face softened. 'But thanks to you I don't have to watch Lulworth falling down, or part with its contents piece by piece. Our son will not have to grow up watching land being sold and farms crumbling because there is no money to repair them.' He put his arm around her and pulled her to him.

Cora was relieved that Ivo's mood appeared to have lightened. She was encouraged by the reference to their child and to the healing power of money. She liked the idea that thanks to her this ancient institution would get up off its knees and walk again. It gave her particular pleasure to think that she would be able to reverse the depredations wrought by the Double Duchess. She smiled to think how her mother-in-law would react when she saw the water terraces she was planning for the south front, or the Canova statues she had bought for the summerhouse. (After the contretemps with the Rubens, she had made sure that the statues of Eros and Psyche and Venus bathing came free of unwelcome associations.)

There was a tap at the door and Bertha entered carrying a tray.

'I brought your hot milk, Miss Cora. The doctor said you should drink it before going to bed.'

'Thank you, Bertha. I had quite forgotten.'

Bertha turned to go, when she heard the Duke's voice.

'Bertha!'

The maid wheeled round to face him.

The Duke said quietly, 'Bertha, I would prefer it if you could address my wife by her proper title. I appreciate that you have grown up in a country without such niceties, but here we set much store by them. Please remember in future.'

Bertha stood motionless, her head bowed.

Cora leapt in. 'It's not her fault, Ivo. I encourage her to call me Miss Cora because it reminds me of home. What does it matter what my maid calls me in the privacy of my bedroom?'

'Bertha, you may go.' Ivo waited for the door to close behind her before he turned to his wife. 'Cora, please remember that everything you say to me in front of Bertha is repeated word for word in the servants' hall.' He turned his back to her. Cora flew at him; the words she could forgive, but not this physical snub. She put her hands on his shoulders and pulled him round to face her.

'What is the matter with you! One minute you say you never wanted to be Duke, and now you are scolding my maid for not calling me Your Grace. I don't understand you.'

Ivo looked down at her tear-stained face. His face had an expression she could not read. He took her hands from his shoulders and clasped them in his own.

'I have been thoughtless, Cora. You are tired. Women in your condition need a great deal of rest. We will talk about this tomorrow.'

Cora tried to respond but he led her to the bed and as she lay down she realised that sleep was all she wanted. She took his hand.

'Stay here with me, Ivo.'

He lay down beside her and she put her head on his chest. She knew there was something she had to tell him but sleep overcame her before she could remember what it was.

In the attic Bertha turned up the gas so that she could get a better look at the seam she was unpicking. All Miss Cora's bodices needed taking out now that she was beginning to show. Cora refused to accept her thickening body and simply ordered her maid to pull the laces harder, but Bertha worried that the tight lacing would harm the baby. By surreptitiously letting out the seams at night, Bertha was able to convince her mistress that she was still able to fit into her wardrobe. These secret tailoring sessions could not go on indefinitely, of course; Bertha hoped that Cora would soon accept the realities of her condition.

Bertha got to the end of the seam, pricking her finger in the process; a bead of red dropped on to the pink silk, soaking into the weave of the fabric, following the threads so that it looked like one of the tiny scarlet money spiders of Bertha's childhood. She spat on the stain and rubbed it with her thumb, turning the spider into a rusty bruise. It was on the wrong side of the cloth, she would be the only witness to what lay beneath the Duchess of Wareham's pink silk. She put the dress down and got ready for bed. Her mind was still turning over the Duke's rebuke and she wondered how long Miss Cora would defend her. She had around three hundred dollars in the chest under her bed, the product of various gifts from Cora, the profits from the sale of used gloves and what she put away from her salary, and she also had the 'boulder'. She had intended to send some of the money to her mother, but now she wondered whether her need might be greater. If only she could be sure of Jim, that he would have the courage to follow her into a new life.

CHAPTER 19

'The Faint Half-Flush'

LOUVAIN'S STUDIO WAS IN CHELSEA, A PART OF London that Cora had only heard of. The coachman had looked astonished when she gave him the address and was forced to consult his fellows before setting off. The fog grew thicker as the carriage got closer to the river, so Cora could barely see the outline of the house through the yellow mist. All she could make out was a red painted door set in a Gothic stone arch. The coachman made to go and ring the bell but Cora stopped him.

'I'll go myself. Come back in an hour.'

She rang the bell and heard it tinkling far off in the distance. After a few minutes the door was opened by a manservant who Cora thought might be Japanese. He bowed to her and gestured for her to follow him down a long corridor lit from above by a skylight. Hanging from the picture rail on either side were black and white prints that looked oriental; Cora stopped to look at one as she went past and saw that it was an exquisitely detailed drawing of a man and woman embracing. Cora felt a quiver of shock mixed with curiosity. She would have liked to have examined the picture more closely but she couldn't risk the servant turning and seeing her. She felt the blood pounding at her temple, she almost turned round and walked away, but she could see the servant holding back the heavy damask portière and she felt herself move forward. Charlotte had said a chaperone was quite unnecessary but now Cora wished she had brought Bertha with her.

The studio was a double-height room with a north-facing window that ran from the ceiling almost to the floor. At the base of the window was a window seat covered in a paisley shawl and velvet cushions. To the right of the window was Louvain's easel and a table covered in brushes, rags and paints. At the other end of the room was a Japanese screen, a chaise longue and a fern in a brass pot. The parquet floor was covered in Persian carpets. Stacked against the walls were canvases and portfolios. Skylights bathed the room in rippling grey light. Cora felt as if she was walking underwater. The impression was reinforced when she heard Louvain's voice echoing through the room. He was wearing a velvet smoking jacket that was flecked with paint.

'Good morning, Duchess, you are late but not unforgivably so. Please give Itaro your things. Good. You have dressed simply.' Louvain stood about four feet away, looking at her through half-narrowed eyes. Cora felt his gaze sweep up and down her body.

'I'm sorry for my unpunctuality, but the fog, you know, slows everything down. We nearly had to give up and go home. My coachman was quite worried about bringing me to Chelsea, he thinks that it is not a respectable neighbourhood.' Cora was talking nervously, aware that Louvain's eyes had not left her for a moment.

'Don't worry, you will be quite safe. There is no one here to molest you apart from a few impoverished artists looking for patronage.' He took her arm. 'Why don't you come and sit down here.' He led her to the chaise longue upholstered in green velvet.

She sat down on the edge, her back as upright as if she was wearing the spine stiffener.

Louvain stood back from her. 'No, no, you look as though you were at a missionary tea. Can't you lie back a little? Here, let me give you some cushions.' He went over to the window seat and picked up some cushions which he placed behind her. 'Now lean back. That's right.' He paced up and down in front of her, looking at her so closely that Cora felt hot with the scrutiny. She sat rather stiffly against the cushions, trying to arrange her arms gracefully.

'Would you like me to fold my hands? I've heard that hands are the hardest thing to paint.'

'Who told you that?' Louvain asked.

'An American friend, who was studying art. He said that the hands always defeated him.'

'Did he paint you? This friend?'

'No, he said he wasn't ready.' Cora thought of Teddy and smiled.

'Not ready for you! He must have been scared.' Louvain shrugged.

'Perhaps.' Cora wished she had said nothing. Louvain had a way of turning every conversation into an intimacy.

He came closer to her and picked up one of her hands which he draped along the back of the chaise longue.

'Yes, that looks better. But it's not enough.'

Cora looked at him nervously. 'I want you – no, I need you, to take down your hair,' Louvain said.

'My hair? I can't possibly.' Cora was firm.

'But why not? You are so young, what could be more natural? I want to paint you as a goddess from the New World, beautiful and unbound. I don't want you trussed up like a society goose. Please take down your hair, I don't think I have ever seen hair quite your colour before.' He reached out a hand to touch one of the tendrils that hung by her cheek.

Cora was alarmed at how close he was to her.

'I think it would look . . . odd.' She could feel his breath against her cheek.

'Then, Duchess, I think you have had a wasted journey.' He turned away from her and started to walk towards the door.

Cora twisted with indecision. She thought of what her mother would say about her taking down her hair and then she remembered Charlotte's cool recklessness. She was not going to be dismissed as a provincial American.

'Wait!' she said. Slowly, Louvain turned round.

She stood up and started to take the pins out of her hair. There were so many of them that she could not hold them all.

'Here, let me take them.' Louvain stretched out his hand.

At last they were all out, Cora shook her head and felt her hair fall heavy and luxurious on to her shoulders. Louvain had been right, she did feel unbound. She looked at him shyly, meeting that ever-present gaze. Although her body was completely covered, she felt naked. She had to stop herself from putting her arms across her breasts.

Louvain said nothing but walked round her slowly. Cora stood still as if pinned to the spot but at last she forced herself to speak.

'Is that what you wanted?'

Louvain still did not speak. Then he moved towards her and quickly and firmly kissed her on the mouth.

'No, Duchess, that's what I wanted. Now, perhaps you would like to resume your pose?'

Cora blinked. Had he really kissed her? Yes, she knew he had because she could still feel the scrape from the bristles of his moustache. And now he was behaving as if nothing had happened. She knew that she was losing control of the situation. She should have slapped him at least.

'I must go. Your conduct is disgraceful.' But Cora did not move.

Louvain, who had walked over to his easel and paints, laughed.

'Oh, don't be in a huff, it was only a kiss. You looked so promising with your hair down. I had to satisfy my curiosity. Anyway it serves you right for teasing me with your American friend and coming here unchaperoned. But I apologise for taking such a liberty and I promise not to do it again.' He made a solemn sign of the cross in the air, and continued, 'If it will help your conscience, I only did it for the sake of the painting. I could see that you were wondering if I was going to pounce and now that I have, you can relax. You know I find you attractive which means you can be sure that the portrait will flatter you.'

Cora was aware that she should leave immediately but she knew that she would stay. She sat down on the chaise longue and lay back against the cushions.

'You see, that's much better, stay just like that.' Louvain had a sketch pad and was rapidly drawing with a pencil.

'Is this the way you behave with all your sitters?' Cora tried to sound nonchalant.

'I don't kiss the men!'

'What about Lady Beauchamp? Did you kiss her?'

'What do you think?' Louvain's tone was dismissive.

Cora fell into her pose. Louvain was right. She did feel more relaxed. She wondered if he would try again and what she would do if he did.

He stopped sketching and looked at her directly. 'Do you want to undo your jacket? You're expecting, aren't you? You might feel more comfortable.'

'How did you know? About the baby? I'm not showing yet, am I?' Cora looked down at her still defined waist.

'My job, Duchess, is to see you and I can see that you are full of expectation. Women in your condition have a certain milky quality. Medieval painters believed that you can see babies in the eyes of pregnant women.'

'And what else do you see, Mr Louvain?' she asked.

'Oh, I'm not going to tell you that, it will all be there in the painting. Which, before you ask, I am not going to show you until it is quite finished. Now, I want you to stop talking so I can concentrate on your mouth.'

As soon as he said this, Cora felt her lips tingle. She looked up at the grey clouds through the skylight.

'No, don't look up there, keep your eyes on me.'

Cora nodded dumbly, there was evidently no escape. The rest of the session was virtually silent, apart from the scratching of Louvain's pencil and the smacking noises he made with his mouth as he rubbed out a line that was less than satisfactory. Every so often there was the muffled sound of a foghorn from a boat on the river and the faint mewings of distant gulls. After a while, despite the kiss, Cora found herself subsiding into a kind of torpor. She found the effort of being looked at exhausting. After about an hour the silence was broken by the crash of a gong being struck. Cora started and Louvain put down his pencil.

'Lunch! Will you stay, Duchess? Itaro is quite a talented cook.'

'No, thank you. I must go home.' Cora rose to her feet.

'I'll see you tomorrow at the same time. And don't be late again, we have a lot of work to do.'

As Cora left, she ran her eyes over some of the other black and white Japanese prints that lined the hallway. She did not dare to linger as Louvain was following her to the door, but he noticed the turn of her head.

'Do you like them? They are called *shunga*. These ones are by Utamaro – they are of the courtesans of the Yoshiwara district where he lived. They apparently thought it was a great honour to pose for him. His pictures are such an exotic mixture of the real and the imagined. Look at this one.' He pointed to one of the prints. Cora came over to look at it. It was a woman embracing a squid. Cora stood back quickly, her face pink with embarrassment.

Louvain laughed. 'That one is called the fisherman's wife. Lovely, isn't it?'

'Unexpected, certainly,' said Cora faintly.

'Till tomorrow then, Duchess.' Itaro opened the door, bowing, She looked round to tell Louvain that in no circumstances would she be coming back tomorrow, but he had gone.

But the next day Cora found herself in the carriage heading towards Chelsea. This time she had brought Bertha with her.

She had decided to make the portrait a surprise gift for Ivo. Something to remind him of the way she looked now, before she was all swollen with the baby. She sensed that his attitude to her had changed since she had started to show; she wanted to remind him that she would not always look like this.

Her mind wandered. Perhaps there would be a party for Ivo's birthday. It was not the season, of course, but there would be enough people in town to have a reception. She would ask Mrs Wyndham.

She tried not to look at the *shunga* as she walked down the corridor towards the studio. Louvain started towards her as she came in but stopped and smiled when he saw Bertha.

'So you have come prepared,' he said.

'Well, I felt awkward yesterday going home with my hair down. If Bertha is here she can make me look respectable first.' Cora smiled.

'Respectability must be preserved at all costs, Duchess. Perhaps your maid would like to sit here.'

He pulled out a chair from behind a screen and placed it so that Bertha would have no view of the painting. Cora went over to the chaise longue and turned her back to him as she began to take the pins out of her hair; she found she did not want to look at him as she did so, it was too intimate somehow. But she spoke to him over her shoulder.

'How long do you think the portrait will take, Mr Louvain? I want to surprise my husband with it for his birthday.'

'It will take as long as it takes. If you sit still and don't fidget, it might be faster,' Louvian said tetchily.

'I will be as still as a graven image, I promise, but would a month be unreasonable?' Cora put a pleading edge to her voice.

'I never give guarantees. But if you are an obedient model, there is a chance the picture might be finished in a month. But you will have to do exactly as I say, mind. Now, unbutton your jacket like you did yesterday. And try to remember how you felt yesterday, the expression on your face was just as it should be.' He winked at Cora who blushed.

'I'm not sure if I can remember how I felt yesterday. I think I was trying not to fall asleep. It is hard keeping still for so long,' she said.

'Would you like me to remind you, Duchess?' Louvain made a step towards her. Cora moved back alarmed.

'Oh no, that won't be necessary. I am sure I can remember enough. Bertha, come here and help me with my hair.'

Bertha started the long process of unpinning hair that she had put up only an hour or two ago. Now she understood why Miss Cora had rushed off yesterday wearing the simplest navy-blue tailor-made and had come back with her hair knotted under her hat. She had scurried into her room and insisted on Bertha fixing her hair properly before going downstairs, but she had not offered a word of explanation. Bertha had been surprised, to say the least. Miss Cora never made morning calls, and as for the hair, that was completely unprecedented. The speculation in the servants' hall had been rife. The coachman, who had seen an oriental servant opening the door, had hinted that Her Grace had been visiting an opium den. He knew all about them as his last employer Lord Mandeville had been that way. Bertha had laughed this off but she had been curious and a little apprehensive.

So she was relieved to find out that Miss Cora was sitting for a portrait, although there was something going on between the painter and her mistress that made her uncomfortable. Miss Cora had always been a flirt, but now she was married she should be more careful. Bertha wondered what had happened yesterday. She looked at her mistress who lay on the chaise longue with her chestnut hair falling over her shoulders to her waist and her jacket unbuttoned to reveal her chemise, her mouth parted in a half smile. She looked as she had on her honeymoon in Venice, her sharp edges blurred. Bertha sat awkwardly between Cora and the painter; every so often she would look up from the mending she had brought with her and feel the heat of their mutual gaze.

On the way home, Cora told Bertha to get in beside her instead of sitting on the box with the coachman.

'What did you think of the studio and Mr Louvain, Bertha?'

'Does he make money from his painting, Miss Cora?' Bertha asked.

'I'm sure.' Cora spoke with the unconcern of a girl for whom money had never been anything but abundant. 'I would imagine he can charge what he likes. We haven't discussed a fee for this painting but I've no doubt it will be exorbitant. Father says that being American adds fifty per cent to everything.' She leaned over to Bertha's side of the carriage conspiratorially. 'This must be kept a secret from the Duke. I want to hold a reception before I get too big and give it to him then. I'd like to do something while I am still respectable.'

Bertha could see some pitfalls to this scheme.

'But suppose you don't like the picture, Miss Cora? Won't it be awkward asking folks to see a picture you ain't fond of?'

'Well, that's not going to happen! Louvain is a genius. This is going to be his last portrait,' Cora said.

'And what if the Duke don't like it? I ain't sure he cares for surprises,' Bertha said carefully. There was something about Louvain that worried her.

Cora remembered the scene in the chapel. Perhaps Bertha had a point. And yet she felt reluctant to tell her husband what she was doing. The thought of him in the studio made her feel quite uncomfortable. And surely this picture was quite different from the Rubens.

'I think he will be delighted to have a portrait of the woman he fell in love with,' Cora said firmly. 'Louvain says he can't work with other people's opinions hanging over him. He says if you want something completely faithful, take a photograph.'

Bertha thought that Louvain had found a way of spending unlimited time with beautiful women without their husbands, and getting paid for it.

Cora was delighted when Charlotte sent up her card that afternoon. She wanted to talk to her about the party. She was determined it should be smart and she needed Charlotte's advice. Mrs Wyndham was always reliable but Charlotte had style.

To her relief, Charlotte approved of all her plans.

'You're so wise not to make it too serious, Cora. London really doesn't need any more high-mindedness.'

'I want to give Ivo the portrait. I thought it should be an occasion.'

Charlotte smiled slyly. 'And there is no harm in reminding the world that Louvain has chosen you as the subject of his last portrait.'

Cora blushed. 'Well, I suppose you could look at it that way. But don't tell anyone, please.'

Charlotte leant forward. 'And how do you like Louvain? Is he being frightfully strict with you?'

Cora busied herself with the tea things. 'He certainly knows what he wants. It's very hard to argue with him.' To her relief Sybil arrived at that moment, gleeful because she had managed to evade her stepmother. Sybil had come to rely on Cora for sympathy when she found life under Duchess Fanny particularly trying.

Charlotte was less warm to Sybil than she had been to Cora. She listened to her complaints for a few minutes and then said a touch impatiently, 'But if Aunt Fanny is making your life so irksome, why don't you get married? You must have had plenty of offers.'

Sybil looked stricken and Cora, seeing her expression, jumped in. 'You must come and stay with me, Sybil. I would love some company at Lulworth and who knows, we might be able to get up a party.' She looked meaningfully at Sybil, who found her smile again. She knew that by 'party' Cora meant Reggie Greatorex, who so far had failed to make her an offer. Charlotte, who had no interest in matchmaking, made her excuses and left.

After she had gone, Sybil sighed. 'Charlotte is so magnificent, isn't she, but don't you think she's just a tiny bit frightening?'

Cora thought for a moment. 'You know, I thought that at first, but she has been quite charming to me. Apart from you, dear Sybil, I would say that she is my only friend here in England.'

Sybil made no reply.

When Cora told Ivo that she wanted to give a reception before, as she put it, she became indecent, he was, rather to her surprise, enthusiastic.

'So you are going to be a hostess, are you? I am delighted. There are some people I would like you to invite.'

The list, when Ivo handed it to her at breakfast, surprised Cora. It was full of politicians, many of them titled, it was true, but politicians none the less. At home, politicians were in the same league as actresses, an unavoidable fact of life but not suitable for the drawing room.

'Ivo, do you really want me to invite all these politicians? I don't want my first party to be dreary.' Cora's tone was light but Ivo replied in his quietest voice.

'So you think politicians are dreary, do you, Cora?'

Cora bridled. 'I don't think they are the ideal guests.'

Ivo turned on her. 'Doesn't it occur to you that I might have a reason?'

Cora looked at him resentfully. She hated the way that Ivo, who made fun of everything, would suddenly become serious without warning.

'I'm sorry, Ivo, I had no idea that you had political ambition. You've always laughed at me when I've asked you about the House of Lords. Forgive me for my ignorance, but in my country, we don't have aristocrats, we have men like my father who go to work.'

There was a pause before Ivo spoke.

'Oh yes, your father, the Golden Miller's son, who came into his first million when he was twenty-one years old. What work, exactly, does your father do? Apart from auditioning promising chorus girls, that is. I thought his only employment was avoiding your mother.'

Cora threw the cup she was holding at her husband. He ducked, and the cup landed on the floor in a mess of china and milk.

'How dare you sneer at my father? What did you ever do before you became Duke except have "friendships" with the likes of Mrs Stanley? My father, on the other hand, runs the biggest mill in North America. Sure, he inherited his fortune, but he has made it grow. Don't forget that his money paid for this house and everything in it.' She stopped, panting with rage.

'Even the china that you just you hurled at my head, I believe. And what exactly is your point, Cora? If you had such a yearning for men who do things, why didn't you stay in America and marry one of them? I am sure a girl like you must have had plenty of suitors. And yet you chose to come to England and marry a duke. What could you have been thinking?'

Ivo stopped as a footman came in with a silver chafing dish.

'Robert, I have been very clumsy.' He pointed at the mess on the floor. 'Can you ask one of the maids to clear it up? And I will have some more coffee while you're about it. Oh, and I believe Her Grace needs a new cup.'

Ivo's tone to the footman was completely neutral, without any of the heat he had displayed a few moments earlier. His self-possession enraged Cora even more than his jibes about her father.

'That won't be necessary, Robert, I am finished.' Cora left the room without looking back.

In her bedroom she picked up one of her silver-backed hair-brushes and hurled it against the wall. Then she kicked the bedpost so hard that she hurt her foot and only after that did she sit down on the bed and cry fat tears of anger and frustration.

Five minutes later, the door opened and she heard Ivo's light tread.

'Go away, I don't want to speak to you.'

'You don't have to say a word. In fact, I would rather you didn't. I just came to tell you that the reason I wanted you to ask Rosebery is that he has been looking for my support in the Lords. I think he may even want me to join his ministry. I don't know if you understand what that means; my family have been beyond the political pale for three hundred years because we are Catholic. You asked me if I had any ambitions, well, I don't for myself but I do for my family. The Maltravers have a chance to be something again and it is my duty to make that happen.'

He paused. Cora knew without looking that he was stroking his chin, which he always did when he was serious.

'Your fortune has made that possible, Cora. None of this would have happened if I hadn't found you that day in Paradise Wood. So let's not quarrel any more.'

She felt his hand touch her shoulder; she rolled over slowly, reluctant to show him her tear-stained face.

'I like you when you've been crying.' He snaked a finger across her wet cheeks. She tried to bat his hand away but he was determined, stroking her face and hair now as if she were a frightened animal that needed soothing. And then his breathing began to quicken.

Cora tried not to look at him but he was already pulling at the buttons on her dress. She was still angry with him, but he had hardly touched her since she had told him about the baby and she could not help but arch towards him as he began to kiss her throat and chest. She was relieved that there was still that same sense of urgency. He began to push her skirts up.

'Oh, Ivo, do you think we should? What about . . .'

But Ivo was kissing her and there was no more resistance she could offer. He pulled away the layers of petticoats and pushed himself inside her there and then. She was surprised at how little difference there was between the rage she had felt earlier and what she felt now; both passions were equally consuming. As she felt her body begin to contract with desire, she opened her eyes and looked at Ivo. His face was stern, concentrating; was he still angry with her? But the thought was lost as she felt the snap of fulfilment and her body went quiet.

The following day she was in Louvain's studio, stretched out on the chaise longue, Bertha sitting in her usual corner. Louvain had barely spoken to her when she came in but when he looked at her, she noticed that his pale eyes were alight with excitement. He was working very fast, almost quivering as he attacked the canvas with his brush.

'Good news, Duchess, this will be our last session. The picture will be ready next week.'

Cora felt a tiny stab of disappointment. She had come to enjoy her hours in the studio, she liked watching Louvain's concentration. She knew there were moments when she ceased to exist for him as anything more than a collection of planes and colours. But she didn't mind, she found his detachment appealing.

'Will you let me have a look, Mr Louvain?'

'Not yet, not yet. But I can tell you I am very happy with it.'

As she left the studio for the last time, Cora dropped her handkerchief in the corridor. As she stooped to retrieve it, she saw the face of one of Utamaro's courtesans, contorted in a spiral of desire.

CHAPTER 20

'That Pictured Countenance'

CORA HAD SENT ONLY A HUNDRED CARDS FOR THE reception but by the day of the event, she had made so many new 'friends' that the likely number of guests had at least tripled. Mrs Wyndham, who had made much of her connection with the new American Duchess, suddenly found herself taken up by the very same people who had vanished so completely from her life after the death of her husband. Some women might have seized this opportunity to exact revenge on those who had slighted them, but Mrs Wyndham was far too pragmatic for that. She knew that people generally behaved only as well as they had to, so she was admirably even-handed in the recommendations she made to her friend the Duchess, only proposing those whom she thought might genuinely add to the evening's entertainment.

To every would-be invitee she said the same thing. 'The Duchess wants this to be an intimate affair, where she can really get a chance to talk to people. I am sure the Duchess would love to meet you. She said to me, "Dear Mrs Wyndham, help me to make a short cut through London society and bring me its best and brightest." I know she is longing to make real friends here in London. She really is a lovely girl, so unaffected and devoted to the Duke. And generous, my goodness. When she saw how shabby my stole had become she insisted on giving me this gorgeous sable. Of course, money means nothing to her, you know, she is the richest heiress of her generation. In the New York papers they call her an American princess and I must say her manners would not be out of place at Windsor. Even Duchess Fanny can't find fault with her.'

Mrs Wyndham thought that Cora was looking suitably princess-like tonight. She was wearing a pink and white striped silk dress with huge bows at the shoulders and at the waist. In her hair she wore a tiara of diamond stars and round her neck the black pearls. The enormous width at the shoulder led the eye away from the thickening waist. Only those women, and it would be women, who looked carefully would guess that she was expecting. Cora and the Duke were standing at the top of the marble staircase greeting their guests. Mrs Wyndham had thought she would be early but there was already a crush of people on the stairs. She could smell that unique mixture of powder, lily of the valley and sweat that always heralded a society event. Just ahead of her was an unusual-looking man with artistic hair that fell almost to his shoulders. She had hinted to Cora that it might be unwise to be too experimental in her guest list, but Cora had been firm that she did not want a stuffy party. As a result there was a greater mixture of guests than Mrs Wyndham was used to seeing: artistic young men, a few members of the Cabinet, idle aristocrats like Ivo's friend Reggie Greatorex and busy ones like Lord Curzon, old money like the Atholls who owned most of Scotland's land and new money like the Tennants who owned most of Scotland's breweries: and the women ranged from the Double Duchess right through to Mrs Stanley. Such a mix would not have happened when Mrs Wyndham had first arrived in London, but these days society was no longer a closed circle. The thing was to have 'tin', lots of it, and then your place in the social firmament was assured.

Mrs Wyndham's small blue eyes criss-crossed the room looking for young men with titles and no tin who might be interested in Adelaide Schiller, from Ohio, who had three million dollars and an accent that could only improve. Mrs Wyndham had hoped to bring Miss Schiller with her tonight, but Cora had been firm. 'No Miss Schiller. I don't care how long she studied at the conservatory, I'm not being unkind but I don't want to give anyone the chance to make scathing remarks about American heiresses. And I don't want anyone who might flirt with Reggie Greatorex. Sybil would never forgive me.' Mrs Wyndham had wheedled but Cora would not budge. 'Ivo's already been through my list twice, I daren't add anyone else. But bring Miss Schiller for tea one day and I will look her over.' It didn't take long, thought Mrs Wyndham, for a girl from New York to turn into a grande dame. She had no doubt that Miss Schiller herself would be equally fastidious when she had landed her title.

Cora and Ivo were standing close to each other, closer than you might expect a married couple to stand. They looked in accord; Ivo was just behind his wife and every so often he would whisper into her ear and make her laugh.

Sir Odo and Lady Beauchamp were next in the procession to be announced. Charlotte was wearing gold satin which made her look literally radiant, everyone around her seemed lacklustre by comparison. Only her husband with his blond curls, red shiny cheeks and elaborately embroidered brocade waistcoat could stand the juxtaposition. Most of the people on the staircase had an air of eagerness, there was a sense of anticipation – a new hostess, a new way of doing things – but the Beauchamps did not hurry up the staircase, they sauntered, creating a pocket of space around them as they stopped to exchange greetings with people in the hall below. They contrived to create a hiatus on the crowded steps, so that it was the Duke and Duchess who stood waiting, while the Beauchamps greeted those around them. And when, eventually, the Beauchamps glided towards their hosts, they had an air of slight fatigue as if the party had already begun to pall.

Cora, who had no choice but to observe these manoeuvres, did not let her smile of welcome falter even as Ivo was muttering in her ear, 'What is that buffoon Odo wearing? The man's absurd.'

'How lovely to see you.' She leant forward to kiss Charlotte on the cheek. 'You must both stand by me tonight. You are, after all, my oldest English friends.'

'Indeed, Duchess,' sniggered Odo. 'Charlotte and I like to claim we invented you!'

'No one could invent Cora, Odo,' said the Duke. 'Not even a man possessed of your imagination. My wife is part of a new and wonderful species that has evolved independently in the Americas. Nothing scares her, except perhaps her mother.'

'Ivo, stop talking nonsense,' said Cora, pleased nevertheless that Ivo had resisted Odo's attempt to patronise her. 'Perhaps you could tell the orchestra to play something else. I must have heard that waltz ten times already. I can see Mr Stebbings wincing at the predictability of it all. Please, Ivo.'

'Is it really that bad? I thought it was rather charming myself, but if you insist. We can't have a party with wincing poets.' Ivo walked off in the direction of the musicians.

Charlotte leant forward so that her husband could not hear. 'Is Louvain here?'

'Not yet,' Cora whispered back. 'I still haven't seen the picture.'

Charlotte touched her on the arm with her fan. 'Don't worry, I'm sure he'll have done you justice.'

The Beauchamps moved into the drawing room and Cora let her smile slip just a little and felt the ache in her cheeks. She could see the line of guests stretching down the stairs almost into the street itself. She wondered when Louvain would arrive. Every time she thought about the picture, she felt her pulse quicken. It had only been one kiss after all, but she could still feel it sometimes – the scrape of his moustache against her lips.

Duchess Fanny was in front of her, her blond head a little on one side as if she was trying to remember who her hostess was.

'My dear Cora, what a charming occasion. I had no idea there were so many people in London in November. You look a little peaky though, dear, I do hope you are not overdoing it. Really, you don't have to stand here any longer, I think half an hour is quite long enough to be in the receiving line.' She gave Cora a gracious smile.

'But I don't know everybody. I would feel discourteous if I wasn't here to greet my guests,' said Cora.

'I suppose you are still young enough to think that you should set a good example. By all means, do the right thing, dear, but don't expect anyone to thank you for it.' Duchess Fanny moved off into the drawing room, the light catching the diamond drops hanging from her ears so that Cora fancied for one moment that her mother-in-law's head had caught fire.

'Don't take any notice of her, Cora.' Sybil was beside her. 'She is furious that you are having a party without asking for her advice. I think everything looks lovely. There can hardly be an orchid left in London. Very forward of you to invite Mrs Stanley, I know there are all sorts of stories about her but I have been dying to meet her since I saw her in *Lady Windermere's Fan*.' Cora could see that Sybil's eyes were searching the room.

'Would you like me to introduce you? I am sure she would like to meet an admirer.'

'No need, I can see she is talking to Reggie.' Sybil sped off, her bright red hair clearly visible in the crowd. Judging by the reddening of an inch of skin between Reggie's collar and his hair, he too was an admirer of Mrs Stanley.

'Your Grace.' The butler was standing beside her. 'Mr Louvain is in the library and everything has been arranged as you asked.'

'Tell him I will be down directly the guests have stopped arriving.'

She wanted to go down at once, but she knew that Duchess Fanny would think she was following her advice, and that she was determined *not* to do.

Downstairs in the library, Bertha was looking at the portrait of her mistress. She had been right, she thought, to suspect Louvain's intentions. Louvain had painted her lying back on the green chaise longue, one arm draped invitingly along its buttoned back, the other demurely in her lap. The abundant chestnut hair fell down over her shoulders as if she had just released it, the jacket of her dress was open with a suggestion of white lace beneath. It was a provocative pose with a hint that Cora had been surprised in the act of undressing, but the most striking feature of the painting was the expression on her face as she looked directly out of the canvas. The only word Bertha could think of to describe it was a word she had heard used time and again in her Carolina childhood: wanton. Louvain had made Cora look wanton. Her eyelids appeared weighed down by the long eyelashes, her mouth was slightly open and on each cheek was a splash of colour. Bertha, who had seen her mistress look like this often in Venice and occasionally since, was amazed at how accurate the painting was. You could almost feel the heat coming from the canvas, from the golden browns and umber tones that Louvain had used for the hair. Cora's grey-green eyes looked unfocused, the pupils dilated. Bertha could almost taste Cora's soft red lips again; Cora had changed so much since she had asked her maid for kissing lessons, but this painting managed to get across something of the innocence of those days as well as the woman she was now. But there was nothing yielding about the picture, it was the image of a woman who wanted satisfaction.

Louvain was watching her with a smile, showing his teeth.

'So, what do you think?'

'It's very like her, sir. I reckon Miss Cora will be pleased.' She could say that in truth; her mistress would like it, she was sure, but she wondered whether the Duke would feel the same way.

'And you? Do you like the picture?' he pressed her.

'That ain't the point, is it, sir?' Bertha looked at him directly.

'Why not?'

'Because you didn't paint it for me. You did it for her and I reckon she will like what you've done.'

Louvain was staring at her with narrowed eyes.

'You know, I would like to paint you, Bertha. You have such beautiful skin, it would be a challenge.'

'I don't think that would be right, sir, and besides, my young man wouldn't like it.' She knew the kind of picture Louvain had in mind, and she had no intention of taking her clothes off.

'Are you sure, Bertha? There are plenty of women upstairs who are longing to pose for me. Wouldn't you like to hang alongside a duchess?' He moved towards her to stroke her cheek, but Bertha saw him coming and took a step aside to look at the picture more closely.

'I don't think the ladies who want you to paint them would be too happy if you start painting their maids,' she said.

'Perhaps not, but no one tells me what to paint,' Louvain said without hesitation.

She looked at him as blankly as she could, thinking that no one could tell her to be painted either. He caught the sense of her silence and smiled.

'Do you realise, you are the first woman ever to turn me down.'

'We all of us need practice in being disappointed, sir.' Bertha made a perfunctory little curtsy. She had to find Miss Cora at once. 'If you'll excuse me, sir.'

'Run away then. You'll regret this one day.' Louvain dismissed her with a wave.

Bertha went out into the black and white checkered hall. There was still a stream of guests coming in from the cold, surrendering their coats and furs to the maids at the door and making their way up the wide curving stairway to where Cora stood. Bertha wondered how she could reach her mistress discreetly. It would have been simpler if she had been in uniform, but as a lady's maid she did not wear a cap and apron. But to her surprise, no one so much as glanced at her as she went up the stairs. Back home it would have been unthinkable for a coloured maid to make her way through a crowd of white folks without leaving a trail of disapproving stares in her wake. Most people in this country didn't realise that she was coloured. The English cared more about class, and here the society people simply did not see those who were not in their world. Bertha wondered what she disliked most: to be noticed for her colour or to be ignored for her class. But right now it suited her to be invisible. She waited until Cora had greeted an older lady wearing some threadbare ostrich plumes in her hair and her two gawky daughters whose kid gloves, Bertha couldn't help noticing, were soiled. That family was sorely in need of a new lady's maid, she thought – or perhaps they did not care. English ladies, she had observed, were a lot less particular than the Americans. Miss Cora would rather stay at home than wear dirty gloves. But at last the grubby family moved on and Bertha sidled up to her mistress.

'Miss Cora,' she said quietly, but Cora was in what Bertha thought of as her 'Duchess' mode.

'Bertha, you must remember to call me Your Grace in public, you know how the Duke feels about it.'

'Your Grace, I think you should come and look at your portrait,' Bertha said.

Cora said impatiently, 'I will be down as soon as all the guests are here. I am going to present it to Ivo.'

'But don't you think you ought to see it first?' Bertha persisted.

'Why, what's wrong with it?' She seized Bertha's arm. 'Does it make me look ugly? Or fat?'

'No, Miss Cora, I mean, Your Grace, you look fine in the picture. I just think you should see the picture, is all.' Bertha was beginning to regret her mission. Perhaps she had imagined things.

'Well, in that case, I have nothing to worry about.' Cora turned away. 'Dear Father Oliver, I am so pleased you could come to my little soirée.'

Bertha left her there. She felt full of foreboding about the portrait, but there was no more she could do. She went downstairs to the servants' hall. Jim was in the pantry eating a piece of cold pie. He looked up guiltily as she walked in.

'Oh crikey, I thought you was Mr Clewes.' He smiled at her. 'But I'm so glad you're not.' He brushed the crumbs away from his mouth and gave her a kiss. She pushed him away.

'Jim, don't. It's not worth it.'

He kissed her again, his lips still greasy from the pie. 'I'll be the judge of that.'

She wriggled away and stood in front of him, her arms folded. 'I'm worried, Jim.'

'Don't worry about Clewes and the others. They're all busy upstairs. I'm meant to be helping but luckily the spare livery didn't fit.'

'No, it's not that. It's about Miss Cora's picture. It ain't respectful, and she don't know it.' Bertha shook her head.

'Why, is she naked?' Jim rolled his eyes.

'No, of course not! Thing is, she looks like she could be, if you know what I mean,' Bertha said.

'Nothing wrong with that. There are lots of pictures of naked women at Lulworth.'

'But not of ladies, Jim. Those goddesses and such ain't ladies.' Bertha looked at him.

'Ladies look the same underneath, don't they, or is there some secret you aren't telling me?'

Jim was whispering in her ear now. Bertha felt his breath tickling her neck. She wanted to fold herself into him, to press her heart against his heart and feel the warmth between them, but she could not contain her worry. There were times when she didn't much care for Miss Cora but she was her mistress and she could not be indifferent. She knew Jim did not understand the connection she felt. He felt loyalty to the Duke but he did not feel responsible for him; the Duke was his employer not his charge. But for Bertha it was different.

'Come upstairs with me, Jim, come and look at the picture. Maybe I'm fancying things that ain't there.'

'Not likely, Bertha! If I go up there, I'll be workin' all night. Ain't a man entitled to a spot of leisure once in a while, with his best girl?' Jim put his arm round her waist and drew her to him. She let her head rest on his chest for a moment but then she remembered the look in the painted Cora's eyes and pulled back.

'I must go, Jim.'

He released her reluctantly, saying, 'Remember, Bertha, all we do is wait on them.'

But she was gone, her dark bombazine skirts rustling against the stone stairs.

Upstairs, the drawing room was now full to bursting. Women were having to turn sideways to pass each other on account of the enormous width of their leg-of-mutton sleeves. Heads crowned with ostrich plumes and diamond aigrettes twisted and craned to get the best view of the new Duchess. There was general agreement that she was pretty, in an American way, 'vivacious rather than soulful', but more interesting was the speculation as to the extent of her wealth. A viscount who had visited the United States on an unsuccessful gold prospecting expedition assured his listeners that every slice of bread that passed American lips was made from Cash's finest flour. Another man said that the Cash family ate all their meals from gold plate, and that in their house in Newport even the servants had bathrooms. There was much talk about the Duchess's settlement. One countess had it on very good authority that she had half a million a year. A silence followed this remark as her listeners tried to estimate how many noughts there were in a million. It was agreed that reviving houses like Lulworth was the very best use for American money, and there was generally expressed relief that the new Duchess appeared to be a woman of some taste. Her gown was much admired, after it had been identified as a Worth, and there was satisfaction that her jewels, though fine, were not overwhelming. There was surprise at the presence of Mrs Stanley, given her previous friendship with the Duke, but the feeling was that inviting her had been a stylish gesture on the part of the Duchess. There was some confusion among the more frivolous-minded guests at the presence of the Prime Minister and the Foreign Secretary – did the new Duchess intend to be a political hostess? It was really too tiresome if that was the case as there were far too many serious-minded hostesses and not nearly enough fun. Mr Stebbings, who had come hoping for a tête-à-tête with the Duchess about his work, was disappointed to see her so firmly hemmed in by philistines, but he had been rewarded by the sight of *The Yellow Book* on one of the occasional tables. He had picked it up and been gratified to find that the volume fell open at the page on which his poem 'Stella Maris' appeared, and as he read it through, he felt the usual prickle of surprise at the felicity of his own expression.

The prevailing mood of satisfaction was rendered all the more piquant by the fact that there were a significant number of people who had not been invited. This was a satisfyingly select gathering. Even those who had previously condemned American forays into English society as impertinent could find nothing to criticise. Only Charlotte Beauchamp looked restless, her eyes constantly straying to the door to see who was arriving. Some of the less generous members of the party put her lack of composure down to being in the house of a rival to her status as the most fashionable woman in London. Charlotte Beauchamp was possibly the more beautiful, that Grecian profile was without parallel, but the new Duchess had such a scintillating smile.

Sir Odo, however, did not think his wife was restless because she was in the presence of a rival. He knew that Charlotte would never allow herself to show weakness. 'You are the most beautiful woman in the room tonight, my dear.'

She turned to him in surprise. 'A compliment, Odo?'

'No, merely a statement of fact. Why do you keep looking at the door?' he asked.

'I was hoping to catch Louvain before he gets mobbed by all his would-be sitters.'

'Are you sure he's coming?' Odo asked.

'Oh yes, he told me he'd be here.' Charlotte stopped, realising too late that she had made an admission.

'Do you have something in mind then, Charlotte?' Odo looked at her closely. 'It really is too bad of you to work alone. You know how I enjoy our little games.'

Charlotte adjusted her glove, pulling the kid leather taut over her knuckles. 'But I wanted to surprise you,' she said, stretching out her fingers. 'I wanted the satisfaction of seeing your face when you realised how clever I'd been.'

'Really?' Odo took one of her hands in his own, folding his fingers around her kid-gloved fist. 'I hope we understand each other, Charlotte, that we are on the same side.'

She pulled away from him, but he held on. 'Don't do that, you'll wrinkle my gloves. Lady Tavistock is looking at us, you don't want her to think that we are having a scene, do you?'

Odo released the hand and she shook it out. And then as if by mutual consent they moved in opposite directions, greeting the people on either side of them with enthusiasm.

Cora had moved from her station at the top of the stairs. The line of guests had dwindled to a few latecomers who had come on from the theatre. She was talking to Mrs Wyndham and Lady Tavistock, telling them how parties in Newport were conducted.

'The balls there never start till at least midnight. It gets so hot during the day there.'

'It sounds too, too exhausting,' sighed Lady Tavistock. 'I can barely stay awake past midnight these days.'

'Oh, I think you might manage to stay awake for one of Mrs Vanderbilt's fancy dress affairs.' Cora said brightly. 'Last year she brought the whole cast of *The Gaiety Revue* from New York to perform after dinner. And the favours were all replicas of jewels worn by the court of Louis the Fourteenth. It was quite spectacular.'

'I still think it sounds exhausting, dear Duchess. You Americans are so energetic.'

'Well, we are still a young nation, we haven't had time to get bored.' And then Cora saw the unmistakable figure of Louvain with his pelt of silvery blond hair, his pale blue eyes assessing the company. He saw her and raised one hand in greeting, but before he could move towards her he was accosted by a trio of ladies, their shoulders raised like hackles.

'Can that be Louvain over there?' said Lady Tavistock, without a trace of her former languor.

'Yes, he has come to show me my portrait. It is so exciting, I haven't seen so much as a drawing yet.' Cora was anxious to get to the painter but Lady Tavistock was still talking.

'Well, that's quite a coup. To be painted by Louvain already. Lady Sale and her daughters have been waiting for years to sit for him. I suppose you must have offered him a fortune.'

'Oh, we never discussed money. He asked me, as a matter of fact. He was really quite insistent.' She caught Louvain's eye again. 'He is impossible to refuse.'

'So I've heard,' said Lady Tavistock, her eyes glittering with malice. 'Louvain always gets what he wants.'

Mrs Wyndham, alarmed at the edge the conversation was developing, looked about her for a distraction. 'I think the Duke might be looking for you, my dear. He is over there with Duchess Fanny.'

'Thank you, Mrs Wyndham. Will you excuse me?' And with a grateful glance to Mrs Wyndham, Cora sailed off towards her husband.

'You've done well with that one, Madeleine,' said Lady Tavistock. 'Quite the Duchess already. You would hardly know she was an American, apart from the voice of course.'

'Do you know, I really can't take the credit for her,' said Mrs Wyndham. 'Some of these American heiresses now are as regal as any of our own princesses. She's certainly better educated than most English girls of her age. But what is so interesting is her fearlessness, she doesn't seem to be afraid of anything.'

'That's just as well, considering that she has Fanny Buckingham as her mother-in-law,' Lady Tavistock said. 'I haven't seen those emeralds in years. I wonder why Fanny decided to wear them tonight? Do you think she might be trying to make a point?'

Ivo met Cora half way across the room. He nodded his head at Louvain.

'Who is that man over there with the peculiar hair surrounded by women? I've seen him before.'

'You mean Louvain,' Cora said.

'The one who painted Charlotte? What on earth is he doing here?'

Cora was puzzled by the sharp tone in his voice. 'I asked him, of course,' she said. She went on quickly before Ivo could protest further. 'In fact, he has brought something with him I want you to see. It's in the library. Come with me now, quickly, before we get caught by Lady Tavistock.'

But Ivo did not move. 'Cora! We can't simply disappear. Not even for Mr Louvain.' Cora caught the edge again in his voice. 'Whatever it is can surely wait.'

Cora could have stamped her foot with impatience. But here was Lady Tavistock bearing down on them.

'My dear Duke, I can't wait to see the portrait, what a coup!' And then, seeing the Duke's face, she tittered and turned to Cora. 'Oh my dear, was it to be a surprise? What an idiot I am.' She looked at the couple curiously.

Cora stood frozen for a moment and then she recovered. 'Not at all, Lady Tavistock. I was just about to show him the picture.' And then to demonstrate she was not intimidated, she made a sign to the butler. 'Clewes, could you arrange to have the picture brought up here.'

Lady Tavistock said, 'To see the unveiling of a Louvain. How exciting! Your wife is so original, Duke.'

Ivo nodded. His eyes were on the object being carried into the room by two footmen, who at Cora's signal set it down in front of him. The picture, which stood on an easel, was covered by a heavy red velvet cloth.

Cora found herself trembling with excitement. She had to stop herself from tearing the cloth down. Instead she beckoned to Louvain who was standing to her left, next to Charlotte Beauchamp. The painter approached the picture, and then hesitated with his hand on the drape. Cora turned to her husband.

'Shall we ask Mr Louvain to do the honours, Ivo? Or would you like to be the first?' She put a hand on his arm and looked at him in appeal.

Ivo did not answer but simply gestured to the painter to carry on. The room went quiet around them.

Louvain pulled the crimson velvet away with a flourish, letting it pool on the floor like blood.

There was a sound as the whole room breathed out. From where she stood, short-sighted Cora could only see a golden blur. She narrowed her eyes to sharpen her vision but all she could identify was the brown sweep of her hair. She needed to get much closer. Bertha had been right, she should have gone to see the picture first so she could prepare herself. Now she would look ridiculous if she started to peer at it. She had forgotten Ivo in her anxiety to see the picture better, but then she heard his voice, quiet but clear. It broke the silence that had frozen the room since the unveiling of the picture.

'May I congratulate you, Mr Louvain, on the likeness. And such a refreshing pose. There will be time for formal pictures later, but you have caught the woman not the title.' Cora tried desperately to see what Ivo meant without screwing up her eyes.

'The Duchess was a pleasure to paint.' Louvain nodded towards Cora. The room which had been so quiet began to hum with conversation again as the guests surged forward to see the picture properly. Cora relaxed a little. The picture was a success. She began to edge forward to have a proper look, but she felt Ivo's hand on her arm, restraining her. He spoke very quietly.

'We will talk about this later.'

Cora looked at him in surprise. 'Talk about it? Why, is there something wrong?' She felt salty bile rise into her mouth as she saw the tension in his face. He was about to reply when Charlotte Beauchamp appeared in front of them.

'I'm really quite jealous, Cora, your portrait is causing a sensation. I think Louvain has excelled himself. It's amazing what a painter sees.' She smiled warmly at Cora and looked up at Ivo. 'And what do you think of your surprise?' She raised an eyebrow. Cora held her breath.

'It is a remarkable picture. I believe you were responsible for the introduction, Lady Beauchamp?' There was an unmistakable edge to Ivo's question, but Charlotte did not flinch.

'All I did was to put your wife and Louvain in the same room. What happened next was between them.' She gestured to the portrait and smiled.

Cora said brightly, 'Charlotte has been so helpful, Ivo. I don't know what I would have done without her.' She put her hand on Charlotte's arm to emphasise the point. Ivo looked at them both, his face expressionless. Cora thought for a moment he was going to quarrel with Charlotte. But then he smiled, not warmly, but enough to make her anxiety subside. Now he was drawing her away. She wondered what he was so anxious to avoid and then she understood. Duchess Fanny was inspecting the picture.

But they were not quick enough. Duchess Fanny turned to Cora and said loudly, 'And what character are you representing, dear? Rapunzel? Or Guinevere? Such abundant hair, and such a charming rustic costume. Really, we shall all have to be painted in character now.' Her blue eyes were very round. Cora heard the malice in her words and felt Ivo stiffen beside her, but it was Louvain who spoke.

He made a little bow. 'Well, I would be happy to paint you as Cleopatra, Your Grace.'

The Duchess inclined her head graciously as if the compliment was only her due, and gave Louvain one of her creamy smiles. Perhaps, Cora thought, it was not the picture that her mother-in-law was objecting to but the lack of focus on herself. She moved a bit closer to the canvas and looked at it properly. Really, it was most flattering; perhaps not very Duchess-like but surely Ivo would rather have this – she saw the warm tones of her painted skin and the attractive curve of her mouth – than some full-length stately thing. She couldn't help smiling. But at the same time she was aware that she was being watched by the guests milling around her. There was something about the atmosphere that reminded her of the night her mother had burst into flames. There was a crackling to the conversations across the room that made her uneasy. But before she could decide whether there was triumph or disaster in the air, Charlotte was beside her, her voice soothing.

'You look so natural. It is almost as if you weren't being painted at all. I can't imagine how you managed to look so relaxed. Louvain was always barking at me if I lost my pose for an instant. But I suppose you were lying down . . .' Her voice trailed off.

Cora said without thinking, 'Well, in my condition, it can be tiring to stand for too long.' Then she blushed, realising what she had done, and put her hand to her mouth. She looked around, hoping that no one had noticed, she did not want to tell the world yet. Once her condition became known she would be expected to retire to Lulworth until the birth, and she very much wanted to stay in London.

She noticed that Charlotte did not look at her but at Ivo, who stood very still, staring intently at his champagne glass. Perhaps he had not heard. But she had forgotten her mother-in-law who said loudly and unmistakably, 'Cora, does this mean there is to be a happy event?' Cora's blush was answer enough. Duchess Fanny looked reproachfully at her son. 'You might have told me, Ivo.'

Ivo looked at her coldly. 'I believe it is usual to wait until the sixth month before making an announcement. And besides, it was really for Cora to tell you.'

Cora broke in, 'Why, I haven't told anybody apart from Ivo. Back home we like to keep these things private. I only wrote Mother last week.'

'But in your country, dear Cora, you are not giving birth to dukes!' The Double Duchess looked at her in astonishment.

Charlotte had remained quite still during this exchange. Cora wondered if it was because she was still childless, and felt a pang of sympathy; Charlotte was clasping her hands together as if frightened they might do some damage. In the end it was Odo who spoke.

'Allow me to congratulate you on behalf of Charlotte and myself. Such a relief to know that there will be a new generation of Maltravers. And such a treat to see your portrait, Duchess, especially as it is such an intimate work.' Odo took Charlotte by the elbow and shepherded her away. But Charlotte stopped and looked back at the group beside the portrait.

'How clever of you, Mr Louvain, to paint the Duchess as a Madonna in waiting. You miss nothing, do you?'

The Duke signalled to the butler to remove the painting. 'Cora, I believe we are neglecting our guests. Mother, Mr Louvain, will you excuse us?' Ivo did not look at Cora directly but put his hand on her elbow to urge her on. She stood for a moment trying to understand what had been said and what had been omitted.

'Cora!' Ivo's voice was soft but urgent. She began to move but as she passed Louvain she stopped.

'Thank you, Mr Louvain. The picture is everything you promised.' She extended her hand to him, intending to shake his, but the painter forestalled her by bringing her hand to his lips.

'No one could do you justice, Duchess, but I have done my best.'

Ivo was pinching her elbow now. Cora disengaged her hand from Louvain and walked on.

Ivo muttered in her ear, 'Please try and remember who you are.'

Cora could not mistake the fury in his voice now. She looked at him but he had already turned away. To follow him now would be too public. She forced herself to smile, as if he had just been murmuring an endearment to her, and then drew her shoulders back and assumed her Duchess pose.

'Did you tell him that I kissed you?' It was Louvain standing behind her, whispering into her ear so closely that she could feel the bristles of his moustache.

'Of course not! There would be no point. You yourself said that it was only to improve the painting.' She kept her smile fixed.

'And you believed me? Do they not have red-blooded men in

your country then, that you believe the excuses of scoundrels like myself?'

'I don't want to talk about it, Mr Louvain. I wonder if sitting for you was a mistake.'

'How can anything that results in a work of art be a mistake? It's a great painting.' Louvain grasped her arm. 'Honestly, what did you think when you first saw it?' He looked directly into her eyes. She lowered her gaze. 'You liked it. You recognised yourself, didn't you?'

She was moved by the urgency of his voice. She realised that he was right.

'Yes, there was . . . something in the picture that I recognised. But perhaps it is something that should not have been painted.'

Louvain laughed. 'There are no secrets in a painting, not a good one anyway. And there is nothing you should keep hidden, Cora.'

The use of her Christian name brought her up short. This conversation should not be happening, not now, not here. He was presuming upon an intimacy between them that should not exist. She tried to compose herself, and said in a bright social voice, 'You know, Mr Louvain, this is my first big party. If I spend the evening talking to you, all of London society will go home saying that I am just another uncouth American. You must excuse me, Mr Louvain, you really must.' And with that she walked away from him. She looked around for Mrs Wyndham. She caught her eye and Mrs Wyndham hurried across the room towards her.

'Are you feeling quite well, Duchess? Do you need some air?' Mrs Wyndham was all concern.

'Yes, perhaps some air might be good.'

At a sign from Mrs Wyndham, a footman opened the long window on to the balcony and Cora leant out, feeling the cold

November air on her face with relief. She longed for a cigarette. At last she asked the question.

'Please, Mrs Wyndham, be honest with me. Is it a disaster?'

There was a pause as Mrs Wyndham composed her answer.

'Oh no, my dear, not a disaster. I think there may be a few people who are surprised by the portrait – it's a very unusual pose for a duchess to adopt. If you had told me that you were sitting for Louvain,' her voice took on a reproachful tinge, 'I would have warned you that he is not a man of unblemished reputation. There have been rumours . . . ' Her voice trailed off. 'But I hardly think that anyone could possibly attach any scandal to you.' She looked keenly at Cora for any sign of guilt. But the girl looked too bewildered. If there had been something between her and Louvain she would hardly have engineered such a very public denouement.

She went on briskly, 'If you behave as if nothing has happened, then nothing will have happened. This is your party, it is for you to set the tone. And if there is a little gossip, that is nothing to be afraid of – at least no one can say you are insipid. But now you must take charge. The real crime is to show weakness.'

Cora whispered, 'My husband is angry. I don't understand.'

Mrs Wyndham looked at her, surprised; could Cora really be so naive?

'Well, Louvain has an unsavoury reputation, and your picture, though charming in every way, has a certain intimate quality that might be open to misinterpretation. But only if you let it, my dear.' She saw with alarm that Cora's shoulders were sagging. It was imperative that the girl kept her head. She must take charge of the situation now or take years to recover her position. Mrs Wyndham shuddered. If Cora failed now then Miss Schiller and her compatriots would find their matrimonial prospects in England much reduced. So she said with a certain sharpness in her tone, 'Come, Duchess, your guests are waiting.'

And to her great relief she saw the young woman pull herself upright, and with her head tilted at an angle calculated to charm, she rejoined the party.

From her post by the door Bertha watched her mistress advance towards her guests. She could see all was not well. Bertha had seen the looks that had been exchanged when the picture had been unveiled and knew her misgivings about the picture had been well-founded. If only Miss Cora had listened to her – but Bertha felt no comfort in being right, she only felt pity for her mistress. She did not want to go back to the servants' hall, she knew they would all be revelling in the scandal. She wanted to be on hand in case Cora needed her. Her mistress had moved out of sight now. Bertha moved along the wall and found a niche where there had once been a statue now covered by a velvet drape. She slipped behind the curtain, pleased that she had found a spot where she could observe her mistress without being overlooked herself.

A couple stood in front of her, Bertha could not see their faces but she recognised the Duke's back.

'. . . Such an intimate pose, what a pleasant change from the grand manner. I suppose that was your idea, Duke – you wanted a boudoir portrait of your new wife.' The woman's voice was probing.

'You make it sound as if I had a whole cupboard of wives stashed away in the west wing.' The Duke's voice was doggedly light.

'And how did you find Mr Louvain to deal with? You hear such stories. But I suppose if you had any doubts you would not have allowed the Duchess to sit for him.'

Bertha stood very still waiting for his reply

'Like most artists he seems more interested in money than anything else.'

Bertha heard the woman laugh. The Duke was hiding his feelings about the portrait in public at least but she doubted whether he had relinquished his anger. Jim had told her that when the Duke was furious he liked to tear a sheet of paper into as many pieces as he could. It was hard to shave his master in the morning, he had told her, because the Duke's jaw muscles were so tight from grinding his teeth all night. No, Bertha did not think that her mistress's husband was a forgiving man.

And then she heard his voice again.

'You did this.' This time his voice was low and private.

'All I did was open the door. She chose to walk through.' A different woman's voice, almost whispering, one Bertha knew but could not place.

'But why?'

'You know why.' There was a silence. Bertha wanted to look through the curtains but she knew that if the Duke was looking that way, he would see her at once.

She heard a sigh and the sound of rustling silk.

'I ... can't ... bear ... this.' The Duke spoke as if the words were being carved out of him.

'There is no choice.' The woman's voice was flat.

Bertha could hear murmuring but was unable to make out the words. And then the music started again and she could hear nothing. After a minute she dared to look through the curtain, but the Duke and his companion were gone.

Cora's head was aching now from the strain of smiling as if she had not a care in the world. She had faced down all the curious stares with her sparkling American smile. She found that brightness acted like an acid on the web of evasion and unspoken thoughts that characterised so much English conversation. If she stood there smiling and looking people in the eye, they were forced to meet her gaze. She began to feel better. Mrs Wyndham had been right, she could set the tone.

She could see Ivo talking to the Prime Minister. She would join him. Ivo was being unreasonable; Louvain was right, she had nothing to hide.

As she walked across the room, she heard Odo's high-pitched voice shrieking, 'A picture of abandonment, my dear, you should have seen his face.' She tried to pass by without noticing, but Odo had seen her and was elaborating. 'So naive, but then I suppose we must make allowances for Americans.'

Cora moved on, her eyes on Ivo, trying not to be distracted. There was nothing she could do about Odo.

At last she reached her husband. He was talking to Lord Rosebery and a younger man she recognised from the party at Conyers, the Prince's equerry, Colonel Ferrers.

Cora put her hand on Ivo's arm. She saw with dismay the expression on his face as he turned to her.

'Cora, may I present the Prime Minister? Rosebery, my wife.' They shook hands.

'And Colonel Ferrers I believe you already know.'

The equerry made her a little bow.

The Prime Minister spoke. 'I was just telling the Duke how delighted I am that he has agreed to accompany Prince Eddy. We need more peers with your husband's sense of public duty.'

Cora smiled blankly. She had no idea what he was talking about but clearly she could not admit that. She glanced at Ivo but could only see his profile.

'It is quite true, Lord Rosebery, Ivo has a strong sense of what is right in his position. But surely he is not alone in that?'

'I wish your husband's selflessness was more common, Duchess. Public service should be the companion of privilege, but so often these days it is not.' The Prime Minister's tone was sombre. He did not, Cora thought, look like a man who enjoyed his role in life. Ivo had told her that the only thing he really liked talking about was his horses.

'I have heard so much about your stable, Lord Rosebery. Have you ever been to America? My father won the triple crown over there last year with his horse Adelaide.'

Ivo broke in. 'I think perhaps the Prime Minister may be too busy to follow foreign horseflesh, Cora.'

But Rosebery was smiling. 'Oh no, Wareham, I am never too busy for racing. Too busy for parliament perhaps but never for horses. Tell me about your father's stable, Duchess. Are the blood lines Arabian?'

Cora began an intricate conversation about the breeding of thoroughbreds which involved a good deal of listening on her part. But at the edge of her vision she could see Ivo fidgeting. Finally Rosebery released her and turned to her husband.

'I must say, Wareham, now that I have met your charming Duchess, I appreciate your sense of duty all the more.' Rosebery smiled at Cora, who managed to smile back.

The crowd was at last beginning to thin out. At midnight two footmen had brought out flowered baskets full of party favours, gold cigarette cases with the Maltravers crest engraved on the front for the men, and mother-of-pearl opera glasses for the women, with the crest in gold filigree on each barrel. This had immediately shifted the party's centre of gravity – like iron filings unable to resist a magnetic field, the guests had clustered around the source of the attraction. Some people, of course, had muttered that this munificence was a vulgar American practice but the baskets had emptied nonetheless. Cora was relieved that she had insisted on importing this Newport custom even though Ivo had laughed when she suggested it; the glittering trinkets had distracted her guests from the affair of the portrait. She was hoarse now from saying goodbye. 'Oh, I am so glad you came – no, thank *you* for coming – I just wanted everyone to have something to remember my first party.' She guessed that the Beauchamps had spread the news of her pregnancy, as many of the women had urged her to get some rest as they pressed her hand in saying goodbye.

Duchess Fanny had been crisp. 'You must go to Lulworth, Cora, at once. You are lucky that everyone is leaving town so the talk will blow over very quickly. You can't afford to have a reputation, at least not until after your son is born.'

'But I have done nothing to deserve one!' Cora was indignant.

The Duchess smiled from a great height. 'Most people who have reputations don't deserve them. I, on the other hand, don't have the reputation I deserve. Just follow my advice, Cora, and there will be no lasting damage. And don't look so martyred, my dear. It's not me who minds these things but my son. He has always worried about the way things look.'

Cora retreated. 'Oh dear, I can see some kind of problem over there with the favours. I had better go and intervene. Goodnight, Duchess.'

'Remember my advice, Cora.'

At last everyone had gone and Cora was able to go to her room. She had not seen Ivo for the last hour, but she was too weary to look for him. So many things had happened that night that she simply could not fit them all in her thoughts. She dragged herself up the stairs to her bedroom. Ivo was not there. She sent Bertha away – she didn't want her presence to annoy Ivo even more. As she started to undress she felt a fluttering in her stomach as if there was a butterfly trapped in her belly. She put her hand there, but she could feel nothing through the layers of petticoats. Impatiently she tugged at her skirts, pulling at the ties which fastened them, but Bertha's knots would not be undone. In a frenzy she found some nail scissors and began to cut at her bonds. By twisting and wriggling she even managed to cut the laces of her corset. At last everything was off. It was still there, that strange light feeling deep inside her. She lay down on her bed and looked up at the ceiling. She put her hands on her stomach just above her groin and waited. Would the flicker come again? Suddenly nothing else, not the picture, not Ivo, mattered. She lay there watching the glow from the dying fire until miraculously she felt it again. She had not quite believed in the baby until now, the soreness in her breasts and the fatigue had simply been unwelcome. But this, this quickening was something else – new life, new hope. This was the bond between her and Ivo. Surely he would be kinder to her now that the line was assured.

The door opened.

'Ivo?'

Ivo said nothing.

Cora tried to stay bright. 'Oh Ivo, the most amazing thing. I felt the baby move, such a queer feeling like a fish darting about. It's doing it now. Put your hand here, perhaps you can feel it too.'

But her husband did not move towards her. He stood in the half-open doorway, his face silhouetted against the light from the corridor.

'Cora, Lord Rosebery has asked me to accompany Prince Eddy on his Indian tour. The Queen and the Prince of Wales are anxious that he takes some part in public life, but Prince Eddy is not, in Rosebery's view, "capable". There have been incidents that . . . He wants me to make sure that the Prince does not cause the government any embarrassment. It is a position of trust and I have agreed to go. I think that after tonight's debacle, it is the best thing.' He paused and rubbed the bridge of his nose with his hand. 'I must go to Lulworth first thing tomorrow to make arrangements with Father Oliver and then straight to Southampton. I suggest that you go to Lulworth as soon you can. I would feel happier if you were there. I am sure that Sybil or Mrs Wyndham would come with you, if you feel you need the company. As you have your own resources, I have not made any financial arrangements for you, but all the wages and estate upkeep will be taken care of.'

Cora sat up and turned on the light, her sleepiness forgotten.

'You're going to India? Now? I don't understand.' She looked up at him. He was still standing in the doorway, his dark face set.

'Really?' He looked at her intently, as if searching for something in her face. 'You sit in secret for a man like Louvain and you don't understand? You may not mind being talked about, Cora, but I do. I don't want people looking at me and wondering about my wife.' His face softened a little. 'I have done my best to contain the scandal by pretending, although it pained me, to like the picture. I don't know if anyone believed me but at least they won't have the satisfaction of knowing that we have quarrelled. By the time I return, it will be forgotten.'

Cora walked towards him and took his hands. He did not resist, but simply let her hold them, inert and unfeeling.

She began to plead, 'I didn't know about Louvain's "reputation". I met him at the Beauchamps, after all. Charlotte almost insisted that I should sit for him. Don't be like this, Ivo, please.' Ivo remained motionless. Cora put her hand to her throat and whispered, 'Look at these pearls you gave me – don't you remember that afternoon?'

'Of course I remember. I thought then that we had a chance of happiness.' His voice was full of sadness.

'But we do.' She put his hand on her stomach.

'Cora, please,' but he did not take his hand away. She put her other hand to his cheek.

He moved away from her and she thought she had lost him, but then with a jerky movement he put his arms round her and held her to him. They stood in silence for a long moment.

Finally she summoned the courage to speak. She could feel his heart beating. 'Do you really have to go?'

'Yes.'

'Because of me?'

'Because of many things. I have agreed to go now.'

'And when are you coming back?'

'In the spring.'

'Before . . . ?'

'Yes, before.' Ivo pulled away from her.

'And are you still angry?'

He looked at her, his face dark. 'I don't know any more what I feel. Sometimes I feel nothing at all.' He turned his face away.

'But I need you to stay. I can't manage all this,' she gestured at her stomach, at the room, at this strange English world that surrounded her.

Ivo's face flickered with amusement. 'Oh, I think you underestimate yourself, Cora,' and then he kissed her on the cheek and closed the door behind him.

She sat after he left her for a long time, feeling the touch of his lips on her cheek; and then just as she thought she would never move again, she felt the slow beating of the life in her womb and she lay down, cradling her belly with her hands, and within seconds she was asleep.

Part Three

The English married ladies ... are the brightest and most venomous politicians in English society.

Titled Americans, 1890

CHAPTER 21

At Sea

BERTHA FELT A TRICKLE OF SWEAT RUN FROM her neck down her back. It had been unseasonably warm for April all week, and the maid wished she had worn something lighter. There was no shade here on the beach apart from her parasol but that could not shelter her from the glare from the sea. She hoped that Cora would get out soon. Bertha did not want her complexion to be darkened by the sun. It was tiring squinting into the glare, following the dark head bobbing through the waves. It was pointless really, her vigil: if her mistress were to get into difficulties, what could she do? Bertha had never learnt to swim. Keeping a watch on Cora was her way of expressing her disapproval. A woman in her ninth month had no business to be swimming in the icy sea. It was undignified, not to mention dangerous, but Cora had ignored all her sighs and tuttings.

Bertha wished that Mrs Cash was here already. The Cashes were due any day now; Mrs Cash had seen no reason to cut short the New York season to be with Cora while she was cooped up at Lulworth, but she had no intention of missing the birth of her grandson, the future Duke (Mrs Cash had not even entertained the possibility that the child might be a girl). But Bertha thought that Mrs Cash should have been here months before. Miss Cora needed some of her own folks at this time. They had been at Lulworth for five months now, time enough to feel homesick. Miss Cora would never admit it but Bertha had seen the piles of letters to the States which went into the wooden post box in the shape of a castle that stood in the great hall. Every day at eleven, two and five, the butler opened the box with a special brass key and gave the letters to the postman. Some days Bertha would see letters to America leaving by every post. There was also the daily letter to India. Occasionally Bertha would send one of her own, but she had told Jim not to reply – a letter from India would cause too much talk in the servants' hall. She knew that every letter was thoroughly scrutinised by the butler and Mrs Softley and she was pretty sure that a letter addressed to her from India would be steamed open before she received it. One of the parlour-maids had been dismissed after Christmas because she had received a love letter from a groom at Sutton Veney. Strictly speaking, it was for the Duchess to dismiss the maid, but Mrs Softley had not found it necessary to consult the mistress. Bertha was not sure now that even the Duchess would be able to protect her if her relationship with Jim was discovered.

Bertha wondered whether her mistress realised how little control she had over the household at Lulworth, how the servants that treated her with such deference in public laughed at her in the servants' hall. Miss Cora had not taken command of Lulworth in the way that Mrs Cash had run Sans Souci. Miss Cora had been full of schemes for 'improving' the house: some things like the bathrooms had been achieved, but her attempts to change the way the house was run – she had been astonished to discover that there was one man who was employed simply to wind all the clocks in the house – had mostly come to nothing. She gave orders but could not enforce them. One of her first orders had been to remove the photographs of the Double Duchess, usually in the company of the Prince of Wales, that were in every guest bedroom. Last time Bertha had looked, the photographs were still there, the silver frames gleaming from constant polishing. Miss Cora had not yet noticed; Bertha wondered what she might do when she did. Probably nothing, Cora's spirit seemed to be waning as the baby grew bigger and there was still no sign of the Duke's return. He should have been back in early February but he had written at the beginning of the month to say that he would be delayed. Bertha had seen her mistress's face crumple after reading that letter and impulsively she had taken her hand. She could see that Cora needed someone to hold on to. These months of seclusion and waiting had made Bertha acutely aware of her mistress's isolation. A few nights ago Cora had asked her to sleep in her bed. She said that it was in case the baby came but Bertha knew that her mistress just wanted a body beside her. Sometimes she felt the same way herself. When she had heard Cora calling Ivo's name in her sleep, Bertha had found herself, rather to her surprise, feeling sorry for her.

Since they had come to Lulworth, Cora had seen almost no one. Father Oliver had been there for a month working on the History. Mrs Wyndham had come to stay for a week, as had Sybil Lytchett, but otherwise Cora had been alone at Lulworth, in as much as you could ever be alone in a house with eighty-one servants. Bertha had been surprised that there had not been more callers from the neighbourhood but when she remarked on this to Mrs Softley, the housekeeper had been astonished at her ignorance. 'No one is going to be calling on the Duchess when she is expecting, not when the Duke's away. It wouldn't be right.' So Cora ate alone most nights, her diamonds sparkling unseen as she picked her way through the six courses that constituted a 'light dinner'.

The sea was much colder than the warm weather would suggest but Cora hardly noticed, she was lit from within by an internal furnace. Her daily swim was the only time she felt relieved of her burden. To float on her back weightless and cool was all she craved. She found the walk down to the beach harder with each passing day but it was worth it to take off all her clothes and step inch by inch into the water, shivering with pleasure and pain as it lapped her ankles, then her calves, her thighs until it reached her swollen belly. When the water was shoulder height she would take a deep breath and plunge her head underwater, blowing out so that a stream of bubbles pierced the surface of the water. Then she would float on her back, kicking her legs sporadically and watching the odd fugitive cloud as it floated over the cove. Sometimes she would turn on her front and on a clear day she would look at the small brown fish that darted beneath the seaweed. She noticed that when she swam, the creature inside her would stop kicking. It was the only time that she could be sure that it would be quiet. Now as she swam across the cove she could imagine that she was the girl she had been two summers before in Newport; although there she had been weighed down with an elaborate bathing costume whereas here she was naked. She had tried swimming with a costume here, but the combination of her pregnant belly and the sodden serge skirts of her bathing dress made her wish that she could swim unencumbered. She had confided this desire to Sybil Lytchett, who had been visiting. Sybil had laughed and said, 'But Cora, nothing could be easier. Tell the servants that the swimming cove is out of bounds and you can swim in whatever you want!' Cora had found it awkward to explain to Bugler that she wanted to be private during her daily swim, she had felt as if she was asking permission instead of giving orders. But in the event, the butler had been quite accommodating and had taken to running up a red flag on the flagpole when Cora set off to the cove, which told everyone on the estate that the beach was out of bounds.

So far, this rule had been observed absolutely; no one from the house would go near the beach while the red flag was flying, but this morning as she surfaced from one of her seal-like plunges underwater, Cora saw a figure coming down the path to the beach. Her poor eyesight meant that she could not see the figure clearly, but from the black and white of his clothes it could only be Bugler. He stood at the edge of the beach hovering, to step on to the beach would be heresy, but whatever it was must have been urgent for the man to have come this far. In compromise he called to Bertha to come over to him. Cora, treading water just out of her depth so that the water concealed everything except her head, watched as the maid picked her way gingerly across the shingle. The butler bent down to speak to her and Cora saw the maid start and then run back down the beach, waving and shouting. The butler retreated up the hill. Cora could not make out what Bertha was saying but she understood that she wanted her to get out. She swam slowly to the shore and started to pick her way across the sharp stones, feeling the wind dry the salt on her skin. She reached gratefully for the linen sheet that Bertha held out to her.

'What's happened, Bertha? Is it Ivo?'

'No, Miss Cora, it is the Double Duchess. She is arriving by the morning train.' Bertha's voice was neutral. She knew that her news would not be welcome.

Cora gasped. 'But I haven't invited her! She can't just arrive like this, without notice. Does she think that she is still mistress of Lulworth?' Bertha said nothing, but held out Cora's wrapper. Cora struggled to get it on over her damp skin.

'I haven't seen her since Ivo went to India and now she is here. She knows he's on his way back, of course.' Bertha knelt down and helped Cora into her slippers. Cora leant on her as they walked slowly back across the shingle beach. Duchess Fanny had written to her several times since she had been at Lulworth, letters full of detail about her visits to Sandringham and Chatsworth and plenty of exhortations to Cora to take care of her unborn child. Cora had long ago stopped reading the letters with attention: she really had no desire to know how many birds the Prince of Wales had bagged or that the Duchess of Rutland, whom she had never met, had quite lost her figure. She had been unpleasantly surprised by how well informed Duchess Fanny was about her life at Lulworth; her last letter had been a lecture on the follies of swimming in her condition. The letter had been so irritating that she had thrown it into the fire. But the arrival of the Duchess in person was far worse. Cora knew that the Duchess had enjoyed the debacle over the Louvain portrait, and she suspected from what Mrs Wyndham and Sybil had hinted that the Duchess lost no opportunity to mock her American daugher-in-law.

At the top of the cliff was the little donkey cart that Cora used to get around the estate now that she could no longer ride or even walk very far in comfort. Cora picked up the reins and gave them an irritable shake as they headed back to the house. She shook her head impatiently as Bertha tried to spread her wet hair out to dry.

'Oh, leave it alone, Bertha.'

'But Miss Cora, supposing the Duchess has already arrived?' Bertha sounded worried.

'Well, what if she has? This is my house now. If I choose to go about with wet hair, it is really none of her concern.' But as they approached the house and Cora saw the carriage already drawn up outside the house, she tried to shape her damp locks into a more seemly braid. She thought for a moment of going into the house through the servants' wing and avoiding the Double Duchess until she had had a chance to change, but she could not face the idea of walking past the servants, who would know, of course, exactly why she was coming in the back way.

As she hesitated at the door, she heard the Duchess's voice already taking possession.

'The Stuart room, I think, Bugler. The Prince was always very happy there, despite its Jacobite associations. So strange to be here and not to sleep in my bedroom.' There was a trace of huskiness in the Duchess's voice and Cora imagined Bugler's sympathetic bow. But the Duchess recovered herself and said, 'Sybil can have her usual room.'

Cora's spirits lifted at the mention of Sybil, and she made herself walk into the room. Duchess Fanny was sitting in one of the carved chairs by the fireplace, flanked by Bugler and her step-daughter. She did not get up when she saw Cora but simply beckoned to her with one long white hand. Cora could see the flash of diamonds as her mother-in-law tilted her wrist.

'Cora, my dear girl.' Duchess Fanny's voice trailed away in reproach. 'When Bugler told me you had gone swimming I was simply amazed. Surely you must understand the risks to someone in your condition. Didn't you get my letter?' As she waved her hands the diamonds flashed again.

Cora felt the baby turn and kick her under the ribs. She gave a little gasp of discomfort, but the prod dissipated the irritation the Duchess had provoked. She nodded to the Duchess and smiled at Sybil.

'Welcome to Lulworth. I apologise for not being here to meet you but then I had no idea you were coming today.' She said this as affably as she could. 'You must excuse me while I change. Bugler will look after you, of course.' She looked over at the butler who, she noticed, did not look at all surprised by the arrival of the Double Duchess.

She turned towards the staircase and started the heavy climb to her room. That was why she swam, to remember what it was to feel light again. She heard a step behind her and felt Sybil's hand at her elbow.

'Let me help you, Cora.'

As they got to the landing, Sybil burst out, 'I am so sorry. I thought you knew we were coming. Mama said she had written to you.'

Cora remembered the letter she had thrown on the fire.

'Don't worry, Sybil, I am always glad to see *you*. How is Reggie?'

Sybil blushed, her skin clashing with her red-gold hair. 'I think he was about to make an offer but then Mama insisted that we come down here.' She realised what she had said and reddened even more. 'I wanted to see you, of course, but I had arranged to go riding in the park with Reggie tomorrow.'

Cora began to feel better. She felt sorry for Sybil, of course, but she was happy to be reminded that as a married woman she was no longer subject to the whims of mothers. She suspected that Duchess Fanny knew all about Sybil's hopes and was determined to thwart them. Reggie Greatorex was a perfectly suitable husband for Sybil but the Double Duchess did not want to lose her companion, particularly one whose youthful charms did nothing to eclipse her own. If Sybil had looked like Charlotte Beauchamp, the Duchess would have married her off without a moment's hesitation, but gawky Sybil was a foil, not a rival.

She smiled. 'Well, perhaps we can prevail on Reggie to come and ride with you here. When Ivo comes back.' Cora paused. 'It can't be long now. His last letter was from Port Said.' She put her hand on her belly and sighed. 'He really should be here. Still, I am delighted you have come, Sybil, even if the circumstances are not ideal. Do you know how long the Duchess intends to stay? It's not a question I can very well ask.'

Sybil looked surprised. 'Well, I think she wants to be here for the . . .' She trailed off and colour mottled her cheeks. Sybil could not bring herself to say the word birth.

Cora looked at her in dismay. 'She plans to stay here until the baby comes? But what on earth for? Is it some kind of custom that she should be present? Another Maltravers tradition that I don't know about?' Cora's voice came out high and strained, she could feel tears gathering behind her eyelids.

Sybil shook her head miserably, 'I don't think it's a tradition, I think it's just what Mama thought was right. She said she wanted to be sure that everything was done properly.'

Cora tipped her head back to hold back the tears. She did not want to cry in front of Sybil. But she felt as if she had been invaded. She had spent the last few months trying to feel at home at Lulworth and now the precarious balance she had achieved was about to be upset. She had spent so much time in these last lonely months imagining the reunion with Ivo. There had been nights when she had cried because she could not quite remember his face. She did not know exactly who Ivo would be when he came home, but she was certain that he would not welcome the presence of his mother.

'Cora, don't you think there should be somebody here? It's not right that you should be on your own at this time.' Sybil put her hand timidly on Cora's arm. 'I know Mama can be overbearing but she is at least experienced.'

Cora forced herself to smile. 'Indeed she is! But I shan't be on my own. My parents will be here next week and I expect Ivo any day now. Your stepmother would have known this if she had asked me.' She put her hand on Sybil's. 'You always call her Mama even though she is only your stepmother. Don't you mind?'

Sybil looked confused by the change of subject. 'She asked me to when she married Father, and actually, Cora, I don't mind. My mother died when I was little. I can hardly remember her now. You can't imagine what it's like to grow up in a family of men, with no one there to tell you what to wear or how to behave. I remember once coming down to tea when Father had guests, wearing a red dress of my mother's. I thought it looked lovely but I knew the moment I walked into the room that it was all wrong. All the women in the room were trying not to laugh. It was Mama – well, she wasn't Mama then, but still Duchess of Wareham – who took me aside and told me that the dress was too grown-up for me, and she actually spoke to Father and told him that I needed some "suitable" clothes. Father didn't see the point of spending money on things that couldn't be ridden or shot, but he couldn't refuse when Mama asked him.'

Cora's surprise must have shown on her face, because Sybil said, 'I know you think she's interfering, Cora, but that's because you have a mother already. You don't need guidance.'

Cora was about to say that she didn't think that Sybil really needed the kind of guidance that stopped her from marrying the man she had set her heart on, but then she thought better of it. She did, indeed, have a mother and while she found little to rejoice about in that relation, when she looked at Sybil with her rounded back and awkward stride, it occurred to her that perhaps her mother had been useful after all.

Feeling sorry for Sybil cheered Cora up and she said briskly, 'Well, I must get changed if I am to have any chance of sitting down to lunch with you all. Not to be late for meals was something my mother did teach me.' She gestured towards her dressing room. 'And afterwards, Sybil, we must see what is in there that will do for you. It will be a season out of date, of course, but I dare say nobody in London will notice.' She smiled at Sybil.

'Reggie certainly won't,' she said.

As there were only ladies present, Cora asked for lunch to be served in the long gallery to take advantage of the afternoon sunshine. She had the satisfaction of seeing her mother-in-law give a theatrical gasp of surprise as she walked in.

'How charming this is! I never thought to eat in here. But for a cold lunch, what could be nicer.' Duchess Fanny swept down the gallery and waited for the footman to pull out her chair. 'Of course, I would have hesitated before giving the servants any extra trouble. Poor Wareham used to say that I was much too soft-hearted to run a house like Lulworth. But I believe that a sympathetic mistress is always rewarded with loyalty.' Cora watched as Duchess Fanny lifted her heavy blue eyes to look at Bugler who was handing round the crayfish soufflé. Bugler did not actually reply but the reverential tilt of his body as he leant in towards the Duchess with the soufflé was assent enough.

Cora ignored this taunt, looking up instead at the vaulted stone roof. Every time she sat in this room she was reminded that everything around her was older than anything in her native country. Whatever was said and done in here would fade away but the room itself would endure.

The soothing nature of this thought was dispelled when she heard Duchess Fanny say, 'But you have changed things around in here, Cora. I remember my wedding bouquet always used to stand here,' she gestured, 'next to the fireplace. I had it cast in wax after I married Wareham. Such a lovely memento. I remember feeling sad about leaving it here but then it would hardly have done to take it to Conyers.' She looked at Sybil. 'You know I would never do anything that would upset your dear father. But Cora, I hope my bouquet is safe and sound?' She raised an eyebrow at her daughter-in-law.

Before Cora could reply, Bugler coughed softly and said, 'I think Your Grace will find that the bouquet is at the other end of the gallery. It was moved at the request of Her Grace.' His tone made it quite clear which Duchess could better lay claim to the title. Cora did not notice the implied insult at first, she was just relieved that the wretched object had not been removed to the attics as she had asked a month ago. How was she to know that it was a wedding bouquet? Then it struck her that the wax bouquet was still in the gallery because her orders had been ignored. She might be the Duchess of Wareham now, but it was clear that, unlike her predecessor, she did not command the loyalty of her servants.

Duchess Fanny smiled serenely. 'It is sentimental of me, I know, but as one gets older, these things become so precious.' She gave a charming sigh and raised a glittering hand to dab her eyes with a tiny handkerchief. There were perhaps not quite enough tears to warrant this gesture.

'But enough of my nonsense.' Duchess Fanny tilted her chin bravely at Cora. 'Tell me, my dear, when does Wilson expect your confinement?'

'But I am not using Wilson. Sir Julius Sercombe will be attending. He thinks it will be another two weeks.' Cora laid a hand across her belly.

Duchess Fanny's wistfulness evaporated. 'Julius Sercombe! But he's in Harley Street. Surely you don't intend to travel to London?'

Cora shook her head, 'Oh no. As I have been told often enough that the Maltravers heirs are born at Lulworth, Sir Julius has kindly agreed to come here. I expect him at the end of next week.' Cora took a mouthful of the soufflé, she felt ravenous.

'Sir Julius is prepared to leave his practice and all his London engagements to await your confinement? How . . . accommodating of him. But if you had asked me I would have told you to use Wilson. He is an excellent doctor and has looked after the Maltravers for years. Why, he was there when Ivo came into the world.' The Duchess's hand began to reach for the handkerchief.

Cora smiled. 'Dr Wilson is most amiable but as this is my first child I wanted to be sure that I had the best and Sir Julius delivers all the royal babies, you know. He was reluctant to leave London to begin with, but he was so pleased with the Maltravers Wing for his new hospital that he changed his mind.' She gestured to

Bugler to bring her a second helping of the soufflé, it really was quite delicious.

'The Maltravers Wing! How magnificent that sounds,' said Sybil who had been following the conversation warily.

'Indeed,' said Duchess Fanny, widening her eyes. 'What kind of hospital is it, dear?'

'For women and children, in Whitechapel. Sir Julius believes that there is a great deal to be done in that part of London. There are women there who are forced to wrap their newborn babies in flour sacks because they have no money for baby clothes. When he told me of his plans and the difficulties he was having raising the money, I was determined to help him.'

A footman passed round the table, taking away the empty plates. When he had finished, Duchess Fanny asked, 'And tell me, Cora, whose idea was it to call it the Maltravers Wing? Yours or Ivo's?'

Cora was shifting in her chair, trying to relieve the pressure on her diaphragm from her belly, so she did not see the alert expression on her mother-in-law's face, or the blush that was beginning to threaten Sybil's freckles.

'Actually, it was my mother's idea. She and Father made the endowment as all my money here is tied up in the estate, and I wanted to do something more substantial than my allowance permitted.' Cora sat up straight, having at last shifted the pressure from her chest. She saw that Duchess Fanny was smiling at her a little too warmly.

'Well, I think it might be wise to let Ivo know before you commit to a name,' said the Double Duchess. 'Donate to good causes by all means, but I think there is something rather . . . unnecessary about putting your name on things.'

Cora took a sip of water and struggled to swallow. She realised, to her horror, that Ivo might react to this use of the Maltravers name as the Duchess had done. He might have another attack of the 'scruples' that made him so peculiar about the Rubens. At last the water slipped past the lump in her throat. But she would not give her mother-in-law the satisfaction of knowing this. She took a deep breath.

'At home there are three hospitals, a college and a library named after my family. My father often says that anyone can acquire wealth, the real art is giving it away.' Cora took a generous helping of the sole veronique. The food seemed especially appetising today; clearly the Double Duchess's arrival was having its effect in the kitchen.

'Your father is such a charming man.' Duchess Fanny's emphasis on the word 'father' implied that such charm did not extend to his wife or daughter. 'But we do things rather differently here. I suppose you are familiar with the phrase, "charity begins at home". Of course, hospitals and libraries are fine things, but I always think it is the simple personal touch that makes such a difference to people's lives.'

The Duchess turned to Sybil for support but her stepdaughter was staring intently at the plate in front of her, cutting her food into smaller and smaller pieces, desperate not to be involved in the duel in front of her. With a little shake of her head, the Duchess continued, 'Why, only last week I spent the afternoon reading to old Mrs Patchett, one of the Conyers pensioners, who is blind. She always says that when I read to her it brings the words to life and she can see all the characters. It's really quite embarrassing how grateful she is, but I feel it is the least I can do – I only wish it were possible for me to visit her more often. Bricks and mortar have their own value, of course, but nothing can take the place of simple human contact, of personal kindness given and bestowed.' Duchess Fanny leant back in her chair, quite pink with the memory of her own benevolence.

Cora put down her fork with a clatter; the other woman's self-satisfaction was intolerable to her, she would not be lectured by this univited guest, family or not.

'Well, that explains why there is no school in the village and why the Maltravers almshouses are permanently damp. As soon as Ivo returns, I intend to set up a proper schoolhouse and to make the almshouses habitable. I think that would be a true kindness to the villagers of Lulworth.' She took a bite of the boneless quail stuffed with sausage meat and noticed that the Duchess had left hers untouched. Sybil was doing her best to look fully absorbed in the process of eating.

Duchess Fanny sighed in mock defeat. 'You Americans are always so practical – no room in your brave new world for our faded notions of honour and duty.' She half closed her eyes as if focusing on a target and sat up a little straighter, readying herself to deliver the *coup de grâce*. 'And when is Ivo coming back, dear? I rather thought he might be here already.'

Cora looked up, surprised by the certainty in her mother-in-law's tone. 'His last letter was from Port Said. So I expect him next week.'

The Double Duchess's mouth curved triumphantly. 'But dear Cora, Ivo is already back in England. I saw the Prince of Wales last night and he said that Prince Eddy and the whole party had docked yesterday at Southampton.'

Cora put down the fork that was halfway to her mouth and forced herself to smile. She would not give her mother-in-law the satisfaction of seeing her consternation.

'Oh, that is wonderful news. I expect he is on his way here now. He must have been hoping to surprise me.' She looked at Sybil, wondering why she, at least, had not told her that Ivo was back, but Sybil was looking at her stepmother in astonishment. The Double Duchess had clearly been hoarding this information.

The Double Duchess put her hand to her mouth in a pantomime of apology. 'Oh no, how thoughtless of me! I will have spoilt his scheme. But after all, in your condition, perhaps that is not such a bad thing. How unfortunate if anything were to happen before the arrival of Sir Julius.' Her voice was sympathetic, but Cora could see the glint of malice in her eyes. She had to get away, so taking a deep breath, she said as calmly as she could, 'I am sorry but I must ask you to excuse me. I am tired and if Ivo is to arrive at any moment I would like to rest now. Perhaps, Duchess, you would be kind enough to tell Bugler that the Duke is to be expected. I am sure all the servants will want to be there to greet him.' She stood up painfully, her body heavy with the shock. She bit her lip, desperate to stop the tears that were threatening to overwhelm her. Ivo was back, this was the moment she had been waiting for all these months, but now it had all been spoilt. She stumbled away down the gallery, the Duchess's voice in her ears.

'Oh, I am sure Bugler knows already. It's uncanny how servants always sense these things.' Duchess Fanny looked up, with a complicit smile, at the footman who was serving the crème brulée. The footman's face did not flicker but his hand shook slightly as the Duchess struck the caramel with a swift sharp blow, plunging the spoon into the yielding custard beneath.

CHAPTER 22

The Homecoming

TOM, THE TELEGRAPH BOY, WONDERED WHAT would happen if he removed his cap. It was expressly forbidden under post office rules but it was a warm day and there was no one to see him here in the Lulworth woods. On the other hand, if Mr Veale was to hear that he had been improperly dressed, he would be sent back to his mother in Langton Maltravers. Mr Veale had fined Tom sixpence the week before for allowing the silver buttons on his tunic to become tarnished; another boy had been dismissed for delivering a telegram with his stiff collar unfastened. Tom decided that the immediate relief of removing his cap, which was too small and rubbed painfully against his temples, was not worth the risk of being discovered. Mr Veale had a way of knowing when rules had been broken. He was fond of saying that he could 'smell an infringement'. Tom had not been clear what an infringement was, until the incident with the buttons, and even now he wondered how they could be smelt. All five remaining telegraph boys reeked of the same things: inky serge, sweat and the bicarbonate of soda they used to shine their buttons. In winter they smelt a bit less and in summer a bit more.

It was three miles from the post office in Lulworth to the house.

Mr Veale always sent Tom because he could walk the fastest. Twenty-one minutes on the way there and seventeen on the return journey, which was downhill. Mr Veale had told him to do it today in twenty minutes because the telegram was from the Duke. Tom was doing his best, bowling along at a loping pace midway between a walk and a run. He had set off at nine exactly and although he did not carry a pocket watch, he knew that he was making good time because he had heard the single chime from the Lulworth church bell which marked the quarter hour. He was at the part of the drive that curved behind a clump of beech trees before emerging into the open and revealing the house itself. There was no longer any question of removing his cap, Tom knew that he could be seen from any one of the glittering windows ahead of him. He loosened the strap under his chin a notch so that there would not be a red welt there, and thought of the glass of lemonade he would be given in the cool kitchen, as he pressed on towards the house.

Bertha spotted him from the window of Miss Cora's room. Her mistress was still in bed, not sleeping but staring up at the canopy as if it was a map. Bertha was unnerved by this, as she was by Cora's silence. She had heard the rumours last night at supper about the Duke's return. Mr Bugler thought he would be home today and had all the footmen put on their dress livery. Bertha herself had put on her best cream silk tussore blouse. It had been Miss Cora's, of course, but she had never worn it. As a rule Bertha avoided light colours because they made her appear darker but after an English winter her skin needed the glow of the pearly silk. She had laid out the pale green tea gown with the swans-down trim for her mistress, which to her mind was the most becoming of Miss Cora's current ensembles. But Cora had refused to entertain the notion of getting dressed, shaking her head when Bertha tried to coax her out of bed. She had even refused Bertha's attempts to do her hair, which lay in limp hanks on her pillow. Bertha was used to her mistress's moods but she had never known them to interfere with dressing her hair before. Miss Cora could be tiresome but she didn't give up on things. Bertha didn't understand why her mistress was moping like this. All she had been doing for the last five months was wait for the Duke to come home, and now he was most likely on his way she was lying there like a corpse.

She turned from the window. 'I can see the telegraph boy, Miss Cora.'

There was no reply.

'I expect it'll be from the Duke. Maybe he is coming on the afternoon train.'

The silence continued. Bertha watched as the telegraph boy started to climb the steps up to the house.

'I reckon Mr Bugler will be bringing the telegram up here in a minute, Miss Cora. Maybe you want to get ready?'

Cora's eyes did not flicker from her scrutiny of the canopy.

Bertha began to feel irritated. If Cora couldn't see the truth of things, she would have to tell her. There were times of late when she felt more like Cora's mother than her maid. She began to speak briskly.

'If I was coming home after five months in India, I would like to see my wife dressed up and looking pleased to see me, not lying in her bed staring at the ceiling. Come on, Miss Cora, you don't want Mr Bugler to see you like this.'

Cora gave a sigh and rolled over on to her side before pushing herself upright. She rubbed her eyes with the heel of her hands.

'All right, all right, you can stop scolding me. You're right, of course, Bertha. Bugler will go straight to Duchess Fanny, and then she will come up here and start interfering. Lord knows I thought my mother was bad enough, but the Duchess really is the end.' She stretched out her hands and then let them drop in her lap. 'I just don't understand why Ivo didn't come straight home.'

Bertha had almost finished pinning Cora's hair in place when Bugler came in with the telegram on a silver salver. Cora opened it without haste and dropped the telegram on to the polished tray when she had finished.

'The Duke will be here for dinner tonight, Bugler. If you could let Cook know, I am sure she will want to prepare something special.'

Bugler bent his head in the shallowest possible bow. 'I believe the Duchess of Buckingham has already spoken to Mrs Whitchurch, Your Grace.'

Bertha was impressed by the way that Cora did not react to this. Instead, she smiled without showing her teeth, and said, 'Indeed! How thoughtful of her.' She put her hand to her hair and brought down one ringlet that she proceeded to curl round her fingers. Bugler hovered, clearly impatient to be gone but unable to move until he had been formally dismissed.

'Will that be all, Your Grace?'

'Yes, I think so, Bugler. No, actually, I do have one request.' She spoke to Bugler in the mirror. 'Duchess Fanny's bouquet, the one from her first wedding. I thought I had asked for it to be removed from the long gallery. Kindly see to it before the Duke arrives.'

Cora caught Bertha's eye in the mirror and tilted her chin. Bertha saw that her mistress's face had lost its sulky heaviness and that there were spots of colour in her cheeks. When she had finished pinning Cora's hair she stood back and said, 'You look quite fine today, Miss Cora.'

Cora looked back at Bertha. 'Do you really think so? I've changed so much though. When Ivo left, I was still in corsets. If he had been here, he would have had time to get used to me . . . swelling.' She put her hands over her stomach. 'When he is confronted with this, I'm afraid he will get quite a shock.' She picked up the black pearl necklace from its green velvet home and handed it to Bertha to fasten.

Bertha slid the gold hook through the eye and pushed it into the diamond clasp. She wondered if the Duke would indeed be taken aback by Cora's appearance. When he left she had been hardly showing; now her whole body had altered; as well as the round globe of her stomach, there were blue veins crossing her décolletage and her face was softer and rounder. Even Cora's voice had changed; as her pregnancy progressed, it had become deeper and huskier, she had quite lost her pert American twang. But at least, thought Bertha, she no longer looks so like the girl in the portrait which had been left leaning unwanted against the wall of the gallery at Bridgewater House. Bugler was fond of describing the picture as shocking, even though to Bertha's knowledge he had never actually seen it. She was the only servant at Lulworth who had set eyes upon the portrait, but when asked her opinion she had pretended ignorance. She knew that Bugler, for one, had not believed her, but she did not want to join them in condemning it. She understood that to do so was really a way of running down Cora herself; Bugler could not allow disrespectful talk of the

Duchess herself in the servants' hall, but the portrait was another matter. There had been times over the last few months when Bertha had wondered whether her decision to hold herself aloof from the gossip in the servants' hall had been the right one, but some loyalty to Cora and a feeling that no concession to her fellow servants would ever make her belong stopped her.

She caught Cora's eye in the mirror and said with more firmness than she felt, 'I think the Duke will be happy enough to see you carrying his child.'

Cora nodded her head. 'Perhaps. It is, after all, the thing only *I* can give him. An heir.'

The Duke's telegram had simply said, 'Arriving this evening. Wareham.' Even allowing for the essentially public nature of the communication which would be read by the postmasters in London and Lulworth, not to mention the telegraph boy, Cora felt the economy of those four words keenly. There was nothing for her there, no hint that he was looking forward to coming home, to seeing her again. Even his letters to her from India had been signed, 'Your affectionate husband, Wareham.' At the time she had found 'affectionate' less than adequate as a term of endearment, but now she would have welcomed anything more conciliatory than this stark statement of facts. She still could not believe that Ivo had been in the country for two whole days without letting her know.

She had been anticipating the moment of his return for so long, rehearsing the conversations she would have with him in her head, planning the food, the company, the flowers. She had ordered the head gardener, Mr Jackson, to force hundreds of jasmine plants so they would be ready for his arrival, as he had once told her that it was his favourite flower. She had been practising the Schubert duets they had played together so that she could play her part from memory. She had spent many hours with Father Oliver trying to piece together the complicated narrative of the Maltravers family so that she could refer casually to the Fourth Duke's stammer or the bloodlines of the Lulworth lurchers. She had done everything she could think of to be a convincing Duchess. An English Duchess, who knew the rules, who knew how to do more than spend money. But it had not occurred to her that Ivo might not be as eager to play his part in the reunion as she was. She had imagined him arriving post-haste from Southampton, salty and fervent. And yet here she was with the sort of telegram he might have sent to his butler. Surely she had done her penance for the portrait affair, sequestered here at Lulworth with nothing to do for months.

She decided that she would not go down to lunch. She had no desire for another skirmish with the Double Duchess. Perhaps she would send for Sybil and sort out some dresses for her.

There was a knock at the door and a footman brought in the second post of the day. There were two letters, one from London, the other from Paris. On one she recognised Mrs Wyndham's handwriting; the other hand also looked familiar but it took her a moment to remember where she had seen it before. Those backward-leaning strokes that betrayed the author's left-handedness she recalled from the ivory tablets that were used as dance cards at the Newport balls. She reached for the paper knife and opened the letter impatiently.

Dear Cora,

I hope I may still call you Cora. I am afraid I still think of you as Cora Cash even though I know that you are now that very august creation, an English duchess. I write to you because I am coming to London for the summer – I have been invited to share a studio in Chelsea and I have been furnished with an introduction to Louvain, whose work, as you know, I admire greatly. But of course the greatest attraction of England is that it is now the country where you live. I imagine that your days and nights are filled with your new duties but may I claim the privilege of an old friend and visit with you? If, in view of our last encounter, this prospect seems painful to you then I can only apologise in advance; but if you can think of me now as a friend whose affection is nothing but disinterested, then please send me word. We have known each other since childhood after all and I hope that our friendship may continue.

Your affectionate friend,
Teddy Van Der Leyden

Cora felt a dull ache at the base of her spine as she read the letter. She started when she saw the name Louvain and wondered if Teddy had heard about the portrait. But as she read on, she realised that Teddy would not have written with such candour if he had known about her contretemps last summer. He was, she reflected, still in Paris and so it was quite possible that the little scandal surrounding the portrait had not reached him. He would learn of it, she was sure, but at least she would have the chance to talk to him first. She thought sadly that the tone of Teddy's letter was more affectionate than anything she had received from her husband. Teddy had written to *her*. Ivo's letters had been well written, full of wry observations about the Indian princes and their courts and the difficulties of anticipating Prince Eddy's erratic behaviour. But though they were letters worth reading, they were not the letters she wanted to read. She had longed for a letter that was for her and her alone, a letter which would give her some glimpse into his heart. But apart from some of the less circumspect remarks about the Prince, there was nothing in Ivo's letters that could not have been published in *The Times*. It was if they had been sent merely as a record of his visit; nowhere did she find a sentence or even a phrase – and she had looked with considerable thoroughness – which suggested that he was writing to a woman he still loved. She had hoped that perhaps this lack of epistolary emotion was one of those English habits that had to be understood and tolerated, like the strange reluctance to shake hands or their pride in speaking in such an exaggerated drawl as to be almost incomprehensible. She knew she was still learning the customs of the country, but Teddy's letter with its open plea for her friendship could only make her wonder if her husband's reserve was not so much a product of his upbringing as a sign that he no longer cared for her.

She wrote a short note to Teddy, inviting him to stay in the summer at his convenience. She extolled the beauties of Lulworth, 'Indeed the light here is softer and more luminous in the late afternoons than anything we have at home,' and hinted at the forthcoming birth, 'When I see you I hope I will be able to introduce you to a new member of my family.' They were, she thought, the words of an English duchess. But at the end she tried to match his candour with her own. 'I look forward to seeing you again very much. My life has changed greatly but not so much that I can discard the friends of my youth. I may be called Duchess now but I am still an American girl who sometimes misses the country of her birth. Please come to Lulworth, it would give me great pleasure to see you again. Sincerely yours, Cora Wareham.' She read the note through and then added as a postscript, 'And I look forward to introducing you to my husband.'

She directed the letter to Teddy care of the Traveller's Club and rang for the footman. When her note had been safely dispatched, she turned to the other letter. This turned out to be a gossipy dissection of the London season so far; Mrs Wyndham was acting as sponsor to the Tempest twins from San Francisco, who were as rich as they were pert and had already acquired a number of aristocratic suitors, 'But my dear Cora,' Mrs Wyndham wrote, 'they are well aware of your magnificent marriage, and have declared themselves indifferent to anyone below the rank of duke. Indeed they frequently speculate whether they should spend the rest of the summer in Europe where it would be considerably easier for them to become princesses. I have pointed out, in vain, that a marquis or an earl of an early creation here in England is quite the equal of any continental prince but now that you have become a duchess they can think of nothing else but outranking you!'

Cora smiled at this. She knew Mrs Wyndham was concerned that she was losing some of her most promising protégées to Paris or Italy where princes and dukes were plentiful. Winaretta Singer, the sewing machine heiress, had gone straight to Paris for her debut and had married the Prince de Polignac eight weeks after her arrival. The only princes in England were of royal blood and they were still beyond the reach of American money. But Cora did not envy the new Princess de Polignac. She had found Parisian society to be even less welcoming than London. Thanks to a succession of French governesses, Cora spoke the language with some fluency but even so she had difficulty in following the brittle chatter of the Parisian *bon ton*. Besides, it was rumoured that all Frenchmen kept mistresses whether they were married or not. She remembered seeing a ravishing woman in the Bois de Boulogne. She had been wearing a striped lilac silk gown trimmed with black lace, but it had been the sinuous quality of her walk that had arrested Cora. She moved so fluidly that Cora found herself staring at her just for the pleasure of seeing her glide along the gravel paths of the Bois. When she had asked Madame St Jacques, their companion in Paris, who the woman was, she had said quite matter-of-factly that she was Liane de Rougement, and that she was currently under the protection of the Baron Gallimard. 'Although there has been talk that she may transfer her favours to the Duc de Ligne.' Cora had tried to conceal her astonishment. She knew that such women existed, of course, but she had not expected to find one so immaculately dressed walking unconcerned through the cream of Parisian high society. No, she did not envy the Princess de Polignac.

She scanned the rest of Mrs Wyndham's letter. Although she understood why the other woman felt she had to include the genealogy of all the people she mentioned – 'I went to the Londonderrys last night, the Marchioness is of course a Percy and is related to the Beauchamps through her mother': knowledge that Madeline Wyndham felt was essential if the American Duchess was ever to blend into her new background – Cora found the skein of connections tedious. But the penultimate paragraph did pique her interest. Mrs Wyndham was describing the *tableaux vivants* given by Lady Salisbury in aid of the Red Cross the day before. The *tableaux* had been of great women of history. The

Duchess of Manchester had appeared as Queen Elizabeth, Lady Elcho had been Boadicea, in a chariot drawn by real ponies, but the *pièce de résistance* was to be Charlotte Beauchamp as Joan of Arc – 'in rehearsal she was quite magnificent dressed as a boy soldier'. But in the interval between the dress rehearsal in the morning and the performance itself, Charlotte Beauchamp had simply disappeared. 'In the end Violet Paget had to take her place but she was no substitute for Lady Beauchamp. I could see that Sir Odo, who was in the audience, had no idea what had happened to his wife although he did say that she had complained of a headache that morning. Personally, I thought she looked the picture of health at the dress rehearsal. Their Royal Highnesses went so far as to express their concern.'

Cora was surprised by this story. She found it hard to imagine what would prevent Charlotte from taking centre stage in front of the Prince and Princess of Wales. She thought it unlikely that anything as trivial as a headache would deter Charlotte from performing at such an event. Parts in Lady Salisbury's *tableaux vivants* were keenly sought after. Leading roles were reserved for the acknowledged beauties of the age. Something, Cora thought, quite momentous must have happened to stop Charlotte from stepping on to the stage in her Joan of Arc costume, her long slim legs clad only in hose.

At the end of her letter, after a gentle hint that Cora might like to entertain her twin heiresses – 'you would find them quite in awe of you' – Mrs Wyndham wrote, 'I have just heard that the Duke is back in the country. You must be so happy to have him home. I trust that that unfortunate business with Louvain is now quite forgotten and you can take up the position in society that is rightfully yours.'

Cora put the letter down and leant back in her chair – the ache in her back was now more pronounced. She was clearly the last person in the country to know that her husband was back. Even Mrs Wyndham knew more about her husband's movements than she did. It was humiliating. She stood up painfully and started to move slowly around the room. When she stopped to gaze out of the window overlooking the lawns down to the sea, she could just make out a pink shape and a green shape moving towards the summer house. It could only be her mother-in-law and Sybil. Her eyesight was too bad to make out their faces, but she felt cheered, imagining the older woman's discovery of the statue of Eros and Psyche by Canova in the pavilion. It was a beautiful piece, but Cora thought it unlikely that her mother-in-law would share that view.

Her train of thought was interrupted by a sudden acceleration of the grumbling pain in her back, as if iron fingers were squeezing her innards. She put her hand on the window frame to steady herself and the pain subsided. Sir Julius had said that if the pain came regularly it was a sign that the baby was coming. She put her forehead against the glass and breathed out slowly, trying to still her bubbling thoughts. She did not want the baby to come today, she wanted to be ready, fragrant and charming, her black pearl necklace round her neck, when her husband returned. Even if he did not care for her any more, she still wanted to look her best. But as the pink and green shapes disappeared into the summer house, she felt another spasm and she understood that this was beyond her control. She rang the bell and was relieved to see Bertha come into the room moments later.

'Bertha, you need to send for Sir Julius. I think it is time.' Cora winced. 'Go down to the post office and send a cable telling him to come at once.'

Bertha looked at her in concern. 'Of course, Miss Cora, but do you think you should be here on your own? Would you like me to fetch the Duchess or Lady Sybil?'

Cora grimaced. 'No, absolutely not. I don't want to see anyone, particularly not the Duchess. I don't want her to start interfering. No, you must take the donkey cart and go down to Lulworth as quick as you can. Send the cable and wait for the answer. With any luck Sir Julius will catch the afternoon train.'

Bertha hesitated. She could see that Miss Cora's face had turned pale and there were beads of moisture along her hairline. But Bertha knew better than to argue with her.

On her way down to the stables, she wondered if she should tell any of the servants, Mabel perhaps; but then she reflected that nobody could be relied on. Bugler would hear of it, and then it was only a matter of time before the Double Duchess knew everything. Nothing that happened at Lulworth could be concealed from the Double Duchess for long. She had Mrs Cash's relentless eye for detail.

There was a flyblown mirror set in the hatstand that stood in the corridor between the servants' staircase and the back door leading out into the stable yard. Bertha caught her reflection and adjusted her hat so that it perched at the most becoming angle, the brim casting a slight shadow over her eyes.

Mr Veale the postmaster was surprised to see Bertha. Normally any telegrams from the house were brought down by the stable boy. He was alert, naturally, to the implications of the maid's arrival: the contents of this telegram were to be kept private. He looked curiously at the Duchess's maid as she handed him the form. He had heard about her from his niece who worked up at the house in the still room. 'The Duchess gives her dresses that are hardly worn, you wouldn't know from looking at her that she was in service.' Mr Veale, as he looked up at Bertha – she was a little taller than he was – thought that this was almost true, only the tinge of her skin meant that she could never be mistaken for a lady.

He tapped out the message – 'Please come at once, Cora Wareham.' When he had finished and had received an acknowledgement from the post office in Cavendish Square, he looked up again at the maid.

'That's gone through then, Miss . . .'

'Jackson.' The maid's voice was deep and her accent was strong.

'I'll send one of the boys up with the reply, Miss Jackson.'

Bertha shook her head. 'The Duchess wants me to wait.'

Mr Veale felt an itch underneath the hard collar of his uniform. He bristled at the implication that his boys were not to be trusted with a message of a confidential nature. He wanted to remonstrate but he reflected that the Duchess and her maid were both foreigners. They did not know how things were done here.

'Well, if you would care to take a seat, Miss Jackson.' He spoke clearly to be sure that she understood and gestured to the wooden bench that stood against one wall of the post office.

'Thank you, but I would prefer the fresh air. I will go for a walk in the village.'

Mr Veale watched as she stood in the doorway, unfurling her parasol. At this angle, with her back to him, she did indeed look like a lady.

Bertha strolled slowly down the village street. She had not been to Lulworth more than once or twice since they had come to the house. On her rare days off she preferred to walk in the park or stay in her room and read illustrated magazines. It was a pretty enough street, the houses all built from the same grey stone, their roofs mostly thatched although some of the larger ones had slate roofs. Bertha had been amazed when she first saw the thatched cottages. Miss Cora had called them quaint but Bertha thought they looked shabby. She thought that the overhanging eaves looked like the hairy eyebrows of old men. She twirled her parasol. Its colour exactly matched the cream of her blouse. Miss Cora had ordered them at the same time; she would only carry a parasol that matched her dress.

Bertha was aware that she was being watched as she walked down the street. There were a few women hanging up washing, as it was a fine day, and the bench in front of the Square and Compass was, as usual, filled with old men. She had been surprised when she had first come to Dorset by how small the villagers were. At home she was tall, but not excessively so, but here in the village she felt like a giant. She regularly saw men, working in the fields, who only came up to her shoulder. Bertha looked at the cottages with their frowning roofs and low doors and wondered whether their inhabitants simply had no room to grow. As she walked past a line of washing, she saw how patched and worn the smocks and petticoats were, they reminded her of the washing lines back in South Carolina. She smoothed her skirts, the silky material reminding her that she had escaped that threadbare existence. If it hadn't been for the Reverend and Mrs Cash, she would have been like those women hanging out rags. She wondered if her mother had got the last letter she had sent her and the money.

She had sent her twenty-five pounds, that was a hundred and twenty-five dollars. How many mothers had daughters who could send them that kind of money? That thought, along with the swish of her silk skirt, distracted her from the knowledge that she had not heard from her mother since she had come to England and the realisation that, no matter how hard she screwed up her eyes, she could no longer visualise her mother's face.

She turned and walked back to the post office. Mr Veale was standing in the doorway waving at her.

'The answer has come through, Miss Jackson.' He handed her the cable. 'Will be on the 5 o'clock train, Julius Sercombe.' Bertha felt her shoulders fall in relief and she put the paper in her pocket.

'Will that be all, Miss Jackson?' Mr Veale hovered curiously.

'Yes, thank you.'

'I trust everything is well at the house. There must be great excitement about the Duke's return.'

Bertha nodded and took up the reins of the donkey cart, aware that Cora would be counting the minutes till she came back. The postmaster cleared his throat nervously.

'Please convey my respects to Her Grace and tell her that we would be honoured if she were to visit the post office. I would be most happy to show her the telegraph machine at her convenience. It is the latest model, quite the equal of anything in the metropolis.'

Bertha said, 'I will do that, and now if you'll excuse me,' and she flicked her switch across the donkey's broad back. Why on earth did that man imagine that Miss Cora would want to poke around his post office? Perhaps he thought there would be money in it.

She set off along the road that ran up from the station to the gates of the house. She heard the church bells strike quarter to – she had been gone for an hour and a half. She hoped Miss Cora was managing. She gave the donkey another flick. She could see a man a few hundred yards ahead of her, walking along the side of the road. He was moving energetically, his arms and legs pumping, his head held high, so different from the old men shuffling outside the pub. He was smartly dressed too, wearing a dark jacket and a bowler hat. A delicious suspicion ran through her as she shook the reins and urged the donkey to move faster. As the distance between them narrowed, she felt a lurching in her stomach and blood rushing to her cheeks.

'Jim,' she called, her voice cracking with excitement. The man stopped and turned round. For a moment she thought perhaps she had been mistaken, he was so brown and his face was much thinner than she remembered. But then he took off his hat and ran towards her.

'I was just thinking about you,' he said and he smiled. There were new creases around his eyes and mouth, but she remembered the look he was giving her now. She smiled back and put out her arms.

After a few minutes he said, 'What a stroke of luck meeting you on the road like this. I'd been thinking all the way down here how I could get you to myself.' He had climbed up on to the cart and was sitting next to Bertha, leg to leg, their hands touching as she moved the reins.

He breathed into her ear, 'Why don't we pull up in the woods for a bit before we go up to the house? Oh Bertha, it's so good to see you again.' He put his hand over hers and she felt his touch flood through her. She leant against him and allowed him to take the reins. He steered them into woods at the edge of the park.

She watched as he jumped down lightly and tied the reins to a tree. His skin was much darker than she remembered, and his hair was fairer, but his expression was still the same, his blue eyes eager and shining. He held out his hand and she hesitated for a second, thinking of Cora's white face, but he was pulling her down now and there was no space in her mind for anything else but the fact of him.

She pulled away from him at last. 'We can't, not . . . not now.' She tried to push him away as he leant forward to kiss her neck.

'I've waited so long for this . . .' Jim's voice was muffled in her hair.

'I know, but Miss Cora's baby is starting and there is no one with her. I must go back.'

But Jim did not release his hold on her. 'Stay with me, Bertha. She's got a husband and a houseful of servants. I only have you. You don't know how much I've wanted you.' She could feel his fingers fumbling with the buttons at her collar.

She arched away from him and looked at him full on. 'But the Duke's not there and she doesn't want anyone else to know until the doctor comes.'

Jim's fingers stopped trying to tease the tiny mother-of-pearl buttons through the tight little loops.

'The Duke's not at Lulworth?' he said reluctantly.

'He sent a cable to say he would be here this evening. You mean you thought he'd be here?' Bertha felt nervous. Had Jim quarrelled with the Duke, lost his position even?

'I thought he must be. When he didn't come back this morning, I thought he must have come down here and forgotten to send for me.' He frowned. 'His Grace won't be pleased if he goes back to the club and finds I've packed up and brought everything down here. Still, it can't be helped.' He smiled at Bertha. 'I'll just tell him that I couldn't stay away from you a moment longer. He'll understand.'

Bertha felt warmed by the smile, but she could not suppress the twinge of pity she felt for Cora. She shook her head. 'I have to go back, Jim. It's her time and she needs me.'

But Jim pulled her to him and held her fast. 'Oh, she doesn't need you like I do.'

She could hear his breath coming fast and strong. She could smell the starch from his stiff collar melting. She let herself relax against him for a moment, remembering how well they fitted together, but then she twisted away from him and jumped up on to the donkey cart. She did not trust him to let her go willingly, and she knew it would take so very little to make her stay.

CHAPTER 23

'A Bough of Cherries'

ERTHA DID NOT KNOCK. SHE WALKED STRAIGHT in and found Cora leaning against the fireplace with her hands outstretched, her face contorted with the effort of not screaming. Sybil was standing next to her with a handkerchief soaked in eau de cologne.

She was saying to Cora, 'Please, Cora, let me fetch Mama.'

Cora gasped, 'No – I – do – not – want – her – to interfere.' And then the spasm passed and she stood up and saw Bertha.

'Sir Julius is coming, Miss Cora. He'll be here soon.' Bertha would have liked to touch her mistress's arm, to reassure her, but she felt constrained by Sybil's presence.

'Oh, thank God. I don't how much more of this I can bear.' She winced as another contraction began.

Bertha said, 'Excuse me a moment, Miss Cora, I think I know what will help with the pain.' She rushed down the corridor to the servants' staircase where she clattered down the uncarpeted stairs to the warren of offices behind the servants' hall. She knocked on the pantry door where she knew Bugler would be. He was in his shirt sleeves polishing a silver candlestick.

'Mr Bugler, the Duchess needs the key to the poisons cupboard.'

She held out her hand. As soon as she did so she realised that this was a mistake. Bugler did not like the presumption: the poisons cupboard was his responsibility.

'Indeed. May I ask why the Duchess did not ring for me herself?'

Bertha swallowed. 'She is indisposed, Mr Bugler. She does not wish to see anyone just at the present.'

Slowly, Bugler put down the candlestick and motioned Bertha to leave the room with him. She hoped that he would not fully understand the significance of her errand. When he opened the poisons cupboard, which was underneath the cabinet where all the most valuable plate was kept, she walked towards it, hoping to see the bottle straight away, but Bugler was too quick for her. He positioned himself in front of the cabinet, forcing her to ask him for the bottle of Hallston's patent cough medicine.

He handed it over grudgingly. 'You will bring it straight back when Her Grace has finished with it, Miss Jackson. I don't like to leave these preparations lying around. Some of the maids can be very foolish.' He looked directly at Bertha. But she kept her eyes lowered and took the bottle as respectfully as she could; she found herself even giving a little placatory bend of the knees. It worked, evidently, as Bugler said nothing more, and turned his back to her, making a great show of locking up the cupboard again.

Bertha walked as quickly as she could without actually running along the corridor to the servants' staircase. As she passed the door to the kitchen, she could hear a clamour of welcome surrounding Jim. He was very popular with the other servants – a local boy who had achieved great things. They would not be so welcoming, Bertha thought, if they knew that she was his sweetheart.

As she scurried crab-like up the stairs – her petticoats wouldn't let her take them two at a time – she misjudged a step and tripped, the bottle falling out of her hand. For a frozen second she thought it would shatter on the wooden boards but the sturdy brown glass was clearly designed to be proof against trembling fingers and had landed unharmed. The cough medicine was famous for containing large quantities of ether which, according to the legend on the front, dulled all pain and blunted all aches. Bertha had taken some for a toothache when she first arrived in England and had been amazed at the way the sharpness of the pain had been reduced. She had not been tempted to go back for more after the initial pain had faded away but she knew that there were many girls who kept a bottle under their mattress. One of the housemaids had taken so much that, before Christmas, her eyes glassy and her hands wet with sweat, she had dropped a whole tea service on to the scullery floor. The girl's wages for a year were a fraction of the tea service's worth so she had been dismissed. When her room was turned out they had found ten empty bottles of Hallston's patent cough medicine under the mattress. Since then all patent medicines were kept in the poisons cupboard.

Cora was pacing up and down holding on to Sybil when Bertha got back. She wrinkled her nose as she drank the medicine but within a few moments Bertha could see her mistress's eyes begin to lose their focus. Sybil led her to the chaise longue and once she was lying down, Bertha began to loosen the ribbons and laces of her tea gown and to undo the buttons on the patent kid boots.

When the ether began to wear off, Cora noticed what her maid was doing.

'Bertha! I want to look nice for my husband when he comes. You will make sure, won't you?'

Bertha smiled. 'Don't worry about that, Miss Cora.'
Cora held out her hand for some more of the medicine.

The arrival of Sir Julius from London some four hours later confirmed the rumours flying around the village that the Duchess had gone into labour. Outside the Square and Compass the long view taken by the clay-pipe smokers was that a healthy boy could only be good news, as money would have to be spent on improving the estate if the heir was to have anything to inherit. They had all heard of the fabulous wealth of the new Duchess but so far they had seen no evidence of it in repairs to their houses, the draining of ditches or the replanting of hedgerows. In the general store, the talk was more short term, concentrating on the new dresses to be worn at the tenants' dinner traditionally held to celebrate the birth of an heir to the Dukedom. There were mothers who wondered if their daughter might be chosen to work in the nursery and fathers of large families who hoped that their wife might gain employment as a wet nurse. Weld, the stationmaster, anticipated a royal presence at the christening and thought about floral displays, and the churchwarden considered which of his team of bell ringers deserved the honour of ringing in the news.

In the house itself, the servants were being pulled between the activity necessary for the imminent arrival of the Duke and the natural desire to congregate in the kitchen and interpret every call for hot water or clean linen from the Duchess's bedroom. Much of this discussion was theoretical as neither the cook nor Mrs Softley had ever given birth – the title of Mrs was an honorific bestowed with the office, and the maids were, of course, unmarried. Mr Bugler had had to come in more than once to remind his staff that their master was expected any moment and there was still no fire lit in the music room.

Upstairs in the Duchess's apartments there were periods of quiet punctuated by screams that became progressively closer together as the evening drew in. The screams might have been louder if Sir Julius had not been a keen supporter of anaesthesia in childbirth. He held no brief for the argument that physical suffering was a necessary part of labour – a punishment visited on women since Eve's tasting of the forbidden fruit – and neither, in his experience, did his aristocratic clients. He had never attended a birth where a woman had refused the blessed relief of chloroform.

The Duchess's labour was progressing slowly, but that was to be expected in a first delivery. He was a little uneasy that the Duke was not present. In case of difficulty it was imperative to have the husband's consent to any procedures that might be necessary. The Duchess of Buckingham, the famous Double Duchess, had already hinted to him that the Duke wanted an heir 'above all else' but Sir Julius had attended enough noble births to know that the mother-in-law's wishes might not always be that of the husband. He sincerely hoped that there would be no choice to make. He liked the American Duchess. When he had told her about the hospital he was building so that poor women could give birth safely, she had listened carefully and had pledged a sum that had made all the difference to his plans. He had other patients, ladies with money and position who had organised whist drives, bazaars and even concerts in aid of the hospital, but he suspected that they did so as much for their own social ends as out of any great devotion to philanthropy. Certainly the sums raised bore no relation to the effort expended or the numbers of frocks that were ordered. So he had appreciated the Duchess's straightforwardness when it came to money, very much.

The evening was drawing in, and there was still no sign of the baby or of its father. Cora was lost in a twilight world punctuated by pain. She would swim towards consciousness on a contraction and then the sweet smell of the chloroform would knock her back into blankness. Finally she woke to a pain so intense that she imagined for a moment that she was being cut open, and then she heard Bertha telling her that it was going to be all right, and then nothing.

As she came round again, snatches of conversation sank into her emerging consciousness.

'. . . the Maltravers nose, definitely.'

'. . . difficult delivery, I had to use the forceps . . .'

'He's dark, just like his father.'

And then a different sound, one that jerked her into full wakefulness, the thin, clear cry of her baby.

She opened her eyes and saw her mother-in-law, like a great blue crow, holding a white bundle. Cora struggled to sit up and there was Bertha on her other side putting a pillow behind her back.

She tried to speak but her voice was scratched and hoarse.

'My baby . . .' and she put out her arms. The Double Duchess looked across the room at Sir Julius and lowered the baby so that Cora could see him.

'Here he is, the Marquis of Salcombe.' Cora tried to take the baby from her but the Duchess drew back a fraction.

'Don't you want to recover a little, Cora?' she said tightly.

Cora shook her head, 'Give him to me,' she whispered.

The Duchess again looked across at Sir Julius and he said, 'I am delighted to tell you, Duchess, that you have a healthy baby boy.' And then he gestured to Duchess Fanny so that she had no choice but to put the child into Cora's arms.

Cora looked at the tiny wrinkled face, the milky unfocused eyes, the surprisingly abundant hair and she folded him to her.

The light had gone and Cora was in a half sleep, the baby lying in the crook of her elbow. The Double Duchess had left and now there was only the nurse Sir Julius had brought with him, busying herself over the carved and gilded bassinet that Mrs Cash had sent the week before. Cora could hardly resist the downward droop of her eyelids when she heard the first bells. The noise carried so clearly over the valley that Cora did not hear the door open; she brought the baby closer to swaddle him against the clamour and then she felt a hand on her cheek, and there was Ivo kneeling beside her, his lips brushing their son's head.

'You have a son,' she said.

He took her free hand and kissed it. She saw at once that his face was soft with tenderness. There was no trace of anger or constraint there. He had come back to her. He would be the husband she had known on her honeymoon, and now the father to her son. All the waiting was over. She forgot everything, all the worry and anxiety, as she recognised the tenderness in his face. She wanted to give him something in return.

'I thought that the baby should be called Guy, after your brother.'

He said nothing and then he stood up and turned his face away from her towards the window. For an awful moment she thought she had blundered. Ivo hardly talked about his brother but she sensed that he was always somewhere in his thoughts. She had wanted to show him that she understood his loss, but all she had done was to remind him of his grief. She was about to call his name when he turned round. His face was in shadow and she couldn't quite make out the cast of his countenance, but there was no mistaking the tone of his voice.

'Thank you, Cora, now I have everything I want.'

And he lay down beside her and at last she could breathe him in.

CHAPTER 24

Protocols

CORA LOOKED AT THE PLACEMENT ONCE MORE. THE red morocco leather blotter with slots for each place round the dining table had been a wedding present from Mrs Wyndham. It was the first time she had used it and she wished that Mrs Wyndham herself was here – she would know whether Lady Tavistock as the wife of a peer ranked higher than Sybil who was the daughter of a duke. Of course Sybil would not mind where she sat, as long as it was near Reggie, but any breach of etiquette on Cora's part would be pounced upon by her detractors, the Double Duchess in particular.

The Prince of Wales was only staying for two nights and he came without the Princess, but he travelled with two equerries, a private secretary and eight servants. Cora had received minute and irritating instructions from her mother-in-law about how to entertain the royal visitor. Lobster thermidor was his favourite dish, he liked to drink brandy after dinner, not port, and he would not tolerate a delay between courses. He would want to play baccarat after dinner, so Cora must ensure that there were enough seasoned players who understood that the Prince should always think that he had won on account of his skill. There were the bath salts he preferred, the cold roast chicken he liked by his bed in case of night-time hunger and the royal standard that must fly from the roof as long as he was in residence.

Cora had been delighted when the letter had come from the Double Duchess saying that the Prince wanted to act as sponsor to her son. Such a sign of royal favour suggested that the Louvain affair had not permanently damaged her social worth. After nearly a year in the seclusion of Lulworth, she was longing to return to London. But Ivo had shrugged when he heard the news. 'More trouble than it's worth, but we can hardly refuse.' As a result Cora tried to conceal her pleasure about the royal visit from her husband but her mother had no reason to. The Cashes, who had arrived a few days after Cora had given birth, had been due to go back to Newport for the end of the season, as Mrs Cash found staying in a house of which she was not the mistress trying; but the prospect of standing next to the Prince of Wales changed everything. Mrs Cash had cabled M. Worth in Paris for new gowns and she had sent her pearls to be restrung.

Cora picked up the card that read 'Teddy Van Der Leyden'. He was to be a godfather to little Guy. When she had suggested this to Ivo he had, rather to her surprise, smiled and said, 'Of course he needs an American godfather. What's this one like? I hope he has a railway, at the very least.' Cora had protested that Teddy came from an old Knickerbocker family that was not the railway-owning kind at all, not that there was anything wrong with railroads, and that he was actually an artist. Ivo had looked at her a touch more closely but then he laughed. 'An American painter, my mother will be *delighted*.' They had agreed that Sybil and Reggie should both be godparents; Cora hoped that it might precipitate a proposal and Ivo saw another opportunity to irritate the Double Duchess. But when Cora had suggested Charlotte Beauchamp, Ivo had hesitated. 'Do you really think Charlotte is a suitable moral guardian? Wouldn't you rather have someone more solid? And what about Odo?' But Cora had insisted.

'I like Charlotte, at least she's not boring.'

Ivo had turned his head away and, looking out of the window, he had said, 'If that's what you want, Cora, I won't stop you.'

Cora decided to put Teddy next to Charlotte tonight. She, of course, would have to sit next to the Prince but she thought that Teddy would find Charlotte intriguing; after all, she had been painted by his hero, Louvain. Her greatest difficulty was where to place her mother. Reggie Greatorex was safe enough but she knew that her mother would be mortified if she was not close to the Prince, but for protocol's sake she would have to put Duchess Fanny next to His Royal Highness. She decided to put her mother opposite but one, so that the Prince would be able to see her good side. And she would place her father next to the Double Duchess, so she could see for herself if there was a flirtation there.

At last the seating plan was finished. She really ought to have a secretary to write out all the cards, some nice girl who would deal with her correspondence and remember the right way to address a baronet. Her mother and her mother-in-law had both suggested it, but Cora did not want to have an English girl with a long nose and droopy clothes pointing out all the things she didn't know. She was tired of being made to feel like a hick by the people who worked for her. She was sick of Bugler's little pauses, by which he indicated that she had crossed an unwritten Rubicon of correct behaviour. When she had asked for all the ladies staying at the house to be brought breakfast in their rooms, he had paused and then said, 'At Lulworth, Your Grace, it is customary for the ladies to come down to breakfast.'

Cora had stared him down. 'Well, it is time that Lulworth had some new customs. I have no intention of coming down to breakfast and I think it unfair to expect my guests to do so.' She turned away in dismissal, but Bugler did not move. 'Thank you, Bugler, that will be all.'

He was looking at a spot somewhere around her knees. She could see a wiry tendril of hair snaking out of his nostril.

'Excuse me, Your Grace, but I wondered if the Duchess of Buckingham was aware of the change?' Bugler kept his gaze lowered and his voice neutral but there was no mistaking the meaning of his words.

'I am not in the habit of consulting the Duchess about my domestic arrangements, Bugler, not that it is any business of yours. You may go.'

Bugler had withdrawn, leaving Cora feeling foolish for allowing herself to be provoked. She comforted herself with the thought that she would dismiss him after the christening. She had wanted to do this for ages but she had not dared to make such a move while Ivo was away. Now he was back she felt that it was time for her to take charge.

Cora looked up at the portrait of Eleanor Maltravers that hung on the wall opposite her desk. She was still getting used to having the picture in her room. It used to hang in the corridor leading to the north tower in a dark alcove. Cora had found her there one day during one of her long perambulations around the house during her pregnancy, and had been intrigued. From the orange satin of her dress and the deep décolleté this likeness had been made before the Grey Lady had earned her soubriquet. Cora thought that Eleanor must have been about her own age when the picture was painted. But it was hard to tell as it was submerged under layers of dust and dirt. After some hesitation she sent the portrait to Duveen's in London to be cleaned, deciding that Ivo could hardly object to her restoring a picture that no one had noticed for centuries. She had forgotten about the picture in the excitement of the birth and Ivo's return, and she had been surprised when the crate was delivered. Ivo had raised an eyebrow when he saw the Duveen stencil on the crate.

'Have you been shopping again, Cora?' he said.

Cora shook her head. She signalled to the footman to open the crate, biting her lip as he prised the nails out of the wood. Ivo lingered at the doorway scratching his dog's head and whistling. Cora held her breath as the footman started to take off the wrappings; Ivo's presence was making her nervous. Then the piece of canvas came off and Eleanor was revealed. Her skin was white now and her dress glowed, the cleaning had revealed the background to be full of details, there was even a lurcher curled up on a green tasselled cushion. Ivo stopped whistling and stepped forward to take a better look.

'Is it really Eleanor?' he said, peering at the picture. 'She's quite something.' Cora listened for a note of disapproval, but then he turned to her and smiled.

'You're a clever girl, Cora. I've walked past that picture all my life but I don't think I have ever really seen it before. Thank you for making me look.' He put his hand on her shoulder and she felt her body sag with relief. She didn't want him to know how nervous she had been, so she said as brightly as she could, 'Mr Fox says he believes this is by Van Dyck. The face certainly, even if the rest of the picture was finished off in the studio.' She took his hand. 'I would like to hang it in my bedroom, you don't mind do you?'

'Of course I don't mind. Lucky Eleanor, you've turned her from a ghost into a beauty. I think we should have all the pictures cleaned, it's time we saw things differently here.' He swung her hand. 'My new broom, that's what you are. I want you to sweep away all the shadows, all the dust. You're the only one brave enough to do it.'

'Brave?' said Cora, 'It's not so very frightening to have a few pictures cleaned.' She put her face close to his, basking in his approval. He touched her cheek.

'Not for you darling, which is why I am so glad that you are my wife.'

She remembered this scene every time she saw a raised eyebrow, or heard a sharp intake of breath from the servants when she suggested changes to the way the house was run. They might not like her ideas but none of that mattered if Ivo approved. If he wanted to make a break with the past then nothing would stop her. She was not going to be a grey lady languishing in corners. She would be the mistress of Lulworth.

She rang the bell for Mrs Softley. She wanted to make an inspection of the guest bedrooms to ensure that they were all as they should be, and that those awful photographs of the Duke and Duchess had been put away. But at that moment Ivo walked in. He had been riding and he was pulling off his jacket as he came towards her. He kissed her lightly on the mouth.

'Good morning, Duchess. How are the battle plans?' He looked over her shoulder at the placement. 'And who am I sitting next to?'

'Between my mother and Lady Tavistock.'

'Scylla and Charybdis, eh? Well, at least my ordeal will be swift. His Highness doesn't like to linger over dinner. Just promise I don't have to play cards with him. He is such a lamentable player, it can be quite tricky sometimes to let him win.' He stroked the inch of Cora's neck that was visible above the high collar of her blouse with his finger. She took his other hand and kissed it.

'I promise to spare you the cards. I am going to take the ladies to the long gallery.'

She could feel his finger tracing the knobs of her spine under the thin silk. He was always touching her now when he was with her. These last few weeks at Lulworth with Ivo and the baby had been the happiest in her marriage since their honeymoon. When she remembered how worried she had been before his return, she almost laughed. Ever since he had come back he had been everything she had hoped for. Even the presence of her parents and the Double Duchess had not spoilt things. The Double Duchess had shown unusual tact in inviting Mr and Mrs Cash to Conyers before the christening. Cora could not have been more surprised by the invitation, but Ivo had said, 'The Double Duchess has clearly got over her aversion to Americans, or American men, I should say. I almost feel sorry for your mother.'

It had taken Cora a moment to catch his meaning, and then she had shaken her head in disbelief.

Ivo had laughed at her. 'I'm sorry, Cora, have I offended your Puritan sensibilities?' And then more seriously, 'It's the way she operates, I'm afraid.'

'Do you think I should tell Mother?'

'Lord, no. Let the situation develop. Besides, I want to be here alone with you.'

Cora could not refuse.

Now Ivo was pulling a strand of her hair out of its chignon. She put up her hand to stop him.

There was so much still to be done. She turned to him and said, 'Come with me to the nursery. I want to show you something.'

He put his hands down in a show of mock surrender. 'As you wish, my dear, as you wish.'

He followed her down the corridor to the nursery. This was not the room where he had stayed as a child, that was on the north side of the house on a higher floor. Cora had chosen to put little Guy and his attendants in the rooms adjacent to hers; she could not bear to think of him being so far away. The nanny had grumbled at first about losing her sanctum which had its own staircase down to the servants' hall, but Cora had raised her wages by ten pounds a year and her objections had vanished.

The baby was lying in the great gilded bassinet that Mrs Cash had bought from Venice. Ivo had laughed when he saw it and said it must have been made from pieces of the True Cross at the very least. Ignoring the flusterings of the nurse, Cora went straight to the cradle and picked up her baby. His body was heavy against her shoulder and his fingers went straight to her hair, just as his father's had done a few minutes before.

'He smiled me this morning, Ivo! Open your eyes wide and see if he'll smile at you too.'

Ivo put out his arms to take his son.

'Were you smiling at your beautiful mother, young man? I see you have taste.' Cora felt herself beaming with pride and happiness. When Ivo was with the baby, she could see that his eyes, usually so dark, were in fact tawny, flecked through with gold. She knew that Ivo had wanted an heir but she had not imagined that he would be so delighted to be a father. Nanny Snowden had said to her, with disapproval in her voice, that she had never known a man to spend so much time in the nursery.

She stood beside him and smiled at the baby lying in his arms. She was rewarded with a flash of gums and sparkling eyes. 'There it is, Ivo, he smiled at us.' And she looked up at her husband's face and saw that it was taut with emotion, his mouth set in a code she could not decipher.

Cora said, 'I think he is going to be a happy boy.'

'Happiness is a talent,' Ivo said slowly and then he kissed the top of the baby's head and gave him to Nanny Snowden who was hovering in the doorway, only just concealing her irritation at their presence.

'Thank you, Nanny,' said Ivo. 'Guy must have his rest for tomorrow.'

'Don't worry, Your Grace, His Lordship will be quite prepared.' Cora felt the same wriggle of surprise every time she heard her baby called 'His Lordship'. Ivo might laugh at her mother's idea of a cradle but surely there was something equally absurd about giving a tiny scrap of a baby a title? She stopped to look at the christening gown which was laid out on a table. The gown had been in the family for generations, Ivo and his father before him had worn it. The silk was yellowed with age and the lace was covered with brown spots, like an old lady's hands. But Cora knew better now than to suggest a replacement.

Ivo was waiting for her in the passage. He took her hand and pulled her into his bedroom. This room had remained untouched during Cora's renovations of Lulworth. The magnificent blue brocade on the tester was dusty and tattered and the curtains hung in limp folds, faded where the sun had touched them.

'Now I have something to show *you*, darling.' He made her sit down in one of the heavily carved wooden chairs. Ivo walked over to the bureau and unlocked a drawer from which he took a velvet pouch. He came over to her and, kneeling in front of her, he emptied it on to her lap. The sun falling in through the window hit the gems as they lay across her skirt, dazzling them both. It took her a moment to realise that she was looking at a necklace that had at its centre an emerald the size of a quail's egg.

'I bought it in Hyderabad. I think it might just be magnificent enough for you.' Cora put her hands to her neck, she was as usual wearing her pearls. 'Take them off and try this on.'

Obediently Cora unclasped the pearls and he put the necklace round her neck. It felt heavy and spiky after the smooth weight of the pearls. He took her hand and stood her in front of the cheval glass. The mirror was foxed with age and her reflection rippled slightly but there was no disguising the splendour of the necklace. The emerald fell just above her breasts; the teardrop facets allowed it to glow like a mossy pool with limitless depths, and the diamond sprays above it looked like a waterfall. It was quite the most spectacular thing she had ever seen, nothing even in her mother's glittering collection could match this.

'It is quite unbelievable, Ivo.' She turned her head from side to side admiring the green rays from the gem. He stood behind her and put his arms on her shoulders. 'Even the Nizam was impressed. He offered to buy it from me for twice what I paid for it. But I said that it could only belong to you, as you were the only woman in the world who wouldn't be outshone by it.'

'I think my mother will be jealous,' said Cora.

'And mine,' said Ivo with a smile. 'It's the perfect present.'

That evening Cora wore a dress of gold brocade overlaid with silver lace. The glowing material brought out the bronze lights in her hair and the emerald hanging round her neck nudged her eyes from grey to green. She was standing by the window in the long gallery talking to her father, and every so often she would move so that the low rays of the setting sun would catch the gems round her neck and scatter their reflections over the vaulted roof. She was standing under this, her own constellation, when Teddy walked into the room. He stood still for a moment, dazzled. The restless girl he remembered had turned into a magnificent force. She seemed taller than he had pictured her. There was a definiteness about her that was new. He sensed that she had taken on her final shape. He was relieved that she had changed so much. This new, grand personage would finally shake the memory of the girl asking him to kiss her that night in Newport.

The footman announced his name and Cora swept up to him, her arms outstretched.

'Dearest Teddy, I can't believe you're actually here.' She leant forward to kiss his cheek and he smelt the foxy scent of her hair that he remembered from the terrace at Sans Souci. He knew then that nothing had changed – Cora could be as grand and as duchessy as she liked but she was still the woman he wanted to hold in his arms.

Still clasping his hands, she smiled at him conspiratorially. 'I guess we are kissing cousins now, us both being Americans abroad.'

'Indeed, Duchess.' Teddy gave her title its full weight.

'Oh please, you of all people have to call me Cora. I am still the same girl.' She was laughing but Teddy thought he heard a shard of anxiety in her voice.

'If you're sure that's allowed.'

He was smiling as he said this but it was a real question. He was not sure what he wanted the answer to be. He noticed the small scar on the underside of her wrist that he had once kissed and wondered, not by any means for the first time, what she had done with the letter he had written her before her wedding. Had she kept it as a memento – folded carefully in the secret compartment of a jewellery box or tucked away into a volume of poetry? Or had she torn it up, or thrown it into the fire? She had not replied, of course, he had not really expected her to, but he wondered about the expression on her face as she had read his letter. Cora met his eyes for a moment and Teddy wanted to kiss her so much that he had to clasp his hands behind his back so that he would not reach out and take hold of her. Perhaps Cora sensed this because she pulled back a fraction and said firmly, 'Come and meet my husband before the Prince comes down.'

Teddy followed her to the fireplace where the Duke was talking to another man and the red-haired girl he remembered from the boat. He wondered for a moment if the Duke would remember his face, but as he came closer he thought that dukes were probably not in the habit of noticing strangers.

Cora fluttered between them, making the introduction. Teddy

could see that she was nervous, which pleased him. He wanted some acknowledgement of their past, to see a hairline crack in her aristocratic composure.

'Welcome to Lulworth, Mr Van Der Leyden. Is this your first visit to England?' The Duke's face was politely curious, Teddy saw no flicker of recognition. The Duke looked somehow different to the man he had seen pacing the deck of the SS *Berengaria*. He looked looser now, as the French said: he looked happy in his skin.

'No, I was here about eighteen months ago, on my way back to America. I believe we may have travelled on the same boat. I remember your name from the manifest.'

Ivo tilted his head to observe Teddy properly. 'What a pity we were not introduced, you could have told me all Cora's secrets. I know remarkably little about her American life.' His gaze met Teddy's and Teddy forced himself not to blink. The Duke was looking at him closely as if he knew just how Teddy felt about his wife. Teddy found himself squaring off against his rival; the Duke was perhaps an inch taller but Teddy felt that he was the stronger.

Cora, who had been following this exchange closely, broke in, her hand closing round Teddy's wrist.

'If I had any secrets, I know that Teddy would never have told! We Americans are the soul of discretion.'

'I don't know about every American, Cora, but this one certainly is,' said Teddy.

Cora's grip on his arm tightened. 'Now, Teddy, you must come and talk to Mother. You can't put it off any longer.'

Teddy nodded to the Duke and said, 'It's no secret that American girls must be obeyed, I think.'

The Duke showed his teeth in amusement. 'In my experience all women expect obedience.'

Teddy allowed himself to be shepherded in front of Mrs Cash, who looked at him without enthusiasm. She hated to be reminded of her accident. She had told Cora that she thought Teddy's presence at Lulworth was in very poor taste.

'And how is your mother, Mr Van Der Leyden, and your sister?' She shifted slightly so that Teddy was facing her good side.

'Both well, thank you, ma'am, though I suspect you may have seen them more recently than I. I have been in Europe for over a year now.'

'Oh yes, I believe I heard you were in Paris – painting.' Mrs Cash let her voice fall on the last word. But Teddy did not waver.

'That's correct. I was studying with Menasche.'

'And do you ever intend to return to New York, Mr Van Der Leyden? It must be hard for your mother to have her only son so far away.'

'Well, I have received a commission from the New York Public Library for a mural, so I am coming home in the fall.'

Cora clapped her hands at this. 'Oh Teddy, that's splendid. I am so pleased. I know you will do something wonderful. What is your subject?'

Teddy saw that she was genuinely pleased and that her mother disliked this.

'I haven't decided yet. There was a thought of doing the Persephone myth. I only wish I could use you as a model, Cora, you would be exactly right.'

Teddy had meant this as a compliment so he was surprised to see the alarm on Cora's face.

'What a pity that I am here then. To be immortalised in a public library, that would be quite something.'

Teddy was about to say that he could work from sketches when there was an intake of breath and a rustling of skirts as the footman announced, 'His Royal Highness, the Prince of Wales.'

Teddy took a step back. He did not want to appear eager to meet the Prince. He hoped that he was immune to the lure of royalty although he could not help looking at the Prince closely. He was smaller than Teddy had imagined and much rounder. Even the dinner jacket which the Prince wore in preference to the more revealing tails could not disguise his girth. His mouth and chin were covered by a pointed Vandyke beard and he surveyed the room through a pair of chilly blue eyes under heavy lids.

The first person he spoke to was a blonde lady, whose curtsy was so abject that her forehead practically touched the ground at the Prince's feet. The Prince smiled at this and kissed the woman's hand when she surfaced. 'Duchess Fanny, such a pleasure to see you here in your old setting.' Teddy noticed that Cora's smile was losing its warmth, her curtsy was stiff, almost jerky – an italic comma in contrast to the other woman's flowing cursive signature. But the Prince appeared not to notice and said, 'Yes, I am verrry pleased to be back here, and in such charming company.' Now Cora was guiding the Prince through the guests to where her mother stood. Mrs Cash's curtsy was a model of dignity, she did not bow her head but kept her back erect throughout and her eyes fixed on the Prince's face. Despite the depth of her curtsy, there was no mistaking, in the regal tilt of Mrs Cash's head, the sense that she was meeting someone of her own rank at last. The Prince was complimenting her on her daughter. 'I don't know where we would be without you Amerrricans.' Mrs Cash half closed her eyes as if to agree.

Cora looked at Teddy and he stepped forward reluctantly.

'Sir, may I present Mr Van Der Leyden, who is one of my childhood friends and is also a godfather to my son.'

Teddy thought for a moment that he might stand his ground but as the Prince stood in front of him, he felt himself bowing as if pulled forward by the inexorable force of royal gravity.

'Whereabouts in Amerrrica are you from, Mr Van Der Leyden?'

'New York . . . sir.' Teddy could not bring himself to say Your Highness.

'Such an enerrrgetic city. I would like very much to go back but it is impossible these days for me to go so far away, I have too many responsibilities. Duty before pleasure, eh.'

Teddy looked at the Prince's rounded form and heavy-lidded eyes and wondered how much pleasure exactly the Prince had sacrificed for duty. It was not, he thought, a face that he wanted to paint.

As the Prince moved sedately on, Teddy looked up and saw that the Duke was looking at him, and to Teddy's surprise he gave him an imperceptible nod as if to say that he had read his thoughts and was in agreement.

The Prince was being offered a glass of champagne but he waved it away and turned to Cora. 'But my dear Amerrrican Duchess, may we not have a cocktail? I met a charming gentleman from Louisiana who showed me how to make a most splendid drink with whisky, marrraschino and champagne. I would so like to taste it again.' The Prince looked wistful although fully aware that his every whim would of course be indulged.

Cora signalled to Bugler. A few moments later two footmen entered carrying a tray with bottles, decanters and a large silver punchbowl.

The Prince busied himself mixing the drink. 'One part whisky to a measure of marrraschino and two parts of champagne. Now, Duchess Fanny, I want you to try this, and you too, Mrs Cash. You can tell me whether it tastes the way it should.' Both women approached, the Double Duchess eagerly, Mrs Cash with due republican reticence. The Prince poured a bottle of Pol Roger into the mixture and then he dipped two glasses into the bowl and offered one to each lady. Duchess Fanny sipped hers and pronounced it, 'Quite delicious, sir, although of course a little stronger than I am used to.'

'Splendid,' cried the Prince, his pendulous lower lip glistening. 'And what do you think, Mrs Cash?'

'I think it would benefit from the addition of some fresh mint.' The Prince looked at her for a moment in surprise; he frequently asked for honest opinions but he was not in the habit of receiving them. There was a tiny pause while he wondered whether there had been any affront to his dignity and then he laughed and said, 'Well now, I know why Amerrrican women make such good hostesses, Mrs Cash. Attention to detail. By all means, let us add mint.'

Teddy tried not to smile. He was used to seeing Mrs Cash prevailing but the assembled company were not. He noticed the blonde woman, whom he now knew to be Duchess Fanny, looking at Mrs Cash warily, as if re-evaluating an opponent.

The Prince was offering a glass to Cora when the footman announced, 'Sir Odo and Lady Beauchamp.' Teddy saw the Prince stiffen; and he remembered Cora's instructions in her letter to him:

'The Prince of Wales breaks all the rules, but he expects perfect behaviour from everyone else. He hates it if people are late, even though the Princess is notorious for her tardiness. So please hurry down to dinner the moment you are dressed. We Americans have to have the best manners of all, of course, as we can get away with nothing.'

The couple that came in, however, did not look at all abashed. The man was flushed, his protruding blue eyes glittering, his lips slightly parted, showing his small white teeth. He bowed gracefully before the Prince, displaying his extravagant profusion of yellow curls.

'You must forgive me, sir, but my wife could not decide between the chartreuse and the mauve. She would not budge until I had advised her, and do you know I just could not make a decision. She looked simply ravishing in both, so in the end she had to wear red, as you see.' He gestured towards his wife who sank into a curtsy that did much to display her décolletage.

'Highness,' she murmured and she raised her shining blond head to look at the Prince with a smile that was quite unrepentant.

'It is your hostess who must forgive you, of course, though I am inclined to agree with you, Sir Odo, that the result was worth the wait.' The Prince gestured towards Lady Beauchamp. Her dress was crimson satin embroidered in black in a repeating motif of bees, ants and scorpions. The neckline and hem were edged with jet beads that shook slightly as she moved. It was a theatrical dress, preposterous even, but Lady Beauchamp was equal to it, Teddy thought. She held her head high, and Teddy could see the strong lines of her neck as it met the collarbone below. She looked beautiful and terrible in equal measure. Teddy thought of Salome holding up the head of John the Baptist. But it wasn't just her perfect, implacable profile that made him stare at her, transfixed. He had seen this woman before, a year ago, standing on the platform of Euston Station with the Duke. He had never forgotten the way she had pulled the Duke's hand into her muff – such ferocious intimacy in that public place. He could still remember the gorgeous curve of her cheek, and the way her eyes were fixed on the Duke's face. It was an image that had never left him, because he knew he had seen the face of a woman saying farewell to the man she loved.

CHAPTER 25

Eros and Psyche

THE DINING ROOM AT LULWORTH WAS IN THE oldest part of the house. The entrance to the room was down a shallow flight of steps and even on a summer's evening the stone walls and floors meant that the room felt a few degrees colder than the rest of the house. Tonight, however, the faintly crypt-like atmosphere was dispelled by the heat from the twelve silver gilt candelabra on the table and the sweet smell coming from banks of jasmine in the window bays. The room glittered as the candlelight hit the crystal glasses, the brilliants dangling from the chandeliers and the diamonds around the women's necks. But the warmth and light were only on the surface, every so often there would be a chill current of air that brushed a bare shoulder or a naked neck and made its owner shiver. Comfort was not the natural order of things here, this room had been built to contain the violent carousing of medieval barons fighting for the favours of the King, not the powdered politenesses of *fin de siècle* aristocrats. The floor was mainly covered by an Aubusson carpet but underneath lay cold hard stone. The footmen who lined the room knew this, they stood on the cold perimeter waiting to pull out chairs, fill glasses and serve food to guests who gave no more thought to their existence than they did to the larks whose tongues lay in aspic before them.

Teddy emptied his glass. He knew that he was drinking too fast. The reappearance of the woman he had seen on the station platform had shaken him. It had taken every scrap of his Knickerbocker composure not to flinch when Cora had beckoned to him to take Lady Beauchamp in to dinner. Charlotte had sensed his confusion but had misattributed the cause, saying, 'Don't worry, Mr Van Der Leyden, the dress is just for show. I won't bite,' and had placed one black-gloved hand on his arm with a great play of docility. At the table, he won a temporary respite as she turned away to talk to the man on her right. Teddy busied himself making agreeable conversation to Lady Tavistock who sat on his left, but he knew that when the mock turtle soup was finished, there would be no escape from Charlotte Beauchamp.

Lady Tavistock was not much interested in him once she had ascertained that Teddy was not a rich American. When he told her that he was an artist, she put on the brightly curious expression that she might have worn on visiting an institute for the blind.

'Oh, how fascinating. You know I have never actually met an artist before, not socially, I mean. Of course dear Duchess Cora has such a fondness for painters. I was at Bridgewater House when Louvain showed the portrait. Such a sensation.' She glanced to the end of the table where Cora was listening to the Prince of Wales and nodded. 'I am so glad to see her back again.'

Teddy did not fully understand the substance of her remarks but he guessed he did not need to. Lady Tavistock was much like one of his mother's cronies: women trained from birth to calibrate social standing. They would follow success like sunflowers tracing the arc of the day, but once the light and heat had gone, they were merciless. He felt a kind of guilty relief. In Paris he had imagined Cora to be invincible, and yet here she was subject to the scrutiny of women like Lady Tavistock.

He was still trying to make sense of the presence of Lady Beauchamp here at Lulworth. Did Cora know about her connection with her husband? He knew that liaisons with married women were commonplace in Paris and he supposed here too, but he could not imagine Cora complacently entertaining her husband's mistress. The idea of a rival would be quite foreign to her – she had been raised to be the prize, not the woman who pretended not to see.

He noticed that Odo Beauchamp, sitting opposite him, was drinking even faster than he was. Teddy wondered how much he knew about his wife and the Duke. From the way his eyes kept flicking between them, Teddy thought that he definitely had suspicions.

A footman came in carrying a silver contraption with a large screw at the side – Teddy thought it looked like a cider press – but from the excited murmurs around him he gathered that this was a meat press and that they were to be given *caneton à la Rouennaise*, a great delicacy much appreciated by the Prince. Teddy watched as the butler turned the screw of the device and collected the blood in a silver jug.

He heard Odo Beauchamp saying, 'The ducks are smothered, you know, so that none of the blood is lost.'

Teddy wondered if Cora, who had always mocked her mother's elaborate dinners, enjoyed all this pomp and spectacle. He remembered the phrase in her letter, 'I am still an American girl who sometimes misses the country of her birth.' He wondered again how much she knew about the currents of deception coursing around the table. She looked so radiant sitting there next to the Prince, yet Teddy felt a certain low satisfaction in knowing that Cora's life was not as perfect as the fabulous jewel that hung around her neck.

The footman was offering him a dish of the pressed duck in its bloody sauce. Teddy looked at the red liquid pooling on his plate and realised that Charlotte Beauchamp was speaking to him.

'So, Mr Van Der Leyden, Cora tells me you have known each other since childhood.' Her voice was low and she turned to look at him as if her entire future depended on his answer.

'New York is a great city but it can be quite small all the same. Cora and I have attended the same parties, picnics and dancing lessons since we were very young. I taught Cora how to ride a bicycle, she stopped me embarrassing myself at the Governor's Cotillion. We were partners in crime.'

'Indeed? Then I am surprised that you let her go so easily. It can be hard to give up your first accomplice.' She half lowered her eyelids and Teddy felt for a moment the intensity of the woman he had seen saying goodbye to her lover.

'Oh, Cora was always destined for greater things,' he said as lightly as he could. 'We always knew that her time with us mere mortals would be limited.' He let his eyes flicker towards the gauzy profile of Mrs Cash.

Charlotte understood him at once and leant over to murmur, 'She is quite regal, isn't she? I think the poor Prince feels quite upstaged.'

'Believe me, in New York Mrs Cash is considered a lightweight.' Charlotte laughed at this and the moment of intensity was gone.

Teddy had no doubt about the intimacy that had existed

between this woman and the Duke. The question in his mind now was whether it still continued. He was used to interpreting people through their body and the mass they displaced around them; there was a certain deliberateness to Charlotte's movements, from the way she picked up her wine glass to the graceful swerve of her shoulder that brought her round to face him, that made him think that she was not a woman who wavered in her feelings.

'I hope you are not tantalising my wife with an ocean-going steam yacht, Mr Van Der Leyden.' Teddy looked across the table at Odo Beauchamp whose shining rosy cheeks were at odds with the set of his narrow lips. 'You Americans with your extravagant toys make it very difficult for humdrum Englishmen like myself.' He lifted his glass and drained it, and Teddy noticed that his hand shook slightly as he put it down.

Teddy laughed. 'I am sorry to disappoint you, sir, but I have no steam yacht, railway line or even a motor car. I have nothing to tantalise your wife with beyond my limited powers of conversation.'

Odo subsided into his seat and Charlotte said, 'Besides, Odo, no one could describe you as humdrum.'

This remark evidently pleased her husband who shook his yellow curls as if to acknowledge the truth of her remark. But Teddy had seen the flash of jealousy and again he wondered about the woman sitting next to him. He could make out a scorpion embroidered on the red puff of her sleeve. He could not decide whether it was a warning or a mark of how often she herself had been stung.

Exactly one hour and fifteen minutes after they had sat down to dinner, Cora was preparing herself to catch her mother's good eye and give the signal that it was time for the ladies to withdraw, when she saw the Double Duchess rising in her seat, her eyes sweeping the room. Cora clenched her teeth; she could hardly believe that even her mother-in-law would make such a brazen play for power. But she knew that she must not let herself be provoked, so she said as sweetly as she could, 'Oh, Duchess Fanny, thank you so much for taking the lead. I was enjoying my conversation with His Royal Highness so much that I declare I would have sat here all night.' She stood up and was grateful for the good two inches she had over her mother-in-law. 'Ladies, shall we?'

The footmen stepped forward and the women got to their feet in a murmur of silk. The men stood. It fell to the Prince to escort Cora to the door as he was sitting on her right hand. As she went past he murmured, 'Are you waging another Amerrrican war of independence, Duchess?'

Cora looked at the fat old man whose eyes were lit up with malice.

'That depends, sir, on whether I have royal approval.'

The Prince swept his eyes over Cora and nodded imperceptibly. 'I have always thought that the New World would one day prevail.'

The men did not linger in the dining room but soon joined the ladies in the long gallery. Ivo came in last and Cora could tell from the stiff set of his shoulders and the lines around his mouth that her husband was not happy. She wondered what had happened when the ladies had retired.

After she had settled the Prince with a game of baccarat, she sought him out.

'I thought you might like to play the piano, Ivo,' and then lowering her voice she said, 'that way you won't have to talk to anyone.'

He nodded. 'Is it that obvious? I'm not sure I can stand Odo Beauchamp a moment longer. I don't care for him when he's sober, but when he's drunk, he's unspeakable. You're right, I shall play for a while until I can bring myself to look at him again.' He walked through the door into the music room.

Cora surveyed the room like a scout on a reconnaissance patrol, looking for signs of trouble. The Prince was happily playing baccarat with Mr Cash, his equerry Ferrers and the Double Duchess. Cora hoped that her father would realise that the point of the game was to put up a gallant fight before losing to the Prince. Teddy was looking at a portrait of the Fourth Duke with Father Oliver; her mother was sitting in another group with Charlotte, Odo and Lady Tavistock, and Reggie and Sybil were sitting in a corner pretending to play chess.

Cora went over to where her mother was sitting. Odo was talking about a play he had seen in London. With his bright red cheeks and round blue eyes, Cora thought that he looked rather like a doll she had once been fond of. He paused for a second and at that moment the piano started in the music room – a Chopin nocturne, Cora thought.

Odo turned towards the music, listening with his head to one side. 'Really, I had no idea that Maltravers was such a romantic, did you, Charlotte?' As he turned to his wife, Cora saw that he was swaying slightly and she realised that he was as drunk as her husband had said.

'He plays with expression, certainly.' Charlotte's tone was neutral.

'Oh, it's more than just expression, Charlotte. To hear him you would think he was a soul in torment.'

There was something in Odo's tone that Cora found unsettling.

'Oh, I hope not, Sir Odo,' she said. 'What kind of wife would that make me?' She laughed and turned to Charlotte. 'Charlotte, I am trying to get a bicycling party together for tomorrow. If it's fine I thought we might have lunch by the folly and those who were so minded could cycle there. What do you think?'

Charlotte shook her head. 'I must be the only woman in England who hasn't yet learnt how to ride a bicycle. Besides, I don't have suitable clothes.'

Cora was about to offer to lend her something when Odo said, 'But what about that charming costume you had as Joan of Arc? Just the thing for cycling. Such a shame that it was never revealed at Lady Salisbury's pageant. Everyone was so disappointed. Remind me again, Charlotte, why you didn't appear that day. What was it now – a headache? It was so bad you wouldn't even let me see you. And yet look at you now, radiant with health.' He took his wife's hand and raised it to his lips. 'There must be something in the Lulworth air that agrees with you.'

Cora saw Charlotte pull her hand away and brush it on her skirt to remove the imprint of his lips. She turned to Cora as if her husband had not spoken.

'If you can lend me something to wear, I will certainly try to conquer the bicycle. What about you, Lady Tavistock, Mrs Cash? Will you join me in my humiliation?'

Mrs Cash said, 'Oh, I learnt to ride a few years ago, but I think I shall leave it to you young people. There are too many hills around here for my liking.' Lady Tavistock nodded in agreement.

Odo leant forward. 'If you are riding, my dear, then I shall certainly be of the party.' Cora felt a damp spray of spittle on her cheek. 'I don't want you to disappear again. It's really quite a struggle,' he leant back to address the assembled company, 'to keep up with my wife.'

He had raised his voice and the challenge in it rang out across the room. Cora saw Teddy turn round and the card players look up. She knew that she must do something to contain the situation – her mother was glaring at her as if to say that it was her duty to take this in hand. Odo was swaying more obviously now, and he was clearly working up to another outburst. She glanced over at Charlotte but she was looking at the floor. This was a test of her mettle as a hostess, she was being watched to see how she would handle this.

She stepped forward and put her hand on Odo's arm, and said with all the charm she could muster, 'Well, there I have to agree with you, we all struggle to keep up with your wife. She is the standard we aspire to. Why, I am sure that in a matter of weeks we will all be wearing dresses that are crawling with insects, because where Charlotte Beauchamp leads, we can but follow. But now I want you to come with me, Sir Odo. We have a new statue in the summer house that I would love your opinion of, and yours too, Teddy. I would very much like to know what you two connoisseurs think of the Canova by moonlight.'

Odo looked reluctant but allowed himself to be led out of the room, Teddy following behind. Charlotte's eyes had not moved from the floor during this exchange. Now she raised her head and looked at Mrs Cash.

'Your daughter has so many accomplishments, Mrs Cash.'

Mrs Cash gave a regal nod. 'I like to think that I raised her so that she could handle any situation.'

The evening air was still warm, Cora could smell roses and the slight whiff of salt coming in from the sea. The moon was a day or two away from being full and lit up the white stone of the summer house. Cora waved away the footman holding a lantern.

'No, I think we should see this by moonlight.'

They walked down the gravel path, the stones scraping beneath their feet, loud in the still garden. Odo had subsided, he was silent until they stopped in front of the pavilion, which had a bell-shaped roof supported on six columns. Behind the dull stone of the pillars, Pysche was being revived by Eros's kiss, her naked torso stretching upwards to meet his lips. Cora had bought the statue from Duveen's sight unseen (after checking its provenance, of course). She had once heard Ivo admire a Canova statue in Venice and she thought it might please him. When it had emerged from the packing case, she had been surprised and faintly disturbed by Eros's muscular arms and the ecstatic arch of Psyche's back as she sought her lover's mouth. By day the statue was arresting but now in the silvery half-light it was unbearably intimate. The flickers of light on the sinuous marble curves made Cora feel as if she was trespassing on a moment of private rapture.

Odo stepped forward and ran his hand down Psyche's naked flank.

'Such a glorious finish, don't you agree, Mr Van Der Leyden? Almost as good as the real thing.'

'The technique, certainly, is faultless,' said Teddy carefully. He felt almost nervous standing in front of the statue with Cora. He knew that she had brought him down here as ballast against Odo but it was hard not to think of that other moonlit night in Newport when she had twisted her face up to his, Psyche to his Eros.

'I'm glad you approve, Sir Odo. I feel it works quite well here in the summer house,' Cora said, wishing that Odo would stop caressing the statue.

'I daresay Ivo likes it,' Odo said. 'There's a man who appreciates the female form.'

Teddy felt for his cigarette case. As he struck the match he saw the yellow flare in Odo's eyes.

'Oh Teddy, may I?' Cora looked at his cigarette.

'Of course, forgive me.' He offered her his case.

'My mother would be horrified if she could see this.' She leant forward into the flame and the emerald around her neck flickered. Teddy watched her put the cigarette to her lips.

'We won't tell her then, will we?' Teddy appealed to Odo. 'We can be depended on to keep a secret.' But Odo wouldn't look at him. He was resting his flushed cheek against the cool marble of Eros's wing.

Cora inhaled gratefully. 'Do you remember, Teddy, the Goelet party where the cigarettes were made out of hundred-dollar bills? Do you think many people actually smoked them?'

Teddy laughed. 'I certainly didn't. In fact, I don't think anyone did. All those Newport millionaires take money much too seriously to see it go up in smoke.'

'It seems vulgar now, doesn't it?' Cora said hesitantly. 'Although at the time I remember thinking it was rather smart.' She blew out a thin stream of smoke.

Teddy said, '*Autre temps, autre moeurs*. I find lots of things feel different over here.' He looked her straight in the eye. 'But there are a few things that feel just the same.'

Cora felt the meaning in his glance and frowned as if he had brought something difficult into her garden of delightful reminiscence. She tossed her cigarette on to the grass and ground it down with her foot.

'I must go in and check on the Prince,' she said.

Teddy watched her disappear into the house and he found that he was holding his breath.

'What a touching little scene.' Odo's voice startled him, and Teddy coughed on his cigarette. 'Sadly for you, the Duchess must be the only woman in England who is in love with her husband. Beautiful, rich and faithful, how foolish of you to let her get away.'

Teddy clenched his fist in his pocket. He knew he should not rise to the bait but he could not help himself saying, 'Funnily enough, I didn't want to be the husband of a fortune.'

'How very honourable of you.' Odo's tone was bitter. His hand was still stroking the Psyche's cool flank. 'I wish I could say the same of my wife. She was beautiful and I was rich. I thought it was a fair exchange, but Lady Beauchamp hasn't kept her side of the bargain. All she had to do was play the wife in public. I guessed, of course, that she had a *tendresse* for the Duke – but then everybody has a weakness, even me,' and he giggled. 'But she had to flaunt her feelings in public. I could have forgiven her everything but not that.'

Teddy lit another cigarette. He didn't offer one to Odo.

'So why have you come here?' he said. 'I would have thought this was the last place you wanted to be.'

'Too good an opportunity to resist, old boy. I knew it would come and here it is. My dear wife is not the only one who can behave badly in public. I intend to cause a nice little scene.' He giggled again and started to move towards the house.

Teddy, catching his meaning, put his hand out to grab the other man's arm but Odo was too quick for him. He darted behind the statue, and said, 'Don't try and stop me, it's really not in your interests to do so. Surely you must see that the sooner your old friend the Duchess knows what's going on under her nose, the sooner she will need the comfort of an "old friend".' Teddy tried to make another grab for him but Odo saw him coming and stepped behind a pillar. They were both very drunk but Teddy had been made clumsy by alcohol while Odo seemed to be quite surefooted. Teddy reached out again to catch his arm but Odo made a sudden movement away and Teddy fell to the ground, hitting his head. He lay on the ground stunned, his mouth tasting the granite. His thoughts and feelings were swirling around his head like quicksilver, unpredictable and reluctant to coalesce. He knew that he must act, that he should stop what was about to happen, but he found himself quite passive, his limbs relaxing into their stone bed, because somewhere he also knew, and hated himself for it, that Odo was right.

Cora surveyed the long gallery from the door. The Prince was still playing cards, Father Oliver was with her mother and Lady Tavistock, Sybil and Reggie had not moved – nor, it seemed, had their chess pieces – and Ivo was still playing in the music room. She wondered where Charlotte was – she wouldn't blame her for retiring to bed so that she could escape from Odo. She tried to imagine what their marriage could be like. Anyone could see they were not happy and yet when they were together they seemed so glittering and powerful that you could not bear to look away. She wondered what they talked about when they were alone. Clearly there must be something that bound them together, some affinity or more likely weakness that they shared. Cora had been shocked when Charlotte had confessed her contempt for her husband, but there was something even more disturbing about the way she was acting up to him tonight, as if they were playing a game, the rules of which only they knew. She shivered with unease as she walked down the gallery towards the music room. She wanted to see Ivo, to remind herself of her own good fortune.

He was playing something she didn't recognise, something fast and showy with cascades of notes. She walked into the music room and saw, rather to her surprise, that Charlotte was standing beside the piano. They were both facing away from Cora. As Ivo came to the end of a passage, Cora saw Charlotte lean across and turn the page of the music. She did this deftly, without fuss, and as far as Cora could see no look passed between her and Ivo, yet there was something in the intimacy of the movement, the anticipation and answering of need without any apparent communication, that troubled Cora more than any look could have done. She stood there in the doorway, trying not to put the dread she felt into words, trying to summon up the bright smile and the outstretched hand, trying to go back to the way she had felt a moment ago – when she felt a gust of hot breath on the back of her neck, and Odo's voice in her ear.

'They make such a lovely couple, don't they? It's as if they understand each other perfectly.'

Cora felt herself go rigid at this revelation of her own unspoken thought. She was about to move away when he went on, 'Such a pity really that you and I are here. So inconvenient.' Odo's voice was hardly louder than a whisper, but he was so close to her that it was impossible to pretend she had not heard.

She turned her head a little and said, 'Oh, but I'm not jealous, Sir Odo. Charlotte and Ivo are old friends. I could hardly expect him to discard all his acquaintances on my account. And besides, I like your wife too. Shouldn't a husband and wife share the same tastes?'

Odo said nothing and Cora waited. Waited for him to advance or retreat – she would not give him the opening, she would do nothing to invite the revelation that she sensed burning up those bright, fleshy cheeks. If he turned away now she would go on as if nothing had happened, pretend that she had never seen Charlotte lean over Ivo as if she owned him, or that Ivo had played on without looking up because he knew that Charlotte would turn the page at exactly the right moment. Cora fingered the emerald on her breast. She could do it, she thought. She would touch her husband on the shoulder and suggest that he played something from *La Belle Hélène* as the Prince was so partial of Offenbach; she would smile at them both without disturbing the surface, and the Prince would compliment her on a lovely evening and they would all go peacefully to bed. That is what she would do and she would not look back.

But then Charlotte leant over to turn another page and her lips half parted. Odo was breathing hard now, and Cora knew even as she saw herself sliding gracefully along the long gallery, a hostess in command of her troops, that he was about to shatter her elegant campaign and that she was glad of it.

He stepped back from her and turned his body so that his next remark could be heard by everyone in the long gallery.

'I don't think you would like my wife so much, Duchess, if you knew where she went on the day of Lady Salisbury's pageant. Slipping away like a bitch on heat to meet your husband at the docks. She didn't even bother to make up a credible excuse. Not that anyone would have believed it, as everybody knew where she'd gone. Perhaps I'm being unreasonable but I really think she could have waited till after the show.' Odo started quietly enough but as his rage overtook him, his voice became higher and louder. The music stopped and Cora felt the silence around her sting. She stared at the floor, she could not bear to look up and see the confirmation in their faces – that everyone knew about Charlotte Beauchamp and her husband, everyone, that was, except her.

And then, at last, the silence was broken.

'It's time you went to bed, Sir Odo. You can apologise in the morrrning, when you've sobered up.' The Prince's voice was thick with contempt. 'Now, Duchess Corrra, perrrhaps you would like to show me your Canova. I feel the need for some fresh air.'

Cora felt a hand on her arm and she looked up and saw that the Prince's pale blue eyes had lost their heavy-lidded indolence and were filled with something approaching concern. She swallowed and managed to say, 'Yes, it is a lovely evening, sir.'

The Prince smiled his approval and steered her down the gallery. She looked straight ahead, trying not to let her American smile falter. As they reached the door she heard the noise behind her swell.

On the steps they passed Teddy, who noticed the angry welts on Cora's chest, flaming red against the dark green gem. He realised that Odo must have made his 'nice little scene'. Cora's face was set, her mouth drawn back into a horrible imitation of a smile; she looked straight through him and she walked down the steps with the Prince as if she was made of glass. Teddy felt his palms go sweaty with guilt. He could have stopped Odo going back inside, he had had the chance and yet he had done nothing. He walked up the stairs into the gallery, trying not to think of Cora's brittle shoulders and that terrible smile. No one looked at him as he walked in, the company had formed into little clumps around the room; only Odo stood alone, bent over with his hands on his knees as if he had just been running. No one was speaking to him or even looking at him, he was like a prizefighter collapsed after losing a bout, his audience indifferent. Teddy hesitated for a moment. Then he caught sight of the Duke at the piano with Charlotte Beauchamp standing beside him. They were not looking at each other, it was as if they were enchanted, as if they were trapped there forever, waiting for the spell to break.

Teddy walked over to Odo and tapped him on the shoulder. Odo looked up at him, his cheeks scarlet, his blue eyes bloodshot, and when he saw Teddy he smiled.

'Too late, Mr Van Der Leyden, you've missed all the fun.'

The force of Teddy's punch sent Odo sprawling on the floor. When he picked himself up his nose was bloody but his smile was still there.

'I'm not sure what I did to deserve that. You should be grateful to me, old boy.'

Teddy reached back to hit him again, but he felt a hand on his arm. He saw it was the Duke's friend, Greatorex.

'Leave him, he's not worth it,' Reggie said. 'Besides, he's drunk. Wait till he's sober.'

Teddy allowed himself to be led away. He heard a woman say

in a low, commanding voice, 'Bugler, help Sir Odo to his room. He is feeling unwell.'

Bugler clicked his fingers and two footmen took Odo by the elbows and marched him the length of the gallery. Odo's smile did not falter for a second.

Teddy said, 'I tried to stop him, coming in, you know. Was it very bad?'

Reggie looked at him and said, 'Bad enough. Beauchamp is a cad.'

Teddy groaned. 'I should have punched him in the garden.'

'Perhaps, but it's not your quarrel, is it?' and Reggie glanced over at the Duke. Teddy followed his gaze and saw the Duke stand up and close the piano lid with a click. Ignoring Charlotte, who still stood with her back to the long gallery, he walked towards the company and looked across them with a mirthless smile.

'Well, I think that's enough entertainment for the evening, so if you will excuse me.' He made a half bow in the direction of Mrs Cash and the Double Duchess and walked down the gallery, his long strides striking the stone flags with metronomic precision.

Teddy looked at Charlotte Beauchamp's profile. How would she react, he wondered, to what had happened? In a moment, she turned and he had his answer – she was smiling and, unlike the Duke's, her smile appeared to be one of genuine delight.

She glided towards him. 'I confess I'm in your debt, Mr Van Der Leyden. I know I am being disloyal, but Odo deserved that. He has a shocking head for drink. I wouldn't mind if it made him maudlin, but he just gets nasty. Poor Cora. I shall make Odo grovel tomorrow, if he dares show his face, that is.' And she put her hand lightly on Teddy's arm to show that they were all connected whether they liked it or not.

Despite himself, Teddy was impressed by her bravura. He glanced over at Mrs Cash and the Double Duchess to see if they would challenge her, but both women looked relieved to see that order had been restored.

Teddy made a little bow to acknowledge his appreciation of her performance and signalled to the footman to bring him a drink. The man brought him a schooner of brandy. He was downing it when Mr Cash walked over to him.

'Well done, Teddy. That son-of-a-bitch got what was coming to him. Would have hit him myself, but my wife would never have forgiven me.' He shrugged to indicate his helplessness.

Teddy finished his brandy.

'It was my pleasure.' He looked at the older man's handsome, acquiescent face and he felt a wave of rage and scorn flood through him. They were all going to pretend that nothing had happened, they would leave the unpleasantness behind and go on serenely like swans sailing over filthy water. And Cora would have no choice but to swim with them, never looking down. He put down his glass but it missed the table and fell to the ground, shattering as it hit the stone floor.

He looked around at the faces that had turned to the source of the noise.

'I think I've had enough,' he said.

CHAPTER 26

'Never to Stoop'

THE NEWS OF ODO'S OUTBURST REACHED THE servants' hall before Cora and the Prince had got halfway to the summer house. The footman was so full of his news that he forgot to put down the heavy silver tray he was carrying and stood there holding it, laden with glasses, as he told them what had happened upstairs. The upper servants were taking their pudding in Mrs Softley's room so they missed the first telling but word soon reached them via the maid when she brought in the Madeira and sponge cake.

'. . . And the new Duchess was standing there the whole time until His Highness came and took her away into the garden. What do you think will happen, Mrs Softley?' the girl said breathlessly.

The housekeeper finished pouring the Madeira into small cutwork glasses.

'That's enough, Mabel. You know I won't tolerate gossip in the servants' hall. Get back to your work.' But when Mabel disappeared, she said, 'Well, I have always said that Sir Odo Beauchamp was a bad lot. She should never have married him. Men like that never get any better.' She looked across at Bertha who was sitting next to Lady Beauchamp's maid.

'You had better go upstairs, Miss Jackson, and you too, Miss Beauchamp. I have some sal volatile in my cupboard if you need it.'

Bertha got up reluctantly, she knew she was being dismissed so that the Lulworth servants could talk about this freely. She tried to catch Jim's eye. But he was looking at his hands, his jaw set. She walked out as slowly as she could but still he did not look up. She lingered in the corridor, telling the other maid that she needed to fetch a new nightgown from the laundry room. She could see the long panel of bells above the door; when Miss Cora rang she would go up, but she wanted to talk to Jim first.

At last he came walking along the corridor with Bugler. Cora thought that the butler was bound to see her but he stopped at the pantry and went inside. As Jim came past the laundry, Bertha caught him by the arm, and he pulled her to him and kissed her. She tried to push him away, but as always she felt the urge to hold him closer.

'Not now, Jim. Not here.'

Jim said, 'So when then, Miss Bertha Jackson? We live in the same house and yet for all I see of you, I could still be in India.' He spoke lightly, but she could hear the frustration in his voice. It had been exciting to begin with: the stolen kisses and hurried embraces in empty corridors, but it could not go on much longer. Jim had not talked of marriage since he had come home, and though Bertha wanted him, she was not prepared to risk her job without at least the prospect of a ring.

'You didn't look at me in there, Jim. Does that mean you knew about the Duke and Lady Beauchamp?'

Jim said nothing and Bertha knew she had her answer. 'But why didn't you tell me? I should have known. I could have . . .' She stopped.

'You could have done nothing, Bertha, and that's the truth. That's why I didn't tell you. What they do upstairs is their business. You don't want to interfere. Anyway, there was nothing to stop you figuring it out for yourself. The only reason you didn't is that you take Miss Cora's side on everything. She's a foreigner, Bertha, and the Duke likes things that are home-grown.'

Bertha began to feel angry. 'What, and that makes carrying on behind Miss Cora's back with that woman all right?' She pushed at him with her hand. 'I'm a foreigner too, remember.'

Jim took her hand. 'Don't take it that way, Bertha. You will never be foreign to me.'

Mollified, she left her hand in his.

'Poor Miss Cora, this is going to be mighty hard on her. She thought she had it all figured out.'

Jim said, 'I don't know that anyone could figure out the Duke. One minute he's throwing shaving water at me because it's cold, next thing he's giving me twenty guineas to get some new clothes. Some days he treats me like dirt, won't say a civil word, and then he'll be as charming as you like, wants to know if I have a sweetheart, if I intend to see out my days in service. There were days on the boat going out when I would have gladly jumped off and swum home – if I'd known how to swim, that is,' he laughed. 'Coming back wasn't so bad, I think he was looking forward to getting home. One thing I do know, he wasn't expecting to see Lady Beauchamp right away. We'd only just got to the club when she sent a note up for him. He looked pretty put out, and threw it on the floor.'

'How did you know the note was from Lady Beauchamp? Did he tell you?'

'Not likely! No, I picked it up after he'd gone and then I saw it was from her. It just said, "I'm waiting for you," signed with a C.'

'But how did you know it was Lady Beauchamp? C could have stood for Cora,' Bertha said.

'It was on plain writing paper, no crest, nothing. And why would the Duchess not sign her name? Anyway, I knew it was from *her*. She came to say goodbye to him before we left for the wedding in America. Rode in the carriage with him all the way to the station. Looked like she was going to a funeral.' A bell began to ring. Bertha looked up from Jim's shoulder and saw that it was the bell for the Duchess's room.

'It's Miss Cora, I must go.' She started to move away from him but Jim held her hand.

'We should leave soon, Bertha. Take our chances. Before it's too late.'

Bertha met his eyes, but then the bell rang again, and she heard footsteps coming down the hall.

She wondered if that had been a proposal. 'I'll need to get my trousseau together first,' she said smiling.

His eyes widened in understanding and he was about to speak when the bell rang and they heard Bugler's door open. 'Later,' Bertha said.

In her bedroom Cora was pacing round the furniture, tearing at the necklace round her neck. The clasp had got caught in her hair and she was desperate to get it off. She gave it one last tug and the necklace exploded, scattering diamonds across the room. Bertha opened the door, and Cora shouted at her, 'Where've you been?

Look what's happened, I couldn't get it off by myself.' Cora knew she was being unreasonable but she was so angry that she had to yell at someone.

Bertha started to pick up the sparkling debris. 'Don't worry, Miss Cora, it shouldn't be too difficult to mend.'

'Oh, just leave it, get me out of this infernal dress.' Cora twitched furiously in the golden brocade. Bertha got up slowly, her movements a reproach. She set down the gems on the dressing table with a clatter, taking a moment to shape them into a neat pile.

Cora screamed with impatience. She felt as if there were ants crawling all over her body. But when, at last, Bertha untied the strings of her corset, her skin felt cold and clammy. She looked at herself in the glass. There were two red smudges on her cheekbones but her lips were pale. She felt herself shivering, all the heat and irritation that had possessed her a few minutes ago had left her and now she felt cold and so weary. She wanted to lie down, close her eyes and obliterate everything that had just passed. She thought of the Prince carefully guiding her round the garden, telling her again about the time he had seen Blondin walk across the Niagara Falls on a tightrope. 'Such a little man, I thought he might be blown away by the sprrray. I confess I had to close my eyes several times.' The Prince had stopped to admire the Canova. 'He was prrresented to me afterwards. He was very composed, as if he had been for a walk in the park. I asked him what his trrrick was, and he said the most important thing was always to look forward and concentrate on the next step and never look down. He was so earnest when he spoke, as if he was passing on a secret. I meet so many people who tell me things but I have never forgotten him.' He paused. 'A fine statue, Duchess, you Amerrricans have such style.' He did not mention Odo's outburst in the gallery but

Cora understood that he had, nonetheless, been giving her advice.

Cora heard the door open. She knew it was Ivo, anyone else would have knocked. She looked up and saw to her amazement that he was smiling. He looked completely at ease as if this was the end to a perfect evening

'So this is where you are hiding. I was beginning to wonder if the Prince had carried you off.' His tone was bantering. 'You really are quite the hostess, darling. No one could complain of boredom at one of your parties.'

Their eyes met. He smiled at her equally; his eyes too dark for her to read. She had the satisfaction of seeing him take in the sparkling rubble of her necklace lying on the dressing table and flinch.

'I don't want to talk to you,' she said quietly. 'Not now, at any rate, not until after the christening.'

Ivo stepped towards her and bent down to put his face at her level, as if he was addressing a child. His smile did not falter.

'Don't tell me you're sulking, Cora. So unlike you. Surely you're not taking Odo's outburst seriously. Everybody knows he lives to make trouble. Most people won't have him in the house, but I seem to remember that it was *you* who insisted on having the Beauchamps to stay.' He shrugged.

Cora took a step back. 'What happened tonight was hardly my fault,' she said angrily.

'Did you know that your American friend knocked Odo down, after you left? Quite a lot of spectres at this particular feast, I'd say.' He was still smiling, but Cora could see that a muscle in his jaw was twitching.

Bertha, who had been standing behind the wardrobe, unseen by Ivo, decided she must make her presence known before the

401

conversation went any further. She coughed and came out with Cora's nightdress and wrapper and laid them on the bed. She tried to keep her expression blank as if she had heard nothing.

'Will that be all, Your Grace?' she said meekly to Cora as she made for the door.

Cora put out her hand to stop her.

'No, I'd like you to stay.' She turned to Ivo. 'The Duke was just leaving.' She wondered if he would protest but he continued to smile, as if nothing was wrong.

'Of course, you will need all your strength for tomorrow. Sleep well, Cora,' and he turned and left them, closing the door behind him softly.

Cora sank back on to the bed. She could not understand what was happening. Ivo was behaving as if nothing had taken place, that if anyone was at fault, it was her. This made her angry but also hopeful. Would Ivo dare to be angry with her if Odo's accusations were true? But then she remembered, almost against her will, Ivo and Charlotte at the piano and the space between them, thick with intimacy. She started to feel cold again and she pulled the wrapper around her. Ivo and she had been so close since his return. All the misunderstandings that had flawed the first days of their marriage seemed to have disappeared. Did Odo's outburst mean that all that closeness had been a lie? Who was she to believe?

Bertha saw Cora huddled on the bed, her hands twisting themselves into a lattice of anxiety. She could see the bewilderment on her mistress's face and she wondered if she should tell her what she knew about the Duke and Lady Beauchamp. But she heard Jim's voice saying, 'It's not our business, Bertha,' and she hesitated.

'You look cold, Miss Cora. Would you like some hot milk?'

Cora looked up gratefully. 'Yes, thank you, Bertha, that would be nice,' and she lay back among the drifts of pillows and closed her eyes.

When Bertha went into the servants' hall, the room fell silent.

'Some hot milk for the Duchess, please,' Bertha asked one of the kitchen maids who was looking at her with round guilty eyes. As the girl scuttled off to get the milk from the dairy, Bertha looked up at a silver cup that stood on a high shelf. Every year there was a cricket match between the house and the village. This year the house had won. Bertha had found the game quite baffling but she had enjoyed watching Jim running down the pitch, his sleeves rolled up, his long arms strong, and she had felt warm with pride when something he did provoked applause. She could not imagine such a scene at home, the masters and the servants on the same team. Then she looked down at the faces surveying her curiously, hungry for scraps about the American Duchess; this was her home now, she thought, but she belonged here as little as she had in Newport. She was always the outsider, the stranger who stopped the flow of conversation, who made people feel uncomfortable. She remembered the cabin where she had grown up but there, too, she knew she would be a stranger with her silk dress and her fancy accent.

She deliberately kept her eyes fixed on the cup until the milk was brought to her by the kitchen maid. She took the tray up the back stairs to the Duchess's bedroom, hoping to see Jim, but no one was about. As she walked along the passage that led to Miss Cora's room, she heard a door shut and a flash of red at the other end. Bertha started. Had Lady Beauchamp really been to see Miss Cora? After all that had happened? She hurried towards the bedroom as fast as the hot milk would allow her and opened the door. But her alarm had been unnecessary, Cora was fast asleep, her face slack, her arms outstretched. Bertha thought she looked hardly a day older than the girl who had asked her for kissing lessons. She put the milk down and pulled the covers around her mistress, tucking her into a linen cocoon. She pushed a strand of hair out of Cora's face.

The room was dark but there was a sliver of moonlight coming in through the gap in the curtains. Cora opened her eyes reluctantly, she did not want to be awake now when everything was still and quiet. She had wanted to sleep through till morning when the bustle and urgency of the day would drive all her thoughts into a small manageable corner of her brain. But she was fully conscious now, her head humming with all the images of the evening before – Charlotte leaning over to turn the page of music, Odo whispering in her ear, the Prince's touch on her arm, Ivo's defiant smile and his opaque eyes. She got up and lit the lamp by her bedside. She pulled on her wrapper – she would go to the nursery. She wanted to feel Guy's small warm body and smell his soft downy head. Her son, at least, was certain.

The nursery smelt of eucalyptus and baby. Cora walked in and put down her lamp. She could hear Guy snuffling in his golden crib. Through the nursery door she could make out the deeper rumbling snores of the nanny. She went over to Guy and picked him up, cradling him against her chest. She tried to think of nothing but the sweet smell of his scalp and the tiny arpeggios of his breathing. But she could not obliterate the image of Charlotte reaching over to turn the page of music. She remembered the way the Double Duchess had looked after Odo's outburst, not shocked or surprised but assessing, as if she were calculating the damage.

Cora held the baby a little closer as she thought how everyone must have known except her. She found the thought of her ignorance almost as distressing as the thought of Ivo's treachery. She felt like a sapling that had begun to put down roots, pushing into the soil for stability and nurture, only to meet with emptiness. She thought of the servants, Sybil, even Mrs Wyndham – had they all known that her husband loved another woman? Had they all smiled and smoothed things over so that Ivo could marry the fortune that had fallen so conveniently at his feet that day in Paradise Wood?

And then she thought of Charlotte, her 'friend', the only woman in London whose wardrobe she envied. She had thought that they were equals – in looks, clothes and position. They had caught each other's eye over the drabness. Had Charlotte been pretending all along? She remembered standing in another room in darkness the night before her wedding, and the note she had found in the dressing case. 'May your marriage be as happy as mine has been.' Even then, she had known the note to be malign and she had destroyed it. She thought back for other signs that she had ignored. Was her ignorance her own fault?

The baby made a shuddering squeak and Cora realised that she was holding him too tightly. She tried to relax her grip and walked over to the window and pulled back the curtain. The moon was over the sea now. She could see the bell-shaped shadow of the summer house stretched out across the silvery lawn. The metal spire sent a long thin stripe like a tightrope over the grass. But could she go forward like Blondin, never looking down?

And then she felt a hand on her shoulder, a breath in her ear. She turned round. Ivo's face was in shadow but she heard him say, 'I told you, Cora, I have everything I want.' And even though she could not see his eyes, she heard the plea in his voice and she could not resist it. She let him put his arms round her and Guy and leant into him as he kissed her hair and her forehead. This was all she wanted too.

CHAPTER 27

'Then all Smiles Stopped'

THE FIRST THING TEDDY FELT WHEN HE WOKE that morning was the throbbing in his right hand, from where his knuckles had met Odo Beauchamp's nose. But the warm pulse of pain was followed by a blush of shame. He did not regret hitting Odo, the man had deserved it, but he knew now that what had seemed noble the night before was, on reflection, quite selfish. He had failed to stop Odo from making his horrible revelation and had assuaged his guilt with violence. He thought of what his mother would say if she knew that he was knocking English baronets about. She would be embarrassed by his lack of self-control but she would be horrified by the emotions behind it. As Teddy tried to stretch out his bruised fingers, he knew that the man he had wanted to hit was not his actual victim but the Duke himself.

The door opened and a footman came in with hot water and towels. He set Teddy's shaving things out in front of the mirror. When Teddy walked over, the footman saw his hand and winced sympathetically.

'Would you like me to get some ointment for that, sir? It looks nasty.'

Teddy understood from the man's knowing look that he had been in the gallery last night.

'Yes,' he said ruefully, 'it is surprisingly painful.'

The footman took this admission as an invitation and continued, 'Never mind, sir, you should see the other fellow! His valet was up and down all night with beefsteak and ice. And then this morning he had to get him all packed up as Sir Odo is leaving on the morning train. He has to go and see a doctor in London, thinks his nose is broken.' From the smile on the footman's face, Sir Odo's injury was clearly a popular one.

Teddy said, 'I didn't realise I'd hit him that hard.'

'Not sure you did, sir. But maybe he thought he wouldn't be welcome any longer.' The footman glanced at Teddy to see if he would be reproved for gossiping, and then he handed him the razor. 'It's Lady Beauchamp I feel sorry for. Whatever she's done, it would be purgatory to be married to a man like that. My cousin was a housemaid there and the stories she told were shocking and I've been in service fifteen years.'

Teddy would have liked to ask what Sir Odo was guilty of, but he was in the middle of shaving and could not speak.

'She said it was a terrible place. Even though the pay was good, she gave in her notice after six months.'

The footman handed Teddy a towel.

'Are you joining the cycling party, sir? Will you be wearing the blazer?'

Teddy nodded.

The footman laid out his clothes and said, 'Is that all, sir?'

Teddy felt in his pockets for a coin and held it out to him.

'That's very kind of you, sir, but I couldn't take it. Reckon you did us all a favour there, punching Sir Odious.'

Teddy took his time getting dressed. Odo Beauchamp might have left but he had no desire to see the Duke at breakfast. He now regretted the impulse which had made him write to Cora and to accept her invitation. He would have done better leaving her alone. He had had his chance in Newport and he had not taken it. She had not replied to the letter he had written to her before her wedding, but it had been too late to tell her then that he loved her. If only he hadn't been so squeamish about the encounter he had witnessed at Euston Station, that would have been useful information for Cora, not some redundant declaration of love. But he had not wanted to get his hands dirty, he had half hoped that Cora would renounce her Duke and confound her mother because he, Teddy, had finally made up his mind that he loved her. And now he was faced with the consequences of his own delicacy: Cora had married a man whose real nature she did not know and, worse still, she had married for love. Teddy remembered the way her face had changed when he went to see her in New York, how she had lost her glorious selfish certainty. And he had seen in the brittle set of her shoulders last night just how much Odo's revelations must have hurt her. He could have warned her. But he had not been interested in protecting Cora then, he had just wanted her to choose him.

He looked out of the window at the water garden on the terrace below, with its statues and fountains. The evening before he had heard Lady Tavistock say to the Double Duchess as she surveyed the glittering parterre, 'So glorious now. Say what you like, Fanny, there are uses for American heiresses and their money after all.'

Had Cora realised, he wondered, exactly what sort of bargain she had made? He was sure not.

And now? Now that she knew what kind of man she had married, how would she proceed? Would she carry on, happy enough with the title her money had bought? Through the window, Teddy saw a man scrubbing one of the fountains, scraping off the slimy legacy of the spring rains. Teddy felt angry on Cora's behalf; she had been deceived so that the marble fountains of Lulworth could be scrubbed clean. She was, he thought, worth a great deal more than that. He could not offer her all this, this panoply of fountains and balustrades and princes, but his feelings for her were at least straightforward: he loved the woman, not the heiress. He could give her a way out. The scandal would be immense for both of them. He would surely have to abandon his commission from the New York Public Library but that was proof of his love. He had given her up before because of his art, now he told himself that he would put Cora first.

Yes, he thought, he would act. The world might be shocked that he would offer his love to a married woman but he did not care for that. He dismissed the thought of his mother's hooded blue eyes and the pious rectitude of her Washington Square friends. He was not an opportunist or an adulterer but a man who would sacrifice everything to rescue the woman he loved.

He caught sight of himself in the mirror and smiled at his own look of resolution. Then he set off down the stairs to join the cycling party.

The Prince of Wales was the first to cycle down the gravel path. His balance was unsteady but he managed to round the first corner without incident. No one dared smile at the portly figure as he wobbled off, he was so sensitive about his weight that anyone who hoped to remain in his favour had to pretend to see the slim young man that the Prince still imagined himself to be. The Prince's equerry Colonel Ferrers rode off next at a pace calculated not to challenge his royal master. Sybil and Reggie followed, Reggie riding close to Sybil, ostensibly in case of accidents. Cora and Teddy were the last in the party as the older ladies had declined to risk their dignity, Charlotte Beauchamp had not yet appeared and Ivo claimed that he had business on the estate.

Cora pushed off quickly. She could see that Teddy wanted to talk to her about last night and she was reluctant to do so. She could still feel Ivo's arm round her when she had greeted her guests that morning, which had allowed her to keep her smile radiant when confronted by so many curious faces. She had ignored all their unspoken questions and had outlined the day's plans as if nothing had happened. Her mother had nodded at her approvingly and even the Double Duchess had given her a gracious incline of the head. But Cora knew that her self-command was fragile, she could not afford to look down. She saw that Teddy was struggling to contain his emotions and she tried to head him off with her best Duchess manner.

'It is such a treat to see you again, Teddy. I am so glad that you are going to be Guy's godfather, I don't want him to be completely British. Don't worry about the ceremony, it will be very simple. The Catholic ritual is pretty much the same as the Episcopalian one.'

Teddy did not reply for a moment and then he said, 'It's not the ceremony I am worried about.'

Cora speeded up a little and pebbles flew out from under her wheels.

Teddy kept pace with her.

At last she said in irritation, the Duchess manner abandoned, 'You only made it worse last night, hitting Odo Beauchamp. I know you meant well, but can't you see that it makes things . . . awkward?' Teddy noticed that Cora was beginning to pick up a British accent. 'I know that inviting Odo was a mistake but I did want Charlotte to be here. She is my particular friend, you see.' Cora slowed down a little, she did not want to get too close to the others.

'Really? What if I were to tell you that she is the last person who deserves your friendship?'

Cora pumped her brakes and stopped with a skid of gravel. She looked at him seriously. 'I would ignore you. Charlotte has not been fortunate in her choice of husband but that doesn't mean that she shouldn't have friends.'

Teddy was annoyed by Cora's composure. This was not the scene he had imagined. He had thought that Cora would be heart-broken by last night's revelations, distraught over her husband's betrayal, but instead she seemed to be blaming *him* for causing a scene. Had she really become part of this British world which seemed to him like a smooth sea on an unlit night, the calm surface concealing the strong currents beneath. He decided to plunge, and putting one hand on Cora's wrist he said, 'Are you just going to ignore the fact that your husband is Charlotte Beauchamp's lover?'

Cora took her hand away and replied boldly, 'And how would you know that, Teddy? You have known my husband and Charlotte Beauchamp for less than a day. If I choose to believe there is nothing between them, how can you possibly say otherwise?'

The sun came out from behind a cloud and Cora had to squint to see him properly. Teddy had never seen her look so plain, her eyes screwed up and her face mottled with anger, her figure hidden in those ridiculous cycling bloomers; but he found this sudden ugliness more endearing than the perfectly dressed woman he had seen last night.

'I have no *right* to say anything. Except for the fact that I care for you and I cannot bear to see you deceived.'

They were both silent for a moment. Cora took a deep breath and resumed her Duchess manner. 'The Prince will be at the picnic tent by now, we should catch up with him, otherwise Mother will be arranging a royal visit to Newport.' She made a show of getting on her bicycle. But Teddy pulled her round to face him. Cora tried to evade him but he held on to her so that she had to listen to him.

'No, Cora, I can't let you pretend that nothing has happened. You are not a girl who can live in the shadows. You deserve to be surrounded by truth and light. Your husband and Lady Beauchamp have lied to you all along. I *saw* them together at Euston Station before he came over for your wedding. I didn't know who they were then, of course, but it made such an impression on me that when I saw Lady Beauchamp last night, I recognised her at once.'

Cora was shaking her hands in front of her in a gesture he remembered. It was as if she was trying to bat away unpleasantness. 'I don't understand you. Why are you doing this?' And he could see that she was blinking fast.

'Because I love you, Cora.' He said it quietly and for a moment he thought she hadn't heard him. 'I *know* you and I love you. I came here ready to be your friend and nothing more but now I see your true situation, the way you have been deceived – all these . . . these vultures hovering around you wanting your money – I have to speak out. This isn't the life you should have, Cora, pandering to princes and worrying whether one raddled old duchess should walk in front of another. None of them *do* anything, except shoot things and gossip. Of course the houses are beautiful and everyone has perfect manners, but how can you live like this in a world built on lies?'

Cora had turned her head away from him but he knew she was listening. He thought briefly of his mother and how disappointed she would be by this squandering of emotion, he felt a flicker of regret for the respectable career he might have as a painter in New York, but with Cora in front of him he had no choice but to press on.

'Cora, come away with me. I love *you*, not your money or anything else. We could have a life with no lies, no subterfuge, where we could be open and honest with each other. We could live in France or Italy among people who don't care about duchesses and rules. You used to care for me once, Cora; I can't believe all that feeling has gone.'

At last she turned her head to look at him. 'Feeling? I wanted to marry you, Teddy, but you were scared. And now it's too late.'

He began to protest but her face was fierce.

'No more, please!' But he was pleased to see that there was a tear escaping from the corner of one eye. She had heard him, he thought.

Then she shook her head and said, 'We must catch up with the Prince. He does not like to be kept waiting.'

And she pedalled away from him, her front wheel jerking from

side to side as if she were not quite able to balance. Teddy followed
behind her.

Lunch had been laid out in the shade of two beech trees. The
white tablecloth was overlaid with the lacy shadows of the leaves.
The meal was to be served in a tented pavilion which Cora had
ordered from London. She knew that the Prince would not
consider dining al fresco, an excuse for inferior food. In the tent
there was a barrel of oysters in ice, lobsters, caviar, tureens of
vichyssoise, lark tongues in aspic, game pies, salmagundi, a variety
of ice creams and a spirit stove for making soufflé omelettes;
and to drink there was champagne, hock, claret, sauternes and
brandy as well as iced tea and lemon barley water. Cora hoped
that there was sufficient ice; in Newport the sun had been so
strong in the summer that meals like these would always end
up lukewarm in a pool of water. At least the weather here was
more temperate. She found that if she concentrated very hard
on the details of the meal, trying to remember exactly what she
had ordered, she could keep out the other thoughts that were
trying to push in. Teddy might dismiss this life as trivial but
right now all she wanted was to get through this day, she wanted
there to be enough ice and no silences. This lunch, after all, was
under her control.

The Prince was already sitting down with Lady Tavistock. Her
mother, to Cora's relief, was being expertly charmed by the Prince's
equerry. Duchess Fanny was flirting with her father, although the
odd flick of her eyes suggested that she was keeping the Prince
under surveillance. Reggie was giving Sybil some cycling 'tuition'

which involved running alongside while she pedalled, his arm firmly round her waist. Father Oliver was sitting back in his chair, his eyes half closed, although Cora suspected that he was listening intently to the conversations around him. She saw Teddy pull up a chair close to him.

Ivo must be on his way. She tried to make out the tiny jewelled hands of her wrist watch: it was nearly one o'clock. When he had left her this morning he had promised he would be here in good time. 'Don't worry, Duchess Cora, I will be present and correct.' She didn't like it usually when he called her Duchess Cora with that ironic glint in his eye, she suspected that he was comparing her to his mother, but that morning she had not minded the connection so much. She peered across the green swell of the park for him; she hoped no one could see her screwing up her nose so that her short-sighted eyes could focus. She thought she could see something moving in the middle distance but she didn't dare stand there for much longer with her face twisted up like a gargoyle. Bugler was standing a few feet away and she waved him over.

'Is that the Duke coming down from the house?'

Bugler nodded and then said, 'He has a lady with him, Your Grace. I can't be certain at this distance but I would say it was Lady Beauchamp.' He permitted himself a flicker of a smile. 'I will make sure there is another place set.'

Cora stared at the figures approaching across the green turf. As they came into focus she could see that Charlotte was wearing white and was carrying a pink parasol in one hand, the other was resting on Ivo's arm. Cora could not see their faces but she fancied they were not talking. She knew she should move but she found their progress towards her mesmerising. It was so deliberate, so steady.

She heard a cough behind her. It was Colonel Ferrers.

'I believe, Duchess, that the Prince is getting hungry.'

Cora started. 'Of course, how thoughtless of me.' She signalled to Bugler to start serving and approached the Prince.

'Forgive me, sir, for keeping you waiting. I would curtsy in apology but I think I would look very comical doing so in this costume. As you can see, the Duke and Lady Beauchamp are on their way over here, but we shall punish them for their tardiness by starting immediately.' She started to direct the company around the table, placing her mother next to the Prince and Teddy next to Sybil. She sat at the head of the table with the Prince on one side and Reggie on the other. Reggie needed no attention and the Prince would be in thrall to her mother; Cora wanted to be able to observe the table without having to talk. She felt numb. This morning she had felt quite sure of Ivo and now he was testing her faith again.

Ivo made a little bow to the table when he arrived. 'What a wonderful sight. I feel as if I have stumbled upon an oasis in the desert. As I have had nothing to do with this, I can say that this is quite magnificent. I always thought that eating outside involved sand and midges. Cora, it never ceases to amaze me how comfortable you Americans insist life should be.'

Cora tilted her head towards her mother. She did not quite trust herself to speak.

'Well, it's true that in my country we see no reason to suffer,' Mrs Cash said, delighted to have a conversational opening. 'In my view there is no excuse for inconvenience if a little thought and planning is exercised ahead of time. At home I ensure that all the picnics and bicycle parties are as well appointed as if they were taking place at Sans Souci. There really is no reason for anyone to be too cold or too hot or uncomfortable in any way. I am quite a martinet in these matters, I daresay, but my guests are always grateful.' She smiled warmly at the Prince. 'I hope we can tempt you back to the United States before too long, Your Highness. We have entertained quite a few members of European royalty. The Grand Duke Alexander of Russia, and the Crown Prince of Prussia among them. I think if Your Highness were to come we could guarantee your comfort.'

The Prince took a large helping of caviar before replying. 'I have no doubt of that, Mrs Cash. I have always thought that Amerrricans were the most hospitable people, at home and abroad. Indeed I think that Amerrrican hostesses like your daughter have done so much to lift the spirits of society. I know when I go to a party given by an Amerrrican hostess that the food will be delicious, the atmosphere warm, the women will be the last word in fashion and the caviar plentiful.' He smiled greedily, his small blue eyes taking in both Mrs Cash's pleasure and the Double Duchess's rage at this speech. 'But sadly, I won't be able to visit Amerrrica in the foreseeable future. The Queen is, thank God, in good health, but I am aware that I may be called upon at any time.' The Prince looked solemn and Ferrers, sensing a change in the royal mood, asked Mrs Cash if she knew anything of the new electric motor cars.

Cora had gathered herself after the shock of seeing Ivo arrive with Charlotte. She tried to dismiss Odo's outburst and Teddy's revelation from her mind. Ivo must, she reasoned, have brought Charlotte deliberately. It was his riposte to last night. There could be no gossip if he was willing to escort Charlotte in public in front of his wife. Accordingly, she smiled at Charlotte, who said, 'I'm afraid I have lost Odo. He had urgent business to attend to in town. He was full of apologies and he insisted that I stay on for the christening. I hope that doesn't throw out your numbers too much.'

Cora hardly heard Charlotte's words, she was struck by how well the other woman looked. Her customary sullen languor had been replaced by a new vigour. She was, again, the woman that Louvain had painted as a beautiful predator.

'I think we can manage. I am sure that Duchess Fanny will happily go in to dinner with Lady Tavistock.' They both laughed and Cora felt that she had done well until she saw Teddy looking at her. She felt a dull ache beginning at the base of her skull.

After lunch Cora decided to go back to the house in the donkey trap. She did not want another tête-à-tête with Teddy and she needed time to prepare herself for the christening. Rather to her surprise she found her mother-in-law being helped on to the seat beside her. Ivo had sent round the barouche landau for the other ladies and Cora had hoped to ride back alone. But the Double Duchess had insisted on Mr Cash riding with his wife and had protested that a ride in the donkey trap would remind her of 'the old days' when she had spent many happy hours wandering around the grounds.

Cora set off in silence. Her head was too full to make conversation with Duchess Fanny.

'This takes me back to my years at Lulworth,' said the Duchess. 'I was so happy here.' She sighed wistfully and Cora responded by giving the donkey a hard tap from her switch. Duchess Fanny continued in her most soothing tones, 'When I first met you, Cora, I have to confess I wondered if you understood what it meant to be mistress of Lulworth. I thought you were too headstrong, too used to your own way to appreciate the sacrifices that would be demanded of you. Ivo is not an easy man and I suspected you wouldn't have the patience to deal with him. I thought that an English girl would understand better what would be required. But it seems that I was wrong. Not many women would have dealt with Charlotte Beauchamp so calmly. You didn't let your own feelings get in the way.'

Cora looked at the flies hovering around the donkey's head and the steady rhythm of its flanks moving in the harness.

'But if I may give you some advice, it is time for you to speak to Charlotte. You must make it clear to her that you will not tolerate such flagrant behaviour. Tell her that you have the Prince's support and mine and that if she and her awful husband cannot be discreet, she will find herself friendless. I think she will understand.' Duchess Fanny put her hand on Cora's arm. 'And don't worry, Ivo won't interfere. He seems quite uxorious now that you have given him a son. After all, women like Charlotte are so exhausting.'

Cora tugged on the reins and pulled the donkey to a grumbling stop.

'Thank you for the advice, Duchess Fanny, but I prefer to handle things in my own way.' She handed the reins to the Duchess. 'I believe I am going to get out and walk now. I am sure you will remember how to manage the donkey.'

She jumped down from the cart and walked away as fast as she could until she could no longer see the cart or the Double Duchess's look of surprise. She sat down on the grass for a moment and put her head between her knees.

When at last, raising her head, she caught a glimpse of the sea filling the gap in the hills, she felt a sudden longing to throw herself into the water and swim free of all the weight that was being piled upon her. But when she looked in the other direction she could see the royal standard flying above the house and hear the chapel clock striking the half hour. The nurse would be dressing Guy in his christening robe now, swathing his wriggling body in the yellowing lace. Guy was part of this too. Soon they would all be gathering round the font in the chapel; the only thing she could do now was to go back, get dressed and smile while they christened her son. She would not look down, not yet.

CHAPTER 28

'The Dropping of the Daylight'

ORA HAD CONSIDERED EVERY DETAIL OF THE christening, from the flowers in the chapel to the white and silver bonbonnières, but she had not given much thought to the ceremony itself. Normally she found herself becoming slightly impatient in church, wishing the repetition and the ritual would go more quickly so that she could be somewhere else. But today, as she stood by the font, she was grateful for the ceremony that demanded nothing from her but a silent nod of the head. She heard the baby's baptismal name read out, 'Albert Edward Guy Winthrop Maltravers'. She had protested about the Albert, but the Double Duchess had told her, 'If you want the Prince of Wales to act as sponsor you will have to name the baby after him. You don't have to call him that; even the Prince doesn't care for the name Albert, but it is a mark of respect.' Cora looked over at the line of godparents: the Prince of Wales very loud with his amens, Sybil and Reggie exchanging complicit glances as they made their vows, Teddy staring at her as he promised to bring up the child in the ways of God – his eyes telling her that he would look after them both. Cora dropped her gaze, she couldn't bear to think about what Teddy was offering her, now. When she looked up again, she saw Charlotte staring at the baby with an intentness that shocked her. It wasn't just the empty gaze of a childless woman looking at somebody else's baby; there was something watchful and predatory about her, as if she was waiting to spring.

Cora felt light-headed, her legs were shaking and she put her hand on Ivo's arm to steady herself. He glanced down at her and put his hand over hers. Cora felt her mouth filling with saliva; she swallowed desperately and looked up at the sky through the glass cupola. She willed her body not to panic, she must keep moving forward.

She saw Father Oliver look at her and she realised that he wanted her to take Guy. For a second she wondered whether she would be able to hold the baby, she felt so weak, but she caught another glimpse of Charlotte's face and put out her arms to take her son.

She kept her eyes fixed on the baby as everyone gathered around her to admire him. He was unmistakably Ivo's child, the tiny face dominated by his father's Roman nose. She heard the Double Duchess saying, 'He has the Maltravers profile of course,' and Father Oliver agreeing that he had 'something about him of the Fourth Duke'.

Deliberately, as if she was conferring an enormous honour, the Double Duchess held out her arms to take her grandson, and reluctantly Cora handed him over. To her secret delight Guy started to howl the moment the Duchess took him in her arms, and she could not soothe him. Cora saw the look of annoyance on the Duchess's face and was about to take Guy back when Ivo intervened, saying lightly to his mother, 'I see you haven't lost your touch,' as he took little Guy and rested him against his shoulder, the long lace skirts of the christening gown flowing like a waterfall over his frock coat.

Guy's sobs faded to hiccups. Cora wanted to laugh and to put her arms round her husband and her son. But she could sense Teddy and Charlotte on either side of her and she could not move.

It was a relief to be outside as the christening party walked back to the house for tea. All the outdoor servants and the villagers were lined up along the path between the chapel and the house and as the Prince walked past talking with Ivo, who was still holding the baby, shouts rang out from the crowd of 'God save the Prince of Wales' and 'God save the Duke of Wareham', and then some wit said, 'It's the Duchess who needs saving.' The Prince and Ivo were too far ahead to hear this last remark but Cora, who was next to Mrs Cash, was not. Cora looked over to her mother to see if she had heard too, but she was on Mrs Cash's bad side so she could not read her mother's expression. Cora's cheeks burned. The thought that her life was being picked over by the villagers was intolerable. She wanted to look round and find out who had been responsible but she could not show them that she minded.

She heard her mother saying, 'I have to congratulate you, Cora, you have arranged this very nicely. Lulworth is improved beyond recognition. Of course the servants here are so good, you don't have to train them the way I do at home. Still, you have made things so much more comfortable. When I think what it used to be like.' She shuddered. 'As the Prince himself said, we Americans have such a talent for hospitality and you can understand when you go about here just why he appreciates it so much. Perhaps Mr Cash and I should take a house in London for the season next year.'

Cora felt the stares of the villagers lining the route like blows. She turned to her mother and said, 'Actually, Mother, I was thinking of coming home for a few months. It would be so nice to see all my old friends again, and I long to show off little Guy. I thought perhaps I could sail back with you when you go.'

Mrs Cash did not reply for a moment and Cora wished she was walking on her mother's other side so she could see what she was thinking.

'Well, of course I would love to have you visit with us. You know I just adore my grandson, the Marquis.' Mrs Cash paused reverently over the title. 'But are you sure that my son-in-law is ready for a trip? He has just come back from one, after all.'

Cora said quickly, 'I was thinking of coming alone, Mother, just me and the baby. Ivo has so much to do here . . .' She tailed off.

'But a wife's place is with her husband, Cora. Whatever your own inclinations are, your duty is to stay by his side. Surely I have raised you to understand that there is more to life than your own pleasure.' Mrs Cash stopped and turned to face her. Cora could see her good eye glittering.

'I don't know, Mother, that Ivo would mind,' she said.

'Nonsense, Cora. It's not a question of minding. You are man and wife and that is all there is to it.'

'But it's so hard, Mother. Everyone here has known each other all their lives, so I am always the outsider. You don't know how much I long to be somewhere where people aren't gossiping about my accent or my latest faux pas.' And her marriage, Cora thought but didn't say.

Mrs Cash took Cora's hand and squeezed it, hard. It was not a gesture of affection.

'And do you think that if you came home after one year of marriage without your husband that you wouldn't be gossiped about? I assure you, Cora, people would talk of little else. There is nothing New York society would enjoy more than the sight of my daughter the Duchess failing in her marriage. I can't have you ruining everything I have worked for because you can't manage your husband. I'm sorry, Cora, but this is your affair, not mine.' Mrs Cash dropped Cora's hand and turned to talk to the Double Duchess and Mr Cash, who had just caught up with them.

Cora stopped so that she could put up her parasol. She would rather be stared at by the crowd than spend one more minute with her mother. She almost broke the parasol's ivory handle in her urgency to get the shade up; her hands were trembling so much that she could not slide the spokes over the catch. There was a moment's respite as the glare of the afternoon sun was filtered by the cream silk. Cora took a deep breath, and tried to compose her face. She should have known that her mother would react this way and yet it was shocking nonetheless that she would put her social supremacy so far ahead of her daughter's happiness. She tested the corners of her mouth, seeing if she could stretch them into a smile. Then she felt a hand on her elbow, and heard a squeak of excitement.

'You are going to hate me for doing this today but I can't help myself.' Sybil took Cora's hand and swung it enthusiastically. 'Dearest Cora, he's proposed and I've accepted!' Sybil was bobbing with delight. 'We're going to announce our engagement at the tea. Please don't be cross with me for stealing Guy's thunder, but if the Prince is there then Mama can't have a conniption fit. Oh, I am so happy, I could burst.'

Cora felt her face soften. 'Dear Sybil, I am glad. I am sure you will be very happy. You two were meant to be together. Where is Reggie? I want to be the first to congratulate him.' Reggie was produced, and the three of them entered the house together. As they walked up the steps to the terrace, Sybil went ahead so that she could fetch a handkerchief. 'I know I'm going to cry.'

As Sybil ran up the steps, Cora said to Reggie, 'I have always hoped this would happen. But what took you so long?'

Reggie laughed. 'Now, I have no idea. I suppose I had some notion that a man should make something of himself before he marries. But then I realised that all I was doing was making Sybil unhappy and really there was no point in waiting. We shall have no money, of course, but I don't think she really cares about that. And last night, well, I realised what could happen if I didn't act. I didn't want Sybil to be thwarted.' Reggie's eyes flickered over to where Charlotte Beauchamp was standing with Lady Tavistock.

Cora followed his gaze. 'No, that would never do,' she said as lightly as she could. 'And now you must tell Ivo. He will want the satisfaction of observing his mother's face when she realises that she is about to lose her lady-in-waiting.'

The news of the engagement gave Cora the lift she needed to preside over the christening tea. The cake was cut and Guy's health was drunk in tea and champagne. After the toast had been drunk, Reggie got to his feet and made a deft little speech announcing his engagement to Sybil. Ivo called for more champagne and the company then drank to the couple – everyone, that is, except for Duchess Fanny who collapsed in a graceful swoon instead. Sybil was about to rush to her side, but Ivo stopped her and called for some smelling salts. He propped his mother against the love seat where she had fallen and waved the sal volatile under her nose. When she started to show signs of consciousness he said, 'Now, now, Mother, you mustn't worry about losing Sybil. With her gone, you will be able to knock a good ten years off your age, so that no one will dare to believe that you are a day over thirty-five.'

The Duchess glared at her son but the Prince of Wales laughed so much that she was forced to join in and her smile did not waver when the Prince said, 'Hard to believe that you are a grandmother now, Fanny. You will always be a slender young thing to me.'

The Duchess put her hands to her tightly corseted waist and said, 'I hope so, sir,' and sighed theatrically. But there was no way back to her previous position and she was obliged to look on nobly while Sybil chattered to Cora about bridesmaids and veils.

The Prince took his leave after the tea; he was taking the overnight train to Balmoral. As Cora walked him to his carriage, he paused to look across the hills to the horizon softening in the evening light. 'It's a glorious spot, Duchess. It has always been a favourite of mine and now that you are here, I find I apprrreciate its charms all the more. I look forward to coming back.'

Cora smiled and curtsied, but when the carriage had at last driven out of sight, she felt herself go limp and if Ivo had not been standing behind her she would have fallen to the ground.

'What was the Prince whispering to you just now, Cora, that made you go weak at the knees? I hope he knows that this Duchess of Wareham, at least, is not his to command. Or were you tempted by Tum Tum? Although judging by his performance on the bicycle today, I doubt that he has much to offer.' Cora knew that Ivo was teasing her but there was a bitterness to his tone that jangled. Surely he could not be jealous of the Prince?

She pulled away from him and said, 'I have a headache, Ivo, I am going to lie down. I am sorry, but you will have to manage without me this evening.'

'Don't worry, I am sure my mother will be only too happy to resume the role of chatelaine. Or shall I ask your mother? What a prospect.' Ivo put his hand against her cheek. 'Shall I send for the doctor, I don't think I can manage without you for long.'

'No, I'm sure I will feel better once I have rested. It has been a long day.'

'The longest,' said Ivo and took her arm as they walked up the steps to the house.

Bertha was just about to join the upper servants who were gathering for their own version of the christening tea when the hall boy stopped her in the corridor, holding out a parcel.

'Miss Jackson, Miss Jackson, this came for you.' He shook it. 'I think it's from America.'

Bertha took the parcel from him. The parcel had been redirected many times. It had gone to New York, to London and now here to Dorset. The return address was the Rev. Caleb Spragge, South Carolina. She felt her mouth go dry. She took the parcel into the pressing room and put it down on the table. She found a pair of scissors and cut the thick twine that held it together. She pulled away the brown paper to reveal a cardboard box about two feet long and one foot wide. Bertha could hear the bustle and clatter of the housemaids in the corridor, she wanted very much to walk out and join them, she did not want to open the box. But then she saw the pile of string and the elaborately tied knots and she knew she could not ignore what lay inside.

She lifted the lid. Inside was a letter and something that looked like clothing wrapped in tissue paper. She opened the letter – the date was 12 March, four months ago.

My dear Bertha,

It is with great regret that I write to tell you that your mother passed away yesterday. She had been sickly for some time and I think she was happy to go to her Maker in the end. She spoke of you often and she often said how proud she was that you were making your way in the world. In the last few months she started to make this quilt for you. She finished it a day or two before she passed. It was evidently a labour of love.

I am sorry to be the bearer of such bad news but be comforted by the thought that your mother is in a better place.

Your affectionate friend,

Caleb Spragge

Bertha leant against the table for a moment. She had known, of course, when she came to England that she would never see her mother again, but the fact of it still made her faint with loss. She folded back the shroud of tissue paper and took out the quilt.

It was not so big, perhaps the size of the table in the cabin, twelve squares, four by three, of interlocking strips of material around a central motif. With a lurch of her heart she saw a strip of blue and white striped cotton from her mother's skirt, and opposite, a scrap of paisley from the shawl that Bertha had sent her. In every square she found some memento of the life she could only dimly remember, a faded strip from some overalls, a scrap of material from a flour sack with the letters *ash's finest flo*. Bertha recognised in the centre of one square a piece of the red and white bandanna that her mother had used to tie back her unruly hair. The stitching was fine and even in some parts of the quilt, but in others the sewing was erratic, rushed as if her mother was desperate to get to the end. She was sending her daughter a message and she would not go until she had finished it. She could not read or write, so this quilt was her last will and testament, her parting gift to her only child. Bertha held it up to her face, feeling her mother's hands on the warm soft fabric. For the first time since she had left South Carolina ten years before, she allowed herself to cry.

A bell rang and Mabel came in.

'The Duchess is down, Miss Jackson. You're wanted upstairs.' She saw Bertha's face and stopped. 'Are you all right? Was it bad news?' She seemed eager for details

Bertha nodded. 'Yes, it was bad news, but it was a long time ago.'

She folded the quilt carefully and wrapped it up in the tissue paper. She went upstairs to her bedroom and laid it out. Only then did she go down to Miss Cora.

Cora was sitting in the window seat when Bertha came in, her face pressed against the glass. She had taken her hair down and the russet weight of it fell over her shoulders like an animal pelt. She had lost her Duchess look, Bertha thought.

'Oh, there you are. I have got such a headache, Bertha.' Her voice sounded weak and uncertain.

Bertha poured some eau de cologne on to a flannel and pressed it to Cora's temples.

'Thank you.' Cora looked up at her for a moment, as if deciding something, and then said, 'Bertha, have you ever been in love?'

Bertha stiffened, she wondered where this was leading. 'I couldn't say, Miss Cora.'

Cora shook her head. 'Well, have you ever known someone who

is nice *and* nasty, who makes you love them one minute and hate them the next? Who makes you feel wonderful and terrible and you never know which one it is going to be?'

Cora's hands were twisting through her hair, rolling it around her fingers so tightly that they went white from lack of circulation. Bertha thought that the only person in her life who fitted Miss Cora's description was Miss Cora herself, who did an excellent job in being nice and nasty. But that was not a thought she could utter. She knew that her mistress was talking about the Duke, so she kept her answer as non-committal as possible.

'I guess the world is full of contrary folks, Miss Cora.'

'Oh, but he's not just contrary, Bertha, it's as if he wants to unbalance me.' Cora stopped. 'I shouldn't be talking to you about this, you're my maid and he's my husband but I don't know what to think any more.' Bertha saw that one of Cora's fingers was turning blue and she gently disengaged it from the hair.

'Why don't you talk to Mrs Cash? She knows a lot more about married life than I do, Miss Cora.'

'Oh, I tried that. All Mother wants is a duchess for a daughter. She doesn't care how I feel.' Cora knocked her head against the glass.

Bertha could say nothing to this as she knew it was true.

'I just don't know who Ivo *is* any more. Sometimes I think – no, I *know* – he loves me but then the next moment he is someone else entirely. Last night, just before Odo made that scene, I saw something between Ivo and Charlotte. I know there is something there, some feeling that I can't be part of. Yet when Ivo says he loves me, I believe him, but he can't love us both, can he?' She looked at Bertha in entreaty as if the maid's answer had the power to decide her fate.

Bertha wanted to wipe Cora's face clean of worry, but she could not lie to her. She knew that Jim would be angry with her for what she was about to do, but she could not stand by while Miss Cora tortured herself.

'Miss Cora, if I tell you something, do you promise not to be angry with me?'

Bertha sat down on the window seat opposite her mistress so that she could look directly into her eyes.

'Of course, why would I be angry with you?'

'Because you won't like what I have to say. Do you want me to go on?'

'Yes, yes, I promise that nothing you say can be worse than I have imagined.' A tear slid out of Cora's eye, but she did not appear to notice.

Bertha fumbled in her bodice and drew out Jim's pearl from its resting place next to her heart.

'Do you recognise this, Miss Cora?'

Cora picked up the pearl and rolled it around her palm. 'This looks as if it could be from my necklace, but it can't be, unless someone has broken it . . .' She looked over at her dressing table in alarm.

'No, *your* necklace is quite safe. This pearl came from another necklace, just like yours.'

Cora tested the pearl against her front teeth. 'It's real enough, but what's it got to do with me?' She held the pearl in one hand and with the other she rubbed her neck where the necklace would have sat. She thought of Ivo fastening it for her that afternoon in Venice.

'All I can tell you, Miss Cora, and I am sorry to be the one to do so, is that Lady Beauchamp had a necklace of black pearls just like yours. It broke one night when we were staying over at Sutton Veney and I . . .' Bertha paused; she did not want Cora to know that it had been Jim who had stolen the pearl. 'It was the night you didn't come back from the hunt. She was wearing it at dinner and it snapped. I guess she picked them all up except this one.'

Cora spoke slowly as if she was trying to add things up in her head. 'Are you saying that Ivo gave Charlotte a necklace like mine?' She frowned.

'Yes, he did.'

Cora stood up and went to the dressing table. She took her necklace out of its green morocco leather box. She compared her pearls to the one in her hand.

'Identical.' She turned and looked at Bertha.

Bertha stood up to face her. She could not tell from Cora's expression whether she was to be blamed for what she had said. She had broken through the invisible wall of deference that lay between them by speaking out. But then she thought of all the things she had never said to her mother and she decided that she could not stop now. She had gone against Jim's advice, her own self-interest even, to tell Miss Cora something that she might very well decide not to hear. But then she remembered how certain and bright Cora had once been and how dim she seemed now. She was only her maid, but Cora mattered to her. She would not just be a bystander.

'There's something else as well,' she said. 'Just before your wedding, you got a letter from Mr Van Der Leyden. Your mother didn't want you to read anything that might upset you so I kept the letter. I didn't read it, and I didn't give it to the Madam, but I thought you should know.' Bertha hoped that Miss Cora would not ask her for the letter, but her mistress did not seem to have heard what she had said. She was rolling the pearls between her fingers.

'Why didn't you tell me about this before?' She gestured with the pearls.

Bertha hesitated. 'It wasn't my place to, Miss Cora. So long as you were happy, what good would it have done?'

'So why are you telling me now?'

'Because now I think you need to know the truth, Miss Cora.'

The pearls clattered against the wood as Cora dropped them on the table.

'Yes, I suppose I do.' She closed her eyes for a moment and then opened them wide, pulling back her shoulders as if she was rising from a long sleep. She looked at herself in the pier glass and made a face. 'I need you to put my hair up again.' She sat down at the dressing table and handed Cora the brush. Her eyes met Bertha's in the mirror. 'And then I want you to find out whether Lady Beauchamp has gone to bed. I think it's time I paid her a visit.'

Bertha nodded and began to brush the conker-coloured hair, which crackled to life with every stroke. When her hair was fully alive like a crown of flames, Cora put her hand on Bertha's.

'Thank you,' she said.

CHAPTER 29

'Taming a Sea Horse'

CHARLOTTE BEAUCHAMP'S ROOM WAS IN THE MEDIEVAL part of the house in one of the towers above the long gallery. Cora had not wanted to put her there, as this part of the house had not yet been modernised, but when she had been discussing the accommodations for the house party with Bugler, the butler had said that Lady Beauchamp preferred the tower room. And when Charlotte had written to her accepting her invitation to the christening, she had said, 'Please can I sleep in my old tower bedroom, Cora? It was my room when I lived at Lulworth and it always reminds me of those happy days.' At the time Cora had thought nothing much of it, besides surprise that anyone would choose to sleep in the coldest part of the house, but now as she walked up the worn stone steps to the tower, she realised that Charlotte had been claiming her territory. It was also true that the tower bedroom's isolation meant that Sir Odo had been housed some distance away.

Cora rubbed the black pearl Bertha had given her between her fingers. She had wanted to pulverise it into dust, but now she held on to it and welcomed the anger it aroused in her. The idea that Ivo had given her and Charlotte the exact same necklace made her kick the stone flags as she walked. She had been deceived, not just about his relationship with Charlotte, but also in his feelings for her. She had held on to that necklace as if to a talisman, she had treasured the memory of that afternoon in Venice through all the long dark months of her exile in Lulworth; at that moment, she had told herself, they had been quite married. But now as she felt her way along the stone corridor, she had no such comfort. Nothing was hers alone. He may have loved her in his way but there was nothing special about it; all he had given her was her allotted ration of love, nothing more, nothing less. He had not cared enough to think of a different present.

She stopped outside Charlotte's door. Next to it was a brass bracket with 'Lady Beauchamp' written in her own best handwriting on the card. Cora took the paper out and ripped it into as many pieces as she could. She knocked on the door and walked in without waiting for an answer.

The room was dark but Cora could see Charlotte silhouetted against the moonlit window. She was clearly waiting for someone, for she turned round expectantly when Cora entered, her arms stretched out in welcome. As she stepped into a patch of moonlight, Cora could see that she was wearing a peignoir made of some silvery material trimmed with swansdown. With her pale hair shining down her back, she looked like some ethereal water nymph.

Cora lit the gas lamp on the table with her candle and adjusted the wick so that the golden flame obliterated Charlotte's shimmering aura. She wanted to look at Charlotte properly. When they had been friends, Cora had enjoyed Charlotte's elegance and beauty, rather as she appreciated her thoroughbred, Lincoln, or the statues of Eros and Psyche in the summer house. Cora liked the best and Charlotte was undoubtedly the most attractive woman in her circle. Too many English women looked weathered, but Lady Beauchamp had skin as smooth and waxy as an orchid. It had never occurred to Cora before to feel jealous of Charlotte's poise or perfect clothes but now she was looking at her not as a friend but as a rival. Charlotte was only four years older than her, but the years had given her face more character. They were about the same height, but despite all the afternoons strapped into the spine stiffener, Cora knew that Charlotte was the more graceful. When Charlotte walked across a room, her movements were so fluid that she appeared to glide. She looks more like a duchess than I do, thought Cora angrily.

Charlotte tried to hide her surprise at seeing Cora instead of the visitor she had been expecting.

'I am so glad you are feeling better, Cora. I heard that you had gone down with a migraine. I was going to bring you a *cachet fièvre* – I have them sent over from Paris as I find they are the only things that work, but I thought you would be asleep.' She spoke in her usual breathy drawl, but her hands were picking at the swansdown trimming of her gown.

Cora held out her hand where the pearl lay in the oyster of her palm.

'I believe this belongs to you.'

Charlotte looked at Cora for a moment. Then she took the black pearl from Cora's hand.

'I thought there was one missing. But I never knew for sure. After they broke I never had the heart to have them restrung.' She tilted her head to one side. 'But you're not wearing your necklace, Cora. I hope finding this didn't put you off,' and she smiled, a fulsome smile that showed her dimples.

Cora wanted to speak but the sight of Charlotte's dimples made her mute with rage.

Charlotte gestured towards her. 'So now you know how it feels, Cora. To be a duplicate.' She gave a little laugh. 'Do you know how rare pearls this size and colour are? God knows where Ivo managed to get a second necklace.'

Cora said almost to herself, 'I can't believe I didn't see this. I have been so stupid.'

Charlotte ignored her; she was pacing up and down the room, her body sinuous even in its agitation. 'I was to wear it when we were apart to remind me of him. I have never understood why he gave you pearls too. Was he trying to torment me? He knows how to be cruel. He never forgave me for marrying Odo, even when he knew I had no choice, even though he knew what kind of man he is.' Charlotte took a deep breath. 'And then you came out of nowhere. An American, who knew nothing and understood nothing. I thought he had done it for your money at first but when I saw you at Conyers wearing your black pearls, I realised that he was punishing me too. But I had my revenge, I introduced you to Louvain. I knew you were exactly the kind of pretty spoilt creature who would find Louvain irresistible. I knew that once Ivo saw you for what you were, he would come back to me.' She turned to Cora and smiled again, showing her small white teeth.

Cora felt that she knew about the kiss in Louvain's studio. She felt ashamed that this woman had known how she would behave. But one kiss was all it had been.

'He's my husband, Charlotte,' she said, 'whether you like it or not. He married me, we have a son. And I believe that Ivo loves me.' Cora thought of the way he had embraced her last night in the nursery.

'Really.' Charlotte's dimples were in evidence again. 'Just because you have bought yourself a title and all this,' she gestured around the tower room, 'doesn't mean that you have bought his love. He's grateful to you, of course, for saving Lulworth and giving him a son. In many ways you have made his life easier, but Ivo's not the sort of man who settles. Yes, you are his wife but I am the woman he loves. Sadly it's not a position you can buy.'

Cora could not bear to hear any more. She picked up the lamp on the table and threw it as hard as she could at Charlotte. But the other woman dodged and the lamp hit the cheval glass behind her, causing the mirror to shatter. The paraffin poured out over the floor and rivulets of fire spread out across the carpet. Cora watched as flames began to lick the bottom of the curtains. Charlotte wrapped the silvery peignoir round herself and walked to the door.

'I see I will have to find somewhere else to sleep', she said as she left the room. 'Perhaps you should ring the bell. Of course, you can afford to rebuild the house from scratch but I know that your husband is rather attached to the place as it is.'

Cora tugged the bell pull as hard as she could, but no one came. Realising that Charlotte could not be trusted to raise the alarm, she picked up the pitcher of water and threw it over the burning material. Only some of the flames were extinguished. Cora snatched up the velvet counterpane from the bed and threw it over what was left of the blaze. The brocade sizzled faintly under the counterpane. The singed material smelt like her hair did when the curling irons were too hot. She remembered the smell of her mother's hair burning, and she stamped on the heaped velvet until she was sure that all the flames were out.

The room was dark now but as she turned to leave, the moon

came out from behind a cloud and the silvery light revealed something small and dark lying on the exposed bed sheet. Cora thought it might be the pearl from the necklace but as she bent to pick it up, she realised that although it was a black pearl, it was a small one. This pearl was framed in gold, with a shank that went through the buttonhole of a shirt to fasten it. Cora dropped it in disgust and ran out of the room. She blundered down the dark corridor without a candle and ran into someone coming the other way.

'Cora?' It was Teddy's voice. 'Is it really you?'

Cora said nothing for a moment, she just put her head against the wool of Teddy's jacket. He smelt of cigar smoke. She leant against his warm solidity, and felt safe.

'You're trembling, Cora, what's going on? I was just going to bed when I heard an almighty crash. But this isn't your room. What have you been doing?' Teddy sounded worried but he was holding Cora in his arms, one hand was stroking her hair and the other was pressing her closer to him. They stood there for a minute in silence and then Cora said, her voice muffled in his jacket, 'I am so glad you are here.'

Then she pulled back and looked at him. Her face was shadowed, her eyes dark sockets.

She said, 'You wrote me a letter before my wedding. But I never got it, Teddy. My mother didn't want me to read it. But now I would like to know what it said.'

Teddy took one of her hands and kissed it. 'It said that my biggest regret was leaving you that night in Newport. It said that I left you out of fear, because I thought that I would always be in the shadow of your money, but when I got to Paris I realised that I had been a coward. Yes, I was following what I believed to be my vocation but the cost of losing you had been too great. And then I offered you my love, Cora, even though I knew it was too late.'

She nodded and put her hand to his cheek. 'I wouldn't have listened to you then. But it's different now. I can't bear it any more. I've been such a fool, Teddy. I thought it was me he wanted. But it could have been anybody, so long as they were rich.'

Teddy squeezed her hands. 'Leave him behind, Cora, leave all of it behind. I want you, only you, and I will take care of you.'

She looked at him. 'But you have to understand that I am not the girl you left in Newport. I have changed. I have a child, and I can't leave him behind. I don't want Guy to grow up like this. Helping me means helping him too.'

He took her hands. 'If that's what you want, Cora. I won't let you down again.'

In the darkness they heard the chapel clock strike one.

Bertha was waiting up when Cora got back to her room. She gasped when she saw that Cora's dress and hands were covered in soot. She looked at her mistress for an explanation but Cora waved away her unspoken inquiry.

'I want you to pack a case for me, just a change of clothes and my nightdress, and leave some space for Guy's things. I am going to London with the baby. But it's a secret, Bertha. I don't want anyone to know I am going.'

Bertha swallowed. 'And do you want me to come with you, Miss Cora?'

'Of course. You will have to help me look after Guy. I can't leave him behind and I am not taking that old trout of a nurse.'

'Will we be gone long?' Bertha put her hand on the table for support.

'For ever.'

Bertha began to shake, but Cora did not notice her agitation and she went on, urgently, 'I will take Guy for a walk in the park after breakfast. I want you to take the donkey cart and meet me in that bend in the drive just before the lodge. From there we can take the cart to the station and get the train to London. Mr Van Der Leyden is going to engage some rooms for me at an hotel. I don't want anyone to be able to find me.'

Bertha sagged. She had set this in motion, but she had not foreseen the consequences. Whatever happened now, she would have to leave someone she loved behind. She had no real family any more, only Miss Cora and Jim. For a long time she had thought she could have them both, but not any more. Now she would have to choose.

Cora, she could see, was too agitated to sleep. Bertha poured some water into a basin and washed her face and hands and brought her a clean nightdress.

'You should get some rest now, Miss Cora. You will need your strength for tomorrow.'

She helped Cora get into bed and said good night.

As she reached the door, she heard Cora say, 'Do you think I am doing the right thing?'

Bertha wondered if she could pretend she hadn't heard but Cora said, 'Bertha?' her voice quavering slightly.

Bertha looked back at her. 'I don't know as I could say it was the right thing, but I know you won't be happy until you do something and I reckon this is your way forward.' She turned the doorknob and walked out. She had no more time for Cora tonight.

Bertha had never visited Jim's bedroom before. The male servants all slept in rooms in the basement, as far as possible from the female servants, who slept in the attics. Bertha was not even sure which was his room. She knew that if she bumped into Bugler down in the male quarters at this time of night, she would be dismissed on the spot, but that was the least of her worries.

The male servants' corridor was lit by one pilot light. She crept along it, listening to the snores and muttering that came from behind the closed doors to see if she could recognise Jim's. But all the snores and muttering sounded the same. She only found his door through his boots which he had put outside his door for the hall boy to collect and clean. Only Jim and Mr Bugler had the privilege of having their shoes cleaned and Jim's feet were much larger than the butler's.

She took one more look along the corridor and pushed Jim's door open and slipped inside. It was a warm night and he was lying face down with only a sheet covering the lower half of his body. She could not resist running her hand down his back towards the swell of his buttocks. He woke with a start and grabbed her wrist.

'Bertha! What are you doing here?' Jim turned to face her. She saw that he was naked under the sheet.

'I wanted to talk to you,' she said. He pulled her down on the bed and started kissing her.

After a moment he said, 'So talk then,' but his hands were fumbling with the buttons of her blouse. Bertha tried to summon the words but she found that she could not say anything. She did not want to think of anything but Jim's hands on her body, and the feel of his skin next to hers. In answer she undid the last button and began to unlace the strings of her corset.

When she had shed all her clothes, Jim whispered in her ear, 'Are you sure, my dearest?'

And she put her arms round him in reply.

But later she would not allow herself the warm comfort of Jim's arms. She started to hunt around in the dark for her clothes. When she was dressed, she shook Jim awake.

'Jim, there is something I must tell you.'

Jim rolled away from her sleepily. 'Not now, Bertha.'

'No, you must listen to me. I came to tell you that the Duchess is going to London today and taking me with her.' She tried to keep her voice a whisper but it was hard not to let the emotion break through. 'She isn't coming back, Jim. She's leaving him. I think she means to run away with Mr Van Der Leyden.'

Jim roused himself at this and grabbed her hand. 'You can't go with her, Bertha. What if she decides to go back to America? Let your Miss Cora ruin her life if she wants to. Your place is with me.' He was whispering, but the anger in his voice was unmistakable.

Bertha twisted away from him. 'I can't just leave her. You see, I made it worse. I showed her the black pearl you gave me from Lady Beauchamp's necklace. I felt sorry for her – everyone was lying to her. I wanted to give her the truth.'

Jim let his hand drop. 'She's got a family, Bertha. You are just her maid.'

'But she needs me. I know she does. She really doesn't have anyone else.'

'So what was this?' He pointed to the bed. 'Some kind of consolation prize?'

She looked away. 'I . . . I wanted you, Jim.' She put out a hand to caress him, but he threw it off.

'And I want you, all the time. But now you are leaving. If you want to go with her I can't stop you, but I don't know if I'll ever see you again.' He turned away from her and buried his face in the pillow.

Bertha put her hand on his shoulder and said, 'I love you, Jim.'

He hit the pillow with his fist. 'Then don't leave.' He sat up and grabbed her by the shoulders. 'Marry me, Bertha. We can go to London. I can get work as a valet in one of those hotels. We can have a new life. Don't leave me because that spoilt mistress of yours can't live without her maid.'

Bertha stood up. 'Miss Cora ain't always easy or pleasant but I can't give up on her now.' She thought of the quilt lying on her bed. Miss Cora was the closest thing she had to family now – they were stitched together by time and circumstance. Miss Cora was part of the fabric of her life. Bertha knew everything about her mistress, from the mole on her right shoulder blade to the way she would blow the hair away from her eyes when she was angry. She could tell Cora's mood from the set of her shoulders, she knew what she was going to say by the curve of her lips. It did not much matter to her that Cora did not observe her in return. Cora was her territory; her home was where Cora was.

She knew she could not explain this to Jim. He would laugh at her; tell her again that they were just there to clean up the mess. She had thought that perhaps she would feel differently after lying down with Jim, but she knew now that desire was not enough. Even his offer of marriage didn't change the way she felt.

There were so many things she wanted to say, but she heard a noise in the passage outside and she could do no more than press her lips against his sullen flesh before scuttling away.

In the corridor she saw the hall boy stooping over Bugler's shoes. She put her fingers to her lips and he nodded. She felt in her pocket and found a sixpence. Silently she put it into the little boy's hands and crept away down the corridor as fast as she could.

CHAPTER 30

'A Nine-Hundred-Year-Old Name'

THE BABY WAS SLEEPING, CORA COULD HEAR his tiny whinnying snores as she pushed the perambulator down the gravel path as gently as she could. She did not want him to start crying now. Nanny Snowden had bristled with disapproval when Cora announced she was taking the baby for a walk.

'But Your Grace, the Marquis is sleeping. He always sleeps in the morning at this time.' But Cora had simply lifted Guy out of his cradle and told the nurse to get the baby carriage ready.

She had passed the summer house now and was about to turn on to the drive itself. She looked up and saw the chapel on its mound. The sight of it made her realise how much she would be leaving behind, this cool grey stone building had housed so much of her joy and her disappointment. She wanted to have one last look but then she heard Guy give a little snuffling roar and she knew that she must press on before he woke up in earnest.

Carefully she pushed the perambulator on to the drive and proceeded as casually as she could. This was the most exposed part of her journey; anyone looking down from the house would be astonished to see the Duchess venturing so far from the house with the baby carriage. The servants might put it down to another example of her American eccentricity but if Ivo saw her he would know something was up. She reassured herself that Ivo always went riding at this time, but she speeded up as she pushed the carriage up the hill; once she got over the crest she would be out of sight of the house. From the top she could see the clover-leaf-shaped lodges of the North Gate on the next ridge; in the dip between lay Conger Wood where Bertha would be waiting for her.

Cora knew that Bertha was not altogether happy about this clandestine escape but there was no other way. She could not bear to see Ivo; she knew that if she did, all her certainty would be clouded by his presence. She would never be able to reconcile what she knew about him now with the overwhelming attraction she still felt for him, and she did not want to soften. She had been used, deceived, humiliated. Every time she thought of the necklaces and Charlotte's dimples, she wanted to smash something. How could she have forgotten that it was always about the money? He had married her because she was rich and he had used her to punish the woman he really loved.

She pushed the baby carriage so hard that Guy woke up and started to whimper. She put her hand to his cheek and tried to soothe him. Reassured by the sound of her voice, he closed his eyes again. She gripped the handle as the road went downhill. She was almost at the track that led through the woods where Bertha would be waiting. She could feel beads of perspiration running down her back; her hair was beginning to stick to her face. And then at last she stepped under the canopy of the trees and smelt the mossy coolness of the ancient forest. She pushed on down the grassy track until she heard the donkey snorting . . .

'Bertha?' she called.

Bertha came down the track towards her on foot. Her steps were slow and her face was swollen and heavy. Cora felt a flicker of annoyance. Why should Bertha take on so? She wasn't leaving her marriage behind.

'I will hold Guy and you can drive, Bertha. Did you get some clothes for him?'

'I had to take them from the laundry. I couldn't get into the nursery.' Bertha's voice was flat. 'They aren't all clean.'

'Never mind, we can get fresh ones in London.' Cora tried to sound bright. She took the still sleeping baby out of the perambulator and climbed on to the back seat of the donkey cart. Bertha got up in front of her and took the reins. The donkey began to amble along the path, but then it stopped. Cora heard Bertha gasp. She turned round and saw Ivo standing in the path, his hand absently patting the donkey's muzzle.

'Going somewhere, Cora? I don't think this fellow here has the stamina to get you very far. But you have a bag, I see. Perhaps you are going to the station.' He stood aside, to let them pass. Cora wondered how he had known where to find them. She looked at Bertha, but her maid's face was set hard.

'Well, I won't stop you if you have a train to catch. But Cora, I am not Bluebeard. If you want to leave Lulworth you are perfectly at liberty to do so. Surely you know that.' He walked round to where Cora was sitting and looked at her, his brown eyes unreadable in the forest gloom.

She shook her head. 'I'm not sure of anything about you, Ivo.'

Guy gave a little cry and she started to rock him in her arms.

Ivo reached over and put his hand on the baby's head. The noise stopped.

'I am not here to stop you. But I would like to talk to you.' He swallowed. 'Come for a drive with me. I have something to tell you.'

Cora had never heard Ivo ask for anything so nakedly. She tried to think about Charlotte's dimples, about the black pearl stud on the white sheet, about Teddy and the letter she had never read. But all she could see was her husband's large brown hand stroking her son's head.

She could feel Bertha's gaze burning into the back of her head and she could hear the donkey snorting and stomping.

'Please, Cora?' Ivo was almost whispering.

'It's too late, Ivo. Whatever it is you have to tell me, it's too late.' She looked down at the baby as she said this, trying to control her face.

Ivo spoke louder now. 'Right from the very first moment we met, I thought you had courage, Cora, but here you are running away from me. Aren't you brave enough to hear what I have to say?'

Cora stood up.

'Bertha, take the baby back to the house in the perambulator for now. I will let you know when I want to leave.'

Bertha got out of the cart and Cora put Guy in her arms. Then she turned to her husband.

Ivo hesitated for moment and then climbed up into the cart and took the reins.

They drove along in silence, sitting side by side, following the road that led to the sea. When they reached the cliffs, Ivo turned the cart to the left.

Cora wondered if Ivo was ever going to speak. The donkey laboured up a steep hill and only when they reached the top did Ivo turn to her.

'I wanted to bring you here, Cora, to explain.'

Cora looked down at the coast spread before her. There was a cove just below them where a spur of rock curved out defiantly into the sea. The waves had responded by tearing into the grey stone, eating away two holes, so that the cliff looked like a coiled sea serpent. The water squeezed in and out of the openings, creating concentric rings which rippled out over the leathery sea.

'That's Durdle Door. Guy and I used to swim here when we were boys. There's a trick to swimming through the holes. You have to go with the wave or you can get smashed on the rocks. We could manage the bigger hole all right but one day when I was eleven or so I dared Guy to go through the smaller one. It's much harder because there are only a few inches for error either way. I could see that Guy didn't really want to do it but I kept on at him, teasing him until he had to go. I remember he went right down under the water so that he would not get smashed by the waves, but the gap was so narrow that I couldn't see him come up on the other side. I waited for a minute, and then another, and I began to worry. Maybe the undertow had pulled Guy against a rock and knocked him unconscious. I shouted for him and got no answer. I remember even now how terrified I was.' He pushed back his sleeve and Cora could see that the black hairs on his arm were standing on end. 'I shouted a bit more but I realised that I would have to go and look for him. I didn't want to, one bit, but I remember feeling that as I had sent Guy in there, I had to go in after him. And if we both died, that was only fair.' He paused and they both looked down at the sea churning through the rocky channels.

'I dived in as deep as I could, my eyes wide open so that I

could see Guy if he was trapped, but the water was murky and I could hardly see a thing. But I stayed down there looking for a fraction too long and I got caught by the undertow which started dragging me along the rocks. My leg got wedged and I couldn't move, my lungs were bursting and I thought I was going to drown. But then I felt an arm under my shoulders pulling me free. Guy had swum back through the bigger hole and when he saw that I wasn't there waiting for him, he guessed what had happened and came to rescue me. If he'd hesitated I wouldn't be here.' Ivo turned to look at Cora. 'He saved my life, but I killed him.'

Cora looked at him in astonishment. 'But I thought he died in a riding accident.'

'Yes, he did, but Guy was a wonderful rider. He wanted to break his neck.'

'You can't know that, Ivo.' Cora was alarmed by the darkness in his voice. Ivo was standing on the cliff now and she thought how close he was to the edge.

'But I do know. It was because of Charlotte.' Cora stiffened. 'You see she was the first, the only thing, to come between us. When she came to Lulworth, she was just sixteen and so lovely.' He caught the expression on Cora's face. 'She was different then. I suppose she still had . . . hope.' He stopped for a moment. 'I was enchanted by her, and she liked me. But then Guy, who took no interest in women, noticed her and he was quite smitten. He didn't flirt with her or even talk to her; he just worshipped her as if she was one of his saints. She didn't realise at first how he felt, but I could see it. I did everything I could that summer to make her mine. I wanted to marry her before Guy ruined it all. I knew, you see, that Charlotte wouldn't hesitate. She loved me, I think, but not enough to give up a chance of being a duchess.'

'My mother noticed what was going on and she took Charlotte to London for the season. She didn't want Charlotte to be the next Duchess any more than she wanted you, Cora.' He almost smiled, and took a step closer to the edge.

Cora said, 'I would much rather hear this story sitting over there.' She pointed to a small chalk outcrop a good ten yards back.

Ivo looked startled. 'Do you really think I would . . . Oh no, Cora, you have that quite wrong.'

But Cora took the reins of the donkey cart and pulled the animal over to the rock. When she looked round she saw that Ivo was following.

'Then my father died and we came back to Lulworth for the funeral. We were all in mourning, there was nothing to do, no one to see. All we could do was look at each other.'

Ivo sat down next to Cora on the rock and started to throw the pebbles at his feet towards the cliff.

'My mother went off to Conyers to secure her next husband. She left Charlotte behind – she didn't want anyone to cloud the Duke's vision, I suppose. And with my mother gone, there was nothing to prevent Guy following Charlotte around like a pilgrim. She noticed and encouraged him. But she didn't drop me – we had gone too far for that. Charlotte would listen to Guy telling her about the Maltravers and their glorious Catholic past and then she would come and meet me, somewhere we wouldn't be found.'

Ivo pitched a larger stone so that it hit the edge of the cliff and curved upwards before disappearing.

'We both knew that Guy was going to propose and that Charlotte would accept and it made us reckless. We couldn't meet in the house because of the servants, so we used the chapel. I should have known better, but I have always wondered whether really deep down I wanted to be caught.'

Cora glanced at his face but he was looking straight out to sea.

'Guy discovered us one afternoon in the organ loft. There could be no mistake. He didn't say anything, he just went away. I should have run after him but I was glad he had found us. He would never marry Charlotte now. Then his horse came back without him that evening and I knew what had happened, what I had done.'

Cora laid her hand on his arm for a moment.

'The day after Guy's funeral, Charlotte asked me when we were getting married. "After all," she said, "there is nothing to stop us now." She couldn't hide her satisfaction and I hated her for it. I told her that we had killed my brother. When she realised that I would never marry her, she went off and married Odo because he was the richest man she could find. I should have stopped her, I knew that Odo was vicious, always has been – his only talent is for making trouble – but I never wanted to see her again. As far as I was concerned they deserved each other. But then a year later I met Charlotte when I was out with the Myddleton. She told me how bad things were and I liked her more because she was suffering. We started again, it was a terrible mistake – we were both trying to find a way out of our misery, but it wasn't a happy thing.' He shaded his eyes with the back of his hand. 'Ironically it was Charlotte that brought us together. If I hadn't been with her that day in Paradise Wood, I would never have found you lying there.'

Cora put her face in her hands; she realised for the first time how hot her face was, she simply had not noticed the sun.

'You had been with her, in the wood.' She started to get up but Ivo pulled her back.

'You can't go yet, Cora. Please let me finish my story.'

She subsided.

'When I met you I felt as if there might be a chance for me. You were so bright and free and . . .'

'Rich?' said Cora.

'Yes, rich, but dearest Cora, you were not the only heiress looking for a title, although you were,' he made a little flourish with his hands and laughed, 'by far the richest. Of course I had to marry a woman with money but it wasn't your fortune I wanted, Cora, it was you. You were never going to be like my mother or even Charlotte. You can't keep secrets and you are a terrible liar. You have no idea how to hide your emotions.'

Cora closed her eyes; she could feel the sun beating through her eyelids.

'Then you will know how I am feeling now.'

'You are angry and humiliated and I can't blame you for that. I should have told you about my past with Charlotte but to do so would mean admitting what I had done to Guy.'

'Your past with Charlotte, or your present?' Cora was surprised at how angry she sounded.

Ivo stood up in front of her, so that the sun was behind him. Cora wondered whether he had done it deliberately because it meant that she could not see his face.

'Don't you understand, Cora? I would give anything, everything, never to see Charlotte again. Do you remember the pearls I gave you in Venice?'

Cora nodded her head a fraction.

'I once gave a necklace like that to Charlotte. I gave you the same necklace as a sign to Charlotte that I loved *you* now. I wanted her to realise that our marriage was not some financial arrangement but a real thing.'

Cora said, almost involuntarily, 'But how *cruel*.'

'Maybe, but I wanted to drive her away. She got her revenge, though, by befriending you and introducing you to that painter.'

'But nothing happened, Ivo.' She stopped. 'Louvain tried to kiss me once, but that was all.'

Ivo shook his head, batting her comment away. 'I was so angry with you that night. That vulgar party, the portrait, everything. I thought the whole evening was about your vanity and that you didn't mind humiliating me in the process. It was as if you were turning into my mother.' Ivo laughed bitterly. 'Charlotte knew that, of course. I should have realised that while you were perhaps a bit vain and certainly a little foolish, you were an innocent in all this mess. It took months for me to understand what had happened. Charlotte wrote to me every day when I was in India, and I began to see what she was about. It was the baby, you see, that made her so desperate.'

Cora remembered the look of hunger on Charlotte's face at the christening.

'When I came back to England, she found me. She begged me to start again. I told her that I could never be with her. There was a terrible scene. And then I came home and found you with the baby.'

Ivo picked a daisy from the bank and started to shred it with his fingers.

'She must have been delighted when you asked her to

Lulworth. I should have stopped you but I didn't know how. And, well, you know the rest. She wanted Odo to make his revelation. I think she would sacrifice everything now if it would guarantee my unhappiness. They have that in common, those two, they both enjoy inflicting pain on other people. If you leave me, then she has won.'

Cora got to her feet. She could see the coast stretching away in both directions and she wondered which way was home. She stood in front of Ivo so that she could see his eyes.

'I went to see Charlotte last night. I found one of your dress studs in her bed.'

'In her bed?' Ivo blinked. 'Are you sure it was mine? Cora, I promise you I have never been near Charlotte's bed. Not since we married. You must believe me. I know that I haven't told you things in the past, but I have never lied to you.'

'I am certain it was yours, Ivo.' Cora pronounced her words slowly and sadly. She got up on to the seat of the donkey cart. 'I am going back. I have a train to catch.' She hit the donkey's rump with her switch and it started to plod in the direction of home.

'Cora, please! Wait.'

She did not look round but gave the donkey another switch. Now Ivo was running beside her.

'It must have been an accident. I never went to her room, but she came to mine, Cora. Just before dinner. I said I had nothing to say to her but she threw herself at me. She – well, she knelt in front of me. I pushed her away but her hair got caught in my shirt. We were struggling. The stud must have caught in her hair.'

Cora looked down at him. She could see a bead of sweat

forming on his forehead. She realised that she had never seen him sweat before.

But she did not stop.

Ivo ran in front of the cart and held the donkey's head.

'That's all there is. All of it. I have no more secrets. If you want to leave and be with your American then I won't stop you.' He saw her surprise. 'I know everything, Cora. Your maid told Harness, who came to me. He's in love with Bertha and doesn't want to lose her.' He shrugged ruefully, acknowledging the similarity between master and man. 'Maybe you can be happy with Van Der Leyden, he looks decent enough. But Cora, he doesn't need you. He is free to go where he likes, do what he pleases, but I can only be the Duke of Wareham. You alone can blow away all the shadows, Cora. Before you came I lived in a world of secrets and lies, but you aren't like that, you live in the light.' He paused as if amazed at his own words. 'I can't imagine life without you now, Cora, I can't go back. If you go now, I am lost.'

He stopped. Cora saw that he was close to the edge. His words had been underscored by the crash and churn of the sea below. His eyes were quite black, the pupils wide open. There was a muscle trembling in his jaw. She put out her hand and pulled him to her.

As soon as the cart had disappeared, Jim found Bertha. He put his hand on her arm but she shook him off and carried on pushing the baby carriage.

'I had to do it, Bertha.'

Bertha did not reply but kept walking, her eyes fixed on the sleeping baby.

Jim walked alongside her, his blue eyes pleading with her. 'I thought she would take you away, Bertha, and then there would be an end to us. I told the Duke that I want to marry you and that if he would give me a reference I would tell him what his wife was planning.'

Bertha looked at him for the first time. 'You had no right to do that, Jim.'

Jim looked at her levelly. 'I want you to be my wife, Bertha. I couldn't just let you leave.'

Bertha stopped pushing the pram and turned to face him. 'But that's my decision, not yours.'

He put his hand on hers where it held the handle of the baby carriage. 'But you were going to do the wrong thing, Bertha. You were going to give me up just because you feel sorry for a woman who doesn't need your sympathy.' Bertha took her hand away. 'Do you think she would do the same for you, Bertha? Do you think that your precious Miss Cora would lift one finger on your behalf?' Jim put his face close to hers. 'You haven't told her about me, have you? Because you know that she won't like it. She doesn't care how you feel, so long as you are there to do what she wants.'

Bertha knew that he was, to some extent, right. Cora would not be pleased to hear that she had a beau.

'Maybe it's not about Miss Cora, maybe it's about me, Jim.' She took a breath. 'I got word yesterday that my mother is dead. She was all the family I had and now she's gone. I have been with Miss Cora every day for the last ten years. Yes, I am only her maid but if I leave her, I leave everything behind. You say you want to marry me but remember I'm a foreigner; things won't be easy for us. Maybe I just want a future I can understand.'

Jim put his hand under her chin to make her look at him. 'Remember in New York, Bertha, you were too scared to hold my hand in public? Do you really want to go back to that? Nobody's going to look at us in London. Everyone's foreign there. I'm scared too, Bertha. I've been in service all my life, but I reckon that together we have a chance.'

She couldn't speak; she started to push the pram up across the gravel towards the house. He didn't move and when she turned her head to look at him he was standing there on the path, holding his hat in his hands, turning it over and over. She stopped. He had been wearing that bowler the day he had come back from India. Only then he had been jaunty, his hair blonder, his skin dark. She realised that she was beginning to fashion her own patchwork of memories, with him at the centre. She called to him, her voice loud and definite.

'Walk with me, Jim, I need to take the baby back to the nursery. And then, maybe, we'll see.'

He threw the bowler up in the air so that it landed on his head, and ran towards her.

There had been three trains that day from Lulworth and Teddy had met every one. Cora had told him that she would send a telegram to his club, but after he had engaged rooms for her at the hotel he decided to go straight to the station. He wanted to welcome her to her new life, he wanted to pluck her out of the steam and confusion of the station and take her straight to the future shining in front of her.

He looked up at the station clock – the next train was due in five minutes. He took out his cigarette case. He thought of Cora smoking in the dark by the summer house at Lulworth, the way she had touched the cigarette with her lips. He remembered holding her in his arms last night, her bony shoulders, her small, delicate ears.

A porter was walking along the platform whistling a tune that Teddy thought was 'Onward Christian Soldiers'. A woman in a straw boater rubbed at a smut on her face with a handkerchief. There was a small square of sunlight on the platform corresponding to a hole in the glass roof. Teddy looked up and saw that there were starlings flying in out and out of the iron beams. In front of him was a poster advertising the delights of Weymouth with 'its health-giving sea air and salubrious surroundings'. He threw his cigarette end on to the platform and ground it out with his heel. He could not stand the waiting much longer. When she arrived, when he actually saw her, he thought he would lose the sick feeling in his stomach warning him that his life was about to be tinted a different colour, telling him that from the moment the train pulled in to the platform, he would always be known as the man who had run away with Cora Cash.

He heard the hoot of the locomotive and the platform began to fill with steam as the Weymouth train pulled in. Teddy stood back as the passengers swarmed towards him, families returning from a holiday by the sea, two men wearing black hats with crepe streamers on their way back from a funeral, an old lady carrying a pug. The crowd began to thin. The doors to the first-class carriages were, Teddy could now make out, all open. He thought he saw a perambulator being taken out on to the platform but as the steam evaporated he saw that the wheels belonged to a bath chair. He held his breath for a moment. If Cora wasn't on this train, it meant that she wasn't coming. His mouth was dry, all his doubts from a moment before now replaced by a lurching hollowness in his heart. And then he saw two women coming down the platform towards him, both of them wearing hats with travelling veils; one of them was Cora's height, the other walked slightly behind with a porter who was pushing a pile of cases on his trolley. Teddy began to walk towards them, his step quickening until he was almost running. Then he stopped, his heart thudding in his chest. It must be Cora, he thought; she was stopping to speak to him and yet he had never seen Cora move so gracefully. The woman lifted her veil and then he saw with shattering vividness the sweep of blond hair.

'Mr Van Der Leyden. What a pleasant surprise this is.' Charlotte Beauchamp gave him a crooked little smile, acknowledging the fact that they were both the losers in this particular game. 'But I am afraid you were not looking for me,' she continued. He looked at her as she said this and she shrank a little from the full force of his disappointment.

'No,' he said, 'I wasn't.' She put a gloved hand on his arm. As she looked up at him, he could see that the whites of her eyes were touched with red. He could see his own pain and loss mirrored in her wide blue gaze. How strange, he thought, that this woman that he had disliked so much should be the only person who could understand him now.

She tilted her head to one side and blinked rapidly as if there were something in her eye.

'I understand your despair, Mr Van Der Leyden. I know what

it is to lose the thing you most desire. But you must be strong and wait. All you have to do is wait.' With that, Charlotte Beauchamp nodded to him and walked off into the station, her maid following behind. Teddy looked after her, wondering how he could ever have mistaken her slippery grace for Cora's urgent stride.

The platform was empty now, but he could not bring himself to move away from the spot where for a few hours he had had the future that he wanted. A pigeon flew down from its perch under the glass roof and began to circle his feet, mistaking him perhaps for a statue. With a great effort he started to move, feeling each step as a betrayal. Charlotte Beauchamp had told him to wait, but what, he wondered, was he waiting for? A quick stride on a platform somewhere one day or the morning when he would wake up without the band of misery that was already beginning to tighten around his chest.

In the nursery, Cora pulled her finger out of her baby's fist. He was sleeping now. The sky was beginning to darken and soon she would go and dress for dinner. In her room, Ivo was also sleeping. She lay down on the bed beside him, putting her face next to his so that she would be the first thing he saw when he woke up. His features were soft now and although his eyes were shut, his countenance was quite open. Cora wondered if at last she had the measure of her husband. Whatever happened, she knew now, and the thought filled her with warmth, that he needed her. Then he stirred, a dream chasing behind his eyelids, and he stiffened as if he had been dealt some unseen blow.

Perhaps she would never really know him. A year and a half ago that thought would have been unbearable to her, but now she had learnt to live with uncertainty, even to love it. Since she had come to England she had learnt to prize the rare bright and beautiful days which broke through the mist and murk, loving them all the more for their randomness. You could buy a more agreeable climate, she thought, but not that feeling of unexpected joy when a shaft of sunlight fell through the curtains, promising a sparkling new day.

Acknowledgements

The characters in this book are by and large fictional, but the circumstances they find themselves in are not. When it comes to the Gilded Age, the more fantastical the circumstance, the more likely it is to be true. There really was a magazine called *The Titled American Lady* and the gossip rags of 1890s New York were every bit as obsessed with celebrity as magazines like *Heat* are today. Here are a few of the books that give a flavour of that overheated era: *The Glitter and the Gold* by Consuelo Vanderbilt Balsam; *The Mrs Vanderbilt* by Cornelius Vanderbilt Jr; *The Memoirs of Lady Randolph Churchill*; *The Decline of the English Aristocracy* by David Cannadine; *The Duke's Children* by Anthony Trollope; *The Shuttle* by Frances Hodgson Burnett; *The Buccaneers* by Edith Wharton; *Consuelo and Alva* by Amanda Mackenzie Stuart.

Anyone familiar with the Dorset coast will know there is a Lulworth Castle, which I have supersized, but the Duke of Wareham and his family are, of course, entirely fictional. Readers who know their nineteenth-century royalty will realise that I have taken one liberty with chronology – Prince Eddy was sent away to India in 1888 rather than 1894 – but I couldn't quite resist borrowing this for my plot.

This book has taken me an age to finish, and I must thank the London Library and the South West Railway London to Crewkerne line for giving me some quiet space to write. Along the way I was encouraged by my faithful and perceptive readers, Tanya Shaw, Emma Fearnhamm, Ottilie Wilford, Richard Goodwin, Jocasta Innes, Caroline Michel, Sam Lawrence, and Kristie Morris. I am eternally grateful to Tabitha Potts for her plot suggestions, and to Paul Benney for his thoughts on portraits. Thanks to Ivor Schlosberg for the pre-orders, among other things. Georgina Moore is a heroine among publicists. Derek Johns is everything you could want in an agent and it was a joy to work with Harriet Evans, albeit briefly. But the real thanks must go to Mary-Anne Harrington who is as brilliant as she is patient and to Hope Dellon whose emails were like getting gold stars for homework. And my thanks to Marcus and Lydia for sending me away right at the end. It made all the difference.

The Fortune Hunter

In memory of my mother
Jocasta Innes
1934–2013

Part One

The Royal Menagerie

July 1875

*W*AS QUEEN VICTORIA A KITTEN OR A CODFISH? Charlotte hesitated. The monarch's chinless face did look remarkably similar to the glassy stare of the fish, but that would mean making the late Prince Consort a kitten, as that was the only animal she had left. It was hard to think of Prince Albert as feline, but now that she had superimposed the image of the fish onto his wife's face, it was undoubtable that the queen made the most magnificent kind of cod. She stepped back for a moment and looked at the overall composition, now that she had replaced each royal face with an animal head. The Prince of Wales was a satisfactory basset hound and Charlotte felt that she had done justice to Princess Alice's mournful demeanour by turning her into a calf. She dipped her brush into the pot of Indian ink at her side and began to shade around her work, blending the edges of the animal heads into the rest of the photograph. Later, depending on what time she could persuade Fred to bring her home from the ball, she would photograph her creation.

She sighed and stretched her folded fingers over her head. The sun had sunk beneath the rows of white stucco townhouses, throwing a warm glow into the room.

Charlotte would have her Royal Menagerie. She thought she would put it on the back wall of the drawing room at Kevill. Properly framed, it would look to the casual observer like any other family portrait; only the people who really looked would see that she had turned the Royal Family into a frock-coated and crinolined 300. It was possible that some of the starchier guests might be a little shocked, but as close observation of anything besides the lace on a visitor's gown seldom took place in the drawing room at Kevill, Charlotte did not feel she had much to worry about. The faint possibility of discovery might be enough to get her through those interminable afternoons spent at home entertaining lady callers. Charlotte hoped that the Bishop's wife, in particular, would look over her long, perpetually dripping nose and be so offended that she never called again.

The thought of the Bishop's wife and the way that she always referred to her as a 'poor motherless girl' was enough to make Charlotte's hand slip, and a drop of Indian ink fell onto one of the ivory silk flounces of her skirt. It was a very small drop of ink, but the silk was so absorbent that it quickly flowered into an unmistakeable stain. Charlotte was annoyed at her carelessness. The ink spot was barely visible, but she knew that her aunt would spot it immediately and would make it into a tragedy of epic proportions. 'What a calamity!' she would exclaim, the lace ribbons on her widow's cap fluttering. 'Your beautiful dress ruined and on the night of the Spencer ball too!' Charlotte's aunt Adelaide liked nothing better than a minor domestic mishap that she could turn into a drama worthy of Sophocles. She would feel it her duty to point out the blemish to everyone they met, and invite them to comment on the tragic twist of fate that had ruined her niece's exquisite dress. Charlotte was dreading the evening's entertainments quite enough without the added humiliation of her aunt's histrionics.

She thought for a moment, and then picked up her watercolour box. Perhaps there was some China White left. She took a clean brush, licked it thoroughly and started to paint over the stain. It wasn't perfect, but it covered the worst of it, and with any luck she might get through the evening without her aunt noticing. She was just giving it another coat when there was a perfunctory knock on the door and her brother Fred walked in wearing his dress uniform.

'Are you ready yet, Mitten? Aunt Adelaide is fretting about the horses and I want to be at the Opera early.'

He saw what she was doing and stopped. 'Why are you painting your dress?' He smirked. 'Is that the latest fashion, hand-decorating your ball gown?'

'Well, if it was the latest fashion, as you never stop pointing out to me, I would be the last one to know. I have spilt some ink on my dress and I am concealing it with paint.' Charlotte pointed at the blemish with her finger. 'There! Good as new.'

'But what on earth were you doing messing about with ink in a white ball gown? I thought girls had better things to do before a ball, like getting their hair arranged or choosing which jewels to wear.'

'If you look carefully, Fred, you will see that my hair has been arranged, and as for jewels, Aunt Adelaide thinks that diamonds are unsuitable for debutantes and so she is wearing Mamma's necklace. I thought I would occupy my time usefully while I waited for you all to get ready.'

Fred glanced over at the work table where the Royal Menagerie lay. He went over to have a closer look, and shook his head.

'You really are a rum one, Mitten.'

'Do you like it?'

'Like it! Of course I don't like it. It's peculiar, that's what it is. Why don't you have any normal accomplishments? Singin', piano playing, needlework, that sort of thing. It's deuced odd for a girl of twenty to be squirrellin' around with cameras and chemicals all the time. You need to be careful that you don't get a reputation. Augusta is quite concerned about you. She says that after we are married, her first task will be to launch you properly. She thinks that with the right approach, you could be quite a success.'

Charlotte smiled. 'How very kind of her.'

Fred looked at her suspiciously, his blue eyes bulging as they always did when he was cross. 'Augusta will be a real advantage to you. She says that making the right sort of marriage is like pilotin' a ship into harbour. It needs a steady hand at the tiller.'

Charlotte thought, but did not say, that despite Lady Augusta Crewe's navigational skills, it had taken her four London seasons to land a proposal of marriage. She decided to change the subject.

'You look very handsome tonight, Fred. Augusta will be proud of you.'

Diverted, Fred pushed his chest out and brushed his hand down the gold braid on his jacket.

'Went to Bay Middleton's tailor. He swears by him, won't go anywhere else.'

'Bay Middleton is clearly very discerning.'

'Best dressed officer in the Guards. It's all about the cut. Had to have three fittings for this.'

'Only three fittings! I must have had ten at least for this frock, and I think your uniform fits you rather better and is altogether more flattering.'

'Nothing wrong with your dress, or at least there wasn't before you started coverin' it with ink.' He put his hand on her shoulder. 'When Augusta and I are married she will advise you. Daresay you could learn something from her. Always very nicely turned out, Augusta.'

Charlotte thought that she had heard enough about the superiority of Augusta Crewe to last a lifetime. Even if her future sister-in-law had been charming and generous, she might have tired of Fred constantly invoking her name, but as Charlotte found her affected and calculating, her presence in every conversation between brother and sister was a scalding irritation.

There was a cough from the doorway. Penge, Aunt Adelaide's butler, looked at them reproachfully.

'Her ladyship has asked to me to remind you that the carriage was ordered fifteen minutes ago.'

Fred became officious. 'Come along, Mitten, nothing you can do about the dress now. Captain Hartopp's not goin' to notice.' He was halfway down the curving staircase before he turned back to look at her. 'And you needn't worry about partners tonight. I know Hartopp will claim the first two, and Augusta has promised to find you some suitable young men.'

Charlotte was silent but thought that she would like nothing more than to dance with an *unsuitable* young man. Despite Fred's solicitude, she was not at all worried about finding partners: although she had only been to a handful of balls, her dance card was always full. Suitable young men and the odd unsuitable one had quickly learnt that although Charlotte was not perhaps the most striking looking girl in the room, she was undoubtedly one of the richest, as the sole heiress to the Lennox fortune, which would be hers when she was twenty-five. The money had not meant much to her growing up in the Borders, but since she had come to London, Charlotte had often heard the phrase 'the Lennox heiress' muttered in conversation or seen it mouthed silently by one new acquaintance to another. She had noticed too that the mutterings and the mouthings made Fred anxious. The money was hers alone – her mother, the original Lennox heiress, had been their late father's second wife – but Fred was as proprietorial about her fortune as if it were his to bestow. Under the terms of her father's will, she could not marry without his consent until she reached her majority, and Fred was enjoying the privileges of this role immensely. There had been some young men in the Guards who had made Fred feel uncomfortable about his tailor or his taste in claret, but those feelings of unease had subsided now that he was the guardian of the Lennox fortune, and, of course, the fiancé of Lady Augusta Crewe.

It was not therefore the fear of being a wallflower that made Charlotte inch down the curving staircase after her brother, one reluctant step at a time. She was probably the only girl in London who dreaded a full dance card. Sitting out a dance was better than being whirled around the room by some pink-cheeked younger son doing his best to secure the Lennox Fortune. Did she hunt? No. Silence. Had she been presented? Not yet. Pause. Did she like croquet? Sometimes she would volunteer that she enjoyed photography. This would generally make Percy or Clarence look anxious, as if being asked a question in an exam that they hadn't prepped for. Then Algernon or Ralph would tell her the story of how he had his photograph taken, 'for Mamma, y'know', and complain about how long it had taken: 'The photographer chap wanted me to stand with my head in a vice, otherwise he said it would come out blurry.' Did they like the results? she would ask, and the young men would pause; sometimes a blush would stain their bewhiskered faces. Despite their confusion, she would persevere: did the photograph look the way they had imagined themselves? At that point her partner would mumble that he never really gave much thought to his appearance, but he supposed that the photographs were accurate enough. Generally after these exchanges the young man would not insist on another dance. Once when a more imaginative young man had asked Charlotte if she would take his photograph, she had demurred, saying that he might not like the result. He did not ask a second time.

At the bottom step Charlotte tried to arrange herself so that her fan and reticule covered the ink stain on her gown. But it was clear that her concern was unnecessary, for Aunt Adelaide was much too preoccupied with her own appearance to give much thought to her niece. She was standing in front of the pier glass in the hallway, turning her head this way and that as the light caught the Lennox diamonds around her throat. Married late to an impecunious baronet who had died six months later, Aunt Adelaide had not had many diamonds in her life and she was enjoying her borrowed finery to the full. Charlotte could see that her aunt, who must be at least forty, was a good deal more excited about the evening ahead than she was.

'How well those pearl earrings go with your dress, dear. Just the right note of ornament without ostentation. I can't bear it when young girls cover themselves with jewels – do you remember Selina Fortescue at the Londonderry ball? She looked positively gaudy, such a shame with a fresh young complexion like that.' Aunt Adelaide looked at Charlotte as she said this but couldn't resist her twinkling reflection for long and turned back to the mirror.

Fred coughed. 'I notice, Aunt, that, unlike Charlotte, you have covered yourself in jewels. Is it quite the thing for you to be wearin' the Lennox necklace? The diamonds are Charlotte's property after all, and I think that as her guardian I should have been consulted.'

Underneath the diamonds, Charlotte saw the skin of her aunt's décolletage redden. She spoke quickly.

'Oh Fred, don't be so pompous. I would feel ridiculous wearing the necklace. It's much too grown up for me, and besides, it looks very becoming on Aunt Adelaide. I would much rather she wore it than for it to be locked up in a vault.'

Aunt Adelaide looked at her gratefully. Fred picked up his gloves and started to pull them down over his fingers, cracking each knuckle as he did so.

'I don't think it is pompous to express some concern about a valuable piece of property that belongs to my only sister. Perhaps you have forgotten the promise I made to Father to look after you, but I haven't. Everything that you do reflects on me. I don't want your future husband to accuse me of mismanagin' your affairs.'

'Well, I have no intention of marrying someone who would complain about me lending a necklace to a member of my family. I was going to offer it to Augusta to wear at your wedding, but if you feel so strongly about it, perhaps that would be a mistake.'

As Charlotte had intended, Fred's indignation subsided.

'Augusta did mention the necklace to me. I will, of course, make sure that she takes very good care of it, as I am sure that you will, Aunt. Now I suggest that we leave, or we will miss the first act.'

Charlotte smiled to herself. Fred's real anxiety was not that Aunt Adelaide was wearing the Lennox diamonds, but that Augusta would see her wearing them at the Spencer ball. Augusta was already planning to wear them to her wedding, and she would be unhappy if their magnificence was diluted by too many public outings on other necks than hers.

As her brother handed her into the carriage, she wondered how she would compose their wedding portrait. There would be the official one, of course, with the bride in white and orange blossom with the diamond collar round her not-quite-long enough neck with Fred standing stiffly behind her – Augusta would be seated as she was practically the same height as Fred. But in the unofficial one Charlotte thought that Augusta, with her flattish nose and wide apart eyes, would make a rather satisfactory Pekinese, and Fred, with his red face and his burgeoning chins, might pass for a turkey. It would not be a picture that she could hang anywhere, of course, not even in the darkest corners of Kevill, but it would give her private satisfaction to look at it when she was being 'launched' by Augusta after the wedding. Unless she could find a husband in the run-up to their nuptials, she faced the prospect of living with the newlyweds. The current arrangement with Lady Lisle suited Fred while he was a bachelor, but when he was a married man he would naturally want his sister to live with him and his wife. Fred's £1,000 a year would not stretch to a house in town, but as Charlotte's guardian, he and Augusta would be able to take Lady Lisle's place as Charlotte's chaperone in Charles Street.

There was a tap at the carriage window. She looked out and saw the large, whiskered face of Captain 'Chicken' Hartopp, Fred's great friend and a devoted follower of the Lennox fortune. Fred was not actively encouraging Hartopp's suit, as he was hoping for a title for his sister, or at least an alliance with one of the older landed families, but as Hartopp's fortune was almost as great as Charlotte's he could not rule him out entirely.

'Miss Baird, I am so glad I caught you before you left. I wanted to give you these; I thought perhaps you might like to wear them tonight.'

He handed her a corsage of white rosebuds through the window and Charlotte gave him what she hoped was a delighted smile.

'Thank you so much, Captain Hartopp. How kind of you to think of me.'

'My pleasure, Miss Baird.' He tipped his hat to Fred and bowed to Aunt Adelaide. 'Good evening, Lady Lisle. What a magnificent necklace. Are those the famous Lennox diamonds, by any chance?'

Adelaide Lisle simpered. 'They are indeed. Dear Charlotte has been kind enough to let me wear them tonight. I hope I can do them justice.'

Hartopp paused just a second too long before saying, 'You can have no doubts on that score, Lady Lisle.'

Charlotte saw the way Hartopp's eyes glittered when he saw the necklace, and thought that even living with Fred and Augusta would be preferable to looking at his face every morning over the breakfast table. She had not yet acquired any photographs of aquatic mammals, but when she did, she was sure that Captain Hartopp, despite his feathery nickname, would make a perfectly splendid walrus.

A Night at the Opera

THE OPERA HOUSE WAS FULL. IT WAS ADELINA PATTI'S last performance of *La Sonnambula* before she returned to New York. Every box was full, every seat from the stalls to the gods was taken. Bay Middleton sat in the second row, so close to the stage that he could see the lattice of blue veins that snaked across La Patti's décolletage, the rivulets of sweat that ran down her painted cheeks.

But though he had his eyes on the stage, Bay Middleton's senses were concentrated on a box in the Grand Tier. He felt Blanche's presence as vividly as if she were sitting next to him; he knew without looking round that her shoulders were bare and that two blond wisps of hair would tremble on the back of her neck. He could almost smell the cologne she used to bathe her temples. Still, he would not look up. He had been aware that he was making a mistake in coming tonight even as he fastened the dress studs in his shirt and adjusted the points of his white tie. But tomorrow Blanche would be gone and he wanted to be near her even if he could not bear to look at her.

The music fed his melancholy. He was not, like most of the audience, here merely to be seen. Bay felt the music; sometimes he would find the hairs on his arm standing on end, just as they did when he knew he was about to win a race, or when a woman looked at him in a certain way. It had happened the first time he had seen Blanche. She had pressed her foot against his at dinner and he had known, at once, that it was no accident. She had looked at him with her heavy-lidded eyes and had smiled, showing small white teeth and a glimpse of pink tongue. It had been the first of many such moments. She had been looking at him across dinner tables and ballrooms for the last year. There had been other women before her, of course, but Blanche Hozier was the first woman he had ever missed a day's hunting for.

She had not been smiling earlier that afternoon as she stood in front of the mirror, tucking away the curls that had come loose a few minutes before. He had been marvelling, as usual, at how quickly Blanche could change back from the woman who had led him by the hand to the chaise longue to the one who stood there now checking that every hair was in place. She was still flushed, but she was once again the mistress of the house and the Colonel's wife. She had caught his eyes in the mirror and had said without expression, 'I am going to Combe tomorrow.'

He had said nothing, sensing that this was a declaration.

'The Colonel is there all the time working on his drainage schemes, and as there is no chance of him coming to London, I must go to him.' She turned to face Bay, tilting her head a little to one side as she looked at him, one of her diamond ear drops catching the light and dazzling him.

He considered this for a moment. There could be only one reason why Blanche would leave London before the end of the Season. His eyes dropped to her waist.

He blinked. 'Are you sure?'

Blanche lifted her chin. 'Sure enough.'

He stood up and walked towards her. She crossed her hands in front of her like a gate. He stood still. 'A child? Oh Blanche, I am so . . .' But she cut him off, as if she couldn't bear the emotion in his voice.

'Combe is lovely at this time of year. Isobel has a cough and I believe the country air will do her good.'

The slight huskiness that he found so beguiling had gone and she had resumed the commanding tones of Lady Blanche Hozier, the daughter of an earl and the mistress of Combe. He looked in vain for some trace of her former softness, but she was as hard as the looking glass behind her. He felt both desolation at the thought of losing her and irritation that he should be so summarily dismissed.

'You will write to me.' It was not a question, but Blanche had shaken her head.

'No letters, not until afterwards. I have to be careful. If the child is a boy . . .' He had seen her twist the wedding ring around her finger.

'I will miss you, Blanche,' he had said, putting his hand out to take hers. But she had shrunk away from him, as if he had become red hot. He had punched his fist into his other hand in frustration.

'I wonder that you didn't tell me, earlier?' His eyes flickered over to the chaise longue.

Blanche looked at him, her drooping eyelids belying the fierceness of her tone.

'I think you should leave now before the servants come back. They have seen too much already.'

He had wanted, very much, to tear her hair down and to shake her porcelain composure, but he had let his arms drop and said, 'Are you sure the child is mine?'

This time she had turned her whole body away from him and had just pointed to the door. He had picked up his hat and gloves from the chair and left without another word.

Now, as he listened to Adelina Patti as Amina singing of her love for Elvino, he felt the blood creeping to his ears as he thought of that last remark. He wanted to look up and show Blanche that he had not meant to wound her, but he could not turn his head. He knew that her retreat to the country was the only prudent course, but he had been hurt by the manner of his sending off. If only there had been some expression of regret, some tenderness. But their liaison had ended as abruptly as it had started. He suspected that he was not Blanche's first lover, but she had always been discreet. Bay knew that her marriage with Hozier was not a happy one. Indeed, there had been a moment when he thought that Blanche had wanted more than their afternoons in the blue drawing room and he had been terrified and excited in equal measure. But that moment had passed and he had felt nothing but relief. To elope with Blanche would have meant leaving the regiment, the country, probably. So he knew he had no right to feel aggrieved, but still – a child. He remembered the way that Blanche had refused to look at him as he left that afternoon, as if she had already erased him from her life.

La Patti hung her head at the end of her aria to receive her applause. The stage was soon covered with flowers thrown by her admirers. Bay looked up at the other side of the theatre from Blanche's box and saw his friends Fred Baird and Chicken Hartopp in a box with two ladies. One he recognised as Fred's aunt and the young girl he thought must be Fred's sister. He supposed that Lady Lisle must be bringing the girl out as the mother had died years ago. He picked up his opera glasses to get a better look at the girl, conscious as he did so that Blanche might be watching him. It would do her no harm, he thought, to see that he had other interests.

But the Baird girl had drawn back, her face was in shadow, and all Bay could see of her was a kid-gloved hand tapping a fan on the side of the box. He held his glasses up for a minute longer, waiting for a glimpse of her face, but she did not reappear. It was almost as if she were hiding from his gaze.

At the interval he decided to leave; he thought he would go to his club and have a brandy. He thought of Blanche looking down at his empty seat. But as he reached the corridor he felt a hand on his shoulder.

'Middleton, what are you doing down here?' Chicken Hartopp looked down at him, beaming. His dundreary whiskers covered almost his entire face, but what skin there was visible was flushed with the heat. 'Thought you would be in a box, old man, not down here with the plebs. Couldn't help noticing a certain lady sitting opposite.' Chicken squeezed one eye in a clumsy wink.

Bay said quickly, 'I thought I'd listen to the music for a change. This is La Patti's last performance before she goes back to America.'

'An opera lover too, eh?' Chicken started to laugh at his own joke. Bay was about to leave him to his mirth when he saw Fred Baird coming towards them.

'Middleton, my dear chap, I thought I saw you down in the stalls. Will you come up to the box and meet my sister?'

Bay was about to refuse, but then he remembered the Baird box was in full view of where Blanche and her companions were sitting. He followed Bay and Hartopp through the crimson corridors to the box.

'Aunt Adelaide, you know Captain Middleton, of course, and may I present my sister Charlotte.'

Bay bowed to Lady Lisle and turned to Charlotte Baird, who was small and dun-coloured, quite unlike her brother, who was large and vivid. She stretched out her hand to him and as he brushed his lips against the knuckles of her glove, he felt her hand tremble slightly.

'How are you enjoying the Opera, Miss Baird? La Patti will be a sad loss to the company here, when she returns to New York.' Bay was standing with his back to the auditorium. He turned slightly to the left so that an observer might notice that he was talking to a young lady. Charlotte Baird looked up at him. Bay was not as tall as Hartopp or Baird, but Charlotte still had to tilt her head up to address him.

'I haven't had much chance to form an opinion about the music, Captain Middleton. I don't think my brother or Captain Hartopp have drawn breath since we arrived.' She gave a crooked little smile. 'Perhaps you can persuade them to be quiet. I should so like to hear the opera as well as see it.' Bay noticed that she had a trace of freckles across the bridge of her nose.

'I will do my best, Miss Baird, but I doubt that even the Archbishop of Canterbury himself could silence Chicken Hartopp.'

She looked at him and he saw that her eyes were the most definite thing about her face: large, with very long black lashes. He could not quite make out the colour in the gloom of the box. She held his gaze.

'But you, Captain Middleton, you like to listen. Is that why you sit down there in the stalls?'

The crooked smile reappeared. He realised she had noticed him earlier. He thought again, how different she was from her brother. Fred was an amiable bully who was happy as long as he was in front. But this girl came up on the inside, in the blind spot.

'I like to look up at the singers, Miss Baird; I want to feel in the middle of things.'

'But that's what I want, and yet here I am, surrounded by distractions.' She waved her hands at the young men who were standing with her aunt and shrugged. The bell rang to signal the end of the interval.

'Delighted to have met you, Miss Baird.' Bay looked over at Fred Baird and Chicken Hartopp and said, 'I hope you are allowed to enjoy the rest of the opera in peace.'

'I hope so too. But Captain Middleton, you aren't thinking of returning to your seat already? There is a lady in blue who has been staring at you these last few minutes while we have been talking; she looks as though she wants to tell you something. Won't you look round and see what it is she has to say?' Charlotte Baird's voice was soft but there was something sharp in there as well. Bay did not look round, but made his way to the door at the back of the box.

'I don't believe anything can be more important than the Second Act, Miss Baird.' He nodded to the others and left. Rather to his own surprise, he found himself making his way back to his seat in the stalls, aware now that he was being observed from two sides. He thought with some satisfaction of Blanche watching his conversation with Charlotte Baird from the other side of the House.

The Second Act was not as good as the first; the music could not push away his swirling thoughts. As he fidgeted in his seat he caught a faint whiff of the gardenia in his buttonhole. The flower had come from a corsage he had ordered for Blanche to wear this evening. He had been going to take it with him that afternoon, but it had arrived too late. It had been lying on the hall table when he had returned to his rooms, a mute reminder, as if he needed one, of how much had changed in the last few hours. His first impulse had been to throw it away, actually to crush the waxy white petals and the dark green glossy leaves under his heel, but as he picked up the flowers to destroy them he had been overwhelmed by their scent. The heavy sweetness was the smell of all their afternoons together in Blanche's blue drawing room. He remembered the dust-laden motes of light that had fallen like sequins on her bare throat. The smell of the gardenias was as abundant as Blanche herself, the waxy smoothness of the petals as dense as the white skin of her shoulders. He could not resist pulling out one spray and fastening it in his buttonhole. But now, as he touched the fleshy white petals, he thought that he had never seen Blanche completely naked and now he knew that he never would. The thought made him shudder, and crush the flower between his fingers.

He was still intending to go to his club, but as he was leaving he saw Fred Baird handing his sister and aunt into their carriage. They must be going to the Spencer ball. He had been sent a card, of course, having been one of Spencer's aide-de-camps in Ireland, but he had decided not to go. He didn't really care for balls; there was so much clamour he could never hear what the girls were saying in their light little voices. Not that it mattered. Those debutante conversations were all the same – did he care for waltzing or polkas? Wasn't the steeplechase most awfully dangerous? Had he ever been to Switzerland in the summer? He was standing on the corner of the Strand, when the Baird carriage passed him and he saw Charlotte's small face looking at him through the glass. He touched his hat and she raised her hand in reply but did not, rather to his surprise, smile.

He hesitated for a moment, before turning north towards Spencer House. Blanche would be there, but then so would little Charlotte Baird. She would be grateful for a dancing partner who was not Chicken Hartopp. He knew that Hartopp was seriously pursuing the girl – she was an heiress, of course, and like all rich men, Hartopp wanted to be richer. But now he had met Charlotte, Bay found that he did not like the idea of Hartopp marrying her. Any girl who went to the Opera to listen to the music was not the right match for the cloth-eared Hartopp. He looked around for a hansom but then decided he would walk. It was a fine evening and it would not hurt to arrive a little late. Perhaps Blanche would be looking towards the door, wondering if he would arrive.

The Spencer Ball

THE BALL WAS AT ITS HEIGHT. IT WAS AT THE POINT where the women were rosy from the dancing, but before the moment when coiffures began to slip – carefully curled fringes flattening in the heat. The guests, who had been delaying their arrival so that it would appear that they had been dining at one of the more fashionable houses before the ball, had finally dared to make their appearance. The parliamentary lobbies on the Suez bill had closed and the ballroom was spotted with MPs and ministers. It was the last event of the season before people disappeared to the country for the summer, so there was an energy to the occasion as the guests tried to make the most of this last opportunity to squeeze what they wanted from the world: a promotion, a liaison, a husband, a mistress, a loan, or simply a piece of delicious gossip. No one wanted to miss this party; it was the final opportunity to acquire the baubles of hope and intrigue that would make the arid summer months bearable before the fashionable world reassembled in the autumn.

As Bay Middleton made his way up the double staircase, he saw that Earl Spencer, the Red Earl as he was known, was still standing by the door to welcome his guests. The last time Bay had seen Earl Spencer in evening dress had been in Dublin at the Vice Regal lodge. There he had been the Queen's representative, and with his great height and golden red beard he had looked the part. But now the political wind had changed, the Whigs had been ousted by the Tories under Disraeli, and Spencer looked a little less burnished. His kingdom was on the hunting field, not here under the chandeliers. But he had daughters to bring out and a Party anxious to manoeuvre itself back into power, so there was no help for it. Still, he hovered on the edge of the festivities as if ready to follow more promising sport at any moment.

Spencer caught sight of Bay at the bottom of the stairs and called to him before the footman could announce him.

'Middleton, my dear fellow. I am uncommon glad to see you here.' He squeezed Bay's hand in his great freckled paw.

'It's not the same as Dublin, eh?' Spencer's pale blue eyes clouded. 'Still, we have royalty tonight. The Queen of Naples, no less, or should I say the former Queen. Very grand, like all these deposed monarchs, but lively enough.' He pointed a stubby finger at Bay. 'I shall rely on you to entertain her. She speaks perfect English but she has a way of sighing that is altogether foreign. I believe the King is not altogether to her taste. No doubt you could bring a smile to those handsome lips.'

Bay smiled. 'I don't think a queen would have much time for a mere cavalry captain, My Lord. But I am at your service as always.'

Spencer laughed and put his arm around his shoulders.

'They were high times in Ireland, eh Middleton? Best hunting in the world. Still, who knows? Disraeli can't last for ever and then we will be back with a vengeance.'

He propelled Bay into the ballroom where the orchestra was playing a polka.

'There she is, Queen Maria, the heroine of Gaeta. They say she took command of the garrison and fought against Garibaldi and the Risorgimento while her husband the little king locked himself in his bedroom.' Spencer pointed to a tall dark woman dressed in white who stood surrounded by a group of men in uniform.

'It appears that she is still in command of her troops.' Bay thought that the Queen looked as if she was posing for a portrait, her arms positioned in a perfect oval and her head turned slightly so that everyone could admire her clear profile and the long curve of her neck. She wore a small tiara that sparkled against her dark hair.

'At least she looks the part,' said Spencer. 'Not like the Widow of Windsor. And a horsewoman too. She came out with the Pytchley last year, led the pack all the way. I suppose a day out with the Pytchley is compensation for losing a kingdom, eh?' But Bay was no longer looking at the Queen in her frame of courtiers. He had seen Blanche's blond head and he could not help following it as it tacked across the dance floor. Spencer followed his gaze and made a small tutting noise.

'I believe you are not listening to me, Middleton. Still, I shall leave you to your own pursuits, even if no good can come of them. It's high time you got married. The right sort of wife would make all the difference.' The Earl moved off towards the supper room, leaving Bay watching Blanche as she danced around the room. He was dismayed to see how very gracefully she was dancing tonight. She was coming around again and he knew that if she were to turn her head she would see him. He stood there, unable to move, and then just as they were about to come face to face, he saw a flash of white to his left and turned his head. It was Charlotte Baird – still small and dun-coloured but just then a most welcome sight.

He pulled himself around to face her. She was standing beside her aunt and another lady, whom Bay recognised as Augusta Crewe, Fred's fiancée. Charlotte looked very small standing beside the other women. Middleton bowed to the group and moved next to her.

'I hope you can hear the music now, Miss Baird.'

She nodded. He thought she looked less sure of herself here in the glittering expanse of the ballroom than she had in the enclosed space of the box at Covent Garden.

'Yes, but this music is not intended to be listened to.' She smiled her crooked smile and Bay could see that her fingers were tapping her fan.

He bowed and asked her to dance. But before Charlotte could answer, Augusta said, 'Oh, but you are too late, Captain Middleton, Miss Baird's dance card is quite full. Isn't that right, Charlotte?' Augusta blinked her sandy eyelashes at Bay.

Charlotte laughed. 'Oh, but Augusta, I *must* make room for Captain Middleton. Haven't you noticed how magnificent Fred is looking tonight? It is all the work of Captain Middleton here who sent him to his tailor. I think I should express our gratitude, don't you?'

Augusta sniffed. 'I can't say that I have noticed anything in particular. Fred is always well turned out.'

'Oh, you are just being loyal. You may have the next dance, Captain Middleton, and Augusta, perhaps you would make my excuses to Captain Hartopp.'

The band struck up a waltz. Bay held out his hand to Charlotte. He was surprised at how small and how light she was. She barely came up to his shoulder, unlike Blanche, who had always been on a level with him. She was concentrating too hard on the steps to look at him at first. He could see her biting her lip with effort. He tightened his grip on her waist and finally she raised her eyes to his and said, 'You are a very good dancer.'

'I have had lots of practice. In Ireland there was nothing to do except hunt and go to parties.'

'But Captain Hartopp was in Ireland with you, was he not? He doesn't dance as well as you.'

Bay smiled. 'It's true, no one could call Chicken a dancer. He can ride, though.'

'Why do you call him Chicken, Captain Middleton? I've asked Fred but he won't tell me.'

'If your brother won't tell you, then you can hardly expect me to, Miss Baird.' He saw her frown and continued, 'Don't be cross. It is rather a sad little story and I am too fond of Chicken to repeat it.'

'But you don't mind taking his dancing partner away?'

Bay looked down at her, surprised. He hadn't expected Fred's sister to be so lively.

'Oh, but that was your decision, not mine. Once you had accepted my invitation I could hardly turn you down.'

'How chivalrous you are, Captain Middleton.' She looked up at him through her lashes and Bay decided that her eyes were grey, almost the colour of the blue roan he had ridden in Ireland last summer. She was not beautiful but he found he liked looking at her face.

'Well, I guessed that you didn't want to dance with Chicken all night.'

'Are you a mind reader then, Captain Middleton, as well as being the best dressed officer in the Guards?'

Bay laughed. 'And on what basis do you call me that? Are you an expert in Guards uniforms, Miss Baird?'

'Not at all, but my brother is. Fred doesn't praise people very often, so I am inclined to believe him. I am only sorry you are not wearing your uniform tonight so I can see what perfection looks like.'

'Oh, I think there are quite enough uniforms here tonight.' Bay's voice was dismissive. He felt there was something ostentatious about wearing uniform to every social occasion.

'Well, I am sure your tails are the epitome of understated good taste, Captain Middleton.'

Bay could not help but glance at his impeccable tail coat with its four jet buttons on the cuff. Charlotte smiled and he checked himself. 'You are mocking me, but I am not ashamed of taking the trouble to ensure my clothes fit properly.'

'I envy your attention to detail. Fred is always berating me for my lack of interest in clothes. He would like me to be a fashion plate like Augusta. But I find the rigmarole of dressmaking so tedious. Standing perfectly still while people stick pins into you is not my idea of an occupation.'

'So what would you rather be doing, Miss Baird?'

She didn't answer immediately and they did a turn around the dance floor before she said rather hesitantly, 'I like to take photographs.'

Bay did not conceal his surprise. How could this curious girl be related to stuffy old Fred? 'Really? What sort of things do you photograph?'

'Oh, a variety of things, landscapes, portraits, animals, whatever I think will make a good composition.'

'Have you ever taken a picture of a horse?'

'Not yet. Did you have one in mind?'

'I would like very much to have a likeness of Tipsy, my hunter. She is a thing of beauty.'

'Horse and rider would be interesting. Have you have ever had your photograph taken, Captain Middleton?'

'Never.'

'Has no one ever asked you for a picture? I am surprised.'

Bay was about to answer when he saw Blanche's golden head and white face inches away from him. He lost his balance for a second and stepped out wildly, then heard a gasp and a faint tearing noise.

'Miss Baird, I am so sorry, what have I done?' Bay looked down and saw that he had put his foot through the flounce of her skirt, leaving a grubby rent in the white silk.

He thought for a moment that Charlotte was going to cry but she shook her head and said, 'It doesn't matter, but I think I should get it sewn up.'

They retreated to some seats in the corner and Middleton told a footman to fetch a maid with needle and thread.

'Unless of course you would rather go somewhere more private like the cloakroom.'

She gave him a sideways look. 'Oh no, I would much rather stay here and try to figure out why such an excellent dancer should lose his balance.'

He made a little flourish with his hands. 'You could make anyone unsteady, Miss Baird.'

She did not reply for a moment, considering his remark, and then said, 'I don't think that was the reason, Captain Middleton.'

Bay was about to protest when the maid arrived and started to sew up the gash in her dress. Bay stood in front of Charlotte, shielding her from the room. When the girl had finished and the dress was whole again he said, 'I daresay you won't dance with me again, but can I take you into supper?'

Charlotte shook her head. 'I am promised to Captain Hartopp. I can't abandon him again.'

'How very irritating. Let me, at least, take you back to Lady Lisle.'

He put out his arm, but she hesitated and then took a flower from the corsage at her wrist. It was a small white rosebud whose tightly furled petals were tinged with pink.

'You've lost your buttonhole, Captain Middleton. Won't you take this instead?'

He picked up the flower from her outstretched palm and put it into his lapel. It was smaller than the gardenia and there was no scent that he could detect.

'You are very kind, Miss Baird.'

'Hardly that. It's just that I notice things.'

'Even without a camera?'

She smiled. 'Once you learn to look at things properly, you never stop.'

'Now I feel thoroughly nervous of having my likeness taken.'

'But I only see what is there, Captain Middleton.'

He was about to ask what she saw, but noticed Chicken Hartopp making towards them across the dance floor.

'There you are, Miss Baird. I have come to rescue you from Middleton. I hope you haven't forgotten that you promised to let me take you into supper.'

'Of course not, Captain Hartopp. I was just on my way.'

'My fault entirely, Chicken. Miss Baird here was furnishing me with a new buttonhole.'

Hartopp looked at the white rosebud on Bay's lapel and flushed. Bay realised that somehow he had offended him. Charlotte looked embarrassed and put her hand on Hartopp's arm.

'I hope you don't mind. Captain Middleton needed a new buttonhole and there are so many flowers in the beautiful corsage you gave me that I could spare one . . .'

'Of course I don't mind,' said Hartopp, who clearly did. 'We should get to the supper room before the ices are all gone.'

Bay knew that it was ignoble of him to enjoy Hartopp's annoyance, but he could not help himself. Hartopp and Fred Baird had never concealed their amazement that despite Middleton's inferior social position and fortune, he was not only a better rider than either of them but was also much more popular with women.

But satisfying though Chicken's chagrin had been, Bay took even more pleasure in the fact that little Charlotte Baird had had no qualms about giving him the flower. She liked him, and though Bay was used to being liked by women, he was pleased that this particular girl had decided to favour him. She was not a girl, he guessed, who was easily pleased.

The band started playing a tune that Bay recognised as one that he had danced to with Blanche. They had not danced together very often, as Blanche was careful of her public reputation, so Bay was able to remember each dance quite distinctly. This particular polka had been playing the night of the Londonderry Ball. They had just become lovers and there had been something intoxicating about being able to hold her in his arms in public. She had hardly looked at him, but he had seen the pulse beating in her neck. He found himself looking across the ballroom for her, wondering if she too remembered that other night, but there was no blond head among the swirling dancers. She must be at supper or perhaps she had gone home. Bay was surprised that she could have left without his noticing. He looked at his pocket watch; it was almost midnight. It was much later than he thought. He had been distracted.

There was a cough behind him. He turned to see a man wearing a dress uniform he didn't recognise.

'Captain Middleton?' The man spoke with an accent, French or Italian.

Bay nodded.

'My name is Count Cagliari. I am equerry to her Majesty, the Queen of Naples.' Cagliari looked over to where the Queen was sitting.

Bay bowed. Cagliari was tall and blond, his chest extensively be-medalled.

'At your service.'

'I believe you may know that Her Majesty will be hunting with the Pytchley this winter.'

Bay nodded. 'I hear that she is an excellent horsewoman.'

'Yes, that is the case. Her Majesty is quite without fear. But she is a queen and there is a feeling that she should have some assistance. She is after all riding with the public.'

Bay smiled. 'I don't think the members of the Pytchley would call themselves the public.'

Cagliari made an apologetic wave of his arm.

'Forgive me, sir, I am aware that the Pytchley is a very superior gathering. But that is perhaps, as you say here, the point moot. The Queen, as you know, is cruelly parted from the land whose name she bears. She has not the opportunity to lead, to shine, that should be hers by birth and upbringing. So it has become very important to her that she should be distinguished, to make her mark.' Cagliari paused, looking for the right words, then he continued.

'The Queen wishes to make her mark on the Pytchley, Captain Middleton. And to that end she needs a guide, someone to help her to take her rightful place.'

'The hunting field is not a court, Count.'

'No indeed, how clumsy of me to have given that impression. It is a place of excellence, of course, but as we know, Her Majesty already is a Diana. All she needs is some direction, from someone like yourself, so that she can be the Queen of the hunting field.'

'Direction? Are you asking me to be her pilot? To open gates and that sort of thing, tell her which way the wind is blowing, help her on her horse if she falls off?'

Cagliari beamed, not picking up on the irony in Bay's voice.

'Yes, precisely, Captain Middleton. A pilot. That is the mot juste.'

Bay paused. The Count did not understand the absurdity of his request.

'Please tell Her Majesty that, while I am aware of the honour she does me, I am sorry to say that I cannot oblige her.'

'Oh, but Captain Middleton, you do not appreciate the situation. The Queen would be extremely grateful . . .' He rolled his eyes as if to convey the extent of her gratitude.

'Really, your mistress would be better off with someone who enjoys making royalty grateful. Why don't you ask Captain Hartopp? You see him over there by the orchestra, tall chap with the whiskers? He is an excellent rider, quite as accomplished as I am and he would like nothing better than to ride out with the Queen of Naples.'

Cagliari looked over to where Hartopp was standing with Charlotte and shook his head. 'I am sure he is an excellent fellow, but Her Majesty has asked for you in particular, Captain Middleton. She has heard so many things about your *particular* talents.'

'I am flattered, of course, but I must still refuse. Even if my own Queen were to command my services as a pilot, I would decline. I love to hunt and I have no intention of spoiling one of the great pleasures in life by acting as a glorified royal nursemaid.'

Count Cagliari looked shocked, and Bay felt that perhaps he had gone too far.

'I have offended you, Count, with my frankness. Forgive me, but you see, I am not one of life's courtiers.'

The Count bowed. 'Her Majesty will be disappointed. Poor lady, she has so many crosses to bear.'

Bay patted the Count on the shoulder. 'Tell her I am rude and uncouth and quite unfit for royal company. I am sure that a man like you can make it seem like a lucky escape.'

The Count smiled wanly. 'Well, I shall do my best, Captain Middleton.'

Bay watched him thread his way back through the dancers towards the ex-Queen. It was time to leave. As he began to walk down the great staircase he looked up and saw Charlotte Baird, closely followed by Hartopp, coming down from the supper room on the mezzanine. He wondered if she would look down and see him. He stood there for a moment until he saw her spot him. She gave him a tiny smile, and Bay touched the rose in his buttonhole. And then Hartopp took her arm and hurried her back into the ballroom.

The Group Photograph

Melton Hall, Leicestershire January, 1876

THE GROUP ON THE STEPS AT MELTON SHIFTED about, trying to keep warm, their breath cloudy against the cold winter air. Lady Lisle looked particularly unhappy; her nose went red in the cold and she had so been looking forward to a delightful morning in front of the library fire, writing letters. But no house party these days was complete without a group photograph, and when Lady Crewe had written to invite Adelaide and her niece and nephew to stay at Melton, the Crewe seat in Leicestershire, over Christmas and the New Year, she had specifically requested that Charlotte should bring her 'equipment'. 'It would be so lovely to have a record of our entertainments,' Lady Crewe had written. 'When Archie went to Balmoral last summer, he said that the drawing room was full of photographs.'

Adelaide Lisle had passed on this message with reluctance. She did not approve of Charlotte's photographic exploits. Her niece had turned her dressing room in Charles Street into some kind of lair, which no one was allowed to enter without ringing a bell. She had remonstrated with Charlotte about the amount of time she spent in her 'dark room' but her niece had simply changed the subject. There was not much else Lady Lisle could do. As both parties were fully aware, it was Charlotte's money that paid for the house in Mayfair, the carriage and the handsome pair of liveried footmen who stood at the back of Lady Lisle's carriage when she paid her afternoon calls, and for the champagne that she liked to serve her guests at her Thursday afternoons. Charlotte would never be so vulgar as to point this out, but then she didn't need to. Adelaide Lisle's husband had died leaving her a title but not the means to support it, so she had lived a meagre existence in a small house in the Close at Salisbury, until she had been summoned by Fred to supervise his sister's debut. It had not been difficult to leave the privations of her Salisbury life for the comforts of Charles Street and the attentions of the liveried footmen; so while Adelaide Lisle did not enjoy standing about on a cold December morning while her niece fiddled about behind the green baize cloth that covered her camera, she was in no position to complain.

The photographic session had been fixed for that morning. When the hunting season got underway the house would be half empty during the daylight hours. All the guests had now arrived. Bay Middleton and Chicken Hartopp had been the last to come, turning up the night before with their strings of hunters. Lady Lisle had been quite surprised that Middleton had been invited to Melton; at the Spencer ball a month before Augusta had been so very definite that he was not a 'suitable' young man. But his unsuitability was not, it seemed, an issue in the hunting season when all the great houses in 'the golden triangle' of the Quorn, Pytchley and Melton meets, competed to attract the best riders. Fred had told Lady Lisle that Bay had turned down five invitations, including one from the Spencers to stay at Althorp, in order to come to Melton.

In her tent of green baize Charlotte peered through the lens and counted the heads again: four, five, six, where was the seventh? She unmuffled herself from the drape and looked from behind the camera at the group. Her hostess Lady Crewe and her aunt dominated the middle of the frame; Augusta sat to the left of her mother, her body turned towards Fred, who stood behind her. Charlotte thought that if she were to tinker with this photograph, Augusta with her pale eyelashes and pinched mouth would be more rabbit than Pekinese, Fred with his high colour and receding chins would as always be an excellent turkey.

The men stood on the step behind, which made the difference in heights all the more evident: Chicken Hartopp's enormous frame towered over the others. Charlotte wondered if she could ask all the other men to go up a step so that the difference in height would not be so great; Lord Crewe was not excessively tall, and Captain Middleton had looked rather slight beside Hartopp. But now Captain Middleton was not there.

'What has happened to Captain Middleton?'

'Don't worry, Mitten, he's just gone to get something. He'll be back directly,' Fred answered.

'But I have the plate all set up. Couldn't he have waited?' Charlotte hated it when her brother called her 'Mitten' in public. He told her it was because she had looked like a mitten without a hand when she was a baby. She had often asked him to call her something else, but of course, the more she protested the more he clung to the nickname.

'Well, can't you just take the picture without him, Charlotte dear?' Lady Lisle said. 'It is is getting rather chilly.'

'But that would ruin my composition,' Charlotte said. This was true – she wanted the four men in the background to frame the women in the centre – but it was Bay's picture she wanted to take. She wanted to see how he would look through her lens.

Just then Middleton came running down the steps and took his position next to Hartopp.

'Forgive me, Miss Baird, I had to adjust my necktie. I thought you would want me to look my best.'

Charlotte put her head back under the heavy drape. She could see Bay's outline upside down on the plate, his head six inches below Chicken Hartopp's. She had told them all to stand perfectly still for as long as it took them to recite the Lord's Prayer in their heads from the moment she raised her hand and squeezed the bulb. Not only was the prayer just the right length, but the act of remembering the words stopped her sitters from fidgeting. Her godmother Lady Dunwoody had told her that taking a photograph of someone captured a piece of their soul, 'So you want to take them in a state of grace, Charlotte, if you can.' *For ever and ever, amen.* Charlotte came out from under the cloth and smiled at the group in front of her.

'Thank you for your patience. I hope you will be pleased with the results.'

The group began to stir, moving stiffly after the enforced stillness. Bay was the first to break ranks. He jumped down the steps to where she stood.

'May I help you carry your things inside?'

'That's very kind of you. I hope you don't mind waiting while I dismantle the camera.'

He watched attentively as Charlotte slid the exposed plate out of the camera and put it into its leather box.

'You have a great deal of equipment, Miss Baird. When you told me that you were interested in photography, I had no idea that you were such an expert.'

Charlotte smiled. 'Oh, I am hardly that, but I enjoy it very much. I am flattered that you remembered our conversation.'

'Of course I remembered. I don't often meet young ladies who tell me they would rather stand behind a camera than have a dress made.'

'No. I suspect that I am in the minority. Augusta, for example, finds it quite incomprehensible. She was very disapproving yesterday when I excused myself from a conversation about her trousseau because I had a print to make.'

Bay laughed, revealing white teeth. Charlotte was glad that he was as sympathetic as she remembered him from the Spencer ball. Even through the lens, he had looked so much more vigorous and alive than her brother or Hartopp. There was a springiness to him that made him a much easier presence than most of the young men she knew with their ponderous movements and their mutton-chop whiskers. He was wearing a suit made out of very dark green material. The jacket had an unusual diagonal facing and elaborate horn buttons. Charlotte recognised the style as the 'university' coat. Fred had told her about it: 'Latest thing, everyone's wearing them at the clubs.' It was not a style that suited Fred, as it accentuated his barrel-shaped torso, but on Bay's lean frame the cut looked stylish rather than absurd. She was relieved too that Bay had not grown the dundreary sideburns that were so fashionable at the moment. Charlotte had spent many evenings trying not to stare at a breadcrumb or tobacco strand adhering to the luxuriant facial hair of her dancing partners. She had once stopped Fred in the middle of one of his homilies about 'feminine behaviour' by finding a sizeable crumb of Stilton in his whiskers. Bay, she was pleased to see, had restricted himself to a neat moustache.

'Here, let me do that. I don't think I can do much damage to this.' He took the tripod out of her hands and began deftly to collapse the extendable wooden legs. 'I hope you haven't forgotten your promise, Miss Baird.'

'My promise?'

'To take a picture of Tipsy, my horse.'

'I don't think I am skilled enough to take a portrait of a horse alone, but I could probably manage horse and rider. Remember that you have to stay very still.'

'That won't be a problem for Tipsy, Miss Baird, she's a very serious horse. I, on the other hand, am a terrible fidget.'

Charlotte smiled. She picked up the camera and the slide case and started towards the house. As they made for the disused nursery that Lady Crewe had allowed Charlotte to use as her photographic studio, they had to pass through the crenellated gloom of the Great Hall. Although Melton was of Jacobean origin, it had just been extensively remodelled in the fashionable Gothic style, and all the windows of the hall had been replaced with stained-glass depictions of the Arthurian legends, so Bay's face was washed with yellow then blue then red as he walked across the hall under the windows depicting the Lady of the Lake, Sir Galahad and Lancelot and Guinevere.

'Will you be hunting on Monday, Miss Baird?' he asked as he followed her up the narrow staircase. He was carrying the tripod, a footman followed with the camera and Charlotte herself held the case with the photographic plate.

'I don't hunt, Captain Middleton, but I shall come to the meet. I am going to take some pictures.'

Bay laughed. 'Not sure you will get anyone to stay still enough to say the Lord's Prayer at a meet.'

He put the tripod down.

'But why don't you hunt, Miss Baird? I suspect that you are an excellent rider, and Fred has a quality stable.'

She laid the plate carefully in the developing tray. She tried to speak as lightly she could, not wanting the circumstances of her life to shadow the conversation.

'My mother was my father's second wife. He married her when

Fred was seven. My mother was very young, very rich and, I believe, very reckless. She died in a hunting accident when I was four years old. My father decided that he didn't want his daughter to run the same risk.' The silence was broken by the noise of the footman putting down the heavy camera.

Bay spoke. 'I think if I was your father I would feel the same.' He looked at her and then gestured around the room which was full of Charlotte's photographic paraphernalia.

'But you have something else to fill your time. I had no idea that photography needed so much stuff.'

'Oh, but this is only some of it. At home I have even more.'

Bay picked up one of the brown holland folders that Charlotte kept her work in.

'May I?'

'Of course. But I should warn you that I am more enthusiastic than expert.'

Bay started to look through the photos. 'They look very accomplished to me. I admire this one of Fred and Augusta, you have managed to make her look quite benign.'

Charlotte laughed. 'Yes, that was quite a test. I had to promise her that I would make her look just like the Princess of Wales.'

Bay chuckled and continued leafing through the photographs, then he stopped and made an exclamation.

'But this is capital.' He held up the Royal Menagerie print. Charlotte had photographed her original collage and set it in a black oval border. 'The Queen as a codfish, there is the most uncommon resemblance. And Bertie makes an excellent basset hound. I see that you have a sense of mischief, Miss Baird.'

'Perhaps. Fred thinks that I am peculiar.'

Bay studied the menagerie photograph closely. 'Well, I think on the evidence of this that he is quite right.'

He looked round and laughed when he saw Charlotte's look of disappointment.

'But much better to be peculiar than to be "fashionable" like Augusta. I, for example, collect porcelain and, as you know, I like to listen to opera rather than talk over or sleep through it. My fellow officers find that peculiar but I am rather proud of my eccentricities. Fond as I am of Chicken Hartopp, I don't want to resemble him more than I have to, and I am quite sure that you feel the same about Augusta.'

'You can't expect me to be rude about my future sister-in-law,' Charlotte protested. 'I am an orphan. Augusta will be my family.'

'You have my condolences.' Bay smiled. 'Tell me, Miss Baird, if you were to make one of these creations with the group you took this morning, which animal would you choose to replace me?'

Charlotte put her head on one side. 'Oh, but that is unfair. If I am truthful I may offend you, and if I flatter you, you will think I am a simpering young lady currying favour.'

'I promise that nothing you could say could offend me, and we have already established that you could never be mistaken for a simpering miss.'

'Well, in that case, let me see . . .' Charlotte half closed her eyes in mock deliberation. She had known from the moment she had first set eyes upon Bay exactly what sort of animal he was.

'I would say that you are something wild but not exotic. A predator who makes his own way. You are not to be trusted around chickens or ducks, but you are capable of giving a day's capital entertainment. I would make you a fox, Captain Middleton. I trust I haven't offended you.'

'On the contrary. I have a great deal of affection for foxes. They have given me some of the best days of my life.'

The gong sounded for lunch.

'We must go, Captain Middleton. Lady Crewe does not tolerate tardiness. And Augusta will be wondering why we have been up here so long without a chaperone.'

'Shall I tell her we have been flirting, Miss Baird?'

'Is that what we are doing, Captain Middleton? Thank you for enlightening me.'

Easton Neston

I T WAS RAINING THE MORNING THAT THE EMPRESS was due to arrive, so the servants were waiting inside. The first thing they heard was the sound of the wheels on the gravel; the second was a weird, high-pitched, pulsating yell. The head housemaid got to the window first.

'She's getting out of the carriage and there's something on her shoulder. It's a monkey. She's only got a pet monkey.'

'Nasty smelly things,' said Mrs Cross the housekeeper. 'My last lady was given one and luckily it died a couple of weeks later. No one missed it, I can tell you.'

Wilmot, the butler, shouted for them all to get into line. The housemaid took her place beside Mrs Cross. She could hear the housekeeper humming under her breath. It sounded like a hymn. Mrs Cross was Chapel and she was not happy about working for a Catholic, even if she was an Empress. She had almost resigned when the letter came from Vienna asking for a room to be set aside for the saying of mass. In the event, she had not given her notice, aware that a letter of royal approval would be valuable whether the monarch was protestant or catholic. But she had assigned the coldest, draughtiest room on the North Front for the popish ritual.

The doors were opened and the housemaid saw the silhouette of a woman walking up the steps against the grey morning light. She was tall, an inch or so taller than the man who was holding an umbrella above her head. As she stood in the doorway, the fur mantle slipped away from her body and the housemaid was astonished to see how slender she was – Mrs Cross had said she was a grandmother already – but she had the waist of a girl. The maid instinctively drew in her own stomach.

The Empress was walking towards them now, the man with the umbrella who, although he wasn't wearing a uniform, looked like some kind of servant following just behind. When she reached Mrs Cross, the housekeeper made a surprisingly graceful curtsey. The maid tried to imitate her, keeping her eyes lowered as instructed. 'Never get in their eyeline, Patience,' Mrs Cross had said, 'foreign royalty can be tricky.' But the Empress was stopping in front of her. Surely it would be rude not to acknowledge her in any way. She glanced up at the veiled face and heard the Empress say in a soft, lightly accented voice, 'What is your name?'

The housemaid tried to speak but found she could not make her mouth work. She heard Mrs Cross say, 'This is Patience, the head housemaid, Your Majesty.'

'Such a charming English face. I feel sure I will like it here.' As the Empress walked away the maid caught a trace of violets and something else that smelt rather like brandy.

There was another eldritch scream as the monkey, who had been lurking in the doorway, scuttled across the hall towards the Empress. She seemed not to notice the racket that the animal was making and continued down the line of servants. The housemaid saw the monkey stop in front of Mrs Cross and watched, horrified, as it squatted down and proceeded to urinate on the housekeeper's skirt. Mrs Cross made a sound like a badly oiled door creaking in the wind, and the Empress looked round just as the housekeeper was kicking the animal across the floor.

There was a moment of quiet and then the monkey started screaming again, this time with a high-pitched chatter that ricocheted around the pillars of the entrance hall. The housemaid saw that the Empress's shoulders were shaking, and she realised that she was laughing. The monkey was rocking back and forth on its haunches; Mrs Cross was muttering under her breath. The maid saw the Empress extend one shaking hand towards the monkey and heard her say something in German, then the little man, who had carried her umbrella, picked up the animal and carried it out of the house. As he turned his back on his mistress, the maid could see that his face was as sour as Mrs Cross's had been.

The Empress sat by the fire in the Great Hall. The monkey had been been sent to the stables, but her favourite wolfhound was lying at her feet. The room was enormous, the double height ceiling as high as a cathedral. Elizabeth felt faintly irritated – everyone imagined that because she lived in palaces that she could not be happy in anything else. Yet really she longed for a room where she could speak without hearing her voice echo. Still it was a beautiful house, and more importantly it was in the heart of the English hunting country.

Baron Nopsca, her chamberlain, came into the room, looking worried.

'Earl Spencer is here, Majesty. I told him that you were indisposed after your journey, but he was very anxious to pay his respects.'

Elizabeth smiled. 'But I am not in the least bit tired, Nopsca. Send him in.'

The Earl, Elizabeth noticed, did not kiss her hand. He bowed rather stiffly when he was presented, but there were none of the sycophantic contortions of a Viennese courtier. He was very tall and Elizabeth had never seen a man with quite such red hair before. She tried not to stare at him.

'I hope Your Majesty is happy with the house?'

'It is hardly a house. In Austria we would call it a palace; even the stables are magnificent.' She smiled and was rewarded by seeing the Earl blush.

'Stables are the most important part of the place in my view, Ma'am. When I was rebuilding Althorp, I had them do the stables first, so at least the horses would be comfortable. The Countess was not happy about it at all. She wanted the kitchen block done, said the food was always cold by the time it got to the dining room, but I said what was the point of eating if you couldn't hunt.'

'I can see that we are destined to be great friends, Lord Spencer. Like you, I would much rather hunt than eat.' Elizabeth laid one hand very briefly on the Earl's arm and watched as his skin darkened to a rich magenta. She enjoyed the Earl's confusion, such a delicious contrast from the perfectly controlled manners of the Viennese.

'I am so looking forward to my first "meet", I think you call it. I am relying on you to teach me all the right hunting argot. I don't want to disgrace myself.'

The Earl interrupted her gallantly, 'Oh I am quite sure there is no danger of that, Ma'am. I have heard what a fine horsewoman you are.'

'And I have heard how fierce the English are in the field.' She looked at him through her lashes. The Earl pulled a handkerchief out of his pocket and wiped his brow, which was beaded with sweat, even though the temperature in the room was chilly.

'What time is the hunt tomorrow? I should so hate to be late on my first day.'

The Earl froze, his massive hand at his temple. 'Tomorrow, Ma'am? But tomorrow is Sunday.' He was now such a regal shade of purple that Elizabeth wondered if he was about to have some kind of seizure.

'Sunday?' she asked. 'I suppose people will attend church first.' But Spencer shook his great head.

'No hunting on the Sabbath, Ma'am. Even though every parson round here is a hunting man, the Church won't have it.'

Elizabeth raised an eyebrow. 'I had no idea that the English were so religious. In my country we hunt every day, in fact the Sunday hunts are usually the best. Everyone rides with a clear conscience.' She laid her hand again on the Earl's arm.

'I am sure, Lord Spencer, that if you were to talk to these, how did you call them, parsons, you could persuade them to bend their rules a little? I have come such a long way, and I would so like to hunt tomorrow.'

Baron Nopsca, who was standing in attendance behind the Empress's chair, began to listen carefully. His English was not perfect but he could hear that note in his mistress's voice which indicated that she had set her heart on something, and he knew all about the repercussions if she did not get what she wanted.

The Earl opened his bulbous light blue eyes wide. 'Can't be done, I'm afraid, Ma'am. Not even Queen Victoria herself could ride out on the Sabbath.'

Nopsca noted with alarm the perfect stillness of the Empress's head. How foolish he had been to stand behind her instead of in the Empress's eyeline. His mistress was not used to having her wishes denied, and he feared for the consequences. Silently he prayed that the Empress would remember that she was a guest in this country and that she could not expect everything to be arranged exactly to her satisfaction as it would be at home. His job was, above all, to save the Empress and the Crown from any embarrassment, and he knew that he would no longer be in employment if he failed to prevent the Empress from breaking the law. Why did the English lord have to be so blunt? Nopsca knew that the way to handle his mistress at these moments was to distract her; an outright refusal would only provoke her.

He held his breath as the Empress replied, 'But I thought Victoria was head of the Church in this country!' She paused. 'But it is not my place to break your funny English laws. I shall have to contain myself till Monday . . .' and she laughed. It wasn't a very warm laugh but the relief of it made Nopsca exhale sharply. To his horror the Empress turned round and looked at him. She saw the relief in his face and this time she laughed properly.

'You worry too much, Nopsca.'

Earl Spencer cleared his throat. 'Your Majesty will need a pilot on Monday. Someone to guide you through the field. Twenty years ago I would have taken on the job myself but I am not the man I was. May I suggest a former equerry of mine, a Captain Middleton. One of the best riders in England and knows the country round here like the back of his hand. Better, if anything.'

Elizabeth tilted her head, her dark eyes narrowed. 'Someone to lead me through the field? But I will not be riding out alone; Prince Liechtenstein and Count Esterhazy have come with me from Vienna. They are both excellent horsemen. I believe they will provide me with all the "guidance" I need.'

The Earl looked down at his boots as if looking for his reflection in the polished leather. He seemed to take comfort from what he saw there because he came back strongly, 'With respect, Ma'am, they may be capital riders but they have not hunted with the

Pytchley. They don't know how things are done here. My purpose in suggesting Captain Middleton was to spare you any of the minor embarrassments that might arise from unfamiliarity with the terrain, or with some of our customs in the field. Middleton knows every ditch and fence between here and Towcester. I suggested him because I feel sure that Your Majesty will want to be at the head of the pack.'

Elizabeth considered this. 'And is he discreet, this captain? Would you send him out riding with your queen?'

'Indeed, Ma'am. He is not absolutely from the first rank of society, but he is a superb rider. And it would put my mind at rest to know that he was at your side. Your presence here is a great honour, Ma'am. But as Master of the Pytchley, your safety is my responsibility.'

Elizabeth smiled. She suspected that this Captain Middleton's real duty would be to report on her activities. But if he could ride as well as Earl Spencer said, he could at least be useful while he spied on her.

'Well, I should hate you to worry, Lord Spencer, so I will accept your pilot. But he should know that I am not some porcelain doll to be protected. I am here because I want to ride out with the famous Pytchley hunt. I hope I won't be disappointed.'

The Earl picked up his hat and gloves from the chair beside him. 'No danger of that, Ma'am.'

Elizabeth held out her hand, and this time the Earl bent over to kiss it, his bushy moustache prickling against her skin. She was surprised to see him turn and walk out of the room. Surely he must know that it was disrespectful to turn your back on a monarch? She heard Nopsca behind her make a noise. She guessed he was thinking the same thing. In Vienna such an act would be inconceivable; a courtier would sooner cut his throat than commit such a grievous act of *lèse-majesté*. But, Elizabeth thought, with a sudden rush of exhilaration, she was not in Vienna now. She had escaped for a moment, from all the layers of custom and faux servility, from the courtiers who were obsequious in public and vicious the moment she turned her back.

'I think we shall have to get used to English manners, Nopsca,' she said.

Clementine

THAT EVENING, LADY CREWE HESITATED FOR A MOMENT before announcing who would take Charlotte into dinner.

The Baird girl was a funny little creature – always fiddling with that camera – but she would be family when Augusta married Fred. Lady Crewe had once hoped for a more glittering marriage for her only daughter, but now she was simply relieved that she was to have a son-in-law at all. The Bairds were a respectable family, not perhaps the smartest, but Augusta at twenty-four could no longer afford to be choosy. Edith Crewe looked at Charlotte, who was standing next to Augusta. She really was no beauty but the fortune, of course, made her attractive enough. It seemed unfair that all poor Dora Lennox's money should have gone to the daughter; Fred was comfortably off, but the Lennox fortune would have made all the difference to Augusta's future position. Fred would gain some benefit from the money now, but when Charlotte married, that would all change. She could see that both of Fred's friends were interested. Hartopp was the more suitable – there was no gossip linking him to married women – but feeling the injustice of Augusta's four fruitless seasons in search of a husband with a shrug almost of irritation, she beckoned to Captain Middleton.

As Lady Crewe announced her decision, Bay heard something

like a sigh somewhere over his left ear. Chicken Hartopp was not happy. But Bay could see from the smile on Charlotte's face that he had been her choice.

He offered her his arm.

'My print has come out well, Captain Middleton,' she said.

'I would expect nothing less, Miss Baird. You strike me as a most competent person.'

She looked up at him, surprised. 'Competent is not a word often applied to young ladies; we are usually called accomplished.'

'But accomplished suggests something rather fanciful and ornamental. You seemed so practical with your cameras and your chemicals, your hobby is hardly that of a young lady,' Bay said.

'Actually, Captain Middleton, some of the finest photographers are ladies. My godmother Lady Dunwoody has had her work exhibited at the Royal Photographic Society.'

'Don't be cross. I was trying to pay you a compliment. I would much rather be competent than accomplished.'

Charlotte paused, uncertain as to the extent of her crossness. A footman pulled out her chair and she sat down. She was about to reply to Captain Middleton when she heard Fred call across to her.

'I say, Mitten, do you remember who the painting of the pheasants in the library at Kevill is by? It's the spitting image of that one in the corner.'

Charlotte tried not to flinch at his use of her nickname. 'Greuze, I believe. Father bought it in Italy.'

Bay leant towards her and said, 'Mitten? Why does Fred call you that?'

'I have no idea,' Charlotte said, 'I hate it.' She glared at her brother, who was trying to impress his future father-in-law with the quality of his picture collection.

'Pity. I rather like my nickname. Much more interesting than

John. I was called Bay after the Grand National winner. We have the same colouring, apparently. Sadly the resemblance ends there.'

'Sadly?'

'I haven't won the Grand National, Miss Baird.' Bay bowed his head.

'Oh, is that what you want?' Charlotte was surprised that he had such a definite ambition. He hadn't struck her as a man who made efforts.

'Of course.' He turned to look at her.

'And will you?'

'I hope so. I might have a shot this year. It's all about the horse, and Tipsy is a contender.'

'Ah yes, the famous Tipsy.'

'I hope you are not mocking me, Miss Baird.' He looked at her with uncharacteristic seriousness. 'You don't ride, of course, so I can't blame you for your ignorance, but believe me when I tell you that horses are remarkable creatures. If you find the right one, as I have in Tipsy, it is like finding the other half of your soul. She understands me better than any woman has ever done. And she will never desert me.' He picked up his wine glass and drained it.

Charlotte said, 'Perhaps you haven't found the right woman, Captain Middleton,' and then, realising how forward that sounded, she blushed and added, 'I believe there are some examples of my sex who may be as sympathetic to your feelings as a horse, even if they aren't much use in the hunting field.'

Bay smiled. 'I shall take your word for it. Perhaps I am better at choosing horses than women. You know what you are getting with a horse, whereas with a woman all you can see is what's on the outside. You can feel a horse's soul the moment you ride out together, but with a woman – well, I don't think I have ever met a woman who says what she means.'

'But Captain Middleton,' Charlotte said, 'let's not forget that horses, even remarkable ones like your Tipsy, cannot actually speak. Who knows what white lies or polite half truths your favourite mare might utter if she could. Or perhaps you would prefer a woman who did not speak at all, but gazed at you in mute adoration, ready to obey your orders instantly. I think you are in the wrong country. I think if you were to go to Constantinople you might find the kind of woman you want in the sultan's harem.'

'I would go like a shot if I thought you were right, but I suspect that even the sultan has difficulty in finding a woman who means what she says.'

'I'm afraid that you are a misogynist, Captain, and that nothing I say will make any difference.'

'Possibly, Miss Baird, but please don't stop trying. I am enjoying your efforts.'

The footman took away the soup plates and Charlotte turned to talk to Augusta's younger brother on her other side. He was round-eyed and earnest and he was soon telling her about his studies at Keble College, where he was an ardent supporter of the Oxford movement. As the soufflé was replaced by the turbot, Charlotte turned again to her right but she saw that Bay was listening to the conversation across the table. He was sitting very still, and Charlotte thought this was the first time she had ever seen him motionless.

Lady Crewe was talking to Fred.

'I am always amazed at the names that perfectly sensible people choose to give their children. Do you remember when everyone was calling their daughters Aurora, on account of Mrs Browning's *Aurora Leigh*? And now I had a letter this morning from Stella Airlie to say that Blanche Hozier has called her new baby Clementine. I mean, what kind of name is that? It sounds like a medicine. You must promise me, Fred, that you and Augusta will choose decent English names that people can pronounce. Nothing worse than a foreign sounding name.'

Fred was nodding enthusiastically, his face flushed. Charlotte could see that he was nervous. Fred's mother's name had been Leonie.

She was about to tell Captain Middleton this – she sensed that he would be more than happy to help her tease her brother – but he was holding himself so rigidly that she felt if she touched him he might shatter. The only thing moving was a muscle that twitched in his eyelid.

For a moment she sat silently, but then, feeling her aunt's eye upon her, she knew she must say something. Her aunt was always scolding her for her lack of conversation, saying, 'A man wants to be soothed by feminine conversation, you don't want to make him work too hard. Your job is to make it easy for him to talk to you.' Charlotte had been surprised at this advice, as in her experience most men were more than happy with the sound of their own voice. But she leant towards Captain Middleton and said, 'What do you think, Captain Middleton? I think Clementine is rather a pretty name.'

Rather to her surprise, Chicken Hartopp, who was sitting opposite them, picked up her remark.

'Yes, what do *you* think, Middleton?' he said, so loudly that the table went quiet.

Bay paused for a moment and then he smiled.

'It's not a name I would have chosen, but then the only thing I am competent to judge is horseflesh.' He turned to Charlotte.

'What do you say, Miss Baird?' She sensed that Chicken Hartopp, her aunt and Lady Crewe were all listening, and she saw that Middleton was labouring to keep his mouth stretched into a smile.

She took a breath and then she said, 'I suppose the question is whether one's name is a self-fulfilling prophecy? My real name is ordinary enough, but I feel quite belittled if Fred calls me Mitten. Perhaps you feel the same, Captain Hartopp, when people call you Chicken?' She saw that Bay's smile had lost its tight rigidity and, encouraged by this, although a little ashamed to have teased Captain Hartopp, she continued.

'When you are at the races, do you bet as confidently on a horse called Treacle as one called Pegasus? How confident would you feel about the diagnosis of a Dr Pain?'

Captain Hartopp was about to answer when Lady Crewe said, 'We have an undertaker here in the village whose name is Coffin. I wonder if he ever contemplated another profession. I must ask him.' The conversation drifted off into maids called Polish, judges called Gallows and a surgeon called Saw. Charlotte felt that the moment, whatever it had been, had passed.

She turned to Middleton, who had slumped back against his chair.

'I hear that there is royalty hunting with the Pytchley this year.'

Middleton laughed. 'If you mean the Queen of Naples, she is ex-royalty. The Italians chucked her out.'

'Still, I should like a picture. My album has nothing grander than an earl. A queen, even a deposed one, would be a coup. Will you help me, Captain Middleton?'

He looked across the table as he replied, his eyes resting for a moment on Chicken Hartopp's red face. 'For you, Miss Baird, I would do anything, even make myself agreeable to one of the vainest woman in Europe.'

'Is she really so bad? I thought she was generally considered rather handsome.'

Chicken Hartopp leant over. 'The Queen of Naples has rather a weakness for Middleton. Wanted him to be her pilot. Not a job I would have turned down, but I suppose you are spoilt for choice, eh Middleton?'

Charlotte felt a tiny brush of saliva on her cheek as Hartopp leant towards her. She sat back involuntarily.

'I didn't fancy being at the beck and call of a woman, even if she is a queen. There are other things I want to do.' Middleton laughed. 'I realise that makes me sound very ungallant.'

'A little, Captain Middleton.' Charlotte was about to say that at least he was honest when Hartopp leant forward again. 'Time was, Middleton, when you liked nothing better than to be at the beck and call of a woman.' This remark hit a pause in the table's hum of conversation.

Lady Crewe clucked audibly, 'I couldn't help overhearing you mention the Queen of Naples, Captain Middleton. Did you know that her sister the Empress of Austria has taken Easton Neston from Lord Hesketh for the season? She is to hunt with the Pytchley. I hear she is coming over with ten horses.'

Lady Lisle spoke. 'Not only horses. Lady Spencer told me that she travels everywhere with a pet monkey, a dairy cow and a pack of wolfhounds. They have had to make all sorts of alterations to Easton Neston. Apparently one of the bedrooms is to be turned into a gymnasium.'

'A gymnasium? What on earth can she want with such a thing?' Lady Crewe was astonished.

'The Empress is so proud of her figure that she does calisthenics every single day,' Augusta said. 'I read in the *Illustrated London News* that she has taken lessons from a circus performer and can make her horses jump through hoops of fire.'

'Honestly, Augusta, how can you be so credulous?' said her mother. 'Empresses don't do circus tricks, even foreign ones. People will say anything to sell a newspaper. But I must say I am looking forward to seeing her. They say she is the most beautiful woman in Europe. '

Lady Crewe rose to her feet and beckoned to the other ladies to follow her.

As Middleton got up to pull out Charlotte's chair, his hand brushed across her bare shoulder. She felt its heat and looked up at him, startled.

'Oh how clumsy of me, Miss Baird, I am sorry,' but Charlotte thought that he didn't look sorry at all. He was staring at her and she stared back, feeling that to look away would be cowardly somehow. At last he laughed. 'Look at me. I have the manners of a stable hand. Will you allow me to escort you to the door, Miss Baird?' He extended his arm with exaggerated deference. Charlotte laid the tips of her fingers on it and they walked in silence to the door. As she walked up the stairs to the drawing room she still felt the touch of his hand on her shoulder, her collarbone to be exact.

Hair Brushing

THE BRUSH STOPPED, ARRESTED BY A KNOT. SO MUCH hair, it came down to below the Empress's knees; the imperial hairdresser had to bend almost double to brush its entire length. To wash it took a dozen eggs and a bottle of brandy. And it was so heavy the hairdresser could see the relief on her mistress's face when she took out the pins at the end of the day. It was like carrying a baby on the back of your head. Sometimes it felt so heavy that the Empress would lie in bed with her hair tied to the ceiling with ribbons to relieve the weight.

The hairdresser stood back, the hair in front of her pacified and smooth at last.

'Shall I tie it up, Majesty?'

Elizabeth put her head on one side and smiled at her in the mirror, 'No, I need it tonight to keep me warm.'

She stood up and shook the hair around her like a cloak. The hairdresser made her deepest curtsey, saying as she always did, 'I lay myself at Your Majesty's feet.'

'Thank you. You may leave us.' The imperial hairdresser walked, as custom dictated, out of the room backwards, hesitating a little as the route was as yet unfamiliar to her.

Elizabeth sat down in front of the mirror. She thought there was a new line underneath her left eye. It was what her mother would call a laughter line: 'Never forget that every smile leaves a crease on your face, girls.' Every time she said that, Elizabeth and her sisters would wipe their faces smooth as china for a minute and then one of them inevitably would start giggling and their mother would sigh and say, 'But your faces are your future, you know.' Her mother had been right, of course. It was Elizabeth's fifteen-year-old face that had changed everything that day in Bad Ischl. She had gone as an afterthought: to be a companion to Helena, her eldest sister and the one who had been chosen by their aunt to marry her son the Emperor. But Franz had seen Sisi, as Elizabeth was known to the family, and after that he was blind to anyone else. For the first and last time in his life, he had acted on impulse. He chose her, Sisi the shy one, not the suitable Helena who was so good at saying the right thing. Helena, who always looked regal, even when she was asleep.

But it was unfair that she should be getting laughter lines. There had not been so very much to smile about. There was a scratching at the door and Elizabeth smelt the monkey as it bounded into the room.

Elizabeth thought of the expression on the English housekeeper's face when she saw the dark stain spreading on her skirt. She knew that it was cruel of her to laugh, but it was such a relief to see something real in the middle of all that stiffness. It had felt like a good omen. Maybe, she thought, she could be happy here. She smoothed the skin round her eyes with her fingertips. The lines would come anyway; perhaps it was more important to find something to laugh about.

There was a knock at the door. Countess Festetics, the thin Hungarian lady-in-waiting, came in, her sleek head down and slightly forward as if she were an otter parting the waves. She was carrying a letter.

'Majesty.' She curtsied and handed the envelope to Elizabeth.

'Dearest Sisi, I hope you have arrived safely and that the house is to your satisfaction . . .'

It was a letter from Maria. Elizabeth felt her face tighten. Of her four sisters, Maria was the nearest to her in age, and they had been very close when they were little, but like so many things the relationship had changed with her marriage. Helena had been dignified about losing the chance to be Empress, but Maria was too young to conceal her envy. Things had improved when Maria had married the King of Naples, but she had barely had a chance to enjoy her status before the Revolution. And now she was a queen in exile, married to a man she could barely tolerate, with no children to comfort her.

The letter went on, 'I have been sorely tried these last few months; when I think of the riches I took for granted in Naples . . . and there are so many minor indignities. Only the other day the Duchess of Savoy was given precedence over me at a Drawing Room.' The letter continued with a catalogue of misfortunes and slights that Maria had been forced to endure. At the end there was a postscript, 'But now that you are here, dearest Sisi, I feel sure that my fortunes must improve. I hope that a little of your imperial glory will reflect on me.'

Elizabeth put the letter down; reading Maria's letter had made her feel weary. She knew that her sister wanted sympathy, but Elizabeth felt something close to irritation. Why should she be made to feel guilty for still wearing a crown?

Festetics was saying something in Hungarian about the dinner tomorrow. Elizabeth felt her spirits lift as she replied in the same language, 'Tell Count Esterhazy and Prince Liechtenstein that my sister is coming for dinner tomorrow.' Her cavaliers could be relied upon to pay court to Maria. Max and Felix were always charming, and so handsome. Of course, she would always be the object of their most intense adoration, but she would not object to a little flirtation with Maria. She was probably starved of that kind of distraction. Judging by the lumbering manners of Earl Spencer, English men had no idea how to flatter a woman. Her life had become considerably more pleasant now that Max and Felix had become her *cavalieri serventi*. The fact that they were inseparable meant that there could be no flicker of scandal in their slavish devotion to their Empress. Her husband, Franz Joseph, had made one of his rare jokes about them, 'I shall call them the dual monarchy – an Austrian and a Hungarian yoked together in the service of a greater cause.'

She looked at the clock; it was a little after ten. At this hour her husband would be sitting in his apartments in the Hofburg going through the state papers with his magnifying glass.

In the early days of their marriage she had been so jealous of those piles of paper. They were always there, waiting for him at five in the morning and still there at midnight when he went to bed. When she had dared to complain, he had looked at her as if he didn't understand what language she was speaking. 'I am the Emperor, this is my work.' She had retreated then in the face of his seriousness, but as time went on she realised that even if the country didn't need him to approve every appointment in the civil service or to sign every document relating to the management of his vast empire, Franz could not wake up in the morning or go to sleep at night without his paper mountain of responsibilities. Once she had resented the time he spent scratching through forestry reports from Carpathia; now she thought of those bundles of paper tied up in red tape with relief. While he had his head down over the paper trail of his empire, he could not look up and reproach her for leaving him alone.

She pictured his study. So spartan for a Hapsburg emperor. Franz slept every night on his iron campaign bed. The only colourful thing was the Winterhalter portrait hanging over his desk, the one of her holding up her hair in a great knot. Not her favourite portrait, but Franz was so fond of it. Probably by now he preferred it to the real woman. In the picture, at least, she was smiling at him.

Sisi picked up her pen and started to write. She certainly found it easier to write affectionately to her husband now that they were safely in different countries. At this distance Franz's inflexible routine seemed comforting rather than irritating. She liked the idea that she always knew where he would be and what he would be doing at any hour of the day. But it was better to know of it than to see it in its daily monotony.

By the end of her letter Sisi felt quite warm towards her husband. She thought that if he were here she would like to put her head on his chest for a moment and feel his warm hand on her shoulder. A moment, though, would be enough.

Franz had not protested when she had proposed this trip to England. In fact he had been almost eager, doubling her allowance and giving her the imperial train to transport her horses. For a moment Sisi wondered whether he actually wanted her to go and felt a little hurt; but then she dismissed the thought as incredible, Franzl would never ever admit even to himself that there was anything untoward about their marriage.

She signed her name Sisi with her usual flourish and sealed the letter. Her duty done, she allowed Festetics to settle her into the vast bed. The day after tomorrow she would be hunting.

The Orchid House

THE NEXT DAY WAS A SUNDAY. THERE HAD BEEN A private chapel at Melton since it was built in the early 1600s. The original had been an austere building, almost Lutheran in its simplicity. But Lord Crewe's enthusiasm for the Gothic had extended to every part of the house, and the architect, who was a disciple – there was no other word – of Pugin, had transformed the chapel into a polychrome tribute to High Anglican devotion. The simple clerestory windows had been replaced with a riot of stained glass depicting Noah's Ark (Lord Crewe had always wanted a menagerie). The flagged stone floor had been taken up and a tessellated pavement of the latest encaustic tiles had been laid down in a design taken from the floor of the Cathedral at Chartres. Every pew had a gilded finial; the ceiling was covered in lavishly painted beams with wooden gargoyles sprouting at every groyne. Lord Crewe had done very well out of the railway boom, so no expense or trouble had been spared. Many visitors had, in his Lordship's hearing at any rate, compared Melton favourably with Keble College in Oxford or even to the Houses of Parliament.

But the Gothic splendours of Melton were not popular with everybody. Every time Augusta knelt to say her prayers on a tapestry kneeler depicting the Miracle at Cana, she would reflect rather bitterly that the lavishness of the chapel was the reason for the modesty of her dowry. As the daughter of an earl, Augusta had expected from childhood to make a Great Match. She had gone into her first season fully prepared to flirt with younger sons, but to save her affections for the heir. To her surprise and chagrin, however, she had found that none of the names she had perused in the nursery copy of Burke's Peerage was finding its way on to her dance card. At the end of her first summer, she had danced with a couple of baronets and had supper with the younger son of a viscount and had taken one heady turn round the conservatory of Syon Park with the nephew of a duke, but none of these young men had come back for more. In her second season she had had high hopes of an Irish peer, who was most attentive until a tenants' revolt had summoned him back to his estates. She had waited for him to return the following year, only to find that he had become engaged to one of the Drummond sisters, who happened to have a dowry of £50,000. When Augusta looked at the gold and lapis mosaic of the Virgin Mary above the altar, she could not help thinking that if the chapel had been left in its original unadorned state, she would now be Lady Clonraghty.

Fred had proposed in her fourth season, just at a point when she was beginning to wonder whether she, like poor Princess Beatrice, was doomed to be the unmarried daughter living at home for ever. She had refused him the first time, of course; it was vital that he realised that she was not an easy conquest and she had not altogether given up hope of a title. But Fred was so excited by the thought of winning an aristocratic bride that he pursued her from ball to ball, claiming every dance that decorum allowed and making sure that he always procured her the peach ices that she coveted from the supper rooms. Although Fred was not aristocratic, or particularly handsome, he was more than respectably connected, and the shortcomings in his face and figure were disguised by the splendour of his Guards Uniform. Kevill, the Baird estate in the Borders, was not as grand as Melton, but thanks to the novels of Sir Walter Scott its location and its ancient pele tower had become quite fashionable. Border society was not so illustrious that it would be indifferent to the importance of a Lady Augusta Crewe. It was not the match she had hoped for, but it was a great deal better to be Mistress of Kevill than to be the domestic angel of some rural deanery. Fred had an estate of 20,000 acres and an income of £10,000 a year. She hoped it would be enough to take a house in town during the season, for while Augusta was an admirer of Walter Scott, she did not want to moulder in the Scottish foothills for ever, like the Bride of Lochinvar.

It was unfortunate that the Lennox fortune would leave the family when Charlotte married. Fred had confessed to Augusta that he had managed to save a substantial amount in the past few years since his father's death by living off the interest on his sister's inheritance. The house in Charles Street and the refurbishment of Kevill had all been paid for with Lennox money, so that the heiress might live in suitable style. Of course, that style would continue if the heiress remained unmarried, but Augusta could not believe that Charlotte, even with all her peculiarities, would be single for long. Hartopp was clearly making a play for her, however Augusta had seen the look on Charlotte's face when Bay had taken her into dinner. Middleton was handsome, of course, and she had observed that he was an excellent dancer, although Bay had never actually asked her to dance. But he was quite unsuitable and only a girl as naive and inexperienced as Charlotte would fail to recognise that.

Augusta thought, not for the first time, how fortunate Charlotte was in having her as a mentor. How easy it would be for Charlotte, without Augusta's guidance, to be swayed by the smooth tongue and nimble feet of a Bay Middleton and diverted from the excellent match that surely lay ahead for her. Not that there was any hurry. Charlotte's prospects would be much improved by spending a season or two under Augusta's tutelage.

Augusta was not the only member of the congregation whose attention was diverted from the young curate, who was preaching a heartfelt sermon on the subject of brotherly love. The Hon. Percy, Augusta's younger brother, was a fervent Tractarian, and he could tell from the priest's elaborate robes and choice of quotations that he too was of the same mind. Lord Crewe was admiring, as he always did, the procession of lions, elephants and zebras making their way up the ramp to the shelter of the Ark. Next to him, his wife was wondering if Lady Spencer would hold a reception for the Austrian Empress; she couldn't help but be curious.

In the pew behind, Lady Lisle was thinking about lunch.

Fred was contemplating whether he should have a coat made up with the new American shoulders as his tailor had suggested. Next to him, Charlotte was trying to decide whether the pricking feeling on the back of her neck meant that Bay was sitting in the pew behind her.

It did. Bay had not woken up with the intention of attending the service, but when he saw Hartopp wearing his frock coat and clutching his prayer book, he realised that he too might benefit from communing with the Almighty. He made a point of sitting directly behind Charlotte Baird and singing as loudly as he could. He wondered if she would turn round. But she didn't.

At the back, the indoor servants enjoyed the respite. If you had been up since dawn laying fires, then half an hour sitting down listening to the importance of Christian charity was divine intervention indeed.

After the service the household dispersed. Lord Crewe went to the gun room; Lady Crewe and Lady Lisle took the carriage to visit a sick villager; the Honourable Percy stayed behind to have a word with the vicar about a recently acquired translation of Josephus; and Augusta and Fred went to see if the lake had frozen. The housemaids stood up, their knees clicking as they got to their feet, and waited for Charlotte, Bay and Chicken Hartopp to leave the chapel.

Charlotte walked quickly. She had no intention of lingering, but if anyone chose to intercept her, well, she could not be held responsible for that. She walked up the flight of steps that connected the chapel to the rest of the house. There were fourteen steps, and on the thirteenth she heard his voice.

'Miss Baird, I think this is the moment.'

She stopped and turned her head.

'The moment for what?' She knew, of course.

Middleton was bounding up the steps towards her, two at a time, as if trying to escape from Hartopp. When he reached her, Bay said, 'You haven't forgotten poor Tipsy? She has been beautifying herself all morning.'

Charlotte laughed. 'I very much doubt that I can do such a paragon justice, but I will attempt to take a picture of you both if you can promise to keep her still.'

'Splendid.' He turned to Hartopp, who stood on the steps below, visibly dismayed by their banter.

'Chicken, old fellow, why don't you help Miss Baird with her equipment while I bring Tipsy round to the front of the house?'

Hartopp hesitated, but when Charlotte said, 'Oh that would be very kind, Captain Hartopp,' he followed her obediently.

As they climbed the stairs to the old nursery, Hartopp said, 'Middleton has some cheek expecting you to take a picture of his horse. He thinks altogether too much of that creature.'

'Oh I don't mind, and besides, I want to take a picture of Captain Middleton, and I suspect that he will be a much better behaved subject if his horse is present.'

They entered the nursery, and Hartopp saw the print of the group photograph that Charlotte had taken yesterday on the table. He looked at it carefully and saw that Bay was the only person in the photograph who was smiling. Hartopp bristled.

'Middleton looks very pleased with himself in this picture.'

Charlotte turned around from the shelf of photographic plates. 'Not many people can smile in a photograph like that. Holding your expression can make even the most genuine expression seem forced.' She took one of the plates over to the window to examine it.

Hartopp did not reply immediately. He stood staring down at the picture, his face filling with colour, one massive hand pulling at his whiskers. His chest heaved and the buttons of his jacket strained at the buttonholes. Finally he spoke, his voice emerging in a rapid mutter.

'Miss Baird, Charlotte if I may call you that, you must be aware that in the last few months I have come to admire you greatly. My admiration is so great that it compels me to take a step which might appear to be premature, but which I, after much deliberation, have decided that I can no longer put off. You see, I am at that stage in a man's life where he feels the need to settle down, and there is no one in the world that I would rather—'

He broke off as Charlotte, who had clearly not heard a word of his speech, gave a squeal of excitement. 'Oh, look at that! Captain

Middleton is making his horse stand on its hind legs, surely he will fall off.' She pressed her face against the window.

Hartopp sighed and cleared his throat, preparing to start again. 'Miss Baird, Charlotte if I may call you that—'

Charlotte, who was picking up her camera and plates, interrupted, 'Come along, Captain Hartopp, we must hurry. I am afraid that if we don't go down there and restrain him, Captain Middleton will break his neck.'

'Oh, there's no chance of that,' said Hartopp with regret.

But Charlotte did not hear him, and put the tripod into his hands.

Outside, Bay was preening and curvetting on Tipsy as if he was in a circus ring. He could see the white faces of the housemaids pressed against the glass, and he couldn't resist jumping up so that he was standing on the saddle as Tipsy cantered around the turning circle. Then he bent down, held onto the edge of the saddle and pushed himself up into a handstand. He managed two circuits before bringing himself upright. He could hear the faint sound of clapping from inside the house, and he gave his audience a little bow.

'Oh, I was hoping that you were going to stay like that a little longer. It would have made a delightful picture.' Charlotte was standing on the front steps setting up her equipment, a thunderous looking Hartopp at her side.

'I'm afraid I was showing off. I don't want to blacken Tipsy's good name with my antics.' Bay jumped to the ground and patted his horse's neck.

Charlotte gestured to Captain Hartopp where she wanted him to set down the tripod. 'If you could just pull out that leg, perfect. Thank you so much, now I am quite ready to do justice to this remarkable horse.'

'Then if you have no further use for me, perhaps you will excuse me, I have letters to write.' Hartopp did not wait for Charlotte to answer before setting off towards the house.

Bay gestured towards the retreating figure with his crop.

'What have you done to Hartopp, Miss Baird? He looks quite fierce. Did he offer to make you Mrs Hartopp and you spurned him with a girlish laugh? I had no idea that you were so heart-less. You must temper your refusals with paltry compliments to assuage a man's pride, y'know. Poor Chicken, he looks quite crestfallen.'

'Don't be absurd. Captain Hartopp has, no doubt, decided that he has more important things to do than to watch you cavorting around on your horse.'

'Well, if you say so, but he looked like a disappointed lover to me.'

Charlotte hesitated. Bay was joking, of course, yet Hartopp's pique was clearly genuine. But having given him no encouragement, she really could not be responsible for his feelings.

'So, Captain Middleton, do you think you can persuade Tipsy to stand still?'

'Absolutely. How would you like us?'

Charlotte looked at them. She had imagined Bay sitting on the horse, but now that she saw him with the animal and observed the way he looked at Tipsy, she knew that was the image she wanted.

'Why don't you stand just there with your hand on the bridle like that?' She pulled the cloth over her head and looked at the upside-down image. She moved the camera a little so that the horse and rider were in the centre of the frame. Coming out from under her shroud she said, 'Remember, when I raise my hand I want to you to keep still for as long as it takes to recite the Lord's Prayer. If you or Tipsy move, the image will be blurred.'

'We will be as still as statues. Won't we, Tipsy?'

Charlotte looked up at the sky and saw a procession of dark clouds heading towards the weak winter sun. She needed to take the picture now, before the light went. She disappeared underneath the baize, steadied herself and raised her hand.

She was at 'Forgive us our trespasses' when Fred's voice broke across her thoughts.

'Oh, what a charming scene, dear Mitten taking a picture of Middleton and the love of his life.'

Charlotte willed Bay not to move; another ten seconds and the photograph would be done. 'The power and the glory . . .'

'A horse is the love of Captain Middleton's life? I am surprised,' Augusta's voice came from behind her.

Charlotte was determined not to lose her concentration. 'World without end, Amen.' She thought she saw Bay flinch. She came out from under her shroud, to see the engaged couple standing behind her. She turned on Fred.

'Really, Fred, how many times have I told you not to disturb me when I am taking a picture? You wouldn't like it if I started talking to you just when you raised your gun.'

'Completely different, Mitten. Shooting is a serious business.'

'And photography isn't? Well, why don't you try and take a photograph, Fred? You might find that it's slightly more complicated than pointing a gun at a bird and pulling the trigger.'

Fred took a step towards her

'Really? It looks to me that all you are doing is pointing a camera at your subject and releasing the shutter. Where's the skill in that?'

Bay's voice broke in with mock plaintiveness. 'May we move now, Miss Baird? Tipsy is getting rather restless. It's feeding time at the stables and she doesn't want to miss her oats.'

'She has been an excellent sitter, I didn't see her move a muscle,' Charlotte said.

'She's terribly vain, didn't want to produce a bad likeness.' Bay jumped on Tipsy's back and, with a touch of his heels, galloped off towards the stables.

Charlotte was left at the top of the steps with Fred and Augusta. There was a little pause and then Fred said, 'You and Middleton seem very pally.'

'I find him amusing.'

'Well, of course he's amusing – he's famous for being amusing and agreeable and an excellent dancer – but I must warn you, Mitten, that he is what is called a ladies' man.' Fred whispered the phrase 'ladies' man' as if somehow to make it less shocking.

'I think you forgot to say, Fred, in your list of Captain Middleton's accomplishments, that he is the best dressed officer in the Guards. Didn't he give you the name of his tailor?' Charlotte asked.

'I don't see what that has to do with anything,' blustered Fred. 'I am simply trying to point out that he is to be treated with caution. I like the man, he's a fellow officer and one of the best riders in the country, but he just isn't suitable.'

Charlotte collapsed her tripod with a sharp snap.

'Suitable for what?' she said.

'For you, of course!' cried Fred.

'So what you are saying is that he is good enough for you, and for Earl Spencer and the Queen of Naples, but he isn't suitable for me. I fail to follow you, Fred.' Charlotte felt herself flushing.

Fred was about to reply, but Augusta put her hand on his arm. 'Dearest Fred, why don't you carry all this equipment upstairs for your sister? I should so much like to show her the new orchid house before luncheon.'

Brother and sister obeyed her with equal reluctance. Fred had a great deal more to say to Charlotte about the unsuitability of Bay Middleton and Charlotte had no desire to look at orchids with Augusta, but neither could think of a way out. Charlotte handed the tripod and the camera to Fred, keeping only the plate she had just taken – she didn't trust Fred not to drop it. Augusta took her arm and propelled her towards the walled garden where the orchid house had been built.

'I daresay you have never seen an orchid house before in a private residence. Papa got the idea after a visit to the botanical gardens at Kew. He is so very fond of exotic plants that he simply couldn't rest until he had created his own orchidarium.'

They walked through the frosty kitchen garden with its blackened cabbages and tall asparagus cloches to the round glass pavilion on the south wall.

Augusta pushed open the door and they both exclaimed at the warm, humid air. A spike of orchids brushed Charlotte's cheek; as she pushed it away she noticed the cold waxiness of the petals and the complete lack of scent.

'Do you like the orchids, Charlotte? My father's collection is famous, of course. There are specimens here that come from as far as the Kingdom of Sarawak.'

'Goodness! I have only a vague notion of where Sarawak is, almost unimaginably distant.'

'Yes, distant to us, but not to my father, who has spared no expense to get the choicest items.' Augusta's tone was unmistakably bitter.

There was a pause. Charlotte decided on closer inspection that Lord Crewe might have better spent his money elsewhere. She did not care for the floral contortions around her; the orchids felt to her like monarchs in exile, their magnificence incongruous with their new surroundings.

Augusta picked up a hot pink flower and began to stroke one of its pendulous lower petals with one kid-gloved thumb.

'As we are going to be sisters, Charlotte, and because you have no mother, I feel that it is my duty to give you some guidance.'

'That is very kind of you, Augusta, but you are forgetting Aunt Adelaide. She is very conscientious.'

'Perhaps. But Lady Lisle has been away from London society for a number of years, and while she is no doubt a delightful companion, her judgement on certain matters is a little rusty. She is out of the swim, and is not quite aware of all the potential hazards that lie in your path.'

'Hazards?' said Charlotte.

'It will be much easier, of course, when you are living with us. I will be on hand to guide you. I have had so much more experience in these matters.'

'But Augusta, you are only four years older than me.'

'Only three years, I think you'll find, but those three years have given me a sense of the pitfalls that lie ahead of you. I know how easy it is to be led astray.'

Charlotte smiled. 'Led astray? Augusta! Are you about to confess to an indiscretion? How very exciting. Does Fred know?'

There was a pop, as Augusta crushed the pink cushion of the orchid's lower lip.

'I am talking about you, Charlotte, as I am sure you are aware. You and Captain Middleton.'

'You really ought to be more careful with your father's orchids. That was a very fine specimen until you started playing with it,' Charlotte said.

Augusta sighed. She spoke slowly and with an air of great patience.

'Fred was perhaps a bit clumsy earlier, but you must understand that he was only trying to protect you.'

'Protect me from what, though? I have danced with Middleton once, sat next to him at dinner once, and taken his photograph twice. He has not made love to me, indeed the bulk of our conversation has been about his horse. Frankly, if he is an example of a dangerous ladies' man, then I am disappointed.'

'Captain Middleton has a reputation. He has been friendly, too friendly, with a married woman. She was mentioned at dinner last night – Blanche Hozier. You must have noticed how Middleton reacted when my mother mentioned her name. I believe the liaison is at an end, but that is hardly the point.'

'But I am not a married woman, and Captain Middleton is not a married man. Our meetings are in public, and as yet, there has been no talk of Gretna Green. I know nothing of Blanche Hozier, but if Captain Middleton's behaviour has been so very shocking then I am surprised to find that he is a guest here at Melton.' Charlotte lifted her chin defiantly.

Augusta gave Charlotte a look intended to convey sisterly compassion.

'Oh dear, this is exactly what I was afraid of. You are taking his side, and that is because he has preyed upon your emotions. You have had so little experience of men, and when an accomplished young man like Captain Middleton makes himself agreeable, you are quite defenceless. You imagine, of course, that he is interested in you. But dear, sweet, innocent Mitten, here is a man who has displayed a fondness for a married woman. Why then would he be attracted by a young girl with no experience or sophistication, if it were not for the fact that you are a considerable heiress? I am afraid that Captain Middleton, who comes, I understand, from a very modest background, is a fortune hunter.'

Charlotte would have liked very much to pick up one of the orchids from Sarawak and poke it into her future sister-in-law's bulging blue eye, but she retained her composure by imagining her instead as an overbred Pekinese holding a parasol.

'A fortune hunter? I fail to see, Augusta, how that distinguishes Captain Middleton in any way. Are you telling me that Captain Hartopp isn't interested in my money, or that you and Fred would be quite so eager to have me share your newly wedded bliss if I were a poor relation? Perhaps Captain Middleton is only interested in my fortune, but if that is the case he does a much better job of concealing it than anyone else.'

Augusta, no doubt thinking of the Lennox diamonds and how distinguished they would make her look on her wedding day, laid a conciliatory hand on Charlotte's arm.

'We mustn't quarrel, Charlotte. I mean no harm. Every girl is entitled to a flirtation. All I ask you to remember is that Bay Middleton may be a wonderful dancing partner and a charming photographic subject, but he is not a serious prospect. I don't want you to be compromised. With your advantages you could marry someone of real standing – a man whose position will give you a role in life. I have such great plans for you next season. If you don't end the year as a future countess or even a marchioness, I will be very disappointed.'

Charlotte felt suddenly weary. She could not hope to explain to Augusta that her disappointment was inevitable. For if the conversation had convinced her of one thing, it was that she would never marry a man who had been procured for by her future sister-in-law.

'You have been very generous with your advice, Augusta, and there could be no better counsel, I daresay, to a girl who wants to make a dazzling marriage. But now you will have to excuse me. I must take this plate back to the house – or I am afraid the humidity in here will affect the result.'

Augusta smiled, revealing her prominent overbite. 'Of course, I know how important your hobby is to you. I just wanted to make sure we had a little tête-à-tête before you took any more "photographs" of Captain Middleton.'

But Charlotte was already at the door, desperate to breathe in the cold winter air.

She didn't consciously intend to go back to the house via the stable block, but somehow she found herself walking through the yard. The stable was the only part of Melton that had not been given the Gothic treatment. Although Lord Crewe had talked about replacing the stable clock with a campanile with revolving figures, his architect had never quite got around to completing the design.

As it was the start of the hunting season all the stalls were full. Charlotte looked for Tipsy's grey coat, but there were so many horses there that she found it very hard to tell them apart. She was almost at the other side of the yard when she saw Bay. He was crouching down on the ground, tying a hunting bandage around his horse's leg. He had taken his coat off and had rolled up his shirtsleeves, revealing sinewy white arms covered in freckles. Charlotte watched him for a minute as he pulled the bandage tight and then soothed the horse, who was stamping and snorting from the indignity. But as Bay whispered in the animal's ear and let it lick the flat of his hand, the horse subsided.

Charlotte willed him to look round. At last he turned his head and saw her and the plate case in her hand. He ran over to where she was standing, just under the stable arch.

'Don't tell me you have done it already? Have you come to show Tipsy the results?'

Charlotte shook her head. 'Even though the printing process is much faster than it used to be, it is not that speedy. You will have your print tonight, if I am not waylaid by something else. No, I came through here to escape from Augusta. She has been giving me sisterly advice, and I find that it is best taken in small doses.'

Bay ran a hand through his hair and Charlotte noticed the swell of his forearm.

'What was the advice about?' he asked, and when Charlotte did not immediately reply, he said, 'I can tell from the way you are blushing that she was advising you about me. Am I right?'

Charlotte looked down at the floor and kicked a piece of straw with her foot.

'She is very concerned about my future.'

'And let me guess, she doesn't think that your future should include reprobates like Bay Middleton?'

'I don't believe she used the word reprobate. I think she might have said that you were "unsuitable".'

Bay laughed and stretched his arms out wide. 'And what do you say, Miss Baird? Do you agree with the Lady Augusta? Am I to be cast into the outer darkness?'

Charlotte raised her eyes to his. 'I find that I agree with Augusta very rarely.'

'Thank goodness for that. But she is right in some respects. I am unsuitable. I am not rich, and while I am a gentleman, you won't find me in Debrett's. I am not the sort of man that makes mamas happy.'

Charlotte interrupted him, 'The one advantage of being mother-less is that you learn how to make up your own mind about people.'

'And have you?'

'I think so.'

They were both silent for a moment and then both began to speak at once. Charlotte was saying that she must go back to the house to change, as Bay said, 'I am really very glad that you are at Melton. I have wanted to see you again since the Spencer ball. If only to make amends for my clumsiness in ruining your dress. I am hoping you have forgiven me for that.'

'I have forgiven you, although my dressmaker hasn't,' Charlotte said lightly, but then, seeing the expression on Bay's face, she lowered her voice. 'I think you were distracted that night, Captain Middleton; something had thrown you off balance.'

Bay put his fingers through his hair again and Charlotte realised to her surprise that he was nervous.

'You are right. I was distracted, but I must tell you, Miss Baird, that I am not distracted any more.' His gaze was steady. Charlotte gripped the plate in her hands tightly. Attempting a smile, she said, 'Oh, my dressmaker will be so relieved.'

But Bay did not smile back. 'I was lucky to meet you that night, I can't tell you how lucky. You were right, I had lost my balance but now I have found it.'

Charlotte felt the blush spread across her face. 'I don't know how I helped you, but I am glad that I did.'

'Are you? I think you may be the only one that can help me. I so wish that I had something to offer you in return.'

Charlotte wanted to tell him that he had already given her so much – a sense of possibility, that her future might be more than she had hoped, but she did not have the words. She looked at his arms and saw that the reddish hairs were standing on end. She wanted to stroke them. She realised that she had never wanted to touch a man before. Almost involuntarily she took a step towards him. He began to raise his arms as if perhaps to embrace her, but at that moment there was a clatter of hooves behind them and they both drew back. A groom in blue livery came to a halt when he saw Bay and dismounted.

'Captain Middleton? I have a letter for you from the Earl. He says I am to wait for a reply.'

The groom pulled a letter out of the pocket of his saddlebag and gave it to Middleton.

Bay broke open the seal and scanned the contents. Frowning slightly, he reached into his breeches pocket and found a coin.

'You must have ridden like the wind to get here so quickly. The Earl says he is writing at twelve o'clock and it is now only quarter past one. Tell his lordship that I will come over to Althorp this afternoon, but I shall go at my own pace. I am not going to ruin my horse on his account.' He threw the coin to the groom.

'Yes, sir, and thank you, sir.'

Bay turned to Charlotte and shook his head. 'We have been monstrously interrupted, Miss Baird. Earl Spencer, who was responsible for bringing us together, is now forcing us apart. He says that he has a matter to discuss with me of the utmost urgency. I don't believe that it is urgent at all, but as the Earl is both my patron and my commanding officer, I have no choice but to go.'

Charlotte was disappointed, but also a little relieved. She knew that Middleton had been on the point of saying something significant, which would tip them from a flirtation into something more serious. She wanted to have that conversation, but she also found the prospect terrifying. Things were happening so quickly. She had no patience with Augusta's view of Bay, but she wanted more time to observe him. She shook her head saying, 'But we are in no hurry, are we, Captain Middleton? Surely we can wait a few hours?'

'Of course we can wait – for you I can be the most patient of men – but it goes against my every instinct.'

Charlotte laughed.

'You are not in a race now, Captain. I will still be here when you return. And who knows? If I can evade the ladies of the house I might even be able to print up your photograph.'

The stable clock began to chime the half-hour, startling them both. Charlotte reacted first.

'Heavens, I must go and change at once and so must you. If we are both late for lunch, I think Augusta will have you arrested for abduction.' She turned and began to walk through the arch.

Bay followed and put a hand on her arm. 'But Miss Baird, Charlotte, am I right to feel lucky that I have met you?'

Charlotte smiled. 'I think we both might be lucky, don't you?'

All the Trimmings

IDDLETON FOUND THE EARL IN THE ALTHORP stables, looking over a handsome chestnut mare. As Bay had found the horse for him, he was happy to agree with Spencer that she was a beauty, but he couldn't believe that he had been summoned to look at a horse he knew better than its owner. Spencer broke a carrot into pieces and offered it to the horse on the palm of his hand. The horse snorted and filled the stable with its steaming breath. The Earl turned to Middleton and clapped him on the shoulder.

'Apologies for summoning you over here on a Sunday, Middleton. Matter of some urgency.'

'So I gathered from your note. But you didn't give me much to go on,' Bay said.

'Too sensitive to put in a letter, Middleton, and besides, some things need to be explained man to man.'

'That sounds a little worrying,' Bay smiled.

'Nothing to worry about. This is what I would call pleasure masquerading as duty.' The Earl took Bay's arm and started to walk around the yard, stopping briefly in front of each horse. 'I don't know if you have heard, but Easton Neston has been let to the Empress of Austria.'

'Lady Crewe mentioned something about it last night at dinner.'

'I called on the Empress yesterday. Remarkable woman, really looks the part if you know what I mean. I am no stranger to royalty but she is quite something. The face that launched a thousand ships and all that . . .'

'But I thought the Empress was a grandmother already.'

'You would never know it, Middleton. She is as slender as a young girl and her complexion is quite perfect. I can't say this in front of the Countess, of course, but I think she is the most beautiful woman I have ever seen.'

Bay laughed. 'You appear quite smitten, sir. Have you summoned me here to act as your Cupid?'

'If only . . .' The Earl shook his massive head. 'She is the sort of woman to turn a man's head. You should see her hair, Middleton, all piled up on her head like a crown – and what a profile!' The Earl fell silent for a moment, lost in admiration.

Bay, who was feeling impatient by now, took out his pocket watch. It was a quarter to four. If the Earl did not get to the point soon, he would have to ride back to Melton in the dark.

'My curiosity is aroused. I hope I shall get the chance to see the Empress in the flesh.'

'You will, Middleton. That's why I asked you over here. The Empress has come here to hunt. She is going to ride out with the Pytchley tomorrow.'

'I shall look forward to seeing whether she is as beautiful as you say,' Bay said with a touch of irritation, 'but I still don't understand why you summoned me over here.'

'Stop interrupting and I will tell you,' the Earl said. 'The Empress needs a pilot, and while I would do it myself like a shot, I am too old to keep up with her. There is only one man for the job.' He pointed his meaty forefinger at Bay.

Bay was silent for a moment and then he shook his head. 'I am flattered, of course, that you would entrust me with such a responsibility, but I am afraid I must refuse. You know very well that when the Queen of Naples asked me to be her pilot I said no. What makes you think that it should it be any different for the Empress? Surely there must be somebody who wants to open gates for royalty? Hartopp, for instance, would jump at the chance to be a royal nursemaid.' He tried to keep his tone light, but he could not prevent his annoyance from poking through.

Spencer simply ignored his outburst, smiling patiently as if talking to a child.

'There is quite a difference between an ex-queen of an Italian principality and the wife of the ruler of the largest country in Europe, Middleton. Refusing the Queen's request, while a touch ungallant, was your own business, but when I ask you to look after the Empress of Austria' – the Earl stopped in front of a pretty grey mare and pulled back her gums to look at the teeth – 'you are not really in a position to decline.' Satisfied with the animal's mouth, the Earl moved on to the next stall.

Bay was silent. Although he no longer worked for Spencer since they had returned from Ireland, the Earl was his patron and supporter. If Disraeli lost the confidence of the House in the next few months, as everyone expected, then Spencer would be back in the Government. Bay had no great desire for an official appointment, but he knew that a position of some kind would make it much easier for him to pursue his interest in Charlotte Baird. As an impecunious cavalry captain on half-pay he was not much of a catch, but if Spencer was to give him some post, he would have a salary and some claim to be a coming man. And while he had no desire to pilot the Empress, there was some consolation in being offered a position that both Chicken Hartopp and Fred Baird would covet.

'But what is an empress to me? How will I look after her?' Middleton looked at his patron's red face, which still held its patient smile, and realised that there was nothing he could say that would change the desire on one side and the obligation on the other. He bowed his head and said quietly, 'I will do it, of course, since you ask me, but I wish you hadn't.' He hit the side of the stall with the flat of his hand and the grey mare snorted in sympathy.

'Oh, don't worry, Middleton, there won't be any gates to open. The Empress is an excellent rider. And as for looking after her, I am sure a man of your experience will have no difficulty in keeping her happy.' The Earl winked at Bay.

'And it is important that she is happy, Middleton. Relations with Austria are delicate at the moment, and we need to keep them as an ally against the Prussians. So anything you can do to further the cause of Anglo-Austrian friendship will be appreciated by the Foreign Office. The word from Berlin is that Bismark is furious that the Empress is here, and anything that riles old Otto is good news for us.'

'I will do my best, of course, but you of all people know that I am no diplomat,' Bay said.

'I think even you will manage to make yourself agreeable to a beautiful woman. What is more, although the Empress has brought her own string of horses, my guess is that she is going to need some new ones, and who better to help her find them than you, Middleton?' Spencer started to shake with impending mirth.

'So . . . don't look . . . a gift horse . . . in the mouth, old man.' When he had finished laughing at his own joke, he said in his normal voice, 'Will you come in for a quick tot of something to keep out the cold? If we go in by the kitchen, we can get to the library without being disturbed by the womenfolk.'

Bay hesitated. He did want a drink, but it was getting dark and he didn't want his horse to lose its footing on the way home, the day before the hunting season started.

'I should like to get back to Melton before the light goes completely.'

'Pity. Still, I am sure you have your reasons, eh Middleton?'

The Earl gave Bay another of his enormous winks.

'My wife tells me that the little Baird girl is staying at Melton.'

Bay looked at him in surprise.

'Nice little thing. I knew her mother, wonderful horsewoman. But absolutely reckless. Would jump anything. The husband tried to stop her but she wouldn't be told. Can't say I was surprised when she broke her neck. She left all the Lennox money to the daughter, so Miss Baird comes with all the trimmings. You could do a lot worse for yourself, eh Middleton? Just the sort of wife a man needs if he wants to win the Grand National.'

Middleton said nothing. He was embarrassed by the Earl's directness. Men and women of Spencer's generation saw nothing wrong in talking about marriages as if they were market transactions, but he found it distasteful. The last thing he wanted was to be thought of as a fortune hunter. He liked Charlotte Baird a great deal. There was the way that she remembered everything he said to her, the way she listened with her head slightly tilted. It was true that he might not have married her a year ago, but he was a different man now. He wanted a quiet place that he could call home. He could imagine Charlotte waiting for him in the drawing room, puzzling over one of her albums but listening all the time for his step on the stair. But then there was the money. He told himself that when he had first met Charlotte at the ball, he had not known that she was an heiress, or rather he had not remembered until a day or two afterwards, when Hartopp had taken him aside at the club and told him about the fortune and his own prior claim to it. 'I was winnin' her over, Middleton, winnin' her over, and then you come along and turn her head. Leave her alone, Bay, she's a nice gel and I want to marry her.' Bay had felt sorry for Hartopp. He knew after one dance with Charlotte that she would never become Mrs Hartopp. But as Chicken was rich, no one would accuse him of being on the make, although Bay knew that Hartopp found the money quite as appealing as Charlotte's other charms.

'It's time you settled down, Middleton. Found yourself a wife of your own.' Spencer emphasised the last word. Bay wanted to punch the Earl's beefy, smiling face, but instead he adopted what he thought of as his courtier demeanour.

'Miss Baird is certainly a charming girl.'

'Charming and rich. Capital combination.' The Earl raised his arm, and Bay evaded the inevitable slap between the shoulder blades by stepping aside and gesturing to the groom to bring his horse up to the mounting block. 'I'll write to the Empress, then, and tell her that she will be in your capable hands.' The Earl winked at him. 'No better hands with a horse, and quite good at handling women too from what I hear.'

Middleton looked up at the sky. A low ray of winter sun was pushing through the swollen grey sky.

'It looks like snow. I hope the Empress is prepared for the going to be heavy.'

Royal Sisters

ℰARL SPENCER'S NOTE WAS DELIVERED TO THE EMPRESS after dinner. Baron Nopsca brought it into the drawing room himself, knowing that his mistress would want to read this right away. The Chamberlain hoped very much that the letter did not contain bad news about the arrangements for tomorrow. Her Majesty was looking forward to taking part in a real English hunt so much, and she did not like to be disappointed. As he walked into the double cube of the drawing room, he realised to his horror that he had forgotten to put on his gloves. He wondered if he should go back and fetch them, but it was too late – the Empress had seen him. She was sitting next to her sister, Queen Maria, on the sofa in front of the fire; her brother-in-law the King, Prince Liechtenstein and Count Esterhazy were standing by the mantelpiece; Countess Festetics was sitting in the corner, sewing.

He put the note in the Empress's outstretched hand as quickly as he could before she noticed his naked hands. But the Empress merely thanked him in German before opening the envelope and then saying in English, 'It is from your friend Earl Spencer, Maria. He says that he has found me a pilot for the hunt tomorrow. His name is Captain Middleton. Do you know him?'

Her sister flushed, 'Yes. I have heard of him.'

'I don't understand why I have to have a pilot, but the Earl insists. He claims that this Middleton is the best rider in England.'

'Only the best rider in England would be able to keep up with you, Majesty,' said Count Esterhazy.

'Oh, don't be such a courtier, Max.' The Empress laughed. 'I am sure that the English ladies ride like the wind.' She turned to her sister. 'What do you think, Maria, will I be able to stand the pace?'

'I don't know why you ask me, Sisi. You know very well that you always come first.'

If Sisi caught the bitterness in her sister's voice, she didn't show it. She carried on, 'And did you see the famous Captain Middleton when you were hunting last year?'

'I did. He can ride, certainly, but I doubt that you will find his manners to your taste,' Maria replied.

Sisi put her hand on her sister's arm. 'Oh dear, was he rude to you? I shall have to scold him. But I have had enough of good manners. Dear Felix and Max are so relentlessly charming that a little roughness will make an interesting change.'

The Empress stood up and moved towards the windows. The curtains were drawn against the dark, but she drew one back and looked out into the night.

'It is snowing.' She turned and asked her sister, 'Will the hunt still go ahead?'

'I guarantee it. The English cannot bear to be deprived of their sport. And everyone will turn out tomorrow to see *you*,' said Maria.

'But I am here incognito. I am travelling as Countess Hohenembs, so it won't be the Empress hunting tomorrow.' Elizabeth stood very straight, her face flushed. 'This is meant to be a private visit. I don't want to be a circus attraction.'

Count Esterhazy and Prince Liechtenstein glanced at each other, hearing a familiar note in the Empress's voice. Countess Festetics looked up from her sewing. Count Eszterhazy was the one to speak first.

'But Majesty, the people tomorrow will be your favourite company – riding folk whose only desire is for a good day's hunting. Perhaps there may be a frisson at having royalty among them, but my guess is that it will be your horse attracting all the attention.'

Elizabeth stared at the Count for a moment and then her face relaxed, her lips almost curving into a smile.

'But which horse? I am worried that none of them are used to jumping these English hedges.'

The men pounced on this conversational opening and began to discuss the merits of the Empress's horses at length. Countess Festetics resumed her sewing.

Elizabeth went back to sit next to her sister.

Maria said, 'You mustn't blame the English for wanting to look at you, Sisi. Their queen has shut herself away since her husband died. And the papers are full of you, even though you are travelling incognito. Everybody wants to see "the most beautiful woman in Europe".' Maria smiled thinly at her sister.

'But I am so tired of being stared at. Can you imagine what it feels like to know that everybody is looking at you, all the time?' Elizabeth spoke in a rush of emotion but kept her voice low. She looked to her sister for sympathy but saw that Maria's face had closed up.

There was a little pause and then the ex-queen of Naples said, 'There are worse things in life, Sisi, than being stared at.'

Silver Nitrate

THE SNOW BEGAN TO FALL JUST AS BAY REACHED Melton. While he waited for someone to come out and open the gates he watched the flakes fall and settle on the gravel underneath the lighted windows of the lodge. Inside he could see a woman feeding a baby in a wooden high chair while her husband looked on. The baby was laughing and trying to pat her cheek as she held up the spoon. The child had managed to smear a good dollop of his porridge on his mother's face and Bay watched as her husband, the gatekeeper, tenderly brushed it away.

Tipsy neighed with impatience and the man looked up and saw Bay. Seconds later he came out.

'Sorry to keep you waiting, sir. Would you like me to light you up to the house?' He held up a lantern.

Bay felt unaccountably guilty for having disturbed the peaceful domestic scene. He found a coin in his pocket and handed it over. 'No need for you to come out on a night like this. I'll take the lamp myself.'

The gatekeeper was delighted. 'If you're sure, sir. Thank you very much indeed.'

At his usual gallop, Bay would have covered the drive from the lodge to the house in minutes, but now the snow and the lantern slowed him down. He felt the flakes settle on his eyelashes and moustache. Charlotte would laugh if she could see him now. He thought that he wouldn't mind being laughed at by Charlotte. When Blanche Hozier had made fun of him for some slip of the tongue or social awkwardness, he had felt the scorn beneath her smiles. Charlotte, though, was different. She might tease him, but there would be no derision in her laughter.

The baby in the lodge had made him think of Clementine, the daughter he had never seen. He could not see Blanche – blonde, immaculate Blanche – feeding a baby with a spoon and having her face smeared with porridge. Instead he imagined Charlotte holding a baby out to him.

Tipsy stumbled, jolting Bay out of his domestic daydream. The snow was laying a blanket of hush over the landscape and there was no light apart from the flickering gleam of the lantern. Then he heard the chimes of the stable clock sounding seven times – if he hurried he might be able to find Charlotte before dinner. Forgetting his concerns about the hazardous snow, he nudged Tipsy into a canter.

The dressing gong was sounding when Bay came into the house. He knew that he should change out of his wet clothes, but he thought there was a chance that Charlotte might still be in her studio. He didn't think that she was the kind of girl who spent more time than she had to changing for dinner. He ran up the stairs two at a time, praying that he would not run into anyone.

He had reached the first landing when he heard a voice.

'Captain Middleton, where have you been in this weather? You must be frozen.' Lady Crewe was standing on the other side of the landing.

Bay chewed his lip. The last thing he wanted was to be waylaid in conversation by his hostess. He said, as curtly as possible, 'I had to ride over to Althorp. The Earl wanted to speak to me.'

'It must have been very important business for you to go all that way, and on a Sunday too.' Lady Crewe sniffed; she was a keen observer of the Sabbath.

Bay knew that if he told Lady Crewe what the Earl had wanted he would never get away. Instead he shook his head and said, 'I am sorry to say that the Earl is not observant. Why, in Ireland, we would sometimes hold amateur theatricals on a Sunday.'

Lady Crewe gasped and Bay shook his head.

'You can imagine my feelings, Lady Crewe. Now, if you will excuse me.'

He did not wait for a reply but dashed off in the direction of the nursery, hoping that she would not remember that his bedroom lay the other way.

Bay sighed with relief when he saw the light under the nursery door. He walked in and saw Charlotte standing with her back to him. She was wearing what looked like an evening dress – white silk trimmed with green velvet – but she had swathed herself in a brown holland apron.

She was examining a print. Bay noticed that her hands were covered with brown stains. As he reached her, Charlotte gave a little shriek of surprise and then smiled broadly.

'Captain Middleton! You are just in time.'

'I am so glad.'

He tried to look at the print, but she held it away out of his view, saying, 'Promise me that you will be honest. I won't be offended if you don't like it.'

'Really?'

'Well, I might be a little piqued, but only a little.' Slowly she held up the print.

Bay had never seen a photograph of himself before. He was disappointed to find that he was not as tall or as broad as he had imagined himself. In the picture his head was level with Tipsy's, the horse nestling into his shoulder. The unspoken bond between horse and rider was quite evident in the photograph. They were undoubtedly a team.

'My dear Miss Baird, Charlotte – can I call you Charlotte? I can't tell you how happy this makes me.' Bay found himself blinking. 'Tipsy is magnificent.'

'And what do you think of yourself?' asked Charlotte.

Bay shrugged. 'Does anyone really like their own portrait?'

'You would be surprised. Fred liked the *carte de visite* he had done at Gaillevant so much that he ordered three dozen and sent them to all his friends.'

'I only want one copy, but I promise you that I will treasure it for ever.' Bay took one of Charlotte's hands in his and touched a brown stain on her forefinger.

Charlotte blushed. 'It's the silver nitrate I use on the plates. I can't get it off. I must put on some gloves before dinner.'

'Not on my account, dear Charlotte. These stains on your hands are like the calluses I get from riding; they are the price we pay for doing what we love.' He stroked her palm with his finger. Her hand trembled a little.

'I don't think Augusta would agree.'

'I don't care in the slightest what Augusta thinks, or her mother, or anyone else for that matter. Do you?'

He held her hand tight. She did not pull it away.

'No, I don't think I do.' There were two spots of red on Charlotte's cheeks.

Bay leant towards her and kissed one of the red cheeks.

'I have made you blush, Will you forgive me?' he said and kissed the other cheek.

'I think so,' Charlotte said softly.

Bay leant forward and kissed her, this time on the mouth. He felt her body soften and lean into his, her mouth opening and the touch of her hand on his arm. He could smell rose water and the tang of chemicals. He wanted to pull her to him, to gather her up completely.

There was a loud creak from the nursery staircase, followed by the sounds of stertorous breathing.

Bay and Charlotte were examining the print when Fred reached the doorway.

'Mitten, I just wanted to . . .' He saw Bay. 'Oh, hello, Middleton.' And then, registering Bay's riding clothes, he said, 'Shouldn't you be changing for dinner?'

'I was just on my way. But I couldn't resist a glimpse of Tipsy.' Bay gestured towards the photograph on the table.

'May I suggest that you hurry up? Lady Crewe does not like to be kept waiting.' Fred fingered the facings of his tail coat, scraping his fingernails against the satin.

'Keeping a lady waiting, that would never do.' Bay made Charlotte a little bow. 'Thank you, Miss Baird, for the photo. For everything, in fact.'

As he left the room, Fred turned on Charlotte.

'I am surprised to find you in here alone with Middleton. You know his reputation.'

'Oh yes. Augusta was punctilious in letting me know about that,' Charlotte replied.

'Then you are either foolish or wilful. A young girl cannot be too careful of her good name. What seems like a harmless flirtation now, could have a major impact on your future.'

Charlotte smiled. 'I hope so. I like Captain Middleton extremely. If he proposes, I shall accept him.'

'Of course he will propose. You are an extremely wealthy woman, but there is no question of you accepting him. You cannot marry without my consent and I have absolutely no intention of giving it.' Fred rose on the balls of his feet to give his point more emphasis.

'That is only true for the next nine months, three weeks and four days, until I am twenty-one. Then I can marry whomsoever I choose.'

Fred rocked back on his heels. 'You forget that I am still your trustee for another four years.'

'Oh, I haven't forgotten, but I don't care about the money. I can wait.'

Fred showed his teeth in a facsimile of a smile. 'You can wait. But what about Middleton?' He pointed to the picture of Bay and Tipsy. 'He is a man with expensive tastes.'

Charlotte said nothing. She was staring at the photograph.

Her brother continued, 'Let's not quarrel, Mitten. I have no desire to play the tyrant.'

Charlotte looked up at him. 'I am not your Mitten. My name is Charlotte.' She unfastened the tapes of her holland apron and folded it neatly, then picked up her reticule and took out a pair of white lace mittens, smoothing them over her hands until all the stains were hidden.

'Come on, Fred. You don't want to keep Lady Crewe waiting.'

'But you do understand me, Charlotte?' Fred put his hand on his sister's arm.

'Of course I understand you. I even promise to think about what you have said.'

'Good girl.'

'But I am not promising to obey you. That will be Augusta's job when she marries you.'

Charlotte was the only one smiling as they both contemplated the likelihood of Augusta being an obedient wife.

Greensleeves

IT WAS CLEAR FROM THE PLACEMENT AT DINNER THAT Augusta had spoken to her mother. Charlotte was taken into dinner by the Hon. Percy and seated at the other end of the table to Bay.

It was not a lively meal. Lady Crewe generally liked to restrict the conversation to topics suitable to the Sabbath. But after an almost silent fish course, she could not contain her curiosity any longer.

'Did you see Laetitia Spencer at Althorp this afternoon, Captain Middleton? She had a chill before Christmas and I am hoping that she is quite recovered. I was thinking that I might call on her this week.'

'I didn't see the Countess, Lady Crewe. But then the Earl and I were in the stables.'

'In the stables? What on earth were you doing there on a Sunday?' asked Lady Crewe.

'I fear that the Earl visits the stables every day. We had some business to discuss,' Bay said, as neutrally as he could.

But Lady Crewe was not to be put off.

'But what business could be so urgent that you had to go over there at once?'

By now the whole table had given up the pretence of conversation and twelve heads were looking at Bay.

'The Earl had an assignment for me.' He paused and, seeing Lady Crewe's expectant eyebrow, he added, 'Of a confidential nature.'

Lord Crewe snorted. 'I hear that Austrian woman is hunting with the Pytchley tomorrow. Daresay Spencer wants you to pilot her.' Lord Crewe had little time for Catholics, even royal ones. 'Am I right, Middleton?'

Bay bowed his head. 'I can't lie to you, Lord Crewe.'

There was a moment of silence as the assembled company digested this revelation along with their turbot à la crème.

Hartopp was the first to speak, attempting but not altogether succeeding in keeping the jealousy out of his voice, 'Quite a last-minute request if she is hunting tomorrow. Do you think someone else dropped out?'

'Very likely,' said Bay.

'Nonsense,' interrupted Lord Crewe. 'Middleton is the best rider in England. Spencer will have been told to get the top man and he has. Congratulations are in order. Quite an honour to pilot an empress, even if she is a foreigner.'

'It is certainly a responsibility,' said Bay.

'I think it is tremendously exciting,' said Lady Lisle. 'But I hope she speaks some English, unless of course you speak German, Captain Middleton.'

Fred snorted. 'Of course he doesn't speak German! But I am sure you will have a way of making yourself understood, eh Middleton?'

Bay said quietly, 'I believe the Empress speaks excellent English, but I don't anticipate much conversation. My job is to guide her during the hunt. There won't be much time for talking.'

'But we ladies expect a full account of the Empress, Captain Middleton, whether you talk to her not,' said Augusta. 'In the *Illustrated*

London News it says that she has taken riding lessons from a circus artist, and that she has been seen to jump through a ring of fire.'

'Well, if I see her jump through a ring of fire when we are out with the Pytchley tomorrow, I will be sure to remember every detail, Lady Augusta,' said Bay.

It was fortunate that the footmen were coming round with the salmis of pheasant, so that the sound of Charlotte's laughter was drowned in the clatter of serving spoons on silver salvers.

Lady Crewe was still thinking about the Empress. 'I wonder if she will be attending dinners while she is here. I am sure Laetitia Spencer won't miss the opportunity to show her off. But it would be a pity if the Empress did not have the opportunity of visiting some of the other important families in the county. Althorp is all very well, but so old-fashioned; it would be such a shame if she went back to Austria without seeing the best examples of the modern style.' She looked up at the hammer-beamed roof of the dining room with its roundels picked out in scarlet and gold, and the frieze of Sir Galahad in search of the Holy Grail, with great satisfaction.

'You must be sure to tell her, Captain Middleton, that Easton Neston and Althorp are quite old-fashioned. If she wants to see an English country house that is really up to the minute, she should come to Melton.'

'If she's hunting with the Pytchley she will be here on Tuesday,' said Lord Crewe, 'as the meet is here.'

'Of course! Well, Captain Middleton, you must tell the Empress that I would be only too pleased to show her around Melton. She won't find a house like this in Austria, I daresay.' Lady Crewe leant forward as she said this and looked directly at Bay, so that he had no choice but to answer.

'If she asks me, I will certainly pass on your invitation, Lady

Crewe. But I suspect that we won't have many opportunities to talk about architecture. And who knows, I may not be to the Empress's taste and I will have lost my post by Tuesday.' Bay smiled.

'Nonsense, Middleton. We all know how good you are with the fair sex.' Fred Baird rolled his eyes at Augusta.

Lord Crewe looked up from his pheasant and let his fork drop with a clang.

'Middleton, you are not to encourage the woman to come inside the house. If she insists, we can't stop her, but I don't want some foreign royal traipsing about Melton. Nothing but trouble. She won't come alone, I am quite sure, and before we know it the house will be full of Austrians.'

'But George, it would be an honour to receive the Empress,' protested Lady Crewe.

'No, it would be an honour to receive *our* queen at Melton. There is no comparison,' said Lord Crewe, his face reddening.

Adelaide Lisle, who hated unpleasantness, turned to her host with her most winning smile. 'Now, you must tell me about the wonderful frieze you have here in the dining room. I am awfully stupid about legends and so forth, and I can't for the life of me figure out who is the handsome young knight with curly blond hair – the only knight whose name I can remember is Lancelot, and that's because I have a cousin called Lancelot, but this young man looks rather different.'

As Lady Lisle chattered away and Lord Crewe began to unravel the Arthurian legends, the other diners began to talk among themselves, tacitly agreeing to avoid all further mention of the Empress.

The men did not linger over their port. Fred and Hartopp felt that they could not talk about the Empress in front of their host and yet it was the only thing they wanted to discuss. Although both men would, if asked, claim to be a friend of Bay Middleton, both of them took the news of Bay's advancement into imperial circles as a profound injustice. When all three of them had been ADCs to Earl Spencer in Ireland, they had jostled for position on a daily basis. Both men could understand why Bay as the better horseman should have been picked to pilot the Empress, but it seemed quite unfair that mere talent should take precedence over superior birth and breeding. How could a man like Bay, be expected to understand the niceties of imperial protocol? True, the father had been an officer who had died fighting in the Crimea, but the mother had remarried some kind of coal merchant in Co. Durham. There was also a lurking suspicion that Bay had been preferred because he was as good with women as he was with horses. Fred felt this a little less keenly than Hartopp; he still reckoned that his successful wooing of Lady Augusta had been the result of his own charms rather than her increasing desperation. So when Bay rose after one glass of port, nobody protested.

But in the drawing room, the conversation among the women was unfettered. Augusta, who had seen the look of surprise on Charlotte's face when Bay had announced his new role, lost no time in asking her what she thought of Bay's elevation into imperial circles, or as she put it, 'to be the Empress's groom'.

'Oh, is a pilot the same thing as a groom? I understood the roles to be quite different. I don't ride myself, of course, but surely the groom looks after the animal and a pilot guides the rider?' Charlotte said.

'It's quite an honour for Captain Middleton,' said Augusta, 'and, of course, he is an excellent rider, but I am surprised that Earl Spencer thought he was a suitable escort for royalty, even foreign royalty.'

'What do you mean, Augusta?' asked Lady Lisle in surprise. 'Captain Middleton seems to be a very personable young man. What objection could there be?'

'I think some people might say that he was altogether too personable,' said Augusta, and, lowering her voice, 'I believe that there are some husbands who would rather he wasn't quite so charming.'

'Augusta!' warned her mother. 'You shouldn't be talking about such things, and on a Sunday too! May I remind you that Captain Middleton is our guest. And I am quite sure that Earl Spencer knows what he is doing. Now perhaps you would like to play for us, instead of spreading slander.'

Augusta, realising that her mother was going to support Middleton so long as there was a chance of being introduced to the Empress, took up her place at the piano and gave her own trenchant version of a Chopin nocturne.

She had moved on to Beethoven when the men came in. Fred went straight to the piano. Bay walked over to the sofa where Charlotte was sitting and stood behind her. Bending down, he said softly in her ear, 'I am just trying to remember where we were before we were interrupted.'

Charlotte looked straight ahead of her and kept her face as bland as if they were talking about the weather. 'I think you were admiring the photograph of you and Tipsy.'

'Tipsy, as you well know, is the apple of my eye, but she wasn't the object of my admiration. Now where exactly had we got to in our conversation?'

Charlotte turned to look at him. 'I think you were about to tell me about your new role as the Empress of Austria's pilot.'

'Why would I waste a moment of our precious tête-à-tête, talking about something so uninteresting? I am being asked to be a nurse-maid on horseback, running after my royal charge and making sure she doesn't get her habit too muddy, or get trampled by the pack,' Bay said, his hand on the back of the sofa, his fingers so close to her bare shoulders that she had goosebumps.

'You can be as dismissive as you like, but it's an honour to be chosen. Fred certainly thinks so.' Charlotte looked at her brother, who was standing next to his fiancée at the piano. 'He was pea green when you made your announcement. Fred would like nothing better than to be at the beck and call of an empress.'

'If you want me to resign my nursemaid duties in favour of your brother, you only have to say the word. I would be more than happy to oblige.'

Charlotte shivered, acutely conscious of the fingers that were now stealthily grazing her shoulders. 'I think even Fred would admit that he is not the rider that you are. And besides, at this moment I am very much in favour of anything that makes him cross.'

'Did he give you a lecture on unreliable cavalry captains, by any chance?' Bay said.

'He was anxious to remind me that I can do nothing without his consent. Which means Augusta's consent, of course. I am not sure Fred is still capable of independent thought.'

'Poor Fred. He is entering into a life of servitude.'

'Oh, he doesn't mind. To be married to a peer's daughter is enough.'

Bay touched one of the vertebrae above her neckline, and Charlotte gasped.

'Are you sure you don't remember what we were talking about before? Perhaps this will remind you.' Bay bent down again and blew lightly into her ear. 'It was such a delightful conversation.'

Charlotte dug her nails into the sofa. 'Perhaps I do remember, just a little. It's not the sort of conversation I am used to, after all.'

'Every conversation is different, but none more charming than with you.' He ran his nail down the groove in the nape of her neck and was gratified to see Charlotte arch forward like a cat. But the sudden movement was noticed by Augusta, who was not so lost in her music that she was unable to monitor the situation of the sofa. It was time to intervene.

She stopped playing and called out, 'I have been playing long enough, it is someone else's turn. Charlotte, won't you give us something?'

Charlotte shook her head. 'Oh, but I am a wretched player compared to you. You are being very unkind to everybody here if you make me perform.'

'Nonsense, Charlotte, there is nothing wrong with your playing that a little practice wouldn't remedy. And I think we would all like to hear you. Isn't that right, Captain Middleton?' Augusta said pointedly.

'Perhaps I might offer to entertain the company too? I can't play but I like to sing.' Bay turned to Charlotte. 'Can you play "Maud"?'

'Yes, if you don't mind a few wrong notes.'

'Perfection is boring. Shall we?' He put out his hand to Charlotte. 'That is, if you don't mind, Lady Crewe.'

Lady Crewe nodded and smiled, while Augusta, realising that she had been outmanoeuvred, left her post at the piano to stand next to her fiancé. As Bay passed she said, 'I had no idea you could sing, Captain Middleton.'

'I am an only child, and as my mother was very fond of music, I had no choice. But as to my ability, you had better reserve judgement.'

Charlotte sat at the keyboard, Bay standing just behind her. As she began to play the introduction, he put his hand on the piano, brushing her shoulder as he did so. She immediately played a wrong note and he looked at her her and smiled.

Come into the garden, Maud,
the black bat, night, has flown,
Come into the garden, Maud,
I am here at the gate alone.

His voice was powerful and true, a warm baritone that wrung every shade of meaning out of Tennyson's lush lyric. When she hesitated over the accompaniment he slowed down so that they were always in step. When he reached the line 'And the planet of Love is on high', he looked at Charlotte with meaning. He was singing, it was clear, to her. On the last line, when the melody went up an octave and he had to sing, 'Come, my own, my sweet', he looked straight into Charlotte's eyes and held her gaze while the final chord died away. There was a moment's silence, which was broken by Lady Lisle, who was dabbing at her eyes with a handkerchief.

'That was one of my dear late husband's favourite songs. But I don't think I have ever heard it sung so well before. Thank you, Captain Middleton, for bringing back so many happy memories.'

Bay made her a little bow. 'My pleasure.'

'Will you sing something else?'

Bay looked at Charlotte, who nodded.

'Play me a G minor chord.'

Charlotte played the chord and Bay sang,

Alas, my love, you do me wrong,
To cast me off discourteously.
For I have loved you well and long,
Delighting in your company.

Charlotte recognised the tune and began to accompany him in earnest, '*Greensleeves was my delight*'.

As he sang the chorus, he gestured at the green velvet ribbons that punctuated the puffed white sleeves of Charlotte's frock. When the song was finished, Bay took Charlotte's hand and kissed it.

'Thank you for playing so beautifully.'

'I think you encouraged me to be better than I am.'

'I don't think that is possible, Miss Baird.'

Augusta broke in, 'You must be sure to serenade the Empress tomorrow, Captain Middleton. She is from Vienna, and we know how the Austrians love their music.'

Bay did not miss a beat. 'I think you may have an exaggerated idea of a pilot's role, Lady Augusta. I doubt if I will be talking to the Empress, let alone singing to her. I am merely a guide, a flag for her to follow, not a troubadour.'

Augusta folded her arms, but made no reply.

Lady Lisle got to her feet, her widow's streamers fluttering.

'What a perfectly splendid evening, but I am ready for my bed. Charlotte, dear, will you hold the candle for me on the stairs? You know how shaky I get in the evenings.'

'Of course, Aunt,' Charlotte said.

They made their way to the door, Charlotte following in her aunt's wake. All the men rose and made a movement to open the door, but Bay was there first. As Charlotte passed him, he touched her elbow. 'Unfinished business,' he whispered.

In her bedroom, Charlotte held up her candle close to the cheval glass so that she could examine her face. It was not, she knew, a beautiful face, and yet Bay had kissed her nonetheless. For a moment she wondered whether he had been kissing her or the Lennox fortune, but she pushed that thought away. If Bay was a fortune hunter, he was very good at disguising his cupidity.

The door opened and Grace the housemaid came in. Charlotte did not have her own maid, since the superior French personage who had attended to her in London had given in her notice after an accident involving silver nitrate and lace. Charlotte did not miss her; she had hated the way Mam'selle Solange had made a sharp intake of breath every time she did her hair.

'I meant to be up here sooner, miss.' Charlotte sighed with relief as the maid loosened the strings of her corset. 'But we were outside in the hall listening to the music and I lost all track of the time. Was that Captain Middleton singing? What a fine young gentleman! He was doing tricks earlier on his horse – standing on his head and all sorts of stuff. Had us all laughing our heads off. He makes it all look so easy.'

'Yes,' Charlotte agreed. 'He does.'

She caught sight of her reflection again in the glass. She looked better now in her chemise, with her hair down.

'Grace?'

'Yes, miss?'

'Do you think you could do my hair differently tomorrow? Perhaps with some ringlets hanging down. Do you think that would look nice?'

'You leave it to me, miss. I will make sure that Captain Middleton has eyes for nobody else.'

A Flawless Complexion

TEN MILES AWAY IN A MUCH LARGER BEDROOM, Countess Festetics was laying strips of raw veal on her mistress's face.

Sisi had been looking at her face in the mirror before she went to bed and decided that her complexion was dull. This was unacceptable, as she wanted to look radiant at her first English hunt. Everyone would be looking at her, she knew, trying to decide whether she lived up to her reputation. Her silhouette was still good; her waist was as small as it had been when she married. She knew that on a horse from a distance, she looked like the dashing Empress that people wanted to see.

She would wear a veil, of course, with the riding habit, but then there was the moment when she lifted the veil. Sisi could not bear that look of disappointment when her audience was forced to replace their mental image of fairy-tale beauty with the worn reality before them. She had hoped that her visit to England might be anonymous, her real identity known only to a few; but that had been a fantasy. Stories about the beautiful Empress with her ankle-length hair sold too many newspapers, even here, for her identity to remain a secret. On the way down to Easton Neston she had spent the night at Claridge's. During the night word had got out that she was staying at the hotel, and when she left in the morning there had been a small crowd outside the door who had come to see the Austrian Empress. She had looked out over the sea of faces, most of them female, and seen that combination of expectation and disillusion that was so difficult to bear. A young woman at the front had held out a bunch of violets to her and Sisi, seeing how desperately she wanted to be chosen, had taken them with a smile. As Sisi got into her carriage, she heard a voice say, 'I thought she was lovely too, but did you see her teeth?'

Sisi knew that it was hopeless to live up to the fairy-tale princess with stars in her hair of the Winterhalter portrait, an image that sold everything from chocolates to liver salts in Vienna, but she found it impossible not to try. Beauty was her gift, her weapon and her power, and she dreaded its passing.

There were some things she could do, like remaining slender. She liked the rigour of her morning exercises, the ache in her arms as she pulled herself up on the rings. But maintaining her nineteen-inch waist had meant that her face had lost its youthful plumpness. There were days when, confronted by an unexpected mirror, she saw a gaunt, middle-aged woman looking back at her. Festetics had found her crying after one of these glimpses of mortality and had told her about the beauty regime of the Princess Karolyi, her grandmother, who at the age of eighty had skin 'as soft and smooth as a baby's'. The veal had to be fresh and pounded very thin, but if used once a week it would keep the complexion radiant for ever.

After she had covered the Empress's face entirely with the raw meat, save for the eyes, nose and mouth, the Countess Festetics took a leather mask out of its case and put it gently in place. She fastened the tapes that tied it at the back so that her mistress could move her head in the night without the meat falling off. The mask was also a necessary protection against the Empress's wolfhounds, who had once mistaken the beauty treatment for an evening meal.

There were times when the Countess had regretted telling her mistress about the secret of the flawless complexion. It had been a family story, much embroidered in the telling, that she had pulled from her memories in a desperate attempt to comfort the weeping Sisi. She knew from ten years' experience that the only thing to do when her mistress was consumed by one of her spells of self-loathing, was to distract her as quickly as possible. Therefore she had turned her vague memories of her grandmother's soft and scented cheek into the elixir of eternal youth. Sisi had insisted on sending for some veal immediately; the next morning she had declared that the treatment was indeed a miracle. Countess Festetics was not as sure as her mistress as to the veal's efficacy, but she had long ago realised that Sisi had only to believe in something for it to be true. If she had convinced herself that veal would restore the lustre to her complexion, then there was no reason to disabuse her.

'I will wear my green habit tomorrow, I think.' The Empress's voice was muffled by the layer of meat and the leather mask.

'An excellent choice, Majesty. You always look so fresh in it and the colour perfectly sets off your hair.'

'And be sure to tell the servants that I will need a very hot bath when I come back tomorrow. I haven't hunted for weeks and I don't want to get stiff.'

'I have already told them, Majesty.'

'Thank you, Festy. I would be lost without you.' The Empress pointed to her face and tried to laugh.

'I am sure that the English milords will be astonished when they see you tomorrow. I have seen pictures of their Queen and she is small and completely round like a *Zwetschkenknödel*.'

Sisi shook her head. 'Oh, I am sure she was young and slender once. How many children did she have? Her husband must have found her attractive.'

'Or maybe he was a Coburger with a taste for *Zwetschkenknödel*,' said the Countess drily.

'I suppose if you are Queen in your own right, it doesn't matter what you look like.'

'Perhaps the English don't know that a queen can be beautiful, which is why you will dazzle them tomorrow. But I think you must sleep now, Majesty. You know that the veal will only work if you rest properly.'

'What you mean is that you are longing for your own bed. Run along then, Festy, but make sure you call me in good time tomorrow. I want my hair to be perfect.'

'Of course, Majesty.'

As she looked at the Empress one last time before closing the bedroom door, Festetics wondered what the world would make of the modern Helen of Troy if they could see her now – wearing a leather mask with veal juices running down her neck, and her hair tied to the ceiling in two long ropes. But no one save the Countess would ever see her like this; it was their secret.

The Lennox Diamonds

HE THREE HOUSEMAIDS SAT AWKWARDLY ON THE nursery sofa. They were trying to hide their work-roughened hands under their skirts, or by twisting them together on their laps. Charlotte wanted to tell them not to worry, she wanted to see the hands in their reddened, chapped reality, but she knew better than to say so.

She waited for them to settle and then she said, 'When I raise my hand, I want you all to take a deep breath and say "bosom" as you exhale.'

The housemaid on the left, the prettiest one, began to giggle.

Charlotte sighed. 'I know it sounds peculiar, but saying the word will put your mouth into the right shape for the photograph. Look what happens when I say it.' She stepped away from the camera and said the word, exaggerating the dignified pout that the final syllable gave her mouth.

'Bosom', 'bosom', 'bosom'; the maids tried the word out, but the giggles were spreading and soon all three were shaking with laughter.

Charlotte walked over to the window to hide her impatience. She wondered when the hunting party would return. She had hoped to go out with her camera that morning and take pictures at the

meet, but there had been too much snow. She turned back to the
maids and clapped her hands.

'Are you ready? I only have you for half an hour, so if we don't
take the picture now it won't get done.'

The maids heard the sharpness in her voice. Sitting up, they tried
to compose their faces. Charlotte looked at them through the
viewfinder. She asked the pretty one, Grace, to sit in the middle
and then posed the other two in profile. Every so often one of
them would shudder with suppressed laughter. She waited for a
moment and then she raised her hand.

'Bosom,' the maids whispered. Charlotte held her breath. Would
they keep still for the whole minute? Twenty-five, twenty-six – she
could see that the maid on the right was going red with the effort
involved in not laughing. Fifty-one, fifty-two – she saw a tear sliding
out of Grace's eye. Fifty-nine, sixty. She dropped her hand and the
girls collapsed together in a quivering heap.

'Thank you, girls, you can go back to work now.' She had wanted
to do several poses, but she could see that they were never going
to stay still for long enough.

'But ain't you going to show us the picture, miss?'

'I have to print it first. Come back tomorrow and I'll show you.'

The maids clattered out, their voices echoing down the back
stairs.

Charlotte looked at the clock on the mantelpiece. Ten minutes to
five. She should be downstairs having tea, but she couldn't face all
the talk about the wedding. Augusta and Fred had settled on a date
in March and Lady Crewe was telling everyone who would listen
that the trousseau would never be ready in time. Charlotte knew

that she ought to be taking an interest in the arrangements, but she found it hard to concentrate on the endless chatter about the best place to buy Valenciennes lace.

Grace returned and put her head round the door.

'Lady Crewe was asking if you wanted some tea sent up, miss.'

Charlotte sighed; the message meant that her absence had been noted and disapproved of. She would have to go down now. Another day she might have pleaded a headache, but that would mean missing Bay at dinner.

'Thank you, Grace. Please tell Her Ladyship I will be down directly.'

Bay had still not returned by the time the dressing bell sounded. Charlotte lingered in the hall till the last possible moment, but there was no sign of him. Fred and Chicken Hartopp had come back halfway through tea. Charlotte had waited till Fred had stopped telling them about the depth of the snow to ask him, 'And Captain Middleton, wasn't he with you?' Fred had laughed. 'Good God, no, we didn't see anything of Middleton all day. He was too busy with the Empress, or should I say, Countess Hohenembs.' Clearly Fred had not been introduced to the royal party, for which he blamed Middleton. Charlotte decided not to press him.

Instead she looked over to Chicken Hartopp.

'What did she look like? Is she as beautiful as they say?'

Chicken shook his great head. 'Really couldn't tell you, she was surrounded the whole time by flunkeys. She must have had at least six men with her. Austrians and such. She could have had her own hunt.'

'It makes you wonder why she needed Middleton,' said Fred.

'Surely the Austrians know how to take an English fence. They ride well enough.'

'Perhaps Middleton's fame has reached Vienna,' said Augusta, 'or should I say his reputation?' She looked hard at Charlotte as she said this, but Lady Crewe lumbered to her feet at this point and the group broke up.

Charlotte thought, not for the first time, that her wardrobe was not adequate for her stay at Melton. She had imagined that three evening dresses would be enough, but she realised her mistake when she saw that Augusta appeared to be wearing a new dress every single night. Her choice was between the blue moire, the pink figured silk or the white with the green trim. She decided on the pink; in truth she would have liked to have worn the white dress that had inspired Captain Middleton to sing 'Greensleeves' the night before, but she knew that Augusta would remember and would make some remark. The pink was pretty enough, and at least the bustle had this season's narrow silhouette.

'There, miss, what do you think of that?' Grace put down the curling tongs and invited Charlotte to look at her handiwork in the mirror. Charlotte usually wore her hair pulled back from a centre parting into a simple chignon, and so she gasped when she saw her reflection. The maid had piled Charlotte's hair on top of her head with loose ringlets hanging down at the back, and curly tendrils framing her forehead.

'Do you like it, miss?' Grace said anxiously.

'I hardly recognise myself,' said Charlotte. It was true, she did look different. She knew that she would never be beautiful, but for once she felt pleased with her reflection. The hairstyle had softened the angles of her face. The curled fringe called attention to her eyes, which tonight looked almost green. Her hair, which was a nondescript shade of brown, seemed to have an unaccustomed lustre. Her mouth, which was too wide to be fashionable, for once did not look too big for her small face. There had been a time when it would have taken all her courage to go downstairs and face the scrutiny of all the other women with their perfect ringlets, but since she had met Bay she no longer felt their stares so keenly.

'I expect Captain Middleton will like it,' said Grace. 'He looks like a gentleman who notices feminine things.'

'Yes, I believe he is.'

Charlotte thought that Bay must propose tonight. He would not have kissed her like that yesterday if he was not serious in his intentions. He could hardly think that she was the sort of girl who could be kissed with impunity. And yet, there was a part of her that was rather taken with the notion that he might think she was 'fast' and worldly enough to take his embraces in her stride. It had been her first kiss, but she hoped that Bay had not known that at once. And if he did propose, what would she say? She thought of the lectures she had received from Fred and Augusta on Bay's unsuitability as a husband. Bay Middleton was not the match they had in mind for the Lennox fortune, but Charlotte suspected that they would only really be happy if she died an old maid leaving the fortune intact to the little Freds and Augustas. No matter what they said, she thought that Bay liked her for herself, and while she had nothing to compare it with, she thought that his impulse to kiss her yesterday had been genuine enough. And for her part, she knew there had been nothing that she wanted more than to kiss him back.

She fastened her pearl drops into her ear lobes and surveyed the effect. They were pretty but not striking. In honour of her new hairstyle, her new look, she needed something more.

'Grace, could you ask my aunt for my jewellery case?'

She would wear the Lennox diamonds tonight. She had never felt equal to their magnificence before, but tonight she felt that she could carry them off. Perhaps not the whole parure, the earrings alone would be dazzling. She had brought the jewels to Melton with her so that Augusta could try them on with her wedding dress, but it would do no harm to remind the world to whom the diamonds actually belonged.

Grace returned carrying the jewellery case, accompanied by Lady Lisle, who started to speak the moment she walked into the room.

'Charlotte dear, when the maid told me that you wanted the diamonds I had to make sure she hadn't made a mistake. Are you going to wear them yourself? Are you sure that's wise? They are quite serious jewels for a young girl to carry off.'

Charlotte smiled. 'Don't worry, I am not going to deck myself out like a Christmas tree. I thought I would just wear the earrings and perhaps the brooch. And if I look ridiculous, well, I hope that no one here will judge me too harshly.'

She opened the box and was gratified by the sparkle within. Charlotte had almost no memories of her mother, but she fancied that she had once kissed her before she went to a ball and had been entranced by the glittering stones hanging around her mother's neck and arms.

The earrings were in the shape of teardrops – the large central stones surrounded by smaller faceted ones. When Charlotte held them up to her ears they flickered and flashed in the candlelight.

Grace smiled at Charlotte in the mirror.

'They look splendid, miss.'

But Lady Lisle looked worried.

'I wonder if it is wise to wear them tonight, Charlotte. I am worried that Augusta might think you are being tactless. After all, dear Fred won't be able to give her jewels like these.'

'I have already offered to lend her the diamonds for the wedding. I think she can't grudge me a night with my earrings,' Charlotte said with some force. Lady Lisle retreated, as always, at any sign of resistance.

'You are probably right, dear. After all, they are your jewels, so why shouldn't you wear them?'

She looked at her niece properly, taking in the new hairstyle, the diamonds and the glint in the grey-green eyes.

'I have to say that you are looking remarkably well tonight.'

'Thank you, Aunt. Grace has worked miracles with my hair.'

'It's very becoming, certainly. But it's not just that, you look different somehow. Perhaps it is the earrings. I always remember your poor mother wearing them. Tonight I can really see the likeness.'

'But she was so lovely. I am not nearly as pretty as her,' Charlotte said.

'Nonsense, child. I don't know where you have got that idea from. You are very like your mother. Not just in your features, but in the way you hold your head, your way of speaking. She would be very proud if she could see you now.' Lady Lisle was a kind woman. Charlotte was so self-possessed that it was easy to forget that she was, after all, an orphan.

'I wish I had a photograph of her. Father had one done of her in her coffin, you know, but I have never been able to look at it. There is the portrait at Kevill, of course, but it's not the same.'

'I have a pen and ink drawing of your mother that I made just after she got married. I shall find it for you. It's not a photograph, of course, but I remember your mother was very pleased with it at the time,' Lady Lisle said.

Charlotte went over to her aunt and kissed her on the cheek.
'That would be very kind.'

Charlotte and Adelaide Lisle were the last of the guests to join the
group gathered under the Arthurian murals in the Great Hall.
The chairs in the room had been designed by Pugin himself, but
they were so ornately carved and exquisitely uncomfortable that
people preferred to stand. Augusta and Fred were huddled by the
fire, looking at the *Illustrated London News*. Augusta's brother,
the Hon. Percy, was talking to the local curate; Lord Crewe was
explaining the significance of the Lady of Shalott mural to an
indifferent Hartopp; and Lady Crewe was sitting on the only
upholstered chair in the room. There was no sign of Bay. As they
approached the group, Charlotte saw Augusta's eyes flicker as she
took in the hairstyle and the earrings. Fred gave her a puzzled look,
as if he couldn't quite decide what was different about her, but then
his fiancée whispered something in his ear. His face clouded, and
for once, Charlotte found herself grateful for Captain Hartopp's
attempts to flirt with her. He seemed to have regained his good
humour and bounded up to her as if nothing had happened the
day before. He was full of a cartoon he had seen in *Punch*,
the humour of which, Charlotte felt, was rather being lost in his
telling. But she smiled and nodded as if it was the most amusing
story in the world.

Augusta, though, was not to be deflected.

'My goodness, Charlotte, you look very splendid tonight. Is there
a special occasion? I feel quite dowdy beside you,' she said, her thin
lips stretched into a tight smile.

'Your maid, Grace, has been so clever with my hair. I am so

grateful to you for lending her to me.' Charlotte's smile matched Augusta's exactly.

'She has a real way with hairpieces, it's remarkable what a little artifice can do.' Augusta carried on, 'But those earrings are all your own, of course. They are quite dazzling.'

'They belonged to my mother.'

Hartopp, who had been listening to this exchange with incomprehension, broke in, delighted to have a point of reference,

'The famous Lennox diamonds, eh? Shame to leave them in a strong box.'

'Exactly my thoughts, Captain Hartopp. What's the point in having lovely things if you don't use them?' Charlotte said.

Augusta was about to reply when the dinner gong sounded. As there was still no sign of Bay, Charlotte put her hand on Chicken's meaty arm.

But just as they were filing into dinner she felt a touch, his touch, on her shoulder.

'Glad to see that Chicken is looking after you in my absence,' Bay said. He looked flushed, as if he had just ridden in from the outside, although he was wearing evening dress.

'I must go and apologise to Lady C. I am damnably late.' He moved ahead into the dining room and Charlotte felt a little sparkle of excitement. Bay was back and he had claimed her.

She looked up at Captain Hartopp and smiled. 'Do you know, Captain Hartopp, I think you must tell me that story again. You do it so killingly well.'

Bay was sitting next to Augusta. Charlotte realised that his status had risen at Melton since he had become the Empress of Austria's pilot.

Augusta might disapprove of him, but she clearly could not resist the glamour of his imperial association. Charlotte listened to her trying to prompt Bay into telling her about his royal charge, but he was clearly enjoying having the upper hand and would only talk about the glories of the Pytchley. Finally Augusta could bear it no longer.

'Captain Middleton, I want no more details of the hounds and the kill. All I want to know is whether she is as beautiful as they say.'

Bay said in mock puzzlement, 'But who do you mean, Lady Augusta?'

Augusta rocked backwards on her chair in annoyance. 'The Empress, of course, who else would I mean? Is she really the loveliest woman in Europe?'

Bay paused for a moment and Charlotte tried not to smile. She was enjoying Augusta's torment.

'Do you know,' he said, 'I really couldn't say.'

Augusta's fork clattered on her plate. 'But Captain Middleton, I thought that you were at her side all day, surely you have some idea of what she looks like. Or is a pilot so far in front that he never sees the person he is guiding?'

Hartopp, who like Charlotte was following this exchange, boomed across the table, 'Come on, Middleton, you are quite the connoisseur of the female form. Surely you have formed an opinion?'

Bay smoothed the end of his moustache with his fingers, making them wait. 'The Empress certainly knows how to ride. I don't think I have ever seen a woman with such good hands. It was hard going today in the snow but she was right behind me the whole way. Took every fence, even cleared the gates. She would have made an excellent cavalry officer.' He smiled across the table at Charlotte.

But Augusta would not give up; information was currency in her world and she was determined to exact her price. She saw Bay smile at Charlotte and so she said, 'Charlotte, please can you help me persuade Captain Middleton to vouchsafe some opinion as to the Empress's looks?'

Charlotte hesitated. She wanted to know just as much as Augusta but she didn't want to side with her against Bay.

'I was hoping to see the Empress for myself tomorrow. I want to take some photographs at the meet, I would so like to have an image of her.'

Bay emptied his glass. 'I am afraid you may be disappointed. The reason I can't give you my opinion of the Empress's looks is that she wore a veil. She only took it off right at the end of the day when it was too dark to see her face.'

Hartopp laughed and said, 'Sorry, Middleton, that's just not good enough. A man like you can take the measure of a woman whether she is wearing a veil or not. You and I both know that beauty has its own smell.'

'Do we indeed?' said Bay. 'I detected no smell from the Empress beyond the usual aromas of the field. All I can tell you is that she is tall for a woman and very slender. Oh yes, and she appears to have a vast quantity of hair of a brownish hue. She holds herself well and she speaks quietly. There were times when I could barely make her out.'

'Tall and slender with good bearing,' said Augusta. 'Sounds as if you were quite smitten, Captain Middleton.'

Bay said, 'You must draw your own conclusions, Lady Augusta. I have merely tried to answer your questions.'

Charlotte said quickly, 'And how is the Empress's English, does she have a strong accent?'

'No, hardly at all. I was surprised at how good it was, much better than that of her entourage. But to be honest, there wasn't much conversation. She is very serious about her sport.'

'Then you are two of a kind,' said Hartopp. Bay smiled in reply but Charlotte could see his hand curling around the handle of his knife. Lady Crewe called out querulously from the foot of the table.

'I want to hear all about the Empress, Captain Middleton.'

'She is tall and slender and has lots of hair, Mama,' said Augusta. 'She speaks English without an accent and she is an excellent horsewoman.'

'Yes, yes, but is she exotic looking? I always think foreign women look so mysterious,' Lady Crewe said.

'There is certainly something mysterious about her, Lady Crewe,' said Middleton, 'but as to whether she is exotic, I really have no other Empresses to compare her with.'

Lady Crewe lost interest and the conversation turned to other things.

When the ladies withdrew, Charlotte lingered in the Great Hall for as long as she dared before joining the others in the drawing room. Luckily for her, Lady Crewe had insisted on playing bridge, so she was able to retreat to a far corner of the drawing room behind an enormous potted palm. She spent an anxious twenty minutes shifting her gaze from the door to her distorted reflection in the brass pot that contained the potted palm. When she turned her head from side to side she could see the earrings sparkle.

The rubber was coming to an end. Any moment now Augusta would be released from her card-playing duties and Charlotte would be forced to talk to her. At last the men sauntered in, and Bay spotted Charlotte at once behind her palm.

'What are you doing hiding over here?' he asked, amused.

'I wanted some shade,' she said.

Bay laughed. There was a pause until Charlotte could bear the silence no longer.

'What do you think of my hair? I hope it is worth the effort. Normally I can get dressed in minutes but this took what seemed like an hour.' She turned her head from side to side.

Bay tilted his head and half closed his eyes as if admiring a painting.

'I think you look charming, but then you always look charming, whether you are wearing ringlets and bedecked with diamonds or wearing an apron with your hands covered in stains. It makes no difference to me.'

Charlotte was both flattered by this speech and faintly annoyed. She had, after all, gone to some trouble on his behalf.

Bay seemed to catch her thought and said, 'But having said that, I think your ringlets and your diamonds are delightful.' He hesitated. 'Charlotte,' she felt a little thrill as he used her Christian name, 'I wish we could go somewhere and talk privately. I can feel Augusta watching me through the back of my head.'

Charlotte looked up at him. 'Is there something particular you wanted to talk about, Bay?' Her voice shook a little as she said his name.

'I think you must – or rather I hope you do – understand that there is. But before that, there are some things I must tell you about my circumstances. I am not a rich man. My stepfather makes me an allowance because he is a generous man and he adored my mother, but when he dies the money will go to his children. I have my army pay and the profits I make from selling horses. I have no debts at least, and I live well as a bachelor, but I am not a man of means. And yet you are an heiress. Tonight I see you in your diamonds and it makes me wonder if the gap between us is too great.' He stopped and looked at the floor.

Charlotte rushed in, 'It's true, I have diamonds. But you have Tipsy, the future winner of the Grand National. It would be hard to say which is the greater treasure.'

Bay looked up and smiled. 'I agree with you, of course, but I wonder if the world will feel the same.'

Charlotte began to pull off one of her evening gloves. 'Look at this hand, at these stains. Do you really think that I care what the world feels?'

Bay took the naked hand and was raising it to his lips when Augusta's patrician drawl shattered the moment.

'Oh dear, am I interrupting something?'

Bay squeezed Charlotte's hand, before releasing it.

'As a matter of fact, Miss Baird and I were discussing a matter of great importance to us both. But as it is a private conversation we should have known better than to start where we would inevitably be interrupted.'

He winked at Charlotte and turning to Augusta he said, 'And as you are so interested in the Empress, I should tell you that the thing that struck me most about her was her lack of pretension. It is a rare quality in a lady of such high rank.'

Augusta's eyes gleamed at this morsel. She was distracted just as Bay had intended, and did not appear to notice the implied insult.

'Really, Captain Middleton, and yet I have heard from Fred that her sister the ex-Queen is very particular about protocol. When Fred was presented to her, he made a quite a faux pas by forgetting to walk backwards out of her presence – even though they were in a ballroom! The Chamberlain came to reprimand him afterwards.'

'Poor Fred,' said Charlotte, 'he must have been mortified.'

'Mortified about what?' said her brother, who had come to join them.

'Your contretemps with the horrid Queen of Naples,' said Augusta.

Fred looked embarrassed. 'I had not intended to cause offence. Didn't think the walking backwards thing applied in the middle of a ballroom – dangerous business.'

'Well, I am sure that the Empress will expect no such niceties tomorrow, Baird,' said Bay.

'Do you think you will be able to present me?' said Fred, unable to conceal his eagerness.

'If the opportunity presents itself. But, of course, I am only the pilot.'

'Perhaps tomorrow, when the hunt is here at Melton, there might be a moment?' Augusta came as close to pleading as her pride allowed.

'I shall certainly do what I can,' said Bay.

There was a general clatter and scraping of chairs from the other side of the drawing room as Lady Crewe announced her intention of going to bed. Augusta made to follow her and beckoned to Charlotte, saying, 'That is our cue to retire. My mother does not hold with late nights.'

Bay bowed to Augusta. Turning to Charlotte, he said, 'We must finish our conversation tomorrow, it seems.'

'I look forward to it.' Charlotte shook her head a little so that her diamonds sparkled.

'So do I, Miss Baird, so do I.'

The Left Foreleg

*W*HEN THE LADIES HAD BEEN ESCORTED TO THE door, Fred turned to Chicken and Bay.

'What do you say to a game of billiards?'

Bay shook his head. 'Not tonight. I want to check on Tipsy.' And he left them before they could protest.

The temperature had dropped and Bay shivered as he stepped outside. But he was grateful for the cold, as he needed to clear his head. He was furious that Augusta had interrupted his conversation with Charlotte just at that moment. They had been almost there. But now his proposal would have to wait until tomorrow. It did not matter really – he was confident that Charlotte's feelings would not change overnight – and yet he would have felt much easier in his mind if the matter had been settled.

For he had not been entirely accurate when he had told Augusta that he had been unable to form an opinion of the Empress's looks. It was true that he could not say whether or not she was beautiful; his impression of her had little to do with her face. Yet he could draw a precise silhouette of the Empress on her horse – the straight back, the tilt of her head – as accurately as if she was standing in front of him.

The day had started badly. When Spencer had presented him to the Empress, she had given him the very briefest of nods and had resumed her conversation with two men, who from the colour and cut of their hunting clothes must have come with her from Austria. These courtiers made no move to acknowledge Middleton at all, evidently taking him for some kind of servant, and Bay found himself hovering awkwardly at the edge of the group, waiting for the hunt to start. When at last the huntsman blew his horn and the pack moved off, Middleton kept himself a few yards ahead of the Empress and her courtiers, who were riding abreast. At no point did she look at him or acknowledge his presence, and as Bay looked out across the sparkling fields crosshatched with black thorn, he cursed Spencer for spoiling a glorious day's hunting. He had no desire to act as some glorified groom.

The hounds had picked up the scent and were travelling at speed towards a small copse. Between the pack and its quarry was a hedge at least twelve foot tall. The hounds had found a hole at the base of the hedge and were squirming through, one at a time, yelping with excitement. The huntsman had stopped, evidently deciding that the obstacle was too high for him to clear, and was making his way further down the hedge, looking for an opening. Bay could see that the rest of the field were following him down to the other end of the field where there was a gate. The hounds were all through now and Bay could hear them squealing from the other side. They would be well into the copse before any of the riders could get into the second field. They were all lining up behind the gate, politely waiting in turn to jump over it.

He hesitated for a second, thinking of Earl Spencer's expectations and the web of obligation he was under, and then he felt Tipsy tremble under him and he felt his spirits lift as he pressed his heels hard into her sides and rode straight towards the hedge. He thought for a moment that Tipsy might refuse, but then she sprang and they were clear of the hedge and, by a whisker, the snowdrift on the other side. His heart was thudding in his chest as he slowed to a canter across the unbroken snow. This was what he loved, to be ahead of the pack with nothing to worry him but the going ahead. He could hear the yips of the hounds in the wood, and as he stood up in the saddle to see which way they had gone, he caught a flash of movement in the corner of his eye. He turned his head, a little piqued that someone else had dared to jump the hedge, and to his amazement saw the solitary figure of the Empress riding a few feet behind. She was sitting quite upright on her horse, looking as spruce as she had done at the beginning of the day, her elegant silhouette precise against the snow. That hedge had been a gamble, even for Bay, but she had taken it with ease and independently, it seemed, of her retinue.

Bay had not believed Earl Spencer when he told him the Empress could ride – he had assumed that this was the kind of hyperbole that hung around anyone of rank. But if anything, Spencer had underplayed it: the Empress could not only ride but she could ride almost as well as Bay himself. He couldn't think of many men who could have taken that hedge, let alone women. He raised his crop to her in congratulation – realising as he did so that he was probably breaching some royal protocol, but he felt the need to acknowledge that, for the moment at least, they were equals.

Bay did not wait to see how she responded, since he could see the rest of the hunt beginning to gallop up the field towards them. He could just make out the green jackets of the Austrian contingent and he urged Tipsy forward into the copse. But as he plunged on into the wood, he did not have to look round to know that she was behind him.

She had been there at the kill. Bay had been surprised to see that the Empress had watched the fox being torn to pieces by the hounds without a tremor. Only when the huntsman offered her the brush did she appear to falter, waving him away.

On the way back, he noticed that she followed him rather than rejoining her own clique. The light was beginning to go, so he let Tipsy subside into a slow trot. He was thinking that Tipsy might be ready for the National in the spring when he heard her say, 'Captain Middleton.' He turned round, surprised and pleased somehow that she should remember his name.

'I think your horse is going lame in the left foreleg.' He had been riding just ahead of her so that he had not heard her to begin with, and she had had to attract his attention by tapping his arm with the leather fan that hung from the pommel of her saddle. Her voice was low and quiet, with almost no accent. It was the precision of her speech that betrayed her as foreign; she didn't have the drawl or lisp of an English society woman. He looked down at Tipsy's leg, but he could see nothing wrong with it.

'I will take a look when we get back to the others, Your Majesty.' She tapped the fan on her saddle. 'I don't think it can wait, Captain.'

He heard the note of command in her voice and he pulled Tipsy in and dismounted to have a better look at the foreleg. The Empress had been right, there was a small rock lodged in the hoof which was making Tipsy limp. He had not even noticed. He dislodged the stone with his pocket knife. The frog of the horse's hoof was red and inflamed; if it had gone on any longer Tipsy could have been lame for weeks, and her National chances would be dashed. He was astonished that he hadn't spotted it earlier. He put the horse's leg down, and when he looked up he saw that the Empress had lifted her veil and was looking down at him.

'Was it something in the hoof?' Her face was pale in the fading light; he could only just make out her features – dark eyebrows against white skin, a straight nose, high cheekbones, a few lines around the eyes.

He held out his hand flat and showed her the rock. She reached over with her fan and poked it. 'It was a good thing you caught it, Captain Middleton. It would be a pity if such a fine horse was to go lame so early in the season.'

'I am in Your Majesty's debt then, for I admit I had noticed nothing.'

'I was brought up with horses, Captain Middleton. My father had not much interest in education but he did teach us all to ride.'

'He was a good teacher, then, Your Majesty, if I am allowed to say that.'

She looked down at him and smiled faintly without showing her teeth.

'If we were in Austria it would not be considered proper for you to talk to me so directly, but then we are not in Austria. I take it that you cannot show sixteen quarterings in your family tree?' Middleton shook his head. He wondered what she would say if she knew exactly how humble his origins were.

'Then you could not be part of the imperial household, Captain Middleton.' The Empress's face was serious.

Middleton got up on his horse. Now their faces were level, and the Empress smiled again, and a dimple appeared in one cheek. 'But that is one of the reasons that I prefer the sport here,' she said as she rode on.

The Leather Fan

CHARLOTTE WAS WOKEN BY A NOISE THAT SOUNDED like a thousand plates cascading onto a stone floor. It took a few moments for her to realise that it was the barking of the fox hounds. As they poured into the stable yard their yelping reverberated around the stone walls, creating a cacophony of sound that made sleep impossible.

She lay in bed listening to the sounds of the house coming to life. There was the clanking of the housemaids with their coal buckets, the hall boy leaving the polished riding boots outside bedrooms, the footmen and valets brushing and starching the hunting coats. The maids when they came in to light the fire were talking excitedly in low voices about the hunt, and the possibility of seeing the Empress. 'Cook says that her hair comes right down to her ankles.'

At home, when the local hunt met at Kevill, Charlotte would bury herself in the innards of the house – developing prints in her dark room or retreating to the linen cupboard, where she liked to check the sheets that her mother had brought as part of her trousseau. Each one was embroidered with her monogram, DAB – Dora Alice Baird – and the little owl that had been her symbol. The second Mrs Baird had not had time in her brief life to make much of a dent on the surface of Kevill – she had been too busy with her horses and her parties – so Charlotte had few reminders of her existence apart from the jewels in the strongbox and an ever-dwindling number of Irish linen sheets. She would look for those small tears that, if snagged by an unsuspecting toenail, could cause a serious rent. It was satisfying work: catching the loose threads before they unravelled. It was her own way of preserving her mother's memory.

Safe in the starchy cool of the linen cupboard, she could allow herself to remember the last time she had seen her mother. Charlotte had been waiting on the landing with her new doll, which she had christened by painting a red cross on its porcelain forehead. At last her mother had come down the stairs, her riding habit looped over one arm. Charlotte remembered the lacy borders of her mother's pantaloons and the shining buttons on her boots. Every detail of her mother's outfit lay crisp in her memory, but not the face. Her mother had laughed when she saw the baptised doll. 'What a solemn little girl you are, Lottie.' Charlotte could still feel the rough grain of the serge riding habit against her cheek and hands when she had pushed her face into her mother's skirts. She could hear the click click click of the riding crop as her mother had trailed it against the banisters as she went downstairs away from her. Her mother had been so young, married at eighteen, dead at twenty-three. Her horse had stumbled over a fence, and Dora Baird née Lennox had been thrown head first into a ditch and broken her neck. They had brought her body back on a hurdle, covered with one of the huntsmen's coats. Charlotte had watched from the nursery window, wondering what the pink speck was that the men were carrying so slowly across the fields, until her nurse had found her and taken her away.

Charlotte's father had said after the accident that he would never hunt again, but the winters in the Borders were very long and the amusements were sparse, so his self-imposed exile from the Orrington did not last beyond the following Christmas. But he had been adamant that his only daughter would not follow the same route as her mother. The Shetland pony was sent away and Charlotte was sent to play in the nursery when the hunt came to Kevill. It was only when her godmother Lady Dunwoody had given her the camera and taught her how to use it, that Charlotte found an occupation that filled the long winter days with meaning.

But there was no escaping the hunt today. Of course, she could have pleaded a headache and kept to her room until the riders set off, but she wanted to see Bay. If she and Bay were to marry, she could not hide in the linen cupboard from November till April. Besides, she wanted to see the Empress.

Charlotte was curious to know if she was as beautiful as everybody said. She had seen an engraving in the *Illustrated London News* after one of the Winterhalter portraits, where she looked romantic and soulful, her long hair studded with diamond stars. But that image must be at least ten years old now, judging by the crinoline. Would Elizabeth still be as appealing a decade later? When questioned at dinner last night, Bay had not been very forthcoming. Charlotte had rather admired him for that. He had so clearly not wanted to descend to Augusta's level by answering her questions. Of course, in matters of feminine beauty, men were not always reliable witnesses. There was, in Charlotte's experience, a great gulf between the charms that men found appealing and the kind of beauty that could withstand female scrutiny. The camera lens was equally ruthless. The kind of women that were all 'wriggle and chiffon', in her aunt's phrase, did not translate well to the photographic plate. All the conventional accoutrements of feminine charm – the pouting, the lowered lashes, the trembling bosom – were deadened by the long exposure time demanded by the photograph. To look unflinchingly into a lens for a whole minute was not easy, and in Charlotte's experience women found it harder than men. Even though the new cameras meant that the exposure time now was shorter, the women who required sleight of hand to dazzle the eye were always disappointing in photographs.

After breakfast Charlotte went up to the old nursery to fetch her equipment. She looked at the photograph she had taken of Bay with Tipsy. His very pale blue eyes shone out of the print. Later, she thought, she would retouch the surroundings so that there was nothing to distract the viewer from the man and his horse.

Carrying her equipment across the Great Hall, she almost collided with a footman carrying stirrup cups on a silver tray. As he opened the door and she could see the red, black and brown mass punctuated by points of silver, hear the shouts and the snorts of the horses and smell the excited animals, she found she could not move. There had been exactly this combination of light, colour and sound the day her mother had set off on her favourite grey. She wanted very much to retreat into the cool gloom of the house and pretend that none of this was happening.

'Stirrup cup, miss?' The footman waved the tray in front of her. Charlotte picked up one of the silver goblets and took a gulp of the steaming liquid. She had imagined it was some kind of mulled wine, but it was stronger than anything she had tasted before, coursing like liquid fire down her throat and melting the butterflies in her stomach. A horse whinnied in the distance and she took another gulp.

By the time she saw Bay cantering across the park with Chicken

Hartopp, the goblet was empty. As they jumped the ha-ha that separated the garden from the park, although she could not really see Bay's face, Charlotte knew that he was smiling.

She took a deep breath and stepped out onto the terrace.

Bay pulled up his horse in front of her. From where she was standing on the terrace, she could look him in the eye. He tipped his hat to her.

'No jewels this morning, Charlotte?'

'I believe diamonds in the daytime are considered vulgar.' Charlotte pursed her lips in her best imitation of Augusta. Bay laughed and leant towards her.

'How I wish you were riding out with me this morning. It is such a glorious day to be hunting. There is really nothing like it.'

'Unless you're a fox, of course,' Charlotte said.

Bay looked surprised at her tone.

'I would love to have your company in my dark room today.' The stirrup cup made it possible for Charlotte to say exactly what was in her head.

'And I would happily attend you in your dark room. But I'm afraid Tipsy wouldn't like it. Look at her, she is dying to be off.'

'And you have an empress to look after as well.'

'Her too.' Bay waved his hand as if to brush the Empress away.

'Is she here yet? I want to see her very much. I am hoping to take a photograph of her. I am becoming quite practised at riders and horses.'

'The Empress isn't here, though I believe she is riding over from Easton Neston. We can't start without her, of course.'

'Of course. But I thought punctuality was the politeness of princes,' Charlotte said.

'But not of empresses, it seems. The hounds have caught the scent twice already this morning. They are working themselves up into a frenzy. They're desperate to be off – they know it's a perfect hunting day.' As Bay looked out over the horses and hounds he shouted a greeting to an elderly gentleman with a face red from years of hard riding and strong drink, mounted on a shiny chestnut horse.

'Good day to you, Colonel. How is Salamander proving?'

The Colonel stopped, his head craning round as he heard Bay's voice. As he turned to face them, Charlotte could see that his eyes were covered by a milky film.

'Is that you, Middleton? Didn't see you there for a moment. Salamander is doing very well. Worth almost every penny I gave you for her.'

Bay laughed. 'I'll take her back any time, Colonel, on the same terms.'

The Colonel patted Salamander on the flank. 'Couldn't part with you now, could I, old girl?' He looked up and Charlotte could see that he was looking for Bay, who was a few feet away. She realised that the man was almost blind.

'Over here, Colonel,' Bay said. 'May I present Miss Baird?' The Colonel looked in the opposite direction.

'Miss Baird, Colonel Postlethwaite – longest serving member of the Pytchley, and the hardest rider in the Shires.'

Charlotte nodded and, realising that was useless, she said as loudly as she could, 'How do you do, Colonel Postlethwaite.'

The Colonel turned his great, blind head towards her.

'Honoured, Miss Baird.'

Bay spoke quickly. 'The scent's well and truly up. I think it is going to be a capital day for it. You can give Salamander her head.'

'Oh, I intend to, Middleton.' The Colonel dug his heels into his horse's flanks and disappeared into the throng.

Charlotte looked at Bay. 'Can he see anything at all?'

'Precious little. But Salamander's a good horse. She'll see him through.'

'But isn't it fearfully dangerous?' Charlotte said.

Bay looked as if he was about to laugh but then clearly thought better of it. Instead he said gently, 'Postlethwaite doesn't think it's dangerous, Charlotte. He's been hunting round here all his life. It's not the danger he's scared of, it's the day when he can't ride out anymore.'

Charlotte felt her eyes fill with unbidden tears. The stupid, blind old fool. She looked down at her camera, and started to fiddle with the shutter so that Bay would not see the emotion in her face. But just then there was a shout and a great murmur ran through the crowd. Charlotte looked up and saw that the royal party were making an entrance. She knew it was the royal party because everyone at the meet, with the exception of Colonel Postlethwaite, had turned to watch the Empress and her attendants cantering down the hill that led to the house.

As a composition it could not be bettered, Charlotte thought. If only they were not moving so fast, it would make a magnificent photograph. The Empress in a dark green habit, slender and erect on her strawberry roan, was flanked by two male riders in coats of a lighter green and silver spurs, with a groom bringing up the rear. Charlotte saw that the Empress rode as if she was glued to the saddle; her slender figure did not waver or wobble as the horse came down the slope. She heard a gasp as the royal party sailed over the ha-ha that Bay had jumped earlier. The male riders flanking the Empress leant forward as they took the ditch, but she stayed quite motionless in the side-saddle, seeming to float with her horse.

'At last,' Bay said. He dug his heels into Tipsy's flanks and with a brief wave to Charlotte, he trotted off towards the royal party.

The Empress had stopped in the middle of the forecourt, still flanked by her escorts. She was talking to Earl Spencer, her face tilted up on account of his immense height, and as she had lifted her veil, Charlotte could see the Empress's profile, a small, sharp counterpoint to the immense weight of hair at the back of her head. The other riders were keeping a respectful distance from the royal party and Charlotte thought she had her picture. She had brought down a plate with a new emulsion that required a shorter exposure time. Lady Dunwoody had said it was quite effective in daylight. She put her head under the cloth and angled the camera so that her subject was at the centre of the frame. It felt strange to be taking a picture without the subject's knowledge, but Charlotte knew that she would probably not get as clear a view again. She moved the viewfinder so that the Empress was in the upper third of the plate; a little asymmetry, she found, always made for a more pleasing effect. She found the bulb and squeezed it. She heard the muffled bang and started to intone the Lord's prayer. At 'Hallowed be thy name', she felt that she had exposed the photo long enough and she unclenched the bulb and came out from her shroud. The Empress was still talking to Spencer, but she had turned her horse a little so that the whole face was visible. She was about fifteen feet away and Charlotte could see that she had regular features, a straight nose, and dark eyes under thick, arched brows. Was she beautiful? Charlotte found it impossible to tell, but there was something intense about the older woman's gaze that surprised her. Charlotte sensed that the other woman was full of emotion, she could almost see her quivering. Charlotte wondered what the Red Earl could be saying to the Empress to create such an effect. But she must capture this moment. As quickly as she could, she put in a new plate and had a look at the composition in her lens. She moved the camera a fraction to the right and squeezed the bulb again. This time she took it as far as, 'On earth as it is in heaven', just to be sure.

Charlotte straightened up. As she looked over to the scene she had just photographed, she noticed two things: the first was that the Empress was holding something that looked like a fan in front of her face. The second was that standing directly beside Earl Spencer was Bay Middleton. The fan was large and unlovely. It was not there for decorative or ventilation purposes. It was being used as a shield.

Although it was a cold day, Charlotte felt the humiliation rise over her like a scorching tide, stinging her face and neck, as if she had just been slapped. She looked over at Bay, trying to catch his eye. Surely he could explain to the Empress that she was just an amateur photographer who meant no disrespect? But Bay did not seem to see her; he was completely held by the face behind the fan.

Major Postlethwaite

ℬAY SET OFF TOWARDS THE EMPRESS, WHO WAS
talking to Earl Spencer. As he approached he could see her
profile clearly, her veil was up. Yesterday he had only seen her face
in the silvery gloom of the twilight; now there was a bright winter
sun and he gazed at her. She was full of contrasts, the dark eyebrows
against the pale skin, the mahogany-coloured hair against the green
habit, the red lips and the white throat. She must have felt the heat
of his glance because she turned her head towards him, but as she
did so she saw something that made her frown and her mouth
compressed into a tight line. She started to tug at the reticule
attached to her saddle with sharp, angry movements and pulled
out what looked like a baton. The Empress gave the object a flick
with her wrist and Bay saw that it was a fan made from smooth
brown leather. She held it up so that her face was hidden from the
front. Bay looked over to see what she was shielding herself from,
and saw Charlotte's small figure standing beside her camera, the
bulb in her hand. Behind Spencer, he could see the Empress's two
companions stiffen and look at each other in alarm.

The Empress now noticed his presence.

'Captain Middleton,' she made an angry gesture with the fan,
'it's too much. Nowhere is safe.'

Earl Spencer, immediately on his guard, said, 'Your Majesty, I can assure you there are no threats to your person at the Pytchley.'

'I am afraid you are wrong. There is a . . . person over there taking photographs of me, Earl Spencer.' She did not raise her voice but Bay thought that the low intensity of her tone was somehow more terrible.

'I came here as a private individual to hunt, not to be hunted. I thought I should be safe here. But once again, I find that I am a fairground attraction to be captured as a souvenir, a prize to sell newspapers.'

The Earl look round, bewildered, and then he saw Charlotte on the terrace, fumbling as she tried to dismantle her equipment.

'Oh, but Ma'am, that is just the Baird girl; she's a guest at the house. I am sure she meant no harm by it. A lot of these young girls play around with cameras now. In my day it was sketchbooks and easels, but I suppose we must all move with the times. Isn't that right, Bay?'

The Earl turned his huge head towards Middleton, the look in his bulbous blue eyes unmistakeable – Charlotte Baird was Bay's responsibility, and as she had caused this faux pas, he must make amends.

Bay saw the hard tilt of the Empress's chin and found it unaccountably attractive. He couldn't understand why she was so angry but he liked the way her temper highlighted her features. He couldn't help himself taking stock of her as a woman, the narrow waist, the mass of hair, the dark, unreadable eyes. He noticed a small mole on the Empress's upper lip. It was the only blemish on the white skin. He found himself wanting to touch it. But then a flick of the fan reminded him that this woman was also a monarch. He hesitated – he knew he should defend Charlotte, but he sensed that the Empress would not like him taking another woman's part.

'If only we *could* move with the times. Literally, I mean. I would so much like to have a record of Tipsy here in full flight.' Bay smiled, willing the woman in front of him to respond in kind. She looked at him directly, clearly surprised by his deflection of her anger, and for a moment Bay thought that she would snub him, but then he saw her face soften and the set of her shoulders relax. 'I have a charming photograph of me and Tipsy, but can you imagine what it would be to actually see her gallop?'

'If it is possible in the imagination, Captain Middleton, then I am sure that one day it will become a reality.' Slowly, the Empress lowered the fan and the corners of her mouth moved upwards into the beginning of a smile. Spencer let out a great sigh and the two Austrians relaxed back into their saddles. Bay saw the courtiers taking him in, registering his existence for the first time.

He was about to reply to the Empress when a great yelping went up from the hounds, who had found the scent. He looked at the Empress and she lifted her crop, gesturing for him to ride on. He pulled Tipsy round and started to follow the others down the drive. At the gate, as the Empress passed in front of him, he turned back to look for Charlotte, but she had already gone.

The day was fine and clear, the thin layer of snow on the ground crisp under the horses' hooves. The hounds had picked up the scent halfway up a hill topped by a small Greek temple, so positioned that it could be seen from the drawing room of the house. As Bay cantered past, he saw that the statue was of Diana the huntress, holding her bow. Bay's classical education had been scant but he recognised Diana – he had taken an interest in the hunting deities. He knew the story of Diana and Actaeon, the hunter who had been been turned into prey for trespassing on the goddess bathing. Spencer had a painting at Althorp of Actaeon surprising upon the deity and her attendants in their nakedness. When Bay had seen it he had thought that the fleshy figure of Diana would have needed quite a substantial mount. This statue, though, was slender, the body taut as it twisted round to take aim. She looked like a woman who didn't miss. There was something in the clarity of its profile that was familiar. He turned his head to take another look and just then the Empress came up on his right flank; the resemblance between the sylph-like statue and the lissom, intent figure beside him was unmistakeable. He raised his crop to show the Empress but she had already passed by, following the hounds ahead.

The going was good. Bay liked a long run at the beginning of the day. He preferred it when the pack thinned out a bit and the riders were strung out in order of ability and courage. He had nothing to prove, but still it pleased him to find himself at the front. There were so many places where he had to curb his instincts, but here in the field there was no deference, no order apart from the natural one. Even the Empress, his social superior in every way, was here to follow his lead.

The hounds had stopped at a stream. They had lost the scent. The huntsman was urging them across, but the animals were confused, reluctant to go through the icy water. Bay looked around for a crossing place. The stream was just too wide to jump and he didn't want to get soaked this early in the day if he could help it. There was a bend in the stream a hundred yards away and Bay urged Tipsy down towards it to see if it offered a better vantage point. He looked back and saw that the Empress was behind him, as was, to Bay's surprise, Colonel Postlethwaite. How the Colonel had followed the Empress, Bay could not imagine. The man might not be able to see a thing, but he could still find the best-looking woman in the field. The Colonel had been one of the many admirers of Skittles, the famous courtesan who had hunted with the Quorn in the Sixties. She had been famous for the tightness of her habits, into which she was rumoured to have been sewn naked, and the ferocity of her riding. The gossip went that she had been quite taken with the Colonel, so much so that she had forgiven him his lack of fortune.

The clamour of the hounds suggested that a few had crossed the stream and had found the scent on the other side. Bay looked at the stream. It was slightly narrower here and there was a sandy slope. He could either try and jump to the other side or take the safer but wetter route and wade through the water. He didn't hesitate, but urged Tipsy into a run and, to his enormous relief, cleared the brook. The Empress landed a moment after and then, with a great bellow, Colonel Postlethwaite, a beaming smile on his scarlet face.

One of the Austrians riding with the Empress was trying to catch up with her and was now readying himself to jump over the stream. Bay watched as the horse stumbled and tried not to smile as the man fell head first into the water. The stream was not deep and the man managed to scramble onto the bank, but he was a comic sight: soaking wet, the gold braid on his coat sodden and his breeches transparent.

Bay heard what sounded like a snort of laughter and turned round to see that the Empress was convulsed. He caught her eye and she shrugged.

'Esterhazy pulled the horse up short. He should have had the courage of his convictions. If you are going to jump, then you must be decisive. There is no room for second thoughts,' she said and cantered after Colonel Postlethwaite, who seemed drawn after the hounds by an invisible thread.

Bay lingered for a moment to watch the unfortunate Esterhazy attempt to recapture his mount and then he turned his own horse in the direction of the pack.

The hounds were swinging around in a great arc – Bay was always impressed by the refusal of foxes to run in a straight line. The endless circling and doubling back was the element that made hunting so endlessly fascinating. There was no logic to it, no order. The railways that now crossed the English countryside might proceed in inexorable parallel lines for ever, but Reynard would never be ruled by Bradshaw. Bay relished the random syncopation of the hunting day; the recklessness of a good run followed by the idle moments as the hounds looked for the scent. All his other days were ordered in a procession of meals, costume changes and ritualised pleasure, but in the field nothing could be predicted. No two days were ever the same. In London, in the season, Bay knew almost to the minute where he would be at any time of the day on any day of the week. The battlefield, Bay supposed, was equally unpredictable, but he was a soldier who had never seen action. The Pax Britannica had made the Shires his battleground.

The rest of the field was beginning to catch up. It had thinned out since the morning; the royal sightseers had given up and gone home when they realised what was required of them to keep up with the Empress. Bay saw Spencer grinding down the middle of the line, the flanks of his horse crusted with a white tidemark of sweat. Spencer was a superb rider but his great bulk meant that he would never be at the front of the pack. Bay turned his head and saw that the Empress was ahead of him, once again. She was riding at full tilt towards a nasty-looking fence, Colonel Postlethwaite at her heels. Bay felt a sick lurch in his stomach as he realised that she was about to take a fence that even he would baulk at. He shouted, 'Look out!' and dug his spurs into Tipsy, hoping to head her off. But the Empress could or would not hear him. He watched as she let her horse's reins go slack and allowed the animal to take off. She cleared it all right, but had she landed safely? Bay could not see over to the other side. He urged his own horse on and over the fence, feeling Tipsy shudder as they cleared the highest bar. And they were down. He looked up and saw the Empress's horse standing in front of him, riderless. He felt his mouth go dry.

Then he heard the awful, unmistakeable shriek of an animal in pain, and turning his head, he saw Salamander, the chestnut mare he had sold Postlethwaite, lying on the ground, the body of her master pinned beneath her legs. The Empress was attempting to soothe the animal, but the horse's leg was bent and broken and it was thrashing about in agony. Bay sat frozen for a moment. He saw Postlethwaite's head bent back at an unnaturale angle. The horse's dreadful screaming grew louder. Bay made himself dismount and walk towards the Empress. She was standing very still. Bay watched as she raised her hand.

At first he thought that the object she was holding was the leather fan, but then he saw that it was a revolver. Slowly and deliberately, her hand quite still, she aimed the weapon at the centre of the horse's forehead and fired. The screaming stopped as the mare's body collapsed. Bay gasped, and the Empress turned her head – the dark eyes burning in her white face.

'The Angel of Death is always with us,' she said and crossed herself, the revolver still in her hand.

Bay walked around the dead horse to Postlethwaite's head. The milky eyes were staring at the sky and the mouth was open in a grotesque smile. Bay knelt down and pushed the old boy's eyelids shut. He tried to pull the body out from beneath Salamander, but the carcass was too heavy. He saw that Postlethwaite's stock was tied with a gold pin in the shape of a horseshoe. He thought of the old man fumbling with the pin that morning and felt tears running down his cheeks. Postlethwaite had been a gallant creature and this was probably the end he would have hoped for, but still Bay felt desolate as he looked down at the bodies of horse and rider. He felt in the pockets of his coat for a handkerchief but could only find his hip flask. He brushed his face as best he could with the rough wool of his sleeve and took a swig from the flask. The brandy tore his throat and made him cough, but at last he could control his tears.

He felt a touch on his arm.

'I am sorry, Captain Middleton. He was a friend of yours?' The Empress held out a small scrap of fabric edged with lace. He realised she was offering him her handkerchief. The gun had disappeared.

'He used to be the Master of the Pytchley. I sold him . . .' Bay found he could not go on. He took the handkerchief from her and tried to wipe his eyes. It smelt of lavender.

'I think, though, that to die like this is a blessing, no? To jump into the next world.' The Empress looked at him directly and Bay saw that there were golden flecks in the dark irises.

Bay nodded. 'He was riding for a fall. Damn fool was almost blind. Shouldn't have been out today.'

'So maybe he chose the manner of his going, Captain Middleton?' She was still gazing at him and he couldn't look away.

'But the waste of it . . .' Bay gestured to the dead body of Salamander, but kept his eyes on the Empress's face.

'No, no. You must think of it as glorious. He died a free man.'

Bay could hear the noise of the field on the other side of the fence. In a moment they would be surrounded. She was still looking at him. He thought of the blind gallantry of Postlethwaite, charging down the field with no thought of the consequences. He took her hand and kissed it.

She did not pull her hand away immediately. It was Bay who pulled back, as if astonished at his own action.

He was about to apologise, when she spoke. 'It is only when I am hunting that I feel free. Perhaps it is the same for you, Captain Middleton?' Her voice was soft and warm but she was not smiling.

'I have taken a liberty, Your Majesty. Forgive me, I forgot myself.'

He waited for the reprimand, but she only tilted her head a little to one side.

'Don't apologise, Captain Middleton. You were paying a tribute to your friend, I believe.' She smiled then.

Bay tried to smile back. It struck him that she was exactly right; he had been inspired by Postlethwaite's recklessness.

'I think Postlethwaite might have kissed both hands,' Bay said.

Elizabeth laughed. Even though smiling made the skin round her eyes crease, she looked much younger. Bay realised that she had neither been shocked nor surprised by his action.

'I see I have had a lucky escape. Now, Captain Middleton, could you help me get on my horse?'

Bay linked his hands and bent down so that she could use them as a step. He saw as she drew up the material of her habit that there were no petticoats, and as she put her foot in its elastic-sided boot in his palm he realised that she was wearing suede breeches underneath the riding dress, and he knew that the glimpse had been quite deliberate. His hands shook as she swung herself into the saddle. As she looked down at him, he saw her face regain its regal composure.

'Thank you,' and she nodded to him as if he had been a servant.

A Proposal

THE HUNTSMEN HAD ARRIVED WITH SPENCER. THE Earl took in the situation and bowed his head for a moment. 'Who's down?' he said to Bay.

'Postlethwaite. Broke his neck,' Bay replied.

'You shot the horse?' Spencer asked.

'The leg was broken.' Bay felt reluctant to admit that it had been the Empress who had administered the *coup de grâce* to Salamander.

'Capital fellow, Postlethwaite,' said the Earl. 'Shame about the horse.'

Bay helped the grooms lift the gate off its hinges. The unwitting cause of Postlethwaite's death would serve as a stretcher for his body. It took five men to lift him from under the dead horse. Bay crossed the old man's hands over his chest and put his silver-handled crop by his side. One of the huntsmen blew a long note on the horn as the grooms picked up the makeshift bier and started to carry it back over the fields.

What was left of the hunt started to make its way back towards Melton. Bay caught up with the Empress but she had pulled her veil down and they rode back to the house in silence. When they reached the house, Count Esterhazy, who had changed into dry clothes, came out to greet her and they rode off together towards

Easton Neston. The Empress did not say goodbye to Middleton, but as she set off down the drive she turned and raised her hand in farewell.

Bay watched the Empress ride away down the drive until she was out of sight. As he pulled Tipsy's head round towards the stable yard he felt the tension in his body. His jaw ached as if he had been clenching it for the last two hours. Dismounting, he felt his legs tremble beneath him. He stood still for a moment, leaning against the wall of the yard, pressing down on his heels, trying to find his balance. Closing his eyes, he waited for the shaking to pass. He had been so reckless earlier, inspired by poor doomed, gallant Postlethwaite.

Bay opened his eyes and saw that Charlotte was standing in front of him, her face screwed up with distress. She put her small white hand on his arm.

'Oh Bay, I am so sorry.'

He tried to make his face into the appropriate shape.

'Poor old Postlethwaite. Still, he had a good run of it. Not such a bad way to go.'

A shadow of surprise crossed Charlotte's face. 'Colonel Postlethwaite is dead?'

'Came off after a jump and his horse rolled on top of him. It was very quick.'

The party bringing Postlethwaite's body back to the house would be arriving soon. Bay took Charlotte's arm and led her out of the stable yard into the park. It would not do for her to see Postlethwaite's broken remains being carried back into the house. He could feel her arm trembling under his hand. They walked in silence towards the vista which ended in the Temple of Diana. When they reached the ha-ha, Bay made to open the wicket gate, but Charlotte stopped him.

'Were you there when Colonel Postlethwaite fell?' she asked.

'I didn't see it happen. I was the other side of the fence, but I was there directly afterwards. He died instantly.' Bay tried to sound reassuring, remembering that Charlotte's mother had died in a hunting accident. 'That kind of thing is over in a second.'

'And the Empress? Was she there too?' Charlotte said.

Bay paused. He thought of the Empress holding the pistol at Salamander's head and his own behaviour after.

He said, 'Postlethwaite was with us at the head of the field. The Empress was there before I was.'

Bay saw, to his surprise, that Charlotte's eyes were filled with tears.

'But what's the matter? Surely you are not crying for old Postlethwaite, a man you met but once, who died a death of his own choosing?' He took her small hand between his two palms. 'Don't cry for him, Charlotte. He was smiling at the end.'

Charlotte shook her head, as if to scatter the tears. She raised her head and looked directly at him.

'Will the Empress will be hunting with you again, tomorrow?'

Bay looked at her. He didn't understand the question, or rather, the urgency behind it. She couldn't possibly know about his foolish gesture towards the Empress.

'Well, yes. Spencer has asked me to be her pilot for the whole visit.'

But at that her face relaxed. Bay felt in his pockets for something to dry her eyes, and pulled out a handkerchief with which he dabbed her wet cheeks. It took him a moment to register that the handkerchief was the one that the Empress had given him beside the body of the Colonel. He wondered if Charlotte would notice, but she was too preoccupied to take in what he was wiping her face with.

Charlotte continued, 'You see, I thought I might have made her angry. When I took the photograph. She put up her fan. And then I saw you next to her, and I was so worried that she would be cross with you, because of me, I mean.'

Bay remembered the hard tilt of the Empress's jaw behind the fan, and the colour in her cheeks.

'And I thought you might be tarnished,' Charlotte burst out. 'With the connection.'

Bay hesitated. He could not admit to Charlotte that he had not acknowledged the relationship between them, that he had entirely failed to defend her, that he had simply changed the subject. She expected more of him, and he rather liked the version of himself that he saw reflected in her eyes. He would like to be that person, not the man who had kissed the hand of the Empress next to the body of a dead friend.

'Dear Charlotte, as if any association with you could do such a thing,' Bay said, and as if to prove it he bent down and kissed Charlotte on the mouth. Her lips were dry and slightly salty from the tears. She trembled so gratifyingly that he kissed her again, pulling her to him with one hand around her waist. It was too late to turn back now. He wanted to jump, without second thoughts.

'I long for the day when you are my wife,' he whispered into her ear. 'I want to marry you. As soon as possible.'

He felt her relax into his arms and she kissed him this time, making it quite clear what her answer was.

At last Charlotte pulled back from him to look at his face. She put one hand to his cheek.

'Bay, you should know that I can't marry without Fred's consent, at least not until I am twenty-one.'

'I shall ask him tonight.'

'And he will lecture you about the virtues of a long engagement. He and Augusta have waited for a year.'

Bay smelt lavender water and a tiny whiff of fear. 'I know there are good reasons to wait, but are they really so very important?' He wanted to kiss the inch of neck that was visible above the boned collar of her dress; he wanted to cover the red blotches that were forming there with his mouth.

'I am afraid that money is always important. Fred is my trustee and at the moment he enjoys the income from my inheritance. When I marry he will lose that money, and that is not something he is looking forward to.' Bay was not listening, he wanted so much to capture that flush. He bent towards her again, but this time he felt a hand against his chest stopping him.

'I can't marry you right away, even if I would like to, so we must be,' she tried to smile as he pressed against her, 'we must be prudent.'

'Prudent?' said Bay, taking the protesting hand in his and finding that inch of neck with his mouth. Charlotte shuddered and for a moment she seemed to surrender, but then she stiffened and this time she pulled away from him in earnest.

But he would not let go of her hand. He looked down into her small, worried face, saw the hectic flush on her cheeks, the filling eyes.

'Do I look like a prudent man? I think you have confused me with somebody else.'

She almost smiled, but his voice was urgent.

'Charlotte, I am . . . unsteady.' His grip on her hand was hard, almost painful.

The look on her face made him regret those words.

'Not in my affection for you, never that. But in myself. I would like to be settled.'

And as he spoke Bay felt that there was nothing he would rather do than settle down with Charlotte in the country.

'Let's elope, Charlotte. We could manage on my income to begin with. I could sell my hunters and we could live very quietly at first.'

Charlotte thought she understood his unsteadiness; she remembered the scene at dinner when Blanche Hozier's baby had been mentioned. But she did not understand Bay's urgency.

'Sell your hunters? Even Tipsy? You would give up your chance of the Grand National to elope with me? Well, I am flattered beyond measure, but are you sure that such a sacrifice is really necessary? I shall be twenty-one in the autumn – surely we can wait nine or so months to be married. I don't see there is any reason for us to behave like fugitives. Fred may not welcome my marriage, but once I have achieved my majority there is nothing he can do to stop me. I see no compelling reason to run away like thieves in the night, when we could be married quite respectably within a year.'

Bay's handsome face turned away from her.

'You're right, of course, it is unreasonable of me to expect you to give up your trousseau and your wedding finery. I know these things mean a lot to a woman. But Charlotte, I so wish it could be done now.'

Charlotte moved so that she could look at him face on.

'But why? I care nothing for wedding finery, but I do care about what family I have left. Fred can be insufferably pompous sometimes, especially now he is engaged to Augusta, but I would still like him to walk me down the aisle.' She paused for a moment, trying to read his face.

'What makes you so desperate to run away? You must know that my feelings for you will be the same in September as they are now. I will not change.'

Bay sighed. He knew that he had done this all wrong. The only reason for haste was his own inconstancy. He could not tell Charlotte that he was afraid for his own heart.

'Forgive me, dearest Charlotte, I am not myself. Major Postlethwaite's death was a great shock. It made me think that we must take our happiness when we can.'

Charlotte kissed his cheek.

'I think we are young enough to risk waiting a few months. Meanwhile you must be nice to Augusta. If she thinks of you as a desirable husband for me, then Fred will hardly dare to object. Perhaps you could present her to the Empress? Have you noticed how much more civil she is to you now that you are riding out with royalty?' She put up her hand and traced his moustache with her fingertip.

Bay nodded.

'I promise to marry you as soon as it is practical.' She smiled. 'And you won't have to sell Tipsy or disappoint the Empress. I think she would be very sorry to lose you.'

A Summons

THE INVITATION ARRIVED AFTER DINNER. THE LADIES had gone to bed and only a few of the male guests were lingering in the billiard room. This, like the rest of Melton, had been fitted out in the Gothic style, with a vast wrought-iron lamp over the table which cast a cathedral-like gloom over the proceedings. Each cue had its own carved niche against the wall, set in a row like truncated choir stalls.

The game was coming to an end. Hartopp was winning and his face was crimson under his dundrearies. Bay and Fred were making half-hearted efforts to catch up with him, but they knew they were beaten. The men had almost finished the brandy that had been left out on the butler's tray, and Hartopp made for the bell to ring for some more, but Fred put his hand on his arm.

'Don't think we can ring for reinforcements, Chicken. Gives the wrong impression.' To make amends he emptied the decanter into Chicken's glass.

'To the victor, the spoils.'

The three men were toasting Hartopp's triumph when the door opened. All three men looked round a little guiltily – they had been quite loud in their toasting – but the figure at the door was not an irate butler but a small boy. In his hand he carried a letter.

'Please, sirs, I have an urgent message.' The boy, who was no more than eleven years old, was consumed by the importance of his mission. This was his first time beyond the green baize door. His normal post was cleaning boots behind the scullery – but when the groom had arrived from Easton Neston with the message, the butler had not thought it worth his while to get dressed again as it was only for one of the young gentlemen, so he had sent the boy. The message had arrived a good half an hour before, but the boy, who was not familiar with the company side of the house, had lost his way in the dark and had blundered into a good number of dark, echoing spaces before he had found the billiard room.

'And who is the message for, boy?' Fred Baird held out his hand.

The boy hung his head. In his panicked stumblings through the dark rooms he had forgotten the name that the butler had told him. He held up the letter in answer, but Fred, who had been largely responsible for emptying the brandy decanter, was feeling playful.

'Well, which one of us three graces is the lucky recipient of the enchanted apple, eh?' he said, laughing immoderately at his own joke.

The boy had no idea what Mr Baird was talking about, but he heard the drink in the man's voice and he knew better than to answer. He continued to stand there, mute, still holding out the letter.

'Surely you can make out the letters – is there an M for the magnificent Captain Middleton here, an H for the heroic Captain Hartopp, or a B for Baird of the Borders?'

The boy shook his head and Baird, on the other side of the billiard table, shook his head too in imitation. His face looked ghostly and mad under the shade of the green light and the boy began to shake with fear. He knew how men could be when they had too much drink in them. He longed to be back beside the kitchen fire, polishing the riding boots until he could see his reflection in the leather.

'Come on, boy, the suspense is too much. Who is the lucky fellow, eh?'

The boot boy said nothing. The writing on the envelope was nothing but a black scrawl to him, as he could not read.

Baird turned to Chicken. 'In my house, a boy like that would speak when addressed by his betters. He would not skulk like a mangy cur when asked a direct question.'

Bay, who until that point had not been paying much attention to Baird's drunken posturings, heard the thin note of cruelty in Fred's voice and he turned to look at the boy. He saw the shake in the outstretched arm still holding out the letter. He put down his brandy glass and began to move round the billiard table to the door where the boy stood.

'Stop, Middleton, damn you. I have asked the boy a question and I will have an answer.'

Fred had tipped over from jocular to bellicose. Bay had seen this before in Ireland, where Baird had been notorious in the mess as a mean drunk. He carried on round the table till he was next to the boy and touched him on the shoulder. The boy's arm was rigid. Bay took the letter and found a shilling in his pocket which he put in the boy's still shaking hand, folding his fingers around the coin like an envelope. The boy stood still for a second longer and then he ran out of the room as fast as he could.

'Insolent little devil. And you, Middleton, what do you mean by interfering? I had asked the boy a question, I was waiting for an answer.' Fred was nearly shouting.

Bay looked down at his name on the letter and turned it over, and when he saw the double-headed eagle outlined on the black sealing wax, he put the letter into his waistcoat pocket.

'Most likely the boy couldn't read and he was too scared to admit it. Didn't you see how he was shaking? But in answer to your question, the letter is for me.'

But Baird's rage was escalating now. Thwarted in his persecution of the hall boy, he turned his fury on Middleton.

'And who is sending you letters in the middle of the night, Middleton? One of your lady friends? Perhaps the Empress herself, eh Chicken?' Hartopp made a noise from beneath his whiskers that sounded like laughter.

Bay smiled. 'More likely a creditor.' He turned to the door. 'And now, gentlemen, I bid you goodnight.' But Baird was not to be deflected.

'Show me the letter, Middleton. I believe it could have been for any of us.'

'But it was, in fact, for me.' Bay put his hand on the doorknob.

'So why won't you show it here? Or do you have something to hide? Don't want us to know that you are getting billets-doux delivered in the middle of the night?'

Bay knew that he should turn the handle and walk out of the room. He knew that once Fred got into one of his drunken rages, there was nothing to be done until the alcohol had subsided. But he hesitated for a moment, and in that moment Fred, with tipsy alacrity, had come round the billiard table and seized him by the shoulder.

'I will see that letter.' And he pulled it triumphantly out of Bay's waistcoat pocket.

Bay stood perfectly still. Fred started pawing the letter – 'Look at this, Hartopp, a fancy black seal. I reckon it is from the Empress. Well, I have to say, Bay, you've lost no time in securing the filly. Fine-looking woman too.' Fred described the Empress's curves with his hands and turned to Hartopp, who drunkenly imitated the same gesture. 'Damn fine looking.'

'Give me the letter, Baird,' Bay said as lightly he could.

'Why? Are you worried that I might tell Charlotte about your royal correspondence? Think it might spoil your romance?'

Fred waved the letter in front of Bay's face, his eyes glittering with drunken malice.

'She might not think so highly of you, if she knew you were getting letters from empresses at midnight.' Bay could smell the brandy on Baird's breath.

'You flatter me, Baird. This letter is undoubtedly some message concerning the meet tomorrow. The Empress thinks no more of me than one of her horses, rather less, in fact, as she is uncommonly fond of animals.'

He spoke confidently, but there was a shade of doubt in his mind. Suppose the Empress made some reference to his presumption that afternoon, perhaps the letter was a note telling him that she no longer required his services as a pilot. He felt his heart lurch and he made to take the letter from Baird, but the other man was too quick for him and darted to the other side of the room.

'Well, I think as my sister's welfare is at stake here, Middleton, it is only right that I should find out whether you are speaking the truth or not.' Baird picked up a cue and started to use it as an improvised letter opener.

Bay said very clearly, 'Don't touch that letter, Fred.'

But Fred was not listening. With one twist of the cue the seal broke. Greedily, he pulled out the letter, while Bay stood frozen. He knew that there could be nothing incriminating in the letter and yet he felt paralysed with guilt. The Empress had moved him today, he hardly knew how much; but he had come back and had proposed to Charlotte. If this letter contained some secret then he would only have himself to blame. In that moment, he knew himself to be a man without character.

Baird threw the letter across the billiard table, where it fanned out across the green felt.

'It's from the Empress's chamberlain, requesting your presence at dinner tomorrow night.' Fred paused, as if he had to adjust to this information.

'Well, you are going up in the world. One minute she's treating you like her groom, and the next moment she's asking you for dinner,' Fred said.

Bay could hear the envy in Fred's voice. He realised, too late, that Fred had never thought for a moment that there could be anything between him and the Empress. It had simply been a drunken taunt. But now Fred was resentful, not for some slight to his sister's honour, but because he had not been singled out for distinction himself. True, he was about to have an earl for a father-in-law, but he was not asked to dine with empresses. What had Middleton done to deserve such marks of distinction? Bay could see these thoughts forming themselves on the other man's flushed face. He tried to keep his own expression neutral. He had felt an unreasonable jolt of pleasure at the invitation – she had not, after all, convicted him of *lèse-majesté*. But there was another part of him that knew that this dinner was the start of something. She had noticed him as a man, just as he had seen her that afternoon, with the gun in her hand, as a woman.

It was not an invitation but a summons, though Bay knew that he should not go. He remembered Charlotte's soft, dry lips and her distress at the thought that she might have angered his patron.

He said aloud, almost without meaning to, 'I can't very well refuse.' He realised his foolishness almost as the words left his mouth, but Fred's rage was deflected in astonishment.

'You can't very well refuse? Why on earth would you? The Empress of Austria, who is also the Queen of Hungary to boot, asks you for dinner and you wonder if you should accept?' Fred turned to Hartopp and said in a falsetto voice, holding out imaginary skirts with his hands, 'Dearest Captain Hartopp, I am the Empress of Austria. Would you do me the honour of favouring me with your presence at dinner?'

Hartopp, who was relieved that the quarrel between Baird and Middleton seemed to have subsided, picked up his cue.

'Well, that would be very nice, Your Majesty, but I promised the Queen of England I would see her tonight, and there's the Empress Eugenie tomorrow. She used to be the Empress of France, you know. I might be able to accede to your most gracious request sometime next week. Would that suit?'

Baird said in tones of mock outrage, 'But don't you know that *I* am the most beautiful woman in Europe?'

Hartopp looked him up and down with lecherous scrutiny and said, 'Well, that's as maybe, Your Majesty, but the others asked first and you will just have to wait your turn.'

Bay made himself smile. He was grateful for the turn in Baird's mood. Of course he had to accept the invitation. Nobody refused an invitation from royalty, even foreign royalty. Perhaps if the invitation had not been made public, he could have written back to say that the honour was too great for someone in his relatively lowly position, but to do so now would be impossible; Baird and Hartopp would consider it swank and would begin to ask themselves why.

He gathered up the letter and stuffed it back into his pocket.

'Do you know what we need, gentlemen? Another drink. I have a flask of brandy in my room. I suggest that we put it to good use.'

As they variously walked and staggered back to the bachelors' wing, Bay felt the awkwardness of his situation. If only Charlotte had agreed to marry him right away. But she had refused, and Bay could not blame her for that. He could not tell her the real reason for his urgency, and so they had agreed to wait until the end of the hunting season before announcing their engagement. Charlotte had been quite clear: 'If we go to Fred now, he will feel bound to refuse, as he has given me so many warnings about your unsuitability. If we wait until the end of the season, then, who knows, maybe the Empress will have given you an Austrian dukedom and then he will have no reason to object to the match except on the grounds of jealousy. And if he won't consent, then I will marry you in September when I am of age and no one can stop me. Of course, I won't be able to touch my inheritance without my trustees' consent till I am twenty-five, but I am sure we will manage. It will be much easier if there is no unpleasantness.'

Bay knew that Charlotte's plan was the sensible course of action. One of the things he found so appealing about her was that strength of character; she was someone who knew her own mind. And yet he wished that he had been able to sweep her off her feet and gallop through the night to Gretna Green. It would be foolish, of course, but it would be irrevocable. There would be a scandal and he would be branded a fortune hunter and a cad, but he thought that he would not mind that so very much if he were actually married to Charlotte. Instead he had received an invitation from the Empress which he could not refuse, even if he had wanted to.

As he climbed the stairs he caught sight of his face in a mirror, and as he turned towards the looking glass the candle he was carrying bathed his face in upward light, casting strange shadows so that his eyes and teeth gleamed and he looked almost devilish. Bay had never thought of himself as a bad person before, but now he wondered what sort of person he really was: the devil in the mirror or the noble-looking young man in Charlotte's photograph?

But before he could decide, Chicken Hartopp lurched up behind him and said, 'Admiring your handsome physog, Captain Bay Middleton, the famous ladies' man?'

'I hope, if I am famous for anything, it is my riding,' said Bay evenly.

Chicken shook his vast head. 'Any man can learn to ride, but not many can make all these women fall for you. How *do* you do it, Bay? Why can't they see what a shallow feller you are?'

'Maybe that's what they like about me,' said Bay.

An Invitation

HE ROOM WAS SO DARK WHEN CHARLOTTE WOKE up, that she thought it was still the middle of the night. But then her door opened and the maid came in with her fire lighting equipment. Charlotte put on her shawl and went over to the window. There were fingers of light just appearing over the hill, turning the temple of Diana a pearly pink. Charlotte put her hand to her lips and felt the dry skin there that yesterday Bay had kissed.

She had gone to bed directly after dinner the previous night, claiming a headache. Part of her, the ignoble half, would have liked very much to have sat in the drawing room with Bay at her side, bursting with the knowledge that this famous Lothario and breaker of female hearts had proposed to Charlotte Baird, the girl with stains on her fingers. But she knew that it would be a short-lived triumph, for if Augusta suspected the truth it would lead to exactly the sort of scene that Charlotte was hoping to avoid.

It was a shame, she thought, that Bay had never flirted with Augusta. If only her future sister-in-law had been able to dismiss Bay as a beau she had toyed with and discarded, then his interest in Charlotte would be much easier to bear. The only way Bay could redeem himself was through the Empress. If he could persuade Elizabeth of Austria to notice Augusta, then anything was possible.

So she had avoided Bay's eye at dinner, only glancing at him briefly as the ladies withdrew, and was rewarded with his most brilliant smile. She had been in her bedroom for a full ten minutes before the blush had subsided.

The maid had got the fire lit at last. The new wood was crackling and spitting. A spark flew out and landed on the hearthrug and smouldered there until the maid stamped it out with her boot. Another spark landed and the smell of burning wool filled the room. The acrid smoke shocked Charlotte out of her reverie.

She plunged her face into the icy water of the hand basin. The maid protested, 'Sorry, miss, I was just going to bring you up some hot water, but I wasn't expecting you to be up and about so early.'

Charlotte felt her skin tingle. 'Sometimes cold water can be just what is needed.'

There was a noise from the corridor, a voice raised, some laughter.

'That'll be the hunting party, miss. The meet's at Greystock today, which is twenty miles off.'

Charlotte looked out of the window; the pink-tinged dawn was now overcast with black rain clouds.

'It's a long way to go, to get wet.'

At breakfast there was a letter waiting for her. It was from her godmother Lady Dunwoody. She was, she wrote, preparing for an exhibition at the Royal Photographic Society in March.

It is both a great honour and an undertaking. The Queen herself is to open the gallery, which is quite an event because, as you know, she hardly goes out these days. But then the Prince Consort was such a keen photographer. I wondered, dear Charlotte, if you would help me in my preparations. You are without question my most talented pupil. Your eye is so good. I would love to include some examples of your work in the exhibition.

*Of course, you may be reluctant to leave Melton if the rumours
I hear of an understanding between you and a certain gentleman
are true, but then this is an opportunity that you could hardly avail
yourself of as a married woman.*

Celia Dunwoody was her mother's cousin. She had married a
wealthy baronet, Sir Alured Dunwoody, who was rather older than
herself, and had used his money and influence to set up an artistic
salon in her house in Holland Park. Celia Dunwoody's Thursdays
were famous as a place where up-and-coming artists could meet
their society patrons. In the last few years Celia had taken up
photography, and her soulful tableaux of young girls dressed as
Circassian slaves, or characters from the Idylls of the King, were
much admired in her circle, and as her circle included everyone of
taste, her reputation was assured. It was true that some of her guests
had preferred Lady Dunwoody's Thursdays before they included
viewings of her latest photographic compositions, but given the
lavishness of her hospitality and the high quality of the lions that
she attracted, these thoughts were only uttered in the privacy of
the carriage going home from Holland Park.

Lady Dunwoody had offered to bring Charlotte out in London,
but Fred had not been happy with idea of his sister becoming part
of 'the Holland Park set'; he had heard too many stories about the
kind of 'artists' that frequented the famous Thursdays. So Charlotte's
debut had been overseen by her paternal aunt, Lady Lisle – whose
artistic ambitions did not extend beyond the odd watercolour of
the Cathedral Close. Charlotte would have very much preferred to
live with Lady Dunwoody in Holland Park, where she could have
spent all day in the studio or the dark room, instead of being
dragged to balls by Lady Lisle. But, of course, she had not been
consulted.

Charlotte was aware that she was being watched across the table by Augusta, who was clearly waiting for her moment to pounce. Augusta had not received any letters that morning. She did not like the sensation, however brief, of being less popular than her mousy sister-in-law-to-be. They were alone in the breakfast room: the men had gone hunting and the older ladies had gone to visit the wife of one of the gamekeepers, who had just had her tenth confinement. The delivery had been complicated and the details had not been thought suitable for the ears of young ladies.

Charlotte kept her head down, studying the letter, hoping that Augusta would leave her alone. But only a minute or two passed before Augusta said in her affected drawl, 'Looks like a very satisfyin' letter. You must have read it through five times at least.'

Charlotte looked up. She saw that she could not escape.

'It's from Lady Dunwoody. She is to be part of an exhibition at the Royal Photographic Society and she has asked me to go to London to help her prepare her prints.'

'The Royal Photographic Society? I never knew such a thing existed. What next, the Royal Hot Air Ballooning Society?' Augusta smirked.

'The Queen and the late Prince were very keen photographers. The Queen is going to open the exhibition herself.'

'Well, I hope Lady Dunwoody won't be too disappointed that you can't go.' Augusta's smile did not reach her eyes.

Charlotte said nothing. Until that point, she had not thought seriously of accepting. But suddenly she saw the next six weeks stretching ahead of her – full of her brother's condescension and Augusta's malice. Bay was the only reason to stay, but he would not be at the house for much longer. He and Hartopp had rented a hunting lodge in Rutland for the rest of the season. And now she had made it clear that she would not elope with him, perhaps it would be better if they did not remain under the same roof. She did not feel very confident of her power to resist him; there had been something unsettling about his urgency yesterday. Furthermore, there was the very appealing prospect that if she were to leave Melton now, it would not only confound Augusta's suspicions about her relationship with Bay, but it would also annoy her very much. Charlotte knew that her main role at Melton was to be the unmarried foil to Augusta's triumphant young bride-to-be.

So with these thoughts running through her mind, Charlotte lifted her chin and said, 'But I have no intention of disappointing her. Lady Dunwoody is my mother's cousin and she has always been extremely kind to me. As she has asked for my help I don't very well see how I can refuse it. I shall go to London tomorrow. The exhibition is in March and I am sure there is a great deal to be done. I am sure your mother will understand how I am placed.'

'I think that Mama will think it very odd, as do I. Why would you go down to London to mess about with some smelly chemicals when there is so much to be done here? Never mind the exhibition, I am getting married to your brother in March. Forgive me if I consider that to be rather more important.'

'But Augusta, as you have often pointed out, I know very little about the fashionable way of doing things. Why do you need me in attendance when I am clearly not qualified? Forgive me, if I would rather go somewhere I can actually be of use.'

Augusta looked at her in surprise. She had never heard Charlotte speak with such vehemence.

'And what will Captain Middleton say, I wonder, to your sudden departure? I thought you were such great friends?'

'I am sure that he will understand.'

Augusta looked puzzled for a moment, and then her eyes narrowed as she took a new tack.

'I suppose Captain Middleton is very busy with his own obligations. My maid told me that a letter came for him last night, hand delivered.' She paused for effect, but Charlotte said nothing.

'It was from the Empress, summoning him to dinner tonight. He has clearly made quite an impression on Her Majesty.' Augusta emphasised the last two words.

'How fortunate,' said Charlotte, trying to hide her surprise, 'as he is her pilot. I hope that the association will be of some use to him. It must be a good sign that she has asked him to dine with her.'

Charlotte spoke with a shade more confidence than she felt, but now she had declared her intention of going to London she was not going to allow Augusta's insinuations to derail her.

'I am not sure I would be entirely happy if Fred was having dinner with the most beautiful woman in Europe,' Augusta said.

'How fortunate then, Augusta, that the Empress did not invite him. And now, if you will excuse me, I must see to my packing.'

Charlotte swept out of the room, her cheeks pink. She knew it was a mistake to engage with Augusta, whose reserves of spitefulness were far greater than her own, but she could not resist the feeling of satisfaction that for once she had had the last word. But now she would have to go to London and leave Bay behind, or Augusta would think that she had changed her mind because the Empress had invited him to dinner.

On the Chocolate Side

A S THE FOOTMAN OPENED THE DOUBLE DOORS OF the Great Hall, Bay felt a surge of relief that he had, after all, decided to wear his dress uniform. It had meant hiring a chaise to get here, an expense he could ill afford after his losses at billiards the evening before; but as he took in the scene before him, he knew that, sartorially at least, he would do. Esterhazy and Liechtenstein were standing by an enormous carved mantelpiece, both wearing the white and gold uniform of the Austrian cavalry, their chests emblazoned with campaign medals and jewel-encrusted orders. Bay wondered how much active service they had seen. Perhaps they had been part of the imperial army that had been so roundly beaten by the Prussians three years ago. All he had was an ADC's ribbon, but he would rather have that, than a chestful of campaign medals from an infamous defeat. He was glad that he belonged to a regiment with the most splendid uniform in the British army – the Hussars were called the Cherry Pickers on account of their red trousers, ornamented with a gold stripe down the outside leg. Bay hoisted his jacket to sit at exactly the right angle on his shoulder and practically marched into the room.

Liechtenstein and Esterhazy did not look round as Bay was announced. Only a slight bristling of the gold-braided shoulders betrayed their awareness of his presence. At the other end of the room there were two women sitting on a sofa talking. Bay could barely see them across the cavernous room, but he knew at once that neither of them was the Empress. He hesitated. The two men clearly meant to snub him, and while he felt confident of a warmer reception by the ladies, he did not know quite how to cross the room to them, imagining the echo of his spurs tapping against the hard floor. In desperation he looked up as if to admire the frescoes on the ceiling. He tried to appear absorbed by the goddesses and cherubs floating above him, but he found it hard to disguise his own awkwardness. He wished now that he had had the courage to refuse the invitation. He should have stayed at Melton and spent the evening being attentive to Charlotte, who had never seemed more attractive to Bay than she did at this moment. But just as his neck was beginning to ache from his scrutiny of the ceiling, he heard the doors open and the footman announcing the Spencers.

'Middleton, what a splendid surprise!' The Earl was clearly delighted to see him. 'Glad to see that you have made yourself indispensable to the Empress.'

Middleton stiffened at the Earl's tone, but a second glance reassured him that Spencer meant nothing particular by his remark. He bowed to the Countess, who gave him a look which suggested that Bay's presence had rather devalued the occasion. She had, Bay noticed, made an unusual effort with her appearance. Her dress was made from a bright magenta silk over which she wore a slightly dingy diamond stomacher. There was a tiara in her fading blond hair. Middleton had never seen her wearing so many jewels, even when presiding over the vice-regal balls in Dublin. The gems were at odds with her weatherbeaten English looks. In her large, beringed hands she carried a fan which she tapped on her skirt like a riding crop.

Her husband, though, betrayed no such nervousness. He surveyed the Great Hall, nodded briefly to the Austrians and clapped Middleton on the shoulder.

'You didn't tell me it was the Empress who shot poor old Postlethwaite's horse. Quite the Amazon. Remarkable horsewoman, too. I don't think anyone but you could keep up with her, Middleton.'

Bay was saved from having to answer by Countess Spencer. Ignoring her husband, she said to Bay, 'Edith Crewe must be so relieved that Augusta is finally to be married. I felt such a weight lifted from my shoulders, when my Harriet was settled, and she was only twenty-two. And Baird is really quite a good match. But then I don't need to tell you that, Captain Middleton – I hear that you have quite an affection for the Baird family.'

Bay spread his hands in a gesture of submission. He knew from experience that the Countess would not be deflected. She addressed her husbands's ADCs in the same tone as she used with her dogs, and she expected the same level of obedience.

'And if you are successful, you can tell Miss Baird that I shall be happy to call upon her.'

Bay bowed again. He sensed that Charlotte might not be over-whelmed with gratitude at this sign of the Countess's favour and that thought made him glad.

'But mind you make sure of her, Captain Middleton. You can't afford to . . .' But the Countess did not finish her thought as at that moment the doors were opened and the Empress entered the room.

Bay made his deepest bow, although he did not click his heels like the Austrians. As he straightened up, he saw the Empress glance at him and then immediately look away. She was wearing a dress of green velvet that exposed her shoulders and décolletage. In her hair she wore several diamond stars, arranged randomly as if they had been sprinkled there by some divine hand.

Her naked shoulders were startlingly white against the forest green of her gown. He found himself almost shaking as she offered him her hand. As he bent over to kiss it, touching her skin with his lips, he had to fight to compose himself. Looking up, he caught her eyes for an instant, but then she had immediately moved on to greet the Spencers.

Her hand had been dry, the skin a little rough, the hands of a horsewoman. But it was something to remember, the first touch of a woman's skin; it was the delicious forerunner of so many things . . . but there he checked himself. He forced himself to think of Charlotte's small, serious face, and the way she had trembled when he had kissed her. It had been her first kiss, he felt sure.

As he stood up he saw that there was another woman following the Empress. This, Middleton realised with an unpleasant lurch of his stomach, was her sister, the ex-Queen of Naples. And for the second time that night Middleton wished himself back at Melton Hall.

He felt a fool for not guessing that this ordeal lay ahead of him. The Queen would, of course, remember the man who had refused even to meet her at the Spencer ball. It had been unwarrantably rude, Bay could see that now, and for a moment he regretted his action. The woman before him was beautiful but everything about her was a little less splendid than her sister. Her face was longer, her lips were thinner, her eyebrows were straight while her sister's rose in graceful curves. She had the same heavy mass of hair, but as she was a couple of inches shorter it seemed to dwarf her. Tonight she wore it in the same diadem of plaits as the Empress, but on her the style looked more like an imposition than a crown.

Baron Nopsca made the introduction. 'Your Majesty, may I present Captain Middleton? He has been acting as the Empress's pilot.'

Once again Bay bent to kiss the hand that was offered to him. The Queen's hand was softer than her sister's but, he noticed, slightly moist. He hoped that the Queen would pass on at once, but she was frowning at him, making an elaborate pantomime of remembering something.

'Captain Middleton, I believe I remember the name.' She looked at him directly and Bay saw that she knew precisely who he was.

'My sister tells me that you are invaluable to her. She says she can't imagine how she could have managed without you.' The Queen smiled with her mouth only. 'I told her that she was very lucky to have secured your services. The famous Captain Middleton is not to be hired as easily as a hackney carriage. He is a man who follows his own inclinations. Sisi has no idea how lucky she is.'

The Queen glanced over at her sister, who was standing now between Liechtenstein and Esterhazy, listening to some story of Spencer's.

Bay wondered if he should make some apology to the woman in front of him, but he sensed that nothing he said could make a difference. Maria would always be the runner-up, in looks, in position, in everything. Instead he said, 'I hope I will have the honour of riding out with the Empress *and* her sister.'

'That will be for my sister to decide. We may be in England, but we are all her subject to her will.'

At this, Baron Nopsca, who had been hovering at the ex-Queen's elbow, looking for a moment to interrupt this worrying conversation, stepped forward and murmured in her ear, 'May I present you to Countess Spencer, Your Majesty,' and to Bay's relief they moved on. The rest of the royal party included the ex-King, a small man with a waxed imperial, who spoke no English and who looked surprised when Nopsca described Bay to him as *'le chef d'équipe de l'impératrice'*. The King looked at Bay and shook his head, as if pondering what the world was coming to when monarchs sat down to eat with their grooms.

Bay was assigned one of the Empress's ladies-in-waiting to take in to dinner. The Baron introduced her as Countess something, but the name sounded thick and foreign to Bay and he stumbled as he repeated it.

'I apologise for my German pronunciation. The only languages I learnt at school were dead ones.'

The Countess, who was a thin woman some years older than the Empress, gave an unexpectedly charming smile.

'I will forgive you, Captain Middleton. My name is Festetics. It is not German but Hungarian, which is famously the most difficult language on earth.' She had a deep voice and spoke with a strong accent, her words coming out fitfully in little staccato gusts.

'Thank goodness then, that you speak such good English,' Bay replied.

'We Hungarians have no choice but to become linguists. We never expect people to speak Magyar. The only person I know who has learnt to speak it fluently is the Empress.' She nodded. 'Yes, the Empress is like a parrot. Sometimes when we are talking, if I am to close my eyes, I am thinking that I talk to one of my own people.'

Bay, whose knowledge of Hungary did not extend much beyond some notion of gypsy violins and Tokay wine, wondered why the Empress had bothered to learn such an esoteric tongue.

'But Captain Middleton, she is Queen of Hungary as well as Empress of Austria. And such a Queen! We Hungarians are for ever thankful that she has married the Kaiser. He is not learning Hungarian, beyond saying "My loyal subjects", but my mistress she wants to understand us. The people say that she has a Hungarian soul.'

The Countess's eyes were shining and she looked over to the Empress, who was seated in the middle of the table between Earl Spencer and her brother-in-law, the little King. As she turned her head to the Earl, the candlelight caught one of the diamond stars in her hair and the refracted sparkles danced across the table, stippling the faces of the other diners.

Bay and the Countess were seated at the end of the table, firmly below the salt as protocol dictated. Bay had not expected anything else and yet he felt uncomfortably aware of his lowly status. In the field, the difference in rank seemed irrelevant; what counted was horsemanship, and in that department he felt the equal of anyone. But here in this vast, coffered dining room, where he had nothing to recommend him but his looks and his cherry picker uniform, he felt awkward. At least he could make himself agreeable to the woman beside him.

'Are you enjoying your stay in England, Countess?'

'It seems to me that it is, how you say, a splendid country,' Bay nodded his approval of her linguistic foray, and the Countess continued, 'if you are a horse or perhaps a dog. The Empress she does not care about food, but I am not so fortunate. Even when we have visited your Queen at her palace, the food was grey like stones, and tasting very much the same way.'

Bay had to laugh at her vehemence. He gestured at his plate, at the perfectly cooked Sole Veronique.

'Not all English food is bad, Countess.'

Countess Festetics leant over to him. 'My point exactly, Captain Middleton. The chef is Hungarian. He comes here with the Empress. Of course, I have to give him the menus. The Empress, she would live on bouillon and pumpernickel if I was to permit it. You are very fortunate that I am here. Because of me you do not have to eat grey food.'

Bay smiled. 'Your presence would be a boon, Countess, whatever the menu.'

The Countess laughed. 'You are very gallant, Captain. The Empress has mentioned to me how fine a rider you are, but she did not tell me that you could also talk so . . .' she searched for the word, 'delicately.' She turned to look at Bay directly as she said this and he felt a prickle of sweat on the back of his neck.

'There hasn't been much time for conversation on our rides together. The Empress likes to ride at the front of the pack. I spend most of my time trying to keep up with her.'

'We are all trying to do that, Captain. But she likes you . . . I am glad, because when she is happy, I am happy.'

'I am not sure all the Empress's party feel the same way,' Bay said.

The Countess saw Bay glance over at Liechtenstein and Esterhazy.

'Max and Felix? No, they are not happy at all to be eating with the stable boy.' The Countess pointed at him and smiled. 'But you must remember that they are Viennese and nobody is good enough for the Viennese. And, of course, they do not like to have a rival. For three years they have been everywhere with the Empress, to Bad Ischl, to Gödöllő, and in Vienna, of course. They are a fine pair of *cavalieri serventi*. The Emperor calls them Castor and Pollux. But now the Empress is talking about you, and asking you to dinner. You have made their noses . . . crooked.'

The footmen came round with the entrée. There was no one sitting on Bay's other side, so when the Countess turned to the man on her left, he was left alone. He tried to make conversation with the woman opposite him, but as she spoke no English they could do little more than smile at each other. He took a surreptitious look at the Empress. She was, as the Countess predicted, not eating, but her wine glass was half empty and there were two spots of colour in her pale face. She turned her head and caught Bay's eye. To his surprise she called out to him.

'Captain Middleton, I should like to hear your opinion of my horses.' She gestured to Spencer. 'The Earl says you are the arbiter of these things. Are they as good as your English hunters?'

The table went silent. To be addressed like this directly was a definite sign of royal favour. Bay felt the shift in atmosphere as the other diners reassessed his status. He hesitated before saying, 'Your horses are magnificent, Ma'am. I would be proud to be seen riding any of them.'

He paused, and wondered if he should continue, but then he saw the expression on Esterhazy's face and decided he would say what he really thought.

'But a great hunter needs more than good looks. To ride out with the Quorn and be in at the kill, you need more than breeding, you need heart. I mean the kind of animal who will ride twenty miles at a gallop over open country and still be ready for more. Your horses, Ma'am, will do anything you tell them, but a great horse doesn't need telling, it will give you everything it has without you asking, and when you think there is nothing left, it will find the legs for that last jump.'

There was a moment before Liechtenstein said, 'Are you really suggesting that Her Majesty's thoroughbreds, the product of five hundred years of breeding, are inferior to the grey mare you were riding yesterday?'

'You may not like her looks, sir, but you have to admit that she covered the distance as well as any in the field,' Bay said, aware that Liechtenstein's horse had refused a gate the day before.

'And these horses, the ones with heart that you speak of, I suppose they are English.' As Liechtenstein turned his head, Bay saw the faint gleam of a duelling scar on his cheek.

'I am sure that there are horses with spirit and courage every-where, but so far I have only found them in England.'

Liechtenstein was about to answer but the Empress broke in, 'Earl Spencer, I must have one of these English horses. Will you help me find one?'

'Middleton's the man for that, Ma'am. No better judge of horseflesh in the country.'

The Empress turned her head towards Bay. He bowed and murmured that it would be an honour. The Empress clapped her hands and turned to her brother-in-law, the King of Naples, and translated the exchange for him into rapid Italian. As he listened the ex-King turned to stare at Bay and shook his head again, still baffled by his presence.

The conversation around the table picked up again, and as the footmen brought round the pudding, the Countess leant over to him and said in a low voice, 'Well, Captain, you are, as they say in German, on the Empress's chocolate side – the one where everything is sweeter. It is where every courtier wants to be.'

'But I am not a courtier,' said Bay, a little too loudly.

The Countess smiled and Bay saw the glint of a gold tooth.

'Perhaps. But you are a man, I think.'

Having made her point, she carried on, 'This is a Hungarian cherry torte, Captain. Even the Empress likes this.'

Bay, who did not really care for sweet things, felt himself obliged to finish every crumb.

After dinner the Empress led the ladies out of the room, but to Bay's relief the men did not stay behind to drink port. The King of Naples left first, followed by the other men, in strict order of precedence, which meant that Bay was the last to leave the room. His face was aching from the effort of appearing agreeable. Alone for a moment in the dining room, he let out a silent scream, stretching his mouth as wide as it would go.

There was a noise behind him, a discreet clearing of the throat. Bay composed his face and turned around. Baron Nopsca was standing in the doorway, his hands clasped together in front of him.

'Captain Middleton, I have a message from the Empress.' He paused and looked down at the floor for a moment. 'Her Majesty would like you to meet her in the stables.' He delivered his message in the expressionless tone of a man who had trained himself not to react to his mistress's caprices.

Bay, though, could not hide his surprise.

'Now? She wants to meet me there now?'

'I am not precisely sure when the Empress will be joining you, but I think her intention is that you should wait for her there.'

The Chamberlain bowed from the waist in the continental manner, signifying that there would be no further conversation, and left the room as quickly as he could. Bay followed him into a corridor that appeared to lead to the servants' wing.

'Baron Nopsca!'

The Chamberlain turned round to face him. Although the corridor was dimly lit, Bay could see that the other man's face was white and sweating.

'The stables? How do I get there?'

Nopsca's face sagged with relief. 'My apologies.' He gave Bay directions, and then said, 'But it is a cold night. And it is possible you will have to wait. Her Majesty can sometimes be unpredictable. One moment, please.'

Nopsca disappeared through a door and came back a few moments later with a footman, who was carrying a decanter filled with a colourless liquid on a silver salver. He poured out a generous glass for Middleton and one for himself.

'Schnapps. In Vienna we call it the sentry's friend. It is very good at keeping out the cold.'

He raised the glass to his lips and emptied it. Bay followed suit, enjoying the hot rush of alcohol as it caught the back of his throat.

The Baron blinked and smiled faintly. 'One more, I think.'

Bay did not refuse. There was a kind of desperation about the Baron. They held their glasses aloft for a moment and the Baron said with a broader smile, 'To the Empress!' Bay repeated his words and felt the schnapps working its way down to his knees.

'Goodnight, Herr Captain, I hope that your wait will not be too long.'

On his way to the stables, Bay caught sight of his reflection in a speckled pier glass hanging in one of the Great Hall's many alcoves. He stepped towards it, unable to resist admiring the splendours of his uniform. Just as he was adjusting his cape to the requisite angle, he caught a flash of white in the corner of the mirror and heard the sound of voices. It was Liechtenstein and Esterhazy. They were speaking German in a low tone but Bay heard his own name spat out by one of them, followed by a harsh laugh. Bay did not dare turn round; he did not want the Austrians to think he had been eavesdropping. It was hard to see them in the foxed and wavy glass; the white shapes kept shifting and buckling. At one point the two white shapes merged into one as if the two men were locked in a fierce embrace. Bay squinted at the glass but it was impossible to make out exactly what was going on behind him. At last the white mass separated into two distinct shapes and he heard the sound of boots and spurs clanking up the great stone staircase. Bay felt a little unsteady, the schnapps was catching up with him. Had he really seen Castor and Pollux in a distinctly unfraternal embrace? He dismissed the idea as an alcohol-induced hallucination. He had been in the army long enough to know that such things took place in the barracks among the men, but between two officers? He brushed the thought away.

He found the stable easily. Like the house, it was a baroque confection – the bas reliefs on the ceiling were equal to the ones in the Great Hall. There were twenty or so animals in the stalls, and Bay felt calmer as he breathed in the familiar smell of horse and hay. He walked down the aisle between the stalls, wondering why the Austrians shaved their horses. He thought the barbering looked unnatural; it offended his notions of the respect due to such noble animals. But then the Austrians, he was beginning to see, cared a great deal about the surface of things – the gold braid on their uniforms, the precise order in which people of different ranks should go into dinner; even the halters around the horses' heads were made of silk rope. He thought of the impossible narrowness of the Empress's waist in her riding habit, her unrelenting carriage. She always looked immaculate, even after a long and muddy day in the field. She was a woman who cared about the way things looked, and yet she had asked to meet him here. What would Lichtenstein and Esterhazy, the ex-King of Naples and even the Emperor himself make of that?

The chestnut horse in front of him switched its tail irritably, kicking out against some unseen demon. The stable clock started to chime, it was ten o'clock already. Bay thought of the hired chaise and wondered how long he would have to wait. The excitement he had felt on receiving her summons, boosted by Nopsca's schnapps, had now began to subside into a feeling of giddy unease.

When, at last, he heard her voice behind him, Bay hesitated a moment before turning round. He wanted to see her face and yet he wondered what he would see there.

The Empress was smiling. She was wearing a velvet cloak with an ermine-trimmed hood over her evening dress. As he turned to look at her, she pushed back the hood and he saw the diamond stars, shining in the chestnut mass of her hair. Behind her was the Countess, sniffing audibly, her nose red from the cold.

'I have kept you waiting.' This was not an apology, but a statement of fact.

Bay bowed, he could think of nothing to say. The Empress turned to Countess Festetics. 'Captain Middleton must be cold. Can you ask Nopsca to bring us something warm to drink?' The Countess looked at her for a second and then left the stables.

The Empress looked around her for a moment and then waved a white hand towards the horses in their stalls.

'Do you really think I need new horses, Captain Middleton?'

Bay swallowed. 'I think, Ma'am, that you need ones that are worthy of you.'

'Worthy? But these are the best horses in Austria.'

'Perhaps, but they are still not good enough for you.' Bay moved a step towards her. 'You are the finest horsewoman I have ever seen. You should have the best.'

She moved a little to her left to stroke a horse's muzzle, and the light from one of the stable's sconces fell across her face and made the diamonds in her hair sparkle. She put her hand under the horse's mouth and let the animal nuzzle at her fingers.

'Does it matter so much? These are good horses. Perhaps I should be content with what I have.'

'Perhaps, Ma'am. We should all be content with what we have. But you deserve perfection.'

She shook her head faintly. 'You sound like a courtier, Captain Middleton.'

Bay felt the sting of this.

'But I am not flattering you for the sake of some advancement.

I speak the truth as I perceive it. If you dismiss what I say as flattery, then I am sorry for your sake, not mine.'

She looked up at this, pleased.

'Well, no one from Vienna would speak to me like that. But if you are not a courtier, then why are you here?'

Bay said very quietly, 'I think you know why.'

'Because I am the finest horsewoman you have ever seen?' she said.

'I came because you asked me to.'

She smiled. 'How very obedient. My sister would be surprised.'

Bay looked down at the straw at his feet. The two things he fancied he knew in life were horses and women. If any other woman in the world had asked to meet him in the stables, alone, at night, he would have been in no doubt as to what was expected of him. At some point he would put his hand on the woman's waist and it would begin. Here, though, any such action seemed impossible. The Empress was not like any other woman. There was her position, of course, her husband the Emperor, as well as the *cavalieri serventi*, but it was not just her rank and status that made him uncertain. He had not seen that slackening, the wide-eyed stare that told him when a woman wanted to be touched.

'Tell me something,' the Empress said. 'Why do they call you Bay?'

He looked up. 'It was was the name of a Derby winner that came in at odds of a hundred to one. After the race my friends started calling me Bay. I suppose they think I am a lucky man.'

'And are you?'

'Sometimes. With a good horse and a clear field I feel as lucky as any man in the kingdom.'

'And now? Are you lucky now, Bay Middleton?'

She was looking straight at him and Bay stared at her, searching for permission in her face for what he wanted to do. She was standing just out of arm's length. To kiss her he would need to step forward. But to move towards her now would make his intentions quite clear – if she recoiled he would not be able to pretend that he had meant nothing by his actions. He wanted to act, to end the uncertainty, to bring that cool, pale face next to his, and yet he knew that if he did, he was lost.

'Lucky and unlucky,' he said slowly.

She shook her head. 'That is a courtier's answer. I want to know, what does Bay Middleton make of his current situation?'

As she spoke, the horse behind her gave an enormous snort and flicked its tail out of the box, swiping the Empress's sleeve. She started forward in surprise and Bay put out his hand to steady her. His hand touched the smooth white skin of her shoulder and before he could think about what he was doing, he was putting his hands behind her head and pressing his mouth to hers. For a moment she was rigid and then he felt her hand on the back of his neck. Her kiss was like a sigh. Bay could smell violets, brandy and the faint musk of her hair. Her head felt heavy in his hands. Behind them the horse whinnied.

At last she pulled away and turned her head to the side. Bay could not see the expression on her face. He took one of her hands in his and said in a low, urgent voice, 'I have taken a liberty. You must forgive me. It was a moment's madness. You are so beautiful and so near. I could not resist.'

She smiled and put a finger against his lips.

'There is nothing to say . . .'

Bay saw the creases at the corner of her eyes and leant forward to kiss her again, but as he did so he heard a cough, a masculine clearing of the throat, and looking up, he saw Baron Nopsca, accompanied by the Countess, with two tankards on a salver. The

Empress saw the look on Bay's face and turned around. She did not falter.

'At last,' she said lightly. 'Poor Captain Middleton, you have been freezing to death. What have you brought, Nopsca? It smells wonderful.'

'It is called negus, Ma'am.'

Bay took the tankard that Nopsca offered him and had a sip of the spicy liquid. It was little more than tepid and Bay wondered how long the Baron had been standing there watching them. The man's face was impassive; if he had seen anything, he was too well trained to show it.

The Empress liked her negus. 'The coffee here is terrible but this is quite good. I think I shall have this every night, Nopsca.'

She turned to Bay and extended her hand. 'Thank you so much, Captain Middleton, for all your help. I am looking forward very much to riding one of your horses. I feel sure that we will get on very well together.'

'Undoubtedly, Ma'am.' Bay pressed his lips to her fingers just a little longer than he should.

'Goodnight then. Where are we hunting tomorrow?'

'With the Quorn, Ma'am. The finest hunt in the three counties.'

'Then I have much look to forward to, Captain Bay Middleton.'

Bay found the way she said his full name as intimate as the kiss that preceded it. He looked to see if the others had noticed. Nopsca had already turned away but Festetics was looking straight at him. As he caught her eye, she smiled and gave him an unmistakeable wink before following her mistress out of the stable.

The Empress's Correspondence

BAY SLEPT IN THE CHAISE ON THE WAY BACK TO Melton Hall, as soundly as he did after a successful day's hunting. The chase was over for the day. There would be time for doubts tomorrow, but for now he closed his eyes, revelling in the memory of the Empress's head in his hands, his mouth upon hers.

But while he slept, the woman who was occupying his dreams was wide awake. She was standing by the window of her bedroom looking out over the snowy fields bathed in moonlight. In the corner of the room Countess Festetics was also awake. She was thinking not of love but of her bed. The Countess was exhausted but she could not retire until she was dismissed, and she knew from long experience that when her mistress was excited, she simply forgot to sleep. Festetics yawned as loudly as she dared and the Empress turned around.

'How you startled me, I had forgotten you were there.'

'Forgive me, Majesty, it has been a long day.'

'But a good one. I thought the dinner went off very well.'

Festetics smiled. 'I had a very pleasant companion, certainly. Captain Middleton is so gallant, he could almost be Hungarian.'

'You must see him ride and then you will be convinced that he was born a Magyar.'

The Empress was wearing a lace nightgown and her hair was loose over her shoulders. Her face softened with pleasure when she talked about Middleton. Festetics thought that she had not seen her mistress look so happy for years.

'He is certainly as devoted to you as any of your subjects. At dinner he praised you at every course. I think you have quite dazzled him.'

The Empress wound a great lock of hair around her hand.

'I did not expect this,' she said quietly. Festetics moved closer to her and put her hand on the other woman's.

'No one desires your happiness more than I do, Majesty. But I beg you to be careful. You know that Nopsca and I serve only you, but there are other people here who do not love you as we do.'

The Empress tossed her head and her hair shifted heavily. 'You know, Festy, I have spent all my life being careful. I have been watched and measured and judged since the age of fifteen. Observed as closely as a wild beast in a menagerie. From the moment I married I have been . . . scrutinised.' She leant forward and the hair fell around her face.

'Do you know that on the day of my wedding, my mother-in-law told me that my teeth were so crooked that when I smiled in public I should always keep my mouth closed? I didn't open my mouth for months.' She smiled then, revealing teeth that were a little crowded, the two incisors pushing out a little. They jarred with the symmetry of her features, giving the mournful perfection of her face a wolfish quality.

'But I am not scared now.' She bared her teeth at Festetics and then, seeing the alarm on her lady-in-waiting's face, she said, 'Oh, don't worry, I am not going to bite anyone. But,' her voice became serious, 'if I see a chance of happiness, even a small one, I will take it.'

The Countess bowed her head.

'My only desire is to protect you, Majesty.'

The Empress squeezed her hand. 'Yes, I know. Now go to bed. I don't need you any more tonight.'

The Countess curtsied. 'As Your Majesty wishes.' She was just at the door, thinking of the bed that awaited her at the other end of the corridor, when the Empress called after her, 'I need some writing paper, I only have a couple of sheets left and I want to write to the Emperor tonight.'

Dearest Franzl,

I have just read your letter of the 15th. You complain that I am a wretched correspondent. But you see, liebchen, I have been so busy that I really haven't had the time to write you the long letter that you so richly deserve. There has been so much to attend to here, and, of course, I have been hunting almost every day. Long hard days where we ride for hours without stopping, when I get home I am so tired that Festetics and Nopsca have to carry me to bed. I sleep so well here, I close my eyes and then, oblivion.

Tonight Maria and Ferdinand were here for dinner, with the Spencers – an English milord with a red beard and many acres and his wife, who has a red nose. Maria is happier here than she was in France but she thinks always of what she has lost. I think Ferdinand is more resigned to his lot. Of course they are still short of money; I believe that Maria relies very much on the generosity of Baron Rothschild. She is pressing me to visit the Rothschilds with her. The stables at Waddeson are, apparently, quite magnificent. Sadly my horses are quite inadequate to the hunting here. But I have a very able advisor in Captain Middleton, who has promised to find me some animals better suited to the conditions. You are always urging me to make friends among the English – I think I shall become very popular among the horse-breeding fraternity!

It was so easy to write to Franzl tonight, she felt buoyant with happiness. Sisi could not suppress a frisson of pleasure as she wrote Middleton's name for the first time. There was no need to mention him really, but she could not resist the urge to bring him into her letter, under her husband's nose. Of course Franzl would not notice; it would take a great deal more to make him look up from those stacks of boxes and feel a flicker of jealousy. But she felt that by writing down Middleton's name she had given warning.

You would be so happy to see your Sisi now. Festetics says that she has never seen me looking so well. The nervous exhaustion that kept me to my bed last summer has gone. What a fine idea this hunting has been. Of course, I miss you very much, but it is doing me so much good to be here. I think of you now poring over your boxes, and it pains me to think of you being alone, but I know you with your great generous soul would much rather that I was here and happy than in the spirits that I was in last summer. So please, dear Franzl, do not press me to give you a date for my return. I am happy here, and as you know, I have not had much happiness since the day we met all those years ago in Bad Ischl. Of course it would be the pinnacle of my happiness if you were to join me here, I think that you would enjoy the hunting enormously. Alas, I know that your devotion to duty means that you are chained to your desk, the father to your people but never perhaps the husband to your wife.

Please kiss my darling little Valerie for me. I would so much like to have her here with me, but I don't want to deprive you of your little dumpling. I know how much comfort she brings you, so I will put aside a mother's needs so that you can have her by your side.

I kiss your hands and your forehead.

your very own Sisi

She folded the letter and sealed it. When Festetics came back with the paper, she laughed and said, 'I didn't need the extra paper after all, I managed to get it all onto one sheet. But you can take the letter to be posted. And then I insist that you go to bed. You look quite fatigued. Get your rest, Festy, you mustn't get ill, as I would be simply lost without you.'

The Countess curtsied again and left the room. This time she managed to get all the way to her bedroom, and despite the tensions that the day had brought, she was asleep in minutes.

Holland Park

*I*T WAS ALMOST DARK WHEN THE CARRIAGE DREW UP
outside the house in Holland Park. Charlotte could see the
round turret of the house silhouetted against the dark blue sky,
the lights from the narrow windows shining out. At this time of
day, the house really did look like an enchanted castle, rising out
of the dark forest of the Kensington streets. The whimsical shape
was comforting to Charlotte; she felt as though she had reached
not just her destination, but a place of refuge.

It had been a long journey. The night before she had stayed up
as late as she could in order to catch a moment with Bay on his
return from Easton Neston. Sitting in the drawing room after
dinner while the gentlemen were at their port had been excruciating. Augusta was barely speaking to her and she had evidently
complained about Charlotte to her mother, who had not, as she
normally did, asked Charlotte to come and sit next to her by
the fire. Even her aunt had been distant; Adelaide Lisle did not
approve of Lady Dunwoody, and when Charlotte had told her that
she was going to Holland Park the next day, the widow had dabbed
her eyes and said plaintively that she had always tried to do her
best by Charlotte, even if her best was clearly not good enough.
Charlotte had been upset by this, until she reflected that one reason

for her aunt's distress was that, as Charlotte's companion and chaperone, all her expenses were covered by the trustees of Charlotte's estate. When Charlotte assured her that she would join her in London after the exhibition, Lady Lisle became noticeably more cordial, since Charlotte's fortune would be paying for the establishment in Charles Street. Adelaide Lisle lived in fear of the day when Charlotte no longer had need of her services as a chaperone and she would be forced to return to her drafty little house in the Cathedral Close.

Charlotte had sat in the corner of the great Gothic drawing room, pretending to be engrossed in a copy of *Punch*. She looked up eagerly every time someone came in to the room, hoping against all rational expectation that Bay would come sauntering in and rescue her from social purdah. But by eleven o'clock there was still no sign of him, and when Lady Crewe announced that she was going to bed, Charlotte had no choice but to follow her.

She did not go upstairs at once, though, but lingered as long as she could in the Great Hall, peering closely at one of the pair of Canaletto scenes of the Grand Canal that an earlier Lord Crewe had brought back from the Grand Tour. She stood in front of the the dimly lit scene of boats and churches for a good five minutes until the butler appeared behind her and asked her if she required a candelabra brought up – was there something in particular she wanted to see? Charlotte realised that this was his discreet way of suggesting that the household was winding down for the night and that it was not altogether seemly for a young female guest to be scrutinising pictures in the darkness. She went up the stairs to her bedroom as slowly as she could, pausing almost at each step as if short of breath, but when she got to the gallery at the top and heard the single chime of fifteen minutes past the hour, she knew that she could not linger any more. Much as she wanted to see Bay on his return, the danger of being discovered lying in wait by Augusta or her mother was too great.

But it was vital to see Bay before she left. She had to explain to him why she was going. He could not be left to think that she was running away from him. He must be told that her feelings for him were undiminished.

As an unmarried woman of limited importance Charlotte had been given one of the lesser bedrooms, on the opposite side to the south-facing facade of the house, so she could not even watch at her window for Bay's return. She would have to send him a message asking him to meet her in the morning. Her train was an early one, but there would still be time for them to see each other before breakfast. She kept the message brief.

I am going to London tomorrow by the morning train. I will be staying with my godmother, Lady Dunwoody. I hope we can meet before I leave. Yours, CB.

She wanted to write something warmer at the end – your very own Charlotte, perhaps – but in a house as big as Melton a letter could so easily be intercepted. Although her 'understanding' with Bay was known, they were not formally engaged, and respectable young women did not arrange meetings with young men without a chaperone. Charlotte wondered how she could get the note to Bay. She was reluctant to trust a servant with it, but as his room was in the bachelor wing on the other side of the house, she could not deliver it to his door herself.

She tugged the bell pull and waited for what seemed like an age, until Grace, the pretty maid who had done her hair the night before, arrived, yawning and rubbing her eyes. She had clearly been in bed because her dress was half-unbuttoned and her hair was hanging down her back.

'I am sorry to disturb you at this hour, but I wonder if you could deliver this note to Captain Middleton.'

The maid stared at her.

'You see, I am going to London tomorrow by the early train, and I am most anxious to speak to him before I go.'

Grace shook her head. 'I am sorry, miss, but I am not allowed to go over to the bachelors' wing at night. If I was found out I would lose my position.'

Charlotte said, 'Can you give it to someone else? One of the footmen? It's very important.'

Grace seemed to consider this, and Charlotte realised that she was waiting for something.

'I am happy to give you something for your trouble.' She looked around for her reticule and took out a guinea; it was too much, she knew – she was giving herself away.

The girl's eyes widened when she saw the coin Charlotte was holding out to her.

'I'll see if I can find the hall boy, miss. He will be doing the gentlemen's boots now. It will be no trouble for him to give it to the Captain.'

'Is he reliable, the boy?'

'I would say so, miss.' But her glance flicked over to the reticule.

Charlotte took out another coin, a sixpence, and said, 'Give this to him, it's very important that Captain Middleton receives the letter.' The maid put the note and the coins in her pocket.

'You see, I don't want to leave Melton without saying goodbye to him.'

Charlotte said this as much to herself as to Grace, but the maid smiled and said, 'I understand, miss. He's a fine gentleman. I wouldn't want to leave him either without saying goodbye.'

Still smiling, she left the room, and Charlotte threw herself on the bed, her face burning. She had always been proud of the fact she was the one who observed other people's behaviour, but now she was turning into one of those people that the servants gossiped about. She was glad that she had made the decision to leave.

In the morning Charlotte was up and dressed by seven. The Great Hall was grey in the morning light and smelt of woodsmoke. It was empty apart from a maid in a brown holland apron who was cleaning out the vast fireplace. Charlotte went into the breakfast room, where the footmen were setting out chafing dishes of eggs and bacon, devilled kidneys, and kedgeree. Lord Crewe was sitting at one end of the table reading *The Times*. The rule at Melton was no conversation at breakfast; everyone ate and drank as if wrapped in individual membranes like eggs. Charlotte drank tea and ate a piece of toast while Lord Crewe dismembered a kipper with lip-smacking thoroughness. One by one the other members of the house party drifted in: only married ladies were allowed the luxury of breakfasting in their rooms. Charlotte had sat with her back to the window so she could see who came in, and she could not help but raise her head every time the door opened. But there was no sign of Bay. She heard the stable clock strike eight o'clock. It was time for her to get ready for the train.

She was standing in the hall in her bonnet waiting for the carriage to be brought round when she felt a light touch on her shoulder. She wheeled around in expectation, only to see the florid face and ginger whiskers of Chicken Hartopp.

'I am so glad I caught you, Miss Baird. Fred told me last night that you were leaving this morning. I didn't want you to leave without saying goodbye.' Hartopp took one of Charlotte's small gloved hands in his huge paw and squeezed it. 'Melton won't be the same without you, y'know. Very much hope I may call upon you in town.'

Hartopp gave her a look that she knew was intended to convey just how much he would miss her.

'Well, I am sorry to be leaving Melton, but my godmother says she really cannot manage without me. The Queen is to open the exhibition, you see, and apparently my presence is essential.' She retrieved her hand. 'Perhaps you would do me a favour, Captain Hartopp. Can you say goodbye to Captain Middleton for me? I was hoping to see him this morning, but I am running out of time.'

Hartopp nodded his great head. 'He must have had a very late night with the Empress. My room is next to his and he wasn't back when I retired for the night. Found the poor wretch of a hall boy asleep outside in the passage on account of having to deliver a message to Middleton. Sent him to bed and told him I would give it to him myself.'

Charlotte felt herself blushing. 'I am afraid the message was from me. You see, I didn't have a chance to tell him I was going away.'

'Haven't seen Middleton myself to talk to in days. Now that he is the confidant of royalty he's got no time for us less exalted beings.' Hartopp was smiling but Charlotte noticed the edge in his voice.

'Being the Empress's pilot is a great honour. I dare say it is very demanding.' Charlotte held out the challenge.

Hartopp tugged at his whiskers. Charlotte thought that rarely had she seen someone thinking so visibly. She fancied she could see his brain bulging with the effort. But his ruminations were interrupted by Fred, who came strolling down the stairs.

'So you are really off then, Mitten? Augusta is not happy with you, you know. Thinks you are deserting her in her hour of need.

Wants me to forbid you to go, but I told her it was no use. I know how much you enjoy hobnobbing with Lady Dunwoody and her aesthetic cronies. Almost as much Middleton enjoys rubbing shoulders with royalty, eh Hartopp?'

'He's quite the courtier. He'll be wearing silk stockings and knee breeches next,' said Hartopp. Both men laughed.

Charlotte did not join in. She saw that the carriage had drawn up outside the door and that the maid who was to chaperone her on the journey back to London was already sitting inside.

'I am sure you will find a way of mollifying Augusta, Fred. Goodbye, Captain Hartopp.'

She walked down the steps to the carriage, where a footman was holding the door open for her. As she climbed into the back beside the maid, she looked back at the house to where Fred and Hartopp were standing. As the carriage set off down the drive, she saw Bay come out of the house and stand between them. Hartopp said something to him and all three men laughed.

Charlotte had tried not to think about that laugh on the train to London. She did not want to see the three men standing loose and complicit on the steps. She did not want to calculate exactly when Bay had learnt that she was leaving, nor to speculate what Fred and Hartopp had said to him to stop him running down the steps to say goodbye. Had Hartopp told him about the note? Or had they been laughing about something quite different, some morsel from the night before? Whatever it had been, Charlotte felt the injustice of that laughter, and it burned at the back of her throat all day. As the carriage had drawn up outside Melton Halt, she had found herself reluctant to take the hand of the coachman waiting to hand her down; she had almost said, 'I do believe that I have changed my mind, please take me back to the house,' but somehow the words would not come. She had walked out onto the platform, half expecting another tap on the shoulder, and to turn round and see not the whiskery Hartopp but Bay. But no one had come. She had boarded the train, choosing a window seat, just in case Bay should make a last-minute appearance, but as the guard blew his whistle and the engine started, there was no sign of him. When the train pulled into St Albans thirty minutes later, Charlotte realised that she had a crick in her neck from looking backwards.

Just as the hansom cab stopped and Charlotte got out, the door to Lady Dunwoody's house flew open and a man came out walking backwards down the front steps as he called out his goodbyes to his hostess. In his haste he missed the bottom step and he fell backwards into Charlotte's unsuspecting arms. He was very tall and smelt of limes and tobacco. He was also heavy and Charlotte was almost winded by the weight of him.

'Oh my. What a situation.' The man, who was young and had an accent that Charlotte thought might be American, righted himself and turned to face her. He was wearing a cloak made out of a dark red velvet and a kind of soft hat that Charlotte had before now only seen in cartoons in *Punch*.

'Now that we have embraced, perhaps we don't need a more formal introduction. But if we are to start as we mean to go on, perhaps I should tell you my Christian name, which is Caspar, although you can call me Dearest if that's too formal.'

Charlotte found herself smiling. Caspar had a wide, freckled face and he beamed at her as if meeting her was the most delightful thing that had ever happened to him in his whole life.

'My name is Charlotte Baird, I am Lady Dunwoody's god-daughter.' She held out her hand and Caspar took it.

Daisy Goodwin

'It's an honour to meet you, Charlotte Baird,' Caspar said. 'Lady D talks about you all the time. You are the photographic paragon, her proudest creation. She showed me some of your plates. If we weren't practically engaged I would be quite jealous. But now that we are almost as one flesh, I am prepared to make allowance for your talents; in fact I think we will be quite a formidable team. We will take New York by storm, Charlotte Baird.'

'But would I ever get a chance to speak, Mr . . .?'

'Hewes!' Lady Dunwoody, who was standing in the doorway, broke in. 'Leave Charlotte alone, she will be exhausted after her journey and in no mood to deal with your nonsense.' She came down the steps and kissed Charlotte on the cheek. 'I am so happy to see you, my dear. Mr Hewes is very skilful in the dark room but he is so talkative!'

Caspar Hewes was not abashed. 'Oh Lady D, you may want to work in silence, but I fancy that Charlotte Baird is a conversationalist. For the dark room is not a tomb but a confessional. I think that as we labour side by side pulling out plates hither and thither, there will be chatter, there may even be confidences. Am I right?' He finished his speech by making Charlotte an extravagant bow.

'I think, Mr Hewes, that you will talk and I will listen, but I think that we will both be content.' Charlotte put her hand to her cheek, suddenly aware that there might be a smut from the train on her cheek.

'Only content? Oh Charlotte, Charlotte, what a decorous English word. You may be content but as a vulgar American I will be irradiated with happiness.'

'That's quite enough, Caspar,' Lady Dunwoody interrupted. 'Go back to wherever it is you live and we will see you in the morning. Miss Baird is not used to Americans.'

'I am not Americans, Lady D. You must not prejudice your divine

204

goddaughter against my race. I am Caspar Hewes, late of San Francisco, California and now resident at twenty-one, Tite Street. You could travel the breadth of my fair country and never come across someone quite like me.'

'Well, that is a relief. Now do go home, won't you, or I shall be forced to shut the door in your face.' Lady Dunwoody led Charlotte up the stairs, leaving the maid to navigate the trunks and boxes.

'Very well, I will accept my banishment. Goodnight, Charlotte Baird, I look forward to entering the darkness with you tomorrow.' Caspar drew the claret folds of his cape around him and walked off down the dark street, his voluminous silhouette fading in and out of the yellow gaslights. Charlotte turned to go into the house.

'Such a particular young man,' said Lady Dunwoody. 'Talented, but so unpredictable. I never know what he is going to say or do from one moment to the next. Perhaps that is an American thing.'

'How did you meet him?'

'He came to one of my Thursdays. I noticed him at once, of course – he looks like a heron in my drawing room – and of course, his ridiculous clothes.' Celia Dunwoody was wearing a red kimono. Charlotte had seen pictures of Japanese geishas wearing this garment, but it looked rather different on Lady Dunwoody, who was tall and barrel-shaped. The kimono, which had clearly been made for a shorter person, ended mid-calf, revealing a rather un-Oriental expanse of buttoned boot. But Lady Dunwoody was not someone who was defeated by detail. She continued talking at rather than to Charlotte in her loud voice, which swooped up and down the octaves like a parrot.

'I assumed that he was one of Violet's aesthetes – you know how she likes to go about with a brace of poets – but then he announces that he is Caspar Hewes of San Francisco and that he has travelled five thousand miles because he wants to see a great photographer at work. Since then he has practically lived here, holding things, making suggestions. He is always saying, "Have you thought about doing it this way?" I don't think I have ever met anyone who asked so many questions.'

Lady Dunwoody swept Charlotte through the hall into her drawing room. 'But enough of Mr Hewes. You must take off your bonnet and I shall ring for some tea. I can't tell you how pleased I am to see you. There is so much to be done.'

That night as Charlotte went upstairs to her room in the turret, she wondered why her godmother had not mentioned Caspar Hewes in her letter. From the work she had seen in Lady Dunwoody's studio, he seemed more than capable of assisting her with the exhibition; if anything he was more skilful than she was. And yet Lady Dunwoody had been so very urgent that she should come.

Charlotte looked around the room which was furnished in the very latest aesthetic fashion. The wallpaper was festooned with peacocks and pomegranates and there was a collection of blue and white china arranged on a shelf that ran all the way around the room just above eye level. It was not a large room, but everything in it was pleasing to Charlotte. She liked the intricacy of the wallpaper and the contrast to the simple bamboo furniture. In most houses, Melton for example, Charlotte imagined herself rather like the drawings in *Alice in Wonderland*, always monstrously out of scale with her surroundings. But she was just the right size for this room.

Her trunk and cases with all her photographic equipment and plates stood in the corner of the room. Usually Charlotte unpacked her plates the moment she arrived at a new place – it was her way of asserting her own order in unfamiliar surroundings – but tonight she felt reluctant to open the leather plate case.

There was a tap on the door and Lady Dunwoody came in. She was ready for bed – the kimono had been exchanged for a paisley wrapper, and her hair was hanging down her back in a long grey plait.

'Are you comfortable, Charlotte, dear? Have you got everything you need?'

'Oh yes, Aunt Celia. It's so lovely to be here.' Lady Dunwoody's eyes swivelled round the room and came to rest on the plate case lying on the bed.

'May I have a look?'

Charlotte was minded to refuse but knew it would be useless. Lady Dunwoody always got her way.

The first plate the older woman pulled from its red velvet casing, was the tableau of the maids. She held it up to the light and examined it critically.

'Good composition.'

The next plate was the group portrait of the house party that Charlotte had taken on the steps of Melton. Lady Dunwoody peered at it. 'Goodness me, Edith Crewe has grown stout. This young lady must be your future sister-in-law – with that chin she has to be Crewe's daughter. Fred looks wonderfully smug, but he has no reason to be: the Crewes have terrible tempers. How old is the girl, twenty-four? Edith must be relieved to have got her off her hands.'

Celia Dunwoody leant forward over the plate and peered at it more closely. 'And I wonder which of these fine young gentlemen is the object of your affections, hmm? Is it this young buck with the splendid whiskers? No, I can tell from your face that he is not the one. Which leaves this elegant creature in the back row.

Can this be the famous Captain Middleton?' Aunt Celia's tone was light but she looked closely at Charlotte.

'I don't know about famous, but yes, that is Captain Middleton,' Charlotte said.

'I can hardly make him out here, do you have another picture? I feel sure that you do.'

Charlotte hesitated, there was something in her godmother's tone that made her reluctant to continue, but Lady Dunwoody was waiting. She reached over and pulled out the plate she had taken of Bay and Tipsy in the Melton stables. He was looking straight ahead, his profile aligned perfectly with that of his horse.

'What a handsome animal. And Captain Middleton too is clearly a fine specimen.' She laughed when she saw the expression on Charlotte's face. 'I don't get many cavalry officers at my Thursdays. I had forgotten how splendid they are. Such good subjects for a photograph.'

'Not all cavalry officers are like Captain Middleton, Aunt,' Charlotte said, taking the plate from her and putting it back smartly into its case.

'Oh, I can believe that. I saw him once at the Airlie ball, in the days when I used to go to balls. I believe he was making himself most agreeable to the younger ladies. He danced with Blanche Hozier three times; so fortunate that her husband wasn't there. Hozier is exactly the sort of man who enjoys a scene.' She paused and looked at Charlotte to see how she was reacting.

Charlotte said slowly, 'I understand that Captain Middleton has a past, Aunt Celia. But I have also met gentlemen without pasts, and I prefer Captain Middleton. And he prefers me.'

'Well, of course he does. You would make any man happy, not to mention your delightful fortune.' Lady Dunwoody laid her hand on Charlotte's and leant over so that Charlotte could feel her warm, clove-scented breath.

'I have nothing against Captain Middleton. I can see that he is exactly the sort of man that a girl would fancy herself in love with.' She saw the expression on Charlotte's face. 'He may be your first love, my dear, but that doesn't mean he will be your last.' She patted Charlotte's hand and stood up.

'Now I must leave you to get some rest. You will need all your reserves of strength to handle Mr Hewes in the morning. I guarantee that he will be here before you have finished your breakfast.'

Charlotte lay down in the narrow brass bed. She had unpacked everything, and now there was nothing to be done except sleep. As she closed her eyes she saw Bay standing on the steps at Melton, laughing. She turned over and pressed her face into the mattress, pulling the pillow over her head, trying to stifle her fears. She breathed in the downy sweetness of the feather bed and forced her thoughts elsewhere until at last they rested on the ungainly figure of Caspar Hewes loping along the pavement in a puddle of red velvet. The contrast with Bay's precise silhouette was so absurd that she almost smiled before falling asleep.

Forest Green

ℬAY WAS HAVING TROUBLE WITH HIS BOOTS. HE LIKED them polished to a high shine, so at the beginning of the day, at least, he could see the red gleam of his coat reflected in the surface. Normally he left them outside his room at night, matt with grime and dust, and in the morning they were miraculously restored to shine and sparkle. But this morning his boots were dull. The boot boy had cleaned off the mud but had not spent the twenty minutes or so that was needed to bring the boots up to their full lustre. Bay was irritated. This was the boy he had protected from Fred's drunken malice that night in the smoking room – it piqued him that this chivalrous act had not been repaid by devoted service. He attempted to polish them himself with the wrong side of his chamois leather waistcoat, but he could not coax a gleam from the cracked leather. He could ring the bell and summon the wretched boy, but then he would miss breakfast, and he was anxious to see Charlotte before setting off for the hunt.

He had come back to Melton the night before in a state of elation – the only time in his life he had come close to feeling like this before was when he had won the Viceroy's Steeplechase in Dublin. He had ridden then with skill and daring that he had not known he possessed. He had taken the outside track, gambling that his horse could outpace the others and that he would not be caught in the melee of riders and men that followed every jump. The risk had paid off; he had jumped free and clear and had finished first. Last night he had been boxed in by those Austrian flunkeys and that sour sister, but he had outmanoeuvred them; he had sailed over all the obstacles and had reached his prize. He had risked everything and he had won again.

Bay did not reflect for a moment that his victory might have been engineered. It did not occur to him that the impediments to his progress had been deftly swept away, that he had been positioned so carefully before the last fence that he could only leap in one direction. Nor did he remember in his triumph last night, what had happened after the victory in Dublin. Agnes, the chestnut mare that had carried him so gallantly, had collapsed afterwards. Her heart had failed her. Bay had cried then. Even now his eyes would fill with tears when he remembered the way that Agnes's legs had simply crumpled beneath her. She had been his finest horse and the race had killed her.

Bay was thinking of Agnes this morning. He could not escape the image of the chestnut mare's crumpled body as he rubbed at the parched leather of his boots. He threw away the chamois leather. The boots would have to do. He must find Charlotte before he set out. He needed to see her small, anxious face.

He pulled the boots on; they were three years old at least and the leather had learnt the contours of his feet precisely. He could ride all day in them and never feel their grip. Most men had several pairs, but Bay had never found any that were as perfect as these, so he wore them every day.

He set off down the long narrow corridor of the bachelors' wing with its narrow oilcloth covering. As he reached the main part of the house, the floor covering grew progressively softer and more luxurious. By the time he reached the main staircase he was walking on fine red broadloom Wilton woven with motifs of gryphons and fleur-de-lis in the best Gothic style.

Bay put his head around the breakfast-room door, looking for Charlotte, but he could only see Augusta and her father eating in the kipper-scented silence. Walking back across the Great Hall he saw that the huge, studded oak door was open onto the porte cochère. He looked out of the window and saw Fred and Chicken standing on the steps. As he joined them outside, he saw a carriage setting off smartly down the drive.

Fred saw him first, and greeted him with a mock obeisance. 'It is Sir Lancelot himself. Surprised to see you here, Middleton. Don't you have royal duties to attend to?'

'If you mean eating cold soup at the end of the table with only an old Hungarian governess with a beard to talk to and those Austrian popinjays sneering across their moustaches at me, then I am quite prepared to join the Republic.' Bay felt a moment's disloyalty to the charming Countess Festetics, but he had to diffuse the envy that he could see on Fred's face.

'What a disappointment. We thought that you would come back with the Order of the Golden Fleece at the very least.'

Bay shrugged. 'The only royal decoration I have is this catch on my sleeve where the Empress's spur caught me when I was helping her onto her horse. Not the highest order of chivalry exactly.' He laughed and Fred and Chicken joined in. This was the laugh that Charlotte had seen as she looked back out of the carriage window and saw the three men together on the steps.

Encouraged by the laughter, Bay went further. 'Do you remember the Queen of Naples, Chicken? The one who asked me to be her pilot at the Spencer ball? And I turned her down. Well, she was there last night and not at all happy to see Bay Middleton. Of course, she is the Empress's sister. So I suspect my days as the imperial pilot are numbered.'

Fred looked rather pleased by this admission and Chicken clapped Bay on the back. 'Never mind, old man, we plebs will stand by you. Never thought you were cut out be a courtier.'

'No indeed. Don't have the knees for it, or the stomach.' Bay turned to Fred. 'I was hoping to speak to your sister. Have you seen her this morning?'

Fred and Chicken looked at each other, and Bay saw something pass between them that he did not understand.

'You've just missed her,' Hartopp said. 'We were seeing her off. Shame you didn't wake up a bit earlier. But I suppose you must be exhausted after your royal visit.'

Bay saw the look of pleasure on their faces. They were enjoying his ignorance. Fred would welcome any setback to Bay becoming his brother-in-law and Chicken Hartopp resented Bay's success with Charlotte. He was torn between his desire to know where Charlotte had gone and why, and his reluctance to admit that she had left without letting him know. He felt his hands grow clammy despite the chill of the morning. Could Charlotte have somehow found out about the scene in the stable? But that was impossible. Besides, in this bright morning air he himself was having difficulty in believing in the events of last night.

He tried to keep the smile on his face, but without success.

'Oh dear, Bay, it looks like you have fallen out with all your lady friends,' said Chicken, grinning broadly. 'You must be losing your touch. Stick to horses, that's my advice. You know where you are with a horse.'

'Well, you should know, Chicken old boy.'

Bay could not resist the retort, but regretted it when he saw the flush creep up behind Hartopp's dundrearies.

The three men stood in silence for a moment until Fred spoke. 'Well, I am going down to the stables. Morning prayers are just about to start and I don't want to be caught by Lady Crewe. Yesterday she made me read the collect for the day, and then told me off for going too fast.' He set off down the steps, followed by Hartopp. Bay could see that the back of Hartopp's neck was dark red.

Bay hesitated for a moment. He needed to go to the stables too, but he did not want to encounter Fred and Hartopp again so soon. He went back into the house, thinking he might find a cigar in the smoking room, but he was intercepted by Augusta so neatly that she might have been waiting for him.

'Did you have a pleasant evening, Captain Middleton? We missed you here, of course, but I am quite sure you didn't miss us.'

Bay bowed stiffly. 'It was a big party, certainly.'

'Oh come, you can do better than that. I think if you desert your friends for the charms of royalty, the least you can do is to come back prepared to recount every last detail.'

'Then I am bound to disappoint you, Lady Augusta. If you wanted me to describe the Empress's horses I could do a creditable job, but when it comes to dresses and jewels you are going to find me sadly deficient.'

'But I thought you had such an eye for the ladies, Captain Middleton. What did the Empress look like in her evening clothes? Was she very splendid? She is a grandmother, after all, so she probably looks better by candlelight.'

'I think all women look better by candlelight, don't you?' Bay said.

But Augusta was not to be deflected. 'Did you see her pet monkey? My maid told me that all the servants at Easton Neston are giving in their notice because the animal is allowed to go round biting people.'

'I saw royalty, but no monkeys, I'm afraid.'

'Well, I think you are very dull. You must have seen something worth repeating.'

'Could you possibly entertain the notion that I might well have seen something worth repeating, as you put it, but that I might prefer to be dull than to be indiscreet?'

Augusta narrowed her pale blue eyes in disbelief. 'Goodness me, how very pompous you are, Captain Middleton. I had no idea you were so attached to the Empress.'

'Perhaps I have a weakness for grandmothers,' Bay said. He took out his pocket watch. 'Is that the time already? Will you excuse me? I don't want to keep the Empress waiting.'

'No, that would never do. How lucky she is to have such a devoted and loyal servant.'

Bay paused. He should, of course, have asked Augusta where Charlotte had gone, but he knew that she would enjoy the fact that Charlotte had left without telling him even more than Fred and Hartopp had done. But it would be foolish to antagonise her completely.

'Perhaps it wouldn't be betraying a confidence to say that the Empress was wearing a green dress and she had some diamond ornaments in her hair. Her sister, the Queen of Naples, was in red.'

'What kind of green?' Augusta said.

'Oh, very dark, the colour of a Scotch pine. The combination of the diamond stars against the dark brown hair and the green put me in mind of a forest at night.'

'A forest at night? Captain Middleton, you are quite the poet. I now have a very vivid picture of your dinner. You must be sure to tell Charlotte. It is the sort of detail we young ladies relish.'

Middleton realised that he had said too much. But he could at least find out where Charlotte had gone.

'I was hoping to see Miss Baird this morning, but I was too late. Her carriage was leaving, just as I arrived.'

'She didn't wait to say goodbye? I am surprised.' Augusta opened her eyes wide. 'I thought you were such good friends. Do you mean she went off without a word?'

Bay said nothing and Augusta continued, her eyes shining, 'I can understand her not wanting to say goodbye to me. She knows I am excessively annoyed with her for deserting me on the eve of my wedding. But you? You must have blotted your copybook, Captain Middleton.' She put a finger to her forehead. 'I wonder what you could have done to upset her? Surely she can't resent your having dinner with the Empress in her forest green dress? What a shame you were back so late last night, as I remember that Charlotte was quite the last lady to retire. The butler found her wandering the Great Hall at midnight pretending to look at the Canalettos.'

Bay said, as evenly as he could, 'Do you know where she has gone? I should like to write to her.'

'I wonder if I should tell you though, Captain Middleton?' Augusta put her head on one side. 'As the lady has left without saying goodbye, it may be that she doesn't want any further communication from you.'

Bay found himself clenching his fists and put them behind his back.

'I find that hard to believe but I won't ask you to betray a confidence. Good morning, Lady Augusta.'

He turned away from her and made his way towards the stables, kicking the paving stones as he walked. He was so full of rage that he took no account of the damage he was inflicting on his favourite boots. He knew that Augusta had been toying with him and that with some cajoling he would have found out where Charlotte had gone, but he could not bear to give her the satisfaction. He was angry with Fred and Hartopp, angry with Augusta and even with Charlotte. Why had she gone away without letting him know? There was probably an innocent enough explanation but still he was angry. He had been quite ready to run away with her, and she had persuaded him that they must wait, and that he should cultivate the Empress to boot. He had merely been doing what she had asked him. It would almost be fair to say that the scene in the stables had been Charlotte's doing.

He would not have been there alone with the Empress if Charlotte had agreed to elope with him. And now, just when he needed to see her, she had disappeared.

Bay had worked himself up quite successfully by the time he reached the stables. Tipsy was waiting for him all tacked up. But as he patted his horse's nose and rubbed her flank in greeting, he remembered the photograph that Charlotte had taken of the two of them in this very spot, and his indignation faltered. He swung up himself up into the saddle and urged Tipsy into a gallop. It made no sense to tire the horse so early in the day, but he needed to shake himself out of his mood.

It had not been a successful morning. Now he had to meet the Empress and his boots were dull.

Part Two

The Quorn

*I*T WAS THE FIRST FINE DAY OF THE HUNTING SEASON. The snow had melted at last. The sky was blue and clear and there was no wind. The members of the Quorn expected no less. They would hunt in any conditions, of course, but it was only fitting that for the biggest meet of the year the weather should be perfect. The God they worshipped in their parish churches on Sunday was undoubtedly a Quorn man, who understood the importance of a good clear run. The railway companies, too, understood the importance of the day ahead and had laid on special trains from London, packed with men and the odd woman who looked forward to a day out with the Quorn all year. The thought of riding to hounds across the trim fields of Leicestershire, their hearts pounding, their muscles straining to be in at the kill, was the talisman they touched in dreary barristers' chambers, or the innermost confines of the Foreign Office, or the committee organising the refreshments for the Lady Mackinnon's *tableaux vivants* in aid of Bulgarian orphans. This already splendid sporting occasion was made all the more piquant by the presence of royalty. The Prince of Wales was hunting with the Quorn this season, and now the papers were full of the equestrian exploits of the Austrian Empress. The idea of a galloping queen was peculiar and splendid to the minds of the passengers on the special trains, so far removed from the image of their own queen, a tiny figure shrouded in black who had kept to the same mournful pace since her husband's death fifteen years earlier. If some of the travellers felt the peculiarity of the wife of one of the most powerful men in Europe laying aside her duties as a wife and sovereign to chase foxes in a foreign country, they did not give the thought much room – this was the Quorn, after all.

Perhaps the only person on the hunting train that morning who did not understand that the claims of the Quorn were paramount, was the Austrian Ambassador, who received regular press reports from Vienna where journalists were less than sympathetic to an absent empress who preferred riding to hounds in a Protestant country than doing her imperial duty. But while he read these reports and in his heart agreed with them, he knew better than to mention his misgivings to the Empress. Her sense of the obligations of her position was, he had discovered, idiosyncratic. She had been in the country for some weeks now and had not yet paid a call on Queen Victoria. When he had suggested, on her arrival in London, that this visit might be politic, she had thrown nuts to that vile little monkey of hers and said that she thought that Queen Victoria did not like her and would be relieved not to have to entertain her. He had tried writing to the Emperor to impress upon him how important it was for the Empress to observe the niceties of royal etiquette, pointing out that there had been several hints dropped by Foreign Office ministers which made it clear that Victoria was 'surprised' that the Empress had not yet called on her. But the Emperor had reproached him for his insensitivity, writing that 'The Empress is travelling incognito to recover her health and strength; her well-being is as you know infinitely precious to me, and I am determined that she must be left in peace until such time that she is sufficiently restored to take up her duties again. I do not wish to sacrifice the well-being of my wife on the altar of diplomacy.' The Ambassador could not help reflecting that a woman who rode to hounds nearly every day was hardly the invalid, broken in mind and body, that the Emperor referred to in his letter.

The Ambassador was enjoying his posting to London – the sport was excellent and he was enjoying a special friendship with Lady Hertford. He did not at all want to be summoned back to Vienna in disgrace, and yet he feared that was exactly what would happen if reports appeared in the British press suggesting that the Austrian Empress was deliberately avoiding Queen Victoria. The Ambassador had been sufficiently perturbed by a conversation he had had with the editor of the *Morning Post* at one of Lady Hertford's drawing rooms to make this journey up to Leicestershire today. The editor had seemed remarkably well informed about the Empress's movements, which suggested that he had been briefed by someone either from the Foreign Office or, worse still, from the court itself. Either way it was a warning – the Queen was not happy and she was letting her displeasure be known. The Ambassador was on the train, not for the sport – although he appreciated the charms of the Quorn – but to persuade his empress to do her royal duty. He was not at all confident of success.

In the crowd gathered outside Quorndon Hall, the glorified kennel that gave its name to the hunt, the Empress was unmistakeable. She sat ramrod straight on her chestnut hunter, with the rest of the hunt arranged in a respectful semicircle around her. She was talking to another rider, who the Ambassador suspected from his girth and the relaxed set of the shoulders, could only be the Prince of Wales. The Ambassador sighed. His mission had just become considerably harder. If the Empress was to ride out with the Prince of Wales today then she would undoubtedly think that she had fulfilled her obligations to the British royal family. But as the Ambassador knew, an audience, or even a day's hunting, with the son was no substitute for a formal audience with the mother. Indeed, if, or rather when, the Queen heard of the day's events, she would fancy herself doubly wronged. Although Victoria was still a semi-recluse, she was not entirely grateful for her son's efforts to keep the monarchy before the public and was sensitive to the idea that his popularity might actually eclipse hers. If the Empress of Austria was seen to be hunting with the Prince of Wales before calling on the Sovereign, then what had been merely a worrying situation would turn into a full-blown diplomatic incident. He must try and talk to the Empress before the hunt set off. The Ambassador knew that as soon as the Empress was in the field he had no chance of catching her.

The Prince of Wales was in the middle of a story. The Ambassador took advantage of the laughter that always followed a royal anecdote, to put himself in the Empress's eyeline. She saw him, frowned and pulled on the reins of her horse as if to move off, but before she could get away the Prince of Wales called out to him, 'Good day to you, Karolyi, so you have come to try the delights of the Quorn as well? Her Majesty is quite the toast of the Shires.'

Karolyi bowed as graciously as he could on horseback. 'I am sorry to say that I cannot hope to represent my country in the field as nobly as the Empress.'

The Empress gave him a brief nod, acknowledging that this was no more than the truth. She turned to the Prince.

'It is such a pity that I cannot persuade the Emperor to join me. He is a magnificent horseman and I know he would enjoy the hunting here as much as I do, but he claims that the country cannot spare him.'

'We must be thankful that he can spare you, to show us how the

Austrians ride.' The Prince stroked his moustache with one gloved hand, as if to show his appreciation of the Emperor's gesture.

'Well, I hope one day you will come to Gödöllő, our estate outside Budapest. That is where I like to ride when I am at home. We don't have the ditches and fences you have here, but you can gallop for miles without stopping.'

'What a prospect. I should like nothing better. My country might be able to spare me for an unchecked gallop across the Hungarian plains, I think.' The Prince of Wales shrugged and then, gathering himself, he said, 'But now, my dear Empress, I must pay my respects to the Master or I suspect we will never set off today.'

Seeing his opportunity, Karolyi brought his horse as close to the Empress as he dared.

'I am so pleased to see Your Majesty looking so well. It seems that the English air agrees with you.'

Although Karolyi's words were automatic, the compliments of a professional courtier, they were for once completely truthful. The Empress did look well. There were pink tones in her pale cheeks and the whites of her eyes were clear. Karolyi was used to seeing her in Vienna where her usual expression was one of simmering boredom, but here she looked as if there was nowhere else she would rather be.

'Yes, I have to say that I am happy here.' As if to prove her point she smiled, and Karolyi, who had never seen her smile before, began to wish that he had not come on this self-appointed errand. But he could see that the hounds were being brought out of the kennels and the huntsmen were beginning to assemble. He would have to say his piece.

'Majesty, I wondered if you had given some thought as to when you might visit the Queen. I know that you are here unofficially, but I fear that she will take offence if you do not call on her soon. Especially now that you have met the Prince of Wales. It would be very unfortunate if the British press was to make some comment. The newspapers here can be quite outspoken.'

Karolyi braced himself for the reproof, but to his surprise the Empress's smile did not waver. She looked not at him but over his shoulder, as if she were looking for someone.

'Poor Karolyi, you worry too much. I promise I shall go and see the Queen. In fact I shall go on Sunday, as there is no hunting then. Please make the arrangements. You are quite right, I cannot put it off any longer.'

The Ambassador almost fell off his horse in surprise. The last thing he had expected to encounter was smiling acquiescence. Clearly the English air agreed with Her Majesty very much indeed.

'Of course, the Queen does not normally receive visitors on a Sunday but I am sure she will make an exception to see you, Majesty.'

But the Empress was not listening. She had seen someone over his shoulder who clearly interested her more. Karolyi turned to see a young man approaching whose hair and moustache were about the same shade as the Ambassador's bay gelding. The Empress raised a hand in greeting.

'Bay Middleton, I was beginning to think you were not coming.' She turned to Karolyi. 'Count Karolyi, may I present Captain Middleton, my pilot. But for him I would probably be lying at the bottom of some Leicestershire ditch.'

Middleton bowed to the Ambassador. 'Is this your first time with the Quorn, Count? Best hunting in this part of the country, but don't try to keep up with the Empress. She rides like a woman possessed.'

Karolyi glanced at the Empress. Middleton's remark struck him as over-familiar. In Vienna he could not imagine anyone talking about the royal family in such a way in their presence. But in England, evidently, things were done differently. This man was clearly not a groom and yet he had no title. Karolyi noted the fact that the Empress had called the man by his curious first name. That too would never have happened in Vienna. He cast about in his memory for what he knew about Captain Middleton. It was a name that had certainly been gossiped about when he had first arrived in London.

'I have had the pleasure of seeing the Empress at the Spanish riding school in Vienna. No Austrian would ever dream of keeping up with her.'

'Well, it is lucky for me, then, that I have an English pilot,' said the Empress and again she smiled.

Karolyi saw that the smile was intended for Middleton and his courtier's sensibilities told him that his presence was no longer required. But he decided to linger. He was interested in the frisson he had detected between the Empress and this young man.

'Very fortunate indeed. I am sure that we Austrians are all grateful to Captain Middleton for keeping our finest ornament safe from harm.'

Middleton smiled. 'I am doing my best, but the Empress is a true sportswoman. She puts the thrill of the chase before her own safety.'

There was a sudden clamour from the hounds, who had picked up the scent. The Empress pulled at her horse's reins.

'We must be off.' She nodded to Karolyi, a clear dismissal.

The Ambassador again attempted a bow. 'Your Majesty can leave all the arrangements with the Queen to me.' The Empress flinched; she had clearly forgotten already her promise, but the bugles were sounding now and she was anxious to be gone.

'Thank you, Karolyi, on Sunday, yes?' Then she and Middleton were off, picking up speed as they joined the gaudy pack of riders and hounds that swarmed across the hillside opposite. He watched as the two figures, the Empress in dark blue, Bay in red, began to cleave their way through the mass of riders. As the hunt approached a hedge, the hounds began to fight their way across it – finding a hole in it and pouring through in a quivering, excited mass. The riders started to move down the field, looking for an easier place to cross, but the Empress and Middleton did not go with them. Karolyi gasped as he saw the Empress, without even breaking her horse's stride, go straight at the hedge. For a moment he thought that she had misjudged it and he had a sudden vision of standing in the Emperor's study in the Hofburg trying to describe to him the precise moment at which his wife had fallen from her horse and broken her neck; but then Middleton was beside her, urging her horse on with his own, and miraculously both horses cleared the hedge at the same time. The Ambassador held his breath as they disappeared from view but then he looked up and he could see them again, the blue and red figures distant specks now, charging up the hill after the hounds.

Karolyi dug his heels into his horse's sides and prepared to join the gaggle of latecomers, mostly 'Cits' from London who had decided to take full advantage of the hunt breakfast. There were some ladies too, who were sitting in carriages ranged around the grounds following the progress of the hunt through their opera glasses. Karolyi was just about to join the riders when he saw that one of the ladies was Countess Festetics, who was his cousin on his mother's side and an old dancing partner. He trotted over to her, but she was so engrossed in following the hunt through her binoculars that she did not notice him. Finally he called out to her in Hungarian and she turned immediately.

'Ah Bela, how lovely to see you. Have you come for the hunting?'

Karolyi jumped down from his horse and went to kiss the Countess, twice on both cheeks as was the Hungarian custom.

'I came to talk to the Empress. It seemed to be the only way to see her. Your vague little notes never actually contained an invitation.'

Festy shook her head. 'I know, Bela, and I am sorry. But you know how she is when she doesn't want to do something. She just shakes her head and says, put him off. I have tried to make her listen but she only hears me when she wants to.'

'Poor Festy, Her Majesty is very lucky to have you at her side.'

'No, Bela, I feel privileged to serve her in whatever way I can.' The little countess gave him a fierce look. 'I know that sometimes to other people she can seem . . . difficult. But I know her kindness and her nobility of spirit.'

She tilted her chin at him as if daring him to defy her.

Karolyi laughed.

'As I said before, Cousin, she is very lucky to have you at her side. But today she has not been difficult at all. I came to ask when she would visit the English Queen, and she said very sweetly that she would go on Sunday and please could I arrange it. I was surprised, to find her so amenable.'

Looking closely at the Countess's face to gauge her reaction he continued, 'Her visit to England seems to be agreeing with her. In fact I have not seen her look so well and in such fine spirits for a long time. Not since the coronation in Budapest, I think. I wonder what it is about England that suits her so well?'

The Countess shook her head. 'Bela, Bela, you know me better than that. I will not gossip about the Empress to you or anyone else. You should rejoice as I do that she is in such good spirits.'

Karolyi took her reproof with a smile. 'Indeed I do. But I have to say that I worry about the hunting. She is perhaps too fearless. I thought just now that she must break her neck at that first hedge.'

'Oh, I know. Every time she goes out I am sick with worry. Today

I had to come and see for myself; somehow that is better than imagining all kinds of accidents at home.' She sighed. 'Sometimes I think that she is really trying to kill herself.'

Karolyi shrugged. 'Yet she has everything to live for. Her husband adores her and lets her do anything she wants. She is still beautiful; in fact I would say she is as lovely now as she has ever been, lovelier even.'

The Countess sighed again. 'It's true. She is still beautiful, but she can't see it. All she sees when she looks in the mirror are the lines and the wrinkles.' She picked up her field glasses and scanned the horizon, but by now the Empress and her escort had vanished from view. She turned back to the Count.

'It is such a waste. She has all the gifts – she speaks six languages fluently, she writes poetry. I sometimes think her mind is like a museum full of great treasures, unseen and unused. If only she had some great cause, some purpose that would occupy her completely – she could do great things.'

'She is an empress, there is no greater position. And she has every opportunity to do good at home, but instead she chooses to come to England and hunt,' Karolyi said.

'I don't mean opening hospitals and giving alms to orphans, Bela, I mean a cause – something for her to believe in. Look how much she did for Hungary. Do you think that Franz Joseph would ever have been crowned King in Budapest without her? I will always be grateful to her for that. But now that time has passed and she has no cause to fight for.'

Karolyi smiled. 'She has the Quorn . . .'

'Exactly. But I wish there was something else.' There was a pause.

'And how are the Empress's *cavalieri serventi*, Castor and Pollux?' Karolyi asked. 'I don't think I have seen them this morning.'

'They are . . . they are indisposed. The Empress made it clear that she wanted to hunt alone.'

'Apart from the gallant Captain Middleton, of course.'

'Apart from him.' The Countess pressed her lips together.

'Her Majesty was kind enough to present him to me. I am glad that she has such an –' Karolyi paused for a moment, ostentatiously looking for the right word, 'such an *able* escort. Captain Middleton is famous for his horsemanship, I believe.'

'He was recommended to Her Majesty by the English Lord with the red hair, Spencer. The Queen of Naples was furious as she wanted him for herself and he refused her.'

'So he is ambitious, then? Why ride with a mere queen, when there is an empress on offer?'

'Ambitious? No, I don't think so. He is not a courtier and he is definitely not a spy. You don't need to worry on that score, Bela.'

'But you have another concern? Captain Middleton has a reputation for more than horsemanship, I hear. He is very popular among the ladies, but not so much with their husbands.' Karolyi had remembered where he had heard Middleton's name before. There had been some tendresse with a married woman, who had left in the middle of the season to join her husband in the country. The lady – what was her name? Blanche, or something like that – had not been seen in town for a while; there had been an addition to the family, which fortunately had been a daughter. The provenance of daughters could stand a little vagueness.

'He is a handsome young man in uniform, why would any husband like him?' said the Countess with a shrug.

Karolyi knew better than to press the Countess any further. She was not a woman who could be flattered into indiscretion. An Austrian lady-in-waiting would have told him everything about the Empress and Captain Middleton, and more, but Countess Festetics was

Hungarian and she felt that it was almost her patriotic duty to resist the swirling gossip and jockeying for position that characterised the Viennese court.

There was a clamour from behind them and the hounds began to pour over the brow of the hill on the other side of the Manor. The Countess picked up her glasses. Realising that the conversation was over, the Ambassador decided that he might as well have his day out with the Quorn and he took up his horse's reins.

'Goodbye, Cousin, I am glad to have seen you. It is so nice to speak Hungarian again. I feel quite rusty.'

'I am lucky, the Empress always talks to me in Magyar, she is very proud of her fluency.'

'And how fortunate that she speaks such good English as well. I assume Captain Middleton does not speak Hungarian, or even German?'

The Countess laughed. 'Enough, Bela, enough. Go away and chase your fox. The exercise will do you good.'

The Ambassador accepted his dismissal. Even though the Countess had told him nothing, as a true diplomat he had gleaned all he needed to know.

Falling

THERE IS A MOMENT TOWARDS THE END OF A DAY'S hunting when the light begins to fail and even the most sure-footed horse begins to stumble; it is a time when hedges loom ominously in the winter light and muscles are cramped from long hours spent in the saddle. After a couple of falls at the end of the last season, Bay had learnt to recognise that sudden waning of his strength, the point at which his mind no longer knew the limits of his body. It was the first sign that, at thirty, he was no longer as physically indomitable as he had been at twenty-one. He was a more skilful rider than he had been then, so his form had been unaffected but he knew the decline had begun. For a while Bay had mourned the notion that life would only get better. But today there were no regrets. The sun had shone and the fox had eluded them for three hours, making it one of the best runs of Bay's hunting career. He found himself hoping that this particular animal might evade the hounds in the end; it deserved some reward for having given them such glorious sport.

The hounds were careering across a ploughed field towards a small copse. He looked across at the Empress, who was riding alongside him; her habit was splashed with mud and a loop of hair had come unpinned and was flapping against her back like a noose.

But her back was as straight as ever and she sat so lightly on her horse that she seemed, to Bay, to hover in the saddle. They had barely spoken that day, the pace had been so fast, but every time he caught her eye Bay felt the thrill of the connection between them. All the anxieties of the morning had been pummelled away by the relentless pursuit of the fox. Now he felt nothing but an intense joy in the moment, hurtling across the Leicestershire earth with the Empress at his side.

They reached the copse. The question was whether to wait to see if the hounds ran the fox to ground, or to skirt the edge of the wood to see if the animals came out the other side. Most of the riders, including the Prince of Wales, were pulling their horses up, grateful for a moment's respite. Bay made to do the same, but the Empress raised her riding crop and urged her horse to carry on. Bay touched Tipsy's flanks with his heels and followed her.

The ground began to rise and Bay's horse faltered at the steepness of the gradient. When he had brought her up to speed and looked up, the Empress had disappeared over the brow of the hill. Bay raised his crop and brought it down on Tipsy's flank. The horse crested the ridge but coming down the steep escarpment on the other side, she stumbled, and Bay, who was looking ahead for the Empress, suddenly saw the earth rising towards him.

In a stupor he heard German and felt a drop of rain falling on his face. A red wave of pain scalded him awake; he opened his eyes and saw the Empress's face very close to his own. He wanted to smile but the pain was too intense. He heard himself groaning.

'Bay? Bay Middleton, can you hear me?'

Bay tried to nod.

The Empress pulled off her glove and put her hand in his. 'If you can hear me, squeeze my hand.' Bay felt the cold, rough fingers, but as he tried to press her hand in return he felt an excruciating jolt of pain in his shoulder and a horrible looseness. The bile rose in his throat. He knew that he must have dislocated his shoulder; it had happened to him once before when he had fallen steeplechasing. Chicken Hartopp had been there and had known what to do. He had given him his crop to bite on while rotating the joint back into place. Afterwards he had teased Bay for the bite marks that had almost severed the pigskin.

Bay tried to speak. But no words came out.

'Are you injured? Can you move your limbs?' The Empress's voice was cracking with tension. She stared intently into his eyes. He tried again to speak, but all he could manage was a moan of pain. The Empress reached into the pocket of her habit and brought out a silver flask. She poured a little brandy between his lips. The alcohol hit the back of his throat and made him cough, but it cleared away the fog in his head and he was able to say, 'My shoulder, dislocated . . . Help me put it back.'

The Empress nodded, 'Tell me what to do.'

'More brandy . . .' She held the flask to his mouth and poured out a few drops, but seeing the expression on his face, she tilted it so the brandy cascaded down his throat. Bay waited for a moment while the alcohol numbed the acute edge of his pain and then he forced himself to speak again.

'Can you feel the joint?'

The Empress put her hand gingerly on his shoulder.

'Yes, I can feel something here that is not right.'

'Can you turn my arm and push it back in at the same time?'

The Empress bit her lip. 'I don't want to hurt you. Perhaps we should wait for help.'

Bay felt himself wobble with nausea. 'Please, just do it now. I can't bear this.'

He felt her grasp his hand and he said, 'Now turn it outwards and push down.'

He heard his own scream as the Empress rotated his arm and pressed the shoulder socket into place. Then suddenly it was all over. The agony had gone, his shoulder, though sore, was no longer the all-consuming centre of his existence. He was still holding the Empress's hand; he tried to raise it to his lips, but the effort was too much.

'Thank you,' he said. She turned her head away. He saw that she was rubbing the hand that he had been holding. He thought of what he had done to Chicken's riding crop.

'I'm sorry, did I hurt your hand? At least you didn't have to shoot me.' He attempted to smile.

She looked at him then, her face white and tear-stained, but she managed to smile back.

'It was I who hurt *you*. You see, I am not so ruthless. If you were a horse, I think I could not shoot you even if you broke your leg.'

'I am grateful for that. I would be even more grateful if I could have some more brandy.'

She gave him some more, and then, without wiping the flask, she took a swig herself.

'I am sorry, you need this more than I do, but you see, when I saw you fall, I thought you must be dead.'

Bay tried to laugh.

'Don't you know that it's very bad form to die at a Quorn meet? I would never hunt again. Have you seen the Master? I am much more scared of him than I am of dying.'

'I think that you are not enough scared of dying. I think perhaps I am the same way. But I was scared when I thought *you* were dead.'

'Then we must be reckless together, or not at all,' said Bay.

'I warn you that I am not so good at being careful.'

She looked at him directly then, and Bay saw that there were shiny trails on her cheeks where the tears had dried.

'Nor me.'

He wanted to touch her, but his arms would not move. They stayed immobile for a moment, Bay lying on the muddy ground, the Empress kneeling beside him, until a gust of noise from the hunt bellowed out over the hill.

The Empress cocked her head in the direction of the sound. 'Should I go and fetch help?'

'I think I will be all right, if you can help me. But I will need some kind of sling.'

'A sling? What is that?'

'Something to hold my arm up.'

Sisi stood up, and picking up the long tail end of her riding habit, she tore it along the seam. As she started to rip it against the grain to make a triangle, Bay saw that she was wearing the chamois leather britches he had glimpsed before. They fitted as tightly as a jockey's, revealing every contour of her slim thighs and long calves. It was both shocking and thrilling to see a woman's legs so accurately represented. Through his pain he felt a frisson of desire.

Now she was kneeling beside him again.

'Can you sit up?'

Bay tried to raise himself with his good arm but the effort was too much for him.

'Will you let me help you?' Her voice was hesitant.

Bay tried to smile. 'I would be very grateful for your help, Ma'am.'

She very carefully slid one hand underneath his bad shoulder, leant over and clasped her arms around him. Her upper body was pressed against his; he could feel her breath on his face.

'Are you ready?' she said. 'I hope I am strong enough .'

He heard her intake of breath, and then a jolt of pain as she pulled him upwards. Now they were looking directly into each other's eyes, their noses almost touching. He only had to lean forward a fraction to kiss her. He tried to read the expression in her dark eyes, but in that hesitation the moment was lost. She drew away from him and started to fiddle with the piece of material she had ripped from her habit.

'If I tie it like this, does it feel right?' She drew the ends of the material into a rough knot behind his neck.

'Perhaps a little tighter.' The sling was already supporting Bay's arm but he liked the cold touch of her fingers against the back of his neck.

'Like this?'

'Exactly.' Bay leant back slightly and felt the swell of her bosom behind his head. He thought how pleasant it would be to remain exactly as he was now. But the light was already beginning to fade and the occasional noises that were carried through the gloom were a reminder that the Quorn could not be far away.

Putting his good hand out to support himself, he scrambled to his feet. He swayed a little as he stood upright. Sisi put out her arm to support him. He gave a rueful laugh.

'As your pilot, Ma'am, I would have to conclude that I am a failure. I am meant to be protecting you from harm.'

'Oh, I have all the protection I want. It is not often that I get the chance to be useful.'

Their horses were grazing together a little further down the bank. Bay whistled through his teeth to Tipsy, who came over and nuzzled his hand. Bay realised his next challenge.

'Now my uselessness is complete. I think I can mount Tipsy with one arm, but I won't be able to help you.'

Sisi laughed.

'Do you think that I am the kind of rider who can't mount her own horse unaided?' She made a clucking noise through her teeth at her horse, which to Bay's amazement bent its forelegs and knelt in front of the Empress. She swung herself lightly onto the saddle and the horse rose to its feet.

'In another life, I could have had a career in the circus.'

Bay considered her. Since she had torn her habit in half to fashion his sling, her legs in their suede britches were quite visible.

'You certainly have the legs for it, Ma'am.'

Sisi looked down. 'It is a mercy it is getting dark. Otherwise we might cause quite a scandal.'

Bay shivered. The impossibility of their current situation struck him. To be seen riding about the countryside with a half-dressed empress was compromising to both of them. If he was to leave her, he would be equally at fault for abandoning a woman in a strange country. But perhaps that might be the wiser course.

'I should really leave you. Easton Neston is only half a mile away. I don't think I should come to the house. Baron Nopsca would have a seizure. If I set off now I can get to Melton Mowbray before dark and find a doctor. I hope you will forgive me if I desert you.' He smiled ruefully. 'I am not much good, am I? First I fall off my horse and then I propose to leave you to find your own way home.' He pulled Tipsy's head round in the direction of the road and started to move off, but Sisi held out her riding crop to bar his way.

'I forbid you to leave, Captain Middleton.' Her tone was light but it was a command nonetheless.

'But I am only thinking of you, Ma'am.'

'It is not your place to worry about my reputation,' she said. And then, softening, 'The thing about my position is that people will talk about me whatever I do. I learnt a long time ago that there was no point in being worried by it. At least this will give them a decent story.' She tilted her chin up. 'You must come back to Easton Neston now; you cannot possibly ride all the way to Melton Mowbray in your condition. I will send for the doctor and you will stay with me until you are quite recovered. We will have your things sent over.' She tapped the horse with her crop and set off smoothly up the hill.

Bay had no choice but to follow. His attempt at chivalry had been definitively countermanded. He was not entirely unhappy about this. There was no reason to go back to the web of rivalry and half-friendships at Melton Hall now that Charlotte had left. Indeed he rather relished the thought of Chicken, Fred and especially Augusta learning that he was now staying with the Empress. Then he wondered what Charlotte would make of the news, and whether he could get a letter to her before Augusta did. But he didn't have her address, and he felt uneasy about the fate of any letter that was sent to her via Melton. Augusta was quite capable of intercepting any missive that she thought was from Bay. That morning's feeling of irritation with Charlotte returned. Why on earth had she slipped away without a word? Was it some mysterious act of feminine caprice? If so, she was not the woman he had thought she was.

A pothole in the road made Tipsy stumble and the jolt sent a stab of pain through Bay's shoulder. He knew that the Empress was right; he was not strong enough to ride ten odd miles in the dark across open country. He would most likely fall off and die of exposure. He could already feel the initial shock of his fall wearing off, and an awful cold weariness numbing his body. He knew that if he was to slide off his horse now, he would be unable to get on it again. It was a relief that she had made the decision for him. His longing to lie down was so great that he did not dwell too much on the fact he was not accepting an invitation, but obeying an order.

The Ex-King's Bedroom

HE JOURNEY BACK WOULD NORMALLY TAKE TWENTY minutes, but though Bay could ride well enough one-handed, anything faster than a walk was too painful for his shoulder, and so the journey took them over an hour. He had urged the Empress to go on ahead, but she had refused.

'If you were to fall again, you would be quite helpless.'

'But I won't fall again.'

'Nobody ever thinks that they are going to fall, Captain Middleton.'

Just after they had had this conversation and were riding slowly along the broad river valley that led to Easton Neston Park, the Quorn came into view, spreading like a scarlet stain down the hill towards them on the other side of the river. The fox was clearly visible in front, running from side to side, trying to shake off the hounds who poured after it. The riders had thinned a little from the morning. As they grew nearer Bay saw the massive figure of the Red Earl and beside him the Prince of Wales. For a moment it looked as though the fox was going to cross the river and bring the whole hunt after it, but at the last moment the terrified animal swerved into a thicket of trees overhanging the water. It must have found some refuge there – possibly in a deserted badgers' sett – as it did not emerge. The hounds set up a terrific row, and the riders began to rein in their horses, waiting for the kill.

The Empress did not stop to watch the hounds at work, riding steadily on, with Bay following. But she was hailed by one of the riders on the other side of the stream who, recognising her, came right down to the water's edge.

'Your Majesty! I was afraid that you were lost.' There was relief in the Austrian Ambassador's voice, but also a note of warning.

The Empress turned her head and said, 'As you can see, Count, I am quite safe. It is poor Captain Middleton who has been injured.'

Bay nodded to the Count. 'Put my shoulder out. The Empress set it for me.'

Karolyi was too well trained to show any surprise at this, although his eyes did widen when the Empress checked her horse and he saw her chamois leather-covered legs gripping the side saddle.

'I am taking the Captain to Easton Neston. Perhaps you would be good enough to send for a doctor.' The Empress gave Karolyi no opportunity for further conversation.

'Of course, Majesty. I will attend to it directly.'

Without another word, the Empress turned her horse towards the road at the end of the valley. Bay nodded again to Karolyi and went after her.

As soon as they were out of earshot, the Empress laughed.

'Well, my new riding costume will be the talk of the Hofburg now,' she said. 'Karolyi would be far better off to keep it to himself, but he lives to gossip, and he won't be able to resist turning this into a story. It will all be about my heroic act in setting your shoulder, but he will find it impossible not to mention the state of my dress.'

Bay said nothing. He had seen the look on Karolyi's face at the sight of the Empress's legs. He hoped that the Ambassador was not a club man. The story of the man wearing a sling made out of an imperial riding habit would keep the gossips of Brooks and White's busy for weeks. It was not an entirely comfortable thought. But his worries about a possible scandal dissipated as he saw the gates of Easton Neston and he started to follow the Empress along the long drive to the house.

When he dismounted he could barely stand. Noticing this, the Empress clapped her hands and ordered the grooms to fetch Baron Nopsca immediately.

The Baron arrived a moment later, looking flushed. He almost managed to conceal his surprise at seeing the Empress's costume. The Empress spoke to him in German and the little man nodded, touching the ends of his moustaches as if to reassure himself that some things at least were unchanged.

Sisi put her hand on Bay's uninjured arm. 'Now you must get some rest. The Baron will take care of you.'

'You are very kind, but I feel that I am an imposition.'

She put up her hand to stop him.

'One of the prerogatives of royalty is that no one is allowed to contradict me. Isn't that right, Nopsca?'

The Baron bowed. 'Majesty.'

Inside the house, the Baron helped Bay up the broad marble staircase to a large bedroom on the first floor.

'This is the room formerly used by His Majesty the King of Naples. The Empress has directed me to accommodate you here.' The disapproval in the Baron's tone did not escape Bay. 'She has told me of your accident and has instructed me to send for the doctor. Please let me know if there is anything that you need.'

As the door closed Bay murmured some thanks, then, sitting down on the bed, he lay back and fell instantly asleep.

He woke with a start. The room was dark apart from the glowing fire. Moving gingerly, Bay felt the ache in his shoulder. It was so stiff that he could hardly move. Someone had taken his boots off and put a blanket over him, but he was still in his riding clothes apart from his jacket. Someone – the doctor, presumably – had strapped up his shoulder. Bay realised that he must have been unconscious.

It was impossible to know what time it was. He could have been asleep for minutes or hours. His head began to fill with worries. Had anyone sent word to Melton about his accident? He knew that he had to send a letter before the hunt gossips turned his accident into the story of the season: 'the pilot who had to be rescued by his royal charge'. He must write to Charlotte before she received some spiteful retelling of the day's events courtesy of Augusta. But even if he could get out of bed, he didn't think he could hold a pen with his injured right arm.

It was an unfamiliar feeling to be powerless – immobile in a strange house, surrounded by foreigners in his own country – yet there was something thrilling about this helplessness. Something was coming, he knew, but would it be pleasure or pain? It was like the moment before jumping an unfamiliar fence, the surge that went with taking off followed by the fear of landing.

Outside a high wind was sweeping across the Leicestershire plain, rattling the panes in the large baroque windows, sending drafts through every chink in the walls and gap in the glazing. Bay felt himself listening to every squeak and groan from the house around him. He tensed when he thought he heard the sound of whispering voices followed by a cry, but then relaxed when he realised that it was a combination of the wind and a squeaking door. Then there was another noise, a rhythmic creaking. Was it his imagination, or did he hear that quick, familiar step outside his door?

He tried to sit up when the door opened, but the pain in his shoulder made it impossible.

Sisi's face was lit from below by the Nightingale lamp she was carrying. The light cast a strange glow upwards on her face. There was something strange about her silhouette, he did not recognise the shape of her head, and then he realised that her hair was down.

'Are you awake?' Her voice was low and covert.

'Yes, over here.' He answered in the same whisper,

As the light came towards him, he saw that she was wearing some kind of white gown, and as she moved her head he saw the great sheet of her hair fall over her shoulders to the ground. When she approached the bed, he knew that he should not, indeed he could not move; to reach out his hand and touch her hair would be the moment of no return – the start of the race. But now she was so close to him that he could smell it – that mixture of violets, brandy and something more animal that he thought of as fox. His hand moved towards it. The hair felt warm and somehow springy, as if possessed with its own life force. He took a lock and wrapped it round his good hand. It was so long that he could wind it three times through his fingers without pulling at the scalp.

'Do you like my hair, Captain Middleton?' The same low whisper.

'Yes, Your Majesty, I do.' Bay tugged gently on the lock in his hand and pulled her face down to his. 'It is very useful to an injured man.' As he put his lips to hers he felt the hair fall around his face like a silken cocoon. He put up his good hand and felt the firm curve of her uncorseted waist under the silk of her gown.

'You may kiss me again, Captain Middleton.'

'Is that an order?'

'Not an order, I think, but a wish.'

'Then, Your Majesty, you will have to lie next to me, if I am to kiss you properly. Remember I am an injured man.'

'Oh, I am very worried about your injuries.' She put one finger lightly on his bandaged shoulder.

'Does that hurt?'

'No.'

'And this?' She leant over and, pushing back his shirt, put her lips to his skin. He felt her tongue touch his flesh, it felt rough like a cat's, and the caress sent a shock of pain and pleasure through his whole body.

'That was the best kind of hurting.'

She licked him again, this time bringing her tongue down to the hair on his chest.

'You taste of salt and something else also, the stable, perhaps.'

'You should have told Baron Nopsca to give me a bath,' Bay said.

She laughed. 'Oh, but I like your taste. I find it interesting.'

'So long as I can amuse you, Ma'am, I shall be content.'

Sisi began to undo the buttons on his shirt and when she had them all open she laid her head on his chest. He felt her breath against his skin and and her hair tickling his armpits.

'Your heart is beating most rapidly, Captain Middleton. Perhaps I should send for the doctor.'

'I don't think that will be necessary. If Your Majesty were to leave now I am sure that my heart rate would soon return to normal.'

'I see. Would you like me to leave? I don't want to endanger your health.' She was leaning over him directly and he could feel her breasts pressing against his chest.

'No, Ma'am, I would not.'

She lay there for a moment, her fingers tracing the outline of his lips.

'But you can't sleep like this, in your riding clothes, like a peasant.'

'It is very hard to undress with one arm.'

'Then you need help. Perhaps I should call Nopsca. No, it would

be too cruel to wake him at this hour. I will just have to help you myself, Captain Middleton. I hope that I am equal to the task.'
She sighed and her breath made the hairs on his chest tighten.

'So do I, Ma'am. But I feel sure that we will both rise to the occasion.'

She laughed and put her finger to his lips.

'Now be quiet, I need to concentrate.'

Later he listened to her breathing in the dark and thought that she had fallen asleep. Her head lay on his chest, her hair covering them like a blanket keeping them warm. He wondered what time it was. Somewhere in the darkness, he heard a clock strike four. There was still time then, before the household began to rumble into life. This was not a house, like some that Bay had stayed in, where they rang a bell in the small hours to summon the unfaithful to their rightful beds.

The Empress moved and Bay felt the blood return to his good arm, the one that she had been lying on. In the darkness he could just make out a glimpse of white as she stood up. He felt the cool brush of the linen sheet as she drew it over his bare skin and he sighed.

'Are you in pain? Did I hurt you?' Her voice was almost anxious in the dark.

'Not exactly,' he paused, 'Ma'am.'

He felt her hand against his cheek. 'When we are here you can call me Sisi. That is what my family call me, and my friends.'

Bay could not suppress the flicker of jealousy. 'Do you have many friends?'

'Not in England. No friends at all, apart from you. You are my

English friend, Bay. And now you must sleep. I need you to get better. I can't hunt without you.'

'What about your courtiers in the gold braid?'

'Max and Felix are not reliable. They can be distracted.'

Bay thought of what he might have seen in the mirror, in the gallery after the dinner at Easton Neston.

'I shall have to ride with one arm then. I hope I can manage.'

'Oh, I think you will manage. You have so far'. He heard the creak of the floorboards as she walked across the room.

'Goodnight, Bay.'

'Goodnight, Sisi.'

In the Dark Room

'WHY, CHARLOTTE, LADY D TOLD ME YOU were a paragon of every conceivable virtue, but she didn't let me know that you had such an eye. I am quite jealous. Such a luscious composition, all these girls tumbled together in one great, wanton heap. It looks so artless and yet every detail is perfect.' Caspar Hewes was holding up Charlotte's print of the Melton maids. They were in the studio of Lady Dunwoody's house in Holland Park, a large room with a great north-facing window, which was rattling in the wind. There was no fire in the studio; Lady Dunwoody believed strongly in living with beauty but was indifferent to comfort.

As he talked, Charlotte could see Caspar's breath condensing in the chilly air, like a dragon or a steam engine.

'When Lady D comes back, I shall tell her that this just *has* to be included in the exhibition. Everything we have is so stiff. This will add the essential note of decadence – loose and languorous, with just a touch of the harem.' Caspar turned to Charlotte and smiled a dazzling, very un-English smile that revealed a gleaming row of sharp white teeth; the puff that followed was definitely dragon-like, thought Charlotte – a Chinese dragon. Today he was wearing a green velvet jacket over a yellow brocade waistcoat and nankeen trousers. The splendour of his outfit was in contrast to the stained linen apron that he wore on top, but somehow he managed to make his costume look exotic rather than absurd. As Lady Dunwoody had predicted, he had barely drawn breath since his arrival at the house that morning. His voice was so different to an Englishman's: when Fred and his friends spoke in their club drawl they sounded as if they really did not have the energy to finish pronouncing their sentences, but Caspar gave every word its own privileged existence, rolling its around in his mouth before releasing it into the world. Charlotte thought that she had never met anyone who enjoyed talking as much as this American. The only word that was not in his extensive vocabulary was silence.

'You are very kind, Mr Hewes, but I doubt if the Queen will be interested in a group of servant girls. All the other portraits are of distinguished personages: Lord Beaconsfield, the Poet Laureate, Miss Nightingale, and members of the court. I am not sure that house-maids, however decadent, would be allowed to hang beside them.'

'Everyone needs youth and beauty, however distinguished they are,' Caspar said, and then, spinning round so that his face was so close to Charlotte's that she could smell the limes in his cologne, 'but why won't you call me Caspar? Mr Hewes makes me sound like a minister of the lord and I have to tell you, Charlotte, dear Charlotte, that I have Doubts, so when you call me Mr Hewes I feel like an imposter. Now I don't believe that a young lady as charming and as personable as yourself would want a poor foreigner like me to feel like a fraudulent man of God, by the constant use of his last name, now would you?'

Charlotte laughed and put up her hands in surrender. 'Enough, enough. I will call you Caspar, but only if you promise to stop talking, just for a minute.'

'But why? What is the point of being in a room with a lovely

and talented young woman if you don't make every effort to talk
to her? To be silent would be a terrible waste of a golden opportunity. Unless, of course, you want me to be silent while I cover
your face with burning kisses?'

'Burning kisses? Well, it is rather cold in here, so only if you
could guarantee they would be burning . . .' said Charlotte.

'You are teasing me now, an orphan all alone and friendless in
a strange country.'

'Friendless! I am quite sure that you have more friends in London
than I do. I suspect that there can't be many people you want to
know who aren't already your intimate friends,' said Charlotte.

'Mere acquaintances. They are not soulmates. If you only knew,
dear Charlotte, how I long for a confidante. I don't feel that I have
had a genuine conversation since I left America.'

As he was talking Caspar took out the other prints from
Charlotte's portfolio and arrayed them on the table in front of him.
Charlotte noticed that, for all his height and lankiness, Caspar's
movements were deft and precise. His hand hovered over the picture
of Bay and his horse and he pointed at it with one long finger.

'Why, Carlotta! I think I like Carlotta more than Charlotte, it
suits you better. You are not the prim little English miss that you
appear; I know by your pictures that you have a dangerous soul.
Already you are making me jealous. Do you know how fearsome
I can be when my passions are aroused?' He held out out his hand
with a thespian flourish.

'I know very little about you, as we only met yesterday,' said
Charlotte.

She could feel a blush reaching her ear lobes. There had been
nothing from Bay at breakfast, no letter, no telegram. But then he
did not know where she had gone. She had a sudden image of Bay
standing on the steps at Melton and laughing with Fred and

Chicken and she felt her mouth go dry. She would write to her aunt and ask her to tell Bay where she was. Adelaide Lisle might have some reservations about Bay, but the prospect of the house in town and the barouche with the matching greys that came with her role as Charlotte's chaperone might overcome her scruples.

Caspar saw the reddening of Charlotte's skin and continued, 'Already you are taunting me with this Adonis on horseback, with his tight breeches and his gleaming boots. But I will not despair, no, I will not lose heart – because as I look at this picture I see that this man is not in love with you. No, he only has eyes for his horse, who is a fine animal, undoubtedly, but compared to you, Carlotta . . . The man must have water in his veins.'

'Do you talk to every lady you meet like this?'

Caspar opened his eyes in theatrical outrage.

'Carlotta, how can you say such a cruel thing? Do I look like a man who makes love to every woman he meets? A rake, a reprobate, a Lothario?'

Charlotte shook her head, laughing. From another man, Caspar's declarations would be not just eccentric but alarming; however, there was something about the smooth fluency of his speech and the way that he was examining all her prints with painstaking care even as he declaimed undying love, that made her think that his extravagance of word and gesture was just as much an affectation as his style of dress.

'I don't know what you look like, an American, perhaps.'

'Oh, Carlotta, you make my nationality sound like an unfortunate disease. And yet I think you would like America. It is the land of the free, you know.' He began to sing 'Yankee Doodle Dandy' in a remarkably true baritone, while at the same time picking up Charlotte's box of undeveloped plates.

He stopped singing. 'You have two plates here that you haven't printed yet. Shall I develop them for you? It would be an honour. I long to see what else you have done. Please allow me to render you this one small service.'

Charlotte hesitated a moment. She felt a little uncomfortable about Caspar's offer – it was as if he was offering to wear her clothes – but she could think of no good reason to refuse.

'If you really want to. And now that you have looked at my portfolio, can I see yours?' she said.

'Oh, Carlotta, nothing would make me happier. I don't have much here. Perhaps one day I can lure you to Tite Street, but Lady D was kind enough to pull out a few things that she thought were worthy of being in the exhibition.'

He pulled a morocco folder down from one of the shelves.

'Here they are. Now I am altogether too bashful to stand by while you look at my work, so I am going to hide myself in the dark room with your plates, and then I won't have to squirm as you try to hide the contempt that it undoubtedly deserves.' Despite his words, Caspar did not look particularly apprehensive. He opened the portfolio with a flourish.

'There you are, Carlotta *mia*, the fruit of my labours. Be merciful, remember that I was not so fortunate as to have Lady Dunwoody as a teacher.'

He picked up her plate box and went into the wooden cubicle that Lady Dunwoody had built in the corner of the studio as a dark room. Charlotte could hear him moving around in there, still singing. She turned her attention to his portfolio, grateful for a brief respite from the torrent of chat. The first batch of photographs was of a desert dotted with huge cacti and strange, eroded rock formations. Charlotte had never seen a landscape like this before – no plants, no grass, nothing but sand and rock and sky. In one picture a young man was standing next to a cactus that topped him by at least two feet. The desert pictures were followed by a series of pictures of Chinese families – ten or more people, from the old men who wore pigtails and traditional costumes to their children who wore western clothes, right down to the babies swaddled in papooses. Some were studio portraits, some were posed outside the family's shop. Charlotte was surprised to see that all the signs were in Chinese characters. She wondered where Caspar had taken these pictures. It was an extraordinary thing to have these images from the other side of the world in front of her – the scenes they showed were so outlandish, and yet they were undoubtedly real.

Charlotte studied these pictures of strange people and savage landscapes and compared them to her carefully arranged pictures of maids and house parties, and she realised that she was jealous of Caspar's freedom and his palette. She felt a longing to go out and record an unknown world with her camera instead of always trying new ways to make the familiar strange. Charlotte had never been abroad – the most exotic place she had visited was the Isle of Wight. Fred and Augusta had offered to take her on their wedding trip to Italy, as a way of defraying the expense, she suspected. But even the prospect of the Colosseum by moonlight had not persuaded her to spend two months travelling with the newlyweds.

The last photos in the pile were a series of portrait heads, all of the same youth, the one who had been standing under the cactus in the desert. He had an angular face with high, flat cheekbones and a square jaw. Charlotte was surprised to see that his dark hair was very long and tied back behind his head. In some of the portraits, the boy, who couldn't have been much more than eighteen, looked straight into the camera, stern and unflinching, but there was one picture where he was looking back over his shoulder and smiling, and Charlotte had a sense of mutual affection on both sides of the camera. To catch a look like that, a moment rather than a pose, was very rare. She wondered who he was. In the last picture he was holding up a bunch of grapes, his head tipped back, revealing his long, supple throat. His eyes were tilted towards the camera and Charlotte saw something in his expression that she recognised. She had seen that look on Bay's face, once.

Caspar was now singing 'Silver Threads Among the Gold', attempting all the parts.

First he sang 'Darling, I am growing old', in a reedy baritone, 'Growing old' again in a sonorous bass, and then 'Silver threads among the gold' in a high-pitched falsetto. It was as if he was trying to recreate the sound of a barbershop quartet single-handed.

Charlotte put the print of the youth with the grapes down, and looked around the room. It was full of the props that Lady Dunwoody used for her photographs. On a chair there was a folded Union Jack and a cardboard helmet and shield which had been used for the famous and much reproduced portrait of Ellen Terry as Britannia. A collection of white pleated muslin tunics was hanging on a lacquered coat stand; on the shelf above was a pile of laurel wreaths. A crystal ball stood on a table next to a skull and a silver candelabra with three candles that had burnt down almost to the wick, with rivulets of wax hanging down like stalactites. On the wall next to the door a heavily embroidered Chinese mandarin's robe hung from a pole; above it on a small shelf that ran the length of the room was a collection of blue and white plates, lustre jugs and a marble cherub, one plump leg pointing towards the floor. Next to the bench where Charlotte was standing, was an easel displaying a photograph of a young girl dressed as Diana the huntress, her bow drawn back as she pointed her arrow at the sky. Charlotte recognised the model as one of Lady Dunwoody's maids. Even the most skilled retouching could not completely disguise the contrast between the girl's reddened hands and the classical white-ness of her neck and bare shoulder. But Lady D had caught something savage in her expression which gave the photograph an unexpected ferocity. This Diana looked as though she would hit her prey. Charlotte wondered what the model had been thinking of to produce that shaft of cruelty. Did she dream of taking up arms and bringing down her enemies, or was she perhaps thinking of Lady Dunwoody's collection of Japanese porcelain that had to be dusted with a single goose feather?

The singing stopped mid-phrase, there was a moment when Charlotte thought she heard a sigh, and then Caspar began to sing again, picking up the song exactly where he had left it.

The verse finished and Caspar emerged from the cubicle, his arms raised in benediction.

'I feel that we have consummated our artistic union, dearest Carlotta. I have brought your negatives into glorious life, and you have seen my humble offerings.'

Charlotte heard her cue.

'Oh, but you have *nothing* to be humble about. Your photographs are exceptional. I have never seen anything like them before. Oh, how I envy you your deserts and your endless light. We have nothing like that here, that's why we have to create little tableaux in studios,' – she gestured to the print on the easel – 'housemaids dressed up as goddesses. But you, you can just go out and find the perfect composition right in front of you.'

Caspar made a little bow of acknowledgement, but he was, for once, silent, and Charlotte realised that she had not said quite enough.

'But only a photographer of great skill and talent could do those astonishing landscapes justice. Don't worry, I know how good you are. Even if you hadn't had such raw material to work with, I would have known it just from this picture.' Charlotte picked up the print of the boy looking back over his shoulder and laughing. 'Only someone with an uncommon gift could have produced something like this. It is so rare to see real emotion in a photograph. But here it is quite naked.'

Charlotte did not know why that last word had come out of her mouth. She felt as if she had said something improper. Caspar looked at her directly for a moment and then he dropped his gaze and made her another sweeping bow.

'I am overwhelmed by your appreciation. To be praised by you is the pinnacle of all my life's achievements. I feel like stout Cortez on the Darien peak.'

Charlotte interrupted him, 'Who is the boy, the one holding the grapes? I can't imagine coaxing a look like that from any of my sitters.'

'But what about the gallant officer and his horse? You captured the love and affection between them perfectly.' Caspar raised an eyebrow.

'Such an unusual face. What is his name?' Charlotte asked.

'His name? Abraham Running Water. His father was a Sioux Indian and his mother was an Irish girl who came west in the gold rush. Abraham was the product of their brief union. I met him in the desert. He helped me carry my equipment, he showed me things. There was the skin of a rattlesnake, completely whole, lying on the sand. I would never have seen it if Abraham hadn't stopped me and made me look.' He paused for a second, and Charlotte asked the question to which she was afraid she already knew the answer.

'Where is he now?'

'Somewhere in the Mojave. I took a picture of the exact location. There were no trees, so I made a pile of stones. Not big ones, there are no boulders there, just pebbles really. He had consumption. I wanted to take him to the city, to see doctors, but he wouldn't leave the desert.'

'I am sorry. But these photographs are better than a gravestone,' said Charlotte.

'That is a delicate thought. I can appreciate it now, but I came very close to smashing the plates afterwards. But somehow, some of my best work . . . I just couldn't bring myself to do it.'

'To have a photograph of someone you cared for must be a consolation.'

'Perhaps, but they are also a permanent reminder of what you have lost. Memories fade, after all, but I will never have to struggle to remember Abraham's face. Is that really such a boon? Perhaps it is better to let things grow dim. Every time I look at one of these pictures I am reminded so vividly of how alive he was once.' He shook his head and waved his hands in front of him as if trying to banish unpleasantness.

Charlotte thought of the photograph of her mother in her coffin that her father had kept in his study. The one she had never wanted to look at.

Caspar clapped his hands.

'But enough of this, we have strayed down a very morbid byway, my Carlotta. We are not here to philosophise, but to work. What would Lady D say if she could see us now? She would condemn us as lilies of the field, gilded parasites, who indulge in idle conversation when we should be toiling.'

'I may have been idle, but you have been developing my plates. Are the prints dry?'

Caspar blinked. 'I suppose they must be. Let me check.' He disappeared into the dark-room cubicle.

Charlotte wondered if it would be too conspicuous to send Aunt Adelaide a telegram about Bay. She decided that it probably would. A telegram would be talked about, and after all, there was no urgency.

She could hear Caspar banging about in the dark room. He was singing Mozart now, '*Ma in Ispagna son già mille e tre . . .*'

The aria finished and Caspar emerged holding a print.

'Here she is, your tragic heroine.' He placed the photograph in front of Charlotte. It was the picture she had taken of the Empress on the morning of Major Postlethwaite's accident. She was in profile.

The focus of the picture was the Empress's narrow waist between the abundance of her hair above and the spread of her skirts below. Her face was tilted away from the camera but it was possible to see the delicate angle of her jaw and the long cord of her neck.

'What makes you say tragic?' said Charlotte.

'She has a melancholy shape. Something about the cast of her head. And she is clearly someone who is at the centre of things – look how everyone around is looking at her. I must say, I am curious. Is she an acquaintance of yours?'

'Hardly. She is the Empress of Austria. She came to a hunt at the house I was staying at.'

'An empress? Yes, I can see that.'

'Do you think she is beautiful?'

Caspar narrowed his eyes at the picture. 'If you had asked me that question before telling me who she was, I would have wavered. But now that I know, well, I have to say I do think she is beautiful, I simply can't separate the form from the function. A beautiful empress is so much more romantic than a moderately attractive one. Even though I am a proud republican, I can't deny that there is something irresistible about a crown.'

He glanced at Charlotte and then said, 'But I suspect from the brittle set of her head that she might be rather . . . taxing. Not like you, dearest Charlotte, you are so easy to be with.'

'That's because I am not an empress.'

'Oh, I know that you would be delightful anywhere.' He made her a little bow and then he took out his hunter from his waistcoat pocket.

'Is that really the time? I promised Lady D that we would meet her at the gallery at noon. We shall have to leave at once. Lady D does not like to be kept waiting.'

Charlotte helped him to pack up all the prints in a portfolio, carefully interleaving each one with tissue paper. Caspar insisted on including her picture of the maids, and the picture of Bay with Tipsy. She countered by putting in his portrait of Abraham Running Water. Just as she was placing the tissue paper over the last print, Caspar picked up the picture of the Empress.

'You can't leave out royalty.'

Charlotte remembered that she had taken more than one picture of the Empress. 'What about the other plate? I wasn't sure if I had the picture or not, because the Empress took out a fan to hide her face.'

'How tiresome.' Caspar put the leaves of the portfolio together and tied the strings. He put his hand on Charlotte's elbow, shepherding her to the door.

Charlotte hesitated. 'But did the other picture come out? I would like to see if I caught her before the fan.' Caspar's grip on her elbow tightened, but she broke away and entered the little dark room. In the darkness she could see one print hanging from string by a single peg. She took it down and brought it out into the light.

The photograph had come out perfectly. But the focus of the picture was not the Empress, who was bringing the enormous fan up to her face, but the rider just behind her. For a moment Charlotte didn't recognise Bay. The expression on his face, which was turned towards the Empress, was one she had not seen before. His pale eyes were completely intent; he was gazing at the woman in front of him as if she were some precious object that would fall and break if he looked away. His mouth was open slightly. It might have been the beginning of a smile, or a grimace of pain, Charlotte couldn't tell. He had never looked at her that way.

She felt a touch on her elbow and the photograph was taken out of her hand.

'Photographs can be so deceptive, don't you think?' Caspar said as he pushed her out of the dark room. 'That fellow there, your captain, looks as though he has seen a ghost. It's the way the light catches his eyes. A sunny day and a short exposure and you can be seeing all sorts of things. I remember once I took a picture of a butcher at work in Chinatown, he was holding up his cleaver in such a way that it looked that he was about to murder his assistant. Just a trick of the light, of course, but so alarming – he could have been Sweeney Todd himself.'

Charlotte allowed herself to be borne along by the torrent of Caspar's chatter out of the house and into a hansom. It wasn't until the cab had reached the Albertopolis in the park that she spoke.

'It wasn't a trick of the light, was it?'

Caspar was looking out of the window at the shiny new statue of Prince Albert sitting under his canopy.

'I can't help feeling that he looks rather morose sitting there. I think if I was a prince, I would want to be remembered as dashing and brave, rather than brooding.' Still looking out of the window, he continued, 'Trick of the light, really I couldn't say. You know the gallant captain, I have only seen the picture. And I have always said that photographs can be very misleading.' He turned to her and smiled.

'Promise me that when I die, you will commission a statue that makes me look like a hero. I really couldn't bear to be a lowering presence like that.'

But Charlotte was not to be diverted.

'If you had to describe the look on Captain Middleton's face; if you thought that expression was a real one, and not a photographic mirage, what would you say?'

Caspar sighed.

'I would say, my dear Carlotta, that the good Captain was enchanted.'

The Widow of Windsor

ISI LOOKED OUT OF THE TRAIN WINDOW AT THE snowy fields rushing by, stained pink by the rising sun. But she did not notice the keen sherbet colour of the snow; if she noticed the landscape at all, it was the fences and hedges that caught her eye. This was not good hunting country. It was typical of Queen Victoria to live in an unsporting landscape. Such a dowdy little woman, with no style at all. The summer before last when she had visited the Isle of Wight, she had been forced to call on the Queen at Osborne. She had been given a grindingly thorough tour of the sculpture gallery and the Swiss cottage where the royal children had their gardens. It had been one of the most tedious afternoons of her life.

But today would be quite different. She looked across at Bay, who was sitting opposite her. His eyes were closed and she wondered whether he had fallen asleep. He must have felt her gaze, even in his dreams, because he opened his eyes and smiled at her. His eyes were such a pale blue, like the stained glass in the Peterhof.

The train went over a junction and Sisi saw Bay grimace as the movement jolted his shoulder, which was still strapped up.

'Is it very painful, Captain Middleton?'

'Only now and then,' said Bay and winked.

'I have a tincture that is very good. From Vienna. The doctors there do not believe in suffering.' She turned to Countess Festetics, who was sitting at the other end of the carriage reading a novel in Hungarian.

'Do you have my solution, Festy? I think the Captain needs it.'

The Countess opened the crocodile skin dressing case at her side. She took out a phial with a silver top and handed it to Sisi.

'Open your mouth, and I will put the drops on your tongue,' said Sisi.

'It is really not so bad,' said Bay. 'Nothing that a little brandy wouldn't cure.'

'Open your mouth, Captain Middleton!'

Bay did as he was told and Sisi put six drops on his tongue. The train shuddered as she was administering the seventh and the drop fell onto Bay's moustache, where it glistened.

'Missed,' said Bay and licked it off with his tongue. He winked again. Sisi smiled and then glanced at the Countess, who was apparently too absorbed in her book to notice them, although she had barely turned a page since the journey began. Her presence in the carriage was necessary to avoid a scandal; the Empress of Austria could not be seen travelling in a carriage alone with her pilot. It did not matter how many hours they had spent alone on the hunting field, a train was different. Sisi had long ago learnt that it paid to observe the outward conventions. Nopsca had winced when she had announced that Captain Middleton would be coming with them to Windsor, but so long as Festetics sat there with her Hungarian novel, he could pretend that all was well.

The train was slowing down now, they must be almost there. The journey had been commendably swift, just under three hours. They had not had the indignity of changing trains; Nopsca had arranged it all very cleverly, procuring a private train which was routed round the outskirts of London. Sisi looked at her pocket watch, it was a few minutes before eleven. It was all quite an effort for a call that would last no more than half an hour, but monarchs could not always follow their inclinations. She put her hands to her hair automatically, to check that her crown of plaits had not slipped.

There was a red carpet at the station, of course, but not a band. This was a private visit by the Countess Hohenembs to Queen Victoria, not a state visit by the Empress of Austria to the Queen of England. Sisi pulled her veil right down; in England there were photographers everywhere.

She turned to Bay. 'There is quite a party to meet us. Are you ready, Captain Middleton?'

Bay stood up and made a little bow. 'Quite ready, Your Majesty.'

There was a knot of men on the platform. The Ambassador, Count Karolyi, stepped forward to kiss the Empress's hand. As he lifted his head his eyes flickered over to Bay, who was standing behind the Empress.

'Welcome, Majesty,' he said in German and then, turning to the man beside him, in English, 'May I present Sir Henry Ponsonby, Her Majesty's chamberlain.'

Sisi nodded and waited as Karolyi introduced the rest of the party who merited introduction, 'Countess Festetics, Her Majesty's lady-in-waiting, Baron Nopsca, her household comptroller, and,' with an almost imperceptible pause, 'Captain Middleton, her pilot.'

There were three carriages waiting outside. Sisi beckoned to Bay to join her in the first carriage with Karolyi and Ponsonby.

The Ambassador gave Middleton his best courtier's smile as they waited for the Empress and then Ponsonby to climb into the carriage.

'Is this your first time at Windsor, Captain Middleton?' he said.

'It is.'

'An exciting day for you, then, to visit your sovereign.' Karolyi lingered over the word sovereign. 'You are moving in exalted circles, Captain Middleton.'

Bay looked Karolyi in the eye. 'It is an honour to be of service to the Empress, Count.' He gestured to Karolyi that he should follow the Empress into the carriage. The older man put one foot on the step and turned to Bay.

'I have spent my life in the service of the Hapsburgs, Captain Middleton. It has been,' he paused for a moment as if searching for the right word, and then said with emphasis, 'the business of my life.'

Bay was about to reply, but the Empress called from the carriage, 'Count Karolyi, did you know that my son is to visit England?' The Count turned his head and the moment of tension between the two men passed.

When they were all seated in the carriage, Ponsonby began to point out the sights on the way. The streets were empty but for a few couples in their Sunday best, hurrying to church. No one stopped to look at the procession of carriages making its way towards the Castle.

As the turrets of Windsor Castle came into view, Ponsonby said, 'Windsor is Her Majesty's oldest residence. The Queen always comes here at this time of year, to remember the Prince Consort. He died here on the fourteenth of December, 1861.'

'So sad.' Sisi sighed. 'Such an enlightened man. I remember we had a long talk once about plumbing. He had a passion for hygiene. And then, poor man, he dies of typhus. I suppose the drains at Windsor are very old.'

Ponsonby nodded. 'Everything at Windsor is old. But with the greatest respect, Ma'am, I would hesitate to say that in the presence of the Queen.'

The carriages drove up the avenue of trees that lined the drive to the Castle. When they arrived at the Great West Door, the Austrian party was shown into an empty drawing room, clearly one of the Queen's private apartments as it was full of silver-framed photographs. There were group portraits of Victoria and her children and grandchildren, on lawns, steps and yachts. Franz Joseph was for ever imploring Sisi to sit for one of these dynastic pictures, so that he too could send out a family photograph that would gather dust in the royal drawing rooms of Europe. But Sisi stood firm; she had stopped sitting for photographs when she was thirty. She hated the idea of her image being pored over by strangers, royal or otherwise, examining her appearance for signs of ageing. '

Sisi looked over at Bay; he caught her glance and smiled. She examined another photograph – this one was of the Queen mounted on a Shetland pony which was being held by a tall, rather handsome man in Highland dress. It was the only picture in the room that showed the Queen with anyone other than a member of her family.

'Who is this?' she asked Sir Henry, pointing at the photograph. The Chamberlain, who had just taken out his watch for the second time since their arrival, said with some nervousness, 'That is John Brown, Ma'am. He is the Queen's personal servant.'

'Her servant?' Sisi could hardly keep the surprise out of her voice. Franz Joseph might have had his picture taken with his groom, but he would never put it in a silver frame and exhibit it for public view.

A series of clocks began to strike the hour, making Sisi aware that she was being kept waiting. She looked at Karolyi and said in German, 'But where is the Queen? Does she know I am here?'

The Ambassador pulled at his whiskers.

'I believe, Majesty, that the Queen did not expect you so promptly. I understand that she is still in church.'

He spoke in German but Ponsonby behind him caught the word *Kirche* and murmured in English, 'The Queen always likes to have a few words with the Chaplain after the service. It's a custom that began when the Prince Consort was alive, and the Queen does so like to carry things on.'

Sisi felt a shiver of impatience. She had come all this way and now she was being kept waiting. Her tone was querulous as she said in English, 'And how long do you think that these "few words" will take?'

Ponsonby exchanged the briefest of glances with Karolyi before replying, 'I believe just a few minutes more now, Your Majesty.' His tone was diplomatic and neutral, avoiding any semblance of retort to her raised voice, but Sisi had caught the look he had shared with the Ambassador, a look which conveyed their common helplessness in the hands of unreasonable women.

Sir Henry kept inviting her to sit down on one of the overstuffed sofas, but Sisi had been sitting down all morning. She began to pace up and down, her button boots making no sound on the thick carpet. It was difficult, though, to pace satisfactorily as the room, though large, was crowded with small tables covered with china models of the Queen's dogs, glass paperweights of Alpine scenes, watercolour albums, and of course the photographs. Sisi found herself threading through the clutter, hoping that her skirts would not knock anything down. Every inch of wall was covered in paintings – some of them by painters Sisi recognised. She thought that the group portrait of the royal family must be by Winterhalter – he really was the most flattering painter; the young princes and princesses looked like angels and while Victoria looked, as ever, like a goose, she was at least in Winterhalter's hands a handsome one. The floor was covered in a violently coloured carpet – Sisi could see patches of burgundy, mustard yellow and carmine red. She thought that it was fortunate that there was so much furniture in the room, as the carpet undiluted would give anyone a headache.

She walked over to Bay, who was standing by a wall. 'I thought we might look at some hunters this afternoon. Some English ones. You will help me choose them?'

'With pleasure.'

'We will go as soon as we are finished here.' Sisi lowered her voice, 'I do not intend to stay long.'

Just then there was a cough from Ponsonby, and Sisi turned to see two liveried footmen throwing open the door for the Queen. She was small, round and dressed entirely in black apart from her white widow's cap. Immediately behind her walked John Brown, who was almost a foot taller than his mistress. Behind him was a selection of ladies, including a young girl whose close-set blue eyes and long nose made her unmistakably one of Victoria's daughters.

There was a rustle as the men bowed and the women curtsied. Only Sisi did not move. She waited until Victoria was halfway across the room before she moved to kiss her on both cheeks.

'Your Majesty.'

'My dear Empress,' the Queen said in her high, childish voice, 'how delightful to see you. And on a Sunday too, such an unusual day for a visit.' There was a glint of steel in her bulbous blue eyes. Behind her Ponsonby cleared his throat nervously.

'This is my youngest daughter Beatrice.'

Beatrice curtsied and Sisi kissed her too on both cheeks. Then she smiled and said in her gayest voice, 'But how lovely you are, Beatrice. One day you must come and stay with me in Vienna. The archdukes will be fighting over you, I guarantee.'

Beatrice blushed and mumbled something about Mama needing her here. The Queen settled herself on one of the vast plaid buttoned-back sofas, and gestured to Sisi to join her.

'Oh, but Beatrice would be miserable away from me. She is such a little home bird.'

Sisi saw that Beatrice was clenching her fists; she wondered how miserable exactly the girl would be to be separated from her mother.

'Oh, but it is so important to travel at that age. I so regret not seeing the world before I married.'

Queen Victoria raised her head and her many chins wobbled. 'How fortunate then that you are able to travel so much now. When did we last meet? I believe it was two years ago at Osborne. You had your little girl with you. Such a dear little thing. Is she travelling with you now?'

'Valerie? No, I left her in Vienna with her father. He dotes upon her, and I couldn't bear to deprive him of her.'

'How is the dear Emperor? Such a *shame* that he is not with you.' Queen Victoria spoke with very definite emphases as if she was underlining the words as she spoke.

'My husband asked me to give you his warmest regards. He is very sorry not to be able to be here in person.'

'I am surprised that you can bear to leave him behind. I know that I was always quite *miserable* when I was parted from Prince Albert, even if only for the night.' The Queen gave a sigh that made her lace tippets flutter and placed one white hand to her breast. After a little pause while she collected herself, she asked, 'Tell me, how long do you intend to stay in England?'

'Till the end of the hunting season, I hope. To ride to hounds here is such a pleasure. We have nothing like it at home.'

The Queen sighed again. 'My dear husband always used to say that there was *nothing* to surpass a day out in the hunting field. If only he had been spared so that he could have enjoyed *more* of them. But he had so many duties here. There was no time for his own pleasure. He always put duty first.' The Queen turned her head to gaze at the portrait of Albert at his desk that hung over the fireplace.

Sisi caught the implied reproach. She replied in the same, slightly pious tone, 'The Emperor is the same, diligent beyond all measure. It was very hard for me to leave him, but he insisted. Dear Franzl, he swears that the only thing that gives him real joy is to know that I am happy and healthy. The winters in Vienna always make me ill, so he was so delighted when I decided to come here.'

There was a little pause as the Queen absorbed this speech. Sisi looked at the boulle clock on the mantelpiece. It was only fifteen minutes past the hour; she would have to stay for at least another twenty minutes. She sat up a little straighter, conscious of the Queen's shapeless black bulk. Only Victoria's head and the bulbous blue eyes had anything regal about them.

'But the Emperor must worry about you so. Hunting is *so* dangerous. The Prince of Wales had such a nasty fall only the other day. Dear Alix was quite beside herself. You must promise me, dear Empress, that you will not do anything *reckless*. After all, we are *grandmothers* now.' Queen Victoria nodded at Sisi, waving a plump white hand to indicate their similarity. Sisi smiled thinly. She did not altogether care to be called a grandmother. It made her sound so old and staid, when she was a mere thirty-eight. The Queen, on the other hand, fully deserved the grandmother label. She was only twelve or so years older than Sisi, but she looked like a contemporary of Sisi's mother. Sisi could not understand how anyone could allow themselves to spread quite so much. And those dreadful clothes. Of course she was in mourning, but even mourning clothes did not have to be so dowdy. Sisi reflexively smoothed the green worsted skirt of her travelling dress.

Victoria continued, 'I have never allowed my daughters to hunt, although Louise *begged* me to let her. But I told her to take up archery, *so graceful*. Really you should consider archery, Empress, such a fetching costume Louise had made, all in green with a peaked hat with a feather. Really quite charming. I believe I shall write to the Emperor and suggest archery. I am sure that he would be very happy to know of a sport that is *perfectly* safe.'

Victoria paused for breath and Sisi broke in, 'Oh, but I am quite safe. I have my pilot, Captain Middleton, to protect me from harm.' She gestured at Bay with her hand. 'Earl Spencer was kind enough to recommend him.' Bay, who had been looking at the floor during this exchange, straightened up and bowed low before the Queen.

Victoria turned to look at Bay, making no attempt to hide her scrutiny. She clearly liked what she saw, saying with almost a regal twinkle, 'We hope you will be *very* careful, young man. If anything were to happen to the Empress on English soil, it would be an *unspeakable* tragedy.'

Bay bowed again. 'You have my word, Ma'am, that no harm will come to the Empress in my care.'

'We are pleased to hear it. You must be *vigilant* at all times. But you seem to have injured yourself? I hope it is nothing serious.' Queen Victoria was all tender concern. There was nothing she liked more than a medical drama.

'Oh it's nothing, Ma'am. I fell from my horse and dislocated my shoulder.'

'Dislocated your shoulder? How dreadful. Was it *very* painful?' Victoria leant forward.

'It wasn't pleasant at the time, Ma'am, but luckily the Empress was able to set it for me right away. It's when the arm is hanging loose that it hurts.'

Victoria looked at Sisi and back at Bay. 'I had no idea, Elizabeth, that you had *medical* training. How very *fortunate* that you knew what to do.'

Sisi laughed. 'I didn't, but Captain Middleton is an excellent teacher.'

Queen Victoria considered this for a moment and then she turned to John Brown. 'I wonder if I would be as useful if anything like that were to happen to you, John?'

'I have nae intention of dislocating anything, Ma'am,' Brown said. 'And I if I did have a mishap then I would not be asking Your Majesty for assistance. My job is to look after you.' He did not look at Bay, but his air of superiority was impregnable.

Queen Victoria flushed with pleasure at this manly declaration. 'Oh, I am sure that Captain Middleton didn't *intend* to hurt himself. A fall like that could happen at *any* time. And besides, John, there have been times when you have been a little *unsteady* on your feet.'

'I've nae broken any limbs, Ma'am,' said Brown.

The Queen tapped him on one kilted thigh. 'You have been lucky then.' She turned back to Bay. 'And which regiment are you with, Captain Middleton?'

'The Eleventh Hussars, Ma'am.'

'Then the Prince of Wales is your Colonel in Chief. I believe he is *very* fond of the uniform. But it doesn't fit him so well these days. Too many dinners and parties. So unlike his poor dear father, who was always so *careful* about what he ate.' Victoria turned to John Brown, who was standing behind her, for corroboration.

Brown nodded. 'The late Prince was always verra dainty with his food.'

Sisi thought that it was a pity that the Queen did not show some of her late husband's restraint. She must be quite as broad as she was tall.

The Queen beckoned to her ladies. 'Can we offer you any

refreshment, Empress? You will stay to lunch, of course. And afterwards we can drive round the park. Fresh air is *so* important at this time of year.'

Sisi looked at her ambassador with reproach. She had made it quite clear that this visit was to be a call and nothing more.

'Oh, that would have been lovely, on another occasion I should like nothing better, but we have to go back. There is some urgent business I must attend to.'

Queen Victoria blinked. There was a muffled gasp from the courtiers behind her. The Queen's invitations were never refused. But Sisi did not flinch. She had kept her promise by paying this visit, but she would not ruin a whole day by staying for lunch. She continued, 'I hope you will meet Rudolph, my son, when he comes. He is such an admirer of all things English. He wants to know everything about your engineering – bridges and tunnels are all he talks about. Not Viennese at all.' She laughed and Karolyi, behind her, did his best to muster a smile. The English courtiers stood frozen, waiting to see how their mistress would react.

Victoria gave a little nod. Her voice was high, clear and unmistakably cross.

'We shall be delighted to see the Crown Prince. Let us hope *he* will not be so *pressed* for time.'

The royal lips were set in a straight line, but Sisi only laughed. 'I shall tell him that he must work very hard to make up for his mother's shortcomings.'

Queen Victoria did not smile back. Henry Ponsonby pulled at his whiskers.

Sisi, seeing Karolyi's pained expression, realised that she must repair the damage. She looked around her in desperation.

'But this is such an *interesting* room. We have nothing like this in Vienna. I know Franz Joseph would admire your decorations exceedingly. So *gemütlich*. He ordered all the furniture for his apartments in the Hofburg from Maples of London.' Sisi pointed at the polychrome carpet. 'What a pity he isn't here to see this. I know he would admire it very much.'

Mollified, Victoria leant forward. 'That is the royal tartan. Dear Albert designed it. He loved Scotland so much, he wanted ·to be reminded of it *at all times*. We were always *so* happy there.' The Queen looked fondly at John Brown as she said this.

'You really must visit Scotland, dear Kaiserin. So *picturesque*. I am never so carefree as when I am in Scotland. Such happy memories of my beloved Albert.'

Sisi thought that, despite her frequent references to her late husband, the Queen looked remarkably content in the company of John Brown.

'Perhaps one day you will visit Bad Ischl in the Tyrol. People say it is very like Scotland.'

The Queen shook her head sadly. 'I am afraid it is too late for me to visit Austria. Dear Albert was never there and I would not like to go anywhere that he had not seen. I would feel disloyal.'

Sisi could think of nothing to say in answer to this. To her relief, the boulle clock started to strike noon, its precise melodious chimes echoed by the deeper notes of the chapel bells outside. There was a brief hiatus as the party waited for the noise to subside.

This, Sisi decided, was her cue. She leant over to the Queen and said, 'I must trespass on your hospitality no longer, Victoria. I shall write to the Emperor today to say that I find you in good health and to convey any other messages you would like to charge me with.'

Sisi wanted to stand up, she was almost rigid with boredom, but protocol meant that she could not rise before the Queen.

Victoria shook her head.

'What a pity you cannot stay longer,' she said again, although she did not look particularly sorry. 'I had hoped we might have more of a chance to talk together. It is not often that I am able to converse woman to woman with another,' a little pause, 'empress.' She made a little pecking motion of her head as she said this, and there was a gleam in her eyes. Ponsonby made a noise somewhere between a cough and a warning.

The Queen ignored him and carried on.

'You may tell your husband that I am to be Empress of India, as well as Queen of England. So you see, we are both empresses now, Elizabeth. Although, of course, there is a difference as I am a *sovereign* and you are a consort.' She beamed, the smile of a child who has been given an enormous box of chocolates.

Sisi saw that she would have to acknowledge this triumph adequately or be condemned to sit in this hideous cold room for ever. Clearly Victoria did not think it was enough to be the Queen of the world's most powerful nation; it had irked her that there was a still grander title that she did not yet possess. Sisi, who had been an empress since she was sixteen, could not share her excitement. To be a queen or an empress, what did it matter? Both titles were gilded cages. Any crown grew heavy. But Victoria would not understand any of this. The little queen was so like Franz Joseph. They both believed that God had chosen them to be monarchs, never doubting their position for a moment. The two monarchs might occasionally tremble at the burden of the duties imposed upon them, but they would not relinquish the tiniest fragment of their powers. Sisi wondered what it would be like to have that certainty, to wake up every morning knowing that you were God's anointed put on this earth to rule over your subjects.

She picked up one of Victoria's hands and pressed it.

'Although mere words can hardly express my feelings, I am so happy to be able to congratulate you in person.'

'Empresses and grandmothers. We stand *alone* on the World Stage, dear Elizabeth.' Victoria was at her most gracious.

'But you are superior to me in this way as in every other. I only have one grandchild,' said Sisi.

This speech seemed to strike the right note with Victoria, and she squeezed Sisi's hand in return and with much rustling rose to her feet.

'You will send my very best wishes to the Emperor. I often think of his poor dear brother. He was such a favourite with us here.'

Sisi lowered her eyes. Maximilian, her brother-in-law, had been crowned Emperor of Mexico eleven years ago, but his brief reign had ended three years later in front of a revolutionary firing squad.

'Poor Max. It was a terrible thing.'

'What a *dreadful* country. You can be sure that we expressed our indignation in the *strongest* terms through the British consul. An anointed sovereign put to death like a common criminal. The Mexicans are little better than *savages*.'

'Yes, we are fortunate to be in Europe,' said Sisi. 'But Max so wanted a kingdom of his own. He wanted to be an emperor like Franzl.'

'Such a mistake to think that a *monarchy* can be manufactured. It is a *sacred* trust.' For affirmation Victoria looked at John Brown, who nodded solemnly.

Sisi did not point out to the new Empress of India that her title was equally artificial, although she would have been liked to see the look on her face.

'Goodbye, Victoria, it was such a pleasure to see you.' She kissed the Queen and Beatrice. Sisi did not think she would say goodbye to John Brown, who after all was only a servant.

The Queen walked with the party to the entrance to the Tower.

'You *must* be *careful*, Elizabeth, I beg you. Please don't take any unnecessary risks.'

She turned to Bay. 'I am relying on you, Captain Middleton, to make sure that no harm comes to the Empress on British soil.'

Bay bowed and said, 'I will watch over the Empress night and day, Ma'am.'

Bay saw a flash in the blue eyes and wondered if he had gone too far, but the Queen smiled and said, 'I feel sure that you will.'

They were halfway down the corridor when the Queen stopped and said, 'Beatrice, you have forgotten the book! Run and fetch it at once.'

The party waited as Beatrice set off down the corridor without evident haste. She returned with a parcel which she pressed into Sisi's hands, 'From mama.'

Ponsonby came back to the station with them in the carriage. This time they were in a landau where the seats were directly behind each other rather than facing. Sisi invited Bay to sit next to her, while the Ambassador and the Chamberlain sat in the seat behind.

'You promised the Queen that you would look after me night and day,' said Sisi, looking straight ahead. 'You will be very busy, Captain Middleton.'

'*Very* busy. But I can hardly disobey my sovereign,' said Bay.

But as they walked up the red carpet to the waiting train, Bay remembered the kilted mass of John Brown standing behind Queen Victoria's chair. He had seen the cartoons in *Punch* of the Queen and her Highland Servant and had laughed in the club at the jokes that circulated about 'Mrs Brown'. There was no similarity, of course, between John Brown's situation and his own, but there had been something about the way that the Queen had looked at him that had made him uncomfortable. It did not surprise him that she had looked. What disturbed him was not Victoria's scrutiny, the slow flick of her blue eyes across his body, but the little turn of her head as she looked over to Brown and back. She had been *comparing* them.

Bay glanced over at Sisi, who was flicking through the book that the Queen had given her. 'Leaves from our Sketchbook of our *life* in the Highlands,' she read, imitating Victoria's emphatically accented delivery. 'What charming pictures. But how dull their life is – just ponies and picnics and those dowdy shawls always. And all the men showing their legs. How do you call the skirt that the Scots men wear? Not a flattering garment, I think.'

'It's called a kilt,' said Bay.

'I am so glad you don't wear a kilt, Captain Middleton, like that great mountain of a man standing behind the Queen. What a brute, and yet she clearly dotes on him. But he is a very odd choice. She needs someone, perhaps, but even at her age she might do better.' Sisi looked over at Bay and smiled. Bay knew that it was a smile of triumph. By choosing him, Sisi had shown her superiority over the dowdy English Queen. He smiled back automatically, the easy smile of a ladies' man. But if Sisi had been observing him closely she would have seen that his pale blue eyes were distant.

But by the time they arrived at Waddesdon to look at the Rothschild stud, the Empress was so reliant on her pilot to tell her which of the many magnificent animals would be best suited to carry her in the field, that Bay's mood lightened. There really was nothing so pleasant as spending someone else's money. And later still when Sisi visited him in his room and together they mocked the hideous carpet, the downtrodden princess and the general dowdiness of Windsor, Bay felt altogether himself again.

The Royal Mail

*I*N HOLLAND PARK CHARLOTTE WAITED FOR A REPLY from her aunt Adelaide. Her letter had been as nonchalantly phrased as she could manage – after the usual enquiries about her aunt's health, Lady Crewe's health and the trousseau preparations of Augusta, Charlotte had said as if in passing, 'Although I find the work here enormously interesting, I do miss our little party at Melton. Do write with some news of Captain Hartopp and Captain Middleton – I suppose they will have left to take up their shooting box.' Then she went on to describe to her aunt the gallery where the exhibition was being held and the heated disputes that were taking place over the hanging. She went into rather more detail about this than her aunt's interest would warrant, but it was necessary to disguise the real purpose of her letter.

Three days after writing to Aunt Adelaide, Charlotte came down to breakfast to find an envelope in Lady Lisle's handwriting. She must have made some sound as Lady Dunwoody looked up from her letters and said, 'I wish I still got letters that made me gasp with delight.'

Charlotte shook her head. 'It is from Aunt Adelaide.'

'Ah.' Lady Dunwoody looked sceptical. 'Well, your aunt must have improved as a correspondent.'

Charlotte waited till her godmother had left the room before opening her letter. She scanned it quickly, looking for Bay's name, but Lady Lisle had never got out of the old habit of crossing the pages so it took her quite ten minutes to decipher her aunt's pinched hand. At last, after detailed, and in Charlotte's view, interminable instructions about the monogrammed tortoiseshell dressing case that her aunt wanted Charlotte to order from Asprey's as a wedding present for Augusta, she finally reached the paragraph she was looking for.

> *The atmosphere here at Melton is not nearly as gay as when you were here, dear Charlotte. Captain Hartopp has gone to hunt on the other side of the county and poor Captain Middleton has not been here since his accident.*

Charlotte felt her stomach lurch. There had been only one accident in her life, and that was the one on the bright winter morning that had left her motherless. She gripped the edge of the breakfast table and for a moment she thought that she might actually be sick, but then her wits returned. It could not be a fatal accident; Aunt Adelaide had said that Bay had not been there, which meant that he must be still alive. She tried to read on, but her hand was shaking so much that she had to put the letter down before she could decipher it.

> *The Empress has quite taken charge of him. Some servants came over to fetch his belongings and his horses. Such livery! We were quite dazzled by the gold braid. But he sent a very charming note to Lady Crewe, saying that his visit had been quite memorable. I think we both know what he means by that! Lady Crewe read the note aloud after dinner and Augusta said that Bay had become*

quite the courtier and that quite soon he would be too grand to consort with his old friends. Lady Crewe wrote back at once to tell him that she would be very honoured to entertain the Empress if she were to suggest a visit. We have not yet received a reply but Lady C has ordered all the footmen to have their wigs repowdered, just in case.

As Charlotte read on and she realised that Bay could not be seriously hurt, she felt the tide of terror that had swept through her body subside and the tightness at the back of her throat ease. She put the letter down and drank some tea, uncomfortably aware that her chemise was clammy with sweat. She would have to go and change. It was unthinkable that she could stand next to the fragrant Caspar like this. It was only when she had got to her bedroom and was trying to unlace her corset (she had felt too embarrassed to ring for her maid), her hand behind her back struggling to undo the corset laces which had been tied into a particularly intractable knot, that she realised that although Bay was not in all likelihood badly injured, he was now staying at Easton Neston with the Empress.

There was a knock at the bedroom door and without waiting for a reply Lady Dunwoody walked in. She looked at Charlotte's state of undress in surprise.

'Do you want me to ring for the maid?'

'If you could just undo this knot for me, I think I can manage.'

Lady Dunwoody gave a sharp tug and the laces came free. Charlotte opened the chest of drawers, looking for another chemise. She felt awkward undressing in front of her godmother, so she turned away from her as she took off the old garment and put on the new one, but Lady Dunwoody carried on talking regardless.

'I came to give you some good news. The hanging committee

has looked at your work and they have decided to show four of your prints. Before you think that there might have been some influence on my part, I must tell you that I submitted the pictures quite anonymously. It is true that I voted for their inclusion, but on a committee of twelve I felt that was quite fair. And to be truthful the votes were unanimous. *Such* an honour for you, Charlotte. I am so very proud of you.'

Charlotte turned round and saw that her godmother's craggy face was quite soft with pride. She put her arms around the older woman's neck and embraced her.

'Not having children myself I have never known what it is to feel a mother's pride, but now that I have seen you succeed, Charlotte, I feel I know something of that emotion.'

Charlotte kissed the leathery cheek. 'If I have succeeded, it is because I had the best teacher.'

Lady Dunwoody straightened up, her briskness returning. 'Well, at least I have managed to put something in your head other than waltzing and cavalry officers. Men are all very well, and a good husband can be enormously useful, but women like us need something to *do*.'

'But you have a good husband, Aunt Celia, you can't blame me for wanting one too,' said Charlotte.

'Of course! But a man will only make you happy for a while, while a skill, an occupation – learning something – will always satisfy you. If only your poor mother could have realised that. She was such a clever, charming creature, but her whole life was about *sensation*. She never understood the value of accomplishment.'

'I believe she rode very well,' said Charlotte, who did not like to hear her mother dismissed so lightly, 'my father always said she had the best hands in the kingdom.'

'She may well have done. But to ride well to hounds is simply a diversion. It leaves no *record*. But already, my dear Charlotte, you have created something, a legacy. When you have children, you will be able to say to them, this is the picture that was picked by the greatest experts in the field, to hang before the Queen. That is something, is it not?'

Charlotte nodded. She did not point out that the inheritance her mother had left her had affected every aspect of her life. Everything she did lay in the shadow of the Lennox fortune. It was true that her godmother had shown her how to take photographs, but it was her inheritance that paid for her cameras, the dark rooms and her freedom to indulge her hobby. If she had been forced to earn her living as a governess she would not have had the time or space to create a legacy.

'Anyway, to show you that I haven't entirely forgotten what it is to be young and foolish, I suggest that if there is anyone you would like to invite to the opening next week, you should do so. I am sure that Fred will want to come with the Crewe girl and Adelaide Lisle, if you must, but I am sure there are *other* friends you would like to ask. I believe that one of the selected pictures is of a very special friend.' Lady Dunwoody raised an eyebrow with an archness Charlotte had not known her to possess. 'Of course you will make Caspar terribly jealous when he sees how handsome your cavalry officer is, but he will survive. The point is that all your admirers should cluster in front of your pictures and acknowledge your talent. That would be a fine thing.'

Charlotte found herself blushing. She had not had enough compliments in her life to know how to acknowledge them. Compliments inspired by her own self, that is, rather than by the Lennox fortune: that kind of flattery she knew exactly how to deal with.

'You are right, Aunt Celia. It is a very great honour and I shall certainly invite people to come. Of course it is very short notice, so I fear that—'

'Nonsense,' interrupted her godmother, 'this is an *event.*' She opened the door and delivered her parting shot, 'Anybody who truly cares for you will be there.'

The door closed and Charlotte picked up her green velvet bodice. Realising that she could not do up the line of hooks down the back unaided, she rang the bell.

While she waited for her maid, she sat down at the bureau and took out some writing paper.

'Dear Bay', she wrote, and then, deciding that was too intimate, she took a fresh piece and wrote, 'Dear Captain Middleton'. She would have liked very much to start with 'My dearest', but she thought of the print that Caspar had been so reluctant to show her, and she knew that this letter must be carefully phrased.

> *My aunt writes to tell me that you have had an accident. She did not vouchsafe the extent of your injuries, simply that it was serious enough to warrant you staying at Easton Neston. So I am writing to you there to wish you a speedy recovery. I was so sorry not to see you before I left Melton. It was rather a sudden departure; my godmother Lady Dunwoody is organising an exhibition of photographs to be presented to the Queen and she needed my help. I thought I would be perhaps more useful to her than to Augusta and her trousseau preparations. Once I had announced my decision I decided to go to London at once – Augusta's reaction made it uncomfortable for me to prolong my stay. I left you a note but I believe that it may have been given to Captain Hartopp by mistake. I hope that he passed it on.*

The maid came in without knocking and Charlotte quickly covered the letter with her blotter. She didn't know if the maid could even read, but she had spent enough time listening to servants' gossip to know that if she could, everything about her letter would be public knowledge below stairs. As the maid did up her bodice with impatient fingers, sighing because she had been called away from her breakfast, Charlotte looked at her reflection with distaste. Her hair looked dingy and her complexion sallow. It was all very well for Lady Dunwoody to talk about achievements, but what use was public approval when what she wanted was Bay's admiration? She thought of Grace, the maid who had arranged her hair so prettily at Melton. She had always resisted having her own maid – it was one of the trappings of heiressdom that she despised – but now Charlotte thought she would like to have someone who could make her look charming. When she had finished her letter to Bay, she would write to Lady Crewe.

When the maid had finished Charlotte picked up her letter again.

The exhibition opens next Thursday, the 18th, at the Royal Photographic Society. The Queen is coming to open the show. There are around four hundred prints on display, and it may surprise you to hear some of my work has been selected. My godmother tells me that this is a great honour and has suggested that I should invite my friends to the opening.

I realise that you must be very busy with your duties as the Empress's pilot, but as you are in one of the pictures to be exhibited, I thought it might be interesting for the spectators to see whether my lens has done justice to the original.

Charlotte wondered whether that last sentence was too obvious an appeal, so she added,

It is a pity that I cannot extend the invitation to Tipsy, who I am sure will be much in demand as a photographic model. I am writing to the Melton party and to Captain Hartopp, and I hope that some of them will find the time to make the journey. I wonder if the prospect of a Royal encounter might tempt Augusta away from her trousseau preparations?

I hope that you are making a good recovery from your injury and that it won't interfere with your plans for the Grand National. You see I remember our conversation . . .

Charlotte paused, wondering if this sounded too significant. She wanted Bay to know that her feelings had not changed, without writing anything that would sound like a reproach. Casting her mind back over their brief courtship, she tried to think of something that would remind him of their past intimacy. She thought of the last time she had seen Bay, standing on the steps of Melton laughing with Fred and Captain Hartopp. Picking up her pen again she wrote,

*. . . and your promise to tell me the story of how Captain Hartopp came to be called Chicken. I will be **most** disappointed if you do not enlighten me. Even if it is an indelicate story I promise not to get the vapours. We women are stronger than you think.*

Hoping very much to see you at the exhibition, and certainly at Fred and Augusta's wedding,

I remain your friend and photographer,

Charlotte Baird

Having read the letter through twice, once silently and once aloud, alert to any suggestion of missishness, she sealed it and addressed it to Captain Middleton, Easton Neston, Northamptonshire. She then quickly wrote to Lady Crewe to beg for the loan of Grace, and to Lady Lisle, Augusta and Chicken Hartopp to invite them to the exhibition.

As she placed the letters in the Japanese bowl in the hallway that Lady Dunwoody used as a post tray, the doorbell rang and Caspar walked in, shaking the snow from his ulster like a wet dog. He began talking the moment he walked through the door.

'Carlotta *mia*, have you heard the news? Your pictures. Unanimous decision. Everyone agog. You are the youngest contributor by far.' He seized her hands and whirled her around for a moment. Charlotte laughed. His delight was clearly genuine and she was touched.

'Aunt Celia told me. I am delighted, of course, but I can't help feeling like an imposter. My photography is just a hobby, I feel embarrassed to be compared to professionals like you.'

Caspar gripped her by the forearms and pretended to shake her.

'Shame on you, Miss Baird, for the crime of false modesty. If you have a talent, why not revel in it instead of protesting against it? Are you are afraid of being unladylike?'

'Not at all,' said Charlotte, pushing him away. 'If I had been afraid of that, I would be painting watercolours of highland scenes and making pictures out of shells.'

'Then you should be proud of your accomplishments. I am delighted that my pictures will be hanging next to yours.'

The faint note of reproach made Charlotte realise that she had forgotten to ask Caspar about his pictures. Quickly, she added, 'Your portfolio is outstanding, I expect the committee wanted to select everything.'

Caspar smiled, mollified. 'They have taken ten pictures. Not bad for an American interloper.'

'Now who is being falsely modest? You know that you are the

equal of anyone here. The society's members must be beside themselves with jealousy.'

'I believe there have been mutterings. Some members tried to exclude me because I was not British, but Lady D would have none of it. She told them that photography was an international medium and that they should celebrate excellence wherever it came from.' As Caspar said this he stuck out his chest to suggest Lady Dunwoody in full flow.

'I hope they chose the picture of your friend. The one with the grapes,' said Charlotte.

To her surprise, Caspar's shoulders dropped, his buoyancy gone.

'Abraham will hang before the Queen of England, a woman he had never heard of,' he said quietly, brushing a snowflake from the sleeve of his coat.

Charlotte saw the pain in his face. She remembered the photograph he had taken of a pile of stones in the desert that was Abraham's gravestone. For all his ebullience, Caspar was, she realised, still in mourning. Even though there was no black band on his sleeve, he obviously felt Abraham's loss as keenly as if it had been a close relative. She tried to soothe him.

'But as your friend, he would have been so happy to have done you this service.'

'No doubt. He was a generous boy. He would have been delighted to make me famous.' Caspar took a yellow silk handkerchief from his pocket and wiped the snow off his moustache. 'No, *I* am the one who minds that he is to be hung before strangers who know nothing more of him than the image I have presented. All they can see is what I have put before them – a savage with a bunch of grapes.'

'But that's not true! Anyone could see that he has a great soul. *I* did. You aren't so great a photographer that you can give your subject a character they don't have,' Charlotte protested.

'Perhaps.' He folded up the yellow silk square carefully and put it back in his pocket. 'But even if they don't see what a remarkable person he was, he will still hang there as an example of my photographic skill.'

Smiling ruefully he continued. 'I do *have* scruples, just not enough of them. Abraham will become a plate in the *Illustrated London News* and I will sigh a little as I cash the cheque.'

To end this exchange Caspar began to look through the letters in the Japanese bowl. Charlotte would have protested but she was relieved that his sudden fit of melancholy seemed to have passed. It struck her that Caspar's high spirits, the torrent of chatter and jokes, was something he turned on to mask his true feelings. It made her like him more, as she knew how hard it was sometimes to disguise the most painful thoughts.

As she watched him flick through the heavy white envelopes, she could see him trying to work himself back to his normal playful pitch. When he spoke, his voice was light again.

'I see you have been busy – these are in your hand, are they not?' He took one out and sniffed it. 'No perfume, Carlotta? Not even for your billet-doux to the handsome captain?'

'Do I look like the sort of girl who sends letters smelling of violets? Lady Dunwoody suggested that I invite some people to the opening, and I have, of course, obeyed her instructions.'

Caspar made a mock bow. 'Lady Dunwoody must be obeyed, certainly, but I wonder if perhaps in this case you might want to consider—'

He broke off as Lady Dunwoody herself burst through the green baize door that led to the servants' hall. She was dressed to go out and fizzing with impatience. She barked at Charlotte, 'Have you forgotten that the carriage is ordered for eleven? The hanging committee meets at twelve. You have exactly two minutes to get ready, Charlotte. I have no intention of being late.'

In the rush and confusion as Charlotte tried to adjust her hat to the least unbecoming angle, find her gloves and button up her boots, she forgot to ask Caspar what he had been about to say before her godmother had interrupted them. Rushing through the hall and down the steps, she didn't even glance at the letters in the blue and white Japanese bowl.

At eleven-thirty the butler collected the letters as he did three times a day and took them to his pantry. There he selected seven penny stamps from his postage book and stuck them to the letters, using a specially moistened pad. The butler did not think it was his place to use his own saliva. After recording the number of stamps used and the destinations of the letters – despite her bohemian leanings, Lady Dunwoody was never vague about household accounts – the butler put the household correspondence in a red velvet bag embroidered with a D. Then he called the footman whose job it was to take the letters to the new red pillar box on the Kensington Road. Despite the snow, the footman was not only the only person converging on the letter box in order to catch the midday collection. There was another footman from Holland House, a maid from Leighton House and a boot boy belonging to the Burne Jones household. The post box had only been there since the new year, so there was still some novelty about watching the letters disappear into its shiny red maw. Sometimes the footman would read out the addresses on the letters in an imitation of an aristocratic accent for the delectation of the Leighton House parlourmaid, who was the reason that he never shirked this particular chore, but today the snow was falling too thickly. Lady Dunwoody's footman watched as the parlourmaid deposited the Leighton House correspondence and then did the same, taking care that the snow did not fall on the envelopes and make the ink run.

Charlotte had not sealed her letter with wax. She had used one of the new envelopes that used dried xanthan gum to stick the flaps together. This made it much easier for the Foreign Office agent whose job it was to intercept all mail to the imperial household at Easton Neston. As it contained no reference to foreign policy that he could detect, he noted its contents in the ledger put aside for this purpose, resealed it and sent it on so that it was loaded onto the 4.10 to Northampton.

The letter was delivered to Easton Neston at seven a.m. the next morning where it was steamed open again, this time by Baron Nopsca, who had made it his business to know everything about the Empress's new favourite. He found its contents marginally more interesting than the Foreign Office man. Although his English was far from fluent, he knew enough to understand that this was a letter from a woman, who if not a mistress was certainly more than a friend. This did not surprise him as he had already assessed Captain Middleton as *ein galant* and a *herzensbrecher*; his only concern was for the happiness of his mistress. For a moment he thought of destroying the letter; the Empress would not be happy about the Captain going to London to visit another woman. In Austria he would not have hesitated to burn the letter, but then in Vienna no woman would be foolish enough to write publicly to the Empress's favourite while he was in residence. After a moment of reflection Nospca decided that there was no need to interfere; the attachment between his mistress and the Captain was too new and too mutually exciting. It would have to be an exceptional woman to summon the Englishman away from the Austrian Empress. He scanned the letter again and decided that there was nothing to fear.

As he got to the mention of Chicken Hartopp, the Baron sighed. Only an Englishman, he thought, would be named after a fowl.

The Monkey's Paw

COUNTESS FESTETICS HAD GIVEN BAY A FLASK OF schnapps as they rode out that morning. 'I think you must have need of this,' she said.

The flask was now empty and for the first time in his hunting career Bay was longing for the chase to end. Every bump, every stumble made his shoulder throb. He needed his good hand to hold the reins so he couldn't use his whip, which made it hard to keep up with the Empress. She was leading the field on one of the new hunters that she had bought at Waddesdon from the Rothschilds. She had bought five horses in all and Bay had made a tidy commission. The blue roan called Liniment, was everything a great hunter should be and showed no sign of flagging after a long day on soft ground, but now Bay was regretting his gift for spotting a good horse.

After clearing one particularly high fence Bay heard her say to Count Esterhazy in English so that he could understand, 'Aren't you jealous of my English Pegasus, Count? You have to admit that the Captain was right about English hunters.'

'The Captain is certainly good at picking winners,' said Esterhazy, also in English.

The Empress did not hear Esterhazy's reply as she had already gone ahead to the next fence, but Bay did. Despite the throbbing in his shoulder he made himself smile at the Count and said, 'If you change your mind about English horses, I would be happy to find some for you.'

'Thank you for your kind offer, Captain Middleton, but I don't think that I need your assistance to choose my horses.'

Bay's smile did not falter. 'I'm always happy to help if you change your mind.'

Count Esterhazy gave him the very smallest inclination of the head, somewhere between a nod and a gesture of distaste.

'Too kind. But unlike the Empress, I never change my mind.' He turned his head to look at the Empress wheeling round the edge of the field on the blue roan. 'I believe I am keeping you from your duties, Captain Middleton.'

Bay gave Tipsy a nudge with his spurs. When he drew alongside Sisi, she turned her head and frowned.

'There you are,' she said.

At the end of the day, the Empress had a carriage to take her home. Normally Bay would have hacked home on Tipsy but he knew he was at the end of his strength. Reluctantly he climbed into the closed carriage, with the Empress, Liechtenstein and Esterhazy. Esterhazy was sitting next to the Empress so he had to take the seat next to Liechtenstein, who shrank into the corner as Bay sat down. The Austrians chatted away in German, the two men doing their best to ignore Bay. The Empress smiled at him from time to time, but she did not insist on speaking English. Bay closed his eyes and instantly fell asleep.

A searing jolt of pain woke him up with a start. Lichtenstein must have poked him in his bad shoulder. To his surprise he saw that the three others were laughing at him.

Sisi said, 'Don't be angry with Felix, Captain Middleton. You were snoring a little loudly, and I asked him to wake you up. I had forgotten about your bad shoulder. Forgive me.'

Bay smiled as broadly as he could. 'I am the one who should be asking forgiveness. To disturb you with my snoring, that is a heinous crime. I deserve the most severe punishment.'

'It is a good thing we are not in Austria, Captain Middleton, as then your punishment really would be severe,' said Count Esterhazy. 'There no courtier would dream of falling asleep in the presence of royalty.'

'How fortunate, then, that we are in England,' said Bay evenly.

'Yes, it is so nice to be here and not in Vienna where everybody takes etiquette so seriously,' said Sisi. 'Everyone must be allowed their frailties. I would have left you to sleep but you were making such a noise that we could hardly hear ourselves talk.' She laughed and Bay could see that she was enjoying teasing him in front of the others, so he forced himself to laugh too.

'And why are you so weary, I wonder, Captain? What are you doing at night that means that you fall asleep in the day?' Sisi said. Bay saw the merest glimpse of her tongue as she licked her lips.

'It can be difficult sometimes to fall asleep in a strange house, Ma'am. Even one as welcoming as Easton Neston.'

'Perhaps you should consider staying somewhere else,' said the Count.

Bay met his gaze without flinching. It was a direct challenge; both men waited to see how the Empress would react. Her cheeks were flushed and her eyes glinted. Picking up her fan, she tapped Esterhazy on the arm, harder than was strictly necessary.

'Do I need to remind you that the Captain is my guest? I have asked him to stay and I will be the one to ask him to leave. We may be in England, but you are an Austrian, and as you were so quick to remind Captain Middleton, a courtier knows the penalty for being rude to royalty. By insulting him you have insulted me. Please apologise at once.'

'I apologise to you, Kaiserin, unreservedly,' said the Count. 'Perhaps I did not understand your feelings completely. But you cannot expect me to apologise to this, this . . .' he was spitting out his words now, 'this groom.'

Bay recoiled from the force of his anger, but he had had years of experience dealing with people who thought themselves superior to him; he knew that the most effective response was deflation. So he smiled affably, the smile of a cavalry officer dealing with a drunken soldier.

'No need to apologise, old man. No need at all. No offence meant, I am sure, and none taken. I don't think either of us would want to embarrass Her Majesty with a petty squabble. That may be the way you do things in Austria, but an English gentleman does not give way to his feelings in the presence of a lady, let alone a queen.'

Sisi clapped her hands.

'Bravo, Bay Middleton. We are not in Vienna now, Count.'

Esterhazy saw that he had been outmanoeuvred. Subsiding into his corner, he was silent for the rest of the journey.

Nopsca was on the steps to greet them, with a footman holding tumblers of negus on a salver. Bay took his and drained it in one gulp. The quarrel with Esterhazy had unsettled him. He did not enjoy being the focus of so much hostility.

Nopsca was distributing the day's letters to Esterhazy and Liechtenstein. The Empress's correspondence was set out in a red morocco casket. Nopsca murmured something about the Crown Prince and the Empress started to go upstairs. Bay, who did not want to be left alone with the Austrians, made to follow her when the Baron called him back.

'One moment, Captain Middleton. There is a letter for you too.'

Surprised, Bay took the letter. Not recognising the handwriting, he put it in the pocket of his coat and had just put his foot on the first marble tread when the whole hall was pierced by a shriek that made the crystals of the great chandelier rattle. A quick grey shape jumped from the top of the balustrade at the top of the staircase onto the stairs and started to bounce from step to step, chattering as it did so. As the creature came nearer to him Bay saw that it was a monkey about the size of a terrier, wearing a red waistcoat with gold braid and a golden collar round its neck.

As it passed the Empress, she cried out, 'My little Florian, you have escaped. Nopsca, we must put him back in his prison or the English housekeeper will hand in her notice.' Behind him, Bay heard Nopsca sigh. Catching the monkey was not going to be easy.

Bay found a sugar lump in his pocket that he kept there to reward his horses, and he bent down and offered it to the monkey. The little animal skittered around him for a moment, coming towards the outstretched treat and then retreating. Bay kept up a a stream of soothing chatter, the sort of small talk he made to his horses.

'Don't be scared, Florian, I'm not going to hurt you, look at this lovely lump of sugar, you know you're hungry.' The monkey's movements began to slow down and at last he came very close to Bay's outstretched hand and one paw darted out to take the treat. Bay let him take the sugar lump and then started to stroke the animal's head and back. Then slowly and carefully he scooped up the little creature with his good arm and held it close to his body.

The monkey, who was blissfully eating the sugar, did not protest, and Bay was about to hand him over to Nopsca's outstretched arms when Liechtenstein said in a stage whisper to the Count, 'Why, even little Florian finds the Captain irresistible.'

Esterhazy gave a sharp bark of laughter which echoed through the vast marble hall and frightened the monkey, which leapt out of Bay's arms and began to dance around him. Cursing under his breath, he dug around in his pocket for another sugar lump, and in doing so he dislodged the letter which fell to the ground. The monkey, who had seen exactly where the supply of treats was coming from, saw the envelope as manna from heaven. He picked it up with both paws and began to scamper up the stairs. Bay went after him, but with only one arm, it was too easy for Florian to jump out of his grasp. He made a grab for the monkey, which had jumped on the handrail, and losing his balance, fell painfully onto the marble steps, narrowly avoiding a headlong tumble down the staircase.

'Florian, you are a wicked creature,' said the Empress, who had been laughing so much there were tears on her cheeks. 'Come here at once and receive your punishment.' The monkey looked at her for a moment, nibbled the envelope he was holding, and then jumped into the Empress's arms.

'Good boy! And now you must apologise to the Captain.' Bay had to pull himself up by the marble banister. At that moment he would have happily throttled Florian. He could see that Nopsca was having similar thoughts. Standing up shakily, he shook the tiny paw that was being held out to him by the Empress.

'Look how sorry he is. But I suppose he is like any caged

creature, desperate to enjoy his freedom.' Bay did not trust himself to reply.

'And here is your letter, only slightly damaged. I hope it isn't too important?' Her tone was pointed.

Bay took the envelope. In a moment of sudden clarity he realised that the letter must be from Charlotte and that the Empress had sensed that it was from a woman.

'I doubt it, Ma'am,' he said, as nonchalantly as he could. He turned the letter over in his hand. 'It's probably from Lady Crewe, wanting to know when I am coming back.'

As Bay had hoped, this distracted the Empress. 'There is no question of you going back. You must write and tell her that I insist that you remain here.'

'Yes, Your Majesty,' said Bay with a mock flourish. Sisi either ignored this gesture or accepted it as her due, Bay could not be quite sure.

Then the Empress swept past him to give Florian to his gaoler, and Bay took his chance to escape.

As he read the letter, he could hear Charlotte's small, clear voice and see the wry tilt of her head. With a pang, he realised that there had been no caprice about her departure from Melton. Hartopp had seen an opportunity to queer things between Bay and Charlotte and had taken it.

He heard the appeal in Charlotte's letter, understanding that she had hedged it around with banter, as if unsure of how he would receive it: he must, he decided, go to the exhibition. It would make Charlotte happy. Whatever happened here at Easton Neston, he liked the idea of making Charlotte happy.

With some relish he thought that he would tell Charlotte exactly how Hartopp had come to be called Chicken – in normal circumstances he would never dream of betraying a fellow officer, but given Hartopp's treachery he felt no compunction. But as he sat down at the walnut writing bureau and tried to pick up a pen he realised that his injured arm was not capable of doing even that, let alone writing a letter. Bay rocked back on his chair. He tried to write something with his left hand, but as he was right-handed his efforts were hardly legible.

In another house, Bay might have asked someone to take dictation for him, but that was not possible at Easton Neston. There was no one in the household whose discretion he could trust. There was the telegraph, of course, but even that would involve getting one of the servants on side.

He was wondering how to solve this problem when the footman who had been assigned to valet him appeared, holding a bowl of hot water.

Bay had cut himself shaving that morning, and it was difficult to hold the razor steady with the wrong hand, so he asked the footman to do the job for him. The footman, who was a tall teenager with a freckled countenance that suggested he had red hair under his wig, was unexpectedly deft.

'Thank you. What's your name?'

'Albert, sir.'

'You could be a barber, Albert.'

'Thank you, sir. Grew up on a farm, so I've been shearing sheep since I was a lad. Got to have a steady hand for shearing.'

'How did you come into service? Doesn't your father need you on the farm?'

'I am the youngest of eight brothers, sir. Would have been ten but two of them died of fever.'

'I see. Do you like it here?'

Albert hesitated.

Bay, sensing this, said, 'Don't worry, I never betray a confidence.'

'Well, sir, I was happy enough here working for Lord Hesketh, but I can't say as I enjoy the current situation. I haven't worked for foreigners before. They've got some funny notions. The housekeeper and the cook are beside themselves. Last week in the middle of the night, the bell rings – Her Majesty's bell. I was still up, so I had to go up there. The Countess, the older lady, tells me to go and fetch some raw veal, quick as I can. So I have to wake up Cook and get the key to the meat safe and fetch the meat up there on a silver salver. Next morning the maid that was doing the room brought it down again. They hadn't touched it.'

Bay thought he had found his man.

'Albert, would you like to earn a sovereign?'

'Yes, sir.'

'Can you write?'

Albert looked puzzled. 'Not copperplate, sir, but I know my letters.'

'If I give you a message, could you write it down and take it to the telegraph office for me?'

'I think so, sir.'

'The important thing is that no one in the household should know anything about it. Not the message, nor the fact that I want to send a telegram.'

Albert looked worried.

'But suppose someone sees me go into the telegraph office, sir. What will I say?'

'If it is one of the English servants you can tell them I sent you, something about a horse. If it is one of the Austrians, just pretend that you don't understand what they are saying.'

The footman smiled. 'That'll be easy enough, sir.'

'Excellent. When you've done it, there will be another sovereign for you.'

'Thank you, sir.'

After Albert had left, Bay picked up Charlotte's letter and tucked it into the inside pocket of his riding coat. Then after a moment he took it out, read it through again and threw into the fire, where it blazed for a moment before crumbling into the ash.

Bay did not go down to dinner that evening. His shoulder was aching and he did not relish the prospect of another encounter with Liechtenstein and Esterhazy. He knew that Sisi would not be pleased by this dereliction of duty, and he wondered whether she would come to his room that night.

By eleven o'clock he decided that she wasn't coming. He rang the bell and asked the footman to bring him some brandy. He had subsided into a pleasant, alcohol-tinged haze, so when he heard the tap on the door just before midnight, he felt a moment of irritation at being disturbed.

Her hair was down, hanging over one shoulder, and she was holding the length of it up with her arm like a train. She was wearing a floor-length velvet gown with a high neck and frogged fastenings all the way down. Bay, as always, found himself moved by the sight of her hair unbound.

She smiled at him. 'I would have come sooner, but I had to write some letters.'

He walked over to her and took the rope of hair and shook it out. The weight of it pulled her head back a little and he kissed her as her mouth tilted up to his.

He slipped his hand under her gown and felt bare skin. He stroked her ribs and the underside of her breast, tiny feathery touches until he could hear her breathing change. He tugged at the fastening of the robe with his good hand but the little knots of silk wouldn't budge.

'Are you trying to keep me out?' he said.

'Aren't I worth a little perseverance?' said Sisi.

She liked to hedge their encounters with these small tests of his patience. After the days spent behaving as Empress and Pilot, it took them both a moment to assume their night-time roles. She always came to him, but she did not instantly surrender. As Bay struggled with the slippery silk fastenings, he knew that in her eyes he was proving himself worthy of the prize.

At last, his fingers aching, he unfastened the last knot at the hem. Kneeling before her, he tugged the robe from her shoulders so that it pooled on the floor.

She looked down at him. 'I don't think that even John Brown would work so hard to possess his queen.'

'But my reward is so much greater,' said Bay.

Later, as they lay side by side on his bed, Bay said, 'I so long to put *both* my arms around you, Sisi.'

'I think you manage quite well.' She laughed.

'I need to see the doctor in London who attended to my shoulder before. I don't think the man here has strapped it up properly.'

'Oh, but you don't have to go all the way to London. What's his name? I will ask Nopsca to send for him,' said Sisi, stroking his injured arm.

'You are very kind, but I think it might be easier if I went to see him myself. I will only be gone for a day and a night.'

'But I will miss you,' said Sisi, pouting.

Bay kissed her. 'You have Liechtenstein and Esterhazy to entertain you. I am sure they won't miss me.'

'No. They are horribly jealous of you. Not because of me, you understand, not in that way – they are more interested in each other. But they are scared that now I have you, I will send them home.'

'And will you?'

'Oh no, they would run back and gossip about me. No, they are better here. They will get used to you.'

'I wish I could agree with you.'

She laughed. 'I thought Max was going to call you out this afternoon.'

'May I remind Your Majesty that duelling is illegal in this country.'

'Oh, it is in Austria too, but it doesn't stop them.'

'Well, I value my life too highly to lose it because someone calls me a groom. And besides, I would rather be called a groom than a courtier.'

'So what do you want to be called, Bay?'

'Your pilot and your friend.' He stroked the length of her side.

'Special friend,' said Sisi, putting her head on his chest.

Bay tried not to flinch as her weight fell on his bad arm. Sisi quite often forgot his dislocated shoulder. He hoped that she would not fall asleep.

The stable clock struck two-thirty and Sisi roused herself. As she stood fastening the blue velvet gown she said, 'Who was your letter from? The one that poor Florian nearly ate.'

Bay was glad he had burnt the letter.

'Oh, it was from Lady Crewe. She wanted to know if I could persuade you to call on her at Melton.'

'But why would I want to do that?'

'The house is an architectural curiosity. It is one of the most famous examples of the Gothic style.'

'Does it have tartan carpets?'

'Oh no. Lord Crewe is a very cultured man. '

'And what is she like?'

'Ambitious.'

'Then I see no reason to call on her. Unless, of course, you have a reason for going there?'

'None at all,' Bay said truthfully.

Sisi seemed satisfied. Fastening the collar, she said, 'I had a letter today too. From my son.'

Bay looked up, surprised. Sisi hardly ever mentioned her children. He had assumed it was from some delicacy about their situation.

'I don't know if he will come here. Rudolph doesn't care for hunting.' She frowned. 'I think perhaps that he is afraid. But I cannot ask him.'

'No,' Bay agreed.

'He has come to look at factories and shipyards. Or so he says.' Sisi paused. 'I think there may be other reasons, but he would not tell his mother those.' She shrugged. 'They took him away from me when he was very young. I had been ill, and my husband's mother did not trust me to bring up the heir to the throne. But I would have managed him better. He is more Wittelsbach than Hapsburg, but they do not listen to me.' She pulled her hair across her shoulder and flicked the ends against her other hand like a switch.

'But if he does come here, we must be discreet.'

'Yes, Your Majesty,' said Bay.

The Crown Prince

THE AMBASSADOR LOOKED AT HIS POCKET WATCH. it was twenty-three minutes past eleven. He had told the Crown Prince that he would come for him at eleven and he had now been waiting in the lobby of Claridge's for twenty-three minutes. He decided that he must chivvy the Prince along. It would not do to arrive at the exhibition after the Queen, who, being an English queen, was always punctual.

The door to the suite was opened by the Prince's valet.

'Where is His Highness? I think perhaps he has forgotten that I was to call for him at eleven.'

'The Crown Prince is still dressing, Your Excellency,' said the valet wearily.

'Perhaps I can be of assistance,' said Karolyi, and followed the valet into the bedroom.

Rudolph was standing in front of a cheval glass, trying to fasten the gold buttons of his uniform. One look at the young man's ashen face told the Ambassador why he had been kept waiting. The Prince had been kept to a strict schedule of improving activities approved by the Emperor – the evening before he had been to a lecture at the Mechanics Institute, but afterwards he had made his own amusement. He was a slight young man, only a little taller than his mother, and this morning he looked weighed down by the gold braid on his uniform. The whites of his black eyes were bloodshot and the Ambassador could see what looked like a bite mark on his throat.

'Good morning, Your Highness.'

'Karolyi.' Rudolph gave him the barest acknowledgement.

The Ambassador sighed inwardly. Although he did not wish to delay their departure any more, he would have to tell the Prince that wearing the uniform of a colonel of the Imperial Guard, while perfectly normal in Vienna, was not appropriate at the opening of a photographic exhibition in London. The Prince, he knew, would not welcome his advice. Like all the Hapsburgs, he loved to dress up, but the Ambassador dreaded the inevitable sniggering about tinpot princes that would follow in the English press if Rudolph was allowed to appear in all his military finery.

'If I might suggest a morning coat, sir . . .'

Rudoph looked at him with distaste, but the Ambassador pressed on.

'The English do not wear uniforms to this kind of event. As you are here on an unofficial visit, I think morning dress is more appropriate.' Rudolph was scowling now and the Ambassador looked around him with desperation. He saw the morocco boxes containing the Prince's impressive assortment of medals and other honours. 'But you could certainly wear one of your Orders. The Golden Fleece, perhaps?'

Like a small child who has been distracted from the edge of a precipice by a glittering bauble, Rudolph picked up the order which signified that he was a chevalier of the Golden Fleece and twirled it around so that the gold- and diamond-encrusted surface of the fleece caught the light.

'Very well,' he said, the scowl subsiding. 'When in Rome.'

Karolyi gestured to the valet, who had been listening to this exchange, and went outside to wait. At eleven forty-five, the Prince emerged wearing morning dress, with the Order of the Golden Fleece prominent on his lapel. He still looked pale and Karolyi could smell last night's alcohol beneath the imperial cologne, but he was presentable.

To the Ambassador's surprise Rudolph smiled at him.

'I am sorry to have kept you waiting.'

Karolyi bowed. 'My time is of no account, but as Queen Victoria is opening the exhibition . . .'

'We must not be late.' The Prince finished the sentence.

'Exactly, sir.' Karolyi said, relieved at the Prince's sudden change of mood.

As the carriage made its way down Regent Street to the Royal Society of Arts just off the Strand, Rudolph stared out of the window at the passers-by.

'The girls are better in Vienna, don't you think?'

Karolyi murmured something non-committal, and tried not to look at the bruise on Rudolph's neck that was only just concealed by his high collar. Then, to change the subject, he said, 'Are you intending to visit your mother while you are here, sir? Easton Neston is very beautiful. One of the finest houses in the country.'

'If my mother asks me I suppose I must go, but I have come here to learn, not to fraternise with my mother's *friends*.'

Karolyi, who had not anticipated this reaction, decided to probe a little further. 'The hunting there is very fine, though. The Empress is very pleased with the sport.'

'No doubt. But I can't stand those popinjays, Esterhazy and

Liechtenstein. I don't know why Mama takes them everywhere. And now Aunt Maria tells me she has taken up with some English groom.'

The Ambassador coughed. 'If you mean Captain Middleton, sir, with respect he is hardly a groom. He is a cavalry officer on Earl Spencer's staff. The Earl asked him to be your mother's pilot. It is true that he does not have a title, but in England this is quite usual.'

'Aunt Maria says that he is insolent and a man of bad reputation. She says that he has been flirting with my mother.'

'I believe that your aunt tried to engage Captain Middleton's services herself before he became the Empress's pilot. As to the flirting, well, your mother is still a great beauty, I am sure Captain Middleton is not the only man to engage her attention in that way.'

'But she is the Empress of Austria.' He should have more respect.'

'Having seen them together, sir, I think that the Kaiserin rather enjoys the attentions of Captain Middleton.'

The Crown Prince relapsed into moody silence, drumming his fingers on the window frame. Karolyi thought how much he looked like his mother.

Charlotte had been at the exhibition since ten o'clock that morning. Lady Dunwoody had been ready to leave from half-past eight, and although her husband and Charlotte pointed out that it would not take more than an hour to reach the Strand from Holland Park, she refused to listen. 'Suppose the carriage's axle breaks? Or one of the horses goes lame? These things do happen.'

Sir Alured, who was not a photographer and had only agreed to attend the exhibition because his wife had insisted, said that he would leave when he had finished his kipper and not before. Charlotte was grateful to him. She had got up at six so that the maid, Grace, who had arrived the day before from Melton, would have time to do her hair, and even at eight-thirty she was not entirely happy with her appearance.

Bay's telegram had arrived a couple of days ago. It had been delivered when Lady Dunwoody was in the dark room so Charlotte had been able to open it alone. TIPSY LOOKING FORWARD TO MEETING THE QUEEN HAS GOT NEW FROCK STOP SHOULDER CROCKED SO CAN'T WRITE BAY. Charlotte had smiled with relief.

She spent the extra minutes afforded by the deboning of Sir Alured's kipper getting Grace to coax a few more curls at the nape of her neck with tongs. She was wearing a new dress in a mauve and white striped silk. It was far more elaborate than her usual day dresses, but Lady Dunwoody had been clear that none of her existing wardrobe was suitable for meeting royalty. The dress had a bustle with a small train, which took some getting used to. She had already knocked over a jardinière in her room by turning round suddenly; she wondered how she would be able to manoeuvre through the crowds at the exhibition.

Charlotte studied herself in the pier glass. She pushed her pancake hat down a little on one side as she had seen Augusta do. She knew from taking pictures that a good image needed just a little asymmetry. She was aiming for jaunty but she pushed it too far, making her look simply dishevelled. She righted it again and stared at herself critically. If she was going to put herself in one of her animal photomontages, she thought, she would be a field mouse – eyes a little too large for her face, nose rather pointed. Her mouth – just the right shape for nibbling. All she needed were some whiskers. In winter, at least, she wasn't covered in freckles. It was not a face to launch a thousand ships. The only thing that she liked about it, the feature that gave her distinction, was her chin. It was firm but with just the suggestion of a dimple.

'Are you sure you don't want to try a false fringe, miss? Lady Augusta wears one, and the Princess of Wales. It softens the hairline.'

Grace held up the curly patch in front of Charlotte's forehead. But Charlotte looked at herself in the mirror, grimaced and pushed it away.

Seeing the maid's disappointed face, she said, 'I am sorry, but I can't wear the fringe. I would feel like a French poodle. I'm afraid I will never live up to your idea of a fashionable lady.'

The toilette was interrupted by a bell being rung violently in the hall. Sir Alured had clearly finished his kipper. Charlotte gave her hat a last-minute adjustment in the mirror and ran down the stairs.

Lady Dunwoody was resplendent in a red and gold figured silk which reminded Charlotte irresistibly of the dragons on the Japanese screen in the studio. There was something quite regal about her – it was the combination of her height and her assumption that she was being listened to with full attention. Charlotte thought that the real Queen could hardly be more intimidating.

Just as they had seated themselves in the carriage, there was a knock at the window and Caspar peered in.

'Good morning, ladies, Sir Alured. I know that I said yesterday that I would meet you at the exhibition, but when I woke up this morning I felt my heart beating like it was fit to burst and the only way to calm my nerves is to be in your company. Will you take pity on me? If there is no room, I will happily walk alongside. I feel that unless I do a great deal of talking now I will splutter like a firework in front of the Queen.'

Ignoring her husband's sigh, Lady Dunwoody opened the carriage door.

'You may ride with us, Mr Hewes, but you must not crush Miss Baird's dress. Or talk too much.'

'I promise to make myself as thin as a pencil and as quiet as a mouse. Miss Baird will emerge unruffled, her ears unsullied by my noisome chatter. But before I embark upon my vow of silence I must just observe the splendour of the feminine apparel in this carriage.'

Caspar climbed in and sat beside Charlotte, making a great play of twisting his lanky limbs into the smallest possible knot.

'That lilac stripe is so à la mode, Charlotte. You look like the most delicious ice, a confection of Parma violets and cream. I don't suppose that anyone will bother to look at the photographs when they have such loveliness before them.'

Sir Alured banged on the carriage roof to give the coachman the signal to drive off and opened his copy of *The Times* with an ostentatious rustle.

'And as for you, Lady D, such splendour. There are not many women who can wear that particular shade of red and emerge the victor, but you have vanquished the colour quite decisively. I bask in your reflected glory.'

Caspar let his ulster fall open a little to reveal that he was wearing a waistcoat of a rose figured silk that did indeed look like a dilution of Lady D's vigorous crimson.

'I think you may be assured of your share of attention in that waistcoat,' said Lady Dunwoody.

'Do you think perhaps that is a little too much for the morning?

I did toy with something a little more discreet, but then I decided that as all the photographs are monochrome it was my duty to add a splash of colour.'

'But Caspar, you don't need a waistcoat to add colour,' said Charlotte, 'your pictures are so magnificent they will attract all the attention you could possibly want.' Caspar smiled. Like all flatterers he longed to be praised in return.

'Now Caspar, if you have the good fortune to be presented to the Queen,' said Lady Dunwoody, 'you bow very low and call her Your Majesty, and if she engages you in conversation you may call her Ma'am. But remember that, hard as it will be for you of all people, you may only speak if you are spoken to. You cannot chat away to the Queen as you would to us.'

'Don't worry, Lady D, even a Republican like me is awed by the presence of royalty. The only unsolicited noise I will make is a sigh as I contemplate Her Majesty in all her pomp.'

There was an audible snort from behind *The Times*.

Lady Dunwoody turned to Charlotte. 'And you must talk to that goose of an aunt of yours, and warn her that the Queen must be allowed to look at the pictures in peace. Caspar is positively taciturn in comparison with Adelaide Lisle.'

'I will do my best,' said Charlotte.

Caspar turned to Charlotte. 'What about the gallant Captain? Is he coming? I am *consumed* with jealousy already. I may have to challenge him to a duel. I am surprisingly good with a pistol.'

'I believe that Captain Middleton is coming, but I shall turn him away at the door if you don't promise to behave,' said Charlotte sternly.

Caspar put up his hands in surrender. 'I will be a model of discretion. I shall fade into the background.'

'Not in that waistcoat, you won't,' said Charlotte.

As the carriage entered the Park, Lady Dunwoody leant forward and said, 'I believe that the Queen will not be the only royal presence at the exhibition. There is a possibility that Crown Prince Rudolph, the son of the Austrian emperor, will be there too. Alured arranged it with the Austrian ambassador. The Crown Prince is very interested in photography, isn't that right, Alured?'

Her husband grunted behind his paper, but after a nudge he put the paper down for a moment and said, 'Apparently so. Although from what I hear about the Crown Prince, his interest in photography may be in its less salubrious forms. I hear that he is quite a volatile young man. Not like a Hapsburg at all. They are stolid to the point of dreariness, but Prince Rudolph clearly takes after his mother.'

'Is the Empress volatile?' asked Charlotte.

Sir Alured folded his hands. 'If our own queen was to behave as the Empress does, I feel confident that we would be a republic before very long. Of course, she is only a consort and there is no doubt that Franz Joseph is the most diligent of sovereigns, but he has indulged his wife in a way that could not be tolerated here. Karolyi says that she can be extraordinarily wilful. In Vienna she hired a circus troupe to teach her to do tricks on horseback. She is most reluctant to go to court functions, but she is quite happy to appear in public jumping through a ring of fire.'

'How splendid,' said Caspar, 'now that would make a great picture.'

Sir Alured looked at him over his half-moon glasses. 'Making a great subject for one of your,' he paused, 'photographs is not the role of an empress.'

'Well, as a Republican, Sir Alured, I would happily trade in one of our presidents for an empress who can do circus tricks,' said Caspar.

'You may joke about these matters, Mr Hewes, but I suspect that as a Republican you do not understand that the mystique of royalty is a precious thing. Majesty cannot be taken lightly. It is inconceivable that our queen would jump through hoops of fire.'

Caspar whispered to Charlotte, 'It would have to be a very big hoop.'

Lady Dunwoody said hastily, 'Have you seen the Queen before, Charlotte?'

'I once saw her riding out in her carriage. But she was a long way in the distance, so the impression I had was of a small black shape. Her lady-in-waiting was about twice her size.'

'But haven't you been presented? Surely Adelaide has arranged it?'

'Not yet. Augusta wants to be my sponsor this season.'

'They are always long afternoons. I remember when I was presented, one of the girls ahead of me fainted from the fatigue. She fell down in a dead swoon and all her feathers were crushed, poor thing. She couldn't be presented after that, of course, and the Queen was asked if the girl could be counted even though she hadn't actually made it to the throne. But the Queen said no, and the poor girl had to do it all over again. We all thought it rather unkind at the time, but I suppose it's very important to stick to the rules.'

Sir Alured nodded. 'How can you doubt it, my dear? That is the difference between our queen and the Austrian one. Our queen knows that she has a divine duty to perform, while the Empress Elizabeth seems to have no sense of the responsibilities that come with her position.'

'I suppose you are right, Alured.'

The carriage was now travelling down Pall Mall and Charlotte had her face pressed to the window in case she spotted Bay coming out of one of the clubs. But a light drizzle had started to fall and the faces of the passers-by were concealed by their umbrellas. She could feel her heart beating so loudly in her chest that she thought everyone else in the carriage must surely hear it. It had been two weeks since she had seen Bay. She tried to picture him in her head but the only image she could summon was the photograph she had taken of him when he had been staring at the Empress. Caspar had tried to persuade her that the photograph should be entered into the competition, but she had resisted. It was a powerful image; the framing and the depth of field was perfect. But Charlotte had felt that it was not a photograph to put on public view. Whatever that expression on Bay's face had been, it was a private matter.

In Harley Street Bay was putting his shirt on. He was in some pain. Dr Murchison had manipulated his shoulder, and while he now had much more range of movement, the deft twist that the doctor had given his scapula had been so agonising that Bay had cried out.

'There, Captain. It's all done. You should be able to use it normally now. But you can't keep doing this. Once a shoulder joint gets loose like this, it could pop out any moment. It's probably useless my saying so, but you should really avoid situations where you are likely to fall and dislocate it again.'

'Perfectly useless, I'm afraid, doctor,' said Bay. 'I don't intend to fall off my horse but sometimes it happens. I can't stop riding.'

'You could stop riding so fast,' said Dr Murchison. 'It is the velocity with which you hit the ground that makes these injuries so dangerous. The next time you fall and put the joint out, I may not be able to fix it.'

'That's a chance I will have to take,' said Bay. 'Meanwhile I am grateful to you, doctor, for giving me the ability to button my shirt.

It's a damned nuisance to be dependent on other people just to get dressed.'

'Well, if you don't take care of that shoulder, you will have your arm in a sling for the rest of your life. And who will button your shirts then?' said Dr Murchison.

'Once again, doctor, I suppose that is another chance I will just have to take.'

It was a quarter to twelve when Bay left the doctor's. He had intended to walk to the Strand but the drizzle was developing into solid rain. He hailed a hansom and then immediately regretted it. The traffic in London was infernally slow in bad weather. He looked out of the window at the women sheltering in shop doorways, trying to protect their expensive new hats.

The hansom had stopped moving entirely. Bay put his head out of the window and saw that a dustcart had lost an axle and was blocking the down traffic along Regent Street. The dustman was trying ineffectively to prop up the cart so that it could be moved out of the way, but the vehicle was too heavy for him to make much headway on his own. The rain was turning the road to mud and the drover kept slipping as he tried to prop up the broken axle. The carriages coming the other way had all slowed down to look at the spectacle. Bay thought that he would have to walk and cursed himself for not bringing an umbrella. Then he saw a group of navvies and other workmen emerging from a public house – he rapped on the carriage roof and said to his driver, 'Tell those men I will give them a sovereign if they will get the cart out of the way.' The coachman climbed down from his box and went to negotiate with the workmen.

As the navvies set to work – clearly too drunk to mind much about the mud – Bay noticed another carriage had drawn up alongside him. It was a private carriage with a coat of arms on the side. The crest was splashed with mud, but Bay recognised the double-headed eagle crest of the Hapsburgs. He could hardly fail to recognise it; the crest was on everything that the Empress's household used at Easton Neston, from the butter pats to the soap dishes. Curious, Bay peered into the carriage. The Empress was hunting with the Cottesmore today after much grumbling about having to ride out 'quite alone' with only Liechtenstein, Esterhazy, and three grooms for company. He glimpsed a profile in the carriage, and until its owner turned and Bay saw the luxurious moustache, he thought for an uncomfortable moment that the Empress had abandoned the Cottesmore to follow him to London. Then the owner of the moustache lit a small cigar and Bay saw that it was a young man not much more than a boy. The high cheekbones and those deep-set eyes were so similar to Sisi's that the man in the carriage could only be Rudolph, her son. Then the other passenger leant forward and Bay recognised Karolyi, the Austrian ambassador. The Ambassador was clearly trying to persuade the Prince of something; he was leaning forward and almost but not quite putting his hand on the Prince's arm. But the Prince was evidently in no mood to be persuaded. Ignoring the other man, he turned his head and stared out of the window, looking directly at Bay. Bay wondered if he should smile or even touch his hat in acknowledgement, settling for a civil nod. But there was no response from the Prince, it was as if Bay did not exist.

There was a shout of triumph from the navvies as the dustcart was pushed to the side of the road. The hansom driver picked up his reins and set off at a brisk clip. Bay threw a sovereign to the mud-splattered men as he passed. As they positively cantered to

Piccadilly, Bay looked back out of the window and saw that the men were brawling in the road, fighting no doubt over Bay's sovereign. The Hapsburg carriage was trapped behind the scrapping navvies. The chill that had come over Bay when he saw the blank, arrogant face of the Crown Prince was replaced by an ignoble flush of triumph.

The rain had stopped by the time the hansom had negotiated its way across Trafalgar Square to the Strand. The queue of carriages stretching down the Strand was stationary, so Bay decided to walk the rest of the way. He skirted the front of the Charing Cross Hotel and turned right onto John Adam Street. The pavements were thick with people. As Bay tried to make his way through to the Royal Society building he could hear a hum from the spectators, 'the Queen, the Queen'. There was a distant noise that sounded like a cheer coming from the Strand. Bay pushed his way to the pillared portico at the entrance of the Royal Society; he knew that he had to get into the building before the Queen arrived or he would be stuck outside for ages. The cheers for the Queen were getting louder. At last Bay squeezed his way through a gap in the crowd and made his way up the white marble steps.

The liveried footman at the door looked at him with suspicion – visitors to the exhibition did not generally arrive on foot and Bay looked a bit dishevelled after his struggle through the crowd. But Bay sprang up the steps with such confidence that the footman did not dare to challenge him.

'What name shall I give, sir?'

'Captain Middleton.'

On the other side of the room, Charlotte heard the words she had been waiting for all morning.

Pictures at the Exhibition

HE TURNOUT FOR THE EXHIBITION WAS VIGOROUS for a wet morning in March. The lure of royalty was enough to draw the politicians from the chamber, the artists from their studios, the writers from their desks and the ladies from their morning calls. The large salon on the first floor had an Adam ceiling and a fine Grinling Gibbons chimney piece, but its eighteenth-century splendours had been eclipsed by the wonders of the modern world. Every inch of wall space was covered with photographs: studio portraits of the great and the good, staged tableaux of scenes from the Bible or the novels of Sir Walter Scott, studies of little girls in white dresses and grizzled old men in kilts. There were photographs of trees struck by lightning and crowds in Piccadilly, the Pyramids in Egypt and the Pavilion at Brighton. The majority of the pictures were monochrome and hung sombrely against the venetian red of the walls, but every so often a spot of colour was introduced by the brush or pen of a photographer who had needed the punctuation of a red lip or a blue sky. Most of the works displayed were no bigger than a family bible, and as there were nearly four hundred pictures crammed together on the walls, the initial effect was almost overwhelming.

Many of the spectators had never seen so many photographs

gathered together before, and as they entered they paused, uncertain where to begin. This was not like the Royal Academy where everybody knew who this year's lions were, and which pictures were to be the talk of the season. Here there were no familiar names to cluster around and no movements to discuss. Most visitors went straight to the portraits of the famous – where at least there was some possibility of judging the photograph against the original. The likeness of Lord Beaconsfield was considered most flattering, making him look so youthful that there was speculation that some artifice had been involved. Several women of a certain age, who had always resisted the pitiless lens of the *carte de visite*, made a note of the photographer's name in their catalogues and resolved to enquire about having their portrait done after the same manner.

A few brave souls who had got all the way to the far wall found pictures that astonished them – women floating in thin air, a girl looking into a mirror and seeing the reflection of an old crone, a man with three legs. A Canon of St Paul's whispered to his wife that he wondered if these pictures were quite suitable, 'had there perhaps been occult practices?' he murmured. His wife, who was ten years younger than him and a keen photographer, told him not to be such a fuddy-duddy. The pictures were 'artistic'. Photographs could be manipulated just as much as paintings, and to achieve the effects in front of them had required an inordinate amount of skill.

Augusta and Fred were looking at a picture of a Highland scene. Or rather, Fred was looking and Augusta was surveying the room. She was not entirely at ease. This was not a milieu that she was comfortable with: royalty notwithstanding, so far she had not seen anyone she considered 'smart'. There were several cabinet ministers in the room, a Poet Laureate and a number of fashionable painters, but none of them met Augusta's exacting standards for smartness. A home secretary was no substitute for a duchess. Augusta was surprised that the Queen should patronise such a ramshackle gathering; it was the sort of occasion that she associated with Charlotte, who had no idea of what constituted 'good form'. Augusta once again felt the unfairness of Charlotte being the heiress to a fortune, while she was marrying a Borders squire who didn't even have a house in town. Augusta knew just what to do with that money – she knew that with sixty thousand a year, she could be one of the foremost hostesses in the land. If only Charlotte wasn't so awkward. She had always wanted a younger sister, but not one like Charlotte. Augusta sighed.

Fred said, 'I say, Augusta. Have a look at this one – ain't those the housemaids from Melton?'

Augusta peered at the photograph through her eyeglass. 'Why, yes. Although you would hardly recognise them; they look quite feverish. This must be one of your sister's photographs. Number forty-seven. What does it say in the catalogue? A group study by Miss Baird. I do think that she might have mentioned Melton. I mean, after Mama went to all the trouble of giving her the old nursery for her photography, she might have had the courtesy to mention that she was at our house.'

'Perhaps she has mentioned it somewhere else, Gus.' Fred sighed; he wished that Augusta wasn't so obsessed with her own position as a daughter of Melton. Although he was happy to be marrying an earl's daughter, it would be more seemly if she remembered that his family had status too.

'I am going to look for all of Charlotte's photographs. I wouldn't be at all surprised to find that she has included the picture she took of us and forgotten to mention our names!' said Augusta.

Fred looked around for a diversion and saw Chicken Hartopp standing behind a bishop. He was stooping to examine a photograph that was hung at waist level.

'Hello, Chicken. Thought you were with the Cottesmore today?'

'Changed my mind. Have you seen this?'

The two men looked at the photograph of Bay and Tipsy in the Melton stables.

'Don't understand how they select the photographs,' said Chicken.

'No. You would think that they would look for interesting subjects.'

'I mean, how is a picture of Middleton and his horse right for a Royal Exhibition? Middleton's a nobody and the horse hasn't won anything.'

'Middleton thinks he'll win the National with that mare.'

'I wouldn't put money on it. Horse is only fifteen hands. You need a big beast for the National. Anyway, Middleton's too busy being a royal horse dealer these days. Someone told me at the club that the Empress bought a whole string of hunters on Middleton's say-so. He certainly hasn't lost any time.'

'Yes,' said Fred, 'Bay has been very busy.'

Lady Lisle was saying to Charlotte, 'And where are your photographs, dear?'

'They are scattered about, Aunt. Only the most distinguished photographers are hung together. I don't even know where all my pictures are, because all the hanging was changed last night. I believe that Mrs Cameron felt that not enough of her photographs were on the line.'

'On the line?' asked Lady Lisle.

'At eye level. That's where they hang all the most important photographs. You won't find any of mine there.'

'But eye level depends on how tall you are,' said Lady Lisle. 'I believe the Queen is quite a small person.'

Charlotte smiled. 'I hadn't thought of that.'

Lady Lisle started to examine the wall behind her. She found the mass of images rather dizzying; watercolours were so much more peaceful. But then she found a picture that punctured her happy blur. This must be one of Charlotte's photographs. That was Captain Middleton, she was almost sure, but who was the lady on horseback that he was staring at so intently? Lady Lisle turned to ask Charlotte, but her niece had disappeared into the crowd.

Charlotte was looking for Bay. After hearing his name announced she had been trying to work her way across to the door, but the room was now packed and the train on her dress made it difficult for her to move through it unimpeded. She saw the back of a head with reddish brown hair and set off in that direction, only for the man to turn around and reveal himself to be wearing a dog collar. Charlotte stopped by a table in the middle of the room that held a stereoscope and stood on her tiptoes to see if she could catch a glimpse of Bay.

'Goodness me, Charlotte, why are you standing here all alone?' Augusta tapped her on the shoulder with her programme. 'Shouldn't you be enjoying your triumph?'

Charlotte was looking at a knot of people clustered around an easel at the front of the room. Was that Bay standing next to a woman in red velvet?

'I am glad you think it is a triumph. I feel rather nervous.'

'I can't think why. It's not as if you are one of the principals. I very much doubt that the Queen will single you out.'

'How kind of you to point that out. I shall stop worrying immediately.'

'I was disappointed to see that you failed to mention that the maids in your photograph belong to Melton. I thought it customary for an artist to thank their patron.'

Charlotte turned round to look at Augusta.

'The photograph is of three young women with their lives ahead of them. It's a study in character and composition. I don't believe there is anything to be gained from knowing that they are house-maids. I wanted viewers to see their characters, not their situation in life.' As she spoke, the chatter in the room dimmed and was replaced by an expectant murmur.

'You will have to excuse me, I believe that the Queen is arriving and Lady Dunwoody has asked me to be in the receiving line.'

Charlotte found her way to the door. At the bottom of the steps she could see a very small woman in black making her way up the red carpeted steps. The crowd in the room drew back to make room for the royal party. Charlotte saw Bay on the other side of the room. She waved to him but he was looking in the other direction. She dug her nails into her palms. To cross that empty floor to greet him now would be tantamount to announcing their engagement in *The Times*. If only he would look her way. She stared at him as hard as she could, willing him to turn his head.

'There you are, Charlotte,' said Lady Dunwoody. 'You must come and stand next to me. I am relying on you to make sure that Caspar behaves himself.'

Charlotte followed her and took her place in the line of people waiting to be presented to the Queen, Caspar on one side, Lady Dunwoody on the other. Caspar whispered in her ear, 'Is that your beau standing over there? Shall we make him jealous? If you smile at me now while I whisper in your ear, he will think that we are having a flirtation.'

'But I don't *want* to make him jealous,' said Charlotte.

'Carlotta *mia*, every romance needs a little tension. If the gallant captain turns his head and sees you gazing at him as you are now, he will know precisely what is in your heart, but if he turns to see you confiding in me, well, he will be confused, and that would not be such a bad thing. Everybody desires a thing more when it is not straightforward.'

'Perhaps that is the way that it works in America, Mr Hewes, but I don't care to play games.'

'What I am suggesting is simply self-defence,' murmured Caspar in a more serious tone than he had used previously.

Charlotte did turn to look at him then, but at that moment the Queen reached the top of the steps and the sounds in the room were muffled by the approach of royalty.

The Queen was even smaller than Charlotte had expected. She barely reached the chest of her Highland servant. But her lack of height was balanced by her considerable girth, the stoutness accentuated by the old-fashioned width of her skirts. The crowd instinctively shrank back another foot as if they hadn't quite anticipated her wideness.

Behind the Queen and John Brown, came a couple of ladies. One of them, who was a little taller but almost as stout as the Queen, must be her youngest daughter, Princess Beatrice. She had the same bulbous blue eyes as her mother. At the rear of the party were two men. Without quite knowing why, Charlotte assumed they must be foreigners – there was something about the younger man's goatee and the cut of his frock coat that made him look quite different to the Englishmen in the room.

Caspar said under his breath, 'Who is the fellow with the gold pin who looks so uncommonly put out?'

'I think that must be Prince Rudolph, the Austrian Crown Prince.'

The Queen was talking now in her high, clear voice with its exaggerated emphasis, and slight German accent.

'What an extraordinary display, Sir Peter,' she said to the President of the Society, who had greeted her at the top of the stairs. 'To see so *many* photographs in one place. How pleased Prince Albert would have been to see this. He was so *interested* in photography. He made us sit for them many times. I remember he would say to me that he always preferred a photograph to an indifferent painting. The camera does not lie, he would say.'

Sir Peter bowed. 'The Society will be for ever grateful to the Prince for his patronage. Such a remarkable man.'

The Queen nodded, satisfied with this tribute. 'Today you have another royal visitor. We are very pleased to see the Crown Prince Rudolph here. The Ambassador was good enough to suggest that the exhibition might form part of the Crown Prince's itinerary.'

The Queen turned to Rudolph. 'What a pity your mother could not join you here today. She came to visit us at Windsor and she looked *very* well. I hope she is still enjoying her visit.'

'I believe so, Ma'am, but you have the advantage of me as I have not seen the Empress since I arrived in England.'

Queen Victoria blinked. 'I trust that she is not overexerting herself. She told me that she rides out every day, but at her age she really should be careful. A gentle ride every day is good for the constitution, but hunting is quite another matter.'

'The Emperor is of the same opinion, Ma'am.'

The Queen was about to reply when Princess Beatrice, who could see the receiving line that was waiting for the royal party, said,

'Perhaps you should move inside, Mama. It is very draughty here, and you might catch a chill.'

The Queen shivered and the royal party moved into the room and began to make their way down the line. Thirty of the photographers in the exhibition were to be presented.

Charlotte was about halfway down. The progress of the royal party was uncommonly slow and she rocked on her heels with impatience. The crowd was still blocking her view of Bay.

'Really, Charlotte. Stop moving about. The Queen won't get here any faster if you fidget.' Lady Dunwoody spoke out of the corner of her mouth, all the while looking straight ahead with a fixed smile on her lips.

Charlotte muttered an apology and tried to stand still, but she could not help craning her head to see if Bay was looking at her. But he had disappeared from where she had seen him last. If only the Queen would move a little faster. At that moment Charlotte would have happily given up her chance of curtseying before royalty if it meant that she could go and find Bay, but she knew that Lady Dunwoody would never forgive her if she left her place in the receiving line, so she balled her hands into fists and tried to count in her head, as if she was playing hide and seek.

Fifty-eight, fifty-nine, sixty, at last the Queen had reached Lady Dunwoody.

'I remember the picture you had at the last exhibition, Lady Dunwoody. It was the Lady of Shalott, I believe. I am so fond of Tennyson.'

'You are too kind, Ma'am. I hope I may be allowed to present you with a print of the picture.'

The Queen nodded, satisfied that her hint had been taken. 'We would be delighted.'

'May I present my goddaughter Charlotte Baird, who has a

number of photographs on display, and my assistant Mr Caspar Hewes, who has given us some splendid views of his native America.'

Charlotte made her curtsey and was gratified to observe that she had been quite right about the Queen's resemblance to a codfish. It was the heavy jowls on either side of the tiny, pursed mouth that quite resembled gills, and the glassy, bulging eyes that glistened moistly as if only recently placed on the fishmonger's slab. Princess Beatrice, who hovered next to her mother, was also fish-like, although not so august a fish as a cod, a haddock, perhaps.

'You are very young, Miss Baird, to be in the exhibition.'

'I have been fortunate to have Lady Dunwoody as a teacher, Ma'am.'

'Your modesty does you credit, Miss Baird. Young women today can be quite *brazen*.' She turned her head slightly to John Brown, who murmured in reply, 'Indeed, Ma'am. Brazen is the wurrrd for it.'

Charlotte bowed her head in what she thought was a reasonable facsimile of demureness. She hoped that Augusta was watching this exchange. Royal favour was not something that Charlotte had ever considered, let alone sought for its own sake, but there was a certain satisfaction in receiving something that would so thoroughly enrage Augusta.

Now Caspar was bowing before the Queen. It was a very low bow, one that would have been more suitable to the court of the Sun King at Versailles than a modern queen, but Victoria nodded with approval, finding nothing extravagant in his gesture.

'Your Majesty,' said Caspar, in a voice that would have filled the Albert Hall.

'Which part of America do you come from, Mr Hewes?'

'I come from California, Ma'am.'

'Such a *romantic* sounding name.'

'It is a spectacular country, Ma'am. I am afraid that my

photographs do not do it justice. There are trees there the height of your cathedral spires and the earth is so fertile and the weather so clement that the settlers call it the land of milk and honey.'

'I am surprised that you could bring yourself to leave such a paradise, Mr Hewes.' The corners of the Queen's mouth were pointing down. Charlotte heard Lady Dunwoody gasp. Sir Peter, who was standing behind the Queen, stood very still, his mouth slightly open as if preserved in aspic. John Brown gave a long rolling sniff.

But Caspar was not deterred. 'Natural beauty is all very well, but there is no culture there. We Americans are forced to travel a long way to find the patina of civilisation that your subjects take for granted, Ma'am.'

He bowed again as if to emphasise the subjugation of the New World to the Old, and this time the Queen's lips flickered upwards.

Sir Peter jerked out of his temporary paralysis and moved to shepherd the Queen further down the line of photographers.

There was a short pause, and then Caspar said, 'Who was the guy in the skirt?'

A Groom

THE QUEEN HAD REACHED THE END OF THE FORMAL presentations and was now making her way around the gallery in the company of Sir Peter. Prince Rudolph and the Austrian ambassador were circulating around the exhibition in the opposite direction. The rest of the crowd were following the royal parties at a respectful distance.

Caspar had been led away by Lady Dunwoody for a scolding. Charlotte scanned the room – she could see Chicken Hartopp's burly frame standing by the door, and Fred and Augusta with Lady Lisle following the Queen, but there was no sign of Bay. Her mouth was dry with impatience.

She felt a touch at her elbow, and a voice murmured in her ear, 'Do I have the honour of addressing the celebrated Charlotte Baird, the promising photographer?'

'Bay! I have been looking for you everywhere.' Charlotte had to stop herself from clutching at the lapels of his coat.

'But I have been here all the time,' he said, smiling down at her.

'I wasn't sure if you would come.'

'Didn't you get Tipsy's telegram?'

'I did, but—' Charlotte broke off. 'Oh, but I haven't asked you about your accident, how thoughtless of me. What happened? Do you feel better? Was it terribly painful?'

Bay held up a hand, laughing at her torrent of questions. 'It was no more than a passing inconvenience, as you can see. My shoulder was sore for a few days and my right arm unusable, which meant that I couldn't write to you. But now I am practically recovered and instead of an illegible letter you have my imperfect self.'

'Oh, I am so glad to see you,' said Charlotte, overwhelmed by how good it felt to stand next to Bay.

'Are you? I would have come to speak to you sooner but you seemed very thick with the fellow in the splendid waistcoat. I didn't like to interrupt.'

'Mr Hewes is a photographer. He also has some pictures in the exhibition.'

'A photographer. How foolish of me to think that he was an admirer.'

'Mr Hewes is my godmother's assistant. We have been working on the exhibition together.'

'And naturally you have become close.'

'We have become friendly, yes. Isn't that often the case when you share an interest with someone? I daresay that you have made many friends on the hunting field.'

'Not with Mr Hewes's taste in waistcoats.'

Charlotte laughed. 'Mr Hewes is an American.'

'That explains a great deal. Now, you must show me where I can find Tipsy's portrait. She is so disappointed not to be here. She has always wanted to meet the Queen.'

'Even though she is riding out every day with an empress?'

Bay looked at Charlotte. He said quickly in a low voice, 'I didn't know what to think when you left Melton. I thought perhaps I had offended you and that our understanding was at an end. There was nothing for me there after you left.'

Charlotte put her hand on his arm. 'But how could you think that, Bay? Why would I change my mind?'

But before he could reply, Lady Dunwoody's voice interrupted them. 'There you are, Charlotte. The Queen is looking at your pictures.' She stopped and surveyed Bay. He bowed and kissed the hand that was held out to him. 'You must be Captain Middleton. I recognise you from Charlotte's photographs.'

'Oh, I am so sorry. Aunt Celia, may I present Captain Middleton. Captain Middleton, Lady Dunwoody, my godmother and mentor.'

'I am sorry to interrupt your tête-à-tête. But, Charlotte, you will want to hear the Queen's verdict on your work.'

'I think we would all like to hear that, Lady Dunwoody,' Bay said.

The Queen's party had stopped in front of a group of pictures that included Charlotte's portrait of Bay and Tipsy. Sir Peter was pointing out compositions by the celebrated Mrs Cameron and Charles Fox Talbot, the son of the man who had invented photography. Victoria had the slightly glazed look of a woman who was being forced to listen when she much preferred being listened to. As Sir Peter talked about the rule of thirds and shutter speeds, Victoria's head snapped forward like a tortoise and peered at a photograph in front of her.

'I have seen this young man before.' She turned to John Brown. 'He was with the Empress. What was his name?'

'Middleton, Ma'am,' said Brown.

'Oh yes. He had had some accident, his poor arm was in a sling.'

Sir Peter coughed. 'This is one of Miss Baird's photographs, Ma'am.' He beckoned to Charlotte, who stepped forward.

'I met the young man in the photograph with Prince Rudolph's mother, the Empress. What a coincidence.'

'Yes,' said Charlotte, 'it is.' Collecting herself, she continued, 'In fact, Ma'am, Captain Middleton is here today.' She stepped aside so that the Queen could see Bay.

The Queen looked at him with interest. Bay made his bow.

'Captain Middleton, did you leave the Empress well?'

'Yes, Ma'am. She is hunting with the Cottesmore today.'

'And you have left your post?' An eyebrow hovered over one bulging blue eye. 'I don't think you have ever left my side, have you, John?'

'Nivverrr, Ma'am,' said John Brown.

Bay said quickly, 'If you remember, Ma'am, I had the misfortune to dislocate my shoulder when I saw you at Windsor. I came to town to consult a doctor.'

'And to admire Miss Baird's photograph of you,' said the Queen, the eyebrow still hovering.

'That too, Ma'am. Although I would say that the true subject of the photograph is my horse Tipsy.'

'What would you say, Miss Baird?' said the Queen, her eyes gleaming with interest. 'You must have had something in mind when you took the photograph?'

'I would say that a good photograph can find favour with spectators for different reasons. I was taking a picture of a man and a horse.' Charlotte spoke as calmly as she could. She was keenly aware that this side of the room had fallen silent to hear her interrogation by the Queen.

'Well, if young ladies are more interested in horses than they are in young men, then the world has changed a great deal since my youth,' said the Queen, smiling at her own joke. 'I only wish my maids of honour were as interested in four-legged animals.'

There was a general murmur of amusement from the people gathered near the Queen. Charlotte felt herself reddening. She could not see Bay, as he was standing directly behind her. She longed to turn her head, but she did not want to give the crowd any more reason to gossip. It was unbearable to be branded publicly as a lovesick girl by the one person against whom there was no defence. In her peripheral vision she could see Augusta whispering to Fred. Charlotte fixed her eyes on the parquet floor, hoping that the Queen would approve of this display of maidenly modesty and move on. But help came from another quarter.

'Your Majesty.' Thirty heads swivelled to see Caspar Hewes on the other side of the room. 'May I show you one of my photographs? I have only one aim when I take a picture and that is to capture a moment.'

The faces of the crowd turned like sunflowers following the sun. Everyone, including the Queen, was now looking at the American who had dared to interrupt a royal conversation. Charlotte allowed herself to look up and caught Caspar's eye; he was smiling broadly.

'I thought you might like to see my picture of the Grand Canyon, Ma'am. It is one of the wonders of the West, almost three miles deep. I don't believe there is anything like it anywhere in the world.'

The company held its breath. Sir Peter put up his hand as if to shield his monarch from the uncouth American. John Brown's ruddy face turned a few shades more towards magenta; Lady Dunwoody wore her most fixed smile; her husband had the smugly moist expression of someone whose worst predictions had been fulfilled. But the Queen, with the capriciousness that can only come from a lifetime of being indulged, surveyed Caspar's improbably lanky form, the pink waistcoat and the unabashed candour in his wide blue eyes, and decided that she liked what she saw.

'The Grand Canyon. What picturesque names Americans give to their landmarks.' She took five steps across the floor, followed by Brown and Princess Beatrice, to where Caspar was standing. He pointed to his photograph, which had been hung above the line, far too high for the Queen to see it.

'John, I can't see this gentleman's photograph.'

'Ma'am.'

For a moment it looked as though the kilted giant was going to pick up his mistress, as you would pick up a child, so that she could put her face quite next to the picture, but then he reached up one enormous arm, took the photograph off its hook and put it in the Queen's hands.

The photograph was taken from a mountain top; it showed the forested slopes of the Canyon's banks bisected by the black snake of the ravine.

The Queen peered at the print.

'Such a *wild* landscape. It reminds me of the Highlands.' She turned her head a fraction and John Brown picked up his cue.

'Sairtainly, Ma'am, verrry like the hills beyond the Dee.'

Caspar leant forward. 'The most extraordinary thing about the Canyon is that it can be snowing on the slopes here, while at the bottom of the gorge the rocks are so hot that you can fry an egg on them.'

'How very convenient for picnics,' said the Queen.

The crowd murmured in amusement and the tension slackened. The Queen demanded to see all Caspar's pictures of America, much to the indignation of the British exhibitors, and as John Brown handed them down to her (all Caspar's pictures had been hung high above the eyeline) she examined them minutely.

Looking at one of the studies of Abraham she said, 'What a handsome boy. Such an exotic face. He looks very like one of my Indian subjects.'

She tilted her head and John Brown followed with, 'He could verra' well be a Hindoo, Ma'am.'

'Abraham's mother was Irish and his father was from the Hopi tribe,' said Caspar, frowning slightly, 'Ma'am.'

'I wish you had brought him with you, Mr Hewes. We would be so interested to meet an *American* Indian.'

'And Abraham, if he were still alive, would have been delighted to meet the Queen of England, not that he had any knowledge of queens or indeed England.'

Queen Victoria stared at the American. A world without royalty was incomprehensible to her. Rather than admit this terrifying prospect, she chose not to believe it.

'I am sure that the American Indians have their own kings and queens. It is the natural order of things.'

'Yes, Ma'am, it is. That is why the Founding Fathers made sure that our presidents have to be re-elected every four years so that none of them could assume the trappings of royalty.' The Queen's eyes protruded from her head like marbles, but Caspar carried on, 'Because, of course, real kings and queens must be born to the purple. A grocer's wife can become First Lady but she can *never* become a sovereign Queen,' and he made another very low bow. The Queen's eyes subsided into their sockets and she blinked, mollified. John Brown, who had begun to swell at the sound of Republican heresy, shrank back to his normal bulk.

Sir Peter, who felt that it would now be safe to intervene, came up on the Queen's other side. 'Perhaps you would like to see some other pictures of picturesque landscapes, Ma'am. Mr Trelawney has made a most remarkable series of photographs of the Holy Land which have been much admired.'

The Queen allowed herself to be shepherded towards a study of the Holy Sepulchre, and the crowd began to disperse a little. Trelawney's sepia-toned photographs of the sea of Galilee were unlikely to provoke an amusing reaction.

'Your American friend has some nerve,' said Bay to Charlotte. 'Sailing very close to the wind there. Thought the Widow might erupt, but he got away with it.'

'Caspar isn't someone you can be angry with,' said Charlotte. 'And I am grateful to him for taking the attention away from me.'

Bay had raised an eyebrow at her use of the American's Christian name.

'You seem to know him very well, for such a short acquaintance.'

'And you are quite the favourite with the Queen. You didn't tell me that you and she were friends already,' Charlotte retorted. 'I thought John Brown looked rather put out.'

Bay smiled. 'I am so very glad to see you, Charlotte.' He leant towards her and she felt his moustache brush her cheek as he whispered in her ear, 'Are you sure you don't want to elope with me? We could take a train to Scotland tonight, and be married by morning.'

'Or we could wait a few short months and get married properly without a scandal,' said Charlotte.

'But how can I be sure that you won't succumb to the transatlantic charms of Mr Hewes?' said Bay lightly.

'And how can I be sure that you won't be swept away by the Empress?' said Charlotte with equal lightness. 'Augusta thinks that I should be jealous.'

'Do you think that we could go somewhere to talk privately?' Bay said. 'I can see Chicken heading this way. And I must spend a moment with you alone.'

Charlotte considered. 'There's a room on the floor above where they frame the photographs. If you go up there now, I will follow as soon as I can.'

Bay started to move across the room, but his progress was impeded by the crowd which had coalesced to the left of the door. The two royal parties had both completed their separate orbits of the exhibition and were now standing together. The Queen was talking earnestly to the Crown Prince, who looked tired and kept fingering the Golden Fleece hanging from his lapel.

'You must be sure to visit the Crystal Palace while you are here. It was my dear Albert's great achievement. I think the opening of the Great Exhibition was one of the happiest days of my life.'

'Indeed,' said Rudolph without animation, 'your late husband was an example to us all.'

'He would have been *so* pleased to see you here. Albert thought it was one of the sacred duties of royalty to promote greater understanding between nations. When my first grandchild, Wilhelm, was born, Albert called me the Grandmama of Europe.'

Rudolph bowed slightly. 'A noble title, indeed. Although it is not one that would please my mother, I think.'

'Well, the Empress was not blessed with nine children,' said the Queen with satisfaction. 'Now tell me, what do you think of the exhibition?'

'It is most impressive. I think we should institute something similar in Vienna. The Imperial Photographic Society sounds very well. I might even design a uniform.'

Victoria's eyes began to protrude. 'A uniform. That is an unusual idea. It might deter the lady members, don't you think?'

Rudolph looked at her blankly.

'Some of the most talented photographers in this country are women. Are there no lady photographers in Vienna?'

'I have no idea.'

'Your mother is not interested in photography then? I suppose she prefers more active pursuits?' said the Queen, looking at the photographs on the wall in front of her.

'My mother has developed an aversion to photography. I think the last one was taken ten years ago. My father the Emperor would like very much to have our photograph taken as a family but Mama refuses.'

'How curious. I always find it such a comfort to know that my children can always have my likeness with them.' She made the little jerk of the head that was John Brown's cue.

'A verra great comfort, Ma'am.'

Rudolph could make no answer to this. He knew that his mother's dislike of photography was because she did not want to be reminded that she was getting older and that her beauty was fading. This was not, clearly, a matter of concern to Queen Victoria.

The Queen was staring closely at a photograph directly in front of her.

'Now this is a curious thing,' she said. 'You say the Empress refuses to be photographed, and yet here is a picture of her and Captain Middleton.'

Rudolph, who had been admiring the ladies in the crowd, turned around sharply.

'A picture of my mother, but that's impossible. You must be mistaken, Ma'am.'

Queen Victoria looked up at him, the jowls on either side of her mouth pendulous, her mouth pursed.

'We are not in the habit of making mistakes.' She pointed one diamond be-ringed finger at the photograph.

'That is most definitely the Empress.'

She tilted her head slightly and John Brown echoed her, 'Most definitely.'

Rudolph's pallor was interrupted by two red patches on his cheekbones. He stood quite still as the Queen pointed at the portrait. When, at last, he moved, it looked at first as if he was going to turn away and walk out of the room. But the Ambassador, who was standing next to him, angled his body so that it would be impossible for the Crown Prince to move in that direction without pushing him aside. Checked, the Prince sighed and walked slowly towards the photograph at which the Queen was still pointing.

'Here is your mother. She is bringing a fan up to her face, but with all that hair, she is quite unmistakeable.'

Rudolph bent down to look at the photograph.

'My apologies, Ma'am. This *is* a picture of the Empress. But it can only have been taken without her knowledge or consent.'

'How unfortunate.' The Queen looked at the picture again. 'Of course, Captain Middleton, the gentleman behind the Empress in the photograph, is here. He will know what happened.' She turned from the photograph to the crowd, looking for Bay.

Bay was at the door on his way to the rendezvous with Charlotte, but stopped when he heard his name spoken by the Queen in that high, clear voice. Stepping forward into the room, he saw that the royal party were clustered around a photograph. As he approached them, he saw Rudolph turn to look at him. It was only a brief glance, but Bay felt the Prince's scorn like a slap. He stopped, wondering if he should go any further, but the Queen had seen him now and was looking at him expectantly.

'Captain Middleton, I hope you can enlighten us about this photograph.' The Queen's voice was not unfriendly. She had been shocked by Rudolph's outburst. A young prince in a foreign country should know better than to make a scene, and certainly should know better than to contradict that country's sovereign.

'If I might look at it, Ma'am?' said Bay. Victoria moved aside so that he could see the picture. Rudolph turned away so that he would not even have to look at Bay.

Bay saw the elegant curve of the Empress's silhouette, the narrow waist, the coronet of hair, the leather fan she was bringing up to conceal her face. He saw the bulky figure of Earl Spencer leaning down towards her, the Roman nose, the thick neck, the massive thigh. But most of all Bay saw his own face – his eyes wide, his mouth slightly open, staring at Sisi. He saw himself as he must look to others and he felt a chill of shame sweeping through him.

The Queen said, 'I am sure you can explain to the Crown Prince how this photograph came to be taken when the Empress is so *very* set against it.'

Bay took a deep breath and bowed to Rudolph. 'Your Highness, I believe there has been an unfortunate—'

But before he could finish his sentence, the Crown Prince put up his hand and without even looking at Bay, said to the Queen, 'I have no interest in "explanations". I do not talk to grooms.'

The room went quiet. The Ambassador laid a hand on the Prince's arm as if to check him but Rudolph shook it away.

'In that case,' said Bay, 'I will not trouble you with my presence any longer.' He bowed to the Queen and backed out of the room.

Queen Victoria looked at Rudolph with distaste. 'This time it is *you* who are mistaken, Prince Rudolph. Captain Middleton is not a groom. How could he be? He is an officer in *our* Army.'

The contrast between Rudolph's scarlet cheeks and his ashen complexion heightened.

'Please forgive me for casting a slur on the British Army, your Majesty. *That* was not my intention.'

'Indeed,' said the Queen, her pale blue eyes as glassy as marbles.

Count Karolyi murmured, 'Your Majesty must excuse the Crown Prince for any infelicity of expression. He is, of course, a most devoted son, and like any son is anxious above all to protect the dignity and honour of his mother.'

Rudolph said, 'On my mother's behalf, I demand to know who took the picture and how it came to be exhibited in public.'

Queen Victoria turned to Sir Peter. 'Who did take the picture, Sir Peter?'

Sir Peter, his face slack with horror at this unforeseen contretemps, made a show of consulting his catalogue.

'This wall was rehung late last night. I wasn't aware that this picture had been selected, there must have been a mistake. What's the number . . .' He fumbled with the card, inserting his monocle so that he could read the label.

'I took the picture, Ma'am,' said Charlotte from the other side of the room. The crowd shrank away from her as she approached the royal party.

'Miss Baird.' The Queen looked at her and smiled. 'You could not resist taking another picture of Captain Middleton, perhaps?'

Charlotte shook her head. 'I wanted to take a picture of the Empress. She is a magnificent subject. I didn't know at the time of her objection to photography. I can only apologise for the intrusion. I never meant for this picture to be displayed; it must have been included in my portfolio by mistake. Let me take it away.' She walked towards the photograph and took it down from the wall.

Queen Victoria gestured towards the Prince. 'Well, there is your explanation, Prince Rudolph. I am quite sure the Empress would forgive Miss Baird for her mistake. Particularly since it is such a *flattering* photograph.'

Rudolph clicked his heels and bowed. 'If you say so, Ma'am.'

'As an empress myself, I *do* say so.'

Having given the final word, the Queen nodded to her entourage, allowed Sir Peter to kiss her hand, and swept towards the door, John Brown following in her wake. Count Karolyi took his charge's arm and propelled him in the same direction.

The room was silent for a moment after the royal exit, and then, as if at a prearranged signal, the hubbub began.

Broken Glass

CHARLOTTE HELD THE PHOTOGRAPH IN HER HANDS so tightly that later that day she found red weals in her hands where the frame had cut into her skin.

Lady Dunwoody put a hand on her shoulder. 'My dear girl, what a drama! But how splendid that the Queen defended you. No one can blame you now that she has so publicly declared herself in your favour.' Lady Dunwoody's smile was wide but she spoke a little too loudly to be completely convincing.

Charlotte said nothing, but Lady Dunwoody did not wait for a reply.

'And how strange that the photograph was hung without your knowledge. We put it in because it was such a striking image; those three heads made such a pleasing composition. I had no idea that it was the Empress.'

'If you'll excuse me, Aunt Celia, I think I should like to get some air.'

'Of course, shall I ask Caspar to accompany you?'

'No. I would rather be alone.'

Charlotte hurried away from her godmother, keeping her eyes on the parquet floor. She had almost reached the door when she heard Augusta's voice.

'I can't tell you how grateful I am to you for asking me here today. Most entertaining. Poor Captain Middleton, though. To be snubbed like that in public.'

Charlotte kept moving, but Augusta was blocking her way.

'Is that the famous photograph? Oh, do let me have a look.' Augusta reached for the photograph, but Charlotte held onto it firmly. Augusta tried to pull it out of her hands but Charlotte would not let go.

'Please show me, Charlotte. I am beside myself with curiosity.' She turned to her fiancé, who was standing a little apart. 'Fred, do persuade your sister to let us have a look.'

Fred shuffled his feet. 'Actually, Augusta, I have seen the photograph and I don't need to see it again. If my sister chooses to keep it to herself that is her decision.'

Augusta almost spat with fury. 'Oh Fred, don't be so tiresome. It's not fair if I'm the only one who hasn't seen it.'

But Fred did not waver and Charlotte walked past Augusta, through the double doors and onto the landing, the photograph still clutched to her chest.

The marble staircase with its red and gold carpet stretched in two directions: down to the street or up to the framing room, where she had arranged to meet Bay.

She hesitated for a moment. Would Bay be waiting for her? Did she want to see him?

'Carlotta, there you are! Lady D said that you wanted to be alone, so of course I came at once. So much excitement. There has been quite a run on the sal volatile among the RPS matrons. The Bishop's wife is having palpitations.' Caspar came round to stand in front of Charlotte, blocking her way to the staircase.

'I don't understand how *this*,' Charlotte held up the photograph, 'came to be in the exhibition at all. *I* didn't submit it.'

Caspar shrugged. 'No. *I* did.'

'But why? I would never have submitted it.'

'I know. But it was too good to be left out.'

'It would have been bearable if you had put in the picture of the Empress by herself. I think there are worse crimes than taking photographs of royalty without their knowledge. But *not* this one.' She tapped on the glass cover of the plate with her nails.

'But why not, Carlotta? It has a much better composition.'

'Damn the composition!' said Charlotte.

Caspar held up his hands in mock horror.

'Why, Miss Baird, that is not an expression I expect to hear from a lady.'

'No. But I don't feel like a lady at this moment. Not only have I been humiliated in front of everyone I know, but Captain Middleton has as well. There would have been no reason for Prince Rudolph to snub him like that, if it hadn't been for this!' Charlotte was trying to keep her voice down, but it rose at the end into something like a sob. She realised to her mortification that tears were pouring down her cheeks.

Caspar pulled out a large silk handkerchief from his pocket and deftly wiped the tears away.

'Now, now, we can't have tears. You don't want that ghastly sister-in-law of yours to see you crying. After all, what have you got to cry about? It's not your fault that Prince Rudolph is jealous of Captain Middleton.'

'Jealous? But why would he be jealous of Bay?'

Caspar sighed. 'For the same reason that you are clutching that photograph to your chest. Because he thinks that Captain Middleton is more than a pilot to his mother.'

'I don't understand you. Bay and I are going to get married. He asked me to elope with him, just now, before all this happened.'

'And what did you say?'

'That I wanted to wait until we could get married properly.'

'Did he know you were going to say that?' Caspar asked.

'Perhaps. I have told him before that I see no reason to run away. Why create a scandal when there is no need?'

'How sensible you are, Charlotte. But I am afraid that Captain Middleton is not as prudent as you. Look at that photograph you are holding. You know what it reveals. He may well want to marry you, why wouldn't he? You are clever, lovely and extremely rich, but you are not the only woman in his life. So I suppose the question is, do you want to marry him?

'That's none of your business.'

'Of course it's my business. I think you have great talents. I don't want you to waste all your promise and potential on a man who isn't worthy of you. If I thought I could make you happy I would propose to you myself, but I know my limitations. However as your friend and admirer, I can't stand by and see you throw your life away. I know he is handsome and I am sure he is charming, but he isn't good enough for you.'

'I suppose you think he is a fortune hunter.'

'Perhaps. Who wouldn't be interested in your money, dearest Charlotte? I am sure he likes you too, but he has been dazzled by that woman. The camera doesn't lie.'

Charlotte looked at the photograph again. She remembered when she had taken it. It was the day the hunt had come to Melton. She had taken the photograph in the morning and in the afternoon Bay had proposed to her and kissed her for the second time. She felt a little pop of anger explode in her head.

Walking to the balustrade, she hurled the photograph down onto the marble floor below. The sound of the glass shattering brought the porter out of his cubbyhole. He looked at the mess of glass and wood in amazement and then looked up and saw Charlotte's face.

'How clumsy of me,' she said, 'I am so sorry.'

'Don't worry, miss, it's only a bit of glass.' He stooped down. 'Here's a lucky thing, the photograph's undamaged.'

Charlotte began to laugh.

Caspar stepped forward. 'I think I am going to take you home now.'

'But he is waiting for me upstairs,' said Charlotte breathlessly.

'Let him wait.'

Caspar took Charlotte's arm and marched her down the stairs. At the bottom, the porter came towards Charlotte holding the photograph.

'Here you are, miss.'

Charlotte took the picture. 'Do you see this man here?' She pointed to Bay's face in the photo. 'His name is Captain Middleton. At some point he will come down the stairs. When he does, I would like you to give it to him with Miss Baird's compliments.'

At Bay

THE FRAMING ROOM SMELT OF VARNISH AND ammonium salts. The windows had the blinds drawn in case the more delicate prints were damaged by the sunlight, so the room was dark, apart from a few stripes on the floor where the wintry light came in through the gaps in the blinds.

Bay pulled out his hunter from his waistcoat pocket. It was twenty-five minutes past the hour. He had been waiting now for thirty minutes. He went to the window and looked down into the street. The crowds had gone now the Queen had left. There were a few people standing on the pavement waiting for their carriages. Bay saw a clergyman hand a younger woman into a carriage and drive off. The woman had been wearing striped silk and for a moment Bay thought that it might be Charlotte, until the clergyman had put an unmistakeably uxorious hand on her waist. There were now two men and a woman standing on the pavement. From his bird's eye view Bay could tell that the woman was not young. The hair falling out from under her hat looked grey. The woman turned her head for a moment and he could see now that it was Charlotte's aunt, Lady Lisle.

He continued to look out of the window as Lady Lisle was handed into her carriage, wondering if at the last moment Charlotte would run down the steps to join her. When the carriage drove off, he looked at his pocket watch again. He would wait another five minutes, in case Charlotte had been waiting for her aunt to leave before coming to find him.

The hunter gave its tiny peal on the hour and Bay finally conceded that she wasn't coming. He opened the door and walked down the stairs to the first floor. The building was silent. Bay put his head around the door of the exhibition hall; it was empty.

He wanted to have another look at the photograph of him and the Empress. It wasn't that he had forgotten the image. It was in the hope that his recollection of the picture was somehow faulty. The glimpse he had got had been terrifying. He had barely recognised himself. The man in the picture was not someone he wanted to be: transfixed by the Empress, eyes wide with desire and – he could barely admit it – greed.

He tried to remember where the picture had hung. He wheeled around the empty salon, trying to identify the scene of his humiliation. But there were so many photographs. He found the portrait that Charlotte had taken of him and Tipsy. She had understood how much the horse meant to him.

At last, accepting that the photograph was no longer there, he realised that there was no point in staying. The hall was clearly empty; only the smell of wet wool remained of the crowd that had been there earlier.

Bay walked slowly down the stairs, towards the door, which was open. Outside, two men were rolling up the red carpet that had been laid out for the Queen's visit.

'Excuse me, sir, but are you Captain Middleton?'

Bay turned to see the porter.

'Yes.'

'Then I have something for you.' The porter went behind his desk and pulled out a package wrapped in brown paper.

'This was left for you, sir. By Miss Baird. With her compliments. I wrapped it up, though, didn't want the print to get dirty.'

'Miss Baird. When did she leave?'

'About an hour or so ago. She left with a gentleman.'

Bay undid the brown paper and string and was confronted with his own face.

'Did she say anything else, leave any other message for me?'

'No, sir. Just her compliments.'

Bay gave the man a half-crown.

'Thank you, sir, thank you very much indeed. Do you want some more paper to cover up the print? Shame that the glass and the frame got smashed.'

'Smashed?'

'Yes, Miss Baird dropped it from the landing. It made quite a mess, but the print's all right. That's the main thing.'

Bay turned out of John Adam Street into the Strand. He stood there for a moment as the crowds milled around him, wondering which direction to take. He could go west to Lady Dunwoody's house in Holland Park and try to speak to Charlotte. He could go north to Marylebone station and take the train back to Easton Neston where the Empress would be expecting him. He could go to his set in Albany but he had shut it up for the winter and had let his valet go. None of these options appealed.

He could not pursue Charlotte. She had decided not to see him and he could not blame her. The photograph had changed everything. Bay could not bear the glimpse of his soul that it had revealed, and he felt ashamed that Charlotte had seen it too. To go there now would be to declare himself a man completely without honour, the fortune hunter everyone took him to be.

Nor could he bear to go to Easton Neston. He did not want to be the man he had seen in the photograph. Besides, the repercussions of his encounter with Rudolph would be profound. He wondered what the Empress would do when she heard about the incident.

In the end, almost without realising it, he found himself walking along Pall Mall to St James's Street and his club. His shoulder was aching and he needed a drink. In the smoking room he ordered a brandy and, not seeing anyone he knew, he sat down and started to leaf through an old copy of *Punch*. But soon the heat from the generous fire and the fumes from the cigars overwhelmed him, and he fell asleep in one of the club chairs.

'Well, if it isn't Bay Middleton, the man of the hour.'

Bay came to with a start. Chicken Hartopp was standing over him, his face ruddy with drink.

'Hello, Chicken.' Bay took out his pocket watch. It was six o'clock. 'Good heavens. I have been asleep all afternoon.' He gestured to Chicken to sit down and called to the club servant to bring them both a drink.

'But what are you doing in town? I thought you would be out with the Cottesmore,' said Bay.

'Same as you, old man – came up to see the photographic exhibition. Charlotte Baird sent me a card.'

Bay understood now why Hartopp looked so exultant.

'So you saw my encounter with the Crown Prince?'

'Infernal insolence. I am surprised you didn't challenge him. I would have been happy to act as your second.'

'In front of the Queen?' Bay said.

'*I* wouldn't have stood for it. I would have called him out there and then.'

'Then you are a braver man than I am,' said Bay

Hartopp finished his drink and signalled for another. He shook his head and said, 'Damn peculiar that the Prince should have taken against you like that.'

'Indeed,' said Bay.

'Maybe he's heard the rumours about you and the Empress,' said Hartopp, slapping Bay on the shoulder, the bad one. Bay tried not to wince.

'As I don't know what rumours you are referring to, it's hard to say,' said Bay as evenly as he could.

'It's all right, old fellow. No need to get on your high horse. You know how these stories go around. One minute you are leading her in the field, next thing we hear you've been to Windsor Castle with her. Royal visits aren't the usual duties of a pilot, maybe old Rudolph thought you were getting above your station and he didn't like it.' Hartopp peered at Bay from behind his thicket of whiskers, clearly hoping for a response.

'The Empress asked me to accompany her. I was not in a position to refuse.'

Bay stood up.

'I have to be going now, Chicken. I have a dinner engagement.'

'Well, don't let me stop you old man. It wouldn't do to keep royalty waiting.' Chicken was guffawing at his own wit as Bay left.

Bay walked across Piccadilly to Brown's Hotel and took a room. He sent a wire to Easton Neston saying that he would not return that night. In the morning he would write to Sisi and explain that, under the circumstances, he could not act as her pilot any longer.

It would spoil the rest of the hunting season but there were still point-to-points and, of course, the National later that month. Tipsy was definitely ready. As he thought of his horse, he felt a little better. But then he remembered the photograph that Charlotte had taken of him and Tipsy in the stables at Melton and felt much worse.

After dinner, he wandered over to Covent Garden, to the Opera House. He thought that music might soothe his miserable state of mind. An opera by Meyerbeer was playing. Bay took a seat in the stalls, hoping that he would not see anyone he knew.

But at the Crush bar in the interval, he realised his mistake. All the ladies who had been at the exhibition in the morning had spent the afternoon paying calls, making sure that their closest friends were aware of exactly how close they had been to the Queen when Prince Rudolph had called Captain Middleton 'a groom'. The news could not have travelled faster if it had been published in a newspaper. As Bay walked through the mirror-lined room he saw the fans go up as the women whispered about him. He decided to leave, making a point of sauntering through the crimson velvet corridor as if he didn't have a care in the world. As he walked down the stairs to the foyer he saw Blanche Hozier, blonde and immaculate, accompanied by her cousin George Spencer. They were coming up the stairs on the other side, so he could not escape them. Bay bowed and waited to see if Blanche would acknowledge him. He was surprised to see that she stopped and smiled at him. Lord George nodded.

'Captain Middleton!' said Blanche. 'I am surprised to see you in town in the middle of the hunting season. Whatever can have torn you away from the Quorn?'

Middleton saw from her expression that Blanche knew precisely why he was in London and had heard every particular of the morning's incident. George Spencer looked embarrassed.

'Oh, I have always been very fond of music.'

'And yet you appear to be leaving. How strange.' Blanche opened her blue eyes wide and Bay was struck both by how beautiful she was and how little desire he felt for her now.

'I find that I have had my fill of sensation for the day. Goodnight, Lady Hozier, Lord George.' And he had to stop himself from running out into the cold night air.

Mother and Son

'FESTY, I AM COMPLETELY CHILLED. I NEED A BATH, a really hot one.' Sisi was pulling off her gloves and unpinning her hat, which she dropped on the floor. She stood still for a moment as the Countess unbuttoned the skirt of her riding habit, revealing the suede breeches beneath.

'It is waiting for you, Ma'am. How was your day?'

'Very tiresome. I can't stand it when no one will keep up with me at the front. It is not the same without Captain Middleton. Everyone else is so slow. Even Max and Felix.'

'Some beef tea, perhaps, with a little schnapps?' The Countess thought that her mistress looked thin and pale.

'My bones are aching, Festy. I need the medicine.'

The Countess went over to the dressing table and opened the wooden case where all the Empress's medicines were kept. The cocaine solution had been made up for the Empress in Vienna, where she used it all the time. Festy had brought a full bottle of the mixture from Austria. In the Hofburg, the Empress would get through one of these vials in a fortnight. They had been in England for weeks now and the bottle was almost unused. The Countess took out the syringe from its velvet-lined compartment, put the needle into the liquid and drew up the plunger.

The Empress took off her bodice and held out one white arm. She looked away as the Countess pushed the needle into one of the thin blue veins.

'Thank you, Festy.' And the Empress smiled for the first time that day.

Countess Festetics waited until the Empress had had her bath and the effects of the cocaine were well advanced before showing her the telegrams. She knew their contents, because Baron Nopsca had already steamed them open. There were two telegrams – one from Bay saying that he was detained in London and that he would not be coming back for dinner. Sisi read it then scrumpled it up and threw it on the floor.

'Captain Middleton is not coming back tonight. It is too bad of him, I have had such a miserable day. I will tell him that he must come back at once. I can't hunt without him.' Festetics did not point out that there was no return address on the telegram.

But the second telegram made the Empress smile.

'Rudolph is coming for dinner, Festy. You must tell Nopsca to have a room made ready.' Festetics nodded, knowing that the Baron had made the arrangements hours ago.

'What a son I have. He doesn't write to me for weeks and now he is coming just like that.' Sisi snapped her fingers. 'Tell the cook to make something with chocolate. Rudolph adores chocolate.'

The Countess nodded again; that too had already been taken care of.

Sisi decided to wear her hair down in a loose plait. She remembered how Rudolph had liked to hide behind her hair when he had been a little boy; that was before he was taken away from her to be 'trained'. They had tried very hard to turn him into the perfect prince, but Rudolph was too like her and not enough like his father to make a good pupil. He would never get up at five every morning, ready to be the 'father of his people'. Rudolph had no sense of duty. He lived simply to be amused. The only thing he had in common with Franz Joseph was their love of uniforms.

Sisi felt her thoughts fizzing through her head. As well as relieving the pain in her joints, the cocaine made her restless. She must send a wire to Bay tonight. If he did not come back tomorrow she did not think she could bear to stay here without him. But why had he not come back? Surely if he had gone to see his doctor he would not be detained for a night. Sisi realised that Bay's life outside Easton Neston was completely unknown to her. He never spoke about his family or his friends and she had never thought to ask him.

At least Rudolph's arrival would relieve the tedium of the day.

There had been another pilot earlier, but he had hung back at every fence as if she had been a china figure. Riding with Bay was like continuing a conversation; she would turn her head and he would be there at her flank. He knew before she did which way she was going. She never hesitated when she was following him. They hardly spoke to each other when they were alone in the field, or later in bed. They did not need to. But now that unspoken thread had been broken. How could Bay bear to miss a day's hunting with her?

'I will wear the green velvet, I think, with the emeralds.'

It was fifty paces from one end of the drawing room to the other. Sisi had taken a thousand steps before Rudolph's carriage finally drew up at Easton Neston.

She noticed at once that he was not wearing a uniform. Just the Golden Fleece decoration. And Karolyi had come with him, which surprised Sisi. She had assumed that Rudoph had come down here to escape from the Ambassador.

'Dearest Rudolph, I am so pleased to see you.'

Rudi kissed her hand, but Sisi pulled him towards her and kissed him twice on both cheeks, in the Hungarian way. Rudolph held himself stiffly and he smelt faintly of alcohol.

'You look taller, or am I imagining it? And even more handsome, surely I am not imagining that. But a little pale. How long is it since we saw each other? Two months?'

'Five months, Mama.'

'Then we must toast to our reunion here in England. Nopsca, please bring some champagne.'

Sisi turned to Karolyi. 'Count, I must thank you for looking after my son and for bringing him here to me. I know that you must have been behind it.'

'Actually, Mama, it was my decision to come. I need to speak to you.'

Sisi saw the red patches on her son's cheeks and heard the urgency in his voice.

'Count Karolyi, I expect you would like to see your room before dinner. Countess Festetics will show you the way.' She turned to Nopsca, Liechtenstein and Esterhazy who were standing in a group round the fire.

'You may leave us.'

When they were alone in the vast room, Sisi sat down on one of the sofas and gestured to Rudi to sit next to her.

But he stood in front of her, legs apart, one hand nervously pulling at his decoration.

Sisi waited. Finally Rudolph burst out, 'I saw your "friend" Captain Middleton today. Did you know that there is a photograph of you and him hanging in an exhibition in London? A picture where he is gazing at you like a lovesick puppy? I was so ashamed. The Empress of Austria and a groom! He even had the impudence to speak to me!'

The Order of the Fleece finally snapped under Rudolph's constant fidgeting and he looked at it in his palm. He was close to tears.

'You saw Captain Middleton? In London?'

'Yes, this morning, at the exhibition. Karolyi made me go because the Queen would be there.'

'Victoria was there?'

'It doesn't matter who was there, Mama! What matters is that you have made yourself ridiculous. Everyone in London is talking about you and this Middleton. You must get rid of him at once.'

Sisi stood up and put her hand on her son's arm. 'Oh Rudi, you have broken the Fleece. Do you remember when you were given that, in the cathedral in Buda? How old were you then? Thirteen or fourteen? I was so proud of you. My little knight.'

'Mama, I am not thirteen now! You cannot pretend that nothing has happened. You must get rid of this man and go home. You are never in Vienna.'

'You want me to go back to Vienna where I am quite miserable? How can you be so cruel to your mother, Rudi? You know what it is like to stand there in those endless receptions, knowing that everyone is whispering about you. Don't you want me to have some happiness in my life? I have been the Empress since I was sixteen, younger than you are now. For twenty-two years I have been watched and measured and criticised every minute of the day. I am so tired of it. You know how hard it is, you feel it too.' She stroked his cheek. 'You are my son.' Rudolph stood for a moment under her touch, but then he broke away.

'But the picture, Mama!'

'Are you so very shocked that someone should admire me?' said Sisi.

'You are my mother.'

'Wait till you are married, Rudi. You will find that not everything is as simple as it seems to you now.'

'I just don't understand how you can be so careless of your position. Aunt Maria says that you and this Captain Middleton are inseparable.'

'Did she also tell you that she wanted Captain Middleton to work for her and that he refused her? Please don't base your judgement of me on what Maria tells you. She is bitter because she thinks that I have all the things that she has lost – a crown, a son like you. You must understand that. She is deliberately trying to make trouble between us.'

'So there is nothing between you and this Captain Middleton?'

'You have no right to ask me that!'

Sisi walked away from him, angry now. This frightened Rudolph, who followed her.

'I'm sorry, Mama. I have no right to ask you anything.'

Sisi stopped pacing and turned to embrace her son. She could feel his breath coming fast and shallow.

After a moment she released him and said, 'Do you like it in England, Rudolph?'

'I don't know. I haven't really had time to take it in. Karolyi keeps me so busy touring factories and visiting printing presses. We have hardly stopped. This will be the first evening where I am not attending a dinner with speeches.'

'I am sure Nopsca can arrange a speech if you like,' said Sisi, smiling.

'Oh, it will be a relief just to speak German and not to have to be polite to Englishmen who talk about their machines.'

'I have asked Festy to arrange for a chocolate cake.'

'Oh Mama, how did you know I have been dreaming of chocolate cake?'

After dinner, Rudi came into his mother's room while the maid was brushing out her hair. The girl had to bend over to take the brush all the way to the bottom. He watched as if hypnotised as the silver-backed brush was drawn through the long chestnut hair, leaving a trail of static crackling in its wake. He addressed his mother's face in the mirror.

'I was thinking that I might stay here for a few days. I have had enough of factories and machine looms. And I thought it would be nice to spend some time with you here, away from Vienna.'

'Of course, my darling. Will you want to hunt? I am sure that Captain Middleton could find you a horse.'

'I don't need anything from Captain Middleton.'

'Oh don't be silly, Rudolph. I thought we had settled this.'

'I don't think the Captain will want to be here with me.'

'But why not?'

'I called him a groom at the exhibition this morning and he was not pleased.'

'Of course he wasn't. How could you be so boorish? He is a cavalry officer, not a servant. Well, you will just have to apologise to him. I am sure he will forgive you.'

'That is beside the point, as I have no intention of apologising. Indeed, Mama, if Captain Middleton returns here then I cannot remain.'

'Oh Rudolph, why do you have to make things awkward? I have come here to hunt. Captain Middleton is my pilot. I cannot hunt without him. So he must come back.'

'But why does he have to stay here?'

'He stays here because I have asked him to.'

'Then you will just have to tell him to go somewhere else,' said Rudolph, standing up.

Sisi heard the petulance in his voice. There could be no reasoning with him in this state. He had drunk heavily at dinner, and he was not a happy drunk. She could not face a scene and besides, there was enough of the little boy he had once been to make her want to protect him.

Sisi signalled to the maid to leave them and she got up, her hair swirling around her, and put her arms around her son.

'My poor boy,' she said.

When she woke up the next morning, Sisi asked Festetics if there had been any word from Bay. When the Countess said there had been nothing since the telegram of the night before, Sisi asked her to fetch Nopsca and the Ambassador to her sitting room. The Crown Prince was still asleep.

As they came in Sisi could see that both wore the all too familiar courtiers' expression of wary neutrality. Neither of them wanted to offend so they would pretend to have no opinions until she did.

'Perhaps you can tell me what happened yesterday, Count Karolyi.'

'Well, Majesty, it was a most unhappy series of events. I took the

Crown Prince to the exhibition in order that he might have an opportunity to meet the Queen. He was not perhaps himself, a late night had left him nervous. I believe that he was very shocked to find a photograph of Your Majesty and perhaps he expressed himself more forcibly than he might otherwise have done. Captain Middleton, prudently in my opinion, decided to leave. But it is fair to say that the Queen, who of course met the Captain on your visit to Windsor, was surprised by the Crown's Prince's rudeness towards him.'

'I see. And can you tell me how my picture came to be included in this exhibition?'

'I believe it was taken by a young lady, a Miss Baird, who appears to be a friend of Captain Middleton. She had taken some other pictures of him which were also at the exhibition.'

'I see. I trust that the picture is no longer on display.'

'No, Majesty, the young lady was very quick to remove it. She appeared to be most distressed by the incident.'

Baron Nopsca remembered the note that he had steamed open the week before and cracked his knuckles with satisfaction, now that the situation was clear to him.

Sisi turned to him.

'Baron, I want you to find Captain Middleton. Tell him that I want him to return as soon as my son has gone. I do not think it would be wise for them to meet again.'

The men nodded in agreement.

'Ambassador, I am relying on you to take my son back to London tomorrow at the latest. *You* must persuade him, I want no part of it. But he must go back. Can I rely on you?'

'Of course, but the Prince can be headstrong and not always open to persuasion.'

'My son is easily bored. I don't think he will find it amusing here for very long. I am sure you can tempt him to return to London.'

Karolyi bowed. He had thought it was his job to keep Rudolph away from those kinds of temptation, but he understood the Empress's predicament. The longer that the Prince stayed at Easton Neston and Bay was banished, the greater the scandal.

'I will do my best, Majesty.'

Sisi nodded to the men. 'You may leave us.'

When the men had gone, she turned to Festetics.

'Did you know anything about this Miss Baird, Festy?'

Festy smiled. 'A man like Captain Middleton will always have female friends, Majesty. He is a *herzensbrecher*.'

'He didn't tell me that he was going to the exhibition.'

'Maybe he was embarrassed to admit that he was going to look at pictures of himself.'

'Perhaps.' Sisi shook herself. 'I am so cross with Rudolph.'

'But Majesty, he is young and jealous. You know how much he loves you.'

Sisi shrugged. 'If he loves me he should want me to be happy.'

The Countess knew it was useless to say any more.

Baron Nopsca's Mission

$\mathcal{B}$AY WOKE UP WITH A SORE HEAD. AFTER THE OPERA he had taken a bottle of brandy to bed with him and now he was feeling the results. He wondered what time it was. He stumbled out of bed and looked at the clock on the mantelpiece. It was past noon. He rang the bell and asked the valet to bring him some shaving things and a pot of coffee.

When he was dressed and shaved he felt a little better. But then he saw the brown paper parcel containing the photograph lying on the writing desk.

Last night, halfway through the bottle of brandy, he had decided that he must go to Holland Park and talk to Charlotte. But sober, he knew that this would be impossible. She didn't want to see him; the message she had left with the photograph had been quite clear. He could write to her, but he did not know where to begin. He could not explain his behaviour to her. Away from Easton Neston, away from the Empress, Bay could hardly explain it to himself.

There was a knock at the door. Thinking it was the valet come to collect the shaving things, Bay said, 'Come in.' But to his surprise Baron Nopsca walked into the room.

'Baron, what are you doing here? I am sorry, that sounded rude, but how on earth did you find me?'

The Baron waved his hands.

'Oh, there are ways, but that is not important.' He coughed. 'The Empress asked me to come. The Crown Prince came down to Easton Neston last night.'

Bay gestured to the Baron to sit down in the hotel room's only armchair. He sat on the ottoman at the foot of the bed.

'So the Empress knows what happened yesterday?' Bay asked.

Nopsca nodded unhappily. 'Her Majesty is aware of the incident. She regrets the Prince's behaviour towards you very much. She would like you to return to Easton Neston, but unfortunately that will not be possible while the Prince remains at the house.'

Bay was wondering how he could explain to the Baron the impossibility of his returning to Easton Neston at all, when the waiter returned with a tray bearing a coffee pot. He set it up on the table and poured out two cups. Bay fumbled for a coin in his dress trousers to tip the man.

The Baron added three teaspoons of sugar to his coffee. He stirred it vigorously, took a sip and grimaced.

'We would not call this coffee in Wien.'

Bay took a sip. 'I am afraid I can't defend it either. So the Empress wants me to cool my heels here until the Prince leaves?'

The Baron plucked at his lapel. 'I would not put it quite like that; she is not happy about the situation but she thinks that under the circumstances it would be better if you were not under the same roof as His Highness.'

'But when he leaves, she would like me to come back and be her pilot just as before?'

The Baron nodded.

Bay stood up. 'Surely the Empress must see that it is impossible.'

The Baron leant forward. 'But nothing has changed, my dear

Captain. The Empress is very happy with your services. She has come to depend on you. You have made this visit very,' he smiled, 'agreeable for her.'

Bay found the Baron's smile infuriating. 'But her son insulted me. He made it quite clear that he did not think that I was a suitable companion for his mother.'

The Baron heard the anger in Bay's voice. He stood up and put his hand on Middleton's shoulder. 'You must understand that the Crown Prince can be . . . volatile. He has not yet learnt to think before he speaks. I feel sure that he will realise his mistake.'

'But I am not to come to Easton Neston while he is there.'

The Baron shrugged. 'The Crown Prince will probably leave tomorrow.'

'I am sorry, Baron, but I want no part of this. You can tell the Empress that I shall stay in town.'

The Baron looked dismayed. 'I cannot possibly deliver such a message.'

Bay felt almost sorry for him. 'Tell her that you did your best to persuade me, but I am a stubborn Englishman. She can't blame you for that.'

'You misunderstand me. It is not for myself that I am concerned but for the Empress. I have been in her service for many years, and I know her moods. She has formed a very strong attachment to you, Captain Middleton. I can see that you have made her happy. She has not had so much happiness in her life.'

The Baron was wringing his hands in real distress. Bay could see that this was more than a courtier's reluctance to be the bearer of bad news.

'Do you really think that I make her happy?'

The Baron nodded. 'You did not see her before. Since she has met you she is eating and laughing. The Countess and I, we both know that you are responsible. And Captain Middleton, I think that she makes you happy too.'

Bay walked over to the window. In the street below a hurdy-gurdy grinder was playing. A small crowd had gathered who were dropping coins into a bag carried around by a monkey.

'Yes, she does,' he said slowly, 'but the situation is impossible. It is not just the Prince, what about Liechtenstein and Esterhazy? They loathe me.'

'Perhaps, but they do not signify. Please, Captain Middleton, do not let your pride make the Empress unhappy.'

The monkey was standing on the peddler's shoulder now, waving his miniature fez in the air.

Bay thought of the Empress that night in the stables with the stars in her hair. He had wanted her so much. The moment when he felt her respond had been so triumphant.

'But I can't lurk about here waiting for the Crown Prince to leave.'

The Baron was silent.

A policeman came along the street and told the hurdy-gurdy man to move along. The monkey tried to pick off one of the shiny buttons on his tunic and put it into his bag.

Bay made a decision.

He turned to the Baron. 'Have you heard of the Grand National?'

The other man shrugged. 'It is a horse race, I believe.'

'It is the best steeplechase in the country, the world, probably. Every hunt jockey dreams of winning the National. I was going to run in it five years ago, but I lost the horse. Since I bought Tipsy I have been thinking of running her, and now I have made up my mind. The race is on the twenty-fourth. The hunting season is almost over and I don't want her to break a leg before the race. If you tell the Empress that I am going to Aintree to train for the National, she will understand.'

The Baron looked dubious. 'Perhaps the Captain would like to write her a letter to explain. I know that Her Majesty will ask me many questions.'

Bay sat down at the desk and began to write, conscious that the Baron was reading over his shoulder.

Your Majesty,

I have decided to enter Tipsy in the Grand National. It is the most magnificent race in the world and to win it has long been my dearest wish. Nopsca has asked me to come back to Easton Neston, but I know you will forgive me if I don't return as I must spend the next days preparing for the race. I can be sure you will forgive me because I know that if you were in my position you would not only enter the Grand National but you would undoubtedly win, as you are the greatest rider I have ever known.

I remain, dear Madam, your most obedient servant,
Bay Middleton

He blotted the letter and gave it to Nopsca, unsealed. He wanted Sisi to know that he had written the letter for public consumption.

'Don't look so worried, Nopsca, the Empress will understand.'

'I hope so, Captain.'

When the Baron had gone, Bay went for a walk in the park. The trees were still bare but the weather was beginning to turn, and every now and then the sun appeared from behind the clouds. The afternoon carriage drives had begun and Bay watched as the ladies went past in their barouches and phaetons. It was not a huge turnout, it was too early in the season for that, but there were a few faces that Bay recognised. It felt strange to be walking in the park instead of riding but on foot there was no danger of running into anyone he knew. The only other pedestrians were nursemaids pushing perambulators.

His mood lifted in the fresh air. The thought of the National made him feel buoyant, and as he walked along the Serpentine he felt as if he was floating above the tangle of his life. Riding in the steeple-chase, for all its dangers, felt ridiculously simple. He had the right horse; if only his shoulder would hold out, then surely he stood a chance of winning.

A woman cantered past on a chestnut mare and for a moment Bay fancied it was the Empress, but then he saw the rider bounce a little in the saddle, looking for a moment as if she would lose her balance. Bay realised that in the weeks he had been riding out with the Empress, he had never once seen her falter.

Mayfair

'LOOK UP, LADY AUGUSTA. SUCH A LONG NECK SHOULD be given every opportunity to be swan-like. And turn your head a little towards me, that's the ticket. Now think of drifting down the Grand Canal on a gondola.'

'But I have never been to Venice,' objected Augusta.

Caspar smiled. 'You don't need to have been there to imagine it, dear Lady Augusta. You are a bride on the eve of her wedding thinking of the pleasures to come. Ah, you are blushing, that is just what I want. Now just keep thinking of the gondola while I take the picture.' He disappeared beneath the velvet cloth and pressed the shutter button.

'Perfect! Now I am going to play with your veil a little, like this. Your eyes have such depths to them, I want the lace to act as a frame. Yes, hold it up a little like that. That is enchanting. I believe you are a natural model, Lady Augusta. In America we would be putting your image on advertising hoardings.'

'How perfectly dreadful,' said Augusta, looking pleased.

She was standing on a small dais in one corner of the Crewe drawing room in Portman Square. Behind her was a painted backdrop of a classical temple, a pair of cherubs blowing their trumpets in the left corner. Charlotte thought that the backdrop was vulgar, but Caspar

had overruled her – 'Women like your sister-in-law-to-be, dear
Carlotta, cannot be flattered enough. She will find it quite appropriate
to be put in a goddess-like setting, believe me.' He had been right.
Augusta was delighted.

Charlotte could only admire the ease with which Caspar handled
Augusta. Despite being an American with no fortune or connections,
he had coaxed and flattered Augusta into regarding him not just as
an equal but as quite indispensable.

It had started after the exhibition. Augusta had come to Lady
Dunwoody's house to see Charlotte, ostensibly to persuade her to
return to Melton, but her real object had been to goad her about
Bay's relationship with the Empress. 'The Crown Prince was terribly
rude to Captain Middleton, of course. But he must have been
provoked. What a difficult position for you, Charlotte. But if you
had stayed in Melton, as I urged you, none of this would have
happened.'

To Charlotte's intense relief, Caspar had interrupted Augusta's
torrent of malice, and had effortlessly turned her into his creature,
by remarking as she turned her head, 'But what a profile! It is quite
Grecian in its purity. I must photograph you, Lady Augusta. To
leave such perfection unrecorded would be a crime.'

Charlotte had expected Augusta to bristle at the impudence, but
instead she had succumbed to his charm and been swept off to the
studio, where Caspar had photographed her looking into a hand
mirror. He had sent the print to Melton the very next day and
Augusta had been so delighted with the result that when Caspar
had begged to be allowed to photograph her in her wedding dress,
she had not only agreed but had asked him to take photographs
of the wedding party, and had even sent him his own invitation.

Now Augusta was standing in her wedding dress and tiara, her
Honiton lace veil arranged by Caspar to hide the jutting Crewe

jaw, looking at the American with a great deal more affection than she ever showed to her fiancé.

'Mr Hewes is so good at putting his subjects at ease,' she had said to Charlotte. 'I had no idea that sitting for a photograph could be such a pleasant experience.' Charlotte had understood the implied rebuke.

'One more, I think, and then I must leave you both to prepare for tomorrow.' Caspar turned to Charlotte. 'Why don't you stand behind the bride and hold up her veil?' Charlotte glared at him, but did as she was told.

'Now that is charming. The bride and her attendant. What would make it perfect is if, Charlotte, you could look a little wistful. As if you were wondering when your turn will come.'

'One day you *will* be the one in the veil and tiara, Charlotte. It takes time to make the right match. I always think it is a terrible mistake to marry the first person who comes along,' said Augusta.

'Evidently,' said Charlotte, 'Fred was lucky that you were prepared to wait.'

Augusta glanced at her, but Charlotte was busy arranging the veil.

'Now that's charming,' said Caspar, 'what a delightful composition. Now I want you both to think about tomorrow. Perfect, I could call this one, Almost Sisters.'

Charlotte dropped the veil as if it had been poisoned.

'I think that's enough, Caspar, you mustn't tire Augusta out.' Charlotte walked over to the table covered in Caspar's photographic paraphernalia and started to put things away.

'Very well,' sighed Caspar. 'You are right, of course, Charlotte, but it is hard to tear myself away when Augusta is looking so exquisite.'

Charlotte looked over at Augusta, wondering if she could really believe Caspar's flattery, but the bride-to-be looked as if she could have listened to the American for ever.

The carriage was waiting outside to take Charlotte back to the house in Charles Street. She had moved back there from Holland Park a week ago when Lady Lisle had come back from Melton. She would have preferred to stay on in Holland Park, but she felt a little sorry for her aunt. When Fred and Augusta returned from their honeymoon, Charlotte would live with them and poor Lady Lisle would soon have to go back to the little house in the cathedral close.

But it was a sacrifice for Charlotte. In Charles Street there was nothing to distract her. Lady Lisle had only two topics of conversation: the forthcoming wedding or the drama of the photographic exhibition. Charlotte could not muster much enthusiasm for the former, and wanted very much to forget the latter.

Fred, who saw no reason to let his impending nuptials ruin his hunting, had only arrived that morning.

Caspar, of course, did not have a carriage waiting. He sighed as he stood on the pavement with his photographic equipment, contemplating the long journey back to Chelsea. He would have to take a hackney cab or even an omnibus. Charlotte knew that Caspar did not enjoy taking public transport. He would happily walk for miles but found the packed buses, or worse, the underground railway, to be altogether claustrophobic. 'In the West you can go for days without meeting another soul. To find someone's nose pushing between your waistcoat buttons on an omnibus is very hard to get used to.'

Despite Caspar's treachery in forcing her to pose with Augusta,

Charlotte decided to ask him to Charles Street for dinner. Since the exhibition, when he had taken her back to Holland Park, Caspar had become an indispensable part of her life. While she had been staying at Lady Dunwoody's he had been there every day – helping at the Thursday salons, printing up Lady Dunwoody's plates, entertaining the ladies during afternoon calls. But Caspar's charm was not confined to Holland Park; since the photographic exhibition he had become the toast of Mayfair too. Augusta had been his first conquest, then he had charmed Lady Crewe with his passionate advocacy of Sabbath Day Observance and had seduced Lord Crewe by taking a picture of him dressed as Merlin. Caspar had been down to Melton for a Saturday to Monday, without Charlotte, and had laid siege to Fred – imploring him to sit as Lancelot to Augusta's Guinevere. Charlotte had blinked in disbelief when she saw the picture being developed in Lady Dunwoody's dark room: Fred had put on the knightly costume that had been hired from Maskelyne's and had gone down on one knee in front of a be-kirtled Augusta with her hair loose. They looked delighted with themselves.

A light rain started to fall and Caspar began to do up the buttons on his plaid ulster. As he reached the penultimate button, Charlotte said, 'Caspar, you can't go home in this weather. Come back to Charles Street and stay to dinner. I am sure my aunt will be delighted to see you. You can leave the camera there and then it will so much easier to pick it up for the wedding.'

Caspar stopped buttoning and made a low bow.

'Thoughtful as ever, my Carlotta. Now you have suggested it, it is clearly the best of all possible arrangements. But I am wary of imposing myself on your brother's last night as a free man.'

'Fred will be delighted, I know.'

As the carriage made its way from the Crewe house in Portland Square across Oxford Street and into Mayfair, Caspar sat opposite Charlotte with his back to the horses, keeping up a steady flow of chatter. But as they turned into Grosvenor Square, he leant forward and said, 'I will only stop talking if you tell me what the matter is. No, let me guess. You see, I can read your mind as easily as I can make the fearsome Augusta invite me to her wedding. You are fretting because you suspect that Captain Middleton will be there tomorrow and you do not wish to see him.' Caspar put his finger to his temple.

'No, that is not right.' He gestured as if he were practising Mesmerism. 'You *do* want to see him, but at the same time you don't. He attracts and repels you equally. And now you are cross with me for reading your mind. But you make it so easy, Charlotte. I don't think I have ever seen someone whose face expresses so exactly what they are thinking.'

Charlotte shifted on the leather buttoned seat. 'Nobody else finds me easy to read.'

'Because they are not as interested as I am. If you would let me photograph you I could show you what I see in your face. But you won't let me because you are afraid of what I will find.'

'I don't know what you are talking about.' Charlotte looked out of the window.

'You see, I am the only one who knows what a remarkable person you are.'

Charlotte put her hands up in front of her face.

'I don't feel very remarkable at the moment,' she muttered.

'That is because you thought that you and the Captain had an understanding. Or rather, he was the man that understood you. And I am sure he did, or rather does. But you are not the only woman that he cares for. And that makes you doubt everything he has ever said to you.'

Charlotte took her hands away from her face. Caspar's analysis of her state of mind had put into words feelings that she had tried not to define. She wished more than anything that she had never taken that photograph, but now it was there it was impossible to ignore. Bay was not, as Fred and Chicken had hinted, using the Empress for his own ends; it was far worse, he was in thrall to her.

Charlotte looked at Caspar. His big, freckled, farm-boy face belied his intelligence. She wondered if a photograph would reveal the shrewdness beneath his flamboyance. In a collage he should be a peacock but she couldn't quite reconcile that small head with Caspar's intelligence. His flamboyance was not an end in itself like a peacock's display. Charlotte thought that it was perhaps a diversion, or even a shield. She could not help remembering the strain in his face when he talked about the short life of Abraham Running Water.

But Charlotte did not want to listen to Caspar talking about Bay. Even though she knew that he was right, at that moment she could not bear to hear it. She leant forward and touched his arm.

'Tell me about America, Caspar. I should very much like to think about something other than my own situation.'

Caspar cleared his throat and held out his hands as if preaching from a pulpit.

'The first thing to realise is that it is a country that is still being imagined. Here every patch of earth has a story, all your places have nuances; if you say Cornwall to an English person, they think of smugglers, and King Arthur and fish. But there are great parts of my country about which Americans know nothing beyond an idea of unimaginable vastness. Of course the Indians that live there know the spirits of these places, but that is not the point. You can't imagine how blue the sky is in the West, Charlotte. So much space. It's really wild, not like your Lake District with its little stone walls. In the West the landscape is unmarked by man.

'That's why I like to photograph it; those landscapes are so strange that they defy the viewer. If I had painted the Grand Canyon, you would not believe me – but with my photograph I have shown you the truth and you will have to find a way to imagine it. Even the cities like San Francisco are making themselves up. They change their character completely in two years – I expect that I shall hardly recognise the place when I go back. Here we are in Mayfair going to Charles Street. An address that has been respectable, respected even, for centuries. Perhaps the buildings may change but to live in Charles Street is something. But we don't have a Charles Street in the West, not yet, anyway. In San Francisco there are fancy streets, of course, but they weren't there five years ago. There aren't any layers yet, the paint is still wet. We don't really have time for the past out West; we are too busy imagining the present.'

With impeccable timing, Caspar brought his speech to a close just as the carriage drew up outside the house in Charles Street.

'There!' he said. 'Did I distract you with my vision of the land of the free? You should come to America, Charlotte, with your camera.'

'Oh, I would love to, but how could I, Caspar? I can't just get on a boat and go.'

'Why not? When Fred and Augusta have gone on their wedding tour, there will be nothing between you and America but your aunt, and I think she is quite manageable.'

'But I can't go to America alone, Caspar. I don't know anybody there.'

'You can take your maid, the one who does your hair so nicely. Oh and of course,' he smiled, '*I* would come with you.'

From any other man that was tantamount to a proposal, but not with Caspar. He was offering her something even more than marriage; he was giving her the chance to escape.

But before she could reply the footman opened the carriage door and there was Lady Lisle standing on the steps.

'What do you know about America, Grace?' Charlotte asked later that evening, as she was changing for dinner. The Melton maid was trying to coax Charlotte's hair around a pad to give it some volume.

'Not much, miss. The blacksmith's son went over there from the village. He is doing very well. Sent his mother a photograph of himself wearing a suit. Mrs Street hardly recognised him.'

'I am thinking of going to America myself. To take photographs. Do you think you would like to come with me?'

'To America? I can't really say, miss. It's too much for me to imagine it. Coming to London was an adventure, but at least everyone speaks English.'

'Oh, I think they speak English in America.'

'Maybe they do, but I wonder how easy it is to understand them. When Mr Hewes starts talking fast I can't barely make out a word he says.'

'I don't think many people in the world speak as fast as Mr Hewes,' said Charlotte, smiling.

'If you go, I think I should like to go with you. But not for ever, Miss Baird, I would miss my mother too much.'

'No, not for ever. I just want to go for a . . . visit.'

'But, excuse me for asking, miss. What about Captain Middleton?'

'What about him?'

'I thought that you and the Captain had an understanding.'

'Sometimes understandings turn into misunderstandings. I doubt that Captain Middleton will care whether I stay or go.'

'Oh, Miss Charlotte, I think you are being too hard on him. He has a good heart. Always popular in the servants' hall. Pleasant with everyone and very generous, even though he isn't a rich man. He didn't keep a valet, but nobody minded polishing his boots or starching his hunting collars, and that can't be said of all the young gentlemen at Melton. I don't know what is passing off between you and the Captain, miss, but he isn't a bad man. He never forgets to be kind to people like me.'

Charlotte wondered if Bay had simply been kind to her in the way that he was instinctively generous with servants like Grace, animals and children. She could not really believe that he had only wanted the money. Avarice she recognised, but kindness was so unfamiliar to her that it was possible she might have mistaken it for love. But as soon as the thought came into her mind, she batted it away. She could not bear to think about him. Caspar had been right, she had thought that Bay had understood her, but it turned out that she had misunderstood him.

Firmly, she made herself think of other things. The idea of going to America was beginning to take shape in her mind. If she had not seen the pictures she would have dismissed Caspar's talk about the West as just another of his gaudy exaggerations. But the pictures were undeniable.

On the other side of Piccadilly, Bay was walking down St James towards his club. He had taken the train down from Cheshire, where he had stabled Tipsy in preparation for the National. In his pocket he had a card for Lady Augusta's Crewe's wedding to

Frederick Baird Esq. He had not expected to get an invitation, but he had reckoned without the social ambition of Augusta, who, despite Fred's protests, saw no reason to banish the most talked about man in London, to spare Charlotte's feelings. 'If we don't invite him, people will say it is because he has jilted Charlotte, but as they were never officially engaged, the best way to put the rumours to rest is to have him at the wedding.' Fred had reluctantly agreed to the sense of this and Augusta had taken great pleasure in telling Charlotte what she had done. 'If he comes, you must just treat him like anybody else. When people see that you are perfectly civil to him, they will stop gossiping about the whole affair.'

At the club Bay found a card game and played until midnight, losing mostly and having to put up with the joshing of the others. 'Unlucky at cards, eh Middleton?' Two of the drunker members had started to whirl each other around the room in an improvised Viennese waltz. Bay had borne it all with an easy smile. He knew how to handle the envious teasing of his contemporaries.

Crombie, a tall major from the Blues who had ridden against Bay at a few point-to-points the year before, accosted him on the stairs.

''Spect you will be too busy with your royal duties for the National, Middleton.'

'Nothing would keep me away this year. In fact I've just been up to Aintree to feel the course.'

'Are you riding that mare of yours? The one you bought in Ireland?'

'God willing. I think we have a chance at getting round.'

'Indeed. I don't think there's a book yet. Maybe I'll take a punt on you. Mind you, it's a bloody course. Might be too much for a mare.'

'Tipsy is a finisher. She will make it past the post even if I don't.'

Crombie nodded. 'Nothing like an Irish horse. Well, I shall look forward to seeing you at Aintree.'

'So long, Crombie.'

Bay was on his way out when he saw Hartopp weaving up the steps. He missed one and would have landed rather heavily if Bay hadn't caught him before his face hit the granite.

'They keep moving the damn steps. Goin' to take it up with the Club Secretary. Damn cheek,' grumbled Hartopp. 'Oh, hello, Bay. What you doin' here? Thought you were too busy bowin' and scrapin'.'

'Came up for Fred's wedding.'

Chicken was brushing the dust from the steps from his evening clothes without much success.

'Well, do me a favour, old man, and keep away from Charlotte Baird. I have a chance there now you are out of the picture. I've had my eye on her for years. Would have got her too if you hadn't come along and turned her head. So stay away from her tomorrow, or you will have me to answer to.'

The threat present in Chicken's words was undermined by his inability to focus properly. He addressed this speech somewhere behind Bay's right ear.

'Can't promise that, Chicken. But I will tell you one thing, if Charlotte won't have you, it has nothing to do with me.'

'Is that so? At least I didn't lead her on and then abandon her when a more attractive offer came along.'

Bay's punch sent Chicken sprawling down the steps. He scrabbled to his feet and tried to have a swing at Bay, but Bay evaded him easily. Chicken's nose was bleeding heavily, staining his shirt front. Bay was already regretting his flash of temper. He went inside and called out the club porter.

'Captain Hartopp seems to have fallen down the steps. Can you see to him?' He pressed a half-sovereign into the man's hand.

The porter touched his cap. 'Certainly, sir. We are quite used to Captain Hartopp.'

Chicken pointed a huge hand at Bay as the other man set off into the night.

'You won't get away with it, you know.'

St George's, Hanover Square

NO CHURCH PEWS WERE COMFORTABLE, BUT THE ones in St George's Hanover Square had been made by a nonconformist carpenter who saw no reason why worshippers, especially rich and fashionable ones, should sit at their ease in the Lord's House. So he had made the bench seats intentionally half an inch narrower than was customary, which made it impossible for the sitter to do anything other than perch. Visiting preachers were always gratified by the attentiveness of the congregation to their sermons; no one ever closed their eyes in St George's, as a momentary loss of attention inevitably resulted in an embarrassing and noisy tumble.

So the congregation awaiting the arrival of the bride did not view her tardiness with indulgence. It was early in the year for a society wedding and quite a number of the guests had come up to town for the day, in order to avoid the expense of opening up their town houses so far ahead of the season proper. The guests who lived near Melton wondered why Crewe had decided to hold the wedding in town when he had that chapel at home that he was so proud of. The women who had come out the same year as Augusta knew exactly why she had chosen St George's; it was a way of showing the world that she was no longer on the shelf but a matron to be reckoned with. It was not a fabulous match for the daughter of an earl to be marrying a Borders squire, but by having the wedding in town, Augusta was making it plain that she did not intend to be written off.

The restless guests had little to do but survey each other as the organ launched into yet another Bach cantata. Captain Hartopp's black eye was a cause of much speculation. There was a rumour that he had been knocked down by Bay Middleton, yet they were today both standing at the groom's side. A drunken tumble seemed a more likely explanation, as Chicken was not a graceful drunk. Those guests who had heard about the now famous incident at the photographic exhibition were most curious to see Captain Middleton. Could the rumours about him and the Empress of Austria possibly be true? Middleton was known to be a ladies' man, but for an officer on half pay to become a royal paramour, well, it was the stuff of novels.

Earl Spencer was particularly uncomfortable. The narrow slat barely supported his massive thighs. It was a beautiful spring day, a perfect day to be out with the Quorn on one of the last days of the hunting season. But Spencer knew his duty. Baird had been one of his adjutants in Ireland, but he might have ignored that tie if it hadn't been for Bay. As far as he was capable of remorse, Spencer felt some responsibility for Bay's current predicament. For that reason he had put on his morning suit and was now perching awkwardly on his pew. There could be no question of people cutting Bay if Spencer was at his side.

Bay stood between Fred and Chicken at the altar steps. He had shaken hands that morning with Chicken, and while neither had forgiven the other, they were now standing side by side as fellow officers, resplendent in their dress uniforms. Hartopp was sporting an eyepatch but the swelling underneath was so bad that it hardly covered the affected area. Because of Chicken's shiner, Fred had asked Bay to hold the ring. 'If Augusta sees Chicken looking like that she might faint.'

So Bay stood next to the groom rolling the ring around in his pocket, listening to Hartopp's stertorous breathing, every exhalation sounding like a complaint.

At long last, the organist pulled out the trumpet stop and the congregation stood up as Augusta came down the aisle on her father's arm. Bay looked over his shoulder at the approaching confection of lace, orange blossom and diamonds, and out of compassion he whispered to Fred, who was shaking with nerves, 'You're a lucky man, Baird.' Fred looked surprised and grateful.

The service took place without incident, although it was noted that, unusually, the bride's vows were considerably louder than the groom's. When it was time for Bay to hand Fred the ring he tried to look at Charlotte, who was standing beside Augusta holding her bouquet. But either by accident or design, Charlotte's face was hidden behind the voluminous folds of the bride's veil. Despite this, Bay had thought it was a good sign that he had been invited to the wedding. He hoped that it was at Charlotte's instigation. As the wedding party formed to make their way down the aisle, Bay thought for a moment that he would be able to take Charlotte's arm, but somehow he ended up with Lady Crewe. Charlotte was behind him with Chicken.

As they came out of the church, the bride and groom made their way through the raised swords of Fred's guardsmen. There was a shout of huzzah for the happy couple, and the congregation were enthusiastic in throwing rice at them as they drove away in the carriage drawn by wedding greys.

Bay tried to find a moment to talk to Charlotte outside the church, but he could not get near her. She stuck close to Chicken Hartopp until she disappeared into the carriage that was to take the bridesmaids to the wedding breakfast in Portman Square.

Bay stood in the throng on the steps, listening to the excited chatter all around him, and wished that he was riding on Tipsy with the hounds in front of him and the wind at his back. For a moment he hesitated, wondering whether he should go on to the wedding breakfast, but before he could decide he felt Spencer's heavy hand between his shoulder blades.

'You managed to hand over the ring then.'

'It was the least I could do,' said Bay, trying to smile.

'Come with me to the breakfast. My wife has gone with Edith Crewe.'

Spencer did not wait for an answer but swept Bay along in front of him, until they were seated in the carriage.

'I saw the Empress last night at the Ambassador's. The Crown Prince was there, which is why, I imagine, you weren't.'

'I wasn't invited.'

'But you might as well have been there, as the Empress talked about you all night.'

'The Crown Prince must have enjoyed that.'

'He glowered like a sulky child. But the Empress wouldn't let him be; she teased him all night until he finally relented and smiled. Funny fellow. The way he looks at her is damned peculiar. Never seen the Prince of Wales look at his mother like that!' Spencer, as always, laughed at his own joke. Bay did not join in.

'The Empress was complaining that you have deserted her for the National.'

'The timing is unfortunate.'

'The Empress means to be at Aintree, so you had better perform.'

Spencer shifted in his seat and tugged at his waistcoat. 'I meant to ask you, how are you getting on with the Baird girl now?'

'She will have nothing to do with me,' Bay said.

'Pity, she's a nice girl, and rich too. But you can't have both, I suppose. Girls can be a bit snappish about these things. Way I see it, you dance to the Empress's tune until she gets tired of you, which she will one day. And then you go back to Charlotte Baird and ask her if she will still have you. My guess is that once she has got over her missishness, she will come round all right. Women like a man who is in demand. Don't think the Countess would have accepted me if she hadn't thought that her sister was keen on me. You mark my words, when the day comes and the Empress decides she doesn't need you any more, you can still have a crack at the Lennox fortune. I think the royal connection will only increase your charms. And if not her, there are plenty of others out there looking for a man like you.'

'Charlotte Baird is the only girl I have ever thought of marrying,' said Bay.

'Understandably. You don't find an heiress like that very often.'

'My reasons for wanting to marry her are not mercenary.'

'Of course not. You like her because she is a sweet young thing who worships the ground you walk on, but would she be so quite so sweet if she didn't have sixty thousand a year? Hard to tell. Man like you is bound to fall for the rich ones. How else are you going to keep a decent string?'

Bay knocked on the roof of the carriage to signal the coachman to stop.

'What on earth are you doing, Middleton?' said Spencer in surprise.

'I am going to walk the rest of the way.'

'But why?'

'Because I don't want to hit you,' said Bay, opening the carriage door.

Baron Nopsca, who had been following the Earl's carriage since Bay had got into it, sat back in his seat so that he wouldn't be seen. But when he saw Bay's face he realised that the Captain was not in a state to notice anything or anybody. He stood on the pavement in his dress uniform, the hilt of his sword gleaming in the spring sunshine, looking as if he might take out the sabre and run through a few pedestrians. The Baron told his driver to wait in a side street. He looked at his pocket watch and observed the hands pass for two minutes, before Bay shook himself and began to walk north towards Portman Square. The Baron waited until he saw Bay disappear into Crewe House, then told the carriage to go back to Claridge's Hotel.

The Wedding Breakfast

'NOW I WOULD LIKE THE NEWLYWEDS IN THE centre here. Perhaps the groom could smile just a little? I know that marriage is a serious business but surely not that serious. You have only been in wedlock for an hour.' Caspar had arranged the wedding party on the orchestra dais of the Crewe House ballroom. The bride and groom were standing slightly in front.

'Miss Chambers and Lady Violet, if you could move a little to your left, I think we want to see those beautiful dresses and their lovely owners. Very nice. Now, Charlotte, if you could move a little closer to your brother. No, there is something wrong with the drape of your skirt, if you will allow me?'

Caspar was fiddling with the volumes of fabric, when the door was opened by a footman and Bay walked in.

'Am I too late?'

'Not at all, Captain Middleton,' said Caspar smoothly. 'I am still arranging my subjects. Why don't you come and stand over here between Lady Violet and Miss Chambers?'

'As the best man, I believe I should stand next to the maid of honour.' Bay found a spot next to Charlotte, who did not turn her head.

Caspar gave a tight smile. 'Oh, the English, such sticklers for etiquette. Please don't worry about the composition of the photograph,

Captain Middleton. What's a little asymmetry if the laws of precedence are being observed?'

Tapping her fan on her head rather menacingly, Lady Crewe said, 'We must get on, Mr Hewes, tempus fugit.'

'Indeed, Lady Crewe, I am practically ready; all I require now is for you all to look at me and imagine that you are ankle-deep in melted chocolate.'

The bizarre image he conjured up broke the stiffness in their faces, and Caspar took the picture.

'Well, I think I have it,' said Caspar.

'Wait,' said Charlotte, stepping forward. 'May I be allowed to take one picture? Caspar, why don't you stand in there, I am sure Augusta would like a picture of you as well.'

Ignoring Lady Crewe's sigh and Caspar's look of horror, Charlotte took a plate from the case and inserted it into the camera.

'Now if everyone could look at me, that's it. Now *I* want you to imagine me going on a tour of North America to take photographs. Remember, quite still, everybody.'

She disappeared under the cloth, squeezed the bulb and took the picture.

When she emerged the bridal party broke up, Lady Crewe hurrying to the drawing room to take charge of the wedding breakfast, followed by Augusta.

But Fred broke away from his wife to say to Charlotte, 'The going to America thing was a trick to shock us like the chocolate, wasn't it?'

'Not exactly.'

'But you can't be serious! You must know that I would never allow it,' said Fred.

'Don't worry, Fred, I understand your objections,' said Charlotte, taking the plate out of the camera and putting it in its case, 'but I am still thinking about it.'

'It's a preposterous idea. You can't go gallivanting round the world on your own just because you've had a disappointment.'

'It's got nothing to do with disappointment. *If* I go it's because I want to take pictures of something more interesting than our friends, their servants, their houses and their animals.' She looked at Fred and smiled. 'And I have no intention of going alone. I am sure Mr Hewes will come with me if I ask him.'

Fred laughed. 'You shouldn't tease me like that, Mitten. For a moment there I thought you were serious.'

But before Charlotte could reply, he was summoned by a shrill cry from his wife, 'Fred, I am waiting.'

As the rest of the wedding party left the room, Charlotte was engaged in conversation by Lady Violet Anson, her fellow brides-maid. Lady Violet had never paid much attention to Charlotte on the few occasions that they had met, but now she seemed eager to make friends.

'Charlotte, my dear girl, I had no idea you were so *skilful,* you must give me some instruction. I long to take photographs. Such a sociable thing to do. You have everybody quite at your command.'

'I wouldn't say that. You can't guarantee that the sitters will like the results,' Charlotte said, wondering how much Violet knew about what had happened at the Royal Photographic Exhibition. But as she saw the other girl's eye flicker towards Bay, who was talking to Lord Crewe, it was obvious that her fellow bridesmaid knew every detail of the story.

'That must be *very* trying. But if you were to take a photograph of me I am sure I would be delighted.'

'If you want a portrait you should sit for Mr Hewes. Everybody likes his pictures. Augusta was thrilled with hers. Come let me introduce you.'

Charlotte shepherded Lady Violet towards Caspar, who was shutting up his camera. 'Caspar, I want to present you to Lady Violet Anson. She wants to have her photograph taken and I told her that you would do a much better job than me.'

'Well, I dispute that entirely, you are easily the more talented, but as I can never resist photographing a beautiful woman, I would be delighted to photograph you, Lady Violet.' He stood to one side considering her.

'With your colouring I think I would pose you as Ophelia.'

Lady Violet, who was so pale that she looked quite spectral in her bridesmaid's dress, looked delighted.

Charlotte left them together and joined the group that was heading towards the wedding breakfast. As she stood in the hall waiting for the clump of guests on the staircase to disperse, she felt a touch on her elbow.

'You can't ignore me for ever,' said Bay.

'But I have nothing to say to you.'

'You aren't really going to America.'

'That's funny, Fred said exactly the same thing. But I suppose he has a reason to ask as he is my brother. You, on the other hand, do not.' She turned to go but Bay stepped in front of her.

'Charlotte, please don't be haughty. Whatever you think of me, it cannot be worse than the opinion I have of myself. You are the person I care for and yet I have wronged you. Won't you let me explain?'

Charlotte tried to push past him. 'There is nothing to explain. I have seen the photograph: it speaks for itself.'

Bay blocked her way, his hand on the hilt of his sword.

'That wretched photograph. It is just a moment – an instant where, perhaps, I was dazzled by the Empress. But it is not a picture of my heart.'

'I am not sure I believe you,' said Charlotte.

'But why not? I am only here because of you. Take a photograph of me now and judge what you see in my face.'

'I just did. But whatever it shows, I am afraid it's too late.'

Bay leant towards her and she could see tears in his pale blue eyes. 'Really, Charlotte? Are you sure?'

She shook her head. 'No, I am not sure about anything. But that's the point. I have to be sure about the man I am going to marry.'

She pushed past Bay and started going up one arm of the double staircase.

Bay followed her. 'Couldn't I just come and talk to you? I miss you.'

'Talk to me?' said Charlotte.

'Tell you stories. Try and make you laugh. I used to be good at that. I could even tell you how Hartopp came to be called Chicken.'

Charlotte tried not to react. She carried on climbing the stairs, her hand gripping the balustrade as if she were afraid she might fall.

'Do you think that I am really so easy to win over?'

'Admit it. You are consumed with curiosity.'

'You don't mind betraying your friend?'

'I don't think he would call me his friend at the moment.'

Charlotte turned her head. 'You gave him the black eye?'

'I am afraid so.'

'But why?'

'Because he told me to leave you alone so that he could "have a crack" at you, as he put it. I told him that it wouldn't make any difference as you would never accept him.'

'Then you have done me a service. Does he really imagine that I would change my mind about him so quickly?'

'You changed your mind about me,' said Bay.

They were at the top of the stairs, behind a throng of guests waiting to go down the receiving line. Some people coming up the other arm of the double staircase looked at Bay and Charlotte with interest. Charlotte noticed this and tried to separate herself from Bay and become part of the group ahead of her. But Bay stayed close.

'People are looking at us,' said Charlotte.

'Let them look,' said Bay.

'It's easy for you to say that, but I don't want to be gossiped about any more than I already am, thanks to you. Please go away.'

'Only if you promise to let me see you.'

'Absolutely not.'

'Then I will tell Chicken that you have confessed to me your overwhelming desire to be Mrs Hartopp and that he should propose to you at once.'

Charlotte could not help smiling, but she put her hand up in front of her like a shield.

'You are not going to win me over, Bay.'

Bay was about to answer, but Caspar and Lady Violet had walked up the other side of the staircase and had drawn level with them.

'Captain Middleton, it is such a pleasure to meet you finally, having seen you on a photographic plate. It is fascinating to observe the original.' Caspar bowed.

'I am afraid I am bound to be a disappointment,' said Bay.

'Not in that uniform. In my country we rarely see anything so splendid. Not man-made, anyway.'

'It's a bit awkward to walk around town in, although it's quite reassuring having a sword.' Bay put his hand on the hilt of his sabre.

Caspar laughed. 'In the West everybody carries a gun. I feel quite naked without mine.'

'But nobody needs a gun in London!' said Lady Violet. 'We are not savages here.'

'We are not savages in San Francisco either,' said Caspar, looking at Bay, 'but we like to be prepared.'

There was a general bustle from inside the drawing room which suggested that the speeches were about to begin. Charlotte hurried inside. One of her duties as chief bridesmaid was to give flower favours from the bride's bouquet to all the female guests. Augusta thought that this was a charming custom, and had told Charlotte it would give her a chance to meet more people. 'You can never have too many female acquaintances. With your fortune you will never lack for male admirers, but it's the women who make the rules.'

She took the bouquet from the table that displayed the couple's wedding presents. Charlotte's gift to the bride of a pearl and topaz necklace was displayed in its red velvet case; but her real gift to the bride had been the loan of the Lennox diamonds. Charlotte had taken a certain pleasure in not conferring this boon until the day before the wedding. It had been enjoyable watching her sister-in-law's delight in snubbing Charlotte, fighting her desire to be resplendent on her wedding day in the Lennox tiara.

Bay's present to the couple was a pair of Meissen figurines of a shepherd and shepherdess. They were exquisite things, standing out from the heavy silver candelabra, pearl-handled fish knives and tortoiseshell dressing cases that made up the majority of the couple's tributes. Meissen porcelain was not something that Charlotte would have expected Bay to choose, but then, she reflected, there was a great deal about Bay that she didn't know.

She picked up the bouquet and circulated, giving out white narcissi and waxy stephanotis to the ladies. As she made her way through the tables and chairs Lord Crewe made a speech on the joys of matrimony, drawing his examples entirely from the Arthurian legends, which perhaps was not the most fertile ground, as Arthur and Guinevere, Lancelot and Elaine and Sir Bedivere had not been known for the felicity of their marriages. Then Fred stood up and made the shortest possible speech, with a great deal of throat clearing and spluttering before and after, but as he looked so genuinely pleased to be married, his awkwardness was forgiven, although Augusta watched him beadily throughout.

Then Bay stood up. Hartopp had been vetoed by Augusta, on account of the black eye.

Bay started off by congratulating Fred for his good fortune in being accepted by a bride as exceptional as Augusta. Charlotte tried not to smile at Bay's use of the adjective. Then he went into flattering detail about Fred's army career, his prowess in the saddle, and his skill at the game of quoits they used to play in the officers' mess with napkin rings and candlesticks. He was a natural speaker and his audience relaxed, satisfied that he would not embarrass them or himself. He told an anecdote about Fred's time in Ireland when as a young adjutant he had been expected to dance with all the young ladies at the vice-regal balls and had to have a consignment of dancing slippers sent over from London because he was getting through the shoe leather so quickly.

Bay took a sip of champagne and continued, 'We are here to celebrate a marriage. There is nothing more noble than the words of the marriage service which pledge to have and to hold from this day forward. I wish Fred and Augusta every blessing in their married life,' and here he looked directly at Charlotte, 'I can only pray that I will be granted the same chance to devote myself to another person's happiness.'

A gust of interest blew through the room at this obvious statement of intent. Charlotte, who had been trying to find an undamaged flower to give to the Dowager Countess of Trent, blushed despite herself. As everyone stood up to drink the health of the bride and groom, she slipped outside to give herself a moment to recover.

As she stood on the stone landing holding onto the balustrade with one hand, the dismembered bouquet with the other, Charlotte looked down into the hall and saw the footman open the door. A man in splendid livery stood outside and there was a muffled conversation between them. At last the footman admitted the man, who gave him a card which the footman carried upstairs on a silver tray. Charlotte watched as the card was handed to Lady Crewe and saw that lady start with surprise and nod violently. She leant over to whisper something in Augusta's ear which made the bride look more animated than she had all day. The footman was sent downstairs again.

This time the liveried servant opened the double doors to Crewe House.

From her vantage point, Charlotte saw the hair first – the medusa-like crown of auburn plaits cascading out beneath the tiny top hat trimmed with peacock feathers.

She tried to retreat into the drawing room but Lord and Lady Crewe were coming through the door to greet the Empress, so Charlotte retreated back onto the landing, trying to tuck herself away behind the double door.

The Empress climbed the white marble steps surprisingly quickly, the Countess Festetics hurrying to keep up with her.

'Lady Crewe,' said Sisi. 'You must forgive me for intruding. But when Captain Middleton told me that he was attending the wedding of your daughter I suddenly thought how nice it would be to see an English wedding. In my country it is the custom for members of the royal house to bless the brides of good families, so I thought you would excuse my visit. I should so much like to offer your daughter my congratulations.'

Lady Crewe had a little difficulty extricating herself from her extremely deep curtsey.

'We are honoured, Your Majesty. Augusta and Fred will feel doubly blessed. Please come in and let me introduce them to you.'

Charlotte thought that the Empress was rather less alluring close to, than she had been as a silhouette upon a horse. From a distance she was an exciting idea; three feet away Charlotte could see the lines around her eyes, the grooves between the nose and the mouth and the red knuckles on her hands. She was graceful, the carriage of her head was impeccable and she moved as if she was on castors instead of feet. But the Empress was a woman whose claim to beauty was now an effort of will rather than a self-evident truth.

The Empress processed into the room and there was much bowing and curtseying. Augusta, pink with excitement, offered the Empress her chair as the place of honour. But Sisi demurred and put her hands to Augusta's face.

'No, my dear child, I wouldn't dream of usurping your place on this your special day. We have brought a wedding gift. Festy!'

The Countess opened her reticule and brought out a small leather box which the Empress presented to Augusta. Inside was an enamelled brooch containing a miniature of Sisi surrounded by diamond brilliants. Taking it out of the box, the Empress pinned it onto Augusta's white satin bosom. 'There, now you will have something to remember my visit by.' Augusta, for once, had nothing to say.

Charlotte, who had crept into the drawing room in the Empress's wake, noticed that everyone in the room looked excited by the new arrival, apart from Bay. He looked, thought Charlotte, as if someone had slapped him in the face. He clearly had not been expecting this. She caught his eye and he shook his head.

She heard Caspar's voice in her ear, 'Do you know, I almost feel sorry for Captain Middleton. I don't think he was expecting a royal visit.'

The Empress was processing throughout the room, with her hosts on either side. When they got to where Bay was standing, Sisi stopped and held out her hand for Bay to kiss.

'Captain Middleton, you did not tell me how charming your friends were or I would have insisted on meeting them before.' Sisi turned to Lady Crewe. 'Easton Neston is close to your house, no?' She smiled without showing her teeth.

Lady Crewe simpered, 'The Melton park runs next to Easton Neston. Such a remarkable house. I hope Your Majesty is comfortable there.'

'Oh, but I didn't come to England to be comfortable, Lady Crewe. I came to hunt your foxes. I would happily sleep in a tent if it meant I could ride to hounds in Leicestershire.'

Lady Crewe looked aghast. 'Oh, I hope there will be no need for that.'

'Ah, here is my great friend, Milord Spencer, and the Countess. How delightful this is. Of course in Vienna we could never be so informal, but what I love about England is that you do not stand on ceremony for its own sake.'

Earl Spencer said with clumsy gallantry, 'Where you are concerned, Ma'am, the normal rules do not apply.'

'You are too chivalrous, but there are some rules that even I cannot break, like hunting on a Sunday.'

'You have to respect the religious affiliations of the foxes, Ma'am.' Sisi laughed.

A suitable chair was produced for the Empress so that she could preside in state over the rest of the reception. As she sat down, she said to Spencer, 'Tell me, where is the young woman who took the picture that made Rudi so angry? I take it that she is here.'

The Earl looked embarrassed. 'I am not sure I know who you mean, Ma'am. I know there was some incident but I was not there.'

'Ah, then I will ask Bay. He will know, of course.'

Remembering the odd scene with Bay in the carriage, Spencer decided it would be better if the Empress did not ask Bay about Charlotte. So taking a chair, he sat down next to the Empress. 'I think you must mean Charlotte Baird, she is the bridegroom's sister.'

'Can you point her out to me?'

The Earl turned his great head to survey the room. He saw Charlotte standing against the wall holding the remains of the bride's bouquet; she was talking to a tall young man who was wearing trousers of a most peculiar cut. He could also see that Bay, who was the only person in the room who was not looking at the Empress, was staring at Charlotte so intently that it was as if he was trying to memorise her face.

'I take it that Miss Baird is the girl holding the bouquet.'

'Yes, Ma'am, I believe it is.'

'I should like to meet her. Would you ask her to come here?'

'It would be my pleasure.'

The Earl walked slowly to the spot where Charlotte was talking to Caspar.

'Miss Baird, the Empress has asked to meet you. May I introduce you to her?'

Charlotte looked up at him. 'Can I refuse, Earl Spencer?'

The Earl said nothing, but Caspar clapped his hands. 'Charlotte, you goose, every girl in the room is dying to meet the Empress. Come along.'

The Earl looked at the American with surprise. Charlotte said, 'Earl Spencer, may I present Caspar Hewes. He is a photographer from America.'

The Earl bowed his head a fraction, in acknowledgement of the introduction.

'Will you follow Mr Hewes's advice and allow me to present you to the Empress?'

'If Mr Hewes may accompany me.'

The Earl nodded. 'But I warn you that the Empress is not fond of photography, Mr Hewes.'

'So I understand, but let's hope that she has nothing against photographers.'

While this conversation was taking place, Sisi turned to Bay, who she had not so far talked to directly, and beckoned to him to come closer.

'This is such a picturesque event. I am so glad to see an ordinary English wedding party.'

'I am not sure that the bride would call this an ordinary wedding, Ma'am, but I am glad you are amused by it.'

'I remember you telling me that the Crewes were very dull, and yet they seem quite pleasant to me. I am sorry not to have met them earlier.'

'You have been busy, Ma'am.'

'Indeed.' Sisi looked across the room, and saw that Spencer was approaching with Charlotte. As they came into earshot she said to Bay, 'Oh Bay, I think I have one of my headaches coming on and I have left my drops in the carriage.'

Bay hesitated for a second and then said, 'Let me fetch them for you, Ma'am.'

'Your Majesty, may I present Miss Baird.' Charlotte made a perfunctory curtsey and Caspar stepped forward so that Spencer had no choice but to say, 'And Mr Hewes, an American gentleman.' Caspar's bow was so low that his forehead almost brushed the Empress's skirt.

The Empress signalled for them to sit, and Caspar pulled up two gilt and velvet chairs.

The older woman's gaze swept over Charlotte.

'I have heard about you, Miss Baird.'

Charlotte lowered her eyes.

'You are the young lady who took the photograph that upset my son.'

'Yes.' Charlotte paused for a moment, 'Your Majesty.'

The Empress laughed. 'Oh don't worry, I haven't come here to scold you. In fact I must apologise if Rudi insulted you. He can be so headstrong.'

Charlotte did not smile back. 'It was Captain Middleton your son insulted. I don't think he noticed me.'

Earl Spencer, who was listening to this exchange, studied the floor with great attention.

Sisi continued, 'Poor Rudi. He is so protective of me, he knows that I cannot bear to be photographed.'

'But how can that possibly be, Your Majesty?' Caspar broke in. 'Someone as lovely as you should be photographed all the time. As a photographer I feel it is a crime to hide your beauty from the public gaze.'

Sisi looked amazed at this interruption, but Caspar's smile did not waver.

'But I do not wish to be gazed on by the public in a photograph. I don't care to be gaped at in magazines, or displayed in shop windows. I am a queen, not a mannequin.'

Countess Festetics broke in, 'Majesty, you sound a little hoarse. May I fetch you some water?'

'No, no, I am fine.' Sisi waved her away.

Charlotte was about to reply, but Caspar forestalled her.

'Well, that is a great pity. The history of art would be much poorer without the great royal portraits – Velazquez, Van Dyck; I believe Your Majesty has been painted by Winterhalter. We photographers only want for the same privilege. How can we ever be respected as artists if we are denied access to the great subjects?'

'A painting is quite different. It is a product of hours of thought and labour. A great portrait shows the soul of the sitter; that is something a photograph can never do.'

Charlotte spoke up now. 'I disagree, Ma'am. A royal portrait is bound by its very nature to flatter its subject, but a photograph cannot lie.'

'You are young, Miss Baird, and if you will forgive me, obscure. You cannot know what it is like to be photographed constantly without your consent. Photographs taken in those circumstances cannot be the truth, as you put it. They are founded on deceit.'

Charlotte considered this. 'I sincerely regret taking your photograph without your knowledge, but the photograph itself was not a lie.'

There was a pause, and then Sisi smiled.

'Ah, but you are young and we all have great opinions when we are young. I think when you are a little older you will see things differently. Here is Captain Middleton. You know Miss Baird, I think?'

'Yes, Ma'am.'

'We have been having a delightful discussion about her hobby.' She turned to Charlotte. 'Tell me, my dear, do you still have the photograph, the one that so upset my son?'

'No. I destroyed the negative. You need have no fears on that score.'

'How very thorough. I feel almost sorry that you had to destroy your handiwork.'

'I had good reasons, Ma'am,' Charlotte said, looking briefly at Bay.

The Empress caught the look and signalled to Countess Festetics that she should gather her things. Having seen the Baird girl, she was no longer worried about her effect on Bay. The girl was insignificant.

'I am afraid I can no longer fight my headache. We shall have to go. Such a delightful occasion, but I am afraid it has quite tired me out.'

The Empress rose, and as the room noticed, they too got to their feet.

'Such a pleasant occasion, Lady Crewe, and such a lovely bride. Thank you so much.' The Empress glided towards the door, followed by Countess Festetics and Lord Crewe. At the door she stopped and said in a clear voice, 'Captain Middleton, I am sure you want to say goodbye to your friends.'

Bay, who had not followed her to the door, stood in the middle of the room – the focus of all eyes. He turned to Charlotte and said, 'You will remember your promise.'

Charlotte said, as evenly as she could, 'If you have time to call before I go to America, then I shall be delighted to see you.'

'You are actually going?'

'I wasn't sure before, but now I am. But you don't have time to stand here talking to me. Your mistress is waiting.'

Bay looked at her, his face contorted with regret. But before he could say anything in reply, Augusta walked to where they were standing and placed herself between them, her cheeks red.

'Captain Middleton,' she hissed, 'the Empress is waiting.'

'Goodbye, Bay,' Charlotte said.

The room fell silent as Bay walked towards the door where Sisi stood, her body turned in motion like Diana fleeing Actaeon. When he was about five paces away, the Empress, seeing that he was coming, turned and went through the door and down the stairs, leaving Bay to follow.

He paused at the door and looked back at Charlotte, before disappearing.

Caspar, who was standing next to Charlotte, said, 'Poor fellow, it can't be easy being an imperial lackey.'

'No, and he doesn't have your talent for flattery either, so it must be harder still.' Charlotte turned her face away from him.

As Bay came down the stairs, Countess Festetics appeared as if from nowhere and took him by the arm.

'Captain Middleton, I am so glad to be seeing you.'

Bay smiled at her.

'How are you, Festy?'

'I am worried, dear Captain. It was not kind of you to disappear like this. It has been most sad without you. The Empress has not smiled, I am thinking, since you left. It is necessary that you should come back.'

'But the Empress asked me to stay away.'

'For one day, maybe two when the Crown Prince was there. She does not want any unpleasantnessess with her son. But since then she has been waiting every day for you to come back. That is why we came here today, not to see some wedding, but to see you.'

Bay looked at the floor. But the Countess dug her fingers into his arm and forced him to look at her.

'I know that you do not love my mistress as I do, Captain, but I think you care for her. You made her happy, now you are making her unhappy.'

Bay said slowly, 'I wish she hadn't come here today.'

'I also. I have tried to stop her, but she is not listening. Now, dear Captain, you must go, she is waiting for you.' The little countess almost pushed him out of the door.

The coachman was waiting to open the carriage door. As Bay climbed in, he saw that Sisi was sitting in the corner opposite him, her face hidden by her fan. The carriage blinds were drawn.

When the coachman closed the door Bay said, 'Sisi?', but still she did not lower the fan. He waited for a moment and then, sitting directly opposite her, he gently pulled the hand holding the fan away from her face.

The Empress was crying.

Bay saw that her even her tears were elegant: they left her eyes shining, but had not made her nose red.

He found a handkerchief in his pocket and started to wipe the tears away from her cheeks.

She caught his hand in hers.

'Oh, I am sorry, Bay. I should not have come today. But I have missed you so.' She looked up at him through wet lashes.

Bay could not resist the appeal in her eyes. Even though he knew it was a mistake, he could not stop himself. He took her other hand in his and began to kiss away the tears until he found her mouth.

The carriage began to move.

'I am not worth crying over, dearest Sisi.'

'I was so happy here in England with you. But then Rudolph has to spoil everything. He doesn't understand. Please tell me that you have forgiven him.'

'There is nothing to forgive,' said Bay.

This time Sisi, her tears dried, kissed him.

'Oh, I am so glad. But I will make sure that your paths do not cross again. Then we can be happy as we were before. We will hunt every day and forget about my crazy son.'

The scent of her hair, that heady mixture of brandy and eau de cologne, made feel Bay feel quite dizzy. He thought that he would like to open the window.

'But I can't come back to Easton Neston now. The National is on Saturday.'

'The National? I know it is a race but is it really so important?'

'The Grand National is the greatest steeplechase in the country.' Seeing that she did not understand, he continued, 'Imagine the fastest ride to hounds you have ever had with a different jump every minute. Four miles, and sixteen fences against the best riders in the country.'

'But *you* are the best rider in the country.'

'Gentleman rider, perhaps, but there are professional jockeys riding too. Irish boys who ride like banshees. I have seen them at Aintree, they have no fear.'

Sisi put her fingers to his lips. 'You will have no fear – because I will be there. I shall come and watch you win your race.'

She was smiling now, her mood light again.

'I will tell Nopsca to make the arrangements.'

The carriage had slowed down, and Bay lifted the blind. He recognised the gates of Devonshire House. A shaft of light fell across the interior of the carriage. He noticed that there were tiny lines forming around Sisi's lips as she smiled.

'Oh Bay, I am so glad that we have no more misunderstandings,' and she held his hand to her breast so that he could feel her heart beating.

As he sat in the carriage, his hand against the Empress's heart, her eyes fixed on his face, Bay heard a paperboy shouting the evening's headlines and it occurred to him what the world would think of Captain Middleton riding around London in the Empress of Austria's carriage with the blinds drawn. Most people would think it was scandalous; some more worldly spectators would think it was perhaps a little ostentatious. All of them would assume that he, Captain Middleton, was the Empress's acknowledged lover. The Empress was smiling at him, her eyes shining, her face radiant under the hat with the peacock feathers. Bay wondered if she was aware of any of this. Had she in fact drawn the blinds to the carriage before starting to cry? But if it had been a trap, Bay thought, then he had walked into it quite willingly.

The carriage came to a halt. Bay looked through the blinds and saw that they were outside Claridge's Hotel.

The Empress said, 'Will you come in?'

'I must go back to Aintree. I don't trust the grooms to feed Tipsy properly.'

'Till Saturday then.' Sisi leant over and kissed him.

'Till Saturday,' said Bay.

The Adelphi

Liverpool

Dear Fred,

I hope that your wedding trip has been everything you hoped for and that Augusta has found Italy to her taste. I must apologise for not being there to welcome you on your return, but by the time you read this letter I will be somewhere in North America. Depending on the length of your wedding trip, I might be in New York, or possibly at the bottom of the Grand Canyon. At any rate I will not be in Charles Street.

I suspect that you will be very much vexed by my departure. I know that you will be worried about my safety and Augusta will be disappointed not to be able to guide me through the season. But I promise you that I will be exceedingly careful. It may temper Augusta's disappointment to know that I enclose the key to my jewel case. I have left the diamonds in the vault at Drummonds, except for the tiara, which I had to pawn in order to pay for my passage. I would be grateful if you could redeem it on your return. I imagine that Augusta might like to wear it. Please do not worry about me, Fred, I shall only be gone for a few months. But if you want me to return you will have to wire me money to New York as I *don't think the tiara will take me across the Atlantic and back. Grace, the Melton maid, is with me — so you don't need to worry about me being unchaperoned, and Mr Hewes will be travelling on the same boat, the SS* Britannic. *He promises to translate American into English for me.*

This is not an elopement, dear Fred, I did not elope with Captain Middleton at a time when I would have been very happy to become his wife, to spare your feelings. I am not eloping now.

I suspect that you may be angry when you read this, but not, I hope, for long. I am sure Augusta will look very splendid in the Lennox diamonds.

I remain, despite my temporary absence, always your affectionate sister,

Charlotte

Charlotte sealed the letter and rang the bell. A page appeared wearing the Adelphi Hotel's red and gold livery. The boy was about twelve but he was small for his age and the uniform swamped him.

She held out the letter and showed him a half-crown. 'I want you to post this for me, and when you've done that I want you to come back here and I will give you this.'

'Yes, miss.' The page took the letter and scampered off.

Charlotte went back to her desk in the hotel library. The room smelt strongly of varnish and morocco leather. The hotel was brand new. Caspar told her that it had sprung up in the year since he had arrived in Liverpool from America. Through the sumptuous red and gold brocade curtains she could see the storm clouds hanging over the horizon and could hear the rain lashing the windows in an endless round of applause.

The library was empty, which was a relief. The train from London had been crowded with parties coming up for the Grand National

Steeplechase, as well as passengers bound for America. Even in the first-class carriage (Caspar had insisted on the most expensive tickets: 'If I have to go back to America I want my last memory of England to be a fragrant one') the atmosphere had been verging on the rowdy. The racegoers had availed themselves of their hip flasks and the America-bound passengers had been voluble about their anxieties concerning the primitive conditions they expected to find there. Caspar had attempted to reassure one particularly nervous lady that most Americans had stopped wearing feathers in their hair, and no longer cooked on an open fire, but both his vocabulary and his waistcoat were so florid that the woman's fears were exacerbated rather than soothed.

Charlotte had no such worries. Her decision to leave had been sudden, but she had not regretted it for one minute. Anything was better than sitting in the drawing room of Charles Street, waiting for something to happen. Or worse still, having to listen to Chicken Hartopp talking about Bay and the Empress.

She picked up her pen and wondered if she could actually bring herself to write to Bay. But as had happened so often before, Charlotte found that she could not find the words. She wanted to write a letter that would both scald him for ever and at the same time bring him to her side. It was easier to pack her trunk, pawn her diamonds and go halfway across the world than it was to know what she wanted to say to him. He had sent a letter to her after the wedding – a note that looked as if it had been written in the dark.

My dearest Charlotte,

I will still call you that in my head even if I can never say those words to you myself. My dearest Charlotte, my offer to explain the truth of how Captain Hartopp earned the name of Chicken still stands. I have nothing else to offer you except my heart and Tipsy's services as a photographic model. The letter broke off here as if Bay had thought better of this jauntiness, and then started again, the handwriting here much less regular. *I wish I could kiss you again: I remember it so clearly – your lips a little dry – the freckles on your eyelids. I would like to kiss every one of those freckles. You see I am quite reckless now; now that it is too late. But you should know how much I want to hold you and how I will always adore you even if we never meet again. You have my photograph but nothing could be clearer than the picture of you that is in my head. A photograph can be destroyed but the image I have of your dear face is* **indelible**. [This last word was underlined several times.]

 I will always remain, now and for ever,
 your own Bay Middleton

It was her first and only love letter. It was the letter that she had longed for after the fracas at the exhibition. But it was, after all, only a letter. If Bay had said these words to her face, Charlotte thought that she would never have been able to resist him, but he hadn't. She had read it so many times that she knew its words by heart, had murmured them to herself as she packed her trunk full of the things she would need for a world three thousand miles away from Bay.

The library door opened and Grace came in. The vivid magenta dye used in the silk trim of her bonnet had run in the rain, so that her face was daubed with amethyst streaks.

'It's terrible out there, miss. I went to buy some hat pins, British ones, you know, but I wish I had stayed here now. I was lucky that there was a gentleman with an umbrella to escort me back to the hotel. He is staying here too on account of the racing.'

Grace caught sight of herself in the mirror over the mantelpiece and gave a little scream. She started to rub at her face with her handkerchief and it came away purple.

'Heavens above! Excuse me, miss, while I go and make myself presentable. And the racing gentleman never said a word. He must have been laughing his head off inside, while all the time he was pretending to be pleasant and talking about the Grand National. He said I should put my money on Dancing Bear at fifty to one. It's a sure thing, he said.'

'You shouldn't trust racing tips from strangers,' said Charlotte.

'Don't worry, miss, I wasn't born yesterday! I told him it was too late for me to bet, even if it was guaranteed, because we were off to America tomorrow. He said if I gave him my address he would keep the money for me. He must have thought I was not right in the head – on account of this,' she scrubbed at her face with her handkerchief.

Charlotte went over to where the newspapers were hanging on the wall on their wooden posts. In the *Manchester Guardian* she found what she was looking for. Halfway down the list of jockeys was Middleton, J.M., riding Tipsy (grey). She felt the jolt of seeing his name in print and realised that she had no idea what his initials stood for. She had only ever known him as Bay.

'Please, miss . . .' It was the page; his scarlet livery was soaked, and the rain had washed his cheeks clean. Charlotte gave him the half-crown and added another shilling.

'I am sorry you got so wet on my account. You should have taken an umbrella.'

'I did, miss, but it got blown inside out, the wind's that strong.'

As the servant went off to get into dry clothes, Charlotte went back to the newspaper. There was an article about the race which she found almost incomprehensible. What she could glean was that there were forty horses in the race. Five of the horses were Irish, two French and only ten of them were mares. She could not see Bay or Tipsy's name in among the list of likely favourites. The shortest odds were being offered on a horse called the Governess, ridden by Ned Beasley.

Charlotte found that she was pleased that Bay had, after all, entered the race. She remembered him telling her about his desire to win that first night at Melton. It meant that he was more than the Empress's creature. It was strange to think that for tonight at least, they would be only a few miles apart. Aintree, the course where the Grand National was held, was, she had gleaned from the racegoers on the train, only a carriage drive away from Liverpool. But tomorrow when Bay was lining up at the start of the race, she would be halfway across the Irish Sea.

She rang the bell to order some tea. Caspar would be back soon. One more night and they would be at sea. It was a terrifying thought but also a great relief to know that for a few months at least she would not be the Lennox heiress or even the girl who was jilted by Bay Middleton; she would simply be Charlotte Baird, the photographer. If things went well she might never come back. She thought that Fred would probably support her till she came of age if it meant that Augusta was able to sparkle through the season in the Lennox diamonds.

Of course, if she did come back there would be talk about her decision to travel with Caspar Hewes. People who did not know Caspar would assume they had eloped. This, Charlotte thought, would be more damaging to his reputation than hers. The worst that would happen to Charlotte was that she would no longer be invited to the smartest parties. There would be duchesses who would no longer think her a suitable match for their younger sons. Augusta would never get over the humiliation of being related by marriage to a social outcast – but these were all consequences that Charlotte felt that she could tolerate. But Caspar's burgeoning success as a society photographer was based on his unique ability to flatter and charm all his sitters into believing that he alone saw their true beauty. If his society sitters thought that his affections were spoken for, especially by someone as insignificant and dingy as Charlotte, he might not be able to cast the spell that made even the plainest of his subjects blossom into the goddess-like being of Caspar's rhetoric.

The night before, as they were eating in the cavernous dining room of the Adelphi, Charlotte had said, 'It feels quite scandalous to be eating alone with you in a restaurant. If Augusta could see us she would die of mortification.'

'But what on earth could be scandalous about a man and a woman having dinner in public? It would be much more shocking if we were having dinner upstairs in your room,' said Caspar.

'Unmarried girls are not meant to be out in public unchaperoned, especially with unmarried men.'

'But you seem remarkably unconcerned, Carlotta, to be consorting with me. Aren't you worried that I might make demands on your virtue?'

It had been a light-hearted question, but Charlotte knew that it had a serious undertone.

'No, I am not worried. Should I be?'

Caspar smiled and Charlotte thought she saw a flicker of relief in his face. He raised his glass to her.

'You are the only woman in the world I could ever imagine proposing to, but even in the unlikely event that you would have me I think I know that I am not the marrying kind.'

'Not even for the Lennox fortune?' said Charlotte, laughing.

'Now I am sorely tempted, but no, not even for that.'

And at that moment Charlotte thought that Caspar was the closest thing she had ever had to a friend.

A waiter brought in the tea.

'Shall I set the table for two, miss?'

'Yes, thank you.'

Caspar should be back from the shipping office by now. Charlotte had bought their passages in London, but Caspar had insisted on going down to the Liverpool office to make sure that they were given decent cabins. This had not seemed to Charlotte like a good enough reason to go out in a thunderstorm, but Caspar had been adamant. 'You have no idea how much these things matter. Trust me, Carlotta, you may be defying convention by running away to America, but you don't want to end up in a cabin next to the engine.'

She was eating her third slice of anchovy toast when Caspar burst into the library, his ulster dripping with rain water. He gave his wet things to the waiter who was hovering in the background and collapsed into a chair.

'Forgive me for leaving you alone for so long. I have bad news, I'm afraid. A timber ship lost its load during the storm and the port is rammed with floating logs. None of the ships can move until the logs have been plucked out of the Mersey. The quayside was full of men with chains shouting their heads off and accomplishing very little, so I suspect that the task may take some time. So we will have to amuse ourselves in Liverpool for another day at least.'

Charlotte handed him a cup of tea.

He looked at her. 'I thought you would be disappointed. And yet you look quite cheerful. Have you changed your mind about going?'

'No, not that. But if we are going to be here for another day, I have an idea as to what we might do tomorrow.'

'And what would that be?'

'I think we should go to the Grand National. The racecourse at Aintree is only a carriage ride away.'

Caspar narrowed his eyes at her. 'I had no idea, Carlotta, that you followed the sport of kings.'

Charlotte blushed. She did not want to admit to Caspar, or even to herself, the real reason for her interest in the Grand National.

'Oh, but this race is famous. It will be a splendid place to take photographs,' she said. 'We could probably make all our passage money by taking pictures of the horses with their owners. There are forty starters.'

'You are remarkably well informed, Carlotta.' Caspar raised an eyebrow.

'Oh, Grace told me all about it,' Charlotte said, as easily as she could. 'It sounds rather interesting. The course is four miles long, and there are sixteen fences.'

'Sixteen fences?' said Caspar. 'Fancy that.'

'Yes, and only about half the horses finish the race. It's tremendously difficult.'

Caspar shook his head. 'It sounds like a supremely English occasion. Incomprehensible and pointless to the uninitiated. But it can't be any worse than a cricket match, so we might as well go.' He looked Charlotte straight in the eye. 'Who knows who we might run into?'

Charlotte could not return his gaze.

The Grand National

THE DAY OF THE NATIONAL WAS FINE. THE STORM had passed over entirely, leaving the sky a watery blue. There was even a weak sun fighting the chilly breeze from the Atlantic. The change in weather was a great relief to the many female racegoers who had bought new trimmings for their bonnets in honour of the great day; it was heralded as a good omen by the seasoned racegoers from London, who knew from experience that the stands at Aintree were not adequately covered; the Prince of Wales was happy because he would be able to wear his new Homburg hat and his view would not be obstructed by umbrellas, which he thought deeply vulgar inventions. The Empress of Austria, who was travelling with him in the royal train, thought that the good weather was entirely in keeping with her present disposition, which was cheerful – she was always irritated when the weather was at variance with her mood. Countess Festetics was happy because her mistress was smiling. For her the only weather that mattered were the clouds that gathered in her mistress's eyes.

Only Bay, who was walking the course that morning, was indifferent to the sunshine. For him the damage had already been done. The ground after two days of rain was soft, and as he led Tipsy round the jumps to show her the treacherous dips and shallows that lay in wait for them later that day, Bay, despite the spring weather, felt a cold ripple of fear. It had been a frosty winter, and the going all season had been hard, but now the ground was muddy and waterlogged. After the first lap of the course it would be a quagmire. Bay hated soft ground: it unsettled the horses and the spray from the puddles made it impossible to see. Horses stumbled on sodden turf; even if they took the fence at the correct angle there was no guarantee that they would land safely.

Bay felt a twinge in his bad shoulder as he walked around Becher's Brook, named after the man who had fallen there in 1856. His doctor had been very stern about the dangers of another fall. He knew that he should have his shoulder strapped up properly before the race, but that would put his whip hand out of action. Was it really worth endangering his whole future for the sake of winning this one race? There was only one possible answer to that. For Bay at that moment, victory at the National was the only thing that mattered. It was the one thing in his life that seemed to be under his control.

A rabbit darted across the ground and Tipsy neighed in alarm. As Bay calmed his horse, he thought that the mare was the only female in his life with whom he was in perfect accord. He was still good with horses, even if he had lost his touch with women. Tipsy nuzzled his ear and Bay tried not to think about Charlotte. He had almost won her over at the wedding before the Empress had arrived and declared her interest. He no longer felt the desire for Sisi that had flooded his senses at the beginning, but that urgency had been replaced by something more insidious; to be so publicly needed by the most beautiful woman in Europe was quite something. But even stronger than the appeal to his vanity was the call on his compassion; he knew he had the power to make her happy.

'Morning, Middleton!' Bay recognised Major Crombie from his club. 'How do you like the course?'

'Too soft for my taste. Could have done without the storm,' said Bay.

'Favours the Irish, they like it boggy.'

'What odds are they giving for Tipsy?'

'Twenty-five to one. Mares are very sticky and a grey has never won the National.'

Bay said nothing.

Crombie laughed. 'Personally I am delighted at the length of your odds. I saw you and Tipsy ride at the Cottesleigh point-to-point last year. Never seen a braver ride. So my money's on you. Some of the Irish horses will give you a run, but none of the jockeys are in your class. I put a monkey on you last week, so don't let me down.'

'I'll do my best,' said Bay.

'The royal box will be full, at any rate. The Prince and Princess of Wales *and* the Empress of Austria. I expect half the crowd will be too busy watching them to pay any attention to the race. But so long as the jockeys don't get distracted, eh Middleton?'

Crombie waved Bay farewell as he turned back towards the stands, which were already beginning to fill up six or so hours before the race was due to begin.

When he got back to the stables, the lads were sitting down to a race day breakfast – porridge, bacon, eggs, ham, devilled kidneys. Bay had ordered it from the local inn the night before but now he found he could not face even a mouthful.

He sat down on a mounting block and pulled out his cigarette case. Perhaps a gasper would help calm his nerves; what he really wanted was a shot of brandy, but even the Irish jockeys never drank before a race. As he fumbled with the match, he heard a familiar voice.

'Feeling a bit shaky, Bay?' It was Hartopp.

'Chicken! This is a surprise.' Bay looked at the other man warily.

'Don't worry, old boy. I haven't come to get my revenge. Anyway, that bird has flown. Paid a call at Charles Street yesterday only to find that Miss Baird has gone to America. To take photographs, if you please. Lady Lisle was in quite a state about it. First thing she knew about it was the note that Charlotte left her on the breakfast table.'

'America?' Bay finally lit his cigarette.

'Desperate measures, I know! That photographer chap she was hanging about with has gone with her.'

Bay took a long draw. 'They've eloped?'

'Lady L says not. But then she would, wouldn't she?'

'Perhaps.' Bay stood up. 'Sorry, Chicken, but I have a few things I must do before the race.' Before Hartopp could say anything more, Bay went round to other side of the stables and was violently sick into a bale of straw.

As the special trains laid on from London and the north-east disgorged their passengers into Liverpool Lime Street, it seemed as if the whole city was migrating north-west. Every wheeled conveyance had been pressed into service and the road was jammed with carriages, omnibuses, governess carts, even a dustcart. Caspar had managed to get seats on one of the special race day omnibuses. Charlotte and Grace were sitting inside; Caspar was clinging to the top deck. It took the best part of the morning to travel the six miles or so to the racecourse as the road was unpaved and the horses and the carriages kept getting stuck in the ruts.

Mud, it seemed, was the great leveller. Even the carriage carrying the royal party found itself defeated by the treacherous conditions and nearly capsized into a hidden ditch. Fortunately for all concerned, the Prince of Wales was sitting on the opposite side of the carriage, and by using his considerable bulk as a counterweight he was able to keep the vehicle from toppling over. When the royal carriage was righted and on its way again, there was a rousing cheer from the spectators, 'God bless the Prince of Wales', as well as more raucous shouts of 'Good old Tum Tum'.

After the second hour of sitting wedged between Grace and a lady who smelt strongly of eau de cologne and who was wearing a hat with orange feathers, Charlotte was ready to get out and walk the rest of the way. But at last the gates of the course came into view and the mass exodus began.

Charlotte felt almost physically assaulted as she walked through the gates. She had never been to a race meeting before and the tumult around her was extreme. The crush was impassable because people moved not as individuals but in packs. There were families, three generations of them in their Sunday best, who had decided that there was safety in numbers and so moved everywhere in a solid clump. Then there were the Irish, who had come over on the boat train and were packed around the show ring waiting for a sight of Glasnevin, the Irish favourite. Charlotte was struck by the gaudiness of the crowd after the monochrome colours of the London streets. Her neighbour on the bus with the orange feathered hat was not the only racegoer who had chosen to wear colours as bright as the jockeys' silks; the milliners of the north-west had clearly been busy. Charlotte saw one woman with a hat consisting of a pheasant in its nest with chicks poking out over the brim. Anyone who could afford it had clearly ordered a new frock for the race, and the array of the latest mauve and lime-green silks was dazzling. Even the men were splashed with colour, sporting spotted silk handkerchiefs, scarlet waistcoats, and suits in mustard check. Charlotte, wearing a fawn travelling dress whose greatest recommendation was that it hardly showed the dirt, felt like a wren in a peacock enclosure.

Caspar, on the other hand, fitted in perfectly. His green and orange check ulster, which in London turned heads, here in Aintree looked exactly right. He had taken out his camera and was setting it up by the owners' enclosure. As he worked, the crowd concentrated around him, and when Sholto Douglas, the celebrated Scottish owner, asked him to take a picture of his horse, the Governess, an excited murmur ran through the racegoers.

The Governess was nervy before the race, and both Douglas and the jockey had to stand on either side to keep the horse still. But Caspar's way with society women seemed also to work on thoroughbreds: he stroked the racehorse on the muzzle and kept up a stream of soothing chatter which had the animal almost hypnotised as he disappeared under the cloth and squeezed the bulb.

Douglas offered to pay for the print, but Caspar said, 'It was a privilege to take a picture of such a magnificent animal. I wouldn't dream of asking for money, but if you could find a suitable place for my companion Miss Baird to watch the race, I would be enormously grateful.'

Douglas looked over at Charlotte, who was looking at the horses being walked round the ring by their lads, and shook his head. 'I'll give you both a pass to the owners' stand. This part of the course is not really suitable for a lady.'

Caspar bowed. 'Thank you, sir. As an American there are so many things I don't understand, and I don't suppose Miss Baird has been to a racecourse before, either.'

'Well, everybody should see the Grand National at least once. It's the finest race in the world. And make sure you place a bet. You can't really enter into the spirit of the thing, unless you have some money down. You can still get decent odds on the Governess and she is definitely going to win.'

Douglas called over one of the race day stewards and asked him to take Caspar and his party up to his box in the stands. Charlotte was relieved to be away from the hubbub. Her one aim, a desire she could barely admit to herself, was to catch a glimpse of Bay, but she was too small to see over the bowler-hatted crowd. But as they were shepherded from the melee of the public grounds to the relative calm of the stands, Charlotte felt a moment of unease. Here the orange feathers had been replaced by mink and sable – the loud checked tweeds by subtle heather mixtures, which meant that it was entirely possible that she would see someone she knew.

As if to prove her point, a tweedy back in front of her turned to wave at a friend and she caught sight of Chicken Hartopp's unmistakeable profile with its dundreary whiskers. She stopped, clutching Caspar's arm to pull him away, but it was too late; Chicken had seen her, and he greeted her with a roar. Even from where she was standing Charlotte could smell the brandy on his breath.

'Charlotte, I mean Miss Baird! What on earth are you doing here? I mean, what a surprise . . . To see you, I mean,' he faltered, checked by the expression on Charlotte's face.

'Good morning, Captain Hartopp, I believe you have met Mr Hewes.'

Chicken looked Caspar up and down in a way that was only a shade away from insolence. 'Indeed.'

Charlotte could see that Hartopp was about to boil over with curiosity. To forestall him she said, 'It is quite an accident that we are here. We were meant to be sailing to America today but there has been a delay. And since we were in Liverpool on the day of the National it seemed that we must come to Aintree.'

Caspar rushed in, 'Such a promising place for photography,

Captain Hartopp. I should like very much to photograph the winner. I have always wanted to capture a moment of total joy.'

Hartopp looked at Caspar in bewilderment. He could not understand how the man could walk around with Charlotte Baird without a trace of embarrassment. Surely if they were eloping, they would not appear in such a public place.

Caspar said, 'Lord Sholto has offered to introduce me to Major Topham, who owns the course. Charlotte, would you mind very much if I left you with Captain Hartopp for a moment? I want to make sure of my place at the winning post.'

Charlotte did mind, but she could see that Caspar was determined to get his picture. She turned to Chicken.

'Captain Hartopp, I would be so grateful if you would go through the race card with me. I am so confused by all the different terms, and I think I should really like to place a bet.' She smiled at Chicken with a charm that made his skin redden under the whiskers. 'Grace, my maid, tells me that I should be backing a horse called Dancing Bear.'

'Your maid is here?'

'Of course my maid is here. Do you think I would come here without a female companion?' Charlotte said in mock outrage.

Chicken looked at the floor.

'Forgive me, Miss Baird. But I don't know what to think. I called on your aunt in London and she said you were going to America with that fellow. She was in a terrible to-do. Everyone in London is talking about it. The word is that you have eloped. But dash it all, you can't marry a creature like that. I don't believe it.'

Charlotte pulled off the kid glove she was wearing on her left hand. She held it up for Chicken to inspect.

'No ring, Captain Hartopp, no ring. Mr Hewes is my travelling companion and colleague, nothing more. I am going to America to take photographs, and he has kindly agreed to act as my guide. So you can tell "everyone" in London that there is no scandal, beyond that of a young woman making a decision about her own life. I don't suppose that will satisfy anyone, but it is the truth. My maid is with me, and while Mr Hewes may not qualify in your mind as a gentleman, he has shown me nothing but kindness.'

Chicken Hartopp could not meet her gaze; he tugged at his whiskers so hard that Charlotte feared that he would pull the hairs out by the roots.

'But dash it, if you are going to America, why are you here? Don't you know that Bay is a runner?'

Charlotte tried to look composed. 'Yes. But coming here was never part of my plan. I should have been on the Irish Sea by now, but when the crossing was delayed and I heard about the race, and I discovered that Captain Middleton had entered, well, I decided to come.'

'But, damn it, I don't understand. The man has treated you monstrously. Humiliating you in public. Carrying on with the Empress like that. I am surprised you can even look at him.'

Charlotte put her glove back on, deliberately smoothing and stretching the leather over her shaking fingers.

'Perhaps you are right to be surprised, Captain Hartopp. But I don't consider myself humiliated, whatever the world may think. Now are you going to be kind enough to explain this race card to me, or will I have to find another guide?'

But Chicken, now that he had begun to speak his mind, could not be diverted so easily.

'But Charlotte, I mean Miss Baird, did you know that the Empress is here too? In the royal box with the Prince of Wales. If you come to the front here you can see her quite clearly.'

He pushed to the front of the stand and pointed to the royal box, which was about twenty feet away. Charlotte hesitated. In her impulsive decision to come to Aintree it had never occurred to her that the Empress might have made the same choice. At first she thought that she could not bear to look, but then a scalding wave of curiosity and jealousy swept her reluctance away. She followed the direction of Hartopp's finger and saw the portly figure of the Prince of Wales in a homburg, a cigar clamped between his teeth. He was flanked by two women. The nearest one Charlotte recognised as the Princess of Wales; the Empress was on the other side. She was wearing a dark blue costume, almost as plain in cut as her riding habit. But the severity of her costume was offset by the sable stole she wore round her shoulders, which even at this distance Charlotte could see was a miracle of softness. The Empress was leaning forward slightly, holding a pair of binoculars which she had trained on the parade ring. The Prince of Wales leant over to her and said something, and the Empress smiled but she kept on looking through her glasses at the horses and riders below.

Hartopp turned to Charlotte with a smile almost of triumph.

Willing herself to sound as light as possible, she said, 'The Empress has a splendid pair of field glasses. I think that they are exactly what I need. Do you know where I might get some, Captain Hartopp?'

'Field glasses?' Chicken seemed not to understand.

'Yes, isn't that what they are called? Like opera glasses, only rather more powerful, I imagine. Fred has some.'

Chicken shook his head from side to side and pulled on his whiskers again, only this time meditatively rather than urgently. Charlotte said nothing while he ruminated. Finally he said, 'Does Fred know you are here?'

'Of course not. He and Augusta are on a boat heading to the Bay of Naples, so he won't come in here if that's what you are worried about. Now, are you able to help me find some field glasses? I can see that something is happening down there, and I really would like to see the race properly.' Charlotte tapped her foot.

'Bay doesn't stand a chance, you know. He's a decent enough rider, but Tipsy doesn't have the stamina for the National. A mare hasn't won at Aintree since the Fifties.'

'All the more reason to find some glasses, so that I can have a chance of seeing him lose,' Charlotte said with some tartness.

Captain Hartopp looked as if he was about to make another protest, but a glance from Charlotte stopped him and he mumbled something about borrowing some glasses from a fellow he knew, and stumbled off.

The stand was filling up by the minute and Charlotte beckoned to Grace to stand by her to protect her vantage point. She wondered if Caspar would photograph Bay in the ring. She hoped he didn't disapprove too vehemently of her desire to come here. After all, it was the purest coincidence that they should be in Liverpool on the day of the National. There was no surrender in coming to watch Bay run in the race of his life. He wouldn't even know that she was there. But even as she rehearsed these arguments, Charlotte struggled to ignore the deep current that had brought her there that day. At a level that she could barely give words to, Charlotte felt that it was fate that had tipped those logs into the Mersey, fate that had led Grace into conversation with the racing stranger. She was meant to be here, that was all.

In the jockeys' changing rooms, Bay stepped onto the scale to weigh in. To his great relief, he was given the lightest possible handicap. He glanced at his pocket watch, the race was due to start in just under an hour. It was time to get changed into his jockey's outfit. When racing, he always wore the scarlet and gold colours of his regiment.

As he took the now rather faded silks out of his Gladstone bag in the changing room, he heard a familiar cough behind him. He turned to see Nopsca holding a flat cardboard box out to him. He took the box and put it down on the boot bench. Nopsca reached into his inside pocket and brought out a letter. Bay did not need to see the crest on on the back to know that it was from Sisi.

'The Kaiserin asked me to give you this before the race.'

'Thank you, Baron.' Bay kept his voice down, as the other jockeys in the room were looking at them curiously. Nopsca, who was wearing a frock coat and spats and was fragrant with attar of roses, was an incongruous figure in the gentleman riders' vestibule, which was strewn with discarded racing stocks and smelt of leather, rubbing alcohol and sweat.

Bay opened the letter first:

My dear Bay,
Please wear these for me when you win,
Your own Sisi

Undoing the string that fastened the box, he saw a set of racing colours in black and gold. As he held them up, he saw that not only were they precisely the right size but the Hapsburg crest had been embroidered on the back.

His horror must have been evident on his face because the Baron shrugged apologetically. 'In Wien, it is the custom for the riders always to wear the arms of their owners.'

Bay turned his head away, and the Baron said quickly, 'I think perhaps I have the word incorrectly. I mean to say patron.'

Bay put the Empress's colours back in their box. He took a deep breath to let out his emotion but still he sounded angrier than he would have liked. 'Tell her that I mean no disrespect, but I can't possibly wear these. Tipsy is my horse and I am not some medieval knight who wears his lady's colours.'

Nopsca held out his hands, about to plead with Bay, but when he saw the other man's face he stopped short, his mouth open, the placating smile frozen. He dropped his arms, picked up the colours and packed them away in their box.

'I understand that you have no use for these. I think, perhaps, that it was impossible to find you here among the crowds.'

He made Bay a stiff bow, clicking his heels together in the Austrian way.

'For my part, Captain Middleton, I wish you good luck.'

A Royal Wager

UNCHEON WAS BEING SERVED IN THE ROYAL BOX. There had been a generous breakfast on the train, but the Prince of Wales felt that was no drawback to the consumption of a sumptuous lunch of the kind he had when out shooting. There were four different kinds of raised pies, salmagundi, chicken in aspic and truffled riz de veau, as well as pheasants stuffed with foie gras, and a terrine of hare and salsify. To drink there was champagne, hock, burgundy and a warm claret cup to which the Princess of Wales was extremely partial.

Sisi, as usual, only toyed with the food on her plate. She knew that if she looked up Festy would be gazing at her, willing her to eat something, but although from time to time she would cut off a morsel and take it to her mouth, it would always return to the plate untouched. This part of the day was taking far too long, she wanted the race to begin.

The Prince of Wales sat on one side of her at the table which had been set up at the back of the royal box, and Earl Spencer on the other. The Princess of Wales sat at the other end of the table, her lovely face unruffled by the conversation that flowed around her as she was almost completely deaf. The Prince was in a benign mood – his lunch had been plentiful and punctual, and he was delighted to have the Empress as his guest. He knew all about Elizabeth's visit to Windsor and he could not help but admire a woman who had defied his mother. '*Not nearly as pretty as dear Alix, and after coming all that way she refused to stay for luncheon.*'

But he thought she was beautiful, and it was a rare treat for the Prince of Wales to find beauty in a woman of his own rank. And she was not Prussian, which was a relief. He knew that the Empress shared his loathing of Bismarck. They had a most enjoyable gossip about the dreariness of the Prussian court and the awfulness of the food at Potsdam. There was an enjoyable frisson when the Empress, in order to emphasise a point about the dowdiness of the Hohenzollern ladies, briefly touched his hand. His eyes flickered to see if Alix had noticed, but she was smiling dreamily at the equerry sitting next to her; she had long ago learnt not to observe her husband too closely.

At a quarter to three, Major Topham, the owner of Aintree Racecourse, came in to let the royal party know that the riders were about to parade around the ring.

The Prince of Wales clapped his hands and said to the table, 'Does anybody want to place a bet before the race begins? This will be your last chance.'

The Empress looked at him sideways. 'I think perhaps that I shall make a bet.'

'Splendid, splendid. Topham will arrange it.'

Topham's bow was a touch reluctant; he had many things to do, and acting as a royal bookie was not one of them.

Sisi beckoned to Festy, who was standing in a corner. 'I need some money.'

Festy nodded. 'How much, Majesty?'

'Let me see, I think five hundred guineas.'

The Prince of Wales exhaled. 'I say, that's brave, which horse?'

'The horse is called Tipsy. But I am not being brave, my dear Prince, Tipsy is being ridden by Captain Middleton.' She smiled at him. The Prince, who, of course, had heard all the rumours about the Empress and her pilot, smiled back.

'In that case, Empress, I shall match your bet.'

Edward waved to his equerry and instructed him to give a note to Topham. The racecourse owner looked surprised.

'I think Tipsy was being quoted at twenty to one, sir.'

'Capital, better get down there before the odds shorten.'

As the Prince's party took their place in the front of the box, a cheer went up from the crowd. The Prince of Wales touched his homburg and the Princess waved one kid-gloved hand. Sisi bowed automatically as she always did when she heard cheering in public, and like her royal companions she stretched her mouth into what she thought of as her public smile. She hoped that there were no photographers in the crowd.

The horses began to come out into the ring. Sisi picked up her field glasses so that she could take a closer look. Earl Spencer, who was standing behind her, was checking the numbers off against his race guide.

'Twenty-three, that's Glasnevin, Leinster's horse, odds-on favourite with Sir William. Listen to the crowd, sounds like half of Dublin has come over to see him run.'

Sisi picked up her own race card, looking for Bay's number. She wished that she could stand down by the ring and speak to him before the race, but it would be impossible for her to go without the Waleses, and the Prince showed no inclination to leave the comfort of his box. But it was of no matter, she would be able to see him after the race. Rudolph had, at last, gone home, so there was no reason why Bay shouldn't return to Easton Neston, although the hunting season was almost over. It might be time to go to Gödöllő. The estate in Hungary was always so pretty in the spring, when the cherry orchards were in bloom. It would be the ideal place to breed horses. How smart it would be to have her own stud farm.

Bay was number thirty-eight. This gave her a little thrill, as it was the age that she was now. It must be a good omen. It would be something to see him wearing her colours. Peering through her field glasses she tried to catch a glimpse of number thirty-eight. But the field was forty strong and although the ring was full of horses, there was no sign of Bay.

Spencer was looking for him too. 'No sign of Middleton yet. Wonder where he's got to. Probably getting some Dutch courage. Fences seem to get higher every year. Last year there were six horses down and two jockeys with broken arms. In 'sixty-nine a fellow died when his horse fell on top of him. Still, makes it more inter-estin', you never know who is going to finish.'

Countess Festetics did not fully understand what the English Lord was saying, but could see from her mistress's face that it was upsetting her. She said quickly, 'Earl Spencer, please to tell me why that man down there is standing on a box and waving his hands like a *puppe*, sorry, I don't know the English word.'

Sisi said, 'Puppet.'

'So who is the man, actually there are many of them, who are the puppets?'

Spencer laughed. 'Oh, you mean the bookies.'

'Bookies?' said Sisi. 'I do not know this word.'

'They take the bets, and set the odds. They wave their hands around to tell each other how people are betting. Once Topham has gone down there and put your bets on Tipsy, they will be waving at each other like crazy, just wait and see.'

But Sisi was no longer listening to him. Through her glasses, she had seen the magic number, thirty-eight. She sighed with relief as Bay rode in on Tipsy, the only grey in the ring. But he looked wrong, not somehow as she expected. It took her a minute to work out the problem: he was not wearing the black and gold colours of the Hapsburgs.

On the other side of the cast-iron and wood partition that divided the royal box from the rest of the stand, Charlotte was also watching number thirty-eight. After her outburst, a chastened Hartopp had found her some field glasses, so now she could see every detail of the riders and their horses as they paraded around the show ring. She spotted Tipsy at once. As she peered at Bay's familiar profile through the magnifying lens, it felt odd to be looking at him when he could have no idea that she was there. He would know about the Empress, of course, and Charlotte watched attentively to see if Bay looked up at the royal box. But to her great satisfaction, so far he had not.

'Big field today,' said Chicken. 'Forty riders. Got to get ahead quickly at the start, otherwise there will be a terrible crush at those fences. I was here in 'seventy-three when six horses went down at Becher's. Only five horses finished that year. Good year for the bookies, that one.'

Charlotte interrupted him. 'How long before the race starts, Captain Hartopp?'

Chicken looked at his pocket watch. 'Oh, not long now. They will go down to the starting line any minute.'

Charlotte wondered what had happened to Caspar; she did not relish the thought of spending the whole race with Captain Hartopp. She thought she might go and look for him, but the stand was now filled with bellowing tweed – suited men and some loud women – and she did not want to lose her vantage point at the rail. Watching the race up here, even with Hartopp, was better than getting lost in the crowd below.

The course steward, who had shown them into the stand, came up to her and handed her a note.

'Miss Baird? The American gentleman asked me to give you this.'

It was a folded betting slip, a receipt for a fifty-pound bet on Tipsy to win at odds of twenty to one against.

Charlotte folded the paper up carefully and put it in her pocket. She understood that the betting slip was a message. Caspar was making it clear that he knew exactly why they were there and where her loyalties lay.

A band started playing 'God save the Queen', and the crowd began to sing the national anthem. Charlotte turned her field glasses on the royal box and saw that while the Prince and Princess of Wales were singing, or at least mouthing the words, the Empress was staring at the riders, her face rapt. Even at this distance, Charlotte could see that the Empress's face at that moment would make a wonderful photograph, there was so much feeling in it. She was looking at Bay, of course, and Charlotte recognised the look. She had never thought, or perhaps she had never allowed herself to think, that the Empress might actually care for Bay. It was easier to think of her as the Snow Queen of fairy stories, a woman with ice in her heart. But the Empress in the sables was not heartless. She was in love with Bay.

This was not a welcome discovery. Charlotte wanted to have the monopoly on feeling. The idea that the Empress might care for Bay as strongly as she did was uncomfortable. The thought that had consoled her as she made her preparations to leave for America was that Bay would be miserable with the Empress. But if the Empress loved him then his misery was not guaranteed. The unfairness of this stung Charlotte, and for a moment she thought she was going to cry.

The strains of 'God Save the Queen' finished and the singing was replaced by a rumble of expectation from the crowd. The horses were making their way to the starting line. They jostled for position, the riders trying to hold back the excited horses who were desperate to get going.

Bay had found a place at the outside edge. It was not a favoured position, but it was a long race and he had been bunched in before when steeplechasing, so he had decided that the only way to win the National was to be as far outside the field as possible. Next to him was one of the Beasley brothers, Ned, riding the Governess. He nodded at Bay. Ned's two younger brothers Jack and Tom were also riding in the race. Bay felt reassured that Ned, the most experienced jockey, had also taken an outside edge position.

Now that he could see the course in front of him, Bay wished that he had taken a nip from his flask. The race caller was announcing the names of all the horses and riders. As their names were called, the jockeys put their whips in the air. There was a great cheer when they got to Glasnevin, the Irish horse, and by now the odds-on favourite. By the time the caller had worked his way down to his end of the field, Bay's hands were shaking as he lifted his crop into the air.

He knew that Sisi would be looking at him from the royal box, waiting for him to acknowledge her, but he kept his eyes straight ahead.

The starter pistol cracked and the line of horses surged forward, Glasnevin leading from the middle of the field. Bay felt his nerves fall away as his horse got into her stride. This was where he was meant to be: riding Tipsy in the Grand National.

Tipsy cleared the first fence effortlessly, but out of the corner of his eye Bay saw a horse stumble and his rider fall. Glasnevin was still at the front of the field. Bay could feel Tipsy straining to get ahead, as she always liked to be at the front, but he restrained her; he did not want to make his bid for the race until the second lap. At Becher's

Brook two horses refused the fence, and several came down at the sharp left-hand turn that took the course back towards the stands. There was a groan from the crowd that lined the course, standing on old railway carriages, when the jockey riding Glasnevin the favourite fell to the ground as the horse made the right-angled turn towards the main stand.

Bay glanced to his right to check on Beasley and the Governess. The big black horse had an easy stride and both horse and rider looked ominously relaxed.

A huge cheer came from the crowd as the horses came into sight of the main stands. The field was about two thirds of its original size. On the second lap the going was much worse; the horses' hooves had churned the soft ground into slippery mud. As Tipsy cleared the second fence Bay felt her stumble on landing, and for a second he thought he was about to fly over the mare's head. All he could do was hope that he would his break his neck instantly and that would be that – but Tipsy found some purchase with her back legs and she managed to get back into her rhythm, Bay clinging not just to her reins but to her mane as well.

'Thank you, my darling Tipsy,' he shouted into his mount's ear, sobbing with relief that his National was not over.

Becher's again, and this time six horses came down as they tried to make the jump and ninety-degree turn. Bay looked up for a moment and saw that while there were about twelve horses left in the race, only eight of them still had their riders on their backs. Glasnevin, the riderless favourite, was still galloping away at the front. But while the stallion was establishing his dominance over the other horses in the field, the racegoers who had backed him to win were crumpling their betting slips, as horses without jockeys were disqualified.

In the royal box, Sisi gasped as the horses came round for the second lap. Where was Bay? She held up her glasses but her hands were shaking so much that she could not hold them steady. She heard the Prince of Wales say, 'Now where is our horse, eh Empress? Hope it hasn't fallen on the first lap. What was the number again?'

'Thirty-eight,' said Sisi.

'Oh, I can't see it. Pity.'

Sisi tried to keep her face still but she was seeing Bay spreadeagled on the ground, his head twisted to the side, his neck broken. She felt a touch on her shoulder and knew that it was Festy trying to give her comfort in her distress.

Then there was a great bellow from Earl Spencer. 'There's Middleton, I can see him, but his horse is so muddy you can hardly tell it's a grey. Time to move up now, Bay. Come on.'

Sisi picked up her binoculars again and fiddled with them until at last she found number thirty-eight. Spencer was correct, horse and rider were so splashed with mud as to be almost unrecognisable. She followed Bay through the glasses until he went round the bend. Tipsy, she could see, was still running well and Bay was as buoyant in the saddle as ever.

'Our horse is still in the running, Empress,' said the Prince of Wales. 'My goodness, the field has taken a battering. Only about ten horses in it now. Your man is good, no doubt about it.'

'Not good. He is the best,' said the Empress softly.

Charlotte missed seeing Bay come into view for the second lap as she had her hands over her eyes. She had picked up the glasses earlier and had focussed on a horse and rider, only to see the horse stumble and fall and the rider being thrown to the side and curling himself into a tight ball as the other horses galloped over him. She knew that it was not Bay that had fallen but the violence of the fall horrified her. The image of her mother's body being carried over the fields on a five-bar gate came into her head and refused to shift.

Chicken nudged her. 'There they are, coming round now. By Jove, Bay is still in there. Glasnevin's lost his jockey, but the Governess is still in it.'

Opening her fingers a fraction, Charlotte saw the horses rush by. Her heart was beating so fast she could hear the blood drumming in her ears. She thought that she could not bear it any more. She turned, thinking that she would push her way out so that she could be somewhere – anywhere – else, but there were so many people pressing down to the rail now that the horses were coming round into the final stretch, that she found she could not move.

Chicken said, 'Middleton is coming up the field now. Now that's a good bit of riding,' he said grudgingly.

Charlotte was making all kinds of bargains with the God she did not much think about, promising anything if only Bay would be delivered safely.

Bay and Tipsy were hurtling towards the last fence. There were three horses ahead of them including the Governess. Now was the time to let Tipsy go. Bay raised his whip to urge his horse on to the final effort and found that he could not move his arm. A bolt of excruciating pain ran down from his shoulder and he saw black spots in front of his eyes, but, gripping Tipsy with his knees, he took the whip in his other hand and gave her a whack.

They sailed over the fence, another horse down. Now there were only two horses in front on the home stretch. Bay, biting his lip so hard that he tasted blood in his mouth, dug his heels into Tipsy's sides. Leaning down, he urged her on. She responded at once and passed the chestnut, so now there was only the Governess between him and the finishing line. He raised his good arm again and felt Tipsy straining forward, desperate to get to the front. But as both horse and rider strained every sinew, they could not edge past the black stallion. The roar from the crowd was coming nearer and nearer as they came closer to the finishing line. Bay saw the four-hundred-yard marker flash and he realised that victory was so close and yet he was about to lose. He saw the gap between the Governess's flanks and Tipsy's head begin to widen; the stallion simply had a longer stride. Bay knew that this was justice. The just punishment for his sins was that the thing he so desired would be held out to him and then snatched away.

His head down, Bay did not see the other horse coming up between him and the Governess but he felt Tipsy accelerate forward in alarm. The riderless Glasnevin was coming to take its favourite position at the head of the pack, and as the bay horse surged forward it veered to the side and crushed against the Governess. The last sound Bay remembered hearing was Ned Beasley's scream as his leg was crushed by the runaway horse, but from then on, as Tipsy galloped ahead to go first past the finishing post, he saw and heard nothing but a blur of faces and sound.

The Prize

THE PRINCE OF WALES SEIZED SISI'S HAND AND
kissed it.

'We won, Empress! We won. We must have champagne.'

'But, I think it was Captain Middleton who won,' said Sisi.

'Of course, but *we* have both won ten thousand pounds. Not
quite a king's ransom, but good enough for the Prince of Wales.'
The Prince was beaming. His win meant some new horses for his
stud and several diamond bracelets for his mistresses.

He held up his glass in a toast. 'To the Empress, who has made
me a very lucky man today. A lady who is as wise about horses as
she is beautiful.'

Sisi smiled back. 'And to Captain Middleton, the best rider in
England.'

More champagne was drunk, and then Major Topham appeared.

'Topham! Twenty to one, eh? All thanks to the Empress here.
Is it time for the presentation?'

'Yes, sir.'

'Well, in the circumstances, I think we might prevail upon the
Empress to hand over the prize to the winning jockey. You don't
mind, do you, Alix?' he said, turning to his wife, who nodded
vaguely, and then back to Sisi. 'Would you do Major Topham the

honour of presenting the cup and what-have-you to the winner, Empress?'

'Nothing would give me greater pleasure!'

The Prince offered Sisi his arm, and the royal party began to make their way down through the cheering crowds to the winner's enclosure. This time the band played 'God Bless the Prince of Wales'.

Charlotte's fingers were stiff from clamping them over her face, and her thumbs from stopping her ears. She had watched Bay and Tipsy come into the home straight but as the noise around her grew louder and the horses got nearer, she realised that she could not bear to see any more. Whether Bay won or lost, it made no difference. He was safe, at least. When she judged from the muffled roar that the race must be over, she put her shield down and looked at Chicken. His expression told her everything. He was loose and shiny from the frequent nips he had been taking from his flask.

'He did it, he damn well did it! Deuced lucky, of course, Glasnevin coming up like that and cutting off the other feller, but then Bay always was a lucky devil.' He shook his head. 'Wish to blazes I had put money on him now. Knew he could ride, of course, but didn't think the mare was up to it. Should have known better, Bay always gets what he wants.'

He looked at Charlotte, his eyes full of drunken meaning.

But Charlotte said nothing. She was watching the crowd retreating like the tide as the royal party came down from the royal box towards the winner's enclosure. There was the Prince of Wales's homburg and at his side the Empress wreathed in sable. There was a dais covered in bunting in the winner's enclosure, with chairs and a stand bearing the silver trophy. The royal party arranged themselves on the dais, the Prince of Wales and the Empress in the middle.

There was a huge cheer as Bay and Tipsy came into the ring. People surged forward to touch the horse and rider, a few holding up their betting slips and kissing them.

Charlotte watched as Bay and Tipsy approached the dais. She watched as the Prince of Wales handed the trophy to the Empress. She watched as Bay was helped to dismount and carried on the shoulders of the crowd towards the Empress. And then she felt she could watch no more. She turned her back on the scene and touched her maid's arm.

'I want to go.'

Grace turned round reluctantly. As the two women began to fight their way out of the stand, Hartopp touched Charlotte on the shoulder.

'You are leaving without saying goodbye?'

Charlotte, still moving, said, 'Goodbye, Captain Hartopp. Thank you for the glasses.' She thrust them at him.

'But hang on! You might need me. It's a bit busy down there.'

Charlotte did not stop, but she looked back over her shoulder.

'I am going back to my hotel. If you would be kind enough to escort us to somewhere we can find a carriage that would be helpful.' She was grateful for Hartopp's bulk as he cleared a path for her through the teeming crowd of racegoers.

'What about your American friend? Would you like me to find him for you?' Hartopp asked Charlotte as they reached the gates.

Charlotte shook her head. She did not want to be there for another second. There was a line of carriages waiting for hire on the road that led back to Liverpool. She signalled to the driver at the front of the queue and he drove up to where they stood.

As Hartopp closed the carriage door, she remembered the betting slip in her pocket. 'I would be very grateful, Captain Hartopp, if you could find Mr Hewes and give him this.' She held out the slip.

Hartopp looked at it. 'By Jove, he will be glad. A monkey at twenty to one, that's a thousand smackers.'

Charlotte tried to smile. 'Then be sure you give it to him.'

Hartopp saw the effort on her face. 'You have my word. And what about Middleton? Do you have a message for him?'

Charlotte put her chin up. 'You may give him my congratulations if you like, Captain Hartopp. My sincere congratulations.' Then she put her hands up over her face to stop him seeing her cry, and Chicken, tactful for once in his blundering life, closed the carriage door and told the man to drive on.

The thing that surprised Bay as he slowly became aware of his victory, was that he felt no elation. All he could think of were the last few minutes of the race when he had known for certain that he was going to lose, and what's more that he deserved to. The pain in his shoulder was intense, but worse was the knowledge that even this, the greatest victory of his life, could not make him happy. As he rode into the winner's enclosure, he saw Sisi standing on the dais, her face lit up with joy. But he could not find the answering emotion in himself.

Hands were picking him up now and carrying him across to where Sisi was standing holding out the trophy to him.

'A splendid victory, Captain Middleton,' boomed the Prince of Wales.

Bay collected himself. 'I was lucky, sir.'

'Nonsense, nonsense, you rode a brilliant race. Now the Empress is going to present you with the trophy.'

Sisi held out the heavy silver cup with both hands. 'It is with the greatest pleasure that I give you this, Captain Middleton.' Her smile was so genuine that she showed all her teeth.

Instinctively Bay put out his hands to take his prize and then realised that he could not move his right arm. He took the cup awkwardly with his left and the weight of it, taking him by surprise, made him stagger slightly. Sisi saw him wince and cried out, 'Bay!' as she put her arm out to stop him falling over.

To the spectators of the scene on the dais and in the crowd it was proof – if any was needed – that the relationship between the Empress and her pilot, the man who had just won the Grand National, was a close one. Even the Princess of Wales, who generally remained aloof from the cross currents of life around her, opened her large blue eyes a little wider and murmured to herself, 'Careful.'

Bay got his balance back and found himself looking directly into Sisi's dark eyes.

'My Bay,' she said silently.

For a moment Bay thought he was going to be happy.

The Prince of Wales turned towards them, 'You kept us guessing right up until the finishing post, Middleton. The Empress and I didn't know where to look. Both of us had placed our shirts on you to win. But you did us proud in the end.'

The Empress smiled. 'I just wish that you had got my colours in time, Captain Middleton. I had them made up in London. It would have been so much easier to pick you out in the field.'

Bay shivered involuntarily. 'Perhaps, but I always race in these.'

The Prince looked at him with something like sympathy and said, 'Regimental colours of the Eleventh Hussars, aren't they? I am proud to wear them myself as your Colonel in Chief.'

'Yes, sir.'

The Prince turned to Sisi. 'An officer always rides under his regimental colours, unless of course, it's not his horse.'

Sisi laughed. 'You English and your rules. Well then, I shall buy your horse, Captain Middleton, and then the next time you win the Grand National, you will be wearing my colours.'

Bay said, 'I would never sell Tipsy.'

'Not even to me?' asked Sisi.

But before Bay could answer, Major Topham appeared at the dais. 'Captain Middleton, I wonder if you would consent to having your photograph taken with your horse. I am sorry to interrupt your celebrations, but I have been told that the light is failing and if we are to take a picture it must be done at once.'

The Empress looked at the Major with distaste. 'I believe that Captain Middleton is otherwise engaged.'

But Bay put his good hand up. 'Actually, if you will excuse me, Ma'am, I would like a photograph of the occasion. These things don't happen very often. But you will have to hold the cup, Major. My shoulder is a bit crook.'

Before Sisi could protest again, Bay followed the Major to where Tipsy was standing. He leant against his horse's flank and closed his eyes, trying to collect his thoughts. Just for a second he had felt Sisi's spell again and he would have surrendered if it hadn't been for the thought of the colours she had sent him. They had been a perfect fit, but he had been unable to put them on.

When Bay opened his eyes, Caspar was standing in front of him.

'May I add my congratulations to those of the entire racecourse, Captain Middleton. It was a thrilling victory. When you are ready, I would like very much to take your picture. I think perhaps you should be on your magnificent horse, do you agree?'

Bay looked at him in astonishment. 'What on earth are *you* doing here?'

'Taking photographs, Captain. That is, I like to think, my calling.'

'But how did you get here? And how can you even think of taking my picture?'

Caspar smiled. 'Because I have been asked by the good major to record your triumph.'

Major Topham came round to where they stood to help Bay up onto Tipsy. 'Are you acquainted with Captain Middleton, Mr Hewes? What a happy coincidence.'

Caspar picked up his camera and tripod and put them at a forty-five-degree angle to Bay and Tipsy. 'Captain Middleton and I have met before in London. I am very familiar with his image.' He fiddled with the camera. 'Now if you would turn your head towards me, Captain. You don't have to smile, unless you want to, of course.'

'I don't,' said Bay.

The Major laughed nervously. 'But perhaps you could look a little happier. After all, you have just won the National.'

Bay turned to look at Caspar, his eyes blazing.

'Splendid. You really are a great photographic subject, Captain Middleton. If you could hold it like that just for a moment.'

Caspar disappeared under his velvet cloth, came out and squeezed the bulb. 'Excellent. That, I can promise you, will be a splendid picture.'

Bay slid down from Tipsy, advanced towards Caspar and used his good hand to shove the other man. 'Where is Charlotte? What have you done with her?'

Caspar, who was a couple of inches taller than Bay, did not flinch. 'Charlotte is where she wants to be, Captain Middleton.'

Bay drew back his fist, but Caspar was too quick for him and caught his wrist. 'You have your prize, Captain Middleton. Remember that.'

Major Topham, who was watching this scene in alarm, came

bustling over. 'Captain Middleton, perhaps you would like to come with me. There is a reception laid on for you in the members' enclosure. After all your exertions I am sure you need a drink.'

Bay felt a profound weariness come over him and allowed the Major to lead him to a room full of cheerful strangers who clapped him on his sore shoulder and gave him glass after glass of champagne. As he had not eaten that day, Bay got swiftly and comprehensively drunk.

He was sitting between Major Crombie and Lord Sholto Douglas, one man celebrating his enormous win, the other drowning his sorrows, when Chicken Hartopp swam into view.

'Well done, Bay. Wish I had put money on you. Can't think why I didn't. You always were a lucky fellow.'

Bay squinted at him.

'Yes, that's me. I'm rich now too. Put a hundred guineas on myself to win. So I'm damn rich and damn lucky.'

But Bay looked so miserable that even Chicken felt curiosity rather than envy.

'What's up, old man? No reason for a long face. You should be on top of the world. What more could you possibly want?'

Bay looked at his boots.

Sholto Douglas nudged him. 'Cheer up, Middleton, you've won the bloody Grand National and the Empress of bloody Austria can't keep her bloody hands off you.'

Bay lunged towards him, fists outstretched, but Sholto ducked easily.

'Steady on, old man, I meant it as a compliment.'

Bay subsided. 'Sorry, Sholto, not quite the thing.'

Sholto got up. 'If you will excuse me, I must go and wring the neck of Glasnevin's jockey.'

Hartopp took his place next to Bay. 'Do you know who I watched you race with, Bay?'

'I don't know, Chicken. Queen Victoria?'

Chicken leant closer and said in his ear, 'Charlotte Baird.'

Bay pulled away from him. 'Of course you did.'

'No really, old man, I did. She told me to give you her congratulations. Her sincere congratulations.'

'She said that?'

'Yes, sincere congratulations, those were her words exactly. But it was damned odd. She came to watch you race but she had her hands over her eyes at the end. I don't think she saw a bloody thing.'

''Spect she was thinking of her mother,' said Bay.

'Her mother?'

'Broke her neck huntin'. That's why she doesn't ride.'

'Oh, is that the reason?'

'That's it precisely.'

There was a silence. Then Bay said, 'Is she still here?'

'No. She went pretty sharpish after the race. Back to Liverpool. Sailing tomorrow.'

'To America?'

'Yes.'

'With that American?'

'Well, he's going with her, but just as her travelling companion. She was pretty clear about that. Says she is going to take photographs and he's going to help her.'

'So they ain't eloping?'

'She says not. No ring, she showed me her hand. No ring.'

Bay went back to contemplating his boots. 'Why'd she tell you that, do you suppose?' he asked.

'Didn't want me to think that she was marrying him. Doesn't

make any difference, mind you. The girl is finished. Even the Lennox fortune won't be enough. No one will marry her now.'

'Is that what you think, Chicken?'

'Yes, that's what I think.'

'So you wouldn't marry her, even supposing she would have you?'

'No, not now. The girl's not respectable. Don't know what Fred and Augusta will say when they come back from their wedding trip. Terrible blow. Newlyweds trying to make a home with a scandal like that in the background. Better really if she *had* eloped with the fellow.' Hartopp started to tug at his whiskers. 'At least she would be married then. All this nonsense about taking photographs. Trouble with Charlotte is that she has been indulged.' He pulled on both whiskers at once so that he looked like a discontented haddock.

'Lady Dunwoody has a lot to answer for, putting ridiculous notions into her head. Photography isn't even a proper accomplishment. It doesn't require any skill, just a lot of equipment.'

Bay tried to consult his watch, and then he remembered that he was still wearing his racing silks and his watch was with his other clothes.

'So let's get this absolutely straight, Chicken, so there is no room for doubt. There is no circumstance in which you would marry Charlotte Baird?'

'None whatsoever, no chance at all.'

'Then, Chicken, you are an even bigger bloody fool than I thought.'

Bay got up and, clutching his bad shoulder to protect it from pats of congratulation from well-meaning racegoers, he stumbled towards the jockeys' enclosure. He needed to get back into his civilian clothes.

The royal party was winding up. The Prince was taking one last draw on his cigar as he looked out over the racecourse, secure in the knowledge that the royal train could not leave without him. His wife was pretending to listen to Major Topham's plans for bringing the railway to Aintree. Sisi was talking to Earl Spencer about her estate in Hungary, Gödöllő. 'You must come and stay with me in the summer, I don't want Bay to feel too lonely with nobody but Magyars for company.'

'I would be delighted, Ma'am. So Middleton is to set up your stable? What a splendid opportunity for him.'

'And then we can come back here in the winter to hunt. It is perfect, no? I must say, Earl Spencer, that I am most grateful to you for giving me my pilot. He has shown me so many things.'

The Earl avoided her gaze. The Empress's passion for Middleton was becoming rather unseemly.

'But where is Captain Middleton, actually? I have not seen him since a man took him away to take his photograph. Why hasn't he come back?'

'He can hardly come in here, Ma'am, without an invitation.'

'Then I shall invite him!'

Spencer coughed. 'I think you might want to consult the Prince. It is after all, his box.'

Sisi smiled. 'Of course, I must not forget that this is not my country.'

She turned to the Prince of Wales. 'I should like to see Captain Middleton before we leave. Would it be possible to bring him in here?'

The Prince blew out a perfect ring of cigar smoke. 'Certainly, Empress. To the victor, the spoils, eh Spencer?'

He waved his free hand at the hapless Major Topham. 'Can you ask Captain Middleton to come up here?'

As Topham set out on his errand, Countess Festetics followed him out onto the racecourse. 'If you please, I should like to come with you. Captain Middleton is my friend.'

The Major shrugged. The royal party was good for business, but he had had enough of being treated like a messenger boy.

They walked across the course, which was scattered with discarded betting slips, chestnut shells and spent cheroots. Now that the racing had finished, the prevailing current of the crowd was towards the gates and the road to Liverpool. Most people were quiet, intent only on getting home, but every so often a little eddy of clamour would erupt. Someone would burst into a snatch of song, or once, loud sobs. Nobody made a sound as two men in white aprons walked through the crowd and onto the course, one of them carrying a stretcher, the other a saw. A woman with drooping orange feathers in her hat, her face shiny with gin, screamed after them, 'Butchers!'

Topham walked fast and the Countess had almost to run to keep up. They went first to the members' enclosure but there was no sign of Bay there, and no one sober enough to know where he had gone. The jockeys' changing room was deserted, too. Major Topham made the Countess wait outside as he looked around, but he could see that Bay had taken his things.

He came out and shook his head. 'Don't know where the feller's got to.'

The Countess said, 'Do you think perhaps he might be with his horse?'

'Anything's possible.' Topham set off grimly towards the stables, but the Countess caught him by the arm.

'The stables are over there, no? You must have so many things to be doing, Major. I think you are too busy to be running everywhere for my mistress, so let me help you. *I* will go to the stables and find the Captain.'

'*If* he's there.'

'Yes, but I think he will be.'

The Major looked irresolute for a moment and then said, 'If you are quite sure, then I will leave you. Thank you.'

The Countess set off towards the stables. Nopsca had told her what had happened when he had given Bay the Empress's colours, and she was worried.

She found him with his arms around Tipsy's neck. He had changed into tweeds. The Countess noticed that his waistcoat was buttoned wrongly, his eyes were bloodshot and his cheeks were pink.

He was singing something into the horse's ear and Tipsy was nuzzling his tweed shoulder. The Countess waited for him to notice her and when he did he looked at her warily.

'Hello, Festy. Have you come to fetch me?'

'In my country we would be giving you leaves to put on your head. When you are the victor.'

'Leaves? You mean a laurel wreath, I suppose. But I am afraid Tipsy would dispatch any leaves in short order. And so she should, she did all the work after all.'

The Countess could see that Bay was not sober, but she did not think he was quite drunk. He was in that dangerous state of intoxication where truth would erupt unimpeded by embarrassment or shame. The Countess could see that he was about to turn; she hoped that she had come in time.

She was considering how she could coax him to come with her, when Bay said, 'You really love her, don't you, Festy?'

The Countess nodded. 'She is everything to me.'

'I understand how you feel. She is . . . intoxicating. But I can't be like you, Festy, in her service. Did you know about the racing colours?'

Festy nodded.

'How could she think that I would wear them? I am not her creature!'

'She was trying to give you something, I think. In return for so much that you have given her. Some happiness. There is not so much for her otherwise.'

Bay sat down on a bale of straw, cradling his head in his good hand. Festy sat down next to him.

'Why did you come, Festy? Nopsca would have been so much easier.'

Festy stroked his head. 'But that is why I had to come. You must understand what you will be doing.'

Bay sat silent for a moment, feeling the Countess's fingers running over his hair, feeling her desire to smooth away his discontent.

'I can't be like you, for ever in her shadow, waiting for a smile. I want something else.'

'You will make her very sad, Captain Middleton.'

'Perhaps for a little while, until she finds another distraction. She still has her monkey.'

Festetics' hand stopped stroking his hair. 'You may leave her, if you must, but do not pretend that it will not matter to her.'

Bay found tears leaking from his eyes. 'I am sorry, Festy.'

Festy patted him on his head and stood up. 'You should be sorry for me, because now I shall have to tell the Kaiserin that you are going away. She will be angry with me, not you, because she will think that I did not say the right words to you. She will think that you can be coaxed to follow me like a horse with a sugar lump.'

Bay looked up at her and smiled. 'Your English is getting quite fluent, Festy.'

The Countess snapped her fingers. 'Any language is easy if you are Hungarian. I suppose now that you are finding the girl with the camera?'

'I am going to try. Though I don't suppose she wants to be found very much.'

'It is enough, I think, that you want to find her.'

'Perhaps.' Bay stood up. He bent to kiss the Countess on her cheek. 'Tell her, the Empress, that I will never forget our rides together, Festy. Please don't forget.'

The Countess touched his cheek. 'Do not worry, my Captain. I won't forget.' And walking back to the royal box, she murmured, 'And neither will she.'

Going West

CHARLOTTE WAS SITTING ON HER TRUNK. GRACE HAD told her that if she sat there for ten minutes, the contents would subside and she would be able to close it. There had been a message from the White Star Line when they had got back to the hotel. All trunks for the *Britannic* were to be sent down tonight, so that the ship could get away promptly on the morning tide.

She sat on the trunk waiting for the moment when the stuff inside would stop resisting and allow her to snap the lid shut. But her possessions remained stubbornly springy; they were not going to settle quietly. The easy thing would be to take some things out, but for some reason, Charlotte could not bear to do this.

Everything had happened so quickly. After Fred and Augusta's wedding it had just been so clear what she had to do. She kept thinking of Caspar's photographic plates of the desert. Those wide expanses of nothingness. Once she had imagined this new Charlotte, the rest had been easy. It was not so very difficult to be free if you had diamonds, and Caspar, of course. He had understood at once. He had even told Lady Dunwoody, which Charlotte could not bring herself to do. Her godmother should approve of her decision – she was the one, after all, who had encouraged her photography – but Charlotte also knew that for all her bohemian affect, Lady Dunwoody was completely conventional about what was suitable behaviour in unmarried girls. Lady Lisle was bribable, but Celia Dunwoody did not change her mind. Charlotte had been afraid that her resolve would wilt under her godmother's disapproval. But while she was quite happy for Fred and Augusta to receive the news by letter, she knew that Lady D would never forgive her if she had not been consulted. So she sent Caspar, who could talk his way in and out of any situation.

But today at the racecourse Charlotte had seen quite how much Caspar was giving up by coming with her. The effortless way that he had put himself at the heart of the event was impressive. Caspar was meant to be at the centre of things, and she was taking him back to the periphery of the world.

There was a tap at the door and Caspar walked in, still in his tweed ulster, brandishing a sheaf of notes in his hand.

'My winnings! One thousand pounds. Captain Middleton has been luckier for me than he has been for you.' He was turning to close the door when Charlotte stopped him.

'Don't shut the door, you shouldn't be in here alone with me if Grace isn't here.'

'Quite right too. I must protect my reputation at all costs. Why are you sitting on your trunk?'

'Because it won't close and it needs to be sent down to the quay tonight.'

'Would you like me to sit on it with you?'

Charlotte nodded. But even their combined weights could not make the lid close.

'Let's sit here for a moment, perhaps something will give way.'

'If you like.'

Charlotte looked at the notes that Caspar was still holding in his hands. 'A thousand pounds!'

'I placed the bet for you, of course.'

'I know.'

'In all it was a most successful day. I took some excellent pictures, including one of the winning jockey.'

Charlotte's sudden movement made the trunk lid sigh and with a click it subsided into line.

'You saw Bay? Did you tell him I was there?'

Caspar stood up. 'I think our work with the trunk is done.' He went over to the doorway. 'No, Carlotta, I did not tell Captain Middleton that you had come to watch him race. I did not want to give him the satisfaction. I thought that he had won quite enough victories for the day.'

Charlotte said nothing.

'Now you are cross with me. But I did it for your own good, and perhaps a little bit for my own satisfaction. He was so very cross. He even tried to strike me. Fortunately he had injured his arm, so I could not retaliate with honour. Which was a shame, as I would have enjoyed it.'

'His arm? What's wrong with his arm?' And then, 'But why would he want to fight *you*?'

'Because I wouldn't tell him where you were, and because I imagine he thinks that you and I have eloped.'

Charlotte turned her head away from him.

'Oh Charlotte, did you really want me to tell him that you had been there all day hoping for a glimpse of him? Far better that he thinks that you have eloped with me and care for him not a jot. It will be easier for both of you. You will have your glorious career in America and he will have his victory and the Empress. That is really the only happy ending.'

Charlotte bit her lip. Finally she said, 'But how do you know what a happy ending is for *me*? Or Bay?'

Caspar took her by the shoulders and shook her, gently but firmly. 'I know, because I understand what it's like to lose something you love. When Abraham died, I thought that I would never be happy again. That I would never take another picture. But I came here and found solace. That is why I agreed to come back to America with you, because you had the courage to start afresh. And you still do, whatever you think now.'

Charlotte looked down at the carpet where a cornucopia of fruits and flowers was erupting across the pile. She poked at a pomegranate with the toe of her boot.

'Now I suggest that you put on your bonnet and we can take a walk down to the quay and see our trunks being loaded onto the *Britannic*. There is nothing worse than discovering that your belongings have gone to Argentina by mistake. So run along and fetch Grace, and then we can observe all the proprieties.'

It was getting dark outside, so Caspar waved for a hackney carriage to take them down to the docks. As he helped Charlotte inside, he said, 'Thanks to the gallant captain, I can indulge myself.'

Charlotte and Grace sat on the seat opposite the driver with Caspar facing them. The streets were emptying now, but every so often they would pass a clump of people obviously back from the races, their best clothes rumpled – the feathers drooping and the neckties wilted – but clinging together with that sense of having shared a great moment. One or two held up their winning betting slips as talismans, proof that for one day only they were fortune's favoured ones. On the street corners, newsboys were still shouting 'Outsider wins National!' and 'Tipsy rides to Victory!', hoping to sell their last editions to the few people left in Liverpool who had not spent the day at Aintree. As they got closer to the docks, the public houses got closer together and every one was crammed with racegoers still enjoying their day out. By the Mersey itself, the Queen Adelaide was overflowing with Irish clans who were waiting for the Dun Laoghaire boat. They were bemoaning the loss of Glasnevin, and the singing had turned mournful.

When they got to the quayside, Caspar went down to the shipping office to find out when their luggage would be loaded onto the ship. 'I am going to tell them that I want to see each one of our trunks being carried up the gangplank. It is, I am afraid, the only way.' Charlotte noticed that Caspar was looking unusually cheerful, as if he had some splendid secret, but then, she thought, he had just won a thousand pounds.

The two women sat in the carriage for a few minutes until Charlotte could stand it no longer. She got out and stood on the cobbled quayside. The light was almost gone now, but the steamships at the dock were lit by lanterns and they loomed like Christmas trees in the twilight, the lights wobbling as the boats rocked on the wash of a passing tug. There were people everywhere; a large crowd had gathered further down the dock to wave goodbye to a boat bound for Canada. To the left of where she stood, a crew of Chinese workers in pigtails were unloading crates from a steamer into a warehouse, passing them from hand to hand in a human chain. The streets around the hotel had already taken on the subdued temper of the Sabbath, but here at the docks the activity was unceasing. It was an utterly exotic scene to Charlotte, and she thought how ironic it was that she was going all the way to America when she had seen more strange sights in the last two days in Liverpool than she had in the rest of her twenty years.

A black sailor was approaching carrying a parrot in a cage, and Charlotte thought what a wonderful picture he would make. How much more exciting to capture life in the raw than to recreate classical scenes in Lady Dunwoody's studio. In an instant the gloom that had enveloped her since her return from Aintree lifted, and she began to look forward to what she might do. To record the world in all its strangeness and beauty, that was a real ambition. It was something that she could actually accomplish. To make a record of the unexpected and the extraordinary, so that other girls like her, less fortunate than her, perhaps, could know that they could expect more than the confines of their drawing room or their kitchens. Standing here on the quayside, with the cold wind blowing off the water and the smell of rotting vegetables and brewing hops streaming past her, Charlotte felt suddenly and unexpectedly happy.

So she was smiling when she first heard the noise from the other end of the wharf. The crowds that had gathered to wave off the Canadian steamer were cheering now and throwing their hats in the air. They were surging around something, but it was too dark now to see clearly what it was. But then the crowd parted and Charlotte saw that it was a man riding a horse, and she realised that she could only see this because it was a white horse.

The crowd was following the white horse and they were singing. Charlotte could not make out the tune, she was staring too hard at the rider. Grace, hearing the singing, got out of the carriage and came to stand beside Charlotte.

'Oh look, miss,' she said, 'it's Captain Middleton.'

She stood there as Bay stopped in front of her, hundreds of hands ready to help the National winner to the ground and to hold the wonder horse's head.

He walked over to where she was standing and hesitated for a moment, then took her hand and kissed it. She remembered the first time he had kissed her hand, the night of the Spencer ball.

There was a roar of approval from the crowd behind them.

'You're smiling, Charlotte. Does that mean you are pleased to see me?' Bay looked so worried that she might have laughed.

'I am happy that you won the National, I know how much you wanted to.'

'You came to watch me?'

'I did.'

There was a silence. Charlotte saw that underneath his greatcoat, one of Bay's arms was in a sling.

'What happened to your arm?'

'My shoulder's gone. The joint is loose. I need to get it strapped up, but I've been busy.'

Charlotte looked him in the eye. 'I am catching a boat in the morning to New York, with Mr Hewes.' There was a cough behind her, and she said, 'And Grace.'

Grace smiled at Bay. 'Evening, sir, and congratulations on winning. I made some money on you, so I am very grateful to you, sir. What a finish! I didn't think you were going to do it, but suddenly that loose horse came out of nowhere and you were there.'

'I didn't think I was going to do it either, Grace, but sometimes things don't turn out in the way you expect. The Governess was a faster horse but I suppose I was lucky, and Tipsy never likes to come second.'

Charlotte could bear it no longer. 'Why did you come here, Bay?'

'To see you, of course. I knew you were here somewhere. Chicken told me.'

'Chicken?'

'Our mutual friend. He told me that you were going to America, but he also told me that you were not yet married to Mr Hewes, which was a relief, because I would like to marry you, dear Charlotte, if there is any chance at all that you will have me.'

There was a whisper through the crowd as the ones at the front, who could hear what Bay was saying, relayed it to the bystanders at the back. Some wag shouted, 'Put him out of his misery, Charlotte!'

Charlotte tried to turn away from him, but she found that she could not actually bring herself to move. 'But I am going to America tomorrow, to take photographs,' she said slowly, not meeting his eye.

'Can married women take photographs?' said Bay.

She looked at him now. 'I don't know.'

'Charlotte, I'm rich now. Well, not as rich as you, but I have enough money to support us both for years. You could give your fortune away to Fred if you wanted and we would still have enough.'

'But what about *her*?'

'I promise you that I will never see the Empress again. No, that sounds as if I am giving something up, when I am not at all. I never *want* to see her again.'

'Poor Empress,' said Charlotte, thinking of the lines around the other woman's mouth.

'I was under her spell, but I am not any more. Can you forgive me?'

There were shouts of 'Go on love, it's cold out here', from the crowd.

'But I am going to America tomorrow.'

'And I want to come with you. I could be the person that carries your camera.'

'Not with your arm in a sling, you couldn't.'

'But apart from that, am I a candidate for the job?'

Someone from the crowd started to sing 'Daisy, Daisy, give me your answer do', and noise swelled as everyone joined in the chorus.

Charlotte put one hand on Bay's good arm and, finding that no words came, she nodded.

'Really, Charlotte?'

She nodded again, and then she closed her eyes as Bay put his good arm around her waist and kissed her.

The cheers from the crowd were so loud that Charlotte did not hear Caspar calling her name, until he tapped her quite hard on the shoulder.

She looked up, her mouth already swollen from Bay's moustache.

Caspar put his head on one side and looked at Charlotte and then Bay, and then addressing Charlotte he said, 'So, I take it there has been a change of plan.'

Bay said, 'Charlotte has promised to marry me.'

'It's not her promise I am worried about, but yours, Captain Middleton. Are you going to keep your word this time?'

Bay tilted his chin at Caspar. 'I deserve that, I suppose. All I can say is that if she will have me, I will marry her tomorrow on the boat.'

Shouts of 'eager beaver' and 'steady on' came from the crowd.

Caspar turned his back on him and bent down to look at Charlotte. 'And you, can you really forgive him?'

'I think so. He is here, isn't he?'

'But do you really want to be a wife?'

'He says he will carry my camera.'

Caspar looked at her for a moment and then he laughed and raised his hands in a parody of benediction. 'Then I have no choice but to give you my blessing.'

It was late when they got back to the Adelphi. Caspar had insisted on riding Tipsy. 'I would rather ride a National winner than play the gooseberry.'

As they stood in the hotel lobby, slightly uncomfortable in their new arrangement, Bay said, 'I must engage a room for tonight. And arrange for stabling for Tipsy. Excuse me for a moment,' and he went to talk to the hotel manager.

Caspar sighed. 'I hope you know what you are doing, Carlotta.'

'He has chosen me, and I think we will be happy.'

'And it's not just because he likes you better than an empress?'

'I loved him first.'

'Then I surrender. And I wish you joy, I really do. I am sure you will take America by storm.'

'You're not coming?'

'No, Carlotta, you no longer have any need for my services, and I have duchesses to photograph. I shall be irresistible when I return to London as the man with all the details of the Lennox heiress's scandalous elopement. Don't worry, I shall do my best to console Augusta for your absence.'

Charlotte laughed and kissed him on the cheek. Then she remembered something. 'But what about your trunk? You must ask them to take it off the boat.'

Caspar winked at her. 'Really, Carlotta, what do you take me for? My trunk never left the hotel.'

The sky was still pink as Charlotte and Bay stood on the deck of the *Britannic* waiting for the ship to sail.

They were standing on the promenade deck, looking back over the city.

Charlotte put her hand over Bay's. 'Now that we are about to be married, you have to tell me.'

'Tell you what?'

'How Chicken got his name.'

Bay laughed and kissed her. 'Darling Charlotte, I am afraid I will have to disappoint you. You see, if it wasn't for Chicken I would never have known that you weren't going to marry your American. I owe him my happiness, so I can hardly betray him by telling you his deepest, darkest secret.'

Charlotte squeezed his hand.

'Besides, if I tell you, what will you have to look forward to?'

Charlotte smiled.

'Oh, I'll think of something.'

Author's Note

My interest in Sisi began when, as a little girl, I was given a jigsaw puzzle of the famous Winterhalter picture of the Empress with diamond stars in her hair. When, many years later I was casting around for a subject on which to base a novel, I remembered Sisi and the more I learnt about her extraordinary bittersweet life, the more I wanted to write about her. This novel is based on fact: the cast of characters: Sisi, Bay, Charlotte, Earl Spencer even Chicken Hartopp are all real, even if their thoughts and feelings have been supplied by me. Sisi did come to England to hunt in 1875/6 and Bay Middleton was her pilot. Her hair did reach to the ground, and she did use raw veal as a face pack. But although the Fortune Hunter is grounded in fact, it is a novel and I have departed from the strict chronology of Sis's life when I felt my story demanded it.

Elizabeth of Austria was the Princess Diana of nineteenth-century Europe: famously beautiful but unfulfilled in her marriage to Franz Joseph, she spent most of her life trying to find the happiness that evaded her. Her early married life was dominated by her overbearing mother-in-law, who tried to mould Sisi (Elizabeth's nickname) into a perfect Hapsburg queen. But Sisi hated the stifling formality of the Austrian court, where every courtier had to come from four generations of aristocrats. She was politically liberal and supported the political aspirations of the Hungarians, who had rebelled against Hapsburg rule in 1848. For these reasons, Franz Joseph was not altogether sorry that Sisi spent so much time abroad travelling though Europe in her private train, or visiting her villa in Corfu on her private yacht. Sisi loved to hunt – partly for the adrenalin rush and partly, of course, because she looked so magnificent in her riding habit.

The second half of Sisi's life was marred by tragedy. Her only son Rudolph ended his life in a suicide/murder with his teenage mistress at his hunting lodge in Mayerling in 1889. Elizabeth wore black for the rest of her life, which came to an end in 1898 when she was stabbed to death by an Italian anarchist as she was boarding a steamer on Lake Geneva. The anarchist was hoping to assassinate a member of the Russian royal family. Franz Joseph lived on until 1916 – the assassination of his nephew and heir Archduke Ferdinand was the event that triggered the First World War.

Bay Middleton (a very distant relation of the future Queen of England) was famous for being the 'hardest rider in England'. He got his nickname from a Derby winner. He spent five years with Sisi 'piloting' her through the hunting seasons in England and Ireland. Their relationship has been the source of speculation ever since. It certainly aroused her son's Rudolph's jealousy. According to the Kenneth McMillan ballet 'Mayerling' it precipitated Rudolph's descent into madness and suicide.

Very little is known about Charlotte Baird apart from the fact that she and Bay did marry. I have given her an interest in photography, an art form which was popular with intelligent young women at that time.

Acknowledgements

I couldn't have written this book without the help and support of some people:

My two outstanding editors, Imogen Taylor and Hope Dellon, my agent Caroline Michel, who is as good as she is beautiful, Georgina Moore and her team at Headline, Dori Weintraub and her team at SMP, Emma Holtz and Silissa Kennedy for expert fielding, Rachel Street who is a brilliant copyeditor as well as being a superlative assistant, Penny Mortimer for the hunting edit, Janet Reibstein for her ability to spot the most important thing, Sam Lawrence who kept me going in a difficult year, Andrea Wong for her enthusiasm and kindness, my friends Shane Watson and Emma Fearnhamm for their patience, Jason Goodwin for the rewrite, my sisters Tabitha, Chloe and Sabine for their support, Richard Goodwin for his excitement on reading the first draft, my daughters Ottilie and Lydia for being my keenest supporters and fiercest critics and my husband Marcus for being the rock on which my flimsy edifice is built.

Francesco Guidicini

Daisy Goodwin is the author of several *New York Times* bestselling novels, including *Victoria, The American Heiress,* and *The Fortune Hunter.* She is a Harkness scholar who attended Columbia University's film school after earning a degree in history at Cambridge University, and was chair of the judging panel of the 2010 Orange Prize for Fiction. The creator and screenwriter of the Masterpiece presentation *Victoria* on PBS, she lives in London.